Translated Texts for Byzantinists

The intention of the series is to broaden access to Byzantine texts from 800 AD, enabling students, non-specialists and scholars working in related disciplines to access material otherwise unavailable to them. The series will cover a wide range of texts, including historical, theological and literary works, all of which include an English translation of the Byzantine text with introduction and commentary.

Liverpool University Press gratefully acknowledges the generous support of Dr Costas Kaplanis, alumnus of King's College London, who suggested the idea of the series to Professor Herrin and has underwritten the initial expenses.

General Editors
Dr Judith Ryder, Wolfson College, Oxford
Professor Judith Herrin, King's College, London
Professor Elizabeth M. Jeffreys, Exeter College, Oxford

Editorial Committee
Jim Crow (Edinburgh)
Mary Cunningham (Nottingham)
Charalambos Dendrinos (Royal Holloway)
Antony Eastmond (Courtauld Institute)
Tim Greenwood (St Andrews)
Anthony Hirst (London)
Liz James (Sussex)
Costas Kaplanis (King's College London)
Marc Lauxtermann (Oxford)
Fr Andrew Louth (Durham)
Ruth Macrides (Birmingham)
Rosemary Morris (York)
Margaret Mullett (Dumbarton Oaks)
Leonora Neville (University of Wisconsin-Madison)
Charlotte Roueché (King's College London)
Teresa Shawcross (Princeton)
Paul Stephenson (Durham)
Frank Trombley (Cardiff)
Mary Whitby (Oxford)

D1104386

Translated Texts for Byzantinists
Volume 1

Four Byzantine Novels

Theodore Prodromos, *Rhodanthe and Dosikles*
Eumathios Makrembolites, *Hysmine and Hysminias*
Constantine Manasses, *Aristandros and Kallithea*
Niketas Eugenianos, *Drosilla and Charikles*

Translated with introductions and notes by
ELIZABETH JEFFREYS

Liverpool
University
Press

First published 2012
Liverpool University Press
4 Cambridge Street
Liverpool, L69 7ZU

This paperback edition published 2016

British Library Cataloguing-in-Publication Data
A British Library CIP Record is available.

ISBN 978-1-84631-825-2 *cased*
    978-1-78138-007-9 *paperback*

Set in Times by
Koinonia, Manchester
Printed in the European Union by
CPI Group (UK) Ltd, Croydon CR0 4YY

CONTENTS

ACKNOWLEDGEMENTS

Work began on these translations several decades ago in Sydney. I should like to acknowledge the support over the years and in different ways of several institutions – the University of Sydney, Dumbarton Oaks, the University of Oxford, Exeter College, Oxford – but especially the Australian Research Council for several generous research fellowships which enabled my explorations of the Byzantine twelfth century to develop. I should also like to acknowledge many fruitful discussions, both formal and informal, over the years with colleagues and students around the world, especially with Panagiotis Agapitos, Roderick Beaton, Carolina Cupane, Michael Jeffreys, Corinne Jouanno, Suzanne MacAlister, Paul Magdalino, Ingela Nilsson, Roderich-Dieter Reinsch, Panagiotis Roilos and Teresa Shawcross; to this list I would now like to add Judith Ryder, the editor of Translated Texts for Byzantinists, and the series' readers, who have frequently saved me from myself. I am grateful to Michael Jeffreys for enabling my access to the most recent revisions to *Prosopography of the Byzantine World* before general release. I owe an especial debt of gratitude to Ruth Harder for her vigilant reading of early drafts. Responsibility for errors and infelicities that remain is, of course, mine alone.

Elizabeth Jeffreys
Oxford, March 2011

ABBREVIATIONS

A&K   Constantine Manasses, *Aristandros and Kallithea*
Ach N   *Achilleis* (Smith 1999)
AnthGr   *Anthologia Graeca* (*Greek Anthology*)
AnthPlan   *Planudean Anthology* (Aubreton and Buffière 1980)
BMGS   *Byzantine and Modern Greek Studies*
BZ   *Byzantinische Zeitschrift*
Charit   Chariton, *Chaireas and Kallirrhoe*
D&C   Niketas Eugenianos, *Drosilla and Charikles*
DigAk   *Digenis Akritis* (Jeffreys 1998)
ΕΕΒΣ   Ἐπετηρὶς Ἑταιρείας Βυζαντινῶν Σπουδῶν
DOP   *Dumbarton Oaks Papers*
GRBS   *Greek, Roman and Byzantine Studies*
H&H   Eumathios Makrembolites, *Hysmine and Hysminias*
Hel   Heliodoros, *Ethiopika*
IG   *Inscriptiones Graecae*
JÖBG   *Jahrbuch der Österreichischen Byzantinischen Gesellschaft*
JÖB   *Jabrbuch der Österreichischen Byzantinistik*
L&K   Achilles Tatius, *Leukippe and Kleitophon*
L&Rα   *Livistros and Rodamne* (Agapitos 2006a)
Longos   Longos, *Daphnis and Chloe*
LSJ   H. G. Liddell, R. Scott and H. S. Jones, *A Greek–English Lexicon* (rev. edn, Oxford, 1996)
MangProd   Manganeios Prodromos
NH   Νέος Ἑλληνομνήμων
OCD   *The Oxford Classical Dictionary*, 3rd edn
ODB   *The Oxford Dictionary of Byzantium*
OHBS   *The Oxford Handbook of Byzantine Studies*
PBW   *Prosopography of the Byzantine World* (www.pbw.kcl.ac.uk consulted 27 September 2011)
PG   *Patrologia Graeca*

PW   Pauly-Wissowa, *Paulys Real-Encyclopädie der classischen*
            Altertumswissenschaft, rev. G. Wissowa
R&D   Theodore Prodromos, *Rhodanthe and Dosikles*
RÉB   *Revue des études byzantines*
RÉG   *Revue des études grecques*
SynChron   Constantine Manasses, *Synopsis Chronike*
TM   *Travaux et Mémoires*
TrGF   *Tragicorum Graecorum Fragmenta*
VV   *Vizantijskij Vremennik*
XenEph   Xenophon of Ephesos, *Ephesiaka*

References to classical authors and editions follow LSJ and *L'Année Philologique*; editions are noted only in cases of ambiguity and obscurity.

INTRODUCTION

Four novels, or romances, were written in the middle years of the twelfth century in Constantinople.[1] These texts are *Rhodanthe and Dosikles* (hereafter *R&D*) by Theodore Prodromos, *Hysmine and Hysminias* (*H&H*) by Eumathios Makrembolites, *Aristandros and Kallithea* (*A&K*) by Constantine Manasses and *Drosilla and Charikles* (*D&C*) by Niketas Eugenianos.[2] These texts share themes and literary techniques that suggest a group of writers operating within the same milieu.[3] All draw extensively on the novels of the Second Sophistic, especially *Leukippe and Kleitophon* by Achilles Tatius (late 2nd cent. CE) and the *Ethiopika* of Heliodoros (perhaps 4th cent. CE), as well as *Chaereas and Kallirrhoe* by Chariton (2nd cent. CE) and *Daphnis and Chloe* by Longos (also 2nd cent. CE).[4] All are written in a mannered style, whether in prose (*H&H*) or verse (12 syllables: *R&D*, *D&C*; 15 syllables: *A&K*), and all are full of 'set-piece' rhetorical displays. The plots deal with the trials of a pair of well-born lovers who are separated by dramatic misfortunes but eventually emerge unscathed to be united in marriage.

For long the standard reaction to these Byzantine novels has been that

1 While the terms 'novel' and 'romance' are virtually interchangeable (in the English-speaking world), the convention has developed in Byzantine studies that the twelfth-century fictional narratives of love and adventure are referred to as 'novels' while those from the fourteenth century are termed 'romances'. Texts of this sort appear only twice in the Byzantine millennium: during the Komnenian twelfth century and the Palaiologan fourteenth. For the historical background to Byzantium in the twelfth century, see the outlines in Magdalino 2002 and 2008, as well as the authoritative discussions of the reign of Manuel I Komnenos (1143–80) in Magdalino 1993, with much of relevance to the first half of the century.

2 All four are conveniently edited with an Italian translation in Conca 1994; they were previously relatively readily available in Hirschig 1856 and Hercher 1859. There are also individual modern editions; *R&D*: Marcovich 1992; *H&H*: Marcovich 2001; *D&C*: Conca 1990; *A&K*: Mazal 1967. Details of older editions, and translations into other modern languages, are given below, in the introduction to each novel.

3 Hunger 1978, vol. 2: 119–42; Beaton 1996: 54–57.

4 These classical models are conveniently available in a collected English translation: Reardon 1989. Modern editions exist of all.

they are insipid, mildly pornographic imitations of their classical models with no intrinsic interest.[5] However, over the last thirty years or so they have been attracting increasingly sympathetic scholarly attention, with studies devoted to individual works as well as general overviews.[6] New editions have appeared to replace the frequently inadequate editions from the nineteenth century and earlier. In part this is a natural consequence of the growing interest in the novel of the ancient world.[7] In part it is due to a greater willingness to explore Byzantine literary products without the blinkers of a classicist's prejudice. In part it is because the novel – which may be defined as a sustained fictional narrative – is the dominant literary genre of the present day and thus all phases of what may be seen as its pre-history attract attention, though this is a dangerous prism through which to observe the twelfth century. The Byzantine novels become particularly significant when it is realized that they predate, possibly by more than forty years, the works of the French poet Chrétien de Troyes,[8] regarded as one of the most significant milestones in the medieval development of the European novel. It is this thought that underlies one challenging study of the history of the novel, Margaret Anne Doody's *True Story of the Novel* (1996), which makes the twelfth-century Constantinopolitan authors pivotal in the transmission of the concept of fictional writing from the ancient to the modern world.[9] One may dispute the detail of the argument, but the fact remains that this Byzantine material is a phenomenon whose genesis and function have yet to be fully explained, for it must be remembered that the writing of romantic fiction of this sort was not a standard element in Byzantine literary culture. Evidence for story-telling, surely a natural human instinct, does survive in Byzantium but has been transmuted into stories about holy men and women,

5 Rohde 1876: 521–22; Mango 1980: 237.

6 Important initial steps were taken in, e.g., Cupane 1974; Alexiou 1977; Hunger 1980; Beaton 1989, revised in Beaton 1996 (Agapitos 1992 should be consulted), was a landmark in bringing these texts to more general attention, and remains useful. See Agapitos 2000 for research desiderata. More recently Nilsson 2001 focuses on *H&H* while Roilos 2005 provides an illuminating and sensitive analysis of the novels' literary techniques; Meunier 2007 attempts a somewhat mechanistic location of the novels in their social context.

7 An initial conference at Bangor in 1976 (Reardon 1977), to mark the centenary of the publication of Rohde's epoch-making study on the ancient novel, had fertile consequences. General surveys have proliferated (see, e.g., Hägg 1983; Bowie 1985; Tatum 1994; Swain 1999; Whitmarsh 2008) as well as conferences and journals (e.g. *Ancient Narrative*) while these texts, after generations of neglect, are now well integrated into university curricula for Classical studies. Byzantium has benefited: see, e.g., MacAlister 1994 and Burton 2008.

8 E. Jeffreys 1980.

9 Doody 1996: 176–81.

that is, into hagiography, of which there are examples in abundance.[10]

Given this interest and the growing number of translations of these twelfth-century novels into other modern European languages, it seems obvious that they should be made accessible to English-speaking students of medieval literature and of the history of the novel. The translations that follow are in prose, though set out line by line for the verse texts as an aid to the reader following the Greek. They deliberately aim at preserving the mannered quality of the Greek, whether verse or prose, and make some effort to keep a consistency of vocabulary, allowing repetitions where English usage would prefer synonyms. The introductions briefly review current opinions on the dates, contexts and nature of each of the novels: much more could be said. The notes are multi-purpose and will probably satisfy no one: they are intended to elucidate references that may puzzle a neophyte Byzantinist or non-specialist; to give some indication of textual issues where these affect the translation and where current editions are at variance; to point up, though without exploring their intertextuality, some of the many quotations that permeate these texts, a feature that has been a major preoccupation of earlier studies; and to give some indication of interesting recent work that opens up new interpretations.

10 Cf. McCormick's deliberately provocative definition of saints' lives as fiction (McCormick 2001: 267–69).

THEODORE PRODROMOS

RHODANTHE AND DOSIKLES

INTRODUCTION

Author

Theodore Prodromos was perhaps the most versatile, inventive and prolific of the writers functioning in the first half of the twelfth century, using both prose and verse to produce a wide variety of texts. These included encomia for imperial events and persons, satire, hagiography, religious poetry, letters and commentaries on texts as disparate as John of Damascus' canons and Aristotle's *Posterior Analytics*. He also wrote the novel *Rhodanthe and Dosikles*.[1]

Little is known of Prodromos' family circumstances. His father apparently travelled and read widely while an uncle, named Christos, held a bishopric in Russia. This suggests a comfortable though not elite background.[2] Prodromos' father advised his son against a life of artisan crafts and soldiering, and – like others of this class in the early years of the twelfth century – provided him with a thorough literary education, expecting a lucrative career to follow.[3] From the range of his works that survive, the texts alluded to and Prodromos' own comments on the sequence of subjects he studied, the education was thorough.[4] However, financial rewards failed to materialize.[5]

1 The authoritative listing of Theodore's literary production is Hörandner 1974: 37–72. The definitive study of his life and works remains to be written; older work is vitiated by confusions between Theodore Prodromos, the poet conventionally known as Manganeios Prodromos and the author of the *Ptochoprodromika* (probably in fact Theodore), with a resulting lack of chronological clarity (see, e.g., Kazhdan and Franklin 1984: 87–114).

2 Hörandner 1974: 22–24; father's travels: *ibid.*, no. 38.19–21; bishopric: no. 59.184–89. Whether the uncle was John II, metropolitan of Kiev, remains debated (*ODB*, under 'John II, metropolitan of Kiev').

3 Hörandner 1974: no. 38.41–56, no. 59.191–203. On the career expectations that a sound education should offer, see Magdalino 1993: 321–23.

4 On the stages through which his education passed, see Hörandner 1974: no. 38.50–56, no. 59.191–203; he refers to grammar, rhetoric, Aristotelian and Platonic philosophy and theology.

5 Hörandner 1974: no. 38, a plea for support addressed to Anna Komnene, makes this anticipation and disappointment plain, as do the Ptochoprodromic poems (cf. Eideneier 1991: no. 3); a similar bitterness is expressed in his *On Poverty* (*PG* 133: 1333–40).

The disappointment may have been partly due to historical accident (as suggested below) and partly to ill health, for it is plain that others with similar training did advance to teaching posts and bishoprics.[6] John Tzetzes was the most signal example of failure.[7] The large number of surviving, mostly anonymous, 'occasional' epigrams from the mid-twelfth century suggest that many others aspired to make themselves known and to translate education into a living by penning literary works, usually in verse, for Constantinopolitan patrons, both imperial and aristocratic.[8] Many of these works would have been presented in *theatra*, literary salons, of which in the first half of the twelfth century the best-known were those presided over by Eirene Doukaina (d. ca. 1133), widow of Alexios I Komnenos (d. 1118); Anna Komnene (d. ca. 1153), daughter of Alexios I, together with her husband Nikephoros Bryennios (d. 1138); and the *sevastokratorissa* Eirene (d. ca. 1152), widowed sister-in-law of Manuel I Komnenos.[9]

Born ca. 1100 in Constantinople,[10] Prodromos' first known datable work was produced in 1122 for the crowning of Alexios (d. 1142) as co-emperor with his father John II Komnenos (reigned 1118–43).[11] Prodromos would presumably have been undergoing his education in the years around 1115–20. Although the Patriarchal School had been newly reformed as part of the efforts by Alexios I to raise the standard of clerical education, small, single-teacher establishments continued at this time to predominate as the

6 Magdalino 1993: 342–43. Among the most obviously successful beneficiaries of high-level education in Prodromos' environment were Stephanos Skylitzes, commentator on Aristotle and later bishop of Trebizond, and Nikephoros Basilakes, teacher in the Patriarchal School until doctrinal disputes in 1157 exiled him to Philippopolis; in the early stages of his career the first had taught Prodromos, the second was widely influential. The epigrams in Marc. Gr. 524 (still most easily accessible in Lambros 1911) are a good witness to the number of mid-twelfth-century educated versifiers in circulation.

7 His problems seem to have resulted from a combination of cantankerousness and a quarrel with his employer's wife: Wendel 1948: 1961.

8 See Magdalino 1993: 336–46, 510–12 on the patrons. The most prolific of these jobbing poets, conventionally known as Manganeios Prodromos, is not to be confused with Theodore Prodromos. For insights into the jockeying for support among these poets, cf. Prodromos' comments in Maiuri 1914–19: 399, lines 17–19. On the incentives to write verse at this time, see E. Jeffreys 2009; for eleventh-century parallels, see Bernard 2010.

9 On *theatra*, see Magdalino 1993: 336–46; on Eirene Doukaina, see Hill 1999: 165–69; on Anna Komnene, see Gouma-Peterson 2000; on the *sevastokratorissa* Eirene, see E. Jeffreys forthcoming a.

10 Hörandner 1974: 22–23, and Kazhdan and Franklin 1984: 100, both with surveys of previous proposals.

11 Hörandner 1974: no. 1.

source of secondary education.[12] Stephanos Skylitzes and Michael Italikos, referred to by Prodromos as his teachers, had connections to the official teaching establishment in the later stages of their careers, but it is not clear that this was the case when Prodromos was their student.[13]

The Komnenian court in the 1120s seems in effect to have been split into two factions – that of the emperor John and that of his dissident mother (Eirene Doukaina) and sister (Anna Komnene), who grudgingly accepted John's status after their abortive coups of 1118–19, which had attempted to place Anna and Nikephoros Bryennios on the throne.[14] In the first decade of Prodromos' career he seems to have placed himself under the patronage of Eirene Doukaina.[15] His Aristotelian commentary suggests that he was also involved with the philosophical group writing at this time under the aegis of Anna Komnene, though the mechanism of her support and involvement is obscure.[16] On Eirene Doukaina's death, which probably occurred in 1133,[17] he appears then to have turned to John as his major patron, carving out a successful career in producing long encomia.[18] Apparently lacking a permanent teaching post, he would have supported himself by writing commissioned work of this sort and by teaching private pupils.[19] By 1140,

12 Magdalino 1993: 328–29.

13 Hörandner 1974: 256. Skylitzes: Prodromos, Letter 6 (*PG* 133: 1255a), and Monody on Skylitzes (Petit 1903: 10–11, lines 141–43). Italikos: Letter 1 (Gautier 1972: 59–65).

14 Chalandon 1912: 2–17.

15 Maiuri 1914–19: 399, lines 21–23. Eirene retired to the Kecharitomene monastery after 1118, and presumably it would have been there that she received her literary protégés and held her *theatron*. The figures associated with her include Nikolaos Kallikles, Michael Italikos and Manuel Straboromanos, as well as her son-in-law Nikephoros Bryennios; see Polemis 1968: 70–74; Kazhdan and Franklin 1984: 97.

16 Tornikes' funeral oration on Anna devotes several pages to Anna's role in developing interest in Aristotelian philosophy (Darrouzès 1970a: 283–93); see also Browning 1962. Though she spent some of her later years in the Pantokrator monastery (where Tzetzes addresses two letters to her; Leone 1972: Letters 74 and 75), after the failed coup of 1118 she initially spent time in her mother's foundation, the Kecharitomene. In his funeral oration George Tornikes claims that Nikephoros and Anna had made their residence 'a home of the Muses' (Darrouzès 1970a: 267).

17 Prodromos' switching of patrons to John in 1133 with his hexameter poem on the capture of Kastamon (Hörandner 1974: no. 8) may well mark the cessation of Eirene's patronage at her death; the alternative death date of 1123 poses a number of problems (Polemis 1968: 71, n. 17; Gautier 1985: 8–9).

18 E.g. Hörandner 1974: nos. 3–10.

19 E.g. Theodore Styppeiotes, who had been a pupil but prior to Prodromos' illness in ca. 1140 and apparently enjoyed his teacher's grammatical exercises (*schede*); Hörandner 1974: no. 71.9–17. On the place of *schede* in Prodromos' work, see Vassis 1993–94.

however, Prodromos' circumstances were at a low ebb – the absence from Constantinople on campaign in Cilicia from 1138 onwards of the emperor and the heads of the aristocratic houses caused the flow of commissions, and the resulting income, to dry up.[20] It was at this point that he addressed a passionate plea for financial support to Anna Komnene,[21] and in despair contemplated abandoning Constantinople for Trebizond in the company of his friend and erstwhile teacher Stephanos Skylitzes.[22] It was at this time too that he suffered a severe illness, possibly smallpox, whose effects were prolonged.[23] In the early years of the reign of Manuel I Komnenos (reigned 1143–80) he sought support from him, claiming that he (Prodromos) had only ever served one family, that of Manuel; encomia resulted.[24] He also looked for support from the *sevastokratorissa* Eirene, writing in consolation on her widowhood (in 1142) and at some point presenting her with an illustrated grammar.[25] He made impassioned pleas to other prominent figures.[26] Eventually he took refuge in a *gerontokomeion* (hospice for the elderly) attached to the Orphanotropheion and the church of St Peter and Paul.[27] He continued to write pieces for Constantinopolitan aristocrats and possibly also take pupils and teach in the Orphanotropheion.[28] He died in 1156–58.[29]

---

20 Positive developments in his career, followed by a collapse and the beginning of 'begging' poetry, can be followed in *PBW* under Theodoros 25001 (http://db.pbw.kcl.ac.uk/id/person/161304; consulted 29 September 2011), under Narrative and Authorship.

21 Hörandner 1974: no. 59.

22 Hörandner 1974: no. 79.

23 Description of symptoms: Prodromos, Letter 6 to Skylitzes (*PG* 133: 1253–58), Letter 4 to Aristenos (*PG* 133: 1249–50); cf. Hörandner 1974: no. 78. On his general miseries, see his address to the *sevastokratorissa* Eirene (Hörandner 1974: no. 46).

24 Maiuri 1914–19: 399, lines 20–32. Encomia, see Hörandner 1974: nos. 30–33.

25 Consolation: Hörandner 1974: no. 45. On the illustrated grammar, see Spatharakis 1985. Eirene's activities are discussed further below, in the introduction to *A&K*.

26 Such as Stephanos Meles; see Hörandner 1974: no. 69.

27 On his entry into the Orphanotropheion, see *PG* 133: 1268–74.

28 For his aristocratic patrons, see Hörandner 1974: nos. 48–51. That he continued to take pupils is suggested by the number of *schede* associated with him: Hörandner 1974: 52, 62–64.

29 His latest datable works are epitaphs for Michael Palaiologos (Hörandner 1974: nos. 66–67), who died in late 1155 or early 1156 (cf. Kinnamos [Meineke 1836]: 151.7–21); in 1158 Manganeios Prodromos referred to Theodore as his deceased colleague (MangProd 37.27–33; pending the fortcoming edition by E. and M. Jeffreys, consult the list of Manganeios' titles, with editions, in Magdalino 1993: 494–500). Two monodies by Niketas Eugenianos shed some light on Prodromos' life and career (Gallavotti 1935: 222–29, in verse; Petit 1902: 452–63, in prose).

Date

It is possible to suggest a reasonably secure date within Prodromos' multi-faceted oeuvre for the composition of *Rhodanthe and Dosikles*. The novel's dedicatory preface is preserved in manuscript H (Heidelbergensis Palatinus graecus 43, f. 38v), an early fourteenth-century manuscript consisting largely of works by Prodromos, and an excellent witness to *R&D*.[30] Though noted by Hörandner and Marcovich, and published long ago by Welz (in 1910), the implications to be drawn from this dedication escaped attention until 1998.[31] The dedicatee is a Caesar (lines 1–4). Subsequent discussion now accepts that this can only be Caesar Nikephoros Bryennios, known for his own literary productions and for whom Prodromos had written other works.[32] Bryennios died in 1138, thus providing a secure *terminus ante quem* for *R&D*.[33] In the interstices of his military career Bryennios had continued to take part in *theatra* (especially that of Eirene Doukaina before her death), as witnessed by Michael Italikos' account of the enthusiastic reception accorded a letter sent by Bryennios while absent on campaign.[34] It was Eirene who instigated his composition of the *Material for a History* ("Υλη ἱστορίας) on the youthful exploits of Alexios I.[35] However, after the death of Eirene Doukaina in ca. 1133 Prodromos, as noted above, would seem to have begun writing for the emperor John. This may have involved a loosening of the ties with the faction that included Bryennios. So, although Bryennios

30 See Hörandner 1974: 151 for a list of the contents. On H as a sound witness to *R&D*, see Cottone 1979: 19–22 and the discussion below.

31 Noted in Hörandner 1974: 151; Marcovich 1992: v; edited in Welz 1910: 15–16. Discussed in E. Jeffreys 1998a, inclining to Caesar John Roger as patron (died after 1166; Varzos 1984, vol. 1: 349–56).

32 Discussion in E. Jeffreys 2000a, and Agapitos 2000a with a new edition of the dedication on which the translation below is based. Other works by Prodromos for Bryennios include a prose epithalamium for the double wedding of his sons (Gautier 1975: 340–55) and a verse monody on the death of his daughter-in-law Theodora (Hörandner 1974: no. 39). On the literary and scholarly environment cultivated by Bryennios and Anna Komnene in their home, see the comments of Tornikes (Darrouzès 1970a: 267).

33 On Bryennios, see Varzos 1984, vol. 1: 179–86; Carile 1968; E. Jeffreys 2003. On Bryennios' death, see *Alexiad*, Prologue 3.4 (Reinsch 2001).

34 Gautier 1975: 376 (letter from Italikos to Bryennios).

35 *Material for a History*: Gautier 1975. On the writers associated with Eirene Doukaina, see n. 15 above. Bryennios continued to work on a history of Alexios' reign, even when on campaign in Cilicia in 1137, until death intervened; see *Alexiad*, Prologue 3.4 (Reinsch 2001). Much of his material is incorporated in the *Alexiad* (see the over-enthusiastic claims of Howard-Johnston 1996, and the rebuttals by Macrides and Magdalino in Gouma-Petersen 2000; see also E. Jeffreys 2003).

maintained his literary interests throughout his life, it is an arguable possibility that *R&D* was presented to him by Prodromos in the earlier rather than the later years of the 1130s. The most likely *terminus ante quem* is 1136; after that date Bryennios, involved with the emperor's campaigns in Asia Minor, was unlikely to have been physically present in Constantinople to receive the presentation copy implied by the dedicatory epigrams. At the earlier end of the possible time-span, the thought that Prodromos may have been stimulated to compose *R&D* by the wedding of the two sons of Nikephoros Bryennios and Anna Komnene, probably in 1122, for which he provided an epithalamium, is attractive, but lacks evidence. The prominence in *R&D* (and the other novels) of marriage and the relation between the sexes in general is insufficient in this case to support a link.[36]

Agapitos has pointed out that the 24 lines of verse in the dedicatory poem are made up of three separate items: lines 1–14 make up the dedication and a plea that the work offered should not be compared to the masters of the past but to recent craftsmen; lines 15–16 are an elegiac couplet claiming Prodromos' authorship; lines 17–24 provide a summary of the vicissitudes that beset Rhodanthe and Dosikles, the central couple. He argues convincingly that these are most suitably interpreted as elements that made up a frontispiece to the dedication copy; a variety of layouts are possible.[37] The epigrams make great play with images of painting. Jeffreys (like Welz before her) interpreted these to refer to illustrations to the text (helped by Welz's insertion of σχεδίοις in line 14),[38] which led to the somewhat unexpected conclusion that Prodromos was author, scribe and painter. While this combination is not unknown,[39] Prodromos' calligraphic abilities are not mentioned elsewhere, and indeed his rejection of the life of an artisan would argue against his possession of such skills. Agapitos proposes that the dedication's imagery belongs to the *topos* of poetry as painting: Prodromos presents his work as a painting, with illustrious literary predecessors and contemporaries concealed behind named sculptors and painters.[40] The identity of the two ancient masters masked by the names Praxiteles and Apelles is of little importance, although Agapitos' suggestion of Heliodoros and Achilles Tatius, the two novelists from late antiquity most referenced in

36 Epithalamium, in Gautier 1975: 341–55; see also E. Jeffreys 2003: 203.

37 For earlier and later parallels and possible formats, see Agapitos 2000a: 178.

38 Where for ἀντίπαλος σχεδίοις Agapitos now reads οὐ πολλῷ χερίων (Agapitos 2000a: 175–76); see below.

39 E. Jeffreys 2000a: 132–33.

40 Agapitos 2000a: 180.

the twelfth century, is reasonable. Much more significant is the identity of the 'recent painters' (line 12: ζωγράφοις νέοισιν) with which Prodromos' own 'recent efforts' (line 9: τἀμὰ ... νεώτατα) are to be compared. Given that his 'recent effort' only makes sense if applied to *R&D*, the reference must be to other comparable sustained narrative pieces of erotic fiction. As is discussed elsewhere in this volume, the fragmentary *A&K* can be placed with reasonable certainty ca. 1145 in the circle (or *theatron*) of the *sevastokratorissa* Eirene, while *D&C*, often stated to be written in imitation of 'the late' Prodromos (on dubious manuscript authority), can be placed on acceptable grounds ca. 1156. Two other texts of this type are known from the twelfth century. One is *Digenis Akritis*; recent work has argued that the first version in a written-out narrative form was put together before 1143.[41] Agapitos rejects *Digenis* as a parallel,[42] although this is perhaps unnecessarily dismissive given the undoubted links to the novel tradition still visible in both the G and the E versions.[43] The other text is *H&H*, whose problematic dating is discussed below. Based on the several *ekphraseis* (descriptions) in *H&H*,[44] the references to the painter craftsman who created the wondrous images in Sosthenes' garden with their iambic inscriptions[45] and the final section in which the author apparently looks to the future creation of a visual monument of his verbal art,[46] Agapitos argues that 'the topos of writing as painting is a central aspect of the poetics of *Hysmine and Hysminias*'.[47] By this argument *H&H* is thus a creation of one of the 'recent painters' with which Prodromos wishes *R&D* to be compared and is, argues Agapitos, the text with which Prodromos' *R&D* is in dialogue. The implications of this for the dating of *H&H* will be discussed further in the next section.

The conclusion to be retained in connection with *R&D* is that it is a product of the 1130s, possibly from early in the decade, from an environment that included the *theatron* of Eirene Doukaina. This *theatron* was attended by

41 E. Jeffreys forthcoming b, arguing that *Ptochprodromika* 1.155–97, by Prodromos and dedicated to Emperor John II (d. 1143), is a parody of *DigAk* G 4.112–38 (E. Jeffreys 1998). The Grottaferrata (G) and Escorial (E) versions of *DigAk* are physically the two oldest recensions of this text, from the late thirteenth and late fifteenth centuries respectively; a good case can be made that G reflects the original attempt to create a unified, biographical narrative based on frontier ballads that retold episodes from the hero's life; on the place of biographical narratives in Byzantine literary culture, see Moennig 2010.

42 Agapitos 2000a: 182.

43 E. Jeffreys 1998: xliv–xlvii.

44 *H&H* 1.4.6: garden; 2.1–11: virtues and Eros; 4.4–18: the twelve months.

45 *H&H* 2.7.5, 2.10.4.

46 *H&H* 11.22.4.

47 Agapitos 2000a: 184.

Nikephoros Bryennios and Michael Italikos, as well as nameless others who would have been seeking to demonstrate their skills and win employment. All would have vied in the presentation of displays of verbal dexterity.

Transmission and reception

R&D survives in four manuscripts, from the thirteenth (V), early fourteenth (H), mid-fifteenth (U) and early sixteenth centuries (L); it also appears in a selection of excerpts, which, though an interesting phenomenon, is not in this case important for the reconstruction of the text.[48] The four manuscripts fall into two families, HV and UL, both derived from the same archetype, to which, in Marcovich's opinion, H is by far the best witness.[49] In recent years the manuscript tradition has been well studied and elucidated by Cottone before being put into practice in the editions of Marcovich and Conca.[50] As with *D&C*, the number of surviving manuscripts does not allow many conclusions about the text's circulation in Byzantium, or among western humanists: it was classified with *D&C*, and appreciated for its rhetorical qualities. In 1625 *R&D* was edited by Gaulmin on the basis of a somewhat inaccurate transcription by Salmasius, and accompanied by a loose Latin translation; thereafter, in spite of two French translations,[51] it was given little attention until Hercher's edition of 1859. Subsequently valuable work was done on *R&D*'s rhetorical style and its sources.[52] When a modern critical edition appeared, by Marcovich in 1992, it proved to be interventionist with an improbably large array of textual parallels.[53] That of Conca, which appeared shortly after, accompanied by an Italian translation with brief notes and parallels, has a limited textual apparatus, and accepts tacitly many of Marcovich's emendations, listing only those that are rejected.[54] Translations into German and Spanish appeared in 1996.

---

48 V: Vat. gr. 121, ff. 22–29v; H: Heidelbergensis Palatinus gr. 43, ff. 39v–83r; U: Vatican, Urb. Gr 134, ff.78v–11pr. L: Florence, Med. Laur. Aquisiti e Doni 341, ff. 1r–50v. U and L also contain *D&C*. The excerpts together with substantial portions of *A&K* are found in Makarios Chrysokephalos' *Rhodonia* (M: Marc. Gr. 452, ff. 245r–246v, dated ca. 1328–36; this manuscript should not be confused with the M of *D&C*).

49 Marcovich 1992: vi.

50 See Cottone 1979 on the manuscript tradition. Editions: Marcovich 1992; Conca 1994.

51 Godard de Beauchamps 1746; Trognon 1822.

52 Grossschupf 1897; Häger 1908.

53 As noted in reviews: Agapitos 1993a; Conca 1994a; Garzya 1993; Grünbart 1996; Trapp 1995.

54 Dawe 2001a offers a number of emendations, some noted in the present translation.

Form

R&D is presented in nine books, using the Byzantine 12-syllable line throughout, apart from a hexameter passage at 9.196–204. From their presence in the manuscripts it is clear that the archetype of *R&D* included headings at intervals in the text, usually to highlight narrative sections or a rhetorical form (e.g. an *ekphrasis* or a lament). These, following Marcovich's marginal notes, have been included in the translation in this volume. For reasons of space these have not been placed in the margin but instead they have been included in the footnotes, introduced by the words 'Marginal gloss'. Apart from its dedicatory frontispiece, *R&D* was probably not illustrated.

Plot summary

Book 1 opens with a scene of devastation on the coast of Rhodes where a pirate fleet has seized many captives, including the handsome couple Dosikles and Rhodanthe. Embarking with their loot, the pirates sail for their homeland. Once ashore, that night Dosikles laments the disaster that has overtaken him and his beloved Rhodanthe in their flight to evade parental opposition to their marriage. He is overheard by a Cypriot fellow prisoner, Kratandros, who relates his own unhappy love for Chrysochroe: an ill-organized abduction had led to her death and his trial for murder; although shown to be innocent after eloquent forensic pleas and an ordeal by fire, he had fled Cyprus but had fallen victim to the marauding pirates. The following morning Mistylos, the pirate chief, singles out Rhodanthe, Dosikles and Kratandros as potential temple servants, sends Stratokles[55] home but condemns four others, including Nausikrates, to be sacrificed. Kratandros asks Dosikles to tell his story.

Book 2 Dosikles explains that he and Rhodanthe had sailed to Rhodes with Stratokles, where they had been entertained to a magnificent dinner by Stratokles' friend Glaukon. On Glaukon asking how Dosikles and Rhodanthe came to be traveling with Stratokles, Dosikles had explained that he had caught sight of Rhodanthe in their home town of Abydos and fallen passionately in love with her; when marriage negotiations between their families failed he had resolved to abduct her, which he did successfully with the aid of friends, whereupon he and Rhodanthe had fled in Stratokles' ship.

Book 3 After the festive gathering Dosikles had observed Nausikrates in a drunken sleep. When everyone else had retired to rest, Dosikles had

---

55 Stratokles' role in the adventures of Dosikles and Rhodanthe is not revealed at this point.

attempted to seduce Rhodanthe, but was rebuffed. The next morning, while sacrifices were being offered for Stratokles' recently deceased child, the pirates had attacked Rhodes and Gobryas, satrap to Mistylos, had taken the travellers prisoner though Glaukon, their host, had died of fright. Dosikles' narrative ends with his encounter with Kratandros in prison. Now, however, Gobryas, Mistylos' second-in-command, amazed by Rhodanthe's beauty, requests her as his prize. Failing to win a logic-chopping argument with Mistylos who had dedicated Rhodanthe and Dosikles to the service of the gods, Gobryas attempts to rape Rhodanthe, but is prevented by Dosikles. Gobryas, assuming Dosikles to be Rhodanthe's brother, wishes to use him as an intermediary in his seduction. Dosikles prevaricates, and he and Rhodanthe lament their ill fortune at length.

Book 4 Mistylos' plans to dedicate the pair in the temple are forestalled by the arrival of Artaxanes, satrap to Bryaxes, emperor of Pissa. Received formally by Mistylos, Artaxanes presents a letter demanding that Mistylos restore the city of Rhamnon to Bryaxes. Furious, Mistylos promises a response and asks Gobryas to offer Artaxanes hospitality. A banquet is prepared, with exotic dishes (notably roast lamb stuffed with live sparrows) and a dwarf jester who rises from an apparent death to sing an ode to Mistylos' greatness. Artaxanes, overwhelmed by his experiences, falls into a drunken stupor, letting slip and shattering an elaborately carved drinking cup. Meanwhile Mistylos, having prepared a letter in response to Bryaxes defiantly declaring Rhamnon is part of his and not Bryaxes' territory, dismisses Artaxanes.

Book 5 Mistylos prepares for battle, sending Gobryas (who had been hoping that his marriage to Rhodanthe was about to be celebrated) to summon his allies. Bryaxes too prepares for battle, while Artaxanes protests that Mistylos possesses supernatural powers, citing his experiences at the banquet. Bryaxes leads out his fleet, and delivers a lengthy exhortation to his men. Battle starts. On seeing the size of the opposing forces, Bryaxes is alarmed and sends a second letter to Mistylos, to no effect.

Book 6 As day dawns Bryaxes sends divers to break holes in the hulls of Mistylos' fleet. In the subsequent battle Gobryas perishes, lamenting his loss of Rhodanthe, while Mistylos commits suicide. Bryaxes' forces leave their fleet and loot Mistylos' city, capturing Dosikles and Rhodanthe, and also Kratandros. They prepare to carry off the booty, separating – to their distress – Rhodanthe and Dosikles. A storm on the second night wrecks the ship conveying Rhodanthe, who is rescued by merchants on their way to Cyprus. Once there, they sell their goods, including Rhodanthe who is bought by

Kraton, Kratandros' father. Dosikles meanwhile laments Rhodanthe's fate at length but is encouraged, without great success, by Kratandros to be positive. Eventually, on the eleventh day, they reach Pissa and are imprisoned.

Book 7 In Kraton's house in Cyprus Rhodanthe laments for Dosikles and is overheard by Myrilla, daughter of Kraton and Stale, who asks for more information. As Rhodanthe recounts her story, she mentions the name of Kratandros, which sets off a general hubbub as the family now knows that their lost son lives, though his whereabouts are uncertain. Next day Kraton departs for Pissa in search of Kratandros. Meanwhile, in Pissa Bryaxes has decided to sacrifice to the gods the best of his booty, which he interprets as Dosikles and Kratandros. There ensues a debate, in Platonic style, as to the justification for this.

Book 8 As Bryaxes ponders the impasse reached in the debate Kraton arrives in Pissa and adds his pleas for the preservation of the youths. Bryaxes, still determined to make the sacrifice, is forced to reconsider when a shower of rain extinguishes the sacrificial flame, indicating the gods' will. Kratandros and Dosikles are set free to return to Cyprus with Kraton, where they are greeted rapturously. Amid the enthusiasm Dosikles pines for his lost Rhodanthe, failing to recognize her as she serves at the banquet until Kraton points to her as his informant. Further jubilation follows, which does not please Myrilla, Kratandros' sister, who had designs on the handsome Dosikles. She gives Rhodanthe a paralytic poison while Dosikles and Kratandros are absent hunting. However, fortuitously they had noted an antidote, observing a bear's healing use of a herb, and employ this to restore Rhodanthe.

Book 9 Dosikles and Rhodanthe discuss their situation and what they should do next, with Rhodanthe explaining how she came to be in Cyprus. Meanwhile Lysippos and Straton, their respective fathers, had consulted the oracle at Delphi. On being told they could find their children in Cyprus they had made their way thither disguised as beggars. Eventually they encounter a dutifully ashamed Dosikles and Rhodanthe. After a euphoric reconciliation and a celebratory banquet the fathers return to Abydos with their children. There, greeted by their mothers, Rhodanthe is united in marriage to Dosikles.

Characteristics and themes[56]

R&D is perhaps best understood first as an exercise much performed in the twelfth century, namely pastiche; examples aping tragedy can be seen in *Christos Paschon* or the light-hearted *Katomyomachia*. In the case of *R&D* the models lie in the novels of late antiquity. *R&D*, which opens *in medias res* and gradually reveals to the reader the characters' situation through enfolded narratives by the protagonists and their confidants, owes much to Heliodoros' *Ethiopika*, while there are also reflections of Achilles Tatius' *L&K* both verbally and in elements of the plot.[57] From Book 3 the plot is linear, with separate strands in Books 6 and 7 when Rhodanthe and Dosikles are separated. The omniscient narrator informs the reader, while flashback speeches (e.g. Rhodanthe at 9.125–79) enlighten the characters' ignorance, although the elaborate structure set up by this narrator does not fold back into itself as neatly as in the late antique examples. Secondly, *R&D* can be understood as a demonstration of rhetorical techniques, presented in a series of set-piece displays of literary virtuosity: *ekphraseis* of heroine (1.39–60) or object (4.331–411: Gobryas' cup); forensic debate (1.329–89); philosophical debate (3.188–264, 7.400–45); lament (1.212–69, 6.264–413); *ethopoiia*[58] (2.206–315, 5.115–414); a song with a refrain in the manner of Theokritos (4.242–308) etc.[59] Roilos aptly remarks that the novels are primarily intended as examples of rhetorical art, though – as he also demonstrates – there are many strands to this art, with *R&D* not the least skilful product of an artful craftsman.[60]

R&D, like the other three novels from this period presented here, survives in written form but almost certainly would initially have been presented in a performance context, in a *theatron*, either book by book or perhaps as a selection of detachable highlights.[61] The audience would have been mixed, consisting of Constantinople's social elite and Prodromos' intellectual peers, his teachers and pupils. The writing is presumably pitched at a level that would not baffle the social elite but would impress the intellectuals

56 The comments here and in the sections on the other novels offer only a sketch of issues that can be explored; see Roilos 2000 for some possibilities that arise from a particular instance, and Roilos 2005 for a broader perspective.

57 Hunger 1978, vol. 1: 128–32; cf. MacAlister 1991: 185–86.

58 For a definition of *ethopoiia*, a character study, and its varieties, see Roilos 2005: 61–65.

59 Cf. the passages listed below in connection with *H&H*.

60 Roilos 2005: 50–57.

61 At ca. 500 lines each the books would be of a manageable performance length, and regular recapitulations would aid the listener.

with its subtle dexterities of composition.[62] There are some hints of class-room humour, suggesting that some of the set-pieces may have begun life as 'fair copies' of school exercises.[63] More interesting is the strand of self-conscious self-referentiality, indicating that Prodromos was alert to ironic aspects of the process of writing: Rodanthe's 'drama' is referred to as a tome (6.280); interpretation of the oracle given to the fathers of the central pair turns on the placing of a comma (9.214);[64] on a more elevated level, Hermes, the Olympian deity associated with eloquence and learning, has a persistent presence in the development of events, underlining the text's rhetoricity.[65]

Prodromos was not unduly interested in exploring amatory psychology. Eros is mentioned as a short-hand personification of erotic passion (at, e.g. 2.421, 2.463, 6.57, 8.192), but there is no discussion of the physiological processes associated with erotic passions that are found in *H&H* (on the role of eyes, on physical sensations on perceiving the beloved) or in the late antique models, notably in *L&K*. In *R&D* 2.191–315 Dosikles' debate on his instantaneous passion for Rhodanthe is expressed as much in terms of social rank as of emotion, and is translated into abduction when a conventional marriage offer is rejected;[66] there are parallels to the abduction in *DigAk* (G 4.300 ff.),[67] with similar hunting terminology (*R&D* 2.400–54) while the motif of 'stolen marriage', that is, a marriage arranged without parental consent, recurs in *H&H* 7.4.2 and 11.6.2. Pointing out that marriage legis-lation was a significant concern in Komnenian Constantinople, arguably a reflection of the dynastic politics of the period, Angeliki Laiou has suggested that this interest in the processes of aristocratic marriage might have been a factor in the revived interest at this time in the novels of late antiquity and the creation of new examples.[68]

This raises the question of the relationship of *R&D* both to its ostensible setting in an antique past and to its twelfth-century context. The relation-ship to the past is demonstrated most obviously by the use of Olympian

62 Cf. the comments in nn. 15 and 16 above.

63 Most conspicuously at *R&D* 8.520 ('never whet my blade on my teachers').

64 Roilos 2005: 50–61. Comments at *R&D* 2.432, 6.148, 6.294 can perhaps be taken as irreverent.

65 E.g. at *R&D* 3.69 (guaranteeing the marriage; cf. 3.432, 8.529), 6.395 and 6.471 (role and veracity doubted), 9.474 and 9.478 (role vindicated).

66 Some of the implications are discussed in Burton 2000.

67 The abduction in *DigAk* is discussed in Mackridge 1993 and Ricks 1989. In *DigAk* the bride is an informed and willing participant.

68 Laiou 1993: 200–18.

deities[69] and their temples, priests and sacrifices, combined with a lack of overt reference to equivalent features of twelfth-century life such as clergy, churches and the liturgy. Nevertheless, the guard slips at times: there are arguably parodic allusions to Christian rituals and texts.[70] The barbarian Mistylos is called emperor (e.g. 1.440, 4.16-17) and given imperial attributes, but these are probably generic: his dealings with Pissa can be seen as an irreverent allusion to Byzantine treatment of foreign embassies and their ambassadors' gullibility. Should the extravaganzas of *R&D* 4.123-70 (the roast lamb stuffed with live birds) and 4.214-49 (the resurrection of Satyrion) be seen as comment on contemporary court entertainments, or just a dense web of rhetorical tropes?[71] Kratandros' ordeal by fire (1.377–89) and the divers' attacking of the ships with hammers (6.7–21) are regularly cited as being prompted by contemporary events.[72] Several recent studies offer suggestive insights into these issues.[73] Interestingly, there are extant examples in stone and fabric of twelfth-century parallels for the 'tetraktys' of bodies formed in the rapturous reunion of parents and children (9.317–34).[74]

Other currents can be noticed that in varying degrees of likelihood reflect contemporary interests. One instance would be the Aristotelian background to comments on Nausikrates' dreams (3.17–42), surely indicating awareness of current commentary work on the *De somniis* in the philosophical movement mentioned above.[75] There is some stress on ethnic identity: for a fellow-prisoner to be a Hellene makes for an instant bond (1.153–55), with the Hellenic subsuming the Cypriot (1.135). Although this may reflect nothing more than the traditional division between Greek and barbarian, the first half of the twelfth century saw the beginnings of a revival of Hellenic consciousness, on which Prodromos may be drawing.[76] The contrast in status

69 Zeus is frequently apostrophized as the supreme deity (e.g. *R&D* 2.468, 488, 3.125, 478. 4.245, 7.141, 8.104 etc.) but also invoked as Zeus Xenios, protector of travellers (and strangers); Hermes (as in n. 65 above), more intricately a part of the author's scenario, perhaps functions as an image of the literary process.

70 E.g. *R&D* 3.103: a eucharistic allusion?; *R&D* 6.253, 749, 8.336, 9.163: Rhodanthe sold for thirty pieces of gold.

71 These passages are well discussed in Roilos 2005: 260–75. On entertainments, cf. Haldon 2002 Manasses' *ekphrasis* of a dwarf at the court of Manuel Komnenos is a suggestive parallel to Satyrion (Sternbach 1902).

72 Fire: Cupane 1973–74; divers: Hunger 1972.

73 E.g. MacAlister 1994; Burton 1998; Kaldellis 2007 and 2007a: 73–76.

74 Maguire 1999: 196–97 and 2007: 26–28.

75 MacAlister 1990. See p. 5 above and n. 16.

76 Magdalino 1991; Beaton 2007.

between the free and the enslaved, though less prominent than in *H&H*, is nevertheless present.[77] Slavery continued to be difficult issue in Byzantine society, as is reflected in Manuel I's legislation at some point in his reign to free those who had fallen into slavery, largely as a result of economic pressures.[78] The prominent role given to pirates and barbarian marauders could well reflect the realities of seafaring in the medieval Mediterranean, while the miserable fate of those they took captive arguably echoes that of the prisoners captured in the Balkan and Anatolian campaigns of the twelfth century.[79]

Of other issues that rise to the surface on reading *R&D* one that has drawn attention concerns the depiction of the women, who range from the self-possessed Rhodanthe through the jealous Myrilla to the shadowy mothers of the central pair. Questions have been asked as to how much these are conventional, due to the genre, and how much they reflect twelfth-century *mores*.[80]

Manuscripts, editions and translations

Manuscripts[81]

H   Heidelbergensis Palatinus gr. 43, ff. 39v–83r
U   Vaticanus Urbinas gr 134, ff.78v–119r
L   Laurentianus Aquisiti e Doni 341, ff. 1r–50v
V   Vaticanus gr. 121, ff. 22–29v

Editions
Gaulminus 1625; Hercher 1859: 289–434; Marcovich 1992; Conca 1994: 63–303.

Previous translations
French: Godard de Beauchamps 1746; Collande 1785; Trognon 1822.
German: Plepelits 1996.
Italian: Conca 1994: 63–303.

---

77 E.g. at *R&D* 6.254–55, 7.81–85, 7.138–40, 7.198–99, 8.354.

78 Dölger and Wirth 1995: no. 1476 (from a non-chronological list of activities recorded under 1167 by Kinnamos [Meineke 1836: 275]). See further discussion below in the introduction to *H&H* (at n. 67) and also Kazhdan 1985; Magdalino 1991; Rotman 2004.

79 On the piratical difficulties of earlier periods, see McCormick 2001. See Meunier 2007 on the twelfth-century social context.

80 See e.g. Garland 1990; Jouanno 2002 and 2006.

81 U and L also contain *D&C*.

Latin: Gaulminus 1625; Hercher 1858: 287–434.
Spanish: Jurado 1996.

This translation
The text translated here is that of Marcovich 1992, though with notice taken of the edition by Conca 1994 as well as of reviewers' comments (notably Conca, Trapp and Agapitos), and comments in Plepelits' translation (1996). Although this is a prose translation it is set out by lines that correspond, as far as possible, to those of the verse original.

TRANSLATION

DEDICATION[1]

My Caesar,[2] for I appropriate the common good for myself,
Caesar best and greatest and thrice brave, Caesar over all,
Caesar the great glory of those on earth, blest Caesar,
gentle Caesar, wise Caesar, <illustrious>[3] Caesar,
your servant Theodore, child of that Prodromos,   5
having grasped these <...> colours in his own hands,[4]
has depicted the image of Dosikles and Rhodanthe,
and begs you to look on it and pass judgment on him.
Do not put my recent efforts to be viewed
with the beautifully drawn panels and charming early works   10
of the great craftsman Praxiteles, or Apelles,
or else I would have endured the burden of my toil in vain;
but compare my skill with recent painters
and it might seem to be not much worse than those.[5]

"The work of Theodore Prodromos, both hand and mind,   15
the mind which begot it and the hand which depicted it."

1 For editions and textual discussions, see Welz 1910; E. Jeffreys 2000a; Agapitos 2000.
The poem falls into three parts; the first section (1–14) offers the book to a Caesar; the second
(15–16) reveals the author's name, possibly beneath a portrait of the Caesar receiving the book;
the third (17–24) summarizes the novel's plot.

2 'My Caesar': almost certainly Nikephoros Bryennios (as discussed above, pp. 7–9); this
phrase is used of Bryennios elsewhere by Prodromos (Hörandner 1974: no. 59.1).

3 'illustrious': following Reinsch's proposal (Agapitos 2000: 175); the manuscript's
crabbed hand is illegible.

4 The hexameter lacks a foot at some point in the line.

5 Following the corrected reading and emendation in Agapitos 2000: 175–76, 180; Welz
1910 had read ἀντίπαλος for οὐ πολλῷ and proposed σχεδίοις for the barely legible χερίων,
the whole to be interpreted as 'rival for these sketches'.

These [are the adventures] of the silvery girl Rhodanthe with the
    lovely garland
and of the valiant and comely youth Dosikles,
the flights and wanderings and tempests and billows, brigands,
grievous eddies, sorrows that give rise to love,   20
chains and indissoluble fetters and imprisonments in gloomy
dungeons, grim sacrifices, bitter grief,[6]
poisoned cups and paralysis of joints,
and then marriage and the marriage bed and passionate love.

THE FIRST BOOK OF THE DEEDS OF RHODANTHE AND DOSIKLES BY THE WISE[7] KYR THEODOROS PRODROMOS

Already the four-horsed chariot of the sun
had traversed the earth with its swift-running circuit
and, dipping beneath it, was bringing on the shades of evening,
leaving the air around us darkened,
when a trireme from the pirate fleet   5
was the first from the entire expedition to dart forward
and put in to the harbour of Rhodes.
It attacked the estates along the shore-line
and was ravaging all the area round about,
for as the barbarians rushed out immediately   10
they trampled the grapes and tore down the vines,
they burnt the cargo-carrying hulks,
tearing the cargo out of their holds,
and incinerated the crew together with their vessels.
One man's head was hewn off by the sword,   15
another was split apart by a whetted blade,
another's wretched heart was pierced
by a well-aimed weapon wielded by a barbarian's fist,

---

6 Following the corrected reading and proposal of Agapitos 2000: 176 (πικρά for πόνοι).

7 *Philosophos*, translated here as 'wise' has ambivalent meanings in Byzantium, implying either a person with extensive training in the ancient intellectual traditions or else someone seeking moral perfection, as a monk; cf. *ODB*, under 'Philosopher'. Although Prodromos became a monk on his deathbed, possibly with the monastic name Nikolaos (Hörandner 1974: 32), the dating of the novel to before 1138 supports the secular meaning. 'Ilyr' is a general term of respect.

others were destroyed by the dagger's edge
that slit their throats like cattle.   20
   While in this way those cruel barbarians
were destroying the coastal areas,
the entire pirate fleet reached Rhodes.
Promptly leaving the ships empty
and all entering the city together,   25
they made it the booty of the Mysians, as the saying goes.[8]
For some of the inhabitants died by the sword
but others died beforehand from fear of the sword.
Some,[9] fearing the barbarian's bitter hands,
hurled themselves into ravines and glens,   30
thinking it better to be deprived of life
than to succumb to piratical heartlessness.
Others they chained by the neck
with hammered iron fetters
and bound their arms behind them   35
and led the miserable slaves away in misery.
Among these Dosikles and the maiden Rhodanthe
were captured by the hand of the savage barbarian.
   The girl's beauty was something extraordinary,[10]
an august figure, a replica of a divine image,   40
wrought in the form of Artemis.[11]
Her flesh mimicked white snow,
the congruence of her every limb was consistent,
each dextrously linked to the other
and every one fitting together gracefully.   45
Her eyebrows were naturally well-drawn
in the graceful imitation of a half-circle,
her nose somewhat hooked and her pupils deep black,
circles were inscribed on her cheeks,

8 A proverbial expression for brutal treatment by an invading force; cf. Zenobios 5.15
(Leutsch and Schneidewin 1839–51, vol. 1); Suda, M 1478; *D&C* 1.22 etc.

9 Keeping (with Conca 1994) the οἱ μὲν of the mss in preference to the emendation οἳ μὴν
('who'; Marcovich 1992).

10 Marginal gloss: 'Description of Rhodanthe'. The first example of an *ekphrasis*
(description); cf. Introduction, p. 14 above.

11 Comparisons of the heroine to a sculpture also occur in, e.g., Hel 1.7.2; XenEph 1.2.6;
and *L&K* 1.4, as well as in twelfth-century contexts such as *H&H* 3.6.1–4; *SynChron* 1157–67.

four on both but two on the one spot;   50
of which the outer and more extensive
one might say were snow drifts
while the inner were, as it were, glowing
with the self-combusting coals within.[12]
A mouth that was quite narrow and closely compressed;   55
elbow, arm and harmony of fingers
were wrought by a natural craftsman;
the posture of her ankles was trim, a support for her legs,
the foundation one might say of the structure.
And all else was proper, and every feature beautiful.   60
     The maiden was so excellent to look at
that the predatory robber Gobryas
suspected it was a goddess who had been captured,
and left her free of all chains,
affected by the not unreasonable fear   65
that some goddess had been caught up among those in Rhodes,
taking on human features.
To such an extent did the wondrous spectacle
cast down even the barbarian's temerity,
and bring confusion to the robber's soul.   70
     Then the expedition embarked into the triremes
those captured in Rhodes,
including the young people Dosikles and Rhodanthe;
they filled the cargo-vessel with a cargo of gold,
and set off for their own homeland.   75
And hymning round about from all sides
their general and leader Mistylos,
and confining in the inner recesses
those held prisoner by the law of captivity,
they returned to their own houses   80
where they refreshed in their beds, but also in carousing,
their bodies that were wearied by toil.
     But what of the multitude held within?

---

12 There are many antecedents and contemporary parallels for this description of the
heroine: e.g *L&K* 1.4.3; *H&H* 2.2.2. For a visual parallel for the vivid circles of colour on
cheeks, see, e.g., Maria of Antioch, in the dedication portrait to the acts of the council of 1166
(Vat. gr. 1176; cf. plate in Mango 2002: 190), or the mosaic portrait of the empress Eirene
Komnene in Hagia Sophia (e.g. Kleinbauer 2004: 70–71).

They slept (sleep of a kind – it was very disturbed),
lying on the ground for a bed,   85
as night covered all after the setting of the sun.
Not so Dosikles, who weeping loudly shouted out:
    "O miserable, savage Fate,[13]
where are you taking me? To what end will you send me?
You have compelled me to migrate from the land that bore me,   90
you have condemned me to flight and wanderings,
you have separated me from kinsmen, friends and loved ones,
from my beloved mother, from my dearly loved progenitor.
And once more a miserable place contains me,
once more a barbarian's hand has control over me,   95
and I lie on the ground instead of a soft bed.
    Yet these are small matters; great fear
about what might happen tomorrow tears at my soul
as it recalls the barbarians' bloodthirsty heart
and the robbers' harsh pitilessness   100
and fierce appearance.
For perhaps when the robber chief sees the girl
he will immediately succumb to the fire of love
and will kindle a burning flame in his heart
and will force Rhodanthe into marriage.   105
And if that happens, there is death for Dosikles,
slain either by the barbarian's sword
or by the intervention of his own hand.
If it does not, then there is death for the maiden Rhodanthe,
for barbarians are hot for love   110
and when thwarted quick to turn to murder.
    Perhaps I would survive the violence,
whether Mistylos accursedly orders
the wretched prisoner Dosikles
to endure chains or the penalty of beating,   115
for I am a man and reared in battles
and I have often contended in unnumbered struggles.

13 Marginal gloss: 'Dosikles' lament'. Cf. Charikles' lament at *D&C* 1.230. This could perhaps be considered an *ethopoiia* (a *progymnasma*, rhetorical exercise, to express what might have been said in a hypothetical situation, in this case: 'What a young man might say on being captured by pirates'), but see discussion at Roilos 2005: 83. This is a lament over present circumstances, as at 3.409–85, 7.17–160.

But how will Rhodanthe endure the pain,
a woman accustomed to a secluded chamber and delicate living,
tender flesh, liable to every disease   120
if the slightest reason arises?
   You endure all this, maiden Rhodanthe,
you endure all this for the sake of Dosikles.
You sleep on the ground and, worn down by hunger,
even so you have Dosikles on your lips.   125
You call out frequently with the appearance of slumber
and you demand that your dreams bring in your slumbers
one vision only, the semblance of Dosikles.
It was I, maiden, who caused you to fall in
with painful fates and dreadful misfortunes;   130
how can you love your foe Dosikles?"
   While the young man was bewailing in this way,[14]
a youth, goodly in appearance, stood beside him;
he had been captured earlier, I think, and imprisoned previously.
And addressing him and seating himself nearby,   135
the prisoner Kratandros, a Hellene from Cyprus,
said, "Cease your groans, stranger,
restrain your floods of tears now.
You have been banished from your own country: bear up,
for you have us who have been banished with you.   140
You are restrained through the greed of harsh robbers:
we have all been restrained by the barbarians' weapons.
You dwell in a prison: we are fellow prisoners.
Indeed and indeed, to share miseries
brings comfort to the sufferer,   145
lightens the burden of pain
and quenches the furnace of distress,
sprinkling the water of consolation.[15]
Cease grieving and weeping at length
(for floods of tears are fit for women)   150
and recount your unfortunate fate,
for you will[16] tell it to a yet more unfortunate man."

14 Marginal gloss: 'Recognition and friendship between Kratandros and Dosikles'.
  15 Sententious moralizing is a feature of novels ancient and medieval; e.g. *L&K* 7.2.3; Hel
1.9; *DigAk* G1.202 (cf. Odorico 1989); and other passages in this text, e.g. 3.135–36.
  16 Translating (with Conca 1994) the mss' εἴπῃς rather than εἴποις (Marcovich 1992).

"A Hellene, saviour gods, this stranger is
a Hellene,"[17] said Dosikles. "But, stranger,
you should rather tell your story first,   155
for perhaps by telling it you will excise the pain
and relieve me of long lamentations."
    "I shall not begrudge[18] telling of my fortunes,"[19]
said Kratandros as be began in his turn.
"I had, Dosikles, Cyprus for my homeland,   160
Kraton as my progenitor, Stale as my mother.
Neighbour to me was the maiden Chrysochroe,
child of Androkles and daughter of Myrtale.
I succumbed to her (for there is no shame to say this
to a fellow sufferer, to one who desires, to a young man),   165
and when I succumbed I revealed the flame that burnt
in my breast to the girl through a messenger.
The girl listened, and gave heed to my plea
and assured me of marriage to her.
    So the appointed evening was fixed   170
on which I was to come to the girl's chamber
and give my pledge and receive pledges;
when I approached the gate at the entrance,
I opened the doors which were shut,
drawing back their wooden bolt,   175
and putting forward a quiet foot
I hastened to make my way to Chrysochroe.
    But I did not escape the attention of the door-keeper Brya,[20]
for she promptly roused her master Androkles
from his bed with an incessant babbling,   180
and her accursed fellow servants too,
and they all immediately rushed off to catch
the escaping intruder and kill him with clubs and stones.

17 Given that Prodromos is writing at the time when there are the first glimmerings of a revived Hellenic ethnic consciousness (see, e.g., Magdalino 1991; Beaton 2007), it is tempting to add this (with *R&D* 1.136 above) to the list of significant examples.

18 Translating (with Dawe 2001a: 12) φθονοῖμι for the φθάνοιμι ('be able') of the manuscripts.

19 Marginal gloss: 'Kratandros' narrative of his adventures'.

20 While one may think that this is an example of twelfth-century domestic practice, guardians (of houses and daughters) are well attested in late antique texts; cf. *L&K* 2.23.5–6 and epigrams (e.g. *AnthGr* 5.262, 290 [Paul the Silentiary], 289 [Agathias]).

One clasped in his hands a club
or rather one or other of the doorposts,   185
another dug up the house or tore it apart
and seized a hand-sized stone in both his hands,
all – armed with whatever they chanced on –
threatened noisy violence to this disturber of the night.
    And nowhere chancing on Kratandros[21]   190
(would that they had; what point is there in my continuing to live?),
their good aim was a mis-hit at the maiden.
For Lestias' ill-judged fist,
hoping for Kratandros,
miserably slew – alas, alas – the miserable Chrysochroe,   195
shattering her head with a huge stone.
And when light dawned in the house
and those present were appalled at the sight
(for how could they not be appalled and terrified
who had slain their own mistress?)   200
they all immediately with one voice together
cried out, they wailed in their consternation
and they summoned Androkles, the girl's begetter,
to see his daughter without breath,
ascribing the murder to Kratandros.   205
    And so the father rent his garments,
cut a lock of hair from his head,
sprinkled dust on his head,
tore at his cheeks,
cast his face into mourning   210
and wretchedly began pitiful dirges, saying:
    'Alas, my daughter, alas, my little one,[22]
so untimely taken from our midst.
My child, offspring of a wretched parent,
you have gone from here through the envy of accursed Fate,[23]   215

21 Marginal gloss: 'Murder of Chrysochroe'.
22 Marginal gloss: 'Androkles' lament over Chrysochroe'. A lament, this time on an actual death.
23 Fate and the Olympian deities are part of the trappings taken over with the genre; how they relate to Prodromos' own Christianity is an interesting question; see Roilos 2005: 271–74 on examples of Prodromos ridiculing the ancient mythology, and cf. Harder 2000; Kaldellis 2007: 7 and 2007a: 271–76.

unwed, unescorted; you have not even glimpsed the bridal
chamber, nor has your progenitor
lit the bridal torch for you
nor has he begun the eloquent bridal hymn,
but the grace of your countenance has been harvested   220
in the bloom of spring-time, and the mortal-devouring Fate
did not wait for the harvest to come.
    O adornment of your mother, heart of your father,
tree of lovely hues, comely, lovely, great,
blooming to no avail, adorned to no purpose   225
— what savage beast,[24] what fiercely roaring lion
emerged from the copse and appeared from the mountain,
its mane bristling, its neck hunched,
and swiftly charged to cut you down in your immaturity?
I had hopes, now to be unfulfilled,   230
to find repose beneath your shade,
to find shelter beneath your fair branches,
but now all that has been miserably overturned
and has undergone a grim alteration.
    And even if the mode of death was natural   235
or[25] you released a most moving sigh
in a true father's embrace,
I would have lamented greatly
(for how could a loving father not do this,
seeing the doom of his dear and only daughter?),
but there would have been an end to the tears   240
and I would have put a limit on the anguish,
for I would have found comfort for my groans
in the natural and normal nature of the suffering.
But now my Chrysochroe's death
is alien to all natural ties,   245
it is quite foreign to the common law.
Where is the beauty of your face, maiden?
Your head has been shattered by a stone,
besmirched with streams of blood

24 Wild beasts also threaten the heroine in *H&H* (10.11.4) and *DigAk* G6.45–102, E1098–
138; cf. MangProd 47.112, 55.12, on the marriage of the emperor Manuel's niece to a 'wild
beast from the West' (E. and M. Jeffreys 2001).
25 Translating (with Conca 1994) the mss' ἤ rather than καὶ ('and'; Marcovich 1992).

is your beauty, your countenance, your seemly bearing   250
and your mortal form is distorted.
    O accursed Kratandros, all-daring insolence,
implacable robber, savage-souled being,
how could you destroy such a maiden
by stealth, craftily, wilfully, heartlessly?   255
I am amazed and astonished
that the rock did not turn back on itself
(having acquired a natural understanding)
to kill the thrower with a just judgment,
but it wilfully struck Chrysochroe.   260
And you, despoiler and slayer of the girl,
may you undergo a deserved death in the future,
when I shall weep with a fitting lament
and I shall enclose the maiden in her tomb
(for you will not be able to despoil the laws   265
or to batter with a stone those who make judgment),
and having slain my daughter
with a dreadful blow from a most accursed stone,
you – unhappy one – will expire pitiably, crushed by stones.'
    While Androkles was thus groaning deeply,   270
I listened to his grim dirge[26]
as I stood hidden behind the door.
Then I returned to my father's abode
and, flinging myself headlong onto my bed
and setting up a bitter wailing from deep within,   275
I began a counter-dirge to her father's for the girl,
saying: 'Alas, august image, maiden,[27]
beauty that can entice the gods
and draw the planets from their orbits
and lure all to desire it;   280
you have departed before your time, maiden Chrysochroe,
leaving Kratandros a living corpse;
you have departed, a lovely sight for those who behold it
and a salutary omen for those who look on you.
You have died, alas, and you have gone before your time,   285

26 'dirge': cf. *D&C* 2.35 and note.
27 Marginal gloss: 'Kratandros' lament over Chrysochroe'. Again a lament on a death
(rather than the speaker's misfortunes).

and now (woe for the inhumanity of Fate)
I have been the cause of your death, maiden.
For when the accursed and evil Lestias
threatened to slay me,
you caught too soon the rock-borne death, 290
harshly dying in place of your beloved.
   Alas, wretched father of a wretched daughter,
it is I who have deprived your offspring,
your maiden, of life and dear existence.
Accuse me of your daughter's death, 295
summon me to the tribunal and seek judgment,
drawing me, dragging me to the lawgivers' houses,
demanding the penalty deemed right by the laws.
It is generally decreed, as you have just said,
that he who strikes with stones should be struck with stones. 300
I myself would yearn for death by stoning
since Chrysochroe died from a stone.
Let the hand of Lestias alone slay me,
which accursedly killed the maiden.
Do not be slow to charge me with murder; 305
for I long to go to where Chrysochroe is.
Since the bonds of the marriage partnership
did not join Kratandros to your maiden,
let death at least join the unhappy ones
in a pitiful union of wretched partnership.' 310
   And so on and so forth up to this point.
Indeed on the ninth day[28]
the unfortunate progenitor of the dead girl
put aside his mourning, checked his tears,
went to the tribunal and the home of the lawgivers, 315
and summoned me, the murderer, to judgment.
   And when both parties were present[29]
(I with Kraton and Stale on one side,
and opposite were Myrtale and Androkles),

---

28 The ninth day after a death was the day for traditional funerary sacrifices, cf. the (non-Christian) Latin 'sacra novendialia' (*OCD*, under 'Dead, attitudes to'); twelfth-century Christian practices would have involved commemorative rituals on the third, ninth and fortieth days (*ODB*, under 'Burial').

29 Marginal gloss: 'Trial between Kraton and Androkles over Chrysochroe'.

Androkles first of us all spoke thus: 320
    'Gentlemen of the jury, advocates of the honourable,[30]
councillors of Justice and upholders of the gods,
it was honourable for me, yes, honourable and fitting
to live always within myself,
for I considered silence and contemplation of my own fate   325
more admirable than public oratory,
not because one would be undertaking a dishonourable task
(for what can be more blessed than justice?),
but judging that the hullabaloo engendered by a law-suit
is to be avoided, detested and abominated.   330
Since the dice[31] of mischievous Fate
has been cast otherwise and fallen adversely
and has forced me towards abominations
and summons me unwillingly to the tribunal and trial,
despite my abstention from public life,   335
behold, I am present at the tribunal and make my speech.
    I had a daughter named Chrysochroe,
beautiful in appearance, yes, beautiful and a maiden,
already prepared for the bridal chamber
and made ready for the marriage yoke.   340
But this robber has killed her with a stone,
entering my house by night.
So now he is present, and let him suffer due chastisement
for the murder by which he impiously wronged us.
Let him at least suffer a rock-borne death,   345
the miserable fellow who threw a stone at the miserable girl.'
    I rushed forward when he had spoken this
to join my own accusation to the accuser's speech
and to call the event to witness against myself,[32]
but Kraton seized the opening before me: 350
    'Gentlemen,' he said, 'revered lawgivers,[33]
it is, I think, proper and in conformity with the laws

---

30 1.321–89: An example of forensic or judicial rhetoric, irrelevant to Byzantine practice
but well known to a twelfth-century writer from examples from classical antiquity; see Cooper
2007.
    31 The reference to dice emphasizes the chance nature of Chyrsochroe's death.
    32 The motif of self-accusation also occurs in Charit 1.5.4–5 and Hel 8.8.4–5.
    33 Marginal gloss: 'Kraton's defence'.

to hear each of the sides
over which divine judgement[34] is to pronounce,
and afterwards to cast the appropriate vote. 355
So now, having received Androkles' words,
accept mine and judge me.
    The murderer (as it seems to Androkles)
came forth from my unfortunate loins,
having lived till this very moment a life of good quality, 360
untainted with murder and free from rapine
and everything shameful and abominated by the laws
(or has anyone laid any such accusations against him?).
Since the august, the generous Androkles,
who cherishes silence and the tranquil life, 365
loving this in more than moderation,
has spewed forth[35] many words against us,
stretching his lips and widening his mouth
as though forgetting silence,
and since he brings a fabricated charge of murder against Kratandros 370
and denounces those who are free of evil,
let fire be brought and judge the case
and provide a complete verdict for us.
    I call to witness the inquisitorial flame
and Selene,[36] the maiden goddess, 375
that Kratandros has no part in the murder.
But let the temple attendants be present,[37]
let them light the fire seven times more fierce than usual.[38]
Behold, let Kratandros step into the midst of the flame
and if he is a ravisher and tainted with murder, 380
let him be fuel for the fire and let him die
(for I hate my son if he is convicted of murder).
If he is no murderer, let him come out untouched by the flames.'

34 Conca (1994: 83, n. 15) points out that justice emanates from the sovereign, who in Byzantine society is vice-gerent of God.

35 Cf. Psalms 44.2, 118.171.

36 This is Selene, the moon goddess, in her most sinister guise as Selene-Hekate, goddess of death (*OCD*, under 'Hecate').

37 1.377–89: For tests by fire, not a Byzantine practice, cf. Hel 10.8–9 (though as a test for chastity, not judicial innocence); for contemporary western parallels, see Cupane 1973–74.

38 Cf. Daniel 3.19 for this phrase, and Daniel 3.19–24 for the episode of the youths unscathed in the fiery furnace.

Kraton's fiercely shouted words
were acceptable to the lawgivers.   385
So the temple attendants lit the fire
and requested the murderer to enter it.
When I went into the middle of the flame,
I trod on the fire and stayed within it, unburnt."
    "You talk of a strange and wonderful matter,"[39]   390
said Dosikles, "if the fire perceived
that you had not committed a murder and did not consume you."
"It was not the fire's but the divinity's deed,"
replied Kratandros; "when I had suffered no harm,
Kraton, taking the stand and his courage,   395
'See,' he said, 'revered lawgivers,
how the fire has made a right judgement
and contains within itself unburnt and unscorched
the young man who is unsullied by murder;
it has condemned, as it were, his accuser.'   400
At that with one voice together
the crowd that was present at the trial called out
and abused the accuser Androkles,
and applauded us with laudatory speeches.
    When this gathering had broken up   405
I went with Kraton to the house,
and being unable to endure living and existing among Cypriots
from whose midst Chrysochroe's beauty had been extinguished,
I resolved to move further afield and make my escape.
And so, going down to the sea at night[40]   410
and immediately finding there a cargo-vessel
about to loosen her prow-cables,
I embarked on her and set off on my flight.
    The morning star was already rising from the world below
and illuminating with its rays   415
the tips of the mountain peaks[41]
when the barbarian fleet drew near.
It captured the vessel with its cargo and crew
as it made its unfortunate voyage,

---

39 Marginal gloss: 'Dosikles speaks'.
40 Marginal gloss: 'Kratandros' flight'.
41 Cf. Hel 1.1.1 and *D&C* 1.1–2 for parallel phrasing and scene-setting.

having already looted a thousand ships.[42] 420
Thereupon it went back towards its[43] own country,
having shut the captives in nether hell
(as I call this cell common to us both),
and turned to a second bout of pillage.
Such are my affairs, fellow prisoner and stranger. 425
Now you tell me of your fate."
"Now is not the time," said Dosikles, "for me to speak,
but if you like, we will curl our legs up on the ground
and relieve our great pains with sleep,
for we are now at the third cock-crow."[44] 430
    So the strangers Dosikles and Kratandros[45]
reclined on the ground as on a soft bed
and partook of sleep until the sun rose.
Mistylos (for he was the robber chief)
came out of his own lodging at dawn 435
and ordered the barbarians under his command
to bring out the imprisoned captives.
Gobryas went into the prison
and immediately brought out all those who were inside
and presented them to the emperor Mistylos. 440
    The robber chief saw Dosikles,
and then saw Rhodanthe immediately afterwards.
He could not have been more astonished,
for both were so handsome in appearance.
Astounded by the grace of their countenances, 445
"This lovely couple," he said,
"and this man", pointing to Kratandros,
"take them back to prison, Gobryas.
I shall make them temple attendants on the gods.
This snivelling old man 450
(weeping all the time for fear of being executed),"

42 Marginal gloss: 'Capture'.

43 Translating (with Conca 1994) the mss' τὴν rather than σὴν ('your'; Marcovich 1992).

44 Although this echoes Matthew 14.30, 14.71 and 26.34, 75 (Peter and the betrayal of Christ), it is difficult to see its relevance to this scene: a meaningless reflection of a familiar phrase?

45 Marginal gloss: 'Dream'. Despite the rubric, though Dosikles and Kratandros sleep they do not dream.

pointing to Stratokles, "send him back to his own country,
freed from a slave's bitter fate.
Those four huddled over there,
whose appearance shows them to be sailors,   455
kill them and pour their blood out as a libation to the gods.
Those who are saved by the providence of the gods
and return to their own city
should sacrifice a thank-offering to those who have saved them.
It is always pleasing to the gods of the ocean   460
to drink the blood of seafaring sailors.
All others, if they have been ransomed by their progenitors
or brothers or loving children,
let them return to their own countries,
or else let them experience a slave's fate."   465
    Having given these orders to Gobryas, Mistylos
turned his attention to the division of the spoils,
and bestowed twice ten *minai* on each man,
taking a fourfold amount for himself ahead of all the others
(for this was his custom in the division),   470
and every image of the gods on Rhodes
he rededicated in the temple of Selene.
    So on Gobryas' instructions Stratokles
was sent on his way to his home
and the quartet of luckless sailors   475
died, slaughtered by Gobryas' sword,
having first shed a bitter tear
for their fathers, their children and their spouses.
One bewailed a wretched infant,
tiny, new-born and still nursing;   480
another wept for his aged father,
he cried out, he wailed loudly;
another pitifully lamented his wife,
the lovely young bride of a young groom.
    But Nausikrates, staunchly, without a tear,[46]   485
hastened to his slaughter as though to a symposium,
saying with a joyful heart,
"Greetings, banquets and symposia of this life

---

46 Marginal gloss: 'Death of Nausikrates'.

and the delicacies of the table.
Nausikrates has had his fill of you   490
and goes gladly to the abode of Hades,
and will investigate the symposia of the dead
and will view the festivities of the underworld."
Thus he spoke and he inclined his neck,
"Come hither, Gobryas," he said, "thrust your sword in me.   495
See, Nausikrates is ready for the slaughter."
And Gobryas stretched out his sword
and pitifully slew the fair Nausikrates.
Those who were present then at those deeds
were all astounded by the dead man   500
and by his undaunted heart.
    But without Dosikles Kratandros
would not return once more to the prison,
nor would he without the beloved girl.
And Kratandros said to Dosikles,   505
"What befalls us is in the care of the gods
(yes, Dosikles, everything is the gods' concern);
you must tell me of your fates,
and bring your promise to its conclusion."
"You are asking from me, fellow temple attendant[47] and stranger,   510
weeping, I know, and floods of tears,"
said Dosikles as he spoke not without tears,
"for you bring recollection of things long past.
Yet (for what may we endure at a friend's request?),
my story may take its beginning from this point.   515

---

47 Reading the mss' συννεωκόϱε (with Conca 1994) rather than συννεώτεϱε ('fellow young man'; Marcovich 1992).

THE SECOND BOOK OF THE DEEDS OF RHODANTHE
AND DOSIKLES BY THE SAME WRITER

The luminary star[48] had just arrayed[49]
its own lamps in the middle of the day
when we sailed safely close by
the harbour of Rhodes with favourable fates
(thus it seemed and was judged by the crew)   5
and we moored the ship in the harbour,
the ship all but battered at the entrance
and broken to pieces and plunged to the bottom.
For the inner parts of the harbour are safe
– there is no tumult from the waves, no peaks and clefts   10
(for the one rises up against the other
in a dense tumult and frequent subsidence,
the peaks cleaving open responsively
and the clefts rising against the peaks),
nor does an interacting rivalry of conflicting winds   15
agitate the current and churn the vessels.
Yet there is one approach only to the entrance,
narrow in its passage and enclosed by rocks.
With difficulty could one of the largest ships
enter unharmed and pass through the opening.[50]   20
    However our ship moored well,
unaffected by evil, safe and sound,
thanks to the skill of the captain Stratokles.
And then, tying the cables at the prow
and fastening the ship with stout anchors,   25
we immediately made for Rhodes, leaving two sailors
only as protection for the vessel.
Stratokles, the ship's commander,
took us to the house of a merchant he knew.
Leaving us outside the gate, on his own he   30
went inside and spoke to his friend
who, amazed at this unexpected sight,
responded to his friend Stratokles

---

48 'luminary star': the sun.
49 Marginal gloss: 'Dosikles' narrative to Kratandros about his own deeds'.
50 2.6–20: This is an accurate description of the harbour at Rhodes.

and clasped him cheerfully round the neck
and, 'Welcome, best of merchants,' 35
he said questioningly, 'Are your babies well,
my good Stratokles? Is Panthia in good health?'
  'A kindly fortune directs my life,[51]
friend Glaukon,' replied Stratokles,
'and oversees all other matters well; 40
but my son Agathosthenes has died
a pitiful death, for the roof fell in on him.'[52]
He made this reply and, groaning deeply,
he shed hot teardrops
as he recalled Agathosthenes. 45
'Tomorrow, accompanied by us,'
said Glaukon, 'you will make a sacrifice
to your dead son of drink offerings, a dedication of tears and libations.
But now call your companions here
to share our hearth with us 50
and to break bread together.'[53]
He ended his speech
and called his wife Myrtipnoe,
saying 'Wife, lay out a banquet,
set up the table in the garden room[54] 55
and invite Stratokles' friends to dine.'
  So we entered at Myrtipnoe's request.
But although Rhodanthe was famished
she did not go in, inhibited by modesty.
With a gesture of her hand she summoned me and said, 60
'Husband, you are well aware of my fate
(for I call my dear Dosikles husband,
although it is not the marriage rite and marriage chamber that have
    united us,
nor the bridal union nor a single couch
nor the conjunction of mutual embraces, 65

51 Marginal gloss: 'Stratokles' reply to his friend Glaukon'.

52 Reminiscent of *Ptochoprodromika* 1.206–12 (Eideneier 1991), where the neighbours rescue a child fallen from a roof.

53 Literally, 'join in the present salt', a proverbial expression for a communal festive meal (cf. 2.92, 9.62)

54 Dining tables in private houses in both late antique and Byzantine society were movable (Oikonomides 1990; Parani 2003: 73–76); cf. *D&C* 7.330.

but a solemn relationship and desire without passion
and the pure bond of bodies that are not linked);
husband, you are well aware of my fate,
for I am both wife and maiden,
and have been shielded from every man's gaze,   70
especially from that of someone completely unknown,
lest anyone should too passionately cast
a demeaning eye on me with unkind intent.
How, Dosikles, can I enter that door
and – a woman on her own – join in a meal with so many men?'[55]   75
    'You have made a very reasonable point,'
I said holding back a little, 'august maiden.
You give me pledges of your passion,
correct, manifest, sure and well-founded
and you introduce the prospect of unkind suspicions,   80
But now come to eat (for what can happen to you?),
since Myrtipnoe invites us.
Otherwise you who are used to
the most luxurious of delicacies at table,
how will you survive without food all day,   85
when, what is more, your body is exhausted
by sorrow, toil and sea-sickness?'
    So the girl was persuaded and we went in.
Seeing everyone coming in, Dryas,
Glaukon's son, a well set-up young man,   90
said, 'Greetings, friends of Stratokles,[56]
and join in our meal together.'[57]
So saying, he brought everyone into the garden
where Myrtipnoe had arranged that we should eat.
And so Glaukon got up from the couch[58]   95

55 Cf. Drosilla's hesitation at *D&C* 6.196, the Girl's in *DigAk* G4.809–11, E1043–46 when she lacks her customary escort, and Kekavmenos' attitude to his women-folk, that they should be kept from public view (*Strategikon* 39; Tsoungarakis 1995). On the legal context for appropriate female behaviour, see Laiou 1993; for some literary interpretations see Garland 1990; Burton 2000.

56 For a discussion of the comic elements, literary antecedents and contemporary references in this banqueting scene, in particular for Nausikrates' dance, see Roilos 2005: 246–52.

57 Here again the phrase used refers to eating salt (cf. 2.51, 9.62).

58 Marginal gloss: 'Glaukon's dinner'. On the significance of 'couch' or 'seat' and Byzantine eating arrangements, see Grosdidier de Matons 1979, especially in connection with

and spoke to us and honoured us with seats.
He was at the head, in the chief place,
seated together with his friend the merchant.
Immediately below them was Myrtipnoe on the right,
and with her Rhodanthe, and the third   100
was Myrtipnoe's daughter, the maiden Kallichroe.
We were opposite, below Stratokles,
I next to him and a little lower Dryas,
and the third with us was the sailor Nausikrates.
This was the arrangement of the seating,   105
and everyone was dining on magnificent provender,[59]
singing sweetly under Stratokles' direction
as he tunefully began a splendid song.
Immediately Nausikrates got up from the symposium
and began a somewhat nautical dance.   110
    For some Stratokles' tune was sweet,
but for me it was Rhodanthe's mouth that was lovely;
and lovely was Stratokles' voice
as it came to Rhodanthe's ears.
For others Nausikrates' twistings and turnings   115
were more desirable than the melody,
a little rustic perhaps (for it was only Nausikrates!),
but not lacking in humour and charm;
but for me it was Rhodanthe's complexion that was lovely.
Some praised the Rhodian wine,   120
saying that it was sweet to taste and sweet to drink,
but I praised it repeatedly
for coming near to Rhodanthe's mouth,
or I thought the cup most blessed
for touching Rhodanthe's lovely lip.[60]   125
Why should I say more or why should I go on?

---

examples in *H&H* 1.6 (cf. also *D&C* 8.246); see also Plepelits 1996: 153–54, n. 15. By the
tenth century the Roman custom of dining in a reclining position was preserved as a conscious
piece of antiquarianism in the ceremonial of the Great Palace while folding chairs or stools
were normal in domestic environments.

59 At this point Marcovich 1992 postulates an (unnecessary) lacuna, in which there will
have been a transition from the dinner to the symposium; but note *L&K* 2.91 where dinner and
symposium are also elided.

60 A motif frequent in epigrams (cf. *AnthGr* 6.171 [Meleager], 261 [Agathias], 295
[Leontius]), as well as other twelfth-century texts (e.g. *D&C* 9.207–11; *H&H* 3.11).

I envied the cup repeatedly
for touching such lips.
For others Dryas, a handsome young man, was desirable,
his chin wreathed with its first down,   130
his skin white, his hair golden
and his curly locks reaching down to his shoulders,
in every respect august and beautiful in his appearance;
but for me Dryas was handsome because of his seat
opposite such a maiden.   135
Some said that Glaukon and Myrtipnoe
were incredible in their hospitality,
but for me the couple were incredible
for the hospitality they gave to such a maiden.
    Such was the banquet's good cheer,   140
but the gentle lad Dryas,
overcome by an unwarranted passion for Rhodanthe,
jumped up in a frenzy and seized the wine bowl,
and mixed a pleasant cup for the guests to drink.
Coming up to Rhodanthe like one possessed,   145
he took a sip from the bowl first and gave it to the girl.[61]
The maiden, recognizing his mischief-making,
returned the dish to Dryas,
but pretended her heart was afflicted.
The young man having done this and received this response,   150
'These well-born young people,' Glaukon said,
to cover up Dryas' tipsy foolishness,
'Stratokles, my friend, where are you taking them, and from where
        have they come?
And from what country are they, and from what family?'
'Let them say,' replied Stratokles,   155
'who they are, from where, where they are going, their circumstances
        and their country.'
And so, turning the conversation to us,
'Strangers,' he said, 'describe your circumstances,
while this good man Glaukon listens.'
    So, briefly clenching my lips,   160

---

61 Flirting over cups of wine at banquets is again a motif found in both late antique and
Byzantine texts (e.g. *L&K* 2.9.2; Longos 3.8.2; *H&H* 3.9), but may indicate Prodromos'
awareness of the scene in *H&H*.

I groaned deeply and responded, 'O Stratokles,
the banquet and the festivity and the mirth –
do you really want to turn these to groans?
And the fair cup of mixed wine,
do you want to fill it with boundless tears?'   165
Glaukon reacted to these words;
'You may speak of your and the girl's experiences,
Dosikles, my child,' he said, weeping a little,
'for it seems that you will tell of bitter fortunes.'
    And then I began to speak.[62]   170
'Abydos is my country, friend Glaukon.
My father is Lysippos, son of Euphrates,
a great general; the maiden's father is Straton.
My mother is Philinna, the girl's Phryne.
Straton, her father whom I have just mentioned,   175
enclosed her in a little tower,[63]
so that she should remain difficult for men to see,
and he did not think it right for her to go out from her prison
except when the girl's soiled flesh
had need of a bath and a cleansing stream.[64]   180
So Straton protected her in this way,
so that she should escape an admirer's curious gaze,
but she could not escape that of Dosikles.
For I was hurrying on one occasion along a path at random,
when the day was already drawing to a close,   185
and behold, there was Rhodanthe being taken to the bath
with an escort and myriads of attendants.
Seeing her, I came near, and coming near I asked
the girls following her who the maiden was and who her parents were;
I learnt they were Straton and Phryne.   190

62 Marginal gloss: 'Dosikles' tale to Glaukon about his experiences'.

63 The enclosed heroine may have literary antecedents in, e.g., Mousaios 187–92 but this became a social reality (cf. Kekaumenos 39, and discussion at *R&D* 2.74–75), a Byzantine cliché (cf. *DigAk* G4.496–99, *L&Ra* and the Argyrokastron), and the subject of later Greek folk songs (e.g. 'The abduction of the king's daughter', part of the Akritic cycle; Spyridakis 1962: 10–15).

64 Large public baths were an integral part of social life in late antiquity but the evidence for twelfth-century Byzantium is ambiguous: monastic establishments regularly contained bath-houses, used with varying degrees of frequency (Thomas and Hero 2000: xxvii and Index), while the satirical *Ptochoprodromika* indicate occasional use of bath-houses by both men and women (1.62, 3.63, 4.90–91; Eideneier 1991); see *ODB*, under 'Baths'.

And so, with my heart shattered as if by a weapon
(for I recognized the maiden by this account,
having heard previously that Straton
was blessed with a very lovely daughter),
I went away, wounded, to my own house,   195
and when Lysippos was asleep (for it was night),
leaving the dinner, the wine bowl and the drinking,
I went to my bed, intending to sleep.
But sleep would not settle on my eyes,
nor did night, that gate-keeper of the gates of sight,   200
make fast my eyelids.
But under the onslaught of conflicting thoughts
I was frantically at odds with myself
and although no grim armies were attacking
I turned the battle on myself.   205
    'Beautiful Rhodanthe, yes, beautiful and a maiden.[65]
August is the motion of your gait,
upright your posture, neat and slender,
like a clinging vine, a young cypress.
Rhodanthe is beautiful: how great is a passion for the beautiful.   210
I am in love with Rhodanthe (what is strange in that?), a beautiful girl.
I desire Rhodanthe (the maiden is well born),
the daughter of Straton, a wealthy man,
a man of significance, and the daughter of Phryne,
a respectable woman, well favoured and comely.   215
I desire beauty, that most beautiful goal for mankind;
beauty is divine and grace is god-given.
Who is so blind, who so despoiled of his wits,
who so ungrateful for the gods' divine gift
that he cannot honour and take possession of beauty?   220
    If only I had conversed with the maiden!
If only she had been led to notice my reaction
and to give a pledge and receive another!
If only the wick from the coals within me
had kindled Rhodanthe's heart!   225
Or perhaps Rhodanthe had often experienced,

---

65 2.206–315: Another instance of an *ethopoiia*: 'What a young man might say when seeing
a beautiful girl'; cf. 3.189–276 (Mistylos to Gobryas). See Roilos 2005: 63–88 on the nature of
ethopoiia, with special reference to this example.

as she beheld me passing nearby,
what I had felt at the sight of her?
Or perhaps she was nurturing deep within her a spark of desire
or, as I met her and looked at her, 230
she had judged me from a mere brief glimpse,
unworthy of further consideration?
   Certainly both the maiden's parents are of good standing,
but neither is my family of ill repute.
Straton is, I know, honourable and of the highest rank, 235
burgeoning with wealth, respected in the council
and the greatest in the city's deliberations.
But in family, respect and good fortune Lysippos
does not take second place to Straton, nor is Philinna
my mother less well-born than Phryne. 240
Time would not have the power
to wipe away so quickly from our midst
Lysippos' many commands
and his many efforts in so many battles,
and submerge them in the abyss and obliteration of oblivion.[66] 245
   Rhodanthe's complexion is beautiful;
for it is not possible to remove or add anything
from its excellent and perfect composition,
for the geometer Nature had constructed it
beautifully and according to the rules.[67] 250
But neither is my face besmirched,
nor is my appearance strange and repulsive.
For masculine beauty has a different quality of steadiness,
powerful strength, bravery in battle,
unshakeable might, a sturdy right arm, 255
a steadfast resistance in the face of battle,
a blade reddened with enemies' blood,
a sword satiated with hostile flesh.
If someone were to make a judgment on beauty by masculine
    standards,

66 To rescue events from oblivion is the regular claim of Byzantine historians (as well as those of the ancient world), in the twelfth century most notably Anna Komnene (e.g. *Alexiad*, Prologos 1).

67 On the rhetorical *topos* behind this phrase see the discussion in Cupane 1984 with a parallel to *D&C* 1.147–49.

he would consider me handsome to look at.[68]   260
For often in many battles
I have received gloriously many crowns.
The bronze-dipped tip of my dagger has fed
on much flesh from many enemies,
has quaffed copious streams of blood,   265
and has feasted on the deaths on many barbarians.[69]
　　I have striven often in many sea-battles
and I have been enlisted in as many battles on dry land.
I know how to command, how to marshall infantry,
to set up ambushes and evade ambushes,   270
to excavate trenches and invest cities,
to block trenches and overthrow cities,
to rally troops and disperse troops,
to demolish walls' lofty heights,
to rebuild walls' shattered heights,   275
to bring up battering-rams, to demolish towers,
in brief, all the arts of generalship,
with my father as an excellent tutor.[70]
This is sufficient to persuade Straton and Phryne
to give in marriage union   280
Rhodanthe the bride to the bridegroom Dosikles.
　　But if Straton does not want this connection,
what dew can I find to quench this fire?[71]
Should I boldly approach the maiden's house
by night and apply force?   285
But, falling on her unexpectedly as she lies asleep,
how should I not alarm and terrify the girl?

---

68 Retaining the mss sequence of lines, and not following Marcovich 1992 in placing
259–60 after 252.

69 The contrasting male and female attributes of the preceding lines reflect the values of
twelfth-century aristocratic Byzantium (Laiou 1992: 92–97), and find parallels in the marriage
songs of, e.g., Theodore Prodromos for the son of Nikephoros Phorbenos (Hörandner 1974:
no. 43), and Manganeios Prodromos, no. 32 for Eirene, granddaughter of the *sevastokratorissa*
Eirene, and no. 33 for Theodora, daughter of the Caesar Roger (Magdalino 1993: 496).

70 2.269–78: This reads like an exercise in the deployment of military vocabulary, in
contrast to the more subtle Homeric vocabulary of 2.255–56 above.

71 From Romanos the Melode to John of Damascus and beyond, Byzantine writers
and hymnographers found the furnace of Daniel 3.50 and its quenching a fruitful source of
metaphor; e.g. in this text 2.349–50, 8.219; and *D&C* 3.320, 9.90–92; cf. Roilos 2005: 268–69.

She would let out a shriek, she would call for Phryne,
who would call for Straton, who would call for the mob,
and would capture the rapist Dosikles. 290
Or[72] else he will not be able to catch me easily
and he will denounce the assault to Lysippos,
who would be full of rage and stirred to anger,
and I would gain my father's fury
and lose all hope of marriage with Rhodanthe. 295
   Do you feel anything too, my sweet maiden?
Do you feel anything for me, are you pained in your heart?
Do you too burn from the fiery darts of passion?
Are you deprived of sleep, do you refuse food?
Are your entrails aflame, do you weep for your lover? 300
Do you call for Dosikles and have his name on your lips,
or perhaps you are unaware of my existence, O maiden?
If the bitter goads of love
you flee quite unwounded,
and you are shielded from the gaze of every man, 305
and you despise words of love
and you reject relationships and passion
and you hate any discourse with males,
the evil must be endured – for it is not directed at Dosikles
(though Dosikles is among those loathed). 310
But if without due thought you prefer another to me
and you have pledged him marriage with yourself,
then either break your pledges to him for my sake
or Dosikles is dead. For I shall thrust
the sword into my bowels and my heart.' 315
   Tormented by so many tempestuous syllogisms[73] of this sort
and battered by conflicting gales
(like a ship without ballast in rough seas),
struggling against so many arguments,
I came at length to the second cock-crow 320
and abandoned myself to sleep.
For an overabundant influx of cares

72 Translating (with Conca 1994) the mss' ἤ rather than the emendation to εἰ ('if'; Marcovich 1992).

73 A technical term in Aristotelian logic. Prodromos' philosophical interests are attested by his commentary on the *Posterior Analaytics*; Hörandner 1974: 48; cf. MacAlister 1990: 211.

which sprinkles darkness on the upper regions
and creates, as it were, a hateful gloom
and deep night and thick murk   325
and obscures the eyes of reason,
is accustomed to bring sleep also,
but sleep that is not without fears and anguish.
   For night fashions many images
and night-hued[74] shapes from the actions   330
and thoughts of daylight, and sketches
only shadows with its shadow-painting finger,
and brings apparitions to the surface in sleep.
This indeed I experienced at that time.[75]
For I immediately saw in my sleep the girl   335
Rhodanthe, and I began to converse with her.
I told her of the heat of my love for her
and I laid bare the yearning that was within me.
And I realized that the girl was laughing at this
and her smile seemed to me to be a favourable token   340
for the passion that was in her breast.
   Thus night, pitying my suffering,
comforted me with visions in my sleep.
Night passed and day came.
And when, parting from my kindly dreams,   345
I no longer saw what I had just been seeing
(for night is a tease and sleep a jester
and dreams mock at spurious pains),
and I could find no means at all of quenching
the fire that was burning my heart,   350
I fell into my mother's embrace and,
'Mother,' I said, 'beloved mother,
save your dear son Dosikles,
save Dosikles. If you don't want to save him,
prepare him for burial with your own hands when he is dead.   355
I call to witness the grace of the Erotes

74 Translating νυκτιχϱόους with the mss (and Conca 1994), rather than μικτοχϱόους ('multi-hued; Marcovich 1992).
   75 On the role of dreams in the romances, see MacAlister 1990 and 1996: 115–64; *R&D* reflects a number of Aristotelian attitudes to the nature of dreams that were under debate in the early twelfth century.

and the image of Rhodanthe that is dear to me,
that if I am deprived of maternal compassion,
I shall plunge my sword into my bowels.'
   Weeping at this because of her maternal concerns   360
(for women are inclined to weep,
but mothers are prone to much weeping),
'My child Dosikles,' she said, 'speak cheerfully
and have confidence, for you may achieve what you have in mind.
Perhaps I have guessed the problem.   365
You are in love with Rhodanthe, by whose beauty you swear.
You are in love with Rhodanthe, whom Phryne bore
and whom Straton brought into the light of day.'
   'Alas,' I said, 'my mother's prophetic word.
I love her, Philinna, I beg you that I might take   370
her in marriage; and if I do not have her,
may I descend unwed to the abode of Hades.'
'No!' she said, 'But I shall send a message
to Straton and Phryne, Dosikles my child.
Certainly Straton will give under the laws of marriage   375
the bride Rhodanthe to the bridegroom Dosikles.
For neither Lysippos nor his father Euphrates
comes second to Straton in family,
and that I am much inferior to Phryne
no impartial judge would ever consider.'   380
   So she spoke to Charissa, a kindly serving-girl
and, sending her to Straton and Phryne,
she requested them that the marriage of Rhodanthe
to the bridegroom Dosikles should be agreed.
The girl went off and spoke to Phryne   385
(for Straton was away, harvesting grapes)
and reported Philinna's message;
she returned, the bearer of bitter tidings.
For, 'Straton,' she said, 'has arranged that at the end of the harvest
Rhodanthe's marriage with the young man   390
Panolbios, son of Klearchos, is to take place.'
   Since I had gone astray along my first path,[76]
I turned to my second device.

---

76 For the metaphor, cf. *AnthGr* 5.302 (Agathias).

What it was I am reluctant to say
for Rhodanthe would blush to hear of it,   395
but I will describe it none the less. And you, lovely maiden,
do not be angry with me for what I say,
for the host is not to be elbowed aside
when he wants to know about what has happened to you and me.
     I went off to my hunting companions,[77]   400
good young men and real friends,
saying, 'Join me in a great affray',[78]
and when they asked me what affray,
I explained about Rhodanthe and Straton and Phryne,
I talked about my devotion, I proclaimed my love   405
and my supplicatory messages to Philinna.
Interrupting my speech,
they said, 'By the gods, you are enraptured
with a lovely, yes, a very lovely girl. But be optimistic about the
     marriage.
Whoever she is and whoever her parents are,   410
let us give the maiden in marriage
to our dear friend Dosikles, as he wants,
either with the agreement of Straton and Phryne
or through the intervention of violent brigandage.'
     'Yes, yes, join me, my hunting companions,   415
in this present pursuit of the girl,'
said I to the good young men.
'For you are young and have not been able,
right up till now, to extinguish the flame of passion.
And if this is so now, there is fear for the future.   420
For Eros wields an irresistible force;
for he is old, even if he thinks like an infant;[79]

77 Marginal gloss: 'The abduction of Rhodanthe'.

78 There are analogies here to the bride-snatching that is the height of Digenis' achievements
(Ricks 1989). Perhaps as a result of heightened dynastic awareness among the aristocratic clans,
marriage legislation was much discussed in the first part of the twelfth century (Laiou 1992:
1–58); note that the emphasis in twelfth-century fiction on marriage–stealing (κλεψιγαμία; cf.
H&H 7.4.2, 11.1.2) has led Laiou (1993: 218) to speculate that a spectacular abduction may
have been behind DigAk; see also Burton 2000.

79 2.421–31: This passage draws on the images and vocabulary traditionally associated
with Eros in the Greek classical tradition, and reappears also H&H 2.10–11, 3.3; D&C 2.135,
3.115, 4.135–48; A&K fr. 95.1; close literary antecedents can be found in Lucian, Dialogue of

he is in a rage, even if he seems to smile.
As he smiles he lets loose the violence of his weapons;
for when he fixes his bow accurately on someone,   425
he strikes right in the very heart.
He lights a flame while he jests for he holds a spark in his hands,
he sets fire to bones, he parches hearts.
He walks on foot but runs as though winged,
he encompasses everything and affects all nature,   430
every kind of swimming or winged creature, wild beasts and flocks.'
    'Stop your pointless speech, Dosikles,'[80]
they said, 'Don't be an orator
(for philosophizing is inappropriate now),
but let us consider sensibly what has to be done.'   435
So we considered and this is what seemed best
– to say nothing to Straton about the marriage
(for if by chance he should reject the proposal
he would surely lock his daughter up),
but to abduct her, willingly or not,   440
as she was going, as her habit was, to the bath-house.
    Which is what happened shortly afterwards.
For as Rhodanthe was going to the bath-house
they leaped with unbridled daring
and unsheathed blades on Rhodanthe's escort.   445
They all then in utter confusion
at the unexpected fight that had developed
scattered through the surrounding streets.
So, on my own and finding the girl on her own,[81]
picking her up from the ground and taking her in my arms,   450
I went down to the sea with all speed,
and embarking immediately on a ship that was about to set sail,
the ship that belongs to the merchant Stratokles here,
I sailed away, abandoning my own country.'
    'You describe the gods' providence,' said Glaukon,   455
'which had made a vessel ready for you,

---

the Gods 6.1; *AnthGr* 9.440, 11 (Moschos); *L&K* 1.2.1, 1.17.1 as well as the Anacreontic poems
(West 1993; cf. Ciccolella 2000).

80 An irreverent undermining of Dosikles' earlier private eloquence (at 2.206–315).

81 The emphasis here (though not elsewhere) on acting alone is reminiscent of Digenis (e.g.
DigAk G4.959, 6.13–14).

so that you were not delayed and overpowered.'
    'All my helpers and friends
came down to the harbour,' said I,
'and they called out "Go in safety, and with benevolent fate   460
as your escort may you proceed on your path,
may you fall in with kindly hosts.
May Eros warm you, and the divine dew of desire
besprinkle your precious union,
and may no obstacle come your way".'   465
    'They were fine, Dosikles,' said Glaukon again,
'they were fine young men, Dosikles.
Would that I too, father Zeus, had such friends.'
    'And Rhodanthe too had something to say,'
I added, continuing my story   470
and returning to the thread of my narrative,
'making what, it seemed, were reciprocal comments
which indeed revealed the fire of love
which she was nurturing for Dosikles in the recesses of her soul:
"Fare you well, brigands who practise sound brigandage   475
and who have carried out my own wishes,
kindly practitioners of a kindly abduction,
excellent despots in an excellent despotism."
"Thank you for these words,
for they describe the love that dwells   480
in your innermost being," said I to the girl.
And then setting off from Abydos
and sailing for four days
we thus find ourselves here and with Stratokles
we are dining luxuriously in your company, friend Glaukon.'   485
    Thus he came to the end of his tale
and the other stretching his hands up high,
'Father Zeus,' he said, 'and senate of the gods,
may you steer these young people
and grant an auspicious conclusion to their passion.'   490
Glaukon wept as he said this
(for he was a hospitable man and discerning
and sympathetic in others' grim circumstances),
and when the table had been cleared from our midst
we removed ourselves from the symposium very late.   495

THE THIRD BOOK OF THE DEEDS OF RHODANTHE
AND DOSIKLES BY THE SAME WRITER

When all the others had ceased their drinking
gentle sleep took complete possession of them.
For wine, if drunk copiously, usually
sends the drinker immediately to sleep,
pouring thick mist over his eyelids   5
and bringing night in the middle of the day.
And this seems indeed to an impartial assessor
a gift of nature and a favour from the gods,
for if a man were to be wide awake on leaving a drinking session
and a festival of the god Dionysos,   10
he would seem to be delirious and quite mad,
because he has obscured his wits and judgement
with the wine-filled and stinking vapour
that has over-vaporized in his head
and muddied the eyes of reason.[82]   15
For excess is destructive of everything.
   Everyone else had succumbed to sleep,[83]
overcome by wine, that great despot,
but Nausikrates who too lay asleep then
appeared even so to be giving the impression of drinking,[84]   20
bringing his right hand up to his mouth
(as though it were skilfully raising a cup)
and gulping down more of his saliva.
For presumably he thought he was quaffing wine,
seeing, I suppose, in his sleep a vision of drink   25
and an over-flowing goblet,
so that Nausikrates should not be deprived of the wine and intoxication
offered even by the apparitions in his sleep.
And, lying in the middle of his couch,
he moved around, twisting and contorting his legs,   30

---

82 3.2–16: A further attestation to Prodromos' interest in Aristotle: cf. Aristotle, *De somno* 457B on sleep and wine-drinking (MacAlister 1990: 207–08). Though presented not unsympathetically here, inebriation was a subject for satire in twelfth-century Constantinople, as in *Anacharsis*, attributed to Eugenianos; see Roilos 2005: 250–52.

83 Marginal gloss: 'Concerning Nausikrates'.

84 3.20–32: Again derived from Aristotle (*De somno* 456A).

depicting by the movements in his sleep
an impression of his dance during the day."
    "Hilarity, Dosikles, in the midst of misery is coming over me,"
said Kratandros, "if the spell of intoxication
so overcame Nauskrates   35
that he gulped down his saliva,
thinking that that he was gulping wine, and did not notice
that he was drinking a cup of saliva and not wine."
"What I am telling you is not peculiar or monstrous,
for the saliva from the handsome Nauskrates,"   40
said Dosikles, "was wine that gushed back up,
as it were, from the wineskin of his belly.
    And so there he was, dreaming of wine.[85]
I held out my right hand to the maiden,
and taking her with me went out of the room,   45
leaving Nausikrates dining[86] there.
Advancing a little way, I examined the vines,
which are a good subject for contemplation.
Looking at them you would say from their nature and not at random
that vines of a certain sort should produce   50
wine of a certain sort, for mothers
display the features that are also found in their children.[87]
When I reached the middle of the vines
(for the branches were everywhere intertwined
in a dense canopy of leaves   55
so that a bystander could see in only with difficulty),[88]
then I began my conversation with the maiden.
    For from the time when I had abducted her from Abydos
and set out on such a great flight and wandering,
I had said nothing to her and had had no word from her,   60
since I was sailing with a band of unknown men.

85 Marginal gloss: 'The first conversation between Dosikles and Rhodanthe'.
86 Translating δειπνοῦντα with the manuscripts (and Conca 1994; cf. Dawe 2001a: 13),
rather than ὑπνοῦντα ('sleeping'; Marcovich 1992); Nausikrates is reliving the past festivities
in his dream.
87 A similar concept, but with reference to fathers, at A&K fr. 86.8–9.
88 Overarching and intertwined branches were an important element in Byzantine
descriptions of gardens, with the *ekphrasis* in L&K 1.1.3, 15.2 standing at the head of the
tradition; for some of the ramifications, see Schissel 1942; Cupane 1974; Littlewood 1979;
Barber 1992.

But then I stepped forward and kissed her mouth
and clasped her truly round the neck,
and as I partook in her sweet kisses,
I asked that the girl become a woman.   65
'Hold back now and know[89] me
from kisses alone,' she replied to me.
'Thus it has been decreed by the ancestral gods.
For Hermes[90] himself, whom a wise stone-mason
carved as is the custom for craftsmen   70
and placed in the forecourts at Abydos,
stood by me at night in a vision in my sleep,
"The marriage of Rhodanthe and Dosikles,"
he said, "will be sealed in Abydos itself,
by the foreknowledge of the gods worshipped there".'   75
And so we, immediately limiting ourselves to kisses,
came to Glaukon's house
and (since it was night) we slept in the garden.
   On the next day we all made our way[91]
directly to the temple in Rhodes,   80
to pour drink-offerings for the sake of Agathosthenes.
So a ram was roasted and a young calf,
sacrificed in the temple porch,
while Stratokles began the dirge.
He cut a lock of hair for the dead child,   85
he shed floods of hot tears[92]
and bewailed the death of Agathosthenes
and wept over the grave of his dear infant.
   Glaukon instructed everyone to remain quiet;
he took a cup brimming full of unmixed wine   90
and sprinkled the sacrificial meat,
'O child,' he said, 'of dear Stratokles,

89 Here, and at 9.486, 'know' is used in the biblical sense as a euphemism for sexual intercourse; cf. Hel 1.8.3, 2.8.3.

90 'Hermes': Olympian god with multiple functions and a tricky character, but known chiefly as the messenger of the gods (see *OCD*, under 'Hermes'); in twelfth-century Byzantium he became a symbol of literary creativity (Roilos 2005: 52). In *R&D* he directs the action.

91 Marginal gloss: 'Glaukon's sacrifice on behalf of Agathosthenes'.

92 A reflection of the mourning traditions of antiquity (cf. Euripides, *Trachiniae* 852, 919; Sophocles, *Antigone* 803) rather than those of Orthodox Constantinople.

handsome offspring of the good Panthia,
snatched so untimely from our midst
and destroying your father's hopes,   95
I have made this sacrifice of drink-offerings to you in your death,
and I make a first offering of this meat for you in your grave.'
He said this and, bending his knee to the ground
and with us seated then around him,
he first before everyone tasted the meat   100
and drank first of the precious mixture.
And when he had tasted the cup and the meat
he allowed all to eat and to drink.[93]
    While the sacrifices were being duly performed,
the barbarian band attacked Rhodes   105
with naked blades and bronze-edged swords;
some of the inhabitants they put to the sword,
pitilessly slaughtering the thrice afflicted,
others miserably captured alive they put in chains.
Gobryas entered the temple   110
(you know, dear Kratandros, fellow prisoner,
the satrap[94] to the pirate leader Mistylos,
harsh in speech, savage in appearance,
bloodthirsty, dragon-headed,[95]
who today killed Nausikrates)   115
and captured us all together as we were making the sacrifice;
he put Glaukon in chains and Stratokles,
and with them us, and with us the girl.
    And now the jaws of prison hold me fast
and the maiden Rhodanthe, as you see.   120
Stratokles has been sent home,
but Glaukon (alas, alas, the inhumanity of Fate)
has died, slain by fear before the sword reached him,
gaining no benefit from his kindness to strangers.
For Zeus the protector of hospitality, perhaps nodding,   125

---

93 Surely a (parodic) allusion to the Christian eucharist; cf. *H&H* 1.11. See Introduction (p. 16) and discussions in Burton 1998; Kaldellis 2007: 6–10.

94 'satrap': a term in use since Herodotos to refer to Persian provincial governors, i.e. with connotations of the barbarian 'other'.

95 'dragon-headed': Conca 1994 refers to Euripides, *Orestes* 256, but note, e.g., MangProd 28.26 for references to the Sicilian Normans as 'dragons'.

allowed the host to die miserably,
unless one were to say that a divine grace from the gods
had been given him in return for his hospitality
to die naturally a natural death
and not to see in advance the bitter barbarian hand   130
about to sever his neck pitiably."
   Dosikles thus finished his account
and partook of food, not without the maiden's participation,
and with the stranger Kratandros joining them both.
Association in many hazards can thus   135
unite those who are clearly alien
and strong desire can develop more easily,
and also an unshakeable affection, in the midst of grief
than amid superabundant banquets
or overbrimming wine bowls.   140
For a not unreasonable fear would arise
that they would be rather friends of their potations
and would love the drink and not the friend,
when they had erected their desire amidst intoxication
– entrusting the entire fabric of their love   145
to rotten foundations which are more friable
than children's huts on the sand.[96]
   Thus far they went in their conversations with each other,[97]
their pain briefly relieved.
However, Gobryas, Mistylos' satrap,   150
saw Rhodanthe with clearer eyes,
and struck by the charm of her face
and hotly desiring (as is the habit of barbarians)[98]
the passion of a more carnal embrace,
he suffered deep within his heart.   155
He went to his master Mistylos,
he clasped both his feet as he was seated
and with hot tears pouring from his eyes,[99]

96 A convoluted sentence, mixing a metaphor from building on shaky foundations into ideas of trustworthy love; translating σαθροῖς θεμέθλοις εὐδιαστροφωτέροις and τῶν ... παιδικῶν ἀθυρμώτων with the mss (and Conca 1994) in place of σαθρῶν θεμέθλων εὐδιαστροφωτέραις and τοῖς ... παιδικοῖς ἀθύρμασι (Marcovich 1992).

97 Marginal gloss: 'Gobryas' lustful attack on Rhodanthe'.

98 On barbarian lust, cf. Charit 5.2.6; see Jouanno 1992.

99 3.159–79: Cf. the scene in Hel 1.19.3–7 in which Thiamis claims Charikleia for himself.

"O robber chief," he said, "fortunate spear,
you know that your satrap Gobryas   160
has striven often in many battles,
has razed many unlucky men's cities to the ground,
has destroyed many ships that sailed against us
and killed the crews in them
and that he has been wounded often and scarred   165
and bears the marks over his entire body.
   So now he approaches his master Mistylos
and clasps your two feet and weeps,
asking one favour in return for all this.
The captive, the girl who is in prison,   170
whose face you immediately admired
and whom you dedicated as a temple attendant on the gods,
I beg for her in the union of marriage.
For I captured her on Rhodes;
the girl is booty from my band of men,   175
plunder from my sword and loot from my dagger.
I will repay you the twenty *minai*, Mistylos,
and I would demand nothing else from the booty
if I can take Rhodanthe alone in marriage."
   In response, clenching his mouth briefly[100]   180
and refraining from speech, the robber chief then
said, "Mistylos is quick to make gifts
to his satraps, if anyone is,
and more than all to one who is better than all.
Gobryas is indeed better than all,   185
and I prefer him to every other satrap;
but for me he should not be considered better than the gods.
   So if I had already promised the maiden[101]
to any other satrap, good Gobryas,
and then you came asking for this favour,   190
I would immediately have given you Rhodanthe gladly,
removing her from the one who had already taken her
(even though he who had first had the girl and then lost her
would have taken the matter badly;

---

100 Marginal gloss: 'Mistylos' reply'.
101 3.188–264: An example of a syllogistic debate, and also another instance of an *ethopoiia* ('What might be said on revoking a dedication').

but it is nothing to us if a satrap is upset   195
when we are giving a chief satrap his due).
But since I have given the girl as a temple attendant
to the gods who have saved us in battle,
how could it not be an impious act
if I were to remove the girl from the temple   200
and give her in union of marriage to a mortal?
How, if what you ask[102] were to happen,
could the gods not be enraged by what has been done?
    For should we act wrongly against others, Gobryas,
the gods are there to act as avengers.   205
Should we inflict the wrongdoing on them,
would they consider that the injustice should be endured?
One cannot say, but much more probably
they would punish us for having acted impiously.
For impiety is worse than injustice,   210
in so much as one might say that impiety concerns the gods
while injustice refers to mortals.
I will quibble somewhat in my present speech:
that the impious do wrong is certainly inevitable
(for impiety is a kind of crime);   215
but why is it inevitable that wrongdoers are impious?
    Examine the argument with application to yourself.
I had already given you the girl you had asked for.
Someone else came up and demanded the gift in exchange,
he is in second place to you and as obscure in his status   220
as you are in relation to the gods, Gobryas.
I acceded to his request
and gave her to him who had asked me,
abducting the girl unhappily from your chamber.
Would you have borne the shame gracefully?   225
Would you have put up with the insult? No, by Justice,
but you would have gone off to take vengeance on the wrongdoer
and you would have let out every reef[103]
to ensure that you ill-treated with appropriate actions

---

102 Translating λέγεις with the mss (and Conca 1994) rather than θέλεις ('wish'; Marcovich 1992).

103 A proverbial expression, meaning to make every effort; cf. 8.249; Zenobios 5.62 (Leutsch and Schneidewin 1839–51, vol. 1); Suda, K 259.

the one who had wronged and harmed you.   230
    So you, a creature of the earth and subject to decay,
have not been able to endure the insult or the injury.
How then would the gods accept the shame,
whose capabilities correspond to their strength,
who need neither supporters nor time   235
to ward off those who abuse them?
For fire kindled below would consume them
or a watery superabundance would sweep them away.
At any rate you would admit in your argument
that the maiden is worthy of more than a husband's bed   240
and is fit to cohabit with the gods."
    "But you have not given the maiden to the gods,"
Gobryas replied to Mistylos,
"for she lives in the prison's gloom
while the gods have the temple for their dwelling,   245
and it is appropriate for the gods' temple attendants
to make the temples their habitation and remain there
(unless you consider the abode of the condemned
a sacred chamber and a place dedicated to the gods)."
    To this Mistylos said in reply,   250
"You have made a truly ignorant response, Gobryas.
I have promised the maiden to the gods.
Even if I have not bestowed the gift with my own hands,
since the profusion of many concerns has disrupted me,
nevertheless a sensible man and one in command of his wits   255
would say that the promise makes the gift,
if it is made to the saviour gods.
But you seem, having taken the maiden
and established her within the bridal chamber
and lit the torches of the marriage procession,   260
to be accusing Mistylos of not explaining
why the union has been delayed.
But Mistylos has already given her to the gods
and Gobryas has taken a girl denied to him."
    Having thus failed to obtain the girl he desired,   265
the satrap changed from his approach as suppliant
to a more brutal method,
one befitting Gobryas, an abominable barbarian:

for he decided to use force by night
and to have intercourse with the girl against her will.   270
So he immediately ran off to the prison
and rushed up to Rhodanthe as she lay there
and, "Greetings," he said, "wife of your husband Gobryas;
come here and embrace me as your bridegroom
and do not be disturbed by my sleeping with you   275
but give thanks to the gods and the fates
who have united you to a great satrap.
For he who captured you in Rhodes
and restrained you with his own hands
has not allowed a maiden of this quality to be bestowed   280
upon any poverty-stricken and lowly barbarian."
    He said this and bent down to the ground
and began to kiss Rhodanthe's mouth.
But the girl escaped from the brute
and rushed away from the rapist Gobryas,   285
and abandoning most of her tunic
in the hand of the violent cur,[104]
ran with all speed to Dosikles.
Her heart filled with great panic,
"Save me," she said, "from the brutish barbarian,   290
save, Dosikles, your dear maiden,
rescue me from the robberly brute.
You have destroyed me; make haste, indeed I am ruined."
    So sleep, which had settled tardily
and with difficulty upon Dosikles' eyes,   295
was thrust aside by the maiden's cry
and flew away and moved off at great speed.[105]
Dosikles, opening the doors of his eyes[106]
and rising up from his bed on the ground
(for the earth was the nearest representation of a couch   300
for the handsome Dosikles as he snatched a little sleep),
said to the maiden in great perturbation,
"Alas, Rhodanthe, what are you frightened of? Speak to me, speak
    to me.

104 A gender reversal of Joseph's experience with Potiphar's wife (Genesis 39.6–20).
105 Hypnos (Sleep) lives on the island of Lemnos (*Iliad* 14.230).
106 See 2.200 for another image involving doors and eyes.

See, here is Dosikles, tell me about the battle.
Surely amidst your sleep and the apparitions in your dreams   305
you have descried new forms of phantoms
(of the sort that night is likely often to transform
as they appear in dreams at that time)?
Surely you have been terrified by some hideous figure,
have you not had a nightmare at the spectacle, as infants do?   310
What has happened? Do stop. Why are you so scared?
The apparition is imaginary and a shadow's deceptive form,
even if (as happens often) it is likely to terrify unmanly hearts
with its strange deformation.
If up till now you have been trembling at the spectacle,   315
now let me arise and prepare to fight
and engage in a battle by night with the dreams
and brandish my sword at the nightly visions."
     Thus Dosikles to the maiden.
Gobryas, Mistylos' satrap,   320
had failed in his second attempt
and he went away in silence to his own house,
terrified, I think, that this should become known to Mistylos
and he pay the appropriate penalty
for having drunkenly insulted the gods' temple attendants.   325
And without caring, his desire urging him on,
he turned to a third way to gain his ends.
For he hurried off to win over with deceptive words
Dosikles, seemingly the girl's brother,[107]
so that he could gain his beloved through him.   330
O utterly useless, utterly deranged heart,
if the satrap expected Dosikles
to betray his own maiden!
But the similarity of their appearance deceived
the barbarian, and so, coming close,   335
he addressed these words to Dosikles,[108]
     "The brilliance of your appearance, Dosikles,

107 There has not yet been any suggestion that Dosikles and Rhodanthe had been taken for
brother and sister.
108 The convention in the novel tradition (e.g. Theagnis and Charikleia in Hel 1.22; cf.
Abraham and Sara in Genesis 20.2) is for the lovers to pretend to be brother and sister in order
to aid their flight; here Gobryas makes the initial suggestion. Cf. *H&H* 9.14–16; *D&C* 4.223.

bears witness to the nobility of both your backgrounds,
that this is far greater than your apparent status
it conspicuously shows and clearly underlines. 340
And the newly blooming charm of your face
you bear as a clearly spoken herald
of your link in kinship with Rhodanthe.
Those whose beauty has corresponding features,
those whose facial features are the same, 345
these surely would also share the same family.
Thus indeed that you are kinsman to the maiden
is inscribed in my mind, as if by some artist,
by the grace that is present in your countenance.
You are perhaps not unaware that Gobryas 350
has greater influence over Mistylos
than any other serving under him,
gaining a myriad of honours.
If you grant me the one favour, and one alone,
of persuading your kinswoman who is imprisoned with you, 355
to come with me and be joined in marriage,
you will receive a far greater favour in return.
For Mistylos' beautiful daughter
I guarantee to you, and the ancestral gods
I take as witness to my claim 360
that Kalippe will be wife of Dosikles
if Rhodanthe is wife of Gobryas.
What marriage could be more fortunate,
or what bridegroom as renowned
as he who is joined with Mistylos' daughter? 365
For such is the maiden in appearance
that surely she is worthy of Rhodanthe's brother.
Such is the beauty of her face
that surely it befits the bridegroom Dosikles.
Add to these considerations the dignity of office, 370
the elevation of your lot, the weight of silver, of gold,
in which those who achieve marriage connections with rulers
exceed more lowly creatures."
   Dosikles, hearing these words
and refraining briefly from reply, said, 375
"You have made a good guess about us, Gobryas,

and you have well recognized my sister's nature
from the appearance of her features.
I am well aware of my own fate,
I understand that I am a sojourner in a foreign land,[109]   382
I am not unaware that I am Mistylos' slave,   380
and unworthy to be Kalippe's bridgroom;
for no man that is a captive would ever be elevated
to such heights and rise above his fate
to share in marriage connections with the rulers,   385
soaring over all ranks of satrap.
But for me this is a thankless gift.
I shall persuade my sister, the maiden,
to take part in a marriage with you, satrap,
only do not look for the promise now.   390
For since she who bore us and nurtured us
has died, alas, and departed from this life
and an ancient law prevails in our city,
that mourning for their begetting parent
should be performed by children for fifty days,   395
restrain yourself until the tenth day,
for that concludes the custom for us,
and I guarantee you marriage with her."[110]
    Hearing these words, Gobryas
succumbed to two emotions simultaneously: 400
the delay twisted his heart
(for he considered the days that had been interposed
would last a lifetime and his whole existence),
but hope eliminated his despondency.
    When Gobryas left the prison,[111]   405
Dosikles immediately ran to the maiden
and amid groans shed tears
and shouted out bitterly from deep within,[112]
"O", he said, "light of my heart,

109 Moving 382 before 380 with Marcovich 1992.
110 The motif of apparent acquiescence in a marriage request while imposing a delay is also
found in, e.g., XenEph 2.23.8; Hel 1.22.6–7.
111 Marginal gloss: 'Dosikles' lament'.
112 3.409–84: A demonstration of a lament for present circumstances (cf. 1.88–31,
7.17–160).

and remedy for my unending woes, 410
O my fellow captive, my fellow prisoner,
O Dosikles' wife in name.
You chose to flee from your homeland,
you have been deprived of your parents, your fellow maidens,
your dear brothers, of Straton and of Phryne. 415
You have seen foreign cities in your long journeying,
you who never saw your own (for how could you, enclosed as you were?).
You have overwhelmed a brutish robber
and to this moment you endure a myriad wrongs.
You dwell within the gloomy jaws of prison, 420
you sleep on the ground, a chilly bed,
you are deprived of much, even of chunks of coarse bread.
Indeed with me and for my sake, maiden,
you have endured hunger, flight and wanderings.
    And now the robber Gobryas, the satrap, 425
has bitterly sundered our passion,
tearing us miserably apart with a pitiful separation,
and he takes[113] Rhodanthe for himself;
he uses force and destroys the marriage
for which Dosikles became a wanderer and an exile, 430
restrained with chains and imprisoned.
Was it thus that the great Hermes in our dreams
assured us of marriage,
was this to be the outcome of the dreams?
    Would that, as you sailed unhappily from Abydos, 435
the depths of the wild ocean had overwhelmed you,
or that Gobryas had done away with you
when he was ravaging all Rhodes
and looting most of the dwellings
and moreover, capturing you alive, kept you alive as a prisoner, 440
saving you for himself and wooing one
who is not his but belongs to Dosikles alone,
an evil saviour offering an unwanted salvation.
    Pitiful, pitiful for Dosikles' eyes would it have been
to see Rhodanthe swept into the deeps, 445

---

113 Translating λαμβάνει with the mss (and Conca 1994) rather than λαμβάνων ('taking'; Marcovich 1992).

into the sea's gaping belly,
achieving a damp and watery grave,
or indeed slaughtered and dying by the sword.
But it is more pitiful than sea and sword
if you are dragged alive, alas, alas, from the midst of my arms,   450
if you are torn away and endure severance
and are given over to a union with Gobryas,
while Dosikles, oh woe, looks on.
     For if you had fallen into the sea's jaws,
if you had been slaughtered by a bronze-edged blade,   455
I would have nevertheless been able to suffer with you, maiden,
flinging myself into the heart of the sea,[114]
or at least thrusting the sword into my entrails,
but now I shall experience death once more
before I see you united in marriage   460
with the most evil barbarian Gobryas,
aiming against myself and my innermost bowels
whatever sword I find.
For I shall not spare my heart,
as long as my arm has life, as long as my sword remains active.   465
     You must join in marriage with the barbarian
and take your sleep on the satrap's couch
and put on the finest clothing,
laden with gold, bestrewn with pearls,
and you will do everything to please Gobryas.   470
You must have no recollection of Dosikles
and the solemn pledge you gave him.
For Fate's abundant good sense,
weighing down on the mind of the compliant,
brings for the most part oblivion of past events,   475
winnowing out the burden of what had gone before
from the threshing floor of the wits.
     Zeus of the thunderbolt,[115] might that wields lightning
and protector of solemn pledges,
will you endure these events?   480
Will you not hurl down hailstones

114 'heart of the sea': a biblical phrase; cf. Ezekiel 27.4, 25, 28 and 28.2; Jonah 2.4.
115 3.478–86: Prodromos combines biblical eschatological phraseology from, e.g., Genesis
28.17; Psalms 77.23; Revelations 4.1 with classical epithets for Zeus.

and fire-winged flames of thunder?
Will you not open every gate of heaven
and lay the earth waste and send out floods,
soaking everything with vast seas of rain, 485
and will you not shake all creation with a huge earthquake?"
    As Dosikles uttered these words,
he shed bitter streams of hot tears,
and although he wanted to cease his dirge,
yet he was eager to continue his speech 490
as the suffering inflamed his heart.
The maiden clenched her lips
and as it were put a fetter on her tongue,
and kept a long and miserable silence.
For an unexpected disaster that arises 495
and a sudden unlooked-for disturbance usually
cause a derangement of the wits
and a dysfunction in the organs of reasoning;
for the heart that suffers is befuddled,
drinking down a strange and newfangled liquor.[116] 500
    With difficulty she struggled from this new intoxication[117]
and ordered her scattered mind
and as it were loosed her tongue and her reason,
"Cease your groans, Dosikles," she said,
"and tell me the origins of this disaster." 505
    "Gobryas is eager to enter into marriage with you,"[118]
was Dosikles' not untearful response,
"and he promises in exchange a bitter favour, marriage
for me with Mistylos' daughter.
For what favour is it, most evil robber Gobryas 510
(for see, I address my words to you,
even if you are far from us, most savage creature),
if you tear me away from my own maiden
and give me another's as a gift?
You slaughter me bitterly and you announce a marriage. 515
What has a marriage to do with those who are about to die?

---

116 3.495–500: An example of a gnomic comment, found in all the novels and sometimes
noted in the manuscripts; see Roilos 2005: 48–49; Odorico 1989.
    117 Marginal gloss: 'Rhodanthe's consolation of Dosikles'.
    118 Marginal gloss: 'Dosikles' reply'.

Grant one favour alone to Dosikles:
do not tear him accursedly away from Rhodanthe."
    "I," replied the girl promptly,[119]
"(the gods certainly hear this pledge),   520
may I be kept pure and preserved either for you
or for the sword, but not for Gobryas.
But I have no little fear in your connection,
that, united with Mistylos' daughter,
you may have not the least concern for a prisoner."   525
    Rhodanthe made these remarks
and she wiped her dear Dosikles' face
clear of his flowing tears,
using her tunic as a handkerchief,
and he gradually ceased from his wailing.   530

THE FOURTH BOOK OF THE DEEDS OF RHODANTHE
AND DOSIKLES BY THE SAME WRITER

Thus they sealed their passion
for each other with confirmatory speeches.
On the following day, putting on a handsome mantle
that was white and reached his feet, befitting a priest,
and taking with him the temple attendants   5
garlanded with pine and laurel,
Mistylos set off to the temple itself,
to consecrate the young people to the immortals.
    Bryaxes' satrap Artaxanes[120]
came before him by the ruler's command,   10
and overturned and upset everything.
For when the fleet commander Mistylos heard
that the great Artaxanes had arrived
he immediately turned back
and put the temple attendants in confinement once more   15
while he himself, seated aloft on a mighty throne
on the tribune, and, glowering like a Titan
with his satrap's army stationed

119 Marginal gloss: 'Rhodanthe's reply'.
120 Marginal gloss: 'Artaxanes' appearance'.

around the throne in appropriate array,
ordered the satrap who had been dispatched to be summoned.   20
    And so the summons was made and Artaxanes presented himself.
The satrap, bowing his head
before the feet of the fleet commander Mistylos,
put a small sealed letter
into the emperor's hands.[121]   25
He in turn gave it to Gobryas,
so that he could read it in the presence of all.
Breaking the seals, Gobryas
read the letter in everyone's hearing:
    "The lord Bryaxes, great emperor of Pissa,[122]   30
greets the great emperor Mistylos.
What Bryaxes' demeanour has been towards Mistylos
and how he has striven to maintain the bonds of love
with him more than anything else
you might learn from many other matters, if you wish,   35
and especially from the fact that by the benevolence of Fortune
I alone have power and have subdued other states
– but it has not been my wish that Fortune's gift to me
should affect your state, Mistylos.
But I would judge it my personal misfortune   40
if your sceptre came to destruction.
May I not be mighty through what I have taken from my friends,
may I not prosper through destroying Mistylos,
may I not be successful through inhuman means,
harming myself when I inflict harm on a friend,   45
robbing myself when I rob Mistylos' possessions.
    So I wish to maintain our friendship
and I am the guardian of my love towards you,
but you overturn this in every way.
Abandoning, as far as I can see, the former terms   50

121 Mistylos is now referred to as 'emperor', and with this has come some of the trappings of official ceremonial, the reception of embassies and treatment of formal communications (especially their being read aloud): these reflect twelfth-century practices, not the late antiquity depicted elsewhere; cf. Roilos 2005: 254–55.

122 Marginal gloss: 'Bryaxes' letter to Mistylos'. It is very tempting to see an allusion here to the Italian city of Pisa, with which commercial agreements were set up in 1111 and 1136 (Hunger 1978, vol. 2: 132; cf. Roilos 2005: 287); note that in the *Alexiad* (e.g. 11.10.1, 12.1.2, 14.3.1) Pisa is spelled as it is by Prodromos.

you break the bonds and ties of friendship
and summon me against my will to battle.
For surely you do not stumble into battle unwittingly
if you remove a city from my jurisdiction[123]
and seize authority over it from us   55
and hold some of the garrison
as if they were enemies, and put others to the sword?
And yet that Rhamnon was entirely my city
and paid me annual tribute
and acknowledged Bryaxes as its only ruler,   60
I would say, Mistylos, that you were not unaware.
    Either restore the city to us
and finally set free those whom you have taken prisoner
and let our friendship continue,
or understand that Bryaxes will take action against you.   65
But without fail I shall set free the city of Rhamnon
and the soldiers who have been captured,
and perhaps I shall lay waste your cities also.
For the eye of all-seeing Justice[124]
never sleeps and never closes even a little;   70
it looks harshly on the unjust
and always supports those who have been wronged.
May you fare well while preserving our friendship intact."
    Gobryas thus read through the letter.
The robber chief and fleet commander Mistylos   75
was both alarmed at Bryaxes' words
and furious and boiling with anger
(for anger and fear both normally
dominate a barbarian's heart);
he was impelled by anger to utter rash speeches,   80
but led to restraint on the other hand by fear;
so he remained silent for no little time
and, possessed by two conflicting arguments,
he was unable to utter a word.[125]

---

123 Translating the mss ἐξαποσπάσεις and ἁρπάσεις (finite verbs), and punctuating with
Conca 1994, rather than ἐξαποσπάσας and ἁρπάσας (participles) with Marcovich 1992.
    124 This image has a long history, starting with Hesiod, *Works and Days* 267–68.
    125 4.84–99: A description, verging on an *ethopoiia*, on how a barbarian would react when
suffering two conflicting emotions.

He sat speechless for a long time, 85
his appearance changing colour frequently
as he was transformed and altered
both by his inner psychic movements
and the excessive volatility of his emotions,
with the variations that appeared outwardly on his face 90
an indication of the tempest[126] within his soul.
Shamed before his own satraps,
but, in fear of Bryaxes' might,
he glowered all over his face and turned pale
as once again he endured an inner contraction. 95
Enraged and engorged with fury,[127]
he was dark with an emotional melancholy
(for bilious and inflammatory passions
are inclined to overheat a sanguine temperament).
Although enduring such anguish at that time 100
Mistylos nevertheless checked his anger and fear
and controlled each emotion
(for he had a firm and unshakeable spirit,
even if he suffered in other respects from barbarian emotions),
"Take Bryaxes' satrap Artaxanes," 105
he said, "and in the meantime, Gobryas,
show him hospitality and remove the weight of much toil
with a banquet and a comfortable couch.
Tomorrow he may take a written response
and convey it to his master." 110
Having said this to Gobryas,
he rose, still with a grim look,
and hastened into the palace.
Gobryas took Artaxanes
and settled him in the satraps' dwellings 115
that had been equipped for such receptions,
and he ordered the barbarians under his command
to set up the wine bowl and to bring in the banquet.[128]
And as Gobryas sat down with Artaxanes

---

126 Translating ζάλην with the mss (and Conca 1994) rather than ἄλην ('distraction'; Marcovich 1992).

127 4.96–99: Marcovich moves these lines after 92.

128 Literally, 'the table'.

the satraps enjoyed the food,   120
and enjoyed the wine even more.
   The dinner was full of delight[129]
and so prepared as to instil amazement.
A roast lamb was set down in front of them
and when Artaxanes was going to take some   125
and started to cut off and remove a piece to eat,
there burst out from its stomach
newly hatched sparrows which, flapping their wings,
flew out above the satrap's head.[130]
Artaxanes was absolutely astounded,   130
and Gobryas was overcome with laughter
at the sight of Artaxanes' amazement.
   Controlling his uninhibited laughter a little,
he said, "Do you see, great satrap,
the might of my master Mistylos,   135
who is able to alter nature
and with fresh changes and devious contrivances
he can rearrange everything and transform it as he wishes.
You see that the lamb is pregnant with sparrows.
Unaware of the law of nature,   140
that a winged bird gives birth to a winged bird,
and obedient to Mistylos' command,
the lamb sprouts winged creatures from its entrails.
What else? Does the fire not reveal a great miracle?
For when it has charred the lamb, as you see,   145
it discreetly hesitates from encroaching further,
so that the sparrows' wings are not harmed.
For the fire is capable of burning
only what Mistylos wants burnt
and, although the flame is able to burn up more,   150
nevertheless it discreetly withdraws
as if afraid to burn contrary to instructions
what it would be against the emperor's instructions to burn.
   See, Artaxanes, best of satraps,
the power of my great master,   155

129 Marginal gloss: 'Gobryas' and Artaxanes' dinner'.
130 This bizarre dish ultimately derives from Petronius, *Satyricon* 40.5 (Beaton 1996: 74).
On the parodic and satirical elements to this rhetorical set-piece, see Roilos 2005: 260–75.

how he can alter and control nature,
and make fire's very being icy
by his mere command and by his will alone;
how he can demonstrate that sparrows are born of lambs,
and he can make lambs extraordinary begetters of sparrows;   160
and that a womb that has just been touched by flame and roasted[131]
can give birth to unsinged offspring, winged embryos,
this he can prove by his word alone –
producing in monstrous shape things which neither nature
nor reason is capable of forming.   165
    Or indeed he might give the order, perhaps, in the middle of battles
and he would make soldiers, hard fighting men,
with their swords and shields,
give birth to swarms of puppies[132]
and he would induce the bellies that are protected by corselets   170
to become pregnant with bizarre embryos,
transforming, manipulating nature at will."
    "Do not, by this banquet, Gobryas,"[133]
said Artaxanes, "do not, by this symposium
at which I am lavishly entertained by Mistylos   175
who, as you say, makes and transforms anything,
do not let the great emperor's command
open up my belly
to give birth to puppies, most abominable offspring.
May he not bestow upon a man who is a general   180
as an unwelcome gift the accursed fate of women
and the grievous pains of childbirth.
For how could I provide the flow of milk,
if indeed the infants should need to be nourished
in the natural way by means of milk?   185
Moreover, how could a man who is a general
be able to endure the dreadful shame
of being despicably pregnant with despicable offspring?"
    Gobryas interrupted and said this in reply,
"Artaxanes, greatest of satraps,   190

131 Roilos 2005: 266–72 points out this vocabulary is found in hymns on the Theotokos.
132 4.166–88: On the rhetorical elements of this *adynaton* (the pregnant man) as an example
of *anaskeue* and *kataskeue*, see Roilos 2005: 261–66.
133 Marginal gloss: 'Artaxanes' response'.

stop doing nothing but insult the blessed gods
when you say that it is no small shame for men
to have a womb that produces embryos.
For if Zeus, the best of the gods,
who gathers the earth up and overturns everything   195
including foundations and groundwork
and who shoots his bolts of thunder,
if he was willing to enfold into his thigh an embryo
that had just been scorched and had completed only half its term
and bring it, quickened by fire, out into the day,[134]   200
and he, the emperor of the Titans, gave shelter
to maternal and womanly pains,
if he put forth Athena from his head
which was sundered by the sword and split in the middle,[135]
how can we say that something is shameful for earthbound men   205
which is honourable for the heavenly gods?
But you need have no expectations of such experiences,
being a friend of the great Mistylos."
      Artaxanes, and indeed Gobryas too,
were occupied with such discussions,   210
Gobryas terrifying Artaxanes
and secretly mocking at his fear,
Artaxanes quaking at what he heard.
But in response to Gobryas' command[136]
the magician Satyrion came into their midst   215
and put an end to the satraps' discussion.[137]
For he girded on a sharpened sword,
stripped to the waist
and then put on a many-hued mantle,
brilliantly coloured with many dyes.   220
He was a little creature, very thin, dark-skinned,

134 In legend Zeus took Semele's premature infant Dionysos (born when she was exposed to Zeus' thunderbolts) and brought him to term in his thigh; cf. Nonnos, *Dionysiaka* 1.1–7. On Prodromos' use of the Dionysos legend in his commentaries on the canons of John of Damascus, see Roilos 2005: 270–75

135 Athene was born from Zeus's head; cf. Nonnos, *Dionysiaka* 1.8–10. The opening lines of Nonnos' immensely long poem seem to be Prodromos' source here.

136 Marginal gloss: 'About the jester Satyrion'.

137 Cf. Manasses' *ekphrasis* on a dwarf who entertained the court in Constantinople (Sternbach 1902).

with his head and beard shaved,
and more often than not he scared infants witless.
And when he had provoked everyone to roars of laughter,
he stood there on his own, an unsmiling Hades.   225
    When he entered and stood in their midst,
with Artaxanes looking on very attentively,
he thrust the sword into his naked neck,
and immediately a fountain of blood bubbled out,
and the unhappy Satyrion lay dead   230
on the ground in front of them all, having gone out of his mind.[138]
And so Artaxanes went up to him, weeping,
and bewailed bitterly from the depth of his soul
Satyrion's suicide.
But Gobryas rose from his seat   235
and, approaching the man who had just died,
"Man," he said, "arise and live;
this is the command of the great Mistylos."[139]
And Satyrion promptly got up
and, taking his usual lyre in his hands,   240
he entertained the satraps with a song to its accompaniment,
singing many things most tunefully as follows:
    "Sun, charioteer of the fiery-wheeled curricle.[140]
        O hail, hail, greatest Mistylos,
        mighty lord, dispeller of misery;   245
        Zeus and the council of the gods converse with you,
        you dine with Pallas the greatest.
    Sun, charioteer of the fiery-wheeled curricle.
        Earth fears you and fire trembles before you,
        the expanse of the sea obeys you;   250
        bitter Hades from his all-devouring throat
        spews forth whole Satyrions.[141]
    Sun, charioteer of the fiery-wheeled curricle.
        By your command you overturn nature;

---

138 False deaths are a feature of the late antique novels; cf. especially *L&K* 3.21.3–5 where
Kleitophon observes what is apparently the murder of Leukippe.
139 There are biblical overtones to this phrase, from the Raising of Lazarus (John 11).
140 Marginal gloss: 'Satyrion's song'.
141 This view of Hades is medieval rather than antique; Plepelits 1996: 146, n. 48 draws a
comparison with the Hades scenes in, e.g., the basilica at Torcello.

you reveal lambs as the progenitors of sparrows,   255
you make sparrows the offspring of lambs
and you chill the fiery nature of flame.
Sun, charioteer of the fiery-wheeled curricle.
    For your trireme the ridges of the sea
    are flattened by mighty Poseidon,[142]   260
    Demetra spreads out the land,
    Ares gives you strength in battle.
Sun, charioteer of the fiery-wheeled curricle.
    For you the earth puts out shoots, for you the world of
        plants burgeons,
    for you the tree blooms, for you the corn sprouts;   265
    for you the vine enwraps great grape-clusters,
    the grape is crushed and brings forth wine.
Sun, charioteer of the fiery-wheeled curricle.
    For you the manifold golden grace of metal,
    for you the gleam of translucent pearls,   270
    for you the Seric thread,[143] for you the mantle of spun flax,
    for you all these labour, all creation trembles before you.
Sun, charioteer of the fiery-wheeled curricle.
    For you labours the wild mountainous beast, for you the
        cattle-nurturing earth,
    for you the winged bird, for you the creatures of the sea,   275
    for you the tiny fish, for you the huge whale,
    for you fire, air, earth, for you the fruitful waters.
Sun, charioteer of the fiery-wheeled curricle.
    For you hail condenses, for you snowflakes fall,
    for you ice hardens into stone,   280
    for you falls a torrent of rain, for you drizzle, for you dew,
    for you the whiteness of snow, for you the dark cloud.[144]
Sun, charioteer of the fiery-wheeled curricle.
    For you the sea's waves become gentle,

---

142 This image (cf. *Iliad* 2.159) recurs in this text at 5.93, 450, 6.211; cf. *D&C* 4.15.

143 Silk, an legendarily exotic import in the early empire but subsequently a vital part of the Byzantine economy and social order; see *OHBS*, 'Silk' and Jacoby 2008.

144 Satyrion's ode to the sun has almost become a version of the Song of the Three Young Men (Daniel 3.52–88, in the Septuagint), one of the nine biblical Odes originally sung during Orthros (Matins) but from the eighth century forming the basis for canons, the new hymnographic form; see *ODB*, under 'Kanon', 'Odes'.

for you the sea is calm for vessels as they sail,   285
for you the ocean gives way, for you the billows die down,
for you the raging surf surges more calmly.
Sun, charioteer of the fiery-wheeled curricle.
    For you the ox at his plough, for you the flocks of sheep,
    for you the Cretan dog, the horse from Arabia,[145]   290
    the race of camels, the leopard, bull and lion,
    for you earth, sea and land yield tribute.
Sun, charioteer of the fiery-wheeled curricle.
    O hail to you, thrice greatest Gobryas,
    consul of Mistylos' satraps,   295
    a sword dyed purple with your enemies' blood,
    a mind undaunted in the midst of battle.
Sun, charioteer of the fiery-wheeled curricle.
    O hail to you, Bryaxes' satrap,
    drinking companion of my master Gobryas,   300
    who when Satyrion expired
    shed a tear from his kindly eyelids.
Sun, charioteer of the fiery-wheeled curricle.
    Hail, banquet and thrice blessed symposium,
    and a second nectar and a new dinner for the gods;   305
    O hail to you also, most musical lyre,
    and Satyrion, the author of the song.
Sun, charioteer of the fiery-wheeled curricle."
Thus Satyrion, skilled on the lyre,
fictitiously slain and collapsing as a false corpse,   310
who rose again at Mistylos' bidding
(exactly like a dramatic performance),[146]
struck his excellent lyre melodiously

145 Dogs from Crete (Xenophon, *Cynegetica* 10.1) and horses from Arabia (*ODB*, under
'Horses'; Hyland 1994: 40–44) are traditionally the best.

146 The nature, even the existence, of dramatic performances in Byzantium after late
antiquity is a matter for discussion (Püchner 2002); however, entertainments were part of
imperial banquets (e.g. the formalized Gothic Games of *De Caerimoniis* 2.92; Vogt 1967)
while fools and jesters became part of the imperial entourage (e.g. Boilas and Constantine
Monomachos: Psellos, *Chronographia* 6.139–50; Garland 1990a; Haldon 2002), surely
trickling down the social hierarchy; see Roilos 2005: 278–84. The scene depicted here arguably
reflects an aristocratic, if not imperial, formal feast. *Theatra*, whatever their format became,
surely also provided occasions for performances, musical and other, akin to that of Satyrion.
For satiric allusions to Christian beliefs, see Burton 2000.

and sang the charming strain of his song.
He drained a huge cup of unmixed wine   315
and quickly left the symposium.
    Gobryas' drinking companion Artaxanes,
his wits battered and reeling
with too much wine and the impact of drunkenness,
seized a goblet brimming with unmixed wine   320
but was overcome by sleep before he could drink it down.
For sleep usually accompanies drunkenness
and is, as it were, a kinsman of lengthy carousals.
So he drowsed off in his sodden state
and the drinking vessel dropped down and was shattered   325
as it fell from his senseless hand.
Gobryas was distressed to see the vessel shattered
and thought this a great disaster;
for it was a delight to behold
and made the drink sweeter.   330
    For it was made from sapphire[147]
which an experienced and cunning stone-worker
had carved with skilled fingers
and given a certain shape;
you can discover what that was, if you have the urge,   335
by looking carefully at triremes.
It was narrow and restricted in breadth
but long and extended in length.
Encircling the mouth of the vessel
was a rim of beaten gold   340
while set beneath this on both sides
were beautiful carvings by the cunning stone-worker,
which displayed thousands of pictured scenes.
    Should you have come close you would have seen

---

147 4.331–411: Another set-piece *ekphrasis*, with ultimate origins in the Homeric Shield of
Achilles (*Iliad* 18.478–608) via Glaukos' cup mentioned at *L&K* 2.3. For the trireme allusion,
Marcovich, in the source apparatus to 4.336, refers to inscriptions on a *krater trieretikos* stored
in the Parthenon in 368/7 BCE (*IG* II, 2nd edn, 1425.361, 1649.3); it is unclear whether the
adjective there refers to the object's shape or the status of the donors. More probably Prodromos
refers to a 'sauce boat', a narrow dish-type with a long history in the Mediterranean, though
apparently no surviving Byzantine examples; for a possible parallel in design if not in shape,
cf. the fourth-century CE Lycurgus cup now in the British Museum. On the *ekphrasis*, see also
Labarthe-Postel 2001; Burton 2006: 551–57 and 2008: 274–77.

on one side grapes as if in the middle of the vines, 345
excellent, ripe, flourishing, about to burst
and as if summoning the harvester,
while on the other side men (almost alive) harvesting and
cutting the grapes from the vines
and putting them in stoutly woven baskets 350
which you would have though were made of cane and not stone.
On seeing this you would have asked, I suspect, for a bunch of grapes,
thinking you were watching the vintage and not a picture of it
– so expertly was the stone carved.
    Others were crushing the clusters from the vines 355
and draining the wine directly into a vat,[148]
others were collecting the wine in small pots 363
and transferring it to fresh storage jars. 364
< ... >
Intertwining their fingers 357
they began a dance, a dancing chorus in stone.
Looking at them more closely you would say
that they were truly singing a real song 360
and you would have a strong desire to join in 361
and hold hands and dance with them 362
    Dionysos, the leader of the harvesters, 365
sitting by the mouth of a new storage jar,
jested with the Bacchai themselves and the Satyrs too,[149]
as is fitting at a grape-harvest.
Tearing grapes from a cluster,
he pelted the Satyrs with the soft missiles. 370
They fell down as though wounded,
one clasping his arm as if it had been sliced into,
smearing the cut with saliva
to complete its cicatrization,
another urinating on his toe 375
which the blow from the grape had inflamed.[150]

148 There are problems of sense and line order in the mss as transmitted, best solved (with Marcovich) by moving 363–64 after 356 and postulating a lacuna before 357.

149 Dionysos, god of wine in Greek mythology, was traditionally escorted by raving women (Bacchai or Maenads) and lusty Satyrs (half-man and half-goat); the classic literary presentation is in Euripides' *Bacchae*.

150 For the efficacy of saliva and urine, cf. Pliny, *Nat. Hist.* 28.35, 66–67; Galen, *De*

Dionysos roared with laughter at them.
   If by any chance you want to know what form
and appearance and visage
the stone-worker had carved for the god,   380
he was a young man, excellent in appearance,
with a ruddy bloom to his cheeks,
though not from nature but from drunkenness.
He was like a girl, he had no down on his chin,
his hair was tied back with a golden band   385
and fluttered in the gentle breezes.
His lips were moist, as though from the goblet,
grinning at everyone, never clenched.
His tunic was hitched up to his knees,
as is right for those who tread grapes.   390
His arm was bare to the elbow,
like that of a man working at the harvest.
He jested and, shifting his position a little
and weaving the twining strands from the vines,
leaves and grapes and all,   395
he surrounded his head with a glorious wreath,
   Indeed the Bacchai entwined their fingers
in a circle and a choral dance;
they seemed to sing a most pleasant melody
and they begged the god to join in the dance with them.   400
One grasped his tunic,
thus summoning him to the dance,
another softly touched his buttock
and gently led the youth away,
another with an even gentler kiss   405
took him off to the leading edge of the dance.
As he was resisting the dictator,
one of them managed to get hold of his wreath
and, throwing it into the circling dance,
compelled him to leave the storage jar against his will   410
and stand forth as a companion in the Maenads' dance.[151]

---

simplicium medicamentorum temperamentis 30.15 (Kühn 1826: 286); Prodromos also shows medical knowledge at 9.464–83.

   151 It is tempting to think that this may reflect contemporary peasant dances; cf. the circle dance at *D&C* 4.324.

With such an extreme of beauty had
Gobryas' shattered goblet been carved.
But Artaxanes, wretched, wretched man, was enshrouded
in a fog of drunkenness like a corpse   415
and was picked up, carried out and tossed onto his bed,
where he slept for hours as if dead.
    Mistylos summoned Gobryas,
and discussed the letter
and what reply should be sent to the most mighty Bryaxes.   420
Mistylos and Gobryas took a decision
and the following reply was made, after due consideration:
    "Greetings to Bryaxes the most mighty from Mistylos,[152]
from the great lord to the lord of the Pissaian fleet.
The warm regard which I truly have for you   425
cannot go unnoticed by anyone, even if they have lost their wits
(and should you ask this of anyone living in darkness,
even there you would find the same response).
And a clear proof of my admiration
are the myriads of support troops   430
that I have sent you in many places and on many occasions.
But you, it seems, put an end to this regard
and admiration and wish to circumscribe it
by seizing cities under my control
and making them completely subservient to you,   435
and by diminishing my own authority
and moreover increasing your own power.
This would seem more an indication of envy,[153]
but not a distinct sign of regard: 439
a clear demonstration of a foolish cast of mind,   442
of a mean spirit, an unloving heart,   440
an impoverished intellect and an ignoble character.   441
    And would I not act most illogically,   443
– having captured the city with an effort
and taken Rhamnon with armies   445
both on dry land and at sea,
and won the fortress at the cost of many casualties,

---

152 Marginal gloss: 'Mistylos' letter in reply to Bryaxes'.
153 Translating φθόνου ('envy'; Dawe 2001a: 14) instead of the mss' φόβου ('fear').

and lost my great satrap,
the protector of the army, my strong right arm –
if I were then, for the sake of an unfriendly friendship, to hand over   450
the rewards of my effort, that one city?
    And yet Mistylos well knows that Rhamnon is not controlled
by Bryaxes but by Mitranes,
and Mistylos has long been an enemy of Mitranes
and has ravaged his miserable territory.   455
So if anyone wants to find fault with me,
it should rightly be Mitranes,
and Bryaxes who has not been wronged
seems to be inventing an injustice.
How can it not be a mischief-making heart   460
and one that has utterly foresworn affection
that demands cities and the possessions of others
or summons to battle those who do not hand them over?
    Turning the argument to you, if you wish,
debate your own position in this regard, and think about it.[154]   465
You have equipped – say – a fleet of a thousand ships on the ocean,
you have gathered a host of naval warriors,
you have collected a formidable shield of land soldiers,
a mighty sword, and myriad-bladed spear;
you joined battle to capture Rhamnon,   470
you saw much slaughter on both sides,
you bloodied your sword, you besmirched your spear,
you reddened your man-slaying right hand
with the dreadful dye of scarlet streams of blood.
You saw the greater part of your army slain,   475
you took Rhamnon with such great toil,
you conquered it as though lord of all,
having endured such an onslaught of disasters.
    Then I came along, I demanded the city back
and proffered friendship as an inducement.   480
Would you have listened to my proposals reasonably?
Would you have restored Rhamnon to the enquirer,
and would you have satisfied the mediators' requests?
No, you would not, if you wish to be truthful.

---

154 4.464–501: The letter has now turned into an example of forensic debate.

You would indeed not have returned the city, 485
but you would have set out the trouble you had endured,
listed your efforts, described the casualties.
And I, should I, having said nothing against your arguments,
should I hand over the city so meekly?
Mistylos is not so small-minded. 490
Why not, Bryaxes, ask for all my territory
for the sake of a meaningless friendship?
    I would not abandon willingly any part,
even a tiny part, of my authority;
if by force or by the tyranny of battle 495
I am deprived of the whole, that is a small matter to me.
The definition of my opinion is this:
a man who possesses territory, whether he holds broad estates,
whether their length cannot be described,
should never willingly give any part away 500
to anyone, but if by the decree of fate
he should be deprived of the whole, he should bear this nobly;
for he remains without reproach, if he suffers against his will.
Farewell, and do not overstep your own boundaries."
    Mistylos wrote this to Bryaxes 505
and bound the letter with his seals.
He put it into hands of Artaxanes, the great satrap
(who with difficulty was reviving after his long bout of drunkenness),
speaking to him in a friendly fashion,
and, giving him no light weight of gold, 510
he sent him back to the great Bryaxes.

THE FIFTH BOOK OF THE DEEDS OF RHODANTHE
AND DOSIKLES BY THE SAME WRITER

Taking the letter and the gold
Artaxanes sailed away to his own country.
Meanwhile, anticipating events, the robber leader
(you understand this to be Mistylos, having heard often about him)   5
gave instructions to his great satrap;   4
he was struck, I think, by a not unreasonable fear   6
that Bryaxes might initiate a battle,
attack unexpectedly and without warning
and win some victory over an unprepared army.
So he told his first satrap, Gobryas,   10
to send orders to the cities under him
so that he could summon to the mustering point
allies who would be well prepared for action,
and who would be well aware
that the battle would not be without reward.   15
   Gobryas was displeased by the order,
for he had marked the following day
as that on which his marriage with Rhodanthe would be celebrated.
However, he obeyed his master's order
(appreciating that his own situation was not without danger   20
should he refuse and neglect his duty)
and hastened to fulfil the order with all speed.
Going round all the surrounding cities,
he announced to everyone with a loud proclamation
the expected battle with Bryaxes: 25
   "Allies of the mighty Mistylos,
take thought for battle and the preparations for battle.
Gird on your iron-clad equipment,
sling your shields onto your shoulders,
whet well your bronze-edged swords   30
and arm your heads with helmets
for a confrontation with the enemy.
For Bryaxes who has in no way been wronged
sets off against us, he puts a numberless fleet in motion,
he sends out many cavalry by land.   35
For servants to fight in support of their masters

is piously permitted by natural law:
your master, being honourable,
guarantees you a great mass of gold."
Thus did Gobryas commit the ruler's allies   40
to battle before the event.
    Bryaxes' satrap Artaxanes came
to Pissa, his own country,
and gave Bryaxes the letter from Mistylos.
When Bryaxes learnt its contents,   45
he raged terribly, he summoned his satraps
who were land-based and also those who fought at sea.
He drew his ships out into the open ocean
and, bellowing savagely against Mistylos,
he set a numberless force in motion against him.   50
    While he was thus making ready for battle
Artaxanes made an apprehensive speech:
"Cease, Bryaxes, preparing a useless battle
and gathering against yourself the force
you wish to collect against Mistylos.   55
Stop your huge bellowing, your great anger,
in case – when battle has broken out against you –
you become bitterly pregnant with shameful infants
and lose your manly abilities
and acquire in exchange a female fate,   60
giving birth and oozing milk from moistureless breasts.
    Are you unaware of Mistylos' power,
that he can overturn nature at will
and enslave creation by his command?
I was overwhelmed by his might,   65
for I saw, indeed I saw coming from some nethermost recess[155]
a corpse rising up holding a lyre
when Mistylos wished and commanded it.
I saw too in the middle of the banquet
a roast lamb become the bizarre father of sparrows   70
and a womb that was recently singed bring to term
unsinged offspring and winged infants."
    When Bryaxes heard these words
he said, "But I did not know, chief satrap,

155 'nethermost recess': i.e. Hades, the underworld.

that Artaxanes could be so terrified by feeble imitations   75
of bogeymen and shadows,
and be frightened of conjuring tricks
which would have no effect even on those infants
whose wits and entire mind had been stolen away
by the deceptions of buffoons and cooks.   80
    And I (but may you look kindly from above,
blessed assembly of all the gods,
and send a helping hand in the battle),
I may learn whether he who is an all-powerful transformer of nature
and miracle-worker, according to Artaxanes,   85
really can raise the dead and transform nature,
if when he succumbs to my sword as a pitiful corpse
he can resurrect himself again."
    He made this speech, and when the whole fleet
had gathered into the same place   90
he set sail, bellowing fearsome threats.
As the fleet got under way
the entire surface of the sea seemed black,
taking its colour as it were
from the blackness of the ships on it.   95
The wise versifier from Smyrna,
talking of 'grey sea' in his epic verses,
would be suspected by many of inaccurate writing
as they looked at the colour of the sea then,
and he would write better if he were to say 'black ocean'.[156]   100
But under the oars of so many vessels
the sea, a crone with wooden fingers, as it were,
tearing at her damp cheeks,
seemed to weep at the shouting and the beating,
and in her rage was forced to spit out foam   105
at great speed together with the oars.
    When Bryaxes' fleet began to come
near those cities of Mistylos,
Bryaxes immediately stepped onto a shield
that was supported from below by men's hands   110

---

156 A self-conscious writerly attitude. Homer's birthplace was disputed; in the twelfth
century a claim for Smyrna was made by Prodromos' contemporary Tzetzes: *Chiliades* 13.624.
'Grey sea': e.g. *Iliad* 1.350, *Odyssey* 2.26; 'black sea': e.g. *Iliad* 24.79.

and which held firm against the pressure of his feet;[157]
he made the following speech as the ships thronged around
and imitated, as it were, an attentive circle
at whose centre the ruler was beginning to speak:
   "Leaders of the army,[158] nurslings of the art of strategy,[159]   115
lovers of battle, illustrious soldiers,
supporters of the skills of Ares,
foster children of the sword, kinsmen of the shield,
dear infants of dear Enyo[160] –
how great is your bravery in battle,   120
how great your daring and what your endowment of temerity,
is borne true witness by all time that has gone before.
May oblivion not lay hold of Bryaxes' heart
and forgetfulness of achievements
to such an extent that my men's sound conduct   125
and abundant bravery in battle
and the fortresses captured by you
and the citadels razed to the ground
and the vessels seized at sea
(together with their cargo and their crew)   130
pass into forgetfulness, the mark of a low-born character.
   But above all do not become conceited or overbearing
as a result of recent prosperity
and think little of the battle that is about to take place,
as if the force you had previously is sufficient.   135
But rather, having learnt more precisely
from previous experiences that victory is a good thing,
make haste to take the necessary pains,

157 Shield-raising, having been part of coronation ceremonial until Phokas, fell into disuse and was not revived until the thirteenth century (*ODB*, under 'Shield-raising'). This passage, not linked to a coronation of Bryaxes, could be a piece of antiquarianism or just possibly a reflection of contemporary debate on ceremonial.

158 5.115–414: This long speech, at the centre to the book, is perhaps the most conspicuous example of an exemplary passage in *R&D*: it demonstrates what a general ought to say on going into battle. It can be seen as acknowledging the military interests of Nikephoros Bryennios (almost certainly the dedicatee and sponsor of *R&D*), and indicates yet again that Prodromos' prime interest is not in erotic psychology (unlike the other Komnenian novelists); contrast the central speeches in *D&C* 4 and 5

159 Marginal gloss: 'Bryaxes' oration'.

160 'Enyo': goddess of war (*Iliad* 5.592, 24.70), variably mother or daughter of Ares, the war god.

being eager to acquire this good benefit.
Or how would you not be afflicted with a new madness,   140
when you have learnt from previous events
that it is good to be superior in battle,
but run further away from this benefit?
   Yet there comes a surfeit in all things:
a surfeit of dining and gourmandise, a surfeit of imbibing,   145
a surfeit of the tuneful sounds of music,
a surfeit of blameless dance.
Someone experiences a quick kindling of a spark of fury,
the flame of anger lights in his heart,
as he is enraged by a slave's indiscipline   150
or provoked by his idleness.
And as fiery projectiles of wrath
kindle in the centre of his heart,
fire bursts out in speech and breath.
Seizing a stout stick in his hands   155
he beats the miscreant violently,
yet when he stops the lashing, even if with difficulty
and after some time, he would have had a surfeit of anger.
As I said, one has a surfeit of all things:
but of victory and of routing the enemy   160
the man who loves good things would never have a surfeit,
for he would be depriving himself of what is good.
   Fighting men nurtured together with your weapons,
do not – even if Mistylos' army is inadequate –
allow your enthusiasm to diminish,   165
for this will blunt the edge of your sword
and will make you more sluggish in the battle itself,
as though suspecting that the enemy will terrify
everyone by their shouts alone.
So rather, impetuous infants of Pallas,   170
for this reason it is right, in my judgement,
for you to stand firm and join battle
bearing in mind this sober judgement,
that if you are victorious, the renown will be small
(for what great trophy or what honour is it   175
if a small, inadequate, easily counted expedition
has been routed by so many marines?).

But if the black doom (but may you avert this
from Bryaxes' indomitable armies,
mighty Ares and victory-bearing Fate),   180
if it should be destined to fall unluckily upon us,
you would undoubtedly acquire great shame
when a huge army, an innumerable fleet,
has been routed by a small army, a small fleet.
   So do not, even if Mistylos is weak,   185
do not be slack in the battle dear to you,
for the old and ancient saying
counsels starting a battle against gnats
as if against all-powerful lions.[161]
What does this mean when more clearly expressed?   190
When we are opening a battle against an inadequate force,
we must not start somewhat sluggishly or unheedingly
in case we are inadvertently put to flight
by those for whom we have contempt,
and we rightly become the object of prolonged mockery.   195
   But indeed, who would say that Mistylos' expedition
is inadequate, that his fleet is small?
For my part, I would call him great and noble,
for I am aware that he has often and on many occasions
proved victorious in many battles   200
and has been fortunate with thousands of warriors at sea
and an innumerable throng of soldiers on land,
entrusting the command to many fine satraps.
Truly I dread this present battle,
knowing Mistylos' army and fleet.   205
Yet, trusting in Fate and the assistance of the gods
and in Justice who takes vengeance on mischief-makers,
I make my move confidently against Mistylos' spears.
   However, the trophies of the opposition
– boldness, daring, steadfastness –   210
should not make you abandon, as it were,
your courage in battle
and your superior power in manoeuvring,
nor should they induce you to fear Mistylos' army
for its quality and size.   215

161 Cf. *L&K* 2.22, ultimately from Aesop, Fable 267 (Hausrath 1959), 255 (Perry 1952).

For Bryaxes wants his allies
to fear the enemy sufficiently
that an end is made to contempt,
and to despise them enough
that the dread emotion of fear is put to flight,   220
overcoming both conditions as they conflict with each other
(one might appropriately call this a civil war).
   Fighting men, nurslings of the art of strategy,
even if Bryaxes has nothing else – no fleet of a thousand vessels,
no sturdy army, no innumerable spears –   225
to assist him in battle,
nor any other element of defence,
does not the hand of the gods, the dagger of Justice,[162]
fend off the law-breaker?
He has destroyed my city,   230
and of the guards whom he captured alive
he has sent some into the jaws of prison
and others he has thrust bitterly and in malevolent fashion
with his bronze-edged robber's sword
to their final leap, to deep darkness.   235
   Fighting men, skilled generals,
the oar that cuts and the blade that rows,
each fitted neatly to the other,
an army that fights on sea, a fleet that campaigns on land,
joining battle partly on water in the full extent of the sea,   240
partly on dry land
as the place and the occasion require,[163]
children of Bryaxes, friends and allies
(for I call you sons and friends and allies
to demonstrate the bonds of my love for you),   245
if you were Bryaxes' mercenaries,
if he were your master and not your progenitor,
when you were preparing battle against the enemy,
you would not have hastened for the sake of your pay
to overrun all the enemies' territory   250
and to seize and capture every city

162 Cf. Aeshylus, *Choephoroi* 647.
163 Marcovich 1992, following Hercher, suggests a lacuna here, for a phrase like 'Fighting men, nurslings of the art of war' as a parallel to 5.115, 163, 223 etc.

and to put on the august purple of victory
as you take prisoners alive or cut the enemies' throats,
gaining nothing at any time
from those who have been stripped by you.   255
For by the law of nature everything is seized
not for themselves but for the paymaster.
   But since you children will benefit
from the entire paternal inheritance,
would it not be a mark of malignant hearts   260
to wish to deprive yourselves of benefits
by not advancing against the enemy
with firm and eager heart and striking up a fierce battle
and seizing your paternal property,
acquiring city after city,   265
to increase your inheritance?
Surely leaving a hostile and alien army
to ravage our cities
while we slumber in our beds
would be the mark of great madness, of great sickness?   270
Alas, alas for the affliction of womanish minds.
   Men nurtured on death-loving battle,
army trained and reared beneath the shield,
let one attitude of mind prevail among you,
may you all agree in the union of your hearts   275
in one united and concordant counsel,
not each arguing differently and with discord among you.
For opponents have no other desire
than to see their opposition split by factions,
with some rising up against others   280
and as it were arming themselves against each other.
And indeed factions lead to disunity,
disunity is kin to party-strife,
party-strife is one and the same as battle,
and victory and rout are daughters of battle.   285
If then we join battle against ourselves,
we are both ourselves victorious and yet defeated.
Can any pain be more grievous than this?
   What other curse would Mistylos' expedition call down
on Bryaxes' myriad commanders   290

greater than this? But, Ares, may you prevent
us from joining battle among ourselves
while they sit and roar with gusts of laughter
and then, because we were helpless, defeat us
with bare hands; for they would not need to use a sword   295
to capture us, if we were already worn out
with fighting each other and softened up.
Therefore, so that this possibility may be kept remote,
let one attitude of mind prevail among you.
    How would you not succumb to the pangs of madness   300
as you took up arms against yourselves
and did not spare your own flesh
but hastened to devour your own true limbs,
as if you had become like demons?
Or like a great boar which rushes out of a thicket   305
and falls on the nimble hunters
and, while someone has already embedded the sword point in him,
thrusts it deep into his entrails,[164]
charging madly at the sword,
and causes a bitter death for himself,   310
a valiant warrior working his own slaughter
– are you too sharpening the blade like this against yourselves?
    Men, even if the power of the gods
were to grant you superiority with Justice as your ally,
even if you were to gain possession of Mistylos' men,   315
do not rush off to seize the spoils
and gulp them down greedily in your eagerness to devour them,
do not swallow the hook as well
(I mean the concealed and abrupt death).
For I have often and in many places known   320
many small, cowardly men who are incompetent in battle
but who even so captured their enemies by a trick.
For they displayed in front of themselves
quantities of vessels, food and clothing
and they killed their enemies pitiably   325
as they came upon on these things when not expecting them.

---

164 Retaining (with Conca 1994) the line ordering of the mss (Marcovich 1992 transposes
308 and 309).

This is how the angler is able to hunt
most sea-creatures,
by offering them food and concealing the barb of death.
   It would be a mere disgrace for Bryaxes' allies 330
to become victims of the enemies' sword,
it would be more of a disgrace should you perish
in the act of carrying off your booty as you loot the city.
Therefore, so that none of these dreadful things befall you,
let no one consider carrying off booty; 335
for he who is preoccupied with booty
offers Mistylos an opportunity to escape
and hence to flee our sword.
By looting he will waste time
in luxuriating in the booty, 340
and out of light-headedness he would succumb completely
to what afflicted a foolish and senseless huntsman.
When he, the huntsman, found not a few partridges
and caught one only out of the large flock,
he lit a fire to roast and eat it; 345
and so the whole flock immediately flew off
and slipped out of the huntsman's hands,
for they found escape very easy
while he was eating the one partridge he had managed to catch.
And he had senselessly wasted on a foolish task 350
time better spent in hunting,
and gained nothing from his expedition.
Or how would you not seem mad
when you robbed your own possessions as if they were others'?
For Mistylos' possessions would become ours, 355
should Fortune grant victory over him.
   Men – but, blessed Justice, may
Bryaxes' allies come off better –,
should we come off the worse since Fortune is maliciously disposed,
should we experience a shameful defeat since Justice does not
    intervene, 360
and should we not be superior since the gods are asleep,
do not turn to flight, do not rush down
the rearward path with unmanned hearts,
do not with ignoble judgment exchange

inglorious safety for a good death,   365
a mean life for a more renowned demise.
It would be better for us, should we be rent asunder,
should we be crushed, should we endure death,
to provide work for the enemies' sword,
yes, it would be better for us to fall in the thick of battle,   370
with our bows and with our shields,
than to be routed, to flee from the field and live.
For it is an attribute of manly daring
to die for one's children and to fall for the sake of one's country,
but to direct one's reins to flight,   375
to cast aside one's weapons and to run away
belongs to an unmanly and womanish soul.
    Moreover, who can guarantee that those who flee
the battle will also flee death,
and above all that Mistylos' fleet   380
will remain quiet in its own country,
allowing passage to us in our flight,
and not pursue and capture the fugitives
and submerge them all in a watery grave?
Or perhaps this is too much for the enemy.   385
For fear, arriving in advance of Mistylos,
would offer us death before it happened[165] and extermination
    before the sword thrust,
slashing away – as it were – at our hopes.[166]
So that you keep all this far distant,
do not rush off in flight in an ignoble way.   390
    For if it were possible to escape from death
and evade extinction completely,
as if one were endowed with unending life,
even then it would be contemptible to run away from battle.
For, tell me, who, terrified by death   395
and endowed by Fortune with unending life,
would even so be pardoned for this state of mind?
Since, were we to flee from the centre of the battle,
we would not be able to evade death,

---

165 Cf. *DigAk* G6.140, derived from *L&K* 3.11.2
166 Translating (with Conca 1994) the mss' ἐλπίσιν rather than ἐμπίσιν ('gnats'; Marcovich 1992).

why should we not fulfil our inevitable destiny　　　　400
with honour for ourselves forthwith?
Or if, ordained as death is by nature,
we should be able to filch a more glorious death,
is it good – by fleeing the sword's edge –
to increase our life and time?　　　　405
But it is shameful, shameful to incur the charge of disgrace,
to live in ignominy and to spend one's life ridiculed.
　　Men, all my intention and my discourse
leads to this and has this conclusion:
that you should have no delusion, no assumption of victory;　　　　410
you should avoid contempt as well as fear;
you should in addition hate factions among yourselves;
you should not charge greedily after loot when you have acquired it
nor should you turn in flight when you are defeated."[167]
　　This is what Bryaxes, a fluent orator,　　　　415
said publicly to the sailors under him.
When the entire speech came to an end,
he took a cup of unmixed wine in his right hand
and another full of sea water
and he raised them both up. Pouring them into the sea,　　　　420
he said, "Poseidon and gods of the sea,
lord Poseidon, emperor of the briny,
who stirs up the broad and deep ocean
with a mere gesture from your trident,
and also institutes and sets up squalls,　　　　425
and smites the angry sea
with the rod of your anger, as it were,
and enslaves the winds' breezes
(they blow where you wish, and where you do not wish them to blow,
they subserviently maintain calm),　　　　430
come, admiral of Bryaxes' fleet,
avenger of Mistylos' sea-battles,
and quaff the unmixed wine that is now poured for you."
　　He said this and he bade the oarsmen
to move the triremes with all speed　　　　435
so that they might reach Mistylos' city
unlooked for and, not being noticed,

167 A well-rounded conclusion to a carefully constructed speech.

might attack unexpectedly like a cloudburst[168]
and bring darkness upon their opponents
and work a myriad deaths upon them.   440
As the expedition made its way forward
and perceived the enemy's fleet in the distance,
drawn up under arms in good order,
it was no small tremor that ran through them,
that they had failed in the expectations they had nurtured.   445
    Mistylos' triremes could be seen;[169]
there were very many of them and they were all fine
and fully equipped and dressed over all, as it were.
As much of the ships as was not submerged
but rode above the sea's ridge,   450
from the second wale as far as the third,
was swathed with thick matted felt
– a device of wise counsel and strategy
so that the majority of missiles that were aimed
stuck there and could not proceed further   455
and fall on those standing midship
but remained embedded in the felt.[170]
Above this array of felt
was suspended a quantity of long shields,
and this too was the device of a far-seeing man.[171]   460
For a man standing between two shields
could from there strike at the opposition,
but he himself, withdrawing behind the shields
unwounded, continued to be unharmed.
The positioning of the shields   465
was like that of the tops of the walls and turrets
from which archers aim their shots
(these are generally called the walls' teeth).[172]

168 A Homeric metaphor: cf. *Iliad* 4.274, 16.66.
169 Marginal gloss: 'Mistylos' battle-line'.
170 Prodromos has an interest in naval technology: cf. the 'frogmen' at 6.8. 'Cilician' matting, which would have been used to protect ships' sides in this way, was part of the equipment provided for the Cretan expeditions of 911 and 949 (Haldon 1999: 227, line 135; Pryor and Jeffreys 2006: 551).
171 Cf. the shields over the sides of the warships (*dromons*) in an illustration to Pseudo-Oppian, *Kynegetika* (Venice, Marc. Gr. 479, f. 23; Pryor and Jeffreys 2006: 273, fig. 26).
172 For a city's walls compared to teeth, cf. MangProd 24.8–12.

Such was the disposition of the triremes.
A host of huge vessels wreathed around 470
Mistylos' entire fleet in a circle
(but they left a narrow outlet
to provide a way out for the sailors),
and on the area beyond these on the cliffs
a great swarm of cavalry had settled. 475
When Bryaxes saw this and the rest of the forces
he was terrified of the enemy's army
and cowardice overcame him in place of his former courage;
he gave a letter to the satrap Artapes
(Artaxanes indeed was not with the fleet, 480
for he had been sent with a force of land-soldiers,
a thousand shields strong, to join battle on foot)
and he sent it to the emperor Mistylos.[173]
The contents of that letter were as follows:
"When I first wrote to you, Mistylos,[174] 485
and denounced your outrage against us
– how you captured my city of Rhamnon,
broke the treaty, tore up the laws
and seized the guards all together,
some of whom you cut down, others you kept in bonds 490
(you cannot say, subverting justice,
that ignorance caused the battle,
that you did not realize the city was Bryaxes') –
there should have been no need of a second discussion,
but we should simply have taken in battle 495
the city of which we had been deprived
and indeed recovered more than we had lost, if possible.
But since the bonds of affection have often and on many occasions
united Mistylos to Bryaxes,
I now begin a second communication: 500
either restore our city to us
and finally set free those prisoners whom you put in chains,
or you will see our expedition under arms."

173 This reflects the regular Byzantine reluctance to join battle unless absolutely necessary;
cf. Maurice, *Strategikon* 8.1. On Byzantine attitudes to warfare see, e.g., Miller and Nesbitt
1995; Haldon 1999.
174 Marginal gloss: 'Bryaxes' second letter'.

When Mistylos read this letter,
he made no written response but replied 505
to Bryaxes' satrap Artapes,
"How accurately would your lord and my friend
have learnt my opinion, satrap,
if he had gone through the letter sent to him a little while ago
and had understood what he had read." 510
When he heard these comments,
Artapes returned to Bryaxes
and reported to his master everything that had been said
and caused his master's heart to be filled with rage.
And he would have joined battle immediately, 515
such was the fury seething in his heart,
had not the shades of evening intervened
and confined the swords in their scabbards.
And so he remained quietly amid his vessels
until he saw day dawning. 520

THE SIXTH BOOK OF THE DEEDS OF RHODANTHE
AND DOSIKLES BY THE SAME WRITER

The giant Helios had just
drawn his untiring chariot up from the world below
and was driving it along the path above us,
when Bryaxes rose from his couch
and solicited the gods of the sea 5
and Ares and Pallas on high.[175]
When he had made his prayer, he went to the front ranks of the battle
and he told the divers, stout-hearted fellows
whom he had had trained in diving,[176]
to take iron hammers in their hands 10
(but small ones, so that the weight

175 'Pallas': Athene (goddess of wisdom) in her warlike aspect; Athene also contested with the sea-god Poseidon for possession of Attica; cf. Apollodoros, *Bibliotheke* 3.12.3, 3.14.1.
176 'diving': another instance of interest by Prodromos in maritime warfare. Hunger 1972 refers to these divers as medieval 'frogmen'; however, this passage is as likely to be a piece of antiquarianism as a reflection of contemporary activities (cf. Herodotos 8.8, on Skyllias diving under the Persian fleet and the sixth-century (?) Syrianus 4.4, in Pryor and Jeffreys 2006: 456–57).

should not drag them down too)
and plunge surreptitiously into the sea
(so that their ploy should remain unnoticed by the enemy)
and swim under Mistylos' triremes 15
and secretly break open their keels[177]
so that the water would pour in
from the holes and fissures there
and a watery grave be prepared for those within.
Instantly the divers brought 20
a favourable conclusion to the instructions,
and Bryaxes got the fleet under way,
since Mistylos was in front of him,
and from that point engaged in a grim battle.
In the first stages and at the beginning of the battle 25
Mistylos' fleet got the better of the conflict,
for Gobryas captured three triremes
from the hostile armada,
together with their weapons and their crewmen,
and all but routed the opposition 30
and put them to general flight.
But the divers, whom I have already described,
swam beneath the ships with their hammers
and destroyed their lower joints,
and brought an unexpected death to many; 35
for they stood tightly packed together,
engaged in battle with iron swords
when a damp-bladed sword slew them.
  It was then that a sight full of tears[178]
and overflowing with pity could have been seen by a tender heart. 40
For a skilful archer
took his bow and drew back the cord
but before he could release the arrow, unhappy victim,
he fell untimely and before his allotted span

---

177 Or 'break off their spurs'? γεῖσσα, translated here as 'keel', is an unexpected word to use in connection with ships: it properly means coping stone or cornice, something projecting from a roof; however, spurs, projecting from the prow and a development of the antique ram, were not an integral part of the hull structure, unlike the antique ram, and so violent removal is unlikely to have damaged the hull (see Pryor and Jeffreys 2006: 203–10).

178 Marginal gloss: 'Mistylos' downfall'.

into the sea's insatiable belly,   45
bow, arrow and all,
with no knowledge of who had smitten him.
Another picked up a heavy rock in his hands
but before he could take aim and throw it
he, thrice miserable, was buffeted by a watery sling-shot   50
and could not gasp out even one final word.
   Mistylos' satrap Gobryas,
whom I have often mentioned in my discourse,[179]
shouted out tersely, "Alas, Rhodanthe,
I am taken from you and with me is taken our marriage";   55
and with that cry he cast forth his soul.
Eros is a most violent force in men of evil disposition
when it flies into the innermost heart
and intends to remain there permanently
and keeps incessant doleful vigils.   60
For the heart, when catastrophe has struck,
scorns everything, including death and the sword,
and attaches itself entirely (even if dragged away by force)
to the vision of the beloved.
   And so almost all Mistylos' men,   65
or indeed the largest part of the fleet at that time,
drank down the briny and departed this life,
vomiting up their souls together with what they had drunk.
And so the lack of a stable force
was balanced by an abundance of good counsel,   70
and it is best to have a weak counsellor
than for someone who is strong in body not to give counsel.[180]
   Such was the end of their life for these men
(for the body of the discourse must continue
although split asunder by a digression).[181]   75
A small contingent, whose station had been by the cliffs,
used vigorous rowing (unhappy oarsmen)
to flee from death on the sea,

179 Does this reminder to the reader, or hearer, indicate a gap in composition or performance?
   180 A curious comment, presumably summing up the success of the divers of 6.8 ff. who
ensured that the battleships were indeed a force that lacked stability on the sea; cf. MangProd
6.26–49 on a rhetorician's amazement that battles can take place at sea on shifting decks.
   181 Again an authorial intervention.

but fell victim unheeded to those from whose traps they had fled
by landing on dry land.   80
For Bryaxes' satrap Artaxanes
had advanced on foot to Mistylos' city
and slew those who had escaped a watery grave.
For so inescapable is the fate that has been decreed;
if the thread of your life has been snapped   85
you will not survive, however far you run;
if you escape the sea, land is nearby,
if you escape the land, then air is present;
the gods are everywhere.[182]
    When the unfortunate Mistylos saw this,[183]
he stood on high on the vessel's sailyard   90
and seized a naked blade with both hands;
he groaned deeply and with a bitter shout said,
"Mistylos, often on many people in many places
you have inflicted death with these hands;
since now the envy of the gods and of Fate   95
have already delivered you to Bryaxes' blade,
do not insist on dying by a spurious sword,
let your own hand and blade kill you.
Do not allow your enemy
to speak words of disdain, nor his neighbour   100
to hear that it was the edge of his knife
that found a target in Mistylos' neck."
These were his words and immediately
he plunged his own sword into his entrails,
and wrought a bitter death upon himself.   105
    When the battle had come to an end in this way,[184]
the sailors who were allied with Bryaxes,
together with the emperor[185] himself and the satraps,
left their vessels empty

---

182 A universal thought, found in Psalm 138/139.7–10, as well as the pre-Socratic philosopher Thales (quoted in Aristotle, *De anima* 411a7) and in Plato, *Laws* 10, 899b; in Byzantine novels and romances it becomes a cliché, cf. *H&H* 2.14.5; *A&K* fr. 8; *DigAk* E 1397–98; *L&Rα* 592–93.

183 Marginal gloss: 'Mistylos' suicide'.

184 Marginal gloss: 'The capture of Mistylos' city and Dosikles' and Rhodanthe's second imprisonment'.

185 It is now Bryaxes who is termed emperor; Prodromos uses the title freely.

and advanced on foot to Mistylos' city   110
to collect all the men up in a group
and to enslave the city itself
since it had been stripped of its lord and its allies.[186]
   Then it was possible to see the temples looted,
the statues of the gods overthrown,   115
the pictures of heroes defiled,
the capture of houses, the murder of their inhabitants,
the laments of women, the wails of children.
A host of bitter Furies danced,
the Titans[187] descanted[188] upon the evils,   120
Pallas sported, Ares was delighted.
The sword devoured much raw flesh,
the dagger drank streams of blood.
   There were improvised couches, rapes of virgins,
a bridal chamber on the ground and an earth-strewn marriage bed,   125
the pregnant belly was torn open;
the dead womb brought forth a dead infant.
The old father lamented for his young son,
the young son lamented for his old mother.
There was no pity, not for the old, not for the infant,   130
not for those in the flowering of their middle years;
the husband wailed as he saw his wife
unwillingly overpowered on the marriage couch.
   Wealthy women (oh, bitter fate)
had their rings cut off with their fingers;   135
the poverty-stricken prospered with a bizarre wealth,
for they retained their bodies; but in the end
neither slave nor master could escape:
there was one fate for all and one law.
One chain dragged on many necks;   140
mother, father, son, children, bride, bridegroom,
adolescent, young man, a man in his maturity, an old man,

186 6.114–46: A set-piece description of a looted town.
187 The Furies, demons who pursue wrongdoers, most conspicuously in Aeschylus' *Oresteia* trilogy; the Titans, the generation of gods preceding the Olympians, with whom they fought fiercely (e.g. Apollodoros, *Bibliotheke* 1.1.7.ii).
188 'descanted': ἐπιτραγῳδέω has overtones of tragic performance; cf. Hel 1.3.2, 2.29.4, 7.6.4 and note at *D&C* 2.35.

rich, needy, master, servant,
sick, healthy, fortunate, unfortunate,
slave-girl, mistress, virgin, old woman, young woman –   145
all were led by the one rope.
   And so, what then? They took Dosikles alive,
together with Rhodanthe. But how was it possible to capture alive
out of them all only the one who was united with the girl?[189]
When the young people were caught   150
and their delicate necks were bound,
they were exceedingly distressed; how could they not be,
since they were enslaved yet again to other masters
and moreover (alas) again to barbarians,
recalling their uncertain fates?   155
But they had this relief to their burden,
though not bound by marriage ties,
that they were bound nevertheless by ties of slavery;
and they had consolation from the fate of Gobryas,
that with his departure from life went also his violence.   160
   Dosikles was distressed, he shed a tear,
he mourned not his own unhappy fate
but that of Rhodanthe, his beloved girl,
as he saw her tender neck in chains;
Rhodanthe was distressed, she uttered a great lament   165
as she saw Dosikles in chains.
Simply forgetful of themselves, as it were,
the couple grieved for each other,
she weeping for Dosikles and he for Rhodanthe.
   Carried off also with them was the foreigner Kratandros,   170
who had been captured and imprisoned with them.
They were all taken to somewhere near the harbour;
when they came close to the place,
Artapes separated the prisoners into two groups
and he filled one vessel with the men   175
and the other with the women.
When Dosikles realized the division
he said, "But if you tear me away
from my maiden sister, leader of the satraps,

---

189 Should this be read as a self-critical comment on an improbable plot?

I shall put an end to the drama[190] of my fate   180
by throwing myself into the midst of the sea."
   As he said this an uncouth barbarian
who was standing nearby, a huge ruthless giant,
struck the handsome young man in the face
and threw him against his will into the middle of the vessel.   185
What then? Dosikles' cheek was grazed,
but Rhodanthe's heart was torn;
he had a wound on his face but her wound
was in her heart and yet she restrained
her welling tears, lest they should reveal the desire   190
that was in her breast and perchance become the cause of evil.
   The pair of vessels sailed away,
bearing the young people's expired union,
the one taking Rhodanthe and the other Dosikles.
For just as a coherent body which has breath   195
(by which you should understand a man, a horse, an ox, a dog),
when it is split by the sword and divided down the middle,
perishes in both parts (and how could it not,
when a coherent whole is cut into two segments?
For creatures which possess sense perception are not   200
constructed like the vegetable world
where a branch cut from a plant puts out shoots again and has life;
but if you cut an ox down the middle in two segments,
you immediately cut out its life),
even so for these young people the separation then   205
was nothing other than death (oh, bitter fate).[191]
   The freighters, as I said, sailed away
with straight-blowing winds as their escorts.
A second night intervened and a vigorous southerly wind
driving up fiercely full from the south   210
immediately mounded up the sea's ridges,
it raised up on it many hills of waves
from the gulfs below as far as the ocean floor.[192]

---

190 On drama and fate, cf. *L&K* 1.3.3, 7.3.1; Charit 4.4.2; see the discussion in Agapitos 1998 on the implications of the term *drama* in the novels. Here the meaning seems to be 'events'.

191 6.195–206: Another example of school-derived (?) philosophical logic-chopping.

192 Storms at sea are a regular hazard in the late antique and Komnenian novels; cf. *L&K*

Poseidon provoked the southerly wind,
and the vigorous southerly in turn roused the sea,   215
and the sea the ships and the ships those within;
the passengers, the sea, the vessels
endured one and the same storm and tempest.
The roaring of the sea's expanse found its counterpart
in the anguished roars of the voyagers.   220
   Not without tears all sent up pleas of desperation,
enduring suffering in common they called on the gods in common,
they sent up their pleas; but it was not possible to see
the envy of Fate placating the storm.
For one of the two freighters we have spoken of   225
(Rhodanthe's ship, the wretched maiden)
was dashed against a concealed rock
and broken in pieces, disgorging its cargo.
And immediately the whole throng of women[193]
who were crammed into the bitter hull   230
found the sea (alas, the suffering) a common grave,
apart from Rhodanthe (oh, the great pity of the gods,
by whom she had already been betrothed to Dosikles).
For, grasping a fragment of the ship,
she lightly rode out the storm,   235
bestriding the plank like a jockey.[194]
   When she had drifted for a long way,
and the storm was already taking a brief respite,
she encountered some merchant vessels
which were making directly for the region of Cyprus,   240
and she begged the merchants who were sailing
in them to rescue her.
They, somewhat overcome by her request,
immediately pulled her on board
and, happening on a more helpful wind,   245
sailed to the island by the third day.
And when they had sold the goods in which they were trafficking

---

3.4.3, 5.9.1–2; *H&H* 7.8–16. On the role attributed to the sea-gods, cf. 6.305–07

193 Marginal gloss: 'Rhodanthe's shipwreck and rescue, and conveyance to Cyprus and sale'.

194 As did Odysseus (*Odyssey* 5.371). Dawe 2001a: 15 suggests drawing on the alternative meaning of κέλης, 'yacht', to read 'rode out the storm like a yacht, bestriding the plank'.

(robes, gems, pearls, aromatic woods,
everything that comes from India and Alexandria)
for not a few talents of gold,   250
they finally gave the girl to Kraton,
the unfortunate begetter of Kratandros,
for a price of thirty golden *minai*.[195]
      And so Rhodanthe embraced a slave's fate
and the light of slavery rather than that of freedom.   255
But what voice, what human speech
is capable of describing Dosikles' grief?
When the sea's turmoil had passed
and the gales had subsided at dawn,
he cast frequent encircling glances from his eyes   260
and gazed all around
but could not see the vessel that was sailing with them,
and immediately thought of a shipwreck.
"Alas, Rhodanthe," he said as he wailed at length,[196]
"alas, Rhodanthe, beloved appellation;   265
is this to be the end of my passion for you?
Is this to be the reward which you win for your pains?
A watery marriage chamber and a liquescent couch,
a watery bridal bower and a sea-girt wedding,
the ocean for your house and a life with the fishes?   270
      You have not appeased the bitter demands of Fate,
you who have been twice taken prisoner by barbarians,
who have had your feet, hands and your very neck bound,
far from your homeland, isolated,
a stranger to your dear father and dear mother.   275
All this has not satisfied Fate's insatiable belly
nor brought surfeit to its gorge
but, gaping greedily out of gluttony,
it has gulped you down shamelessly,
shattering the massive tome of your drama.[197]   280

---

195 *Mina, minai*: an ancient (Greek) unit of weight, equivalent to one hundred drachmas.

196 Marginal gloss: 'Dosikles' lament for Rhodanthe's shipwreck'. 6.264–413: Another exemplary lament (for a presumed death), again with elements of an *ethopoiia* ('what a lover might say when his beloved is shipwrecked').

197 A further instance of writerly self-consciousness? As indicated above (6.180), 'drama' has multiple meanings in a Byzantine context.

Two robber bands have caught us,
the enemy Bryaxes and another enemy, Mistylos;
but hope came upon me, and gave me the comfortable thought
of seeing again the light of freedom
when the fog[198] of slavery had been removed.   285
But now the bitter enemy, hostile nature,
the barbarian sea, the harshness of men
have enclosed you viciously in a new prison,
have enthralled you with a new coil of chains,
from which there is little hope of escape.   290
   Alas, Rhodanthe, where is the springtime of your youth,
the cypress of your fair figure,
the roses of your cheeks and your lips,
the ivy of your locks (that strange adornment)[199]
which weaves around your head as if round a plane tree?   295
Where are the lilies of your fair kisses,
the myrtle of your body, the verdure of your flesh,
the flowers of your eyelids? Alas, maiden,
the apple has shrivelled, the pomegranate has withered,
the trees have lost their leaves, the lilies have drooped;   300
the fruit lies on the ground, the charm has perished,
autumn has come too soon upon the year.[200]
Alas, your body is food for fishes,
your flesh is a banquet for the denizens of the deep.
How jealous is the nature of winds: 305
Zephyr slew Hyacinth
and envious Notos[201] has just thrown a spell over Rhodanthe.
   It seems, despicable Gobryas, that
in your death you were to join Rhodanthe in marriage,
whom you were eager to acquire when alive but were prevented,   310

198 Translating (with Conca 1994) the mss' νέφους rather than κνέφους ('darkness'; Marcovich 1992).

199 Literally 'strange grace', or 'charm': a self-aware comment that this is a bizarre conceit?

200 The fruits mentioned here are symbols of fecundity, both biblical and in classical literature and mythology; cf. *D&C* 6.66–74. Conca 1994 points out that roses are a possible play on Rhodanthe's name, and that apples can stand for breasts.

201 Zephyr (west wind) and Notos (south wind); Hyacinth was killed when Zephyr, jealous that Hyacinth preferred the god Apollo, blew Apollo's discus off course, which then struck Hyacinth (Lucian, *Dialogue of the Gods* 16 (14).2; Nonnos, *Dionysiaka* 10.253-3); the same examples appear at *D&C* 4.250–53.

while Fate mocks at my misfortunes.
Because you share a common means of death,
because you have been allotted a common grave in death
and have been granted a common bridal procession –
drowning, waves, the Nereids –   315
you may be happy there, robber Gobryas;
but you will not possess love for ever,
for I will join Rhodanthe with all speed;
indeed you will discover what is a pure passion
and you will learn the strength of a jealous heart.   320
    You, the maiden Rhodanthe, golden girl,
eye and light and breath of Dosikles,
you were often driven by the upheaval of the waves,
you were gusted along by the blasts of the winds,
tossed up to the airy heights   325
and thrust down to the furthest deeps;
whirled lightly from hither to yon
as the wind and the wave took you.
You brought Dosikles to your lips,
calling on the wretch to save you,   330
and you recalled his former speeches
and you shouted out his sworn pledges
except the waves barred your mouth.
    I, the tormented one (for how could I look
on such suffering, Zeus and all the gods?   335
Who could have foretold and predicted the fates?
Or who in his predictions could have expected to seem correct?
For a man's soul which has a rather sincere desire
for a certain thing and a vehement attachment
usually thinks those who agree with what he wishes to say   340
are correct and those who say the opposite are
hostile, hateful, miserable, writers of falsehoods),
I lay in silence (what highmindedness),
not blushing at these words,
leaving you to struggle alone in the storm,   345
and I remained in cowardly quiet in the freighter,
as if you embraced for another and not Dosikles
the unending torments you were enduring.
    O charm, O beauty, O grace from the gods,

it is I who am your murderer, not the tempest.   350
Why did I steal you from your dear land and
your dear habitation and your kinsmen's blood?
Why did I convey you to a foreign land and
foreign dwelling and piratical malevolence?
Did I not know that the fates are mischievous?   355
Did I not know that ambushes and robber bands
await travellers, that storms and
pirate fleets encounter those who sail?
Why then, since I know the upsets that life brings,
did I bring you miserably to this foreign land,   360
tearing you away from your kinsmen's embraces?
    They were no mean expectations that comforted us
as we set off on our journey from Abydos to Rhodes,
expecting our wedding in alien places,
dreaming of our beds in foreign lands   365
and imagining our marriage couches and bridal procession;
the anticipated pregnant belly delighted us,
the expected infants pleased us,
we set up the splendid bridal chamber that was to be,
we invented fruit of our loins that did not yet exist,   370
feeding on a fictitious fruit; for envy
did not allow our hopes to be fulfilled.[202]
For you have the sea in place of your bridal chamber,
the crashing of waves in place of the beat of drums,
the flash of lightning in place of torches,   375
the lord of the watery deeps in place of your bridegroom;
and you the bride are the banquet (oh, bitter marriage),
set out as nourishment for those set aside for food.[203]
    Did you enjoy your daughter well,
mother and father of Rhodanthe, Phryne and Straton?   380
Did you set up together a lovely chamber for the marriage,
did you weave together a lovely garland for the girl,
did you light a brilliant torch,
did you have this joy from your guardianship?
Have you seen the result of the invocations   385

202 An insight into Byzantine family feelings.
203 Rhodanthe's imagined corpse is now feeding the fishes.

which you sent to the gods, hapless Straton?
Have you seen your child in the midst of her wedding
and have you greeted your daughter's garland
(which is the first prayer of affectionate fathers)?
Have you seen your daughter's child, Phryne,   390
and have you preserved the continuation of your family during
    your lifetime?
Oh, all this is in vain and the word is an empty custom;[204]
the yawning ocean has swallowed up your hopes.
    Is this the truth of the god-delivered words?
Has not Hermes' utterance been disproved,   395
which foretold the marriage of Rhodanthe and Dosikles?
To whose speeches then should one listen,
whose pronouncements should be considered correct,
or should one believe that there is a limit to speech
when the gods falsify their promises,   400
they who are the upholders of a guaranteed truth?
Who then would not turn to telling lies
to become like the immortals?[205]
    O abyss of the ocean and heart of the sea,
do you have no perception? You should   405
at least have been aware of Rhodanthe lying there
and you should not have buried a treasure of this sort,
which is too precious, in your own depths.
So be it; you are already dead, maiden,
abandoning your Dosikles to this life;   410
yet Dosikles cannot abandon you,
but, if you have any sensation in the world below,
look on me as I share the shipwreck with your graceful self."
    These were his words and, shouting out "Envy, take your fill",
he rushed towards the waves;   415
and he would swiftly have acquired a rapid death
and an immediate end through his reckless daring,

204 Translating (with Conca 1994) the mss' νόμος rather than μόνος ('only'; Marcovich 1992 and others).

205 Presumably one should not look for the authorial voice in this comment; however, the interplay between the roles of the Olympian deities in *R&D*'s plot and the expectations of the Christianized society of Prodromos' Constantinople is interesting; cf. Burton 1998; Roilos 2005: 203–23; Kaldellis 2007.

had he not been restrained by Kratandros' intervention
both with his hands and his persuasive words.
"Why, Dosikles, in such confused circumstances[206]   420
do you hasten so precipitously to die?" he said.
"Indeed, by the gods, listen to what I have to say.
   If while Rhodanthe were still preserved in this life
you were to fall hazardously into the ocean,
would it be possible to rise up from the deep   425
and cohabit with the girl and be united with her
and escape from such a chasm (O gods, how great it is)
and flee from the darkness,
while the bonds of death are laid aside?
It is not possible for those have once left this life,   430
who have turned to dust, who have mingled with those below,
who have sailed across the Acherousian lake,
who have sipped one cup from Lethe
or drunk from the goblet of Kokytos or Styx,[207]
it is not possible for them to see the day dawn again.   435
   If indeed your maiden has died
(let this be put plainly and brought into the argument),
why do you welcome death?
Cut the tip of your hair on behalf of the dead girl,
shed a bitter tear from your eyelids,   440
rend your tunic, groan deeply,
hurl yourself face down on the ground,
put ashes on your head, if that is your wish;
these are not manly actions but must be accepted
when a soul has been captured by love.   445
   I suffered the same affliction in similar circumstances,
when I was captivated by a well-born maiden
(you have already heard from me about Chrysochroe);
the girl died when her head was crushed;
I wept for the dead girl as I should,   450
I absented myself from gatherings of my kin,
from my friends, from my dear land, from my ancestral clan;
but I would not have responded to the girl with death.

---

206 Marginal gloss: 'Kratandros' speech of encouragement'.
207 The rivers Styx (Hateful), Kokytos (Wailing), Lethe (Oblivion) and the Acherousian Lake are features of the underworld of classical Greek mythology.

If there was perception among the dead,
or if there was knowledge of what we do in our lives,   455
or a glimmering of a mind or the slightest hint of speech,
you would be pardoned for dying for your beloved.
But since those who have fallen lack perception
and are altogether unaware of life,
grief, sickness, tears, lamentation, pain,   460
drink-offerings, first fruits, the meat of sacrifices,
brothers' mourning, mothers' pitiful weeping,
lovers' deaths, seas, swords,
what benefit would you gain from death?[208]
    You are to be chided for your petty spirit,   465
even if we grant that your maiden is dead;
but I, stranger, am a prophet for you,
that Rhodanthe survives and lives, not happily
(how can she, when separated from Dosikles?),
and so she lives, I conjecture, a tearful life.   470
But Hermes could not be false in his promises,
a god by nature and the attendant of gods."
    Such was Kratandros' speech,
by which he intended to settle Dosikles,
but he did not realize that he was speaking to deaf ears;[209]   475
for Dosikles began his tale of woe again,
as if he had heard nothing of what had been said,
and fitted his words to his previous lament.
"Alas, Rhodanthe, what place conceals you?[210]
How fortunate is that place," he said, "maiden.   480
Do you remain within the deep itself,
or has the ocean found you and tossed you aside, a corpse,
and thrown you out, a naked body?
And who either passing by along the sandy shore
or sailing on the edge of the sea   485
has seen you, O gods, unveiled?
    Have fishes torn you apart and ravaged you

---

208 In contrast to the lyrical account of the young lovers' expectations from their anticipated marriage, nothing softens this bleak picture: there is no hint of a Christian philosophy of death.

209 A realistic comment (but proverbial: Matthew 13.13; Apostolios 10.36 [Leutsch and Schneidewin 1839–51, vol. 2]).

210 Marginal gloss: 'Dosikles' lament'.

or have the waves battered you with their pebbles
and dashed you onto submerged rocks?
Or are you breathing a little and still gasping,   490
or are you recently drowned and swallowed by a sea-monster?
How terrible is all this, and beyond terror;
and yet my grief would be more bearable,
should your body not be thrown up naked by the cliffs." [211]

    Such was the tempest for Dosikles,   495
when the freighter of his mind was
all but hurled into an ocean of pain;
the ship into which he was loaded
reached Pissa on the eleventh day,
having wrestled with many wild tempests.   500
So when everyone disembarked from the vessel,
they were flung into gloomy prisons
together with the friends Dosikles and Kratandros,
until Bryaxes should enter the city
and announce the verdict that had been passed on them.   505

THE SEVENTH BOOK OF THE DEEDS OF RHODANTHE
AND DOSIKLES BY THE SAME WRITER

For Kratandros and for Dosikles too
there was once again imprisonment, once again captivity,
iron fetters and forged manacles,
and as well fear from vain hopes.
But what of Rhodanthe? Even if she suffered a slave's fate,   5
even if she had Kraton as her new master,
she was not ignorant of her former master Eros;
even if, through Fate, she had Stale as her mistress,
she was not ignorant of her former mistress Aphrodite;
even if she found a huge swarm of new fellow slaves,   10
she knew that Dosikles was also a slave;
she mourned his absence frequently,
uttering a solemn lament in secret,
lest she be noticed by her new masters

211 The possibility of nudity (about which Byzantines were ambivalent) has added to the
horror of the situation; cf. *ODB*, under 'Nude, the', and Zeitler 1999.

and draw many punishments on herself.   15
    So, flinging herself on the ground in the middle of the night,[212]
"Alas, Dosikles," she cried out miserably,[213]
"Dosikles, my husband in speech alone,
what land bears you, what sea, what abyss?
What ship, what vessel, what prison, what darkness?   20
What barbarian hand, what inimical violence?
What fame, what couch, what new life?
What house, what rod of office, what jest of Fate?
What bliss, what betrothal, what new passion?
What bridal chamber, what marriage, what maiden?   25
What forgetfulness of sworn pledges?
Are you still alive for me, Dosikles, and do you breathe the air?
Do you see the light of slavery or the day of freedom?
Are you throttled with bonds, have you shed your chains?
Do you serve the lord Bryaxes as satrap?   30
Have you found another barbarian to be your new master?
Do you dwell in Pissa, do you sail the sea?
Tempest or calm? Billows or a smooth passage?
Opposing winds or unruffled waters?
Is your ship sound or rotten, its hull whole or perished?   35
    Did you see Rhodanthe carried off to the deep?
Did you not see her, as the cloud came up over us?
Did you see the plank that saved me?
Did you see the ocean that carried me off?
Did you see the vessel that gathered me up?   40
Did you see nothing – neither ship nor plank?
Did you weep, or did you not weep? Was there anguish, a tear?
Or no anguish, no tear, no brief pain?
Are you still alive for me, Dosikles, and do you weep for Rhodanthe?
Or are you no longer living, Dosikles, and do not weep for Rhodanthe? 45
Did the sea swallow you up, or did it not?
Did the dry land gulp you down, or did it not?
Have you heard that they have sold me in Cyprus
for a mere thirty *minai* of gold?
Have you heard that I have found a mistress in Stale?   50

212 Marginal gloss: 'Rhodanthe's lament for Dosikles'.
   213 7.16–160: The parallel set-piece to the male lover's lamentation in the previous book,
and a lament on present circumstances (cf. 1.88–131, 3.409–85).

Or do you know nothing of Cyprus, an island, *minai* and Stale?
    Alas, Dosikles, this is a long speech
and the foolish prattlings of an erring heart.[214]
But perhaps you, seeing me in the midst of the abyss
and expecting my watery and bitter fate,   55
drowned yourself in anticipation, a suicide?
And if by chance you are dead (alas, my bridegroom)
for the sake of me, the distressed Rhodanthe,
should I see the light and breathe the air,
without blushing at the light or the air   60
which you have ceased to breathe and ceased to see for my sake?
I look on the sea, and am I not ashamed before the sea
which you possess (alas) as both tomb and wedding chamber?
I tread without dishonour on the earth's back,
on which you (woe, ye gods) do not walk, for whose sake?   65
For mine. Why did you not burn me alive?
Is it right for Dosikles to have left this life
and for Rhodanthe to go on living and live unnoticed?
Where are the pelting sheets of hail,
where are the lashing squalls, the distant flashes of lightning, 70
the peals of thunder, the rain, the jaws of fire?[215]
Where is the sun on the ground, the heaven rent asunder,
a fresh cleft in the earth, a strange blast of wind,
the sea piled up to the heaven,
everything overthrown, life transformed?   75
    Alas, Dosikles, have confidence in me;
why did I leave my dear country, my ancestral estate,
him who begot me, her who bore me, my dear brothers,
the group of my unwed peers,
the weight of gold, pearls, silver, gems,   80
and to mention the greatest, the fate of freedom?
Why did I leave these and choose a mockery of life
and exchange them for wandering with Dosikles
and embrace chains in place of comfortable living?

214 A reflection of Hebrews 3.10
215 'jaws of fire' (cf. Aeschylus, *Coephoroi*, 325; *Prometheus* 368) following, with
Marcovich 1992 and Conca 1994, Hercher's emendation γνάθοι for the mss' νόθοι ('bastard').
There is a biblically apocalyptic tinge to the phrasing of these lines; cf. Luke 23.45; Matthew
27.51.

And now shall I not abandon the fate of slavery   85
and all this on your behalf, alas, on Dosikles' behalf,
alas, on whose behalf I chose so much pain?
Shall I not abandon breath and heart
for your sake, who are my very breath and heart?
    Shall I not be false to your sworn pledges   90
(even if the gods are false to their promises),
if I were to continue in this life when you are dead?
Shadows cannot exist without bodies,
nor can Rhodanthe exist apart from Dosikles.
Or who would need vessels and nets   95
when the sea has drained away completely
(unless the surface of the earth were to become sea
and some miracle-worker were to fish it and sail over it
and ensnare a fresh draught of other types of fish,
and were to cut through a dry ocean rather than a watery one),   100
who would buy an ox for ploughing
or would acquire a tool for tilling the earth
unless land existed which needed cultivation?
(Unless anyone wished to cultivate water
or scatter seeds over the air.)[216]   105
How would anyone respire without air,
and how would Rhodanthe respire and what life would she live
were her dear Dosikles not alive with her?
    Have confidence, Dosikles, about my marriage couch;
I was your companion even in exile, even in wanderings,   110
I will be your companion even in the abyss and the ocean deeps.
I will not be false to my oath, nor to my pledge;
I will not defile my ardour, nor my love;
I will not outrage my gifts of kisses;
I will not shame our marriage that is of lips only   115
or the couch that permits only an embrace.
Have confidence, throng of fellow maidens,
who desire lovers, beloved young men
and who are desired by lovers, by beloved young men;
you will not be hated by those most dear ones,   120

---

216 Proverbial expressions for futile activities: cf. Diogenianus 7.67; Zenobius 3.55
(Leutsch and Scheidewin 1839–51, vol. 1). The whole paragraph expresses a series of *adynata*
(absurd impossibilities) or paradoxes.

who have suspected that women kiss duplicitously;
for I have now given a good example to women who are adored.[217]
Emulate, yes, emulate me.

    But you, Dosikles, when you embarked on the freighter
(which you did by an ill fate, by the envy of the Moirai)   125
and expected to join Rhodanthe,
you endured many blows because of her,
struck in the face by the reprobate.
O that hand, the accursed hand of the beast,
the hand of a savage serpent, did you not contract into yourself,   130
did you dare to strike out? Yes, the fire is cold,
yes, the gods' sword cannot cut;
the Erinyes' bows shoot over the smoke,[218]
the Titans doze,[219] O divine judgement.
The mischief-makers never drowse   135
on our behalf but, ever alert,
keep a sharper watch than Lynx himself.[220]

    You have suffered this, and more than this;
do I prefer a slave's fate in Cyprus
to dwelling with Dosikles?   140
No indeed, no, by Zeus, no, by the assembly of the gods.
Alas Dosikles, O my fair vision,
if you have already breathed out your life
and you have run aground in your marriage with Rhodanthe,
my condition will be the same and I go to meet you in death;   145
the law of love does not permit
any lingering in life whatever.

    For if you have not expired, who am I, what shall I do?
I am a slave, my master is Kraton
and he controls my fate.   150
And if I should somehow secretly escape from my master
and wander everywhere seeking for you,

---

217 Byzantine (and general medieval) misogyny emerges here.

218 'Erinyes': avenging Furies. 'over the smoke': a proverbial expression; cf. Hesiod, *Works and Days* 45; Eustathius, *Iliad Commentary* (Van der Valk 1971–87, vol. 2: 711.12–13).

219 The Titans, fearsome giants, never rest: these are *adynata* to express the temerity of those who dared strike Dosikles.

220 Lynx, one of the Argonauts, was proverbial for his acute sight (e.g. Aristophanes, *Plutus* 210; Suda Λ 775).

my first fear is that he should find me
when I had escaped and capture me
and I would completely fail in my purpose   155
and all I would gain would be a flogging.
Then in which city should I search?
To which country, to which place should I go
to look for Dosikles? I do not know where I should run,
or where, once I had arrived, I should come upon your dear
    countenance."   160
The girl sobbed out all this and much else
but no one (not Kraton, not Stale)
heard her bitter lament
(for their hearing was barred,
with sleep guarding its entrance).   165
But Rhodanthe's grief could not escape the notice
of Myrilla, Stale's daughter,
and all night as she lay awake
what was said came to her watchful ears.

    And this is nothing extraordinary; for when love   170
enters a maiden's heart[221] and the image of marriage
and the thought of bridal chambers,
this bestows many cares on the girl,
this provides the wretched girl with many concerns.
Tormented by such thoughts and unable to sleep   175
she gets up in the middle of the night as though it were day,
and although a small portion of her worry has been laid aside
and sleep has briefly overcome the distressed girl,
the wakeful maiden whose anguish is the same
pares slumber away from the sleeper,   180
by her words, her tears, her wailing
and she rouses the squall that had been calmed
and rekindles the fire that had turned to ash.

    This was the affliction that befell Myrilla;
for as she, lovely enamoured maiden,   185
overheard the other enamoured maiden,
as if pricked by a goad
she quickly got up from her bed,

---

221 For a similar picture of female concerns, cf. MangProd 56, and his musings on a dress
for a young girl.

and went to the sobbing girl
and asked what was the sorrow for which she wept,   190
who was Dosikles, where was he from and how did he die;
and she swore to guard all that she should be told
in the deepest recess of her soul.
When Myrilla vouchsafed this utterance
Rhodanthe groaned deeply from the bottom of her soul   195
and, weeping, uttered this speech:
     "My mistress, Myrilla (yes, for through Fate
Rhodanthe is the slave and Myrilla the lady);
for me a slave to tell of my fate
and indeed to my mistress demands much courage.   200
But since, however, it is necessary for servants
to do their masters' bidding,
I would not wish to conceal my fate.
But take care that you do not weep;
for it is not permitted, it is not decreed by the gods   205
that a mistress should weep over a slave's pains.
About my family or country or begetters
or abundant gold or prosperous hearths
or everything else that belongs to yesterday and my prosperity
it is superfluous and long-winded for you to hear;   210
but learn about the main points of my griefs
and consider whether I do not weep with reason.
     There was in my country a noble youth,[222]
Dosikles by name, comely in appearance,
with his beard just blooming on his chin   215
and his face gracefully surrounded
by the first down on his jaw,
with hair, ye gods, beautiful to see
(how it curled!); the blond hue –
its beauty is amazing; his whole complexion –   200
incredible beyond description; his whiteness –
quite astonishing; his redness –
altogether impossible. What should I say
of his eyes, his cheeks, his eyebrows, his lips,
his sturdy, well-proportioned figure   225
close kin to a cypress,

222 Marginal gloss: 'Description of Dosikles'.

his shoulders, his ankles, his hands, his feet;
his hand is beautiful, but much more beautiful
when it has made advances, moved by forces of nature
(I blush to speak of advances,   230
but yet I am in love, Myrilla, and what have I to lose?),
and it is clinging enthusiastically to my neck.
His lips are lovely, but so too is his mouth;
and when they move and make sounds,
calling and laughing and kissing me,   235
oh indeed how great is their beauty.
But why should I go on and why should I speak at length?
His whole bearing was that of a god.
    That young man for reasons of which I am ignorant
was smitten by me, the thrice wretched;   240
it was not Eros whom he summoned as his accomplice
(for his mere appearance was a sufficient substitute for Eros)
but some young friends, fellow huntsmen;[223]
and he seized me and put me in a freighter
and sailed in flight as far as Rhodes.   245
There a robber fleet attacked us,
whose emperor was Mistylos and under him was Gobryas;
Mistylos captured us and put us in a vessel
and carried us off to his own country;
and we endured chains and prison and darkness.   250
Amidst this had been imprisoned previously a young man,
Kratandros by name, who boasted of Cyprus as his homeland,
child of his father Kraton and his mother Stale,
as he himself recounted to us;
we were enriched by one benefit in our troubles,   255
when we fell in with an honest fellow prisoner."
    Rhodanthe's mouth uttered the name Kratandros
and a new sickness took hold of Myrilla;
for struck by the word[224] as if by a hurricane
and letting out a long and harsh wail,   260
she moved like an ox stunned with a club
and looked like victim of black bile

---

223 Cf. Dosikles' hunting vocabulary at 2.400 ff.
224 Translating (with Conca 1994) the mss' λόγον rather than γόον ('grief') with Hercher and Marcovich 1992.

(for unexpected news,
whether it comes for good or for bad,
inebriates souls and turns minds),[225]   265
she sprang up from the ground and went to Stale,
"Kratandros lives, mother, to the present time,
mother, Kratandros lives," she cried out,
"enquire from this young slave girl,
enquire and learn about your son."   270
    At this there was a general commotion, a general hubbub,
a tumult mixed with tempests of tears.
All begged Rhodanthe to say indeed
where Kratandros was and what life he was living.
"But where he is and what his life is,"   275
said Rhodanthe, "you cannot now discover from me.
For from the time when my rescuers purchased me
I live in Cyprus and do not see what is far away.
What I do know I tell my masters who have asked this of me.
Mistylos had him shut up[226]   280
in a dark prison and a gloomy dungeon.
A short and brief time passed
and a certain Bryaxes attacked Mistylos
and joined battle against him
and his entire state was overthrown.   285
    And after that Artapes, under the command
of lord Bryaxes, captured Kratandros
and a huge swarm of other prisoners
and with them me and some other fellow maidens;
and filling one vessel with the men   290
and another with the women,
he set off for Pissa, his own city.[227]
So of the two ships I mentioned, one,
the one to which I had been entrusted, Kraton my master,[228]
was split and torn apart in the middle of the abyss   295
and took the life of all, apart from me.

225 Further moralizing; cf. Odorico 1989.
226 Marginal gloss: 'Rhodanthe's declaration about Kratandros to his father'.
227 φιλὴν in the possessive, Homeric sense, rather than 'dear' or 'friendly'.
228 δεσπότης is used in several senses, e.g. as 'master' (in a slave–master relationship) or
'lord' in the political and military hierarchy.

The other survived (whether completely
I do not know, but one may hope), for then
turmoil immediately spread over the sea.
And now, I suppose, my master Kratandros   300
has reached Pissa and is either confined once more
or perhaps sees the light of freedom,
as his captor Bryaxes may decree."
    With this Rhodanthe concluded her speech;
and Kraton, saying, "Greetings from me, child,"   305
went back with Stale.
When the day dawned, they both made their decision;
Kraton took a not immoderate mass of gold
and, boarding a Cypriot ship with favourable fate,
set off to Pissa in quest of his son.   310
O paternal compassion, O fatherly heart,
there is nothing greater than a father's affection.[229]
    Kraton (for he was a father) thus thought
little of the voyage made for his dear son's sake.
But what of Kratandros and Dosikles, the wanderers?[230]   315
Did Fate look kindly on them
and did Envy remove its scourges?
It is impossible to say, but the malicious thread
span many forms of evil.
For when Bryaxes entered the city   320
and granted a brief time of respite
(bodies might be restored that were
already weakened by long hardship),
he intended to offer a sacrifice to the gods of the region,
and to sacrifice the best of the booty he had captured   325
(for the gods should be honoured with the first-fruits);
he had nothing better than Dosikles
and Kratandros, the handsome couple.

229 Should this be read as an expression of the strength of family bonds in twelfth-century society? On the prevalence of slavery, see McCormick 2001: 244–53, 733–77; Rotman 2004: 94–98.

230 'wanderers': here translating ξένος, a word of multiple meanings; 'foreigner', 'stranger', 'exile' as well as 'guest' are all part of its semantic field expressing 'otherness', not necessarily with a pejorative sense. In *DigAk* G8.129–30 the hero's wife is still a ξένη (E. Jeffreys 2000)

(Oh shameful beauty, oh evil gift from the gods;
may no one be beautiful in life   330
if they are to be slaughtered because of their beauty.)[231]
    Since thus was the decree of violence
(lawless laws of grim tyranny)
and all remaining time was barred to them
(for the temple attendants had kindled the pyre),   335
the youths were unloosed and led forth;
they stood before the gates of the temple
at the place where Bryaxes sat on high
and they displayed two states of mind.
For one of them, Kratandros, bowed down to the ground,   340
was clearly taking the matter badly,
his face pale, his neck bent,
his gaze bitter, his limbs trembling,
so that Bryaxes said to them all,
"We have no need of a sword, men, for this one;   345
he will put an end to himself before the sword does."
The other was cheerful in appearance
and stood there with a bright countenance
as if going to a festival at his death,
thinking it good and beyond every good thing   350
if he could leave this life together with Rhodanthe;
for an unfortunate hope beguiled him
that love and marriage existed even in the grave[232]
(such a blind and foolish thing is desire).
    Seeing this and more, Bryaxes   355
summoned both young men to him
and, ordering his subordinates to be silent, said,
"That a prisoner's fate is yours
(whoever you are and from whatever family),
it is not necessary to teach you who know this from your
    circumstances –   360
nor that masters are permitted to take any action,
nor that might is right where the defeated are concerned
– and you obey the natural order of things.

231 Note that Theagenes and Charicleia (prisoners of war) are intended to be sacrificed by Hydaspes at Hel 10.1.4.
232 A reflection of Matthew 22.30, that 'in the resurrection' there is no marriage?

For if all things lived together in the one fate,
and no one was a slave but everyone was free,   365
there would be no rule, no measure, no standard of life,
no overall command, no discipline,
everything would be in confusion and corrupted.
Since natural reason controls everything,
it is necessary that there should be slaves and masters.[233]   370
   Or how would cities be inhabited at all,
if no man needed another?[234]
Or does not a doughty warrior in the heat of battle
seem in need of a bridle maker?
Or a smith of a miner?   375
Does not everyone who gives need someone who takes, and does
    not everyone
who takes need someone who gives? Does not the helmet need the
    hoplite
and again does not the hoplite need the helmet?
Should we not then say that everything is in need of everything else?
What is a valiant man without his sword,   380
or what is a sword without a valiant man?
Since all this is clear (for who cannot understand this
if he lives in the world and dwells among men?),
it is right for me to obey the laws of masters
and, whatever has been decided, to bring it to its conclusion.   385
   But this is not Bryaxes' decision; for the sword must not
devour human flesh without a trial.
It is permissible, indeed, but even if it were permissible for me,
I prefer the laws and decrees of Justice.
All this is so, and I am right;   390
but if I am wrong, someone should cross-examine me.
But since I wish to put some brief questions,
let one of you two give the answers.
I had intended to ask your religion and your family,
but I do not insist, relying on your garb and speech   395
to instruct me in these matters,
nor shall I ask if you reverence the gods and these in particular;

233 Cf. Aristotle, *Politics* 1.1 2352a; 2.1254a; 3.4 1278b.
234 Cf. Plato, *Republic* 2.369b and *Laws*, 3.676a–680.

instead I put another question which
whichever of the two young men chooses may try to solve.
    Is it fine to revere the divine, or what is your response?"[235]   400
"Fine," replied Dosikles succintly.
"You may be pleased," he said, "that you have replied well.
What then? Would you say that sacrificing and revering are the same thing?"
"And how would they not be the same thing?", he replied.
"Congratulations, Dosikles, on your speed," he said again,   405
"for you do not give dilatory answers.
What then? Would you not sacrifice a sturdy fat ox
if you wanted to make an ox sacrifice?" "Of course," he said.
"What then? Would you not pour out the best of the libations
and besprinkle the meat of the sacrifices?"   410
"And in this too," he said, "you are surely correct;
for indeed the best is worthy of the best."
    "What then? Do the gods not love what is fine?"
"Of course they do," he said, "how could they not?"
"What then? Is not beauty fine, or what is your response?"   415
said Bryaxes; "if this is not the case, say so."
"This is so," he said; "ask something else."
"And therefore they do not love what is ugly,[236]
for it is evil?" he said. "They do not," he replied.
"And if someone were to sacrifice a small ox," he said,   420
"surely they would be enraged with him?"
"It could not be," he said, "other than you have said."
"What then? If I were to chance upon an immeasurable weight of gold
but then offer a clay pot,"
he said, "would they welcome and accept me?"   425
"No, indeed," came the reply, "on the contrary, they would be furious
    with you."
    "If then, I am not offering an ox to the gods," he said,
"but I am sacrificing a man, surely I would not sacrifice a cripple,
a blind man, a sniveller, an old man,[237]

---

235 Marginal gloss: 'Debate between Bryaxes and Dosikles'. 7.400–45: Another set-piece demonstration of a Platonic dialogue (in verse), comparable with Prodromos' other pastiches, both in the novel (e.g. the oracle at *R&D* 9.196–204) and elsewhere (e.g. tragedy in the *Katomyomachia*).

236 Literally, 'the form [or, idea] of the Ugly', using Platonic phraseology.

237 Cf. Lucian, *Dialogues of the Dead* 16.2, on not sacrificing the aged.

one with withered limbs, a man with the palsy, a hunchback,   430
with bleary eyes, or his teeth half gone,
or with gout and a bald head,
and a beard hanging from his chin,
long and white and stinking of goats?
Which of these do you think the gods would accept?"   435
"None of them under any circumstances; how could they?" came
     the reply.
"What then? Should a corpse be sacrificed?"
"You're joking," he said, "if you sacrifice a corpse."
"What then is left," he said, "except to sacrifice to the gods
handsome young men in the prime of their life?"   440
"It seems, emperor," he said, "that this is surely the case."
"What then is the conclusion of our debate?" he said.
"That you should be sacrificed to the gods of victory,
the first fruits of my spoils."
"Make your sacrifice then," was the reply, "if it seems fine to offer
     sacrifices."   445
     When Bryaxes heard these words
and looked at Dosikles more carefully,
he knotted his brows
and his brutal heart was touched.
Turning to his satrap Artaxanes,   450
he said, "Greatest of all my satraps,
such pity for this youth
has just entered my heart
that it moves me to tears;
such as he is in beauty, in youth,   455
in character, in understanding, in his responses,
he will depart miserably from this life,
exchanging his beauty for a tomb.
I would have set this youth free
and liberated him from his present difficulties,   460
if this would not seem folly to the gods.
And now I stand between two states:
pity for him and fear of the gods.
I do not know which to favour more,
I do not know where to tip the balance and to what I should turn.   465
I am concerned for Dosikles as for a son,

but I fear the gods as my masters."
   Having said this, he turned round again.
"And what, pray, Kratandros, is your response?"
he said, "Why have you succumbed to such great fear, 470
why do you shudder, grow pale, bow your neck,
why do you tremble before death in such an unmanly fashion?
Do you not see Dosikles' courage,
how he has zealously striven towards the sacrifice?
And with good reason; for he wishes to approach the gods 475
and thinks the intervening time a penalty.
If therefore you think that what has already been said is sufficient
and you do not wish to add anything more,
let us not punish the handsome Dosikles
by postponing the deed; but if you wish to say 480
something more, come forward and have the courage to speak."
   "Dosikles' words are fine, emperor,[238]
they are fine, emperor," responded Kratandros,
"and everyone concurs; I contribute one thing more
to them, since you allow me to speak. 485
Sacrifices of bulls, emperor, are pleasing to the gods,
as well sacrifices of calves and of roast oxen,
and grains of frankincense in the heart of the flame;
but sacrifices of men and fresh murders are,
I think, hateful to the gods.[239] Indeed, which city, 490
governed by laws of pious intent,
makes sacrifices of men and reveres the gods in this manner?
   If therefore, emperor, he who is beautiful in form,[240]
is worthy to die because of his appearance
and can bring pleasure to the gods though being sacrificed, 495
tell me why did he ever appear on earth?
Was it to die and entertain the gods?
Why then did the gods bring him into this life?
So that he could be struck down and provide them with a banquet?
What then? Is it because they have done wrong that those who are
   beautiful in form 500
prepare to be a feast for the gods?

238 Marginal gloss: 'Kratandros' reply to Bryaxes'.
239 Cf. Hel 10.9.6, 39.2–3 on human sacrifice as being hateful to the gods.
240 Platonic vocabulary once again.

If they die because they are beautiful (I shrink from saying this;
I will speak nonetheless, but listen to me kindly),
an emperor is a beautiful thing and exceeding all beauty;
why should he not be sacrificed to the immortals?   505
If beautiful men are slaughtered for the sake of the gods,
what will be the result of this new law,
once all beautiful objects have perished?
– that only the evil walk the earth and only the evil live,
receiving life in exchange for their depravity.   510
Could there be a more wretched law than this?
It is shameful that it is the face that justifies survival.[241]
This seems to me to be a reasonable comment;
as for you, O emperor, whether I make a just statement
or unjust, you would, I know, make a judgement without bias."   515
    When Bryaxes heard these words,
he said, bursting out with a huge guffaw,
"Prodigious Zeus, what prodigies I see;
he who just now was terrified and dying of fright
to what heights of valour has he brought himself."   520
Saying this and looking at the ground
he seemed to be pondering over the youths.

THE EIGHTH BOOK OF THE DEEDS OF RHODANTHE
AND DOSIKLES BY THE SAME WRITER

Bryaxes pondered what was to be done;
knotting his eyebrows in a frown,
he sat in silence for no short time.
While he was debating what he should do,
a hullabaloo from a man in their midst, in mourning,   5
terrified, yes, all of them with a fresh fear.
It was Kraton; he had reached Pissa,[242]
disembarked from his ship and gone up to the city;

---

241 Keeping the line order of the mss rather than placing 512 before 511 with Marcovich
1992.

242 Marginal gloss: 'Kraton's arrival in Pissa and supplication to Bryaxes concerning
Kratandros'.

chancing on an old man, a barbarian,
he asked him about Bryaxes   10
and, when he learnt about the sacrifices and the murders,
he immediately made for the temple, shouting loudly
(clawing, scratching at his pleasant face,
tearing his white and reverend locks),
and clasping Bryaxes' feet   15
he began this most pitiable lament:[243]
   "Do not, most high emperor, do not do this;
do not, do not remove so untimely from this life
the son who is the support of his father's old age
and remove at the same time the old man's hopes.   20
Do not do this, do not hand Kratandros over to the sword;
do not do this, do not cast Kratandros into the flame.
Let grey hair and old age importune you;
let a wrinkled brow and trembling gait
incline you from wrath to pity.   25
In vain would I have accomplished so great a journey,
if leaving Cyprus I hastened uselessly in this way
and in vain clasped your sacred feet
so that I, an aged father, might see my child alive;
do not do this, divine emperor, by the gods, do not do this.   30
You have me; if you wish, cut me down, consume me with fire,
give to the gods the flesh of an old man
(if indeed the gods take pleasure in human deaths).
You have me; pull out my teeth
(if any still remain in this aged creature).   35
   You have me; gouge out my eyes
(if time has not already done so).
Let a forlorn father pay the penalty in place of his son;
sacrifice an old man, not a handsome young one.
For an old man a sword is a matter for brief debate   40
since in a short while he will die even without a sword;
but for a young man the delights of life are still to come.

---

243 The speech that follows is the conclusion to the extended *ethopoiia*, on what should be said if threatened with sacrifice, with response from the prospective victim, the victim's friend and now the victim's father. The exemplification of rhetorical exercises is arguably the purpose of Prodromos' novel since depictions of amatory psychology or the relations between the lovers, while a necessary element in the genre that is being imitated, are not the main focus.

It is terrible, when a comely youth dies,
that a decaying old man still yearns for life.
Truly, emperor, I shall not rise from my lowly position,   45
I shall not cease embracing your imperial feet,
I shall not check the constant throb of my groans,
nor shall I restrain my flow of tears,
unless you allow me to have my son alive.
    Offer the gods pity in place of sacrifice;[244]   50
benevolence is a fine banquet for the gods,
a man who escapes death a fine wine bowl.
In this way the gods dine on salvation,
in this way shared joy is the gods' feast,
but not mortal flesh, not wholesale murder,   55
not welling blood, not a satiated sword,
not roast meat and a stench in the air.
For if the immortals had a body
and a constitution very like ours,
if they had a tongue, teeth, a mouth,   60
if they had the belly's receptacle, the bowels' position
and all the other things connected with my physique,
you would give then tables and drinks
and roast meat and cups of honey and milk;
but since the gods' divine nature is incorporeal,   65
they would not be able to eat meat or to drink wine.
Surely, anyone who roasted human flesh
would enrage the immortals.
    What then? A potter who made a pot[245]
and then saw it smashed to pieces   70
would not be pleased at the breakage and roar with laughter,
as neither would the carpenter who built a three-storey building
and then saw the roof fall in.
Do you think that the gods would take pleasure in my death,
who are my carpenters, my potters?   75
Would the craftsmen allow this situation to continue,
when the shards are quite shattered?[246]

---

   244 Cf. Matthew 12.7. The emphasis on human sacrifice, which is also present in the late
antique novels, is striking.
   245 Pots and potters are a biblical image (Jeremiah 18.6; Romans 9.21).
   246 Re-punctuating, with a question mark, with Conca 1994.

They would be able to maintain a livelihood,
making a new pot when one is smashed.
But they do not laugh at the damage — quite the opposite;   80
by analogy, would the gods be pleased with a man's death?
    Grant the son to his father, victorious emperor,
grant the son his father, the youth the old man,
allow me in my old age to be rejuvenated.
For a long time, emperor, a very long time indeed,   85
deprivation of my son has gnawed at me;
may he not perish now, an unhappy captive;
do not now, when I have briefly opened my eyes
and looked quickly towards the light of day,
then finally gouge them out."   90
    In response to these comments, which amazed the emperor,[247]
he made the following reply to the old man:
"Your streams of tears, old man,
have touched me to the heart, by Themis;[248]
I did not come from a stone, I was not born of a rock,   95
it was not an oak[249] that brought me to the light, to life,
to be unaffected by a man's sorrows
and to be unmoved and unappeased by distress.
I want to bestow a worthy son on his old father,
freed from the fate that awaits him   100
(the gods are witness to my word),
but I am afraid that Poseidon will storm,
Ares rage, Kronos fling down hail
and Zeus blast me with a thunderbolt.
And it is expedient that Kratandros alone meets death,   105
rather than all of us and the gods be angered.[250]
Do you see that young man near Kratandros,
the one with the good-looking face, old man?
You can see just how handsome he is;
he will be sacrificed, and what am I to do?   110
It is the act of a madman to start a war with the gods,

247 Marginal gloss: 'Bryaxes' reply to Kraton'.
248 'Themis': goddess of Justice.
249 A topos, for which examples can be found from Homer (*Odyssey* 19.163) to Prodromos'
contemporaries (e.g. *D&C* 1.343, 4.244; *H&H* 6.11.1; *A&K* frags. 17.2–3, 42.6, 71.8).
250 Biblical overtones; cf. John 18.4 (Caiaphas to the Jews, with reference to Christ).

so do not ask what is beyond my power."
Saying this, he rose up from his throne
and approached the edge of the fire;
grasping the young men with his hands he said,   115
"O almighty Zeus, O Kronos,[251] father of Zeus,
Ares, Poseidon and the assembly of the gods,
Bryaxes sacrifices these young men,
he offers these to you as the first fruits of his booty."
He had not brought his speech to its conclusion   120
when a sudden shower flooding down from on high
revealed that the pyre was dowsed,
that not even the smallest flame remained
or a part of a flame or its wick.[252]
At this all Bryaxes' satraps,   125
Bryaxes himself, Artapes, Artaxanes,
the rest of the horde let out a confused cry,
"May you be gracious, lord gods,
since you have clearly granted the young men life."
Bryaxes gestured for silence and said,   130
"May you be saved, children, and may you breathe
the breath of freedom and see the light of day.
Aged father, you possess your son through the gods;
Dosikles, you possess life through Zeus,
and through Bryaxes the fate of a free man.   135
Approach your fathers with confidence,
let your loving mothers see you,
and the throng of your dear brothers and your kinsmen.
Make your way homeward with good cheer
and offer sacrifice to the gods who brought your salvation."   140
Having spoken thus to the young men, Bryaxes
dismissed the gathering with this speech.
Kratandros, Dosikles and Kraton[253]
went on board the Cypriot ship.
They made their departure with a benign fate   145

251 'Kronos': Kronos, son of Heaven and Earth, was father of Zeus by his sister Rhea
(Hesiod, *Theogony* 254 ff.).
252 Imminent death by execution is averted also in *L&K* 3.19–22; XenEph 2.13, 4.2; Charit
4.2–3; the dowsing of an altar flame was a potent portent.
253 Marginal gloss: 'The arrival of Kraton, Kratandros and Dosikles in Cyprus'.

and, after spending no long time on their voyage,
with the gods' assistance they beheld the island.[254]
   But when Myrilla and Stale learnt
that Kratandros had arrived, that Kraton had come,
they immediately went out onto the headland itself   150
and what joy they felt, indeed what great joy,
when they both saw setting foot on Cypriot soil
– mother, sister, daughter, spouse –
their brother, son, father, spouse.
When they had met all the usual obligations,   155
when they had embraced and wept over the young man,
they set off for the house. When the city
learnt of what had befallen and taken place,
there came pell-mell out of their houses
a horde of men and women, striplings and youths,   160
old men and not so old, the fortunate and the poor,
a crowd of old women, maidens and those no longer maidens.
Kraton's delight and that of Stale
became the common joy, the common applause,
the common triumph and the celebration of all.   165
Every man clasped the young man,
every woman embraced the youth who had been saved.
They wept, they grieved, they burst into laughter;
mixing a wine bowl mingled with happiness and tears
they quaffed to the point of drunkenness.   170
   Thus Kratandros, by being discovered, discovered fame,
and he held a most magnificent celebration.
For absence and the removal of the beloved
is liable to enflame those who are in love.
For no one is consumed with passion for the beloved   175
when he can enjoy their company by being present,
seeing them and having daily conversation.
But if he is removed and time passes,
the heart of those in love is eaten up,
as though hungering for the beloved.   180
And if Fate is kind and permits a reunion,

---

254 Dosikles (and Kratandros) have been saved by participating in a Platonic dialogue with their captor, while Rhodanthe suffers the passive female fate of being married off, with no threat of sacrifice to the gods.

then with one gulp he gorges insatiably on his love.
    Thus the city held a festival for everyone
to mark the young man's return to it.
Nor did Kratandros abandon Dosikles   185
when he found himself involved in a parade of such dimensions;
putting his hands in his,
he made him share in the happiness and applause.
But Dosikles could not take part with him
in the happiness or the applause, for he could not see Rhodanthe.   190
    While the young men were being thus honoured,
fierce Eros had his sport,[255] as is his custom,
aiming many arrows from his fiery bow
at the young men and the young women.
For the entire throng of maidens in the procession   195
who gazed at Dosikles with wide-open eyes
received a massive arrow in their souls
(the kind that Eros always shoots –
poisoned, bitter and enflaming hearts).
For one, abandoning modesty,[256]   200
came up close and gazed at him with insatiable eyes,
as if by looking from close by she would really see[257] clearly;
another came up and touched his tunic,
and received a second arrow from the contact;
another, in a far greater frenzy than the other two,   205
breaking all the restraints of decency
and losing her sober wan complexion,
came up and kissed the youth,
and was pierced in every part of her soul.
    Then it could be seen that Dosikles was suffering   210
when he recalled Rhodanthe,
for, being put in mind of his own maiden
by these, he wept within his heart;
being kissed, he remembered their kisses,
and as he remembered them he let out a secret groan.   215
So this was the conclusion of the festivity.

255 Back, at very long last, to Eros.

256 This provocative behaviour has parallels in Hysmine's teasing of Hysminas in, e.g.
H&H. 1.8 ff.; cf., again, MangProd 56.

257 Reading βλέποι with the mss, rather than φλέγοι ('inflame'; Marcovich 1992).

The maidens in the procession returned
wounded to their own homes,
and no balm existed for the burning fire.
And even if there were, they would have rejected it;   220
for the more they were aflame with the torch,
the more they clasped its golden flame;
the closer the fire came to their hearts,
the more fuel they fed to the flames.
O fire that soothes, O balm that enflames.[258]   225
     As Kratandros, and Dosikles too,
both entered the house,
Stale received them with glorious food.
So all tasted what was set before them
and quaffed pleasurably from the wine bowl,   230
all partook of the mirth.
Only Dosikles out of all the company was despondent,
only Dosikles out of all the company pined,
because he was eating a banquet of his own flesh,
because he was drinking a cup of his own blood.   235
Thus anyone who saw him so pale and tense
would perhaps have been puzzled;
was it that by taking part in such a strange and dreadful banquet
he was eating his flesh and drinking his blood,
and sated with nourishment from within   240
he had no need of the external repast?[259]
     Myrilla joined with the stranger in pining,[260]
nourishing her eyes only in the intensity of the gaze
which she turned on Dosikles.
So, seeing him deep in misery,   245
eating nothing of what was set before him,
drinking not even the smallest drop from the cup,
she became thoughtful, she kept up a dizzy chatter,
hauling on every proverbial rope,[261]

258 For this oxymoron, cf. *D&C* 2.382 (identical line); *A&K* fr. 11, 165.9; George of Pisidia, *Hexaemeron* 1747 (Gonnelli 1998), a phrase with a biblical and liturgical background (Daniel 3.49–50; Romanos the Melode, Kontakion 46.21 [Maas and Trypanis 1963: 390]).
     259 A strange, cannibalistic concept (with parodic eucharistic overtones?)
     260 Cf. Kleitophon's situation in *L&K* 1.5.3.
     261 The same proverb as in 3.228.

contriving every device,   250
leaving no stone in the adage unturned,[262]
to persuade Dosikles to eat what was in front of him.
Then, approaching her begetter,
she said, "Father, do you not see how the stranger
is sitting listlessly at dinner   255
and his face, marked by the fate that has befallen him
(and which would blossom under the cosmetic of joy),[263]
in its gloom casts a shadow over the symposium and disturbs it,
as he sits on his chair without eating?"[264]
    Kraton went over to him and said,   260
"Why are you doing this, Dosikles, child?
Why are you doing this? It is not good in the midst of rejoicing
to be so gloomy, this is not permitted.
Abandon your gloom, for Fate is smiling;
it is shameful not to applaud loudly when you have fared well   265
and, when you have escaped the band of robber barbarians,
for you not to eat and not to drink from the wine bowl
makes you ungrateful to the gods your benefactors.
I am your father, since you are deprived of yours,
and this is your mother, in place of her from whom you are separated, 270
and this is your brother (if you weep for a brother),
whom the fates bestowed on you before we did.
Nothing can be missing from your happiness and entertainment."
    To this Kratandros said with a sigh,
"I am not ignorant of Dosikles' sufferings,   275
I am not ignorant of the grief which makes you weep;
I am aware of my brother's fate,
how burdensome it is, how fit for lamentation,
how far it exceeds all limits for tears;
but when will the mourning have an end,   280
and when will your breast-beating groans cease?

---

262 Another proverb; cf. Zenobius 5.63 (Leutsch and Schneidewin 1839–51, vol. 1).

263 On the metaphor, cf. Themistius, *Oratio* 27 (Downey and Norman 1970: 160.16); for cosmetics and blooming, cf. Philostratos, *Epistles* 22; also *D&C* 5.83; cosmetics as aid to attraction: e.g. MangProd 24.26–27, 214 on the emperor Manuel adorning the aged city of Constantinople with the cosmetics of his victories (in 1148).

264 In contrast to *H&H* 1.6 and *D&C* 8.46, or *R&D* 2.95, there is no question of reclining (rather than sitting) here.

A manly heart, best of men,
does not grieve unendingly for those who have suffered misfortune.
You have wept, you have pined for no short time;
taste a little food and drink."   285
He ended his words and forcibly persuaded Dosikles
to eat a small portion of what was before him.
     This is how things were with Dosikles, for he saw
but did not recognize the maiden who was standing close beside him.[265]
But how could he not have failed to recognize the golden girl,   290
clothed in a shabby tunic,
her body wasted away, merely a slave girl?
But Rhodanthe did not fail to recognize Dosikles,
and although she was urged by passion
to cling to him and to kiss his mouth,   295
she was forced to do the opposite by modesty and fear.
In the meantime, however, she did all that was in her power
to make her beloved recognize her;
she stood in front of Dosikles,
she sighed, she began to weep a little   300
and she bared her arms to the wrist
so that he might take notice of the shape of her fingers.
She hovered about the youth so much
that she thought she could not be Rhodanthe,
if he himself did not discover that it was she.   305
So Dosikles thought about the girl
and recreated Rhodanthe's image
so that it resembled the girl that had appeared,
but he still could not be certain.
For where could he have got the idea that   310
Rhodanthe was living in the middle of Cyprus,
brought there from the ocean deeps,
escaped from the sea's expanse?
     So this is how matters stood with the young people;
and when the dinner drew to its close
and there was an end to the lavish cuisine,   315
"Mother," said Kratandros to Stale,

265 A major improbability: surely the rescuers and rescued would have discussed the reason for Kraton's appearance in Cyprus, and the mysterious slave-girl would have been mentioned. However, this demonstrates the passivity forced on females in the conventions of this genre.

"the gods' compassion has united us
once more with each other, as we see,
and rescued your son from lengthy wanderings
and restored him to his begetters' bosom.   320
Yes, yes, the gods' foresight, yes, the gods' might
(and may you gods have care for me in the future)
– but from whose announcement of my fate
did my father learn that it was in Pissaian territory
that I dwelled as slave of lord Bryaxes,   325
and come and save me in the middle of an execution
and rescue me from the tyrant's hand?"[266]
"Well spoken, my child, well spoken,
you have spoken well," said Stale;
"you bring to mind what had been passed over;   330
for the abundance, the sheer greatness of our happiness
has made me completely overlook what has happened already."
She made this comment and then, leading Rhodanthe
into the centre of the festivity, said,
"This girl, Kratandros, by a good fate   335
I bought for thirty golden *minai*
and I have received more than that in exchange from her
by finding you, Kratandros, my son.
But may she not reveal you without reward
(for she will receive the fate of a free woman in exchange), 340
and how and when she encountered you
and could announce to us that you were safe;
behold, here she is – enquire about everything."
    Rhodanthe anticipated the request   345
and seized on Kratandros' question,
"O lord Kratandros," she said with a noble air,
"O lord Kratandros (for lord, yes,
you were formerly my fellow prisoner by the hand of Fate);
I would never have suspected (the gods are my witnesses) that you   350
would not have recognized Rhodanthe, standing thus before you,
and Dosikles even more than you.
He swore that he had engraved my appearance
in the very tablet of his heart;[267]

266 A somewhat belated enquiry.
267 Cf. 2 Corinthians 3.3.

for his sake I dwell in Cyprus with a slave's fate,
and he knows what country I abandoned,   355
what house, what wealth, what parents,
even if he now pretends not to know me when he looks at me.[268]
Since you want to know how I recognized you
and, having recognized you, how I told your parents,
I will tell you everything, beginning from that point ..."   360
    Rhodanthe finished her remarks, and Dosikles immediately,
lacking breath and speech,
sat like a corpse, his head bowed;
and he would have died of joy
had not Myrilla put smelling-salts under his nose   365
and revived the youth.
When he stood up and got his breath back,
"What, gods, is this bizarre spectacle?
What is this overwhelming dream," he shouted out.
"Do I see Rhodanthe? Envy, you are playing a joke;   370
Fate, you are making a jesting mockery of my tears,
revealing the image of my beloved.
Are you alive for me, Rhodanthe, and do you see the day?
Are you alive for me, Rhodanthe, are you alive, do you see, do you breathe?
This is no phantom; yes, gods, I see clearly;   375
what is here is a waking dream, the spectacle is no mirage;
it is a waking dream, saviour gods, and no deception;
it is not a deception and an apparition;
it is not an apparition and another act of Fate.
Oh, come hither and touch me, fair maiden,   380
oh, come hither and embrace your bridegroom."
    To this Kratandros cried out in response,
"Alas, alas, what is this, what indeed, triumphant gods?
Rhodanthe lives, and Dosikles weeps?
What are wine bowls and feasting to me? What is drinking?   385
Alas, father and mother, O all my friends,
what was the happiness of the feast that has just taken place?
Let us hold another even more cheerful celebration.

268 Other recognition scenes occur in *L&K* 5.18.3–5; *H&H* 9.9; literary conventions for
the recognition of long-lost family members go back to fifth-century tragedy (e.g. Aeschylus,
Choephoroi; Euripides, *Ion*); one might speculate to what extent the scene here would resonate
with twelfth-century societal expectations.

Let the rejoicing be complete and the cheerfulness,
and let the gratitude to the gods be most profound.   390
So let us leap for joy, let us leap, men, all together,
let us make thank-offerings to the gods who are our saviours.
    Dosikles, behold, here is Rhodanthe, do not cry;
Rhodanthe, behold, bid your tears farewell,
let your frequent wailing be hurled far away.   395
Cast off your shabby garment, maiden,
and put on a robe worthy of Rhodanthe.
Come with us, rejoin your beloved's company,
seat yourself next to Dosikles.
You are served and you eat the same bread,   400
but you are not the one to serve those who are feasting;
you drink the same wine, if you wish to drink.
Mother, let us hold a second banquet,
let us set up a more magnificent festival,
let us rejoice, let us enjoy the new gladness;   405
the young people's earlier misfortunes have been put aside."
    As he said this he rose up from his seat
and, taking hold of the girl by her tunic
(which Stale had immediately provided for her,
a pure white one,[269] worthy of Rhodanthe),   410
he brought her to sit next to Dosikles.
What rejoicing there was at this, what delight.
Who did not revel in what had happened?
Who did not offer thanks to the gods?
All shared in the delight over everything, all shared in the applause,   415
only for Myrilla, Stale's daughter,
was the delight turned into grief.
For since the fortunate marriage which she had decided on
and the handsome bridegroom she had anticipated
(for through a bond of amatory expectation   420
she had made a pledge to Dosikles),
since this marriage couch and this wedding
had been snatched away and she had been deprived of all expectation
when her slave-girl had stolen her dear marriage,[270]

---

269 Cf. *L&K* 5.17.10 where Melite provides Leukippe with a white tunic.
    270 The term 'stolen marriage', a noticeable sub-theme in the Komnenian novels, normally
refers to a marriage transacted as the result of abduction; see note 78 above.

she took the mishap badly, she could not accept it,   425
she became envious of the girl who so recently had been a slave,
she eyed her bitterly and jealously.[271]
    So for these the tumult came to an end in this way,
and yes, indeed, the tumult together with the banquet;
but Myrilla's envy did not end,   430
and from henceforth she constantly
wove malicious plans to contrive a web of deceit[272]
in which she could ensnare Rhodanthe.
So when every outlet for her envy had been blocked
(for though pursuing every possibility she failed in them all),   435
finally what did she do, what trick did she devise?
She filled a cup of poisoned drink
and when Kratandros, and Dosikles as well,
had set out on a hunt,
she produced this drink during a meal.[273]   440
The effect of the potion was not a swift death,
nor an abandonment of the wits, nor any other disease,
only a paralysis of the entire body.[274]
    So when Rhodanthe had drunk from the cup
her entire being immediately lost its coordination.   445
Her entire body slackened and, like a corpse,
lacked movement, being unable to move.
O jealous and malignant heart;
in order to gain love, to achieve marriage
(which would not have happened if just judgements prevailed),   450
in order to be united with the bridegroom Dosikles,[275]
she brought paralysis on the maiden's body.
There was no hand there that could move or take action,
no fingers that could ever do anything,
no foot that could stand trimly on a path,   455

271 Cf. Arsake's jealous behaviour in Hel 7.7.7, 8.7.1.

272 For the image, cf. *Iliad* 15.16; *Odyssey* 2.236.

273 Cf. XenEph 3.5.11, 6.5, 7.4 where Eudoxos also uses a drink to prevent a marriage.

274 A variation of a Snow White folk-tale motif, translated into the lurid adventures and false deaths of the novel tradition; the fourteenth-century romances also made use of folk-tale elements such as poisoned apples and magic rings, especially *Kallimachos and Chrysorrhoe* and *Livistros and Rhodamne*.

275 Retaining the line sequence of the mss and not repositioning, with Marcovich 1992, 451 before 450.

no tongue to speak, no mouth to move.
Why should I talk at length and in detail?
It is sufficient to say succinctly
that none of the maiden's limbs could function.
   These were Myrilla's malignant actions.   460
What of the hand of the gods and the bonds of Justice?
Were they not immediately repulsed by her wickedness?
Of course; for they hate a malevolent creature.
So while Dosikles and Kratandros, as I said,
were off hunting in a dense thicket,   465
they found an ailing and half-paralysed bear,
with its right side withered and incapable of movement
and able to drag itself along only on its left side.
When it came to a grassy spot,
it fell down onto a most delightful plant   470
(whose roots were white, and whose leaves were like roses,
red roses and not white ones,
which had many earth-hugging stems
with a purplish covering;
briefly the charming plant was tri-coloured);   475
rubbing this onto its withered limb
the natural craftsman (the bear, I mean)
revivified its entire withered body
and, newly cured, went off on its way.[276]
Dosikles saw this extraordinary spectacle   480
and was amazed at it (how could he not be,
if animals know by natural instinct
things of which we, despite our education, are often ignorant?)
He stooped down and picked the healing herb;
and without delaying longer   485
he turned with Kratandros towards the house.
   A slave met them as they came in
and began miserably a pitiful message,
announcing, alas, the maiden's paralysis.
The anguish which Dosikles then felt,   490

---

276 Marcovich (1991: 401–02) proposes Dioskorides (*De material medica* 2.175) and
Paul of Aegina (*Handbook of Medicine* 3.18.3 [Heiberg 1921]) as sources for this episode;
Prodromos had medical interests. Note that Rhodanthe is again a victim and is rescued by the
efforts of others, not her own.

the laments he uttered as he heard this,
no one can describe who has not suffered as he has.
"Alas, Fate, again more tragedies begin,
again yours is the mockery and the pain comes to Dosikles.
Rhodanthe ails from a paralysis of the body   495
and endures a living death, unable to move;
Rhodanthe ails, and the horseman Dosikles
charges off to the hunt and the pursuit of wild beasts.
Yesterday I saw Rhodanthe, oh bitter Envy,
yesterday and not the day before or the day before that, accursed Fate." 500
    He spoke and went to the girl
and, shedding appropriate tears,
he searched in his pouch for the herb.
When he found it, he took it out and, rubbing it in,
he brought strength back to the paralysed girl's entire body,   505
he revivified it (oh divine grace).
She who had not been able to make the slightest movement
leaped up, she approached her beloved,
she restrained the tearful young man's lamentations.
    When Dosikles saw her alive, standing up,   510
speaking as she wished and moving,
"I knew, saviour gods," he shouted out,
"that you are concerned for what happens to me and the girl.
To you I entrust myself in everything;
on you I make dependent my expectations of marriage.   515
As for you, bear, what favour can I offer
in return for the precious herb which you produced?
Except (let the gods be witnesses to my vow)
that I never draw my sword against bears
and never whet my blade on my teachers."[277]   520
    Making such comments he embraced the plant
and "Welcome," he said, "blest daughter of the earth,
that restores life to the dying race of men,
that re-animates a soul declining into lifelessness,
bond of joints that are unjointed and of limbs that are paralysed,   525
and mover of that which cannot move.

---

277 While it is possible to interpret this line, as Conca does, with reference to masters of the hunt, it is tempting to link it to other allusions to a teaching environment (cf. 483 above) and a self-consciously writerly situation: Prodromos is making a joke.

Gods, may you thus save Dosikles;
Fate, may you thus protect Rhodanthe;
eloquent Hermes,[278] remember your word
and bring to fruition the marriages that you have promised."   530

THE NINTH BOOK OF THE DEEDS OF RHODANTHE
AND DOSIKLES BY THE SAME WRITER

Such things, more or less,
said Rhodanthe's exceedingly handsome bridegroom,
as joy enabled him to be most eloquent,
joy in which Kratandros and Kraton participated
with Stale herself and all members of the household.   5
Only Myrilla, consumed with envy,
and especially as she had failed in her mischief-making,
found in the common delight, the common mirth
her private grief, her private tear.
   When night approached with the displacement of light   10
and all were drowsing in their beds,
Rhodanthe on her own to Dosikles on his own
said, "Dosikles, Stale is good,
Kratandros is excellent and so too is Kraton,
saving, sheltering and rescuing those who have gone astray.   15
May Zeus Xenios[279] graciously repay
my host and my hostess
for enabling me to address Dosikles
and for bestowing the fate of freedom on me.
But we must discover what will be expedient,   20
we must escape by every device from the wicked,
we must plan our own salvation
and decide where we may remain hidden.
Meanwhile we must journey away from Cyprus,
and hastily depart from Myrilla   25
and avoid her envy by all means possible,

278 It was Hermes who at 3.69–75 had guaranteed their betrothal. Hermes is regularly
eloquent (e.g. Lucian, *Gallus* 2; *AnthPlan* 321.2); on the role given Hermes in the novels, see
Introduction, p. 15, n. 65 above.
   279 Zeus in his role as protector of strangers (ξένοι) and travellers, and hospitality.

if we do not wish to succumb to our previous fates.
What they were and the extent of their bitterness
you well know, having had experience to teach you.
 Or has Myrilla's envy escaped your notice?   30
Do you not know whence and for what reason
came the cup of poison given to me
and through which my circulation was paralysed?
Were you not able to perceive the plot against us,
the machinations of a jealous heart?   35
Or did you notice it but perhaps support the deed
and, as if Rhodanthe had become an abomination,
preferred instead to be Myrilla's bridegroom?
If this is so, be united with your beloved
and let Rhodanthe take death as her bridegroom.[280]   40
For, divorced from Dosikles,
she will not lack a bridegroom, but will be united with darkness
and will enjoy the bridal chambers of Charon.[281]
 But if you were not aware of Myrilla's plot,
let us flee from Cyprus,   45
lest we be condemned to suicide
by not having fled from the death of which we had foreknowledge.
Kratandros is excellent, yes, excellent; Stale is excellent,
yes, she is excellent, and so too Kraton is excellent;
but not more excellent in my view than Dosikles.   50
That it will be expedient to flee from Myrilla
is to me clear; but the means by which we flee
and where, having fled, we build our bower[282]
(yes, bower, for so Fate has decided)
requires Dosikles' consideration."   55
 Encountering these words Dosikles said,
"That Kratandros is excellent, that Stale is excellent,
that Kraton is responsible in all matters, that he is good –
I indeed agree with your statement, maiden.

---

280 For death as bridegroom, cf. Euripides, *Iphigeneia in Aulis* 461; *Iphigeneia in Tauris* 369; Sophocles, *Antigone* 654, 816; and elsewhere in ancient Greek tragedy.

281 'Charon': ferryman in the Underworld, transporting souls across the river Styx, and a personification of death in Byzantium; cf. *D&C* 2.171, with note.

282 καλύβη is ambiguous – both 'hut' and 'marriage chamber'; cf. Hesychios, under καλύβη· σκηνή, παστάς (κ 523 [Latte 1953–2009]).

Let us not drink so deep of Lethe's cup   60
that we subsequently suffer from ingratitude
and forget our hosts' salt.[283]
That envy entered Myrilla
together with the new disease of jealous madness,
I am aware (for a person in love easily recognizes   65
hearts that are in love and has learnt what they suffer);
what at the beginning of the exquisite banquet
she endured and did, did not pass me by;
but that she was propelled to such a depth of envy
so that she would pour out a cup of poison for Rhodanthe   70
from which paralysis would extend over her body
so that I might turn my desire towards her
while Rhodanthe, alas, lay with limbs unmoving,
all that I had never suspected (Justice be my witness).
For how would Dosikles have expected   75
that Myrilla could be so far out of her mind
as to expect that she could seduce Dosikles
if he were to see Rhodanthe paralysed,
I who would have instantly seized a sword
and would have plunged it into my entrails?   80
I had not had foreknowledge of Myrilla's plot;
I had no knowledge, no, by this mouth,
no, by this lip," (and as he said this
he enfolded them both and embraced them).
    "But since I now know of the mischief-making   85
through conversing with you, Rhodanthe, my teacher,[284]
I will ask you a question and you must reply to me.
If you intend simply to flee from Cyprus
to bring this one intention to its conclusion
and to learn more accurately about Dosikles   90
(if you are indeed ignorant of him up till now),
I will follow you. For what can I do?
If you concentrate entirely on planning and deliberation,
I will give this counsel, and may God look kindly on the plan.
And you, take counsel with me and deliberate with me,   95

---

283 Again, salt as a mark of hospitality as at 2.51, 92 and cf. Hel 4.16.5, 6.2.2.
284 Another gratuitous reference to a teacher.

lest what will be expedient passes me by unnoticed.
For we are dealing with the salvation of both of us.
   The first thing that needs planning and consideration
is where we should go on escaping from Cyprus
(for we do not know the nearby cities),   100
whom we should use as guides
if by chance we should wish to run away
(for we have no real friend).
And then, should we flee to another city,
who would be our guarantor and take oaths before the gods for me,   105
that no robber band or barbarian fleet
or the wretched emperor Bryaxes
should come and bind me with unbreakable chains
and send me back to his country as a slave?
And should he wish to sacrifice me to the gods,   110
what second Kraton would rescue me from the fire
and establish me in his own house
and enable me to gaze on Rhodanthe's face?
   For me Cyprus is more secure
than any unknown city   115
(and I have seen it, I have traversed it, I have experience of it),[285]
until the gods reveal where we should turn aside.
And it is relevant that only Myrilla is angry,
one woman only, not whole armies of men,
brigands in pursuit, ravaging furies,   120
savage murderers, bloodthirsty barbarians.
If, however, you do not agree that I am making a good decision,
we will discuss the matter next year.
But now, tell me how, and from where, and when,
and who brought you at some time to Cyprus?"   125
   "We should not, Dosikles," the girl responded,
"enquire about previous fates
but rather consider the present circumstances,
how these might be brought to a good conclusion and find a useful ending.
For whatever ending the past was to find, it has found it,   130
but the present needs planning and counsel

---

285 Translating (with Conca 1994) the line sequence of the mss, not moving 116 before
115 with Marcovich 1992.

to come to an auspicious conclusion.
And some fates we have brought to a close (by what route?
if I were to say evil, I would be wary of the word,
but were I to say good, I would not speak the truth),   135
so we have come to the closure that Fate granted.
Two scales balance our hopes,
one holds what is disastrous (may you avert this, Fate),
the other what is not disastrous (may the gods bring this to fruition).
It was good to consider the present circumstances   140
as they have come to a happy conclusion;
but when you investigate a previous fate,
it is necessary to speak of it (and what else should I do
when my dear Dosikles gives the order?).
     What was the wave and what the squall   145
when the vessels were entrusted with us
and sailed to Pissa with an accursed fate,
it is not necessary for you to learn for you both experienced and learnt it.
What followed was nothing other than Envy's evil weaving
and the gods' hand unwinding the web.   150
For the ship in which I had embarked was immediately broken up,
all its cargo was hurled into the deep,
and I too was dragged along by the tempest
but clinging astride a small plank,
by means of which, though fearfully, I nevertheless floated along –"   155
"You mean that the providence of the gods saved you,"
said Dosikles, breaking into the narrative,
"flying safely above your head
and giving a helping hand with the plank."
     "I went on for a little," continued the girl,   160
"and suddenly a crowd of merchants rescued me
and exchanged my salvation for a price
of only thirty golden *minae* –"
"A bargain price, august maiden,"
said Dosikles, "you had good fortune in the transaction   165
if you purchased your entire life for thirty *minae*;
who can be a better shopper[286]
than one who has purchased his life for gold?"

---

286 There is surely ironical humour here, as well as a parodic reference to the Gospels.

"How I lamented for you in the depths of night",[287]
Rhodanthe resumed, "how I wept for you,   170
how I pulled the hair from my head,
how I endlessly tore at my face,
how I reddened my cheeks" (and as the girl spoke
Dosikles bent and kissed the places)
"with stains from my blood,   175
how I bewailed you bitterly, hugely,
it is superfluous to describe; but you should know this one thing,
that my tears, my bitter lament,
are the reason that Dosikles is dwelling in Cyprus."
     So these (for they were young and the servants of passion)   180
consumed the entire night with their talk,
but meanwhile the Moirai[288] were spinning with their golden thread
the end of the young people's wandering and the commencement
     of their union.
For Lysippos, and in addition Straton,
the well-born progenitors of the lovers,   185
who had had their children snatched from their bosoms
(Lysippos had lost Dosikles and Straton Rhodanthe),
when they had pursued long searches
(on land, on sea, in all neighbouring areas)
but found no trace of the fugitives anywhere,   190
they had finally decided to go to Delphi,[289]
to enquire of the god about their children.
So they went to the Pythia[290] and put their enquiry,
and without the slightest delay the tripod
uttered this response to the aged fathers:[291]   195
     "Why, paired parents, do you seek the twisting paths[292]

287 For mourning rituals and the resemblance of these to Byzantine actions, see Roilos
2005: 93 ff. (with references to twelfth-century comments).

288 The Fates, who in Greek mythology spun each person's thread of life; cf. *A&K* fr. 137.

289 Site of the most renowned oracle in the ancient Greek world.

290 The priestess who was the mouthpiece of the oracle, which she delivered while seated
on a three-legged stool (hence 'tripod') over a vaporous vent; *OCD*, under 'Delphic oracle'.

291 A pastiche, in appropriate hexameters, of the contorted vocabulary typical of oracular
utterances. On the role of oracles in late antiquity, and their linguistic style, see Lane Fox
1986: 168–261; awareness of the Chaldaean Oracles (Majercik 1989) had been revived in the
eleventh century by Psellos.

292 Marginal gloss: 'Oracular response'.

of your much-loved calf and tender heifer?
By the sea-girt land, by the animal-nurturing island
which fell to the Cyprus-born begetter of Desire, Aphrodite
(a name either bestowed or taken),   200
there beholding them, you will see where they were living, but in
    that country
crown them with the wreaths of the trophy-bearing Kytherean;[293]
for Eros and Desire and the foam-born Kytherean
have subdued them with the indissoluble bonds of iron bound on
    by the gods."
Thus spoke the Pythia to the old men;   205
the oracular decree, expressed ambiguously
(with the phrases the tripod always uses),
caused much cogitation for the miserable beings.
For the one who had brought Rhodanthe into this life
(called Straton, as you know)   210
judged the god's response unfavourable
and wailed, groaned and began to weep,
expecting his child[294] to have been found dead,
ignorantly placing a full-stop after "were living"[295]
and then passing over what followed.   215
But the tripod did not elude Lysippos,
and since he understood he explained its meaning to Straton,
well comprehending the Pythia's intention,
"That indeed the young people are in Cyprus,
that indeed we might be able to see living   220
those whom we never expected to see alive,
that indeed when united with each other in marriage
they might forget us, and what the tripod meant by death
was their forgetfulness of their progenitors."[296]
Straton was convinced by Lysippos' remarks   225
and said, "Come, let us set off for Cyprus,

---

293 'Kytherean': i.e. Aphrodite, born on the island of Kythera according to Hesiod
(*Theogony* 192), though also associated with Cyprus, and the cult centre at Paphos (e.g. Homer,
Odyssey 8.362).

294 Rhodanthe is oddly referred to as υἱὸν, 'son'.

295 A self-aware reaction to the processes of composition, and their possibilities; see
Introduction, p. 15, n. 64.

296 A somewhat garbled interpretation: 'death', after all, is not mentioned in the oracle.

and if the fugitives continue to live,
let us contrive a bridal chamber for them,
since this has been decided by the immortals."
   His remarks convinced Lysippos' heart; 230
and when they had expended time on no small excursion
and hastened to Abydos from Delphi,
they immediately set off to Cyprus together.
When they had reached the island,
they went into every man's house, 235
putting on beggars' disguises
(for the oracle had not indicated the house).
When, after the passage of many days,
they came at last to Stale's dwelling,
behold – there was Dosikles in the courtyard of the house. 240
   As he leant out and saw the elderly men
and recognized who they were from their appearance,
he experienced joy mingled with fear
and fell upon Rhodanthe who was seated there;
he said, "Is this a dream, august maiden? 245
Is this," he said, "a dream and a vision?
A hallucination, a lie, a deception of the eye?
Or am I looking at Lysippos in my sleep
and inventing Straton's image?
For I saw both of them entering the door. 250
If you do not believe me, come here too and look;
if you do not see them, then the image was an apparition.
And even if it were not an apparition, how it should be approached
would need thought and wise counsel.
   Should we flee or should we confront it? 255
It would be shameful to flee and abandon our fathers,
who have undertaken a long journey on our behalf;
to greet them face to face would be shameful and terrifying.
So then (what awaits us?) we must approach
and greet our parents respectfully. 260
You blush, I know, before your begetter,
you blush and are ashamed to come before him,
lest Straton accuse you of forsaking your country;
but indeed one must not disregard one's parent.
You have an overwhelming reason for your flight; 265

he addressed Dosikles insultingly,
calling him a brigand, a violator, abductor, a thief who stole you;
for yes, I had acted violently using the rules of brigandage,
yes, I abducted Rhodanthe by force."[297]

Saying this and other similar things,   270
and with Rhodanthe persuaded by his argument,
together they came up to their fathers;
and falling at the feet of each
(Dosikles before Lysippos, the girl before Straton),
they washed them with another bath of tears,   275
the girl in silence and kept from speech by modesty,
the youth imploring the immortal gods,
his father's compassion and benevolent disposition,
to overlook his folly completely,
saying, "Sufficient punishment, father,   280
comes from the band of brigands, the tyranny, the wandering
and also from the chains, the darkness of prison,
the flame, the shipwrecks, the flashing sword,
the thousand deaths, the endless murders;
father, Fate the avenger has done enough,   285
harsh Fate, yes, harsh on Dosikles
(how harsh may you learn from words and not from experience).

And I say this to you, lord Straton;
I stole your daughter from you
and deprived you of your beloved child;   290
now be gracious to me, although I have offended you.
If you wish to take action against my offence,
I accept responsibility for the wrongdoing.
See, I am here before you, beat me, punish me,
consume my flesh, take your fill of my blood.   295
The thief, the brigand is in your hands; bind my feet,
contrive every torture – except one.
Do not take Rhodanthe from me,
sundering with a pitiful and bitter division
those whom the gods have united in a dream."[298]   300

297 On marriage by abduction in twelfth-century novels and legislation, see note 78 above.
298 The dream is at 3.69–75. The theme of the indissolubility of marriage, based on Matthew 19.6 ('Those whom God has joined, let no man put asunder'), recurs in *D&C* 3.12, 7.264, as well as in *DigAk* G4.143, E1179, 1305.

Thus Dosikles by speech and tears
urged the progenitors to be merciful.
Straton anticipated Dosikles
and, raising Rhodanthe to her feet,
"Oh, come hither, children," he said, "kiss me;[299]   305
come hither, clasp your progenitor
and put your arms around my neck;
O child, O daughter, embrace me.
Come here, bride, come here, glorious bridegroom;
How fortunate is your marriage, children,   310
which has the gods as bridal attendants.
Your wanderings have had a happy conclusion for us:
Dosikles, you have two fathers in the place of one,
Rhodanthe, you have a brace of mothers."
Shouting this out, both aged men   315
embraced the young people,
and depicted a new design:
for four bodies could be seen
beneath what appeared to be the one head.[300]
And I have often seen on many robes   320
(which the silken craft of weaving fabricates,
of one substance by definition
but tinted with multi-hued dyes)
such a design from an inventive painter,
truly an invention of the art of weaving;   325
one head dispersed on the tetraktys
of the bodies or the tetraktys of the bodies
as it were merging into the one head;
a four-bodied animal, or the other way round –
a single-faced creature made up of four animals,   330
a lion and lions; for the necks
filled out as far as the tail
the remainder of the body with the bulk of the beast,
but, for the face, all were a single lion.

299 Retaining (with Conca 1994) the line sequence of the mss, not placing 308 after 304 with Marcovich 1992.

300 On tetramorph images of this sort in stone, in a manuscript or woven in a textile from twelfth-century Byzantium (as well as the West and especially the Veneto), see Maguire 1999: 196–97 and 2007: 26–28; also Roilos 2005: 54–56.

Some such design the hand of joy, 335
the wise geometer, attempted to sketch for them,
the design of the fathers and the children,
when they joined in their embrace.
And it would have been easier to disentangle
two branches for long intricately intertwined 340
than the parents entwined with their children.
But the young people were none the less young;
the girl, while ostensibly kissing her progenitor,
was secretly kissing Dosikles;
and he was also in sundry ways doing the same, 345
kissing Lysippos with the edge of his lip
but giving the whole of his mouth to Rhodanthe,
as though giving a greeting of recognition.
And the stolen kisses gave greater pleasure
than those that had been achieved openly; 350
so great a stimulation did the embrace offer.
Hence, I think, the fables of the ancients
say that Desire is beardless,
pointing to the god's precocious development.
    So when the embrace came to its leisurely conclusion, 355
Dosikles let out a loud shout,
"O hosts and friends and masters,
Kraton, dear Kratandros, excellent Stale,
come hither, come here, celebrate with me."
When Kratandros came down with fleet-footed speed 360
and discovered the reason for Dosikles' joy
and learnt who were Straton and Lysippos,
he approached both and kissed them on the mouth
and took them and brought them to his father
and, "Father," he said, "the fates that have preceded 365
will appear, I think, small reason for happiness
if you want to compare them with the latest events;
these men here, whom you see present,
are the father of Rhodanthe and the father of Dosikles."
    Kraton, not able to restrain himself
and to allow the message to continue further, 370
stood up and addressed both honourably,
"Fellow fathers, welcome, fellow elders

and co-participants in my twofold fate,
that was unhappy at first but happy in its conclusion.   375
Kratandros, we must summon your mother,
we must prepare the wine bowl and the table,
we must be hospitable and take good care
of these men whom Xenios[301] has sent to me;
we must hold a banquet and we must hold a festival   380
with food, with wine bowls, with cymbals, with sacrifice of oxen,
in short with every means we can.
It is shameful for us to pass by as a gift given in silence
the best of what is bestowed by the gods
and not to make the event a reason for joy."[302]   385
    He said this, and the banquet was prepared;
and they all sat down in a circle
and delighted in the delicacies that had been prepared.
When neither Lysippos nor Straton
ate, Kraton laughed pleasantly   390
and said (not unaware of their demeanour),
"Since you do not wish to eat what is set before you,
I propose to make some humorous remarks,
so perhaps I can feast my friends in this way.
For in the course of my childhood   395
I learnt many frivolous stories,
acquired in abundance with my elderly nurse as teacher.
When once I asked her in puzzlement
why those who are happy do not eat,
my teacher made this reply: 400
'The heart consumes the joy;
and if it eats excessively and to satiety,
it grows in length, it swells hugely
and extends in all directions and fills up the space
(the belly, the chest and the neck);   405
and when every limb has been filled,
the person who is happy eats nothing all day;
for the hollow of his interior is no longer empty
and even if he wanted to eat he would not have room for his food.'[303]

301 'Xenios': Zeus Xenios; cf. 9.16.
302 An exemplification of the principle that every romance ends with a feast and a wedding.
303 A piece of Byzantine nursery lore?

When my nurse taught me this 410
she made me laugh right up till now;
but now, it seems, the tale is likely
to be turned completely around,[304]
even though it is quite right and correct
and has hit on an accurate truth. 415
For if it were otherwise, you, my friends,
would not have ended the banquet fasting;
but, so it seems, the abundance of joy
has filled the whole of your interior's receptacle,
so that it cannot hold even one crumb 420
or scrap of meat or drop of wine
or a bit of pastry or a slice of sesame cake.
Yes, thank you, nurse, most wise old lady,
for solving my problem by natural means.
Or perhaps you have read Empedokles' book 425
or Anaxagoras' pamphlet,[305]
and from your investigation in the lists of natural phenomena
you have thus arrived at a solution to the problem?
But in that case, it seems to me, you have become bleary-eyed,
through poring so much over books." 430
   Breaking in on Kraton's speech,
"I have fed on so much meat of happiness,
I have drunk so much wine of pleasure,
that even if I had space for a thousand stomachs,"
said Lysippos, "for a thousand bellies, 435
I would have filled them all with my rejoicing,
my heart swelling up, as you say.
Yet it keeps a space for friendship,
so that Kraton should not be distressed." And saying this
he picked a little at the meat before him. 440
   Kraton thus provided hospitality to the old men
until two whole days were completed,
when he could hold them back no longer,
praying for the best – favourable winds,

304 Because the guests' lack of eating makes the hosts sad.
305 Pre-Socratic philosophers, now extant only in fragments (see, e.g., Kirk, Raven and Schofield 1983), in which form they would have been known to Prodromos, who refers to Empedokles in, e.g., *Amarantos* (see Roilos 2005: 187, n. 285).

a favourable sea, the calmest of voyages; 445
finally coming forward and kissing them on the mouth,
he despatched them on the third day to their own region,
with Kratandros as excellent fair escort.
Lysippos and Straton considered
sending him back to his ancestral establishment 450
when he came with them as far as Rhodes;
but they could not induce him to return to his country
until he had trodden with them the soil of Abydos
and seen the marriage of Rhodanthe and Dosikles.
When they sailed up to that city 455
and were about to see their own homes,
they had an argument as to which should take the other
home and who should prepare the feast,
and where indeed they should contrive the bridal chamber
and the children's marriage that had been decreed by the gods. 460
    While they were disputing with each other in this way,
the situation became known to Philinna and Phryne,
and brought both to the seashore with giant strides
(if you had seen them you would have said that wings and not feet
wafted them along, as if not touching the ground); 465
and when they had embraced their offspring
(who had, as it were, risen from their graves like corpses)
and had shed another tear of joy,
what huge rapture overcame them
– the greatest, ye race of gods, there was. 470
    Their mothers, their companies of friends,
the mass of fellow citizens all exulted
with the visitors in what had been accomplished.
The priest of Hermes, becoming the inspired
messenger of the mysteries' evocations, 475
allowed all to enter the temple
when Rhodanthe was united with Dosikles;
"Hermes permits this to be so," he said.
He made this pronouncement and, holding out two branches of ivy
in his hands to the bridal couple, 480
he led the entire crowd into the temple.
From there the young people, now united,
were taken to their house with such a din,

such hubbub and dancing and cymbals.
And the conclusion of the feast that was celebrated: 485
Rhodanthe had full knowledge of her bridegroom Dosikles.[306]

---

306 i.e. carnal knowledge in the biblical sense; cf. the last line of *D&C*.

EUMATHIOS MAKREMBOLITES

HYSMINE AND HYSMINIAS

INTRODUCTION

Author

The majority of the manuscripts that transmit the text of *Hysmine and Hysminias* refer to the author in their headings as Eustathios; one thirteenth-century manuscript (K) names him as 'Eumathios'; all give him the rank of *protonobelissimos*.[1] This has led to an identification with the Eumathios Makrembolites who was the subject of a funerary epigram by the canonist Theodore Balsamon and also the recipient of two letters from him in the latter years of the twelfth century;[2] Eumathios was in addition the author of a set of riddles.[3] Balsamon's epitaph, written in the persona of the deceased, outlines this Makrembolites' illustrious background and the steps of his distinguished career: ultimately he was twice eparch of Constantinople, with the rank of *sebastos*. However, an ambivalence about an identification of the novelist with this figure has remained, and most editors and translators have used the name 'Eustathios'.

Recently this issue has been revived, and apparently settled, by Herbert Hunger's publication of one seal, and re-publication of another, with the name Eumathios Makrembolites, both clearly belonging to the same individual.[4] The use of the title *eparchos* on one of these seals, combined with the rarity of the name, makes the association of the seals' owner with the subject of Balsamon's epigram secure. Hunger argued that this individual is also to be seen in the *megalepiphanestatou protasekretis tou Makrembolitou* who was a signatory to the Synod of 1166. He concludes that we have here the author of *H&H*, and – basing himself on the now discredited reading of *notarios* – that the novel was written at an early stage in his career. This argument is

1 See the textual apparatus to the title in Marcovich 2001. The reading of *notarios* that has been attributed to K results from an incorrect resolution of an abbreviation: Cupane 2000: 54.

2 Funerary epigram: Horna 1903: 206–09, no. 13. Letters: Miller 1884: 18–19, nos. 8 and 11; of letter 11 only the addressee's name survives; letter 8 is an elegant discussion of the repayment of a debt, indicating an amiable connection between the canonist and his correspondent.

3 Treu 1893.

4 Hunger 1998.

no longer tenable, but the revised reading of *protonobelissimos* does fit with the career path implied for the signatory in 1166, as the name appears in the Synod's protocol after the last *protonobelissimohypertatos* and before the first *protonobelissimos*.[5] The rank of *megas chartophylax* that appears in a group of later manuscripts is to be discounted, given that this office did not appear until the mid-fourteenth century.[6]

It nevertheless remains true that the earliest manuscript witnesses to the author's name, dating from the thirteenth century, are divided: one (K) reads Eumathios, another (J) Eustathios, another (E) is illegible and the fourth is acephalic (G). While it is possible to argue that, despite Eumathios Makrembolites' apparent status as a married man,[7] Eustathios represents the monastic name that he may have taken at some point, perhaps on bereavement, it remains true that there is no secure connection between the activities of the eparch and the novelist: Balsamon's epigram makes no reference to literary achievements and while the wording on the seals betrays literary sophistication,[8] this cannot be a clinching argument. The name Eumathios is not only rare but the four examples in *PBW* belong to only two families, the Philokales and Makrembolites.[9] The fact that the novelist comes from one of these increases the likelihood that this was indeed his name, though it is best to retain a certain degree of doubt. However, while the most recent editor of *H&H* has retained the form Eustathios, this translation uses Eumathios.

Whether Eustathios or Eumathios, the surname of the author of *H&H* shows that he came from one of the elite families of Constantinople. The Makrembolites clan included an empress in the eleventh century and several highly placed civil and ecclesiastical officials in the twelfth.[10] Young males from such a background were regularly the recipients of a thorough literary education.[11]

5 Hunger's suggestion is the more convincing now that the reading of *notarios* from K can be disregarded; cf. Hunger 1998: 5–6.

6 Darrouzès 1970: 111–12; Hunger 1998: 7, n. 13.. Note the comment by Cataldi Palau on the names and titles given to Makrembolites that the later the manuscript, the longer the title (Cataldi Palau 1980: 107, n. 2).

7 Horna 1903: 183, no. 13, line 33.

8 Hunger 1998: 8.

9 *PBW* (consulted 27 September 2011): Eumathios Makrembolites 101 http://db.pbw. kcl.ac.uk/id/person/107061 and 20102 http://db.pbw.kcl.ac.uk/id/person/152723; Eumathios Philokales 102 http://db.pbw.kcl.ac.uk/id/person/120119 and 20104 http://db.pbw.kcl.ac.uk/id/person/152725.

10 *ODB*, under 'Makrembolites'.

11 Magdalino 1993: 320–23.

Date

As with the name of its author, the date at which *H&H* was written remains problematic. There are two elements to be taken into account: first, the relationships between the four novels from the Komnenian period and between these and other contemporary texts; and secondly, the putative career of the author Makrembolites.

Taking the second issue first, there is nothing that can be said about Makrembolites' career if he is taken to be the otherwise unknown Eustathios. Should he be Eumathios – the more likely alternative – then he would have died around 1185,[12] after a reasonably distinguished life of public service. In the words Balsamon puts in his mouth: 'I gained many luxuries from office, and many distinctions from my rank' (lines 19–20).[13] He progressed in a regular fashion and attained the dignity of *sebastos* (line 24). There is no indication of his age at death: we can only judge that he would not have been young. Should he have been 60, this would put his birth ca. 1125 and he would have been a full generation younger than Theodore Prodomos, generally taken to have been born ca. 1100.[14] If he should be identified with the Makrembolites who signed the protocol for the Synod of 1166, at that point he would have been aged about 40, holding the office of *protoasecretis* and ranked with the *protonobelissimoi*. Should he have died at the age of 80, then he would have been more or less Prodromos' contemporary. Theodore Balsamon (1130/40–95) and Eumathios Makrembolites were on friendly terms as can be concluded both from the funerary poem and from a letter that refers elaborately to a debt;[15] but no conclusion can be drawn from this about an age differential. From the fact that the manuscript tradition refers to him as *protonobelissimos* and not as *sebastos*, with no reference to present or past tenure of the office of *eparchos*, the novel would have been written before the last stages of his career, and arguably before 1166.

Although it is plain that the four Komnenian novels were composed by writers who were aware of each other's work, the sequence of writing is disputed. The problematic relationship is that between *R&D* and *H&H*. It will be argued below that Manasses' *A&K* was written ca. 1145 and Eugenianos' *D&C*, ca. 1156, self-confessedly (it might seem) modelled on Prodromos' *R&D*. As for *R&D* and *H&H*, the conventional position was for

---

12 Horna 1903: 207, although no reason is given for this claim. The format of the seal is consistent with a date in the latter part of the twelfth century.

13 Horna 1903: 207.

14 As discussed above, p. 4.

15 Miller 1884: no. 8.

a long time that *R&D* was written in the 1140s[16] and *H&H* in the latter part of the twelfth century, or even later.[17] More recently it has been argued that *R&D* can be seen conducting an intertextual dialogue with Achilles Tatius' *L&K* through the intermediary of *H&H*, which thus must have been written earlier.[18] Furthermore, recent investigations of the poem by Prodromos in which he dedicates *R&D* to a 'wise Caesar' have led to two conclusions. The first, discussed above, is that this Caesar must be Nikephoros Bryennios (the only Caesar with considerable literary interests to whom this epithet was applied, who was dead by 1138). The second, to which we must now turn, is that the dedication poem, with its interplay of metaphors for writing and painting, is a deliberate reaction to the themes and style of *H&H*.[19] By this argument *H&H* as well as *R&D* were written in the 1130s.

There are, however, difficulties. *H&H* also demonstrates affinities with the work of Nikephoros Basilakes (ca. 1115–after 1182).[20] It has been argued that Basilakes' *progymnasmata* (rhetorical exercises), especially his *ethopoiiai*, show many of the preoccupations of the novels.[21] More strikingly, however, some seventy or so phrases from Basilakes' monody on his brother Constantine are also found in *H&H*. Constantine Basilakes, a career diplomat, died in 1155/6, in South Italy.[22] The two genres – a funerary lament and a sustained erotic narrative – are very different, though in *H&H* many of the shared phrases appear in a context of lament. While it is not easy to argue that either set of phrases fits one context more appropriately than the other, at least two are expressed more fully in Basilakes' lament and more enigmatically in *H&H*.[23] To complicate the issue, there are also one or two phrases in speeches of Basilakes that have recognizable parallels in *H&H*; these speeches date from 1138 and 1150 but were possibly revised for his collected edition made ca. 1160.[24] These dating criteria are not absolute: a plausible suggestion remains that the parallels are the result of schoolroom

16 On no very clear grounds: E. Jeffreys 1980: 475–76; Beaton 1996: 70.

17 See e.g. Beaton 1996: 79–80, 211–12; Alexiou 1977; Cupane 1974.

18 MacAlister 1990.

19 Agapitos 2000a: 86.

20 Pignani 1983: 235–52; see also Garzya 1969.

21 Beaton 1996: 25–26, 88, but especially Roilos 2005: 61–65 on the place of *ethopoiiai* in the formation of the Komnenian novels.

22 Monody: Pignani 1983: 235–52, with a discussion of its dating at 61–65.

23 Socrates' followers: *H&H* 1.3.15, cf. Basilakes' lament (Pignani 1983: 236.30–34); Abradates' hand: *H&H* 7.14.2, cf. Basilakes' lament (Pignani 1983: 250.340–45).

24 *H&H* 2.3.3, cf. Basilakes to John Komnenos (Garzya 1984: 52.3–24, 54.4); *H&H* 2.10, cf. Basilakes to John Komnenos (Garzya 1984: 56.19); *H&H* 5.10.5, cf. Basilakes to Nikolaos Mouzalon (Garzya 1984: 75.10).

exercises. Since Basilakes was a charismatic teacher for much of his life,[25] it is a defensible proposition that the parallels with *H&H* represent Basilakes' pedagogical stock-in-trade that could be drawn on at any stage in his career, while the phrases in *H&H* are the product of an attentive pupil's notebooks.[26]

There remains one other proposal, which draws attention to the erotic imagery applied, with considerable daring, to the emperor Manuel by the poet conventionally known as Manganeios Prodromos.[27] In three poems to be dated between 1152 and 1156 Manuel is referred to as Ἔρως βασιλεύς (*Eros basileus*), and pictured in erotic settings, most notably a bath-house surrounded by the Graces.[28] Paul Magdalino has made an interesting connection of this theme to the striking imagery of an imperial, and tyrannical, Eros in *H&H*. He concludes that the passages in Manganeios and *H&H* must both belong to a new fashion, dating the composition of the novel to the early 1150s; he does not discuss possible intertextual connections between *H&H* and *R&D*.[29] Magdalino's conclusion is, however, not inevitable. The three relevant poems date from the years around the birth of Manuel's first child, whose birth is alluded to in them (the primary subject is praise for recent military victories), and could also be seen as an allusion to the emperor's recently proven virility through a sly reference to his many amorous adventures. Mention of a dominant Eros is not infrequent in Manganeios' poems, especially (appropriately) in *epithalamia*, of which the earliest datable example is from 1145,[30] or in other more surprising contexts, such as an *ekphrasis* of the decoration on a young girl's dress.[31] Manganeios' inclusion

25 Basilakes, Prologue 3–4, 11 (Garzya 1984: 3, 6–7).

26 Hunger 1998: 7, n. 16, referring to Polyakova 1969.

27 Manganeios Prodromos, as noted earlier, is not to be confused with Theodore Prodromos; otherwise anonymous, he acquired his modern nickname from a long-running campaign for admission to the *adelphaton* in the Mangana monastery. Published only in part, an edition of his not inconsiderable corpus in Marc. Gr. XI.22 is in preparation by E. and M. Jeffreys; this new edition will keep the poem numbers used in the Venice catalogue (Mioni 1973: 116–25). For a convenient listing of titles, bibliography and some suggestions on poems' dates, see Magdalino 1993: 494–500.

28 MangProd nos. 4 (dated to 1152), 17 (1153), 14 (1155–56).

29 Magdalino 1992: 257–74. It should be noted, however, that 'imperial' and 'imperially' are used in *H&H* not only of Eros himself but also of the wedding chamber, wedding songs and processions and even of Hysmine at the concluding marriage ceremony (5.8.2, 6.7.2, 11.19.3).

30 MangProd no. 52 (partially edited in Miller 1875–81, vol. 2: 771–72, mentioned further below in connection with *A&K*), for John Kantakuzenos on his marriage to Maria, eldest daughter of the recently deceased *sevastokrator* Andronikos and the *sevastokratorissa* Eirene (Varzos 1984, vol 2: 156).

31 MangProd no. 56: an elaborate brocade with Erotes shooting carefully aimed arrows.

of Eros in his poetic armoury indicates that interest in themes found in the novels remained current in the 1140s and 1150s, witnessed also by a reference to Achilles Tatius in his own verse[32] and by the composition of *A&K* and *D&C*. It does not necessarily impose a close temporal connection to the composition of *H&H*.

Equally, an argument by MacAlister, with which Agapitos concurs, that *R&D* reveals an acknowledgement of key scenes in Achilles Tatius' *L&K* through a reading of *H&H* is not fully convincing. There is probably a connection between the equivalent scenes in *R&D* and *H&H*, but there is no reason to assume that one or the other must have been a completely 'published' work. They can as readily be taken as independent reactions to a model text, perhaps moulded by discussion in a *theatron* or rivalry in a classroom. Agapitos' proposal, discussed above in connection with *R&D*, that the dedication epigrams to *R&D* reveal a response to themes in *H&H* is suggestive, but again the connections may be explained in a similar way. They are as likely to be the result of rivalry with contemporaries' inchoate works as with a completed and 'published' text.[33] The suggestion that Prodromos chose verse for *R&D* in order to restore dignity to narrative fiction after the salacious prose of *H&H* acknowledges the prestige attached to verse writing but does not provide a persuasive argument for the priority of *H&H*.[34] Far more persuasive in the question of intellectual priority in the revival of the composition of novels is the fact that Prodromos is demonstrably an inventive, productive and ingenious writer while the only other known writings that can be ascribed to Makrembolites, a career bureaucrat, are a short set of riddles. The novel is a genre where oral publication in a *theatron* may regularly have preceded circulation as a written text, while the writers may all be connected as teacher and pupil: in such a situation textual similarities need to be used with special care in attempts to establish chronological priorities.

It is plain that the novels of late antiquity were read throughout the middle Byzantine period.[35] The simple answer as to why this literary form

32 MangProd no. 52.67, in the epithalamium referred to above, suggesting a perceived link between the themes of late antique novels and wedding festivities.

33 Other elements that suggest mutual awareness by the authors of *H&H* and *R&D* include the all-pervasive role of Hermes, scenes involving amorous exchanges over drinking cups, and the motifs of slavery and 'stolen marriage'.

34 Salacious prose: Agapitos 1998: 146; status of verse: E. Jeffreys 2009; Bernard 2010: 97–156.

35 As argued by Agapitos 1998, pointing to Photios and Psellos; cf. Roilos 2005: 40–50.

was revived in the twelfth century is that many other types of literary form from antiquity were revived – or, more accurately, given pastiches – at this time, often by Prodromos, as part of the rivalry between aspiring writers.[36] As discussed above, the novels may be deconstructed as a series of rhetorical displays, strung into a simple narrative framework.[37] Given that the overall theme celebrates an aristocratic wedding, it is not implausible that an initial impulse came from a wish to celebrate a wedding held in the household of a potential, or actual, patron.[38] As indicated above, it is tempting to look to the double wedding of the sons of Nikephoros Bryennios, dedicatee of *R&D*, and Anna Komnene in 1122, but this is an uncomfortably early date even for Prodromos, though possible, and probably impossible for *H&H* given the material shared with Basilakes (born ca. 1115). Information for weddings in the reign of John II Komnenos, like everything else, is sparse for the 1120s and early 1130s. There is, however, evidence for a spate of weddings in 1139, when the emperor and his generals returned to Constantinople after campaigns in Syria;[39] but these are too late to be relevant to Bryennios and *R&D*.

There is thus no straightforward fit of careers and dates for the writing of *H&H*. If the identification of the author of *H&H* with the Eumathios defined by Hunger is accepted, as is likely, it has also to be accepted that it is very difficult, though not impossible, to attribute a pre-1138 date to the composition of the novel. A date in the 1140s or 1150s is much more likely, with the evidence from Manganeios Prodromos suggesting a *terminus ante quem* of 1145.[40]

---

36 E.g. tragedy: *Christos Paschon, Katomyomachia*; Lucianic satire: *Philopatris*. On rivalry, see E. Jeffreys 2009: 223–24; on literary innovations at this time, see Magdalino 1993: 393–400; Roilos 2005: 4–7. On poets' rivalry in the eleventh century, see Bernard 2010: 201–33.

37 As apparent from Roilos 2005: 26–112.

38 See discussion above in connection with *R&D*. As indicated above (n. 29), imperial terminology in *H&H* is not confined to Eros but applied to the bride and the bridal chamber. Wedding crowns were part of the Orthodox marriage liturgy from the sixth century onwards; see *ODB*, under 'Marriage crowns'.

39 As witnessed by epithalamia by Theodore Prodromos (Hörandner 1974: nos. 13, 14, 16).

40 Marcovich, the most recent editor of *H&H*, dates Prodromos' death to 1156–58, finds clear echoes of *R&D* in *H&H*, dates Basilakes' monody to 1157, and concludes without further argumentation that Makrembolites wrote in the reign of Manuel (1143–80) (Marcovich 2001: vii). Nilsson 2001: 92, without detailed argument, finds a date of 1130–40 not unreasonable.

Transmission and reception

The transmission of *H&H* is an interesting case study. *H&H* has been preserved in a comparatively large number of manuscripts, which suggests that it was widely read. However, the audience was not always the expected Byzantine one. Of the 43 manuscripts, only nine can be considered Byzantine; of these, four (K, E, J, G) are from the thirteenth or early fourteenth century, and are given priority in Marcovich's edition.[41] Little can be said about the wider reception of *H&H* in the twelfth century, apart from pointing out that, as suggested above, Prodromos and Makrembolites were writing with awareness of each other's work, perhaps in competition. In the thirteenth century, *H&H* was included in the compendia of Komnenian court rhetoric produced as part of the revival of learning fostered by the emperors in exile in Nicaea (in, e.g. Oxford, Barocc. 131). The influence of *H&H* on the authors of the Palaiologan verse romances is palpable, notably on *L&R*, particularly in passages of *ekphrasis* of months, Virtues and fantastic gardens.[42] It is clear that little distinction was made by later readers and copyists between the novels of the Second Sophistic and this Byzantine imitator: eleven of the manuscripts copied in the sixteenth century and later combine *H&H* with Achilles Tatius or Heliodoros. A similar mingling can also be observed in the translations into French and German.[43] Furthermore, it is also clear that an appreciable number of the later copies were produced within a comparatively short space of time in two environments: Rome and Venice. Ms K (Vat. Gr. 114), held in the Vatican Library by 1475, was borrowed three times between 1486 and 1546; each time it is clear that it was wanted for *H&H* and not for any other of its contents.[44] L (Vat. Gr. 1350) was copied directly from K by Giovanni Orsini (active 1536–55) and owned by the noted humanist Fulvio Orsini (1529–1600).[45] A further five copies were made over the next fifty years. Of the 19 manuscripts that make up the β group in Cataldi Palau's categorization, the sixteenth-century copies were made between 1538 and 1545 from Par. Gr. 2915, once owned by Markos

41 K: Vaticanus gr. 114, ff. 3r–53r; E: Oxford, Barocc, 131, 487r–507v; J: Vaticanus gr. 1390, ff. 138r–158v; G: Vatican, Barberinianus gr. 29, ff. 2r–48v. See Cataldi Palau 1980; Marcovich 2001: xi–xiii.

42 Lambert 1935: 33–40; cf. Schissel 1942; Cupane 1974; Cupane 1992; Dolezal and Mavroudi 2002.

43 E.g. in the collocations in LeBas 1822 and Reiske 1778.

44 Cataldi Palau 1980: 87, n. 2.

45 Cataldi Palau 1980: 8.

Mousouros.[46] It is also striking that copies of *H&H* were owned by major collectors and significant scholars of the sixteenth and early seventeenth centuries: Markos Mousouros, Guillaume Pellicier, Hurtado de Mendoza, Fulvio Orsini and Henri Estienne. The attraction of *H&H*, for whatever reasons, is attested by the number of translations into European languages from Carani's Italian translation of 1550 onwards;[47] especially intriguing is the transformation of *H&H* into a tragic masque performed in 1770 at the court of Louis XV of France.[48]

In his authoritative edition of 1876, Hilberg knew and used 22 manuscripts; this number was almost doubled in 1980 by Cataldi Palau, who listed 43, drawing attention in particular to a thirteenth-century manuscript (Oxford, Barocc. 131 = E) hitherto ignored.[49] Her analysis distinguished two families of manuscripts that descend from the same archetype, in essence the conclusion to which Hilberg had come, though after Cataldi Palau's work both families now have sound early witnesses. Cataldi Palau also demonstrated that many of the 43 witnesses may be removed from consideration in a critical edition since they are copies of manuscripts still extant. The essentials of this categorization are followed by Marcovich in his 2001 edition, where he uses 14 witnesses to make the text, giving particular weight to the four from the thirteenth century.[50]

Form

Alone of the Komnenian novels *H&H* is written in prose, in 11 books. The style is straightforward and paratactic, with many redundant phrases and adverbs. In this, as in much else, it is closely modelled on Achilles Tatius' *L&K*.[51] The lexical range is relatively restricted.

---

46 Cataldi Palau 1980: 93.

47 Made from a manuscript of the β family; Cataldi Palau 1980: 99.

48 Laujon 1770.

49 Cataldi Palau 1980: 108–09.

50 Marcovich 2001: xiv; cf. Cataldi Palau 1980: 113. The text printed by Conca to accompany his 1994 Italian translation is based on Hilberg's edition, with emendations, but is not a full critical edition. Note that, as with his 1992 edition of *R&D*, Marcovich's edition of *H&H* has been criticized for its interventionist and, at times, cavalier approach (Nilsson 2001a; Cupane 2003).

51 On the extent and nature of *H&H*'s indebtedness to *L&K*, see the excellent analyses in Nilsson 2001.

Plot summary

Hysmine and Hysminias tells how the hero, Hysminias, meets and falls
in love with the heroine, Hysmine, and the adventures they go through
before they are able to achieve marriage. It is narrated in the first person
by Hysminias to a certain Charidoux, who is mentioned at the beginning,
possibly alluded to once more (at *H&H* 5.7.1), but then makes no further
appearance. Much of the first six of the 11 books into which *H&H* is divided
is taken up with descriptions (*ekphraseis*) of paintings, while a significant
proportion of the remainder involves recapitulations of previous events. The
action moves between the cities of Eurykomis, Aulikomis, Daphnepolis and
Artykomis at some unspecified time in the pre-Byzantine past.

Book 1 The story opens when the chaste Hysminias has just been chosen
by lot to serve as herald from his home city of Eurykomis to the nearby
city of Aulikomis at the time of the Diasia, the festival of Zeus. He is given
hospitality in Aulikomis by Sosthenes, in whose house there is a magnificent
garden with a beautiful well. At a banquet wine is poured for the guests by
Hysmine, Sosthenes' daughter, who makes it plain that she is attracted to
Hysminias. After the meal, Hysmine assists in washing Hysminias' feet, and
makes amorous advances before leaving. Kratisthenes, who has accompanied Hysminias from Aulikomis, demands an account of what had happened.

Book 2 On the next day Hysminias and Kratisthenes go into the garden
and admire the paintings on the wall. There are two sets – of the four Virtues,
Prudence, Fortitude, Chastity and Justice, and of Eros lording it over all
creatures. Kratisthenes comments on the power of Eros, which Hysminias
insists he intends to resist. Another banquet takes place and Hysmine again
pours the wine and indicates her interest in Hysminias. When Kratisthenes
remarks that Eros has enflamed her, Hysminias reiterates his indifference.

Book 3 That night Hysminias dreams that he is dragged before Eros for
spurning Hysmine, but is spared punishment when Hysmine pleads for him.
Hysminias wakes in horror and tells Kratisthenes that he is no longer chaste
but has fallen in love; he describes his dream. The two friends then return to
sleep and Hysminias has an even more vivid dream of an erotic encounter
with Hysmine. He awakes and discusses this with Kratisthenes. Sosthenes
appears; another banquet is held at which Hysmine pours the wine.

Book 4 The usual byplay between Hysmine and Hysminias takes place
at the banquet, at the end of which Sosthenes announces that, the three
days of celebration at Aulikomis being now at an end, on the following day
he will accompany Hysminias back to Eurykomis for sacrifices to Zeus.

Hysminias is devastated at the thought of separation from Hysmine. He and Kratisthenes examine the other paintings in the garden, which are of the 12 months. They interpret the symbolism of these as a further exemplification of the all-encompassing power of Eros. Hysmine reappears, and Hysminias' attempts to make love to her are thwarted by her resistance and the arrival of a servant.

Book 5 Hysminias has another erotic dream, in which he and Hysmine are interrupted by her mother. Sosthenes then summons Hysminias to leave with him on the ceremonial journey to Eurykomis. Once there a banquet ensues, attended by the parents of Hysmine and Hysminias. Kratisthenes acts as wine-pourer, but erotic byplay takes place between Hysmine and Hysminias. That night Hysminias is again tormented by a dream of Hysmine. Later in the night both sets of parents make sacrifices to Zeus, and in their absence Hysminias again attempts to make love to Hysmine, who again resists.

Book 6 Hysminias wakes late. Sosthenes announces at the next meal that on their return to Aulikomis Hysmine is to be married. The young couple are devastated. That evening the parents again go to make sacrifices while Hysmine and Hysminias meet to express their devotion and suggest an elopement. Hysminias, unable to sleep, goes to watch the sacrifices and sees an eagle swoop down and remove the offerings, to the consternation of all. There is no agreement over the meaning of the eagle's intervention, much discussed over yet another meal. Kratisthenes tells Hysminias that he has organized a ship on which he and Hysmine can escape. Hysminias dreams again of Eros, who this time bestows Hysmine upon him.

Book 7 Hysmine and Hysminias meet when their parents have gone to make further sacrifices. He persuades her to elope with him by ship. They set sail but when day dawns a storm blows up. The ship's captain decides that a passenger has to be sacrificed, and the lot falls on Hysmine, who is duly thrown overboard. Calm follows, but Hysminias' laments so irritate the crew that they put him ashore. There he has another dream in which Eros restores Hysmine to him.

Book 8 When Hysminias awakes, rather than discovering Hysmine he is captured by a band of Ethiopians and added to their war-spoils. The barbarians make their way to Artykomis where their female captives who had come through the virginity test at the temple of Artemis are put up for sale. The barbarians then continue on to another harbour, where they camp and are attacked by Hellenes. The Hellenes take captive the barbarians and their prisoners and bring them to Daphnepolis. There Hysminias is allotted a master and made to serve as his slave. A year elapses, in the course of which Hysminias' new mistress extracts the story of his love for Hysmine and proposes herself as a substitute. Hysminias' master is elected to be herald at a festival of Apollo and to go to Artykomis, accompanied by Hysminias.

Book 9 Hysminias' master is welcomed in Artykomis and given hospitality by Sostratos. A banquet takes place, mirroring the banquet at Aulikomis, with Rhodope, daughter of Sostratos, pouring the wine and washing the herald's feet. She is assisted by a serving-girl who reminds Hysminias of Hysmine. The next day this girl gives Hysminias a letter that reveals that she is indeed Hysmine. On the following day Rhodope realizes that something is going on and questions Hysminias, who tells the story of his flight with his beloved (whom he does not name). Hysmine is present and when Rhodope sees her distress Hysmine claims Hysminias is her brother. At the banquet Hysmine kisses Hysminias openly, claiming that she is doing so not only as his sister but on behalf of Rhodope who is in love with him. After the banquet Hysmine and Hysminias meet in the garden.

Book 10 There Hysmine gives Hysminias a letter from Rhodope that proposes their marriage and offers freedom to Hysmine. That night Hysminias again dreams passionately of Hysmine. The next day Sostratos with Hysminias' master and Hysminias leaves for Daphnepolis. While his master goes to the altar of Apollo Hysminias, left in the house, is only saved from an erotic assault made by his mistress when her husband returns. A banquet follows, at which there is much flirtatious byplay between Hysminias and the three women in love with him (his mistress, Rhodope and Hysmine). Later that night all, both masters and slaves, go to keep vigil at the altar and there find the parents of Hysmine and Hysminias lamenting the loss of their children and seeking an oracular response about their fate. The oracle pronounces that their marriage is approved, Hysmine and Hysminias reveal themselves, Hysminias' master and Sostratos claim that they are still their slaves and the ensuing pandemonium is only resolved when Apollo's authority is invoked. Hysmine and Hysminias are declared to be free and a celebratory banquet is held. Hysminias is asked to tell of their adventures, but puts this off until the next day.

Book 11 Another banquet is held, and Hysminias relates what had happened to him. Hysmine then reluctantly does the same. The next day there is an excursion to Artykomis to test Hysmine's virginity at the spring of Artemis. She emerges triumphant and a magnificent wedding takes place. Hysminias ends his narrative with a fervent wish that the adventures of Hysmine and Hysminias should not be consigned to oblivion.

Characteristics and themes[52]

Like *R&D*, *H&H* is structured as a variation on a novel from late antiquity, in this case *L&K*. The relationship between these two has been fruitfully explored from a narratological standpoint by Ingela Nilsson (2001).

The construction of *H&H* is somewhat simplistic, with embassies arbitrarily moving the protagonists from one locality to another and inter-action between characters taking place at a succession of meals.[53] There are no complex sub-plots, although, for example, in *H&H* 9 and 10 Rhodope, Hysmine's mistress, falls in love with Hysminias. Given the first-person narration, there is no exposition of parallel events and Hysmine's separate experiences are finally reported by Hysmine in person (11.13–16). One noticeable feature is the reduplication of plot elements, the most striking being the embassy in *H&H* 8 when the master of the now-captive Hysminias goes as herald to a neighbouring city to encounter a host, Sostratos, with a similar name to Sosthenes, Hysminias' earlier host.[54] Smaller elements – actions and phrases – are also repeated within reduplicated scenes. Nilsson sees this technique as a deliberate device to delay the action and make the text more artful, while admitting that it may have contributed to the modern assessment of *H&H* as laboured and artificial.[55] More puzzling is the dupli-cation of names: that Hysmine and Hysminias share a name is stressed (e.g. 1.9, 1.14, 2.12), while the motif reappears in connection with the nymph Daphne, the homonymous plant and the associated, fictional, city (8.18); in the final paragraphs (11.22) these elements are bound up together in the narrator's plea for the immortality of his tale.[56]

H&H, like *R&D*, can be deconstructed as a set of literary exercises strung together as a narrative.[57] The exercises are in pastiche, or *mimesis* (largely of Achilles Tatius' *L&K*), making extensive use of *progymnas-mata* (preliminary rhetorical exercises) and the conventions of late antique amatory writing. That *H&H* is a pastiche of *L&K* is immediately obvious

52 For general discussions, see Hunger 1978, vol. 2: 134–42; Beaton 1996: 78–87; Roilos 2005: passim; Jouanno 2005; Meunier 2007: passim.

53 On the significance of banquets, see Roilos 2005: 242–46 in addition to Jouanno 1996 and Harder 1997.

54 On the nature and function of these reduplications, see Nilsson 2001: 56–74 and also Meunier 2007: 104–09.

55 Nilsson 2001: 74; cf. Marcovich 2001: x, note 6.

56 See Nilsson 2001: 155–59, also pointing out the similarity of names to those in *L&K*.

57 Note again Roilos 2005: 26–112 on the place of rhetorical structures in the novels; cf. Meunier 2007: 183–219.

from the opening paragraphs: the indebtedness is much greater than the genuflexions in *R&D* to Heliodoros. In *H&H* not only have wording and syntax been imitated but also the use of first-person narration as well as whole episodes and motifs (although *H&H* functions on a smaller scale than *L&K*).[58] Makrembolites also makes extensive use of tags or quotations from classical authors, chiefly Homer, Hesiod and the tragedians (especially Euripides), Aristophanes and Theokritos, probably reflecting the main texts read in the course of his education; some of these allusions seem a little perfunctory.[59]

The rhetorical set-pieces include *ekphraseis* of works of art[60] (and their elucidation (Kratisthenes at 2.11, 4.18), speeches of lament,[61] and embedded examples of *ethopoiia*.[62] There is also much small-scale rhetorical inventiveness: use of chiastic phrases, paradoxes and oxymoron. Every possible variation is wrung from each situation. As with Prodromos in *R&D*, this literary dexterity demands an audience that would appreciate the author's versatility.

However, unlike Prodromos in *R&D*, Makrembolites is interested in exploring a range of amatory motifs. These include descriptions of images of the personified Eros (2.7, 3.1), accounts of dreams in which Eros demonstrates his powers over all nature (2.9–10), and accounts of the physiological effects of erotic passion (3.7; a 'wet dream').[63] Eros is depicted as an autocratic lord, an emperor who tyrannizes those subjugated to him, a motif that has famously been attributed to influence from Western courtly literature of the twelfth century (and later).[64] Although this has become widely accepted the issue is by no means clear cut: most of Eros' physical attributes (wings, feathered feet, nudity etc.) lie within the Greek tradition of amatory

---

58 The plot indebtedness of *H&H* to *L&K* is particularly apparent at *H&H* 6.2.2, cf. *L&K* 1.7.4–5; *H&H* 6.10.1–2, cf. *L&K* 2.12.1–2; *H&H* 7.12.4, cf. *L&K* 3.15.2–6; *H&H* 10.9.1, 11.13.2–3, cf. *L&K* 5.9.1, 6.13.2; *H&H* 11.14–16, cf. *L&K* 5.9.3, 5.17.5, 8.16; *H&H* 8.7.2–5, 11.17.2–18.1, cf. *L&K* 8.12.8–13.2, 8.14.2–4. See Nilsson 2001: 166–260.

59 These authors formed the staples of Byzantine classroom reading; Markopoulos 2008: 788–89.

60 Virtues: *H&H* 2.2–6; months: 4.5–16; the figure of Eros and his retinues: 2.7–11.

61 E.g. *H&H* 6.6–7, 6.10, 7.9; cf. Roilos 2005: 79–111.

62 E.g. *H&H* 5.3: what a mother would say when she found her daughter being assaulted; 6.6: what a young man would say when his beloved is to be married to another.

63 Alexiou 1977. There are parallels for this motif: MangProd 14.5–86 (Bernadinello 1972: poem 7) and 147.26–49, and Zonaras (*PG* 119: 1020).

64 Cupane 1974, 1984, 2000. Note, however, that the dating of some of the French parallels is incorrect, while the re-dating of *H&H* invalidates much of the argument.

writing, especially verse, while his imperial attributes (throne, retinue) come from the Byzantine court environment, as shown by the use of this framework by Manganeios Prodromos in connection with Manuel I, as discussed above.[65] It is worth noting again that at, for example, 6.8, there are references to imperial elements in Hysmine's wedding dreams.[66] The vocabulary of enslavement to Eros, which also is strongly reminiscent of the vocabulary of the contested Western concept of 'courtly love', is, however, embedded in the Greek vocabulary of emperor–courtier, master–servant relationships, or even those of God and worshipper. It is part of a tension visible in *H&H*, as well as to a lesser extent in *R&D*, arguably arising from contemporary anxieties over concepts of freedom versus slavery, as witnessed by legislation by Manuel I.[67] While there can be no doubt that the fourteenth-century Greek romances were written with awareness of recent and contemporary fashions in Western amatory conventions,[68] the situation for the twelfth-century novels is questionable.

Many other themes that can be picked out in *H&H* merit exploration. The emphasis on slavery is one. Prominent in *H&H* in connection with Eros, as just mentioned, the motif also appears in comments on the tragedy of captivity, the irony of the reversal of social positions (9.16) and the nature of double and triple servitude.[69] When Hysmine and Hysminias are discovered by their parents, a dispute with their former masters over lawful ownership – with implications of servile status – erupts at 10.14. A key passage elaborating these topics is at 8.10–11. There is also much exploration of the interplay between art and craftsmanship, with a blurring between painterly and writerly skills as evidenced by uses of *grapho* ('write' but also 'paint') and its compounds, culminating in the author/craftsman's aspirations in the closing paragraphs of *H&H* for his work's longevity and endless re-copyings.[70] There is also a thread of allusions to drama and acting,[71]

65 Magdalino 1992. One must beware of circular arguments over cause and result.

66 As already noted, this may be connected with the use of marriage crowns in the marriage service; see *ODB*, under 'Marriage crowns'.

67 For details see n. 78 in the introduction to *R&D*. The date of Manuel's legislation is unclear. See also Kazhdan 1985; Magdalino 1991; Rotman 2004.

68 See, e.g. Beaton 1996: 154–64; Agapitos 2004; E. Jeffreys 2013. The fourteenth-century vernacular verse romances were also aware of their predecessors in the twelfth-century novels.

69 Vocabulary of servitude and triple servitude: e.g. *H&H* 2.9, 3.1, 3.10, 7.9, 7.18, 8.10. 8.11, 10.8, 10.14, 9.22, 11.5, 11.9, 11.16 where forms of *doulograph-* are used in both an amatory and a legal sense; on triple servitude, see Nilsson 2001: 117–22.

70 *H&H* 11.21, as discussed in Agapitos 2000a.

71 E.g. at *H&H* 2.6.1; 5.4; 5.8; 8.10; 8.14; 11.12; see Agapitos 1998; Roilos 2005: 38–39.

although the meaning of 'drama' – probably not implying more than 'deeds done' but with possible dramatic implications – needs further exploration. Much the same could be said of *tragodo* and *tragodema* ('sing' and 'song'), although *tragodia* retains its reference to a theatrical genre.[72] In the oldest manuscripts the title of *H&H* refers to the work as a *poiema* by Eumathios, or Eustathios, Makrembolites: '*poiema*', a word of multiple meanings, is perhaps best understood here as 'work' or 'product'. This statement may thus be simply a statement of authorship without indicating the nature of the text.[73] That Makrembolites is a self-aware writer in tune with such ambiguities is apparent from his final paragraphs, while there are passages elsewhere of self-referentiality and acknowledgement of the rhetoricity of his work.[74]

As with *R&D*, *H&H* is set in an antique past, using rituals associated with the cult of the Olympian deities and civic festivals as fundamental to the scene-setting and the plot. Thus the exchange of heralds resembles the Hellenistic practice of sending *theoroi* as representatives to a neighbouring city's festival.[75] However, the sacrifices at night may well reflect the practices of twelfth-century *agrypniai*, vigils that were held regularly before church festivals.[76] As with *R&D*, there are biblical echoes and hints of Christian rites: the cup offered by Hysmine has undeniable overtones of liturgical phrasing (1.9, 1.14), as does the scene at the banquet for Apollo (10.16).[77] There are Christological and New Testament resonances in the *ekphrasis* of the months (4.5–18) which have been explored at length by Plepelits (1989), though his case for a particularized Christian allegory is not completely convincing; more useful is Roilos' approach, which argues for a flexible Neo-Platonic undercurrent.[78]

It could be argued that the main theme of *H&H* is the importance of chastity. Both hero and heroine are virgin, as is stressed repeatedly; Hysmine maintains her virginity despite constant assaults; Sophrosyne (Chastity) is the most emphasized figure in the painting of the four Virtues; the Spring of Artemis is used twice to test disputed virginity; Hysminias laments inces-

---

72   E.g. at *H&H* 6.13, 8.11, 8.14, 10.17; contrast 6.15, 8.20, 9.23.

73   Cf. Agapitos 1998 and 2000a.

74   E.g. at *H&H* 5.7, the narrator refrains from 'glory-mongering' in his account of the processions in his honour; see Roilos 2005: 57–61.

75   See *OCD*, under 'Theoros'. Note, however, that *keryx*, 'herald', is the term used in *H&H*, not *theoros*.

76   See *ODB*, under 'Vigil'; cf. MangProd 68, written ca. 1145, which is set during a night-time service before a feast of the Theotokos.

77   See the points made in Burton 1998; Kaldellis 2007.

78   Roilos 2005: 137, and the section (113–224) on allegory in the novel tradition as a whole.

santly that his erotic experiences (especially his dreams) have left him techni-
cally unchaste; his master comments on the importance of chastity (8.14).
Is this an allusion to a currently important social issue, or an indication that
religious and moral sanctions concerning marriage were being flouted, as
it is plain they were in the imperial court in the early years of the reign of
Manuel? The Komnenian preoccupation with marriage legislation and its
possible role in instigating the novels has already been noted. In *H&H*, as
in the other novels, 'marriage stealing' appears as a motif (7.4.2, 11.6.1).

Banquets are structurally significant for *H&H*.[79] Given that the seating
arrangements for Sosthenes' banquet have led to discussion of twelfth-
century practice,[80] the question might be extended to whether the conventions governing meetings between unmarried youth of high social status are
in any way reflected in *H&H*. Hysmine's presence at her parents' banquet
is acceptable, while at 8.4 the presence of women at the pirates' banquet is
disgraceful; there is a clear distinction drawn between the treatment to be
accorded virgins and other women (8.3–4).[81]

Again as with *R&D* dreams are used conspicuously as a device in plot
development, reflecting past experiences and foreshadowing future events –
as in the first dream at 3.1, when Hysminias' attitudes to Eros are challenged
and his future with Hysmine laid out.[82] It was suggested in connection with
Prodromos' use of dreams in *R&D* that this reflected current interest in
Aristotelian dream theory; while no such textual connections are immediately apparent in *H&H* Makrembolites does seem to be tapping into a
fashionable motif in the dream in 3.9, which, as pointed out earlier, has
parallels in his (approximate) contemporaries, Manganeios Prodromos and
Zonaras. Arguably, then, the dreams in *H&H* reflect a current interest, and
are a further point of dialogue between Prodromos and Makrembolites.

79 In addition to Jouanno 1996 and Harder 1997, see Roilos 2005: 242–46.

80 Grosdidier de Matons 1979 in connection with *H&H* 1.6.1.

81 See discussions in Jouanno 2002 and Garland 2006a. Note there is a certain prurience
about nakedness (e.g. in the stripping of Hysmine at *H&H* 7.15 and prisoners at *H&H* 8.3) which
contrasts with the physical frankness of the erotic dream at *H&H* 3.7; for some approaches to
Byzantine attitudes to nudity, see, e.g., *ODB*, under 'Nude, The', and Zeitler 1999.

82 The place of dreams in *H&H* and the novel tradition in general has been well discussed
in MacAlister 1996; see Nilsson 2001 passim on *H&H*. Dreams occur in *H&H* 3.1, 3.4–7,
5.1–2, 6.18, 7.18, 10.4.

Manuscripts, editions and translations

Manuscripts
For a full account of the manuscripts of *H&H* see Cataldi Palau 1980; see also the discussion at pp. 166–67 above. The thirteenth- and fourteenth-century manuscripts given most weight in Marcovich 2001 are:
K   Vaticanus graecus 114, ff. 3r–53r
E   Oxford, Baroccianus, 131, 487r–507v
J   Vaticanus graecus 1390, ff. 138r–158v
G   Vatican, Barberinianus graecus 29, ff. 2r–48v

Editions
Gaulminus 1617; Lampanitziotis 1791; Teucher 1792; Le Bas 1856, reprinted in Hirschig 1856: 523–97; Hercher 1859: 161–286; Hilberg 1876; Conca 1994: 499–687; Marcovich 2001.

Previous translations
Latin: Gaulminus 1617; Teucher 1792; Le Bas 1828
Dutch: Nispen 1652
English: Le Moine 1788
French: Louveau d'Orleans 1559; Colletet 1625; Godard de Beauchamps 1729; Laujon 1770 (verse drama based on Godard de Beauchamps 1729); Le Bas 1822; Meunier 1991
German: Schirmer 1663; Reiske 1778; Plepelits 1989
Italian: Carani 1550; Conca 1994: 499–687
Russian: Polyakova 1965

This translation
This translation is based on Marcovich's edition; differences between this and that of Conca (1994) are noted only where the translation is affected significantly. Notice has also been taken of comments in Nilsson 2001a and Cupane 2003 on the details of Marcovich's edition, though many of these points influence passage from Greek into another language only obliquely: this is not the place in which to supply the detailed textual and linguistic discussion that *H&H* still needs. One constant translation issue is that of shifting tenses: especially in passages of description (*ekphraseis*) Makrembolites makes much use of a historic present which has often, though not always, been respected in this translation.

TRANSLATION

THE WORK OF EUMATHIOS MAKREMBOLITES CONCERNING THE ADVENTURES OF HYSMINE AND HYSMINIAS[1]

BOOK ONE

[**1.**1] The city of Eurykomis[2] is excellent in many respects, not only because it is garlanded by the sea and watered by rivers and luxuriates in meadows and flourishes with bounteous food, but also because of its piety to the gods and even more than golden Athens it is entirely given over to altars, sacrifices and offerings to the gods. It proclaims celebrations, it holds festivals, it sacrifices offerings to Zeus and the other gods. [2] In this Eurykomis the

---

1 At the head of the text several manuscripts present four sets of 12-syllable verses, none likely to be attributable to Makrembolites. 1. *Verses to Eros.* Hysminias, his heart pierced by Eros, I bids all young people to flee Eros, I for Eros wounds more sharply than a dart. 2. *Other [verses].* Wounded by Eros' sharp soul-destroying I bows to the depth of his heart, Hysminias I urges young people to flee the unruly onrush of passion I with vigour for it is the cause of harm. I Whatever passion Eros induces with his gaze, may I escape his goad. 3. *Other verses.* Solomon, writer of odes and psalms, I declared in his scriptural proverbs, I "Never, my son, let desire for a woman I overcome you, except for your own wife. I For even if sweetness flows from her lips I at first, even if she seems to you, my son, I as sweet as any honey, I later – alas – she will induce bitterness, I taming your heart with incessant arrows." I And this Solomon's tongue uttered also: I "Contemplate, spectator, the erotic style I and expression that makes up this book I and describes the course of physical love; I at first it is unalloyed sweetness I but later a bitterly caustic dart. I Consider the end of every beginning." 4. Hysminias, wounded by the dart of love, I urges young people to enlist against Eros.

For the name Eumathios rather than Eustathios, see Introduction, pp. 159–60.

2 'Eurykomis': literally 'Broad village'; the place names in *H&H* all have suggestive etymological elements (e.g. Aulikomis: 'Village of the court'; Artykomis: 'Village of Artemis'; Daphnepolis: 'City of Daphne'), but attempts to see these as symbolizing Alexandria, Constantinople, Ephesus and Antioch are not supported by the narrative and are ultimately unconvincing (cf. Plepelits 1989: 24–29). These opening paragraphs are very closely modelled on the first paragraphs of *L&K*.

time of the Diasia is also the time when lots are cast for the heralds;[3] for it is both the city's custom and also an unwritten law that, whenever it is the time for the sacred festival, lots should be cast among the unmarried men in the prominent families in the city; and the man on whom the lot falls is sent as herald to the city allotted to him, having first been garlanded with laurel.

[**2**.1] Thus the lot falls on me, and I am garlanded, my handsome Charidoux,[4] and become the sacred herald to Aulikomis. I come out from the temple, garlanded with a laurel wreath, wearing the sacred chiton and august buskin,[5] and the bystanders welcome me with a glittering escort of torches, cymbals, flares, processional songs, an entire sacred parade. [2] The city is in a hubbub and all because of me; one man embraces me, another kisses me, yet another dances before my feet and in one way or other, another contrives a triumph for me. Seeing this, you would have said that a raging flood of river-water was pouring over me, the herald. [3] One cry alone is heard throughout the whole city: "The herald is Hysminias, and he goes as herald not to any city but to Aulikomis."

[**3**.1] And so I come to that city. Why should I dwell at length on what had taken place in the meantime? My good friend, I come as a herald, and I am received in the city not as a herald but as a god. The population comes running out, they decorate the streets, they strew the road before me with myrtle, they cloud the air with perfumes, they sprinkle the bystanders with rose-water; [2] they crowd round me and they whirl around in a brilliant throng, just as the devotees of Sokrates[6] crowded around him. Everyone tries

3 'Diasia': a major Athenian festival in honour of Zeus Melichios, celebrated on 23 Anthemios (late February/early March), until the second century CE. 'herald': The rituals ascribed to the choosing of heralds, their role in moving between cities, their performance of rites to honour the Olympian deities, their robes and garlands are the chief way in which the novel conveys its setting in the antique past. These have something in common with the embassies sent in *L&K* 2.15 to sacrifice in another city, though the term 'herald' is not used, and reflect the Hellenistic *theoroi* sent to attend festivals (*OCD*, under 'theoroi'); see Joannou 2005: 23, n. 34.

4 'Charidoux': The suggestion at Plepelits 1989: 3 that this conceals the name John Doukas, brother of the emperor Constantine X Doukas, cannot stand, on chronological grounds. If there is a reference here to an individual – a patron – there are several mid-twelfth-century figures of this name with literary associations who could be proposed, though none with any conviction (see the lists in Magdalino 1993: 510–12). However, this addressee provides a reason for the first-person narrative, though he does not reappear; one might expect a reference in the novel's final paragraphs, to complete the narratological illusion.

5 'sacred chiton and august buskin': i.e. a tunic and sandals in the antique manner.

6 'devotees of Sokrates': a phrase found also in Nikephoros Basilakes' lament for his brother (Pignani 1983: 236.28–31), as are many other phrases in this passage. For possible Platonic implications, see Nilsson 2001: 182–86.

to carry me off for themselves, thinking that I would bring good fortune to the one with whom I end up, since I have been sent as herald on great matters from a great city. [3] Sosthenes is the victor and, bringing up his chariot, leads me off and brings me to his house and takes most generous care of me and shows me round his garden.[7]

[**4**.1] This was full of grace and pleasure, brimming with plants, completely full of flowers. The cypresses are in rows, the myrtles form a dense covering, the vines are wreathed with grape clusters; the violet leaps out from its leaves and beautifies the vision with perfume; as for the roses, one is emerging from the bud, another is swelling, yet another has already emerged; and some which have already reached maturity are spread on the ground. [2] Lilies decorate the garden, they sweeten the nostrils, they attract the spectator and contest with the roses; if you[8] had to sit in judgment on them, you would not know on which to bestow the prize.

[3] Seeing this, I thought I beheld Alkinoos' garden and felt that I could not take as fiction the Elysian plain so solemnly described by the poets.[9] For laurel and myrtle and cypresses and vines and all the other plants that adorn a garden, or rather that Sosthenes' garden contained,[10] had their branches raised like arms and, as if setting up a dance, they spread a roof over the garden, but they permit the sun to filter through to the ground [4] in as much as the zephyr blew and rustled the leaves. When I saw this I said, "Sosthenes, you have woven me a golden cord."[11]

[**5**.1] A well had been dug about four cubits deep, circular in form; a hollow column made the central point of the circuit of the well; the column was of marble, marble of a hundred hues. [2] On top of it was a basin of

7 The garden with its protective walls and abundant fertility can perhaps be taken to stand for the protected chastity of its maiden owner; see Littlewood 1979; Barber 1992. On the complex role of the gardens in *H&H* see Nilsson 2001: 97–103, 209–11.

8 'you': perhaps a reference back to the Charidoux of the last paragraph, not merely a generalization.

9 'Alkinoos' garden': proverbial for its beauty (*Odyssey* 7.112–31). Here Makrembolites is especially indebted to the garden description in *L&K* 1.15.1–6. 'Elysian Plain': where the Olympian deities reposed; cf. Lucian, *True History* 2.5–6.

10 'or rather [...] contained': perhaps to be deleted as a gloss (Plepelits 1989: 79).

11 'golden cord': cf. *Iliad* 8.17–27, 15.14–33, where Olympian gods are bound in a golden cord or chain, the source of an immense allegorical literature and discussed in Byzantium by Psellos, under Neoplatonic influence, as the chain binding the spiritual and sensible worlds (Lévêque 1959; Cesaretti 1991: 72–74; Nilsson 2001: 211). For Plepelits 1989: 32–33 this phrase, found also in Basilakes (Pignani 1983: 244.195), justifies his Christian allegorical interpretations of the whole novel; Roilos 2005: 175–83 demonstrates Makrembolites' awareness of current Neoplatonic preoccupations which diffuse *H&H*.

Thessalian marble, and on it a golden eagle was spouting water from its beak.[12] The basin received the water; the eagle stretched out its wings as if it wanted to bathe. [3] A goat that had just given birth crouches over its fore feet to drink the water; the goatherd sits by the teat, feeling the udder. The goat drinks the water, the goatherd squeezes out the white milk; [4] and as long as the goat gulped down the water, the goatherd does not abandon his milking but the wooden shepherd's bowl that he had placed under the teat does not have the opening at its base firmly closed and it does not hold the stream from the teat. [5] And a hare joins in the circle and, dipping his right forepaw in, he makes a stream of water spurt up into his mouth and wets all his face.

[6] Perched around the coping of the well are a swallow and a peacock and a dove and a cockerel, all of which Hephaistos had cast in bronze and Daidalos' hand had crafted.[13] Water poured out of their beaks, with a flowing sound which endowed the birds with song. The leaves of the trees, stirred by the zephyr, whispered; hearing this you would have said that the birds were singing sweetly.[14] [7] The flowing water through its clarity took on the colours of the marble. Island marble decorated the base of the well; it was white but with a black hue in places and the black imitated the painter's art since the water seemed to be in constant motion and to billow up and almost burst out. The well's surround was decorated with marble from Chios, coming from Lakonia,[15] and on the other side with Thessalian marble and the central section had multi-coloured marble of a hundred hues, fitting in alternately with each other. [8] This was a novel sight and full of charm – the well with its variegated colours, the birds spouting water, the Thessalian basin, and the golden eagle with the fountain in its beak.

[**6**.1] There were seats[16] set round about in a row, not made from wood or from ivory but from costly gleaming marble; Thessalian marble made up the base while the sides were decorated with marble from Chalkidike.

12 Cf. the fountains constructed by Basil I in the imperial palace (Theophanes Continuatus 5.85; Bekker 1838), which also had animals in bronze around the rim; note the bucolic tones (Burton 2006: 571–77). The mixture of tenses in this passage reflects the Greek.

13 Hephaistos, the blacksmith for the Olympian gods; Daidalos, the legendary craftsman; cf. *Iliad* 18.391.

14 'birds were singing sweetly': cf. Lucian, *True History* 2.5.

15 'from Lakonia': a nonsensical phrase derived from *L&K* 2.2.2, where it is used in its proverbial sense ('from a Lakonian cup') with reference to Chian wine, not marble.

16 'seats': already by the tenth century it was no longer customary to recline for meals, except for certain ceremonial feasts in the Great Palace, so κλίνη should be translated as 'seat' rather than in its classical sense of 'bed' or 'couch'; see Grosdidier de Matons 1979; here Hysmine's game with the cup and later with her feet can only be envisaged if the diners are upright round a table. Cf. *R&D* 2.95; *D&C* 8.246.

There were hemispheres close by the couches, [2] which the craftsman had hewn entirely from Pentelic marble as foot rests; myrtles, cleverly trained upwards, overshadowed the seats on all sides, intertwined with each other and shaped into a kind of roof.

[**7.**1] When, by Zeus, I saw all this, I fastened my entire gaze on the spectacle, and stood all but speechless. Sosthenes said to me, "Lay aside your office of ambassador, lay aside your role as herald, and sit down with us." [2] So I laid aside my garland and the herald's chiton and the sacred sandals, and sat down. And there sat down with me Kratisthenes, my cousin, my other self (for so I define a friend), who had sailed with me from Eurykomis. So we sat down, I and Kratisthenes and Sosthenes and Panthia, his wife.

[**8.**1] And what need is there for me to make careful distinctions over delicacies and delights? Sosthenes instructed his daughter, the maiden Hysmine, to pour the wine. She girt up her tunic, she bared both her arms to the elbow, she tied with a fine cord about her neck the light fabric[17] that was round them and, sitting by the dove, washed her hands, using the bird's beak as an aid in this action. [2] Then, taking a silver pitcher, she holds it to the eagle's beak and in an instant filled it with water, so vigorously did the water gush forth. She sets cups around the pitcher and, after washing them carefully and attentively, she applies herself to the task.

[3] And so Sosthenes drank, for he could not persuade me to drink before him. Then Panthia too drank before me, and the drink came to me as the third. So the girl came up and, placing the cup beside me, whispered, "Welcome." [4] I heard her, though I made no reply but drank with great pleasure, because the cup was very delightful and the wine very sweet and the water clear and very cold: nothing can be more agreeable than this for a man who is thirsty and very hot and sweaty. And after me Kratisthenes drinks the nectar, for this is what I call the wine from Aulikomis.

[**9.**1][18] We had made a little progress with the dishes, which were abundant and very choice, when we drank again. So the maiden came and said to me, in a very quiet voice, "You are receiving the cup from a maiden with the same name." And she placed her foot against mine, and kept it there for as long as I drank from the cup. I blushed, by the gods, and I might have made a joke of it, except I thought that this had happened accidentally.

17 'light fabric': Hysmine's garment presumably has long, loose sleeves; cf. Parani 2003: 73–74, and plates 81, 83 (cf. also Vat. Urb. Gr. 2, f. 167v, detail of the attendant at the birth of John the Baptist).

18 See Jouanno 1996 for a discussion on the extent to which scenes of this sort can be taken to reflect twelfth-century practice.

[2] Then we ate once again and then we drank again. The girl came up, she mixed the wine for me and held out the cup. I held out my hand to take it and grasped the cup, but she did not let it out of her maidenly hands. For the maiden both offered me the cup and kept hold of it and though she was apparently offering it, in reality she was holding on to it. [3] So there was a contest between our hands, and the hand of the virgin girl is victorious over the hand of the virgin herald.

I was shamed by the defeat and addressed the girl in my herald's mien, with my full voice, with a virgin soul, "'Do you not want to give it to me? What do you want to do?" [4] At this she snatches her hand away from the cup and was quite abashed and her cheek grew more red than was natural; she kept her eyes completely on the ground and looked as if she had been struck by a thunderbolt, with her shame visible all over her face.

[**10.**1] Panthia turns her eyes on the girl, eyes which are full of fury, full of wrath and full of blood; she sweeps her eyes over the girl's head, her hands, her feet, her neck; looking over the whole girl, she is utterly furious and utterly enraged with her, and her cheek grows red (it strikes me as paradoxical, that blushing should be engendered by rage),[19] but she soon grows pale as if the blushes are draining away to Hysmine's face.

[2] Sosthenes too looks sharply at his daughter and, shaking his head, immediately pulls his eyes away from her and says, "It is the time of the Diasia, let us make merry at the Diasia; let us give ourselves up entirely to the festival and the celebration. [3] Zeus joins in the banquet and the banquet is Zeus's since this is Zeus's herald," pointing to me with his hand.[20]

And Kratisthenes, who is sitting by me, tells me with a gesture to be quiet, pressing his foot on mine and saying in a whisper, "Be quiet." [4] I did not know what would become of me; I blushed, I grew pale, I kept quiet, I was terrified, I trembled, I was ashamed of myself, of Sosthenes, of Panthia, of the girl, of the company, even of my Kratisthenes, I fixed my eyes on the table, and I prayed to get away from it.

[**11.**1] The girl, as she was bidden, once again offered the wine to her father, and after her father Sosthenes and her mother Panthia she approached me, the herald. Sosthenes says, "Hysminias the herald, this is the cup of the festival; drink in honour of Zeus and rejoice.[21] [2] Rejoice as you eat, rejoice

19 'paradoxical': cf. Kallistratos, *Ekphrases* 11.2 (where blushing is engendered on bronze).
20 'banquet': on banquets in *H&H*, see Roilos 2005: 239–45.
21 One of several scenes arguably alluding to Christian rituals; cf. *R&D* 3.103. See Introduction p. 174 and discussions in Burton 1998; Nilsson 2001: 280–82; Roilos 2005: 203–23; Kaldellis 2007: 6–10.

as you drink, rejoice as you proclaim the Diasia." I responded, "May you rejoice too, Sosthenes, for you have taken most generous and lavish care of me." The girl stands beside me, putting the cup with her hand into mine and entwining her eyes intently with mine. [3] I hold out my hand to take the cup and she presses my finger, and as she does so she moans[22] and breathes a gentle sigh as if from her heart. I kept quiet, obeying Kratisthenes, and so the symposium came to an end.

[**12**.1] Sosthenes, Panthia, the maiden Hysmine and three female attendants conducted us to our chamber. One of the servants brought water from the well, another brought in a silver bowl on her shoulders, and the third brought linen as white as snow. [2] We entered the chamber and Sosthenes said, "Farewell," and went off with Panthia. Kratisthenes and I sat down on the beds, which were magnificently appointed and very comfortable. [3] The servant who was holding the bowl placed it by the end of my bed, while the other poured water into it. The maiden Hysmine, crouching down by my feet and taking hold of them, washes them in the water (this is an honour accorded to heralds); she holds them, she clasps them, she embraces them, she presses them, she kisses them silently and sneaks a kiss; eventually she scratches me with her fingernails and tickles me.[23]

[4] I put up with all the rest in silence but at this I could not suppress my laughter; the girl shook her head and, looking at me intently, smiled slightly and nodded her head again, even though I had done nothing to encourage her amorous advances. She dries my feet with the towel, taking it from the attendant's hands, and saying, "Farewell, herald," she left.

[**13**.1] I promptly readied myself for sleep, being somewhat befuddled with food and drink and my heraldic duties. About the third watch of the night the good Kratisthenes wakes me up, saying, "A herald should not sleep all night long."[24] [2] So I tried to tear myself away from sleep, obeying respect and friendship, but sleep would not let itself be torn from my eyes for food and drink and hard work are the sources of sleep. "What do you mean, Kratisthenes?" I said, "Why do you tear sweet sleep from my eyelids?" He wanted to know what had happened at dinner, and why I had burst out laughing, and he reproaches me for chattering too much, saying,

22 'presses […] moans': cf. *L&K* 2.4.4.

23 'tickles': Conca 1994 speculates that the tickling is a sign of the presence of Eros; cf. *Anacreontea* 6.5–6 (West 1993), used at *D&C* 3.142–43.

24 'third watch': night was divided into four periods of three hours each (the length of the hours varying with the season); so this would be roughly between midnight and three in the morning. 'A herald […] long': cf. *Iliad* 2.24.

"Men's best treasure is a tongue that is
niggardly, the greatest benefit comes from its moderate use."[25]

[**14**.1] I said to him, "You know all about the rest of the dinner, Kratisthenes, since you were sitting next to me and drinking the nectar, but this is what went on with the girl. The first time she brought the cup she whispered, 'Welcome'; the second time she said, 'Receive this cup from the hands of a maiden with the same name', rather quietly and concealing the sound; and all the time I was drinking she was pressing her foot on mine. The third time she brought the cup, although she seemed to be offering it she was holding on, and so I said what you heard.

[2] The rest you know, Panthia's anger, the father's wrath, the nodding of the head, the maiden's shame, the silence, the astonishment, the blushing and all the other things she went through, as if struck by a bolt of lightning. By my herald's sacred wand, I was rather abashed by all this, especially at your warning me to be quiet. [3] We drank to Zeus the Saviour for the fourth time, and once again Hysmine pressed my fingers.

This is what went on at the table; what about what happened by the bed? She washes my feet, she embraces them, she squeezes my fingers, she kisses them, she sneaks a kiss as she kisses them and finally she scratches the sole of my foot – hence the burst of laughter you heard."

[4] Kratisthenes shouted out, "By all that is fortunate, the maiden is in love with you, and what a lovely maiden! Are you not in love with her too?" But I said, "What is this being in love?" [5] And Kratisthenes shouted out again, "By Herakles, what an idiot, what a dolt! May Eros and his mother Aphrodite and all the bewitchments of passion be kind to you." I said to Kratisthenes, "Who are these? Who will instruct me in this?" And he replied, "What is innate to living creatures cannot be taught."[26] And with that we returned to our slumbers.

---

25 'niggardly [...] use': Hesiod, *Works and Days* 719–20.
26 'What [...] taught': cf. Hippocrates, *De alimento* 39.1 and *L&K* 1.10.1.

BOOK TWO

[**1**.1] On the following day we went into the garden again, and fed our eyes with its charms, drawing the pleasure down into our souls. For the garden was the abode of all good things, a dwelling place for the gods, and was all charm and pleasure, a delight to the eyes, comfort to the heart, consolation to the soul, repose for the limbs and rest for the body. [2] So much for the garden. The surrounding wall was another marvel; of sufficient height to prevent invasion of the garden by eyes and feet, it was graced everywhere by the hand of a skilled painter.

[**2**.1] Four maidens had been depicted in a row. On the head of the first was a brilliant crown;[27] the gems round the crown gleamed brightly, flashing fire and giving off light, yet full of water. [2] On seeing them, you might say that the immiscible, fire and water, were mingled in the gem, and both were delightful and both were charming. The one glows with its red hue while the other sparkles – so accurately did the craftsman imitate the nature of the gems. [3] Pearls surround the gems, white as snow, circular in shape, of an unnatural size. I fixed my eyes immovably on them and said with amazement and pleasure, "Hail and coals of fire." Kratisthenes (for he was with me) burst out laughing at my misuse of language.[28]

[4] The maiden's locks were spread lavishly over her shoulders and curled in the usual manner; the curls were fairish in colour. A necklet of silver with flecks of gold was around the maiden's throat;[29] its clasp was of aquamarine. [5] The maiden's hands were white and truly virginal; her right hand was stretched out and curved back and touched her head and the ruby on her forehead with her finger;[30] her left hand held a most delightful sphere. [6] The maiden's right foot had no sandal, the left was covered by her tunic. The whole tunic was rather ugly and somewhat crude, for the craftsman had expended all the decoration on the girl's head, and painted the rest rather haphazardly.

[**3**.1] The maiden that came after her, second in line, was entirely military, apart from her face, except that her eyes were somewhat wilder

27 'four maidens': on these allegorized personifications, see Roilos 2005: 145–75. 'crown': στέφανος and related words can mean both 'crown', as here, and 'garland'.

28 'Hail [...] fire': cf. Psalms 17(18).13, with reference to the Almighty's wrath; hence Kratisthenes' laughter.

29 'flecks of gold': cf. Song of Songs 1.11, quoted also in Basilakes' lament (Pignani 1983: 245.13–14).

30 For the gesture, with reference to a dance movement, cf. Athenaeus, *Deipnosophistae* 14.629 F.

than a maiden's should be. [2] A helmet flashes on her head and adorns it. A square shield is on her chest, a tunic of scales on her back, and a belt around her waist; her feet, hands and all the rest of her body were protected by armour in military fashion. [3] Her arm was as sturdy as an oak, yet her fingers had been painted as those of a maiden. Wherever her limbs were bare, the soldier was entirely a maiden but wherever she wore armour, you see that the maiden was entirely a soldier. The maiden, or, if you prefer, the soldier, had a shield in her left hand, and in her right a long spear, Ares' pen.[31]

[**4**.1] The figure that came after her was entirely maidenly, entirely stately as to her face, her appearance, her tunic, her sandals, with her head crowned, not with gems like the first, not with pearls like the girl at the beginning, but entirely with leaves, entirely with flowers. [2] There were no roses in the crown, either because the craftsman had made a mistake or had decided against it or because his colours were defeated by the hue of roses. The girl's locks were tied back a little and also restrained by the crown. [3] A white veil was over her head and covered part of her forehead. The maiden's tunic was gossamer thin, white in colour, reaching to her feet and very full.[32]

[4] Her right arm is laid dextrously on her bosom, covering the homonymous breast, while her fingers rest on her left breast, concealing it completely and guarding it; looking at the girl you might have said that she had been painted without breasts. Her other hand held her tunic around her thighs; for the north wind seemed to be blowing full in her face and most of her tunic was billowing around her heels. [5] Thus the girl was stately, the wind strong, and the tunic light; but the north wind, scion of clear skies, did not whistle through the maiden's tender flesh.[33] Her right leg is twisted round the other, and clings there and is entwined, thigh with thigh, and foot completely over foot, so that her body could not be spied through the light tunic. She had black sandals on her feet, very sturdily made and not at all appropriate to a young girl.

[**5**.1] The fourth and last maiden seems to be falling from a cloud that had just been rent apart, and she looks as if she is peering down from heaven. She was entirely aethereal, stately in appearance, yet with a charming face. Her tunic is red but with a touch of white; if it is the white of her body that

31 'Ares' pen': Ares, god of war; cf. Basilakes' lament (Pignani 1983: 243.179). This figure, like that of Goliath in the wall-paintings in *DigAk* G 7.73–78, is envisaged in *kataphrakt* armour; see *ODB*, under 'Kataphraktos'.

32 'tunic': girls' tunics are often gossamer thin: cf. *L&K* 3.7.5; *DigAk* G 6.782.

33 'scion of clear skies': cf. *Odyssey* 5.296. 'whistle through': cf. Hesiod, *Works and Days* 519, also at *H&H* 4.18.13,

appears through the tunic, the craftsman did not allow this to be glimpsed. [2] The girl's hair was all tied elegantly at her back; her eyes are completely turned to heaven. She has a set of scales and a flame in her hands, the one in her right hand, the other in the left. Her tunic left both her legs visible as far as the knees.[34]

[**6**.1] So this is what the women looked like; what their role was and who they were we sought rather diligently to discover. Then we notice some writing above the maidens' heads, an iambic line divided into four and giving the maidens' names; it went like this: "Prudence, Fortitude, Chastity and Justice."[35]

[2] Then we discussed the women's appearance and we comprehended what till then had been incomprehensible to us: the first maiden's brilliant crown, the gems around the crown, the pearls, the gold around her throat, the silver, the aquamarine, [3] the girl's appearance, the gesture of her right hand which seemed to say that "I have my wealth here on my head," the sphere in her left hand which indicated that she encompassed the universe, and the tunic's lack of decoration, showed that Prudence is unadorned except for her head.

As for the soldierly appearance of the next girl, the maiden in guise of a soldier and the reverse, she who was entirely a soldier and yet entirely a maiden – bravery is by nature a soldier, but by name a maiden – [4] as a result wherever she is not protected by armour, she appears to be entirely a maiden, both in name and in body; in the aspects which hint at strength, the maiden is entirely a soldier, and as the painter had preserved the name in the nature, so even in the name he depicted that nature as a whole.[36]

[5] As for the next, the third girl – the crown of flowers, of unfading leaves, the braiding of her locks, the veil over her head, the covering of her chest, the protection of her breasts, the placing of thigh over thigh, the chastity before the wind, all this the craftsman had adapted most harmoniously to my own dear maiden. [6] I embrace your hand, painter; I kiss your brush; I thank you in addition that you did not weave a rose into the crown of this true maiden, for chastity has nothing in common with a rose, which is dyed most disgracefully and whose countenance blushes red with shame.[37]

---

34 In this paragraph, as at 1.5.5 and elsewhere, the mixture of tenses reflects the Greek.

35 'Prudence [...] Justice': the four cardinal virtues. The names form a 12-syllable tetrameter, with a caesura after the fifth syllable.

36 The convoluted personification described here embodies Fortitude; Ἰσχύς is a feminine noun while 'name' (κλῆσις) is also the grammatical term for 'nominative case'.

37 Hysmine is envisaged here as the embodiment of chastity.

[7] As for the fourth girl, there was the peering out of heaven, her aethereal appearance, her lack of veiling, the brilliance of her face, the balances
of justice and all the other things which the craftsman had adapted appropriately to Themis;[38] for justice peers down from heaven and weighs her
judgements and directs eyes to heaven and has nothing human about her.

[7.1] We turn our eyes to the picture that came after the maidens, and we
see a lofty throne, that is brilliant and truly imperial – the throne of Kroisos
or of some lord of Mykenai rich in gold.[39] [2] On this was seated an awesome
young lad,[40] with every part of his body naked. Looking at him I was abashed
and remembered the saying: "To be unaware is a painless evil."[41] [3] There
was a bow and a torch in the lad's hands, a quiver at his loins and a two-edged
sword; the lad's feet were not human but were entirely winged;[42] as for his
head, the lad was so charming that he outdid every other lad, every maiden,
he was an image of the gods, a statue of Zeus, he was entirely Aphrodite's
girdle,[43] entirely the garden of the Graces, entirely pleasure.

[4] If Thetis' marriage were to take place, if Hera were to make her fuss
about the wedding, if Aphrodite, if Athena, if this lad, if Eris were to disturb
the symposium, if she were to make the apple, if she were to ask a beauty
to take the apple, if Paris were the judge, if the apple were the prize for
beauty,[44] you, my lad, would have it. [5] And I said to Kratisthenes, "What
a clever thing is the painter's hand. It creates wonders that surpass nature,
it devises imaginary objects with its intelligence and then brings them into

38 'Themis': in Greek mythology a goddess personifying Justice.

39 'throne': δίφρος, more usually meaning 'chariot', is also used here (and at 3.1.2, 6.18.3)
in its other sense of a magisterial seat; in biblical terminology it refers to the Throne of Majesty
(Ezechiel 1.15; Daniel 7.9). 'Kroisos': there is no surviving literary reference to a throne for
Kroisos, ruler of Lydia ca. 560–546 BC; his wealth was proverbial. 'rich in gold': cf. *Iliad*
7.180; *Odyssey* 3.304. In the Homeric poems Mykenai was ruled by Agamemnon, leader of
the Greek expedition against Troy.

40 'awesome young lad': on the symbolism and historical and literary context of this
passage, see Cupane 1974; Magdalino 1992; Dostalova 1993.

41 'To be [...] evil': Sophocles, *Ajax* 554b.

42 'winged': Eros normally has wings on his shoulders, not his feet; Cupane 1974: 255, n.
33 suggests that this is a metaphor for the speed of love, but see Roilos 2005: 163–65 (and note
201) for a Platonic parallel (*Phaedrus* 252 b) which would allow Eros to be assimilated to the
personification of Time (season) at 4.20.1.

43 'Aphrodite's girdle': a magically seductive girdle given to Aphrodite by Hera; *Iliad*
24.214–21.

44 'If Thetis [...] beauty': this passage lists all the elements in the Judgement of Paris,
where Paris' presentation of the prize to Aphrodite was the ultimate cause of the Trojan War;
cf. Apollodoros, *Epitome* 3.1–5; *OCD*, under 'Paris'.

being with its art. If you like, let us discuss the lad.

[**8**.1] 'The vices are neighbours to the virtues and are annexed to them.'[45] The lad was devised to exemplify this maxim, and art brought what had been devised to life. [2] I can grasp, craftsman, your riddle, I can grasp what you have done, I can immerse my mind in yours;[46] even if you are Sphinx, I am Oidipous;[47] even if you utter riddling prophecies from the Pythia's hearth and tripod,[48] I am your priestly attendant and I can interpret your riddles."

[**9**.1] But what about what came next?[49] An entire army surrounded the lad, whole cities, a mixed crowd of men, women, old men, old women, young lads, maidens. Emperors, usurpers, lordlings, masters of the earth, stand like slaves[50] around him, not as if he were an emperor but a god; and there were two women with linked hands, of more than female stature and older than Iapetos,[51] with unusual faces, unusual wrinkles, unusual appearance and unusual colouring.

[2] One was like the sun and entirely white, with white hair, white eyes, white tunic, face, hands, legs – everything white; the other was entirely black – hair, head, face and hands and feet, and tunic. [3] They were identical in age but different in colouring, identical in wrinkles but different in race, the one was as if she came from Achaia fair in women,[52] the other as if from scorched Ethiopia.

A host of birds is present, their wings free yet they are present as slaves. The whole race of Amphitrite's footless creatures[53] are recruited as the lad's

45 'The vices [...] them': a gnomic saying, much used in patristic literature: e.g. Gregory of Nazianzos, *Carmina* 1.1.27, 13–14 (*PG* 37, 499a); *Vita Cyril Phileotae* 29.2 (Sargologos 1964: 29.2); see Plepelits 1989: 181–82, n. 20; Roilos 2005: 160, n. 194.

46 'I can [...] yours': cf. Basilakes' lament (Pignani 1983: 243.286).

47 'Sphinx [...] Oidipous': Oidipous of Thebes solved the riddle on the three ages of man set by the monstrous Sphinx; best known through Sophocles' *Oidipous Tyrannos*, but also included in the Byzantine chroniclers.

48 'Pythia's hearth and tripod': Pythia was the priestess at the ancient oracular shrine of Apollo at Delphi.

49 2.9.1–10.4: These paragraphs on the attributes and effects of Eros, god of Love, draw on the Greek amatory tradition: e.g. *AnthGr* 9.440; *L&K* 1.1.13 ff.; Longos 2.7.1–2; cf. also *R&D* 2.421–31, 8.191–99; *D&C* 2.130–43, 3.114–18, 6.365–81; *A&K* frags. 96 and 165.

50 'slaves': the first appearance of the concept of enslavement, to Eros or to a master, which is an all-pervasive element in *H&H*; see Nilsson 2001: 111–23, and Introduction, p. 173.

51 'Iapetos': one of the Titans born of Gaia and Ouranos; Hesiod, *Theogonia* 132–34; Aristophanes, *Clouds*, 998.

52 'Achaia fair in women': cf. *Iliad* 3.75, 258; also used at *H&H* 5.7.2 of Aulikomis.

53 'footless creatures': fishes; cf. Oppian, *Halieutica* 1.2. Amphitrite was wife of Poseidon, god of the sea.

slaves, and the savage emperor of beasts is present as a fellow slave with all other savage animals.

[**10**.1] I said to Kratisthenes, "Why do the birds not spread their wings in unfettered flight but instead are so strangely and unnaturally recruited as slaves? The savage lion, emperor of beasts, is slave to the lad, who is moreover stripped naked, yet the wild beast although fully armed is terrified of him. [2] Where are his claws, his beetling gaze,[54] his shaggy chest and above all his fearsome and angry roar? The race of armed warriors[55] (for they are present too) and every emperor, every lordling, every usurper – are they not strong enough against this quite naked youth who is on his own? [3] But why do the fishes or every sea monster tremble before the lad? Is it the fire? But indeed they control every sea, every deep, and these are hostile to fire. The bow, the wings? Are these not blunted by the deep?

[4] Oh the women, the wonder, their great age, their wrinkles, their appearance, their slavish garb! Zeus and the gods, how truly portentous is the painting, the mind's contrivance, the artist's masterpiece. [5] But let us look, if you like, at what is written about the lad's head." There were iambic verses, which went as follows:

This lad is Eros, with his sword, torch,

bow, arrows, nudity, a dart aimed at fishes.[56]

[**11**.1] And Kratisthenes said, "My words to you will no longer lack support. You were asking me who is Eros; now look – you can see him. [2] But may your experience of him be kindly." I replied to him, "Explain the meaning of the picture to me then and show how the epigram is relevant to it." Kratisthenes responded, "Eros is naked, he carries a sword, he carries fire, he is an archer, he is winged. [3] He wields his sword against men, fire against women, bows against wild beasts, wings against birds, his nudity against the denizens of the sea and against it in its entirety. Day and night, as you see, serve Eros, for these are the women by the sight of whom you were amazed." I said to Kratisthenes, "May I never know him!"[57]

[**12**.1] Sosthenes came up, and we sat down for dinner. And once again the maiden assisted with the serving, and once again she fixes her eyes on

54 'beetling gaze': more usually used of men but cf. Hesiod, *Shield* 175f. in connection with lions.

55 'armed warriors': a similar phrase in Basilakes' lament (Pignani 1983: 242.150–51).

56 'sword': literally 'weapon', but *H&H* 2.7.3, 2.11.2–3 and 3.2.4 make it plain that 'sword' is meant. 'nudity': the 'dart' is in apposition to 'nudity'; that Eros' nakedness is to be used against the inhabitants of the sea is clear from *H&H* 2.11.3 and 7.17.7.

57 'May [...] him': cf. Euripides, *Hecuba* 255.

me and stands in front of me; quietly inclining her neck a little she gives me a stealthy greeting and putting her fingers to her lips bids me be silent. [2] I said to Kratisthenes, "Do you see that? What does it mean?" He said, "Be quiet." The girl came up to pour out the wine and, "Welcome, herald with the same name as mine," she whispered and pouring out wine for Kratisthenes after me she said, if indeed her whisper could be called speech, "I owe you thanks."

[**13**.1] Once more there were delicacies on the table, not simply from the land or the sea such as might delight a landsman or a sea-board dweller, but everything that chefs' hands and skills could devise, such as fish from the land and a peacock from the ocean – so luxurious, so brilliant, so charming was the banquet that it was delectable both to the eyes and the gullet. [2] And we drank again (for exquisite food demands appropriate drink), and once again the girl mixes the cup and drinks from it before me and as she gives it to me again she says in her usual voice, "As I share your name through chance, so I share this drink with you through love."

[3] When we have consumed sufficient at the table from the different dishes and multitudinous sauces and drink and varied sweetmeats, we end the symposium. Sosthenes said, "It is good to obey night.[58] Let us make due offerings to the night," and saying "Farewell," he went off with Panthia.

[**14**.1] Hysmine pretended to stumble over her foot and, going out slightly after her father Sosthenes and her mother Panthia, "Farewell," she said, and "Obey my father," as she too went off. [2] Kratisthenes and I sat down and talked about what had happened at dinner and about the girl, how she greeted me surreptitiously, how she put her fingers to her mouth, telling me to be silent, how she whispered "Welcome, herald with the same name as mine" as she gave me the cup, how she drank first from the wine when she had mixed it, [3] how she said again to me with the second cup, "I share this cup through love as I share your name through chance," and finally the pretence with the foot and "Obey my father."

[4] Kratisthenes said, "Eros has set this maiden entirely on fire for you; Eros has mastered her; her soul is in love and her tongue is aflame with love. How long are you going to be condemned for deserting Eros?[59] [5] Where will you escape him?[60] In heaven? But he will reach you with his wings. In

---

58　'Good […] night': cf. *Iliad* 7.282, 293; a favourite Byzantine tag (cf. *Alexiad* 7.8.10). The phrase appears again at *H&H* 4.19.5, 10.4.1.

59　'deserting': this vocabulary sets up a military metaphor for Eros.

60　'Where […] him': cf. Psalm 138/139.7–10. This phrase had a long history in the Byzantine romances; cf. *R&D* 6.88; *A&K* fr. 8; *DigAk* E 1397–98; *L&Rα* 592–93.

the sea, by stripping off your tunic?[61] But he has stripped off before you. On land? But he will shoot you with his bow. [6] Have you seen Eros? Have you seen his fire, his bows, his nakedness, his wings? Are you alone free from love – you alone?" I said to Kratisthenes, "Allow me to be chaste, my good friend,

for the chaste
the gods love and hate evil men."[62]
So we fell silent and gave ourselves up to slumber.

BOOK THREE

[**1.**1] And then about the middle of the night, while I was sleeping, a vision came to me, a rather terrifying dream;[63] for I see a crowd of inestimable size entering the chamber, a mixed throng of men, women, youths, maidens. All held torches in their right hands while their left they placed on their breasts in a servile manner. [2] And in the middle was the lad who was painted on the wall around the garden, Eros, the emperor, that terrifying figure, seated on his golden throne once more.[64] [3] His voice was unleashed against me like thunder, "Bring to me the upstart, the one who is free,[65] who does not fear my dart, who is not frightened of my wings, who reviles my fire, who is embarrassed by my nudity, who mocks at me for being a young lad, who congratulates the painter for besmirching the rose, who spurned my beloved Hysmine and whom the gods love for his chastity."

[4] I was dragged along pitiably, quite trembling, quite dumb, quite dead, and lay on the ground. "Spare him, emperor," I hear a voice saying, and coming to myself a little and raising my eyes I see Hysmine, her head crowned with roses, a rose in her right hand and her left hand clasping the emperor's feet;[66] she is saying, "Spare Hysminias, spare him for my sake,

---

61 'by stripping off': translating Marcovich's emendation to a participle.

62 'for the chaste [...] men': cf. Sophocles, *Ajax* 132–33 where, however, the meaning is 'prudent' rather than 'chaste'.

63 'a rather terrifying dream': for an analysis of this dream instigated by the garden's paintings, see Nilsson 2001: 103–11; on dreams in the novels generally, see MacAlister 1996.

64 'Eros': the depiction of Eros in *H&H* has generated much debate; see Cupane 1974 (where the French parallels are now generally discounted); Magdalino 1992; Nilsson 2001: 202–08; see also Roilos 2005: 161–66, 175–81.

65 'free': i.e.. free from love; cf. 2.14.6.

66 'clasping the emperor's feet': the classic gesture of supplication; cf. *Iliad* 1.500–01.

emperor; I will enroll[67] him in your service."

[5] And the emperor said to the maiden, "It is for your sake that I was angry, so for your sake I receive him back in favour." She immediately took my hand and made me stand up, telling me to be confident. The emperor summons me with a gesture and crowns my head with roses. All the bystanders cried out and applauded, [6] and danced around, saying, "Hysminias has become our fellow slave, the bold, the unwed,[68] who spurned the lovely Hysmine." Then saying to the lovely Hysmine, "You have your lover," the emperor Eros flew away from my eyes and plunged deep into my heart.

[**2.**1] And immediately sleep too flew away from me, and I sat upright on my couch in great perturbation, and was quite overcome, revolving the dream endlessly in my mind. My heart was pounding in my chest and I gasped for breath. I said to Kratisthenes, "O Kratisthenes, O Kratisthenes." [2] He leaped up from his couch and I said again, "I am ruined, Kratisthenes." He leaped barefoot on to my bed and, taking me by his right hand, said, "What is the matter, good Hysminias?" I was silent. [3] He said to me in tears, "What is the matter, Hysminias? Hysminias, why are you silent?"

I replied, "I am ruined, Kratisthenes. Hysmine destroys me, Hysmine saves me. Eros has emptied his entire quiver into my soul, he has burnt up my entire heart. [4] If you had been there to see it, you would have seen him penetrating my soul with his sword, his quiver, with all his fire. I am no longer herald of the Diasia, I am no longer Zeus's attendant, I am no longer chaste.[69]

War has broken out[70] in my heart because of Eros and Zeus. [5] Zeus thunders loudly from the heaven, as it were, and his thunder re-echoes; Eros raises up his siege engines on the earth, as it were, and assaults my citadel; the one hurls down lightning from the clouds, the other kindles craters of fire against me from the earth. [6] I am a city, the city of Zeus, but Eros lays siege[71] to me and draws everything towards himself. I am the fountain of Zeus, full of the graces of chastity, but Eros diverts me towards the fountain of Aphrodite.

67 'enroll': this neologism (δουλογραφέω) on analogy with πολιτογραφέω, creates an impression of a social hierarchy (Hunger 1980: 24), ostensibly analogous with French and Provençal concepts of servitude in the Court of Love.

68 'the unwed': omitting with Marcovich 2001 'crowned with laurel'.

69 'chaste': note that παρθένος has several implications; in connection with Hysmine it is usually best translated as 'maiden' but for Hysminias 'unwed' or 'chaste' seem the more appropriate possibilities.

70 'War has broken out': cf. *L&K* 1.11.3 on the lover's internal conflicts.

71 'lays siege': military metaphors are frequent in late antique and Byzantine amatory literature (e.g. Alciphron 3.26.2; Charit 2.8.1; *AnthGr* 5.294 [Agathias]).

[7] I came from Eurykomis as herald of the Diasia but now I shall leave Aulikomis as the herald of Aphrodite's festival. My head was crowned with laurel then, but is crowned now with roses. Whose soul is so bold, whose heart so steadfast, whose chest made of such stout iron that he can resist[72] the gods in battle and withstand them all as they lay siege and smite him? I have not the strength, Kratisthenes."

[**3**.1] He said, "How is it that, from being entirely chaste and a herald of Zeus and entirely virtuous, everything you now breathe out is Eros, having been initiated spontaneously and yourself become an instructor?" I said to Kratisthenes, "It was Eros himself who initiated me,[73] Eros who transformed me. It was Eros's hand that crowned this head of mine and changed its crown."

[2] And I told him all about my dream, the god's procession, the diverse escort, the hand-held torches, the god on his throne, his anger against me, the voice that pealed down from heaven, my being hauled away, what I suffered, Hysmine's speech, her supplication on my behalf, the god's pardon, and to finish it all off, the crown.

[3] "What you have experienced," he said, "is nothing out of the ordinary. You are in love; you are not alone in this but share the experience with many mortals.[74] And you are fortunate in matters of love, for your beloved is so beautiful and so completely responsive, and you have Eros at your service.[75] [4] It was good that you were able to sleep; for eyes that are wakeful from love reveal a soul that is in love[76] and, just as a sarcastic tongue cannot keep a secret, so eyes that are deprived of sleep betray love."

[**4**.1] So Kratisthenes promptly dropped off to sleep again and began to snore, but sleep had fled from my eyes and I seemed, by the gods, to have my ribs gouged out and, by Eros, I was lying on a bed of thorns and I tossed and turned as though I was being roasted on coals, like some strange sacrifice being cooked up for Eros.

[2] I longed to see the day; I went into a dream about the banquet and Hysmine mixing the wine, saying, "If she squeezes my finger, she will be squeezed more firmly in return. But she did squeeze it yesterday! Very well,

72 'Whose soul [...] resist': cf. *L&K* 5.22.5.

73 'initiate': for this and cognate terms cf. *L&K* 1.9.7, 2.19.1, 2.37.5, 5.26.10, where, as here, they can be interpreted as a metaphor for sexual experience.

74 'share the experience': a variation on Euripides, *Hippolytus*, 439.

75 'at your service': Eros has sanctioned the union of Hysmine with Hysminias.

76 'eyes [...] love': an amatory topos; cf. *L&K* 1.7.3. See discussion in Jouanno 1994; Nilsson 2001: 199–200.

let her squeeze it yet again; if she does, she will be squeezed; but if she doesn't, she will still be squeezed. [3] If she puts her foot on mine, I'll add my other foot to the two already there. If she says, 'Welcome', she will hear, 'A hundred times welcome.' If she greets me surreptitiously, she will be greeted openly. If she drinks from the cup before me, I'll drink the whole girl down myself. [4] If she holds the goblet back, I'll grab hold of her hand as well as the goblet. And if she keeps hold of my feet and squeezes them as she holds them, and as she squeezes them kisses them, and as she kisses them steals other kisses, then I too will keep hold and squeeze and as I squeeze will kiss; except that I will not steal my kiss. [5] If she tickles my foot, I too will tickle the girl, and I will make her burst out laughing from pleasure and passion. If after dinner her foot hurts, if as she goes out following her father she is separated from her mother, I will take hold of the sore foot, [6] I will kiss the hurt, I will make a fuss of the wound, I will ask for the right ointments, I will put them on, I will massage the scar like a doctor, I will make a professional examination and I will make it all better.

[7] I won't put up with Eros's wrath any more, I won't be reproached any more for my virginity, I won't be made fun of any more for my chastity, and all the other things, by Eros, that I have put up with. If she is looking for what is appropriate for the night, I will go and sleep with the maiden and I will proclaim in poetic manner that sleep is sweet.[77] But sleep is already making its peace with me, I am already falling asleep."

[5.1] So while I was preoccupied with sleep and the girl was preoccupied with me, night outstrips day and the banquet, and everything that I had sought to see, feel and do I saw and felt in my dreams as if in mirrors, for the divine being did not allow me action.[78]

[2] My dream creates the entire banquet for me, and I seemed to be seated in my customary position and watching the girl mixing wine. Whether Sosthenes and Panthia drank before me as usual I do not know, by Eros whom I saw in my dreams; but the girl came towards me, mixing the wine, and I drank her down completely with my eyes and I quaffed the girl entirely, and I took her entirely into my soul. [3] And she said to me, "Take the cup." And I gazed at her intently again, and stretch out my hand even so to take it, and I squeeze the maiden's finger and press her foot with

77 'poetic manner': that is, in the Homeric manner; Makrembolites has used an adjective regularly applied to sleep in the Homeric poems, cf. *Iliad* 2.2.

78 'action': i.e., would not allow him to bring his desires to fruition. For a discussion of the role of this and other dreams in *H&H* and their reflection of Aristotelian dream theory, see MacAlister 1990.

mine, whispering quietly to the girl "Welcome," just as she had whispered previously; she made no reply, she did not react but blushed as if from modesty.

[4] The customary variety of food was spread around the table, and I paid true honour to my dream and was thoroughly fed in my dream; the maiden Hysmine, to whom alone I turned my gaze so intently, was food and drink for my eyes and soul.[79]

[5] The girl came up once again, offering the cup, for the time for drinking summoned us. I took it and sipped a little and then returned the whole vessel to the maiden, saying, "I share the cup with you."

[6] An end came to the banquet which in my sleep a dream had made erotically ready for me, or rather which Eros had prepared in my dreams. And we went off to our chamber and Sosthenes and Panthia took their leave of us as usual. Kratisthenes and I lay down. [7] But I see Hysmine by my bed and without the least shame I draw her by the hand and sit her beside me on the bed; for Eros is the father of shamelessness.[80] But the girl, being a virgin, is abashed, and at first pretends to be reluctant but finally is overcome, as happens to a virgin when with a man, for she has been defeated by Eros even before the touch of my hand.

[6.1] She fastened her eyes to the ground, while I impaled mine entirely on the girl's face, for it was full of light, full of grace, full of delight.[81] Her eyebrows were black, curved like a rainbow or a crescent moon; [2] her eyes were black, lively and very bright and her eyeballs had a certain sharpness and her eyes were cone-like in shape, or rather circular. The lashes on her eyelids were quite black, and the girl's eyes were truly a mirror for Eros. [3] Her cheeks were white, unblemished white where there was no mixture of red; the centre was red, red that was separated off and imprinted there, not drawn by hand or painted by art and fading over night and washed off in water.[82] Her mouth was parted evenly, most of the flesh from her lips was pressed back and both her lips were tinted red. [4] Seeing her you would say that the girl had crushed a rose with her lips. The chorus of her teeth

---

79 'Hysmine [...] was food and drink': cf. *L&K* 1.5.3.

80 'father of shamelessness': cf. Euripides, *Ion* 895–96.

81 3.6.1–4: For comparable descriptions of a beautiful heroine, cf. *L&K* 1.4.3 and *DigAk* G 4.349–56, as well as *R&D* 1.39–60.

82 'washed off in water': it was customary for Byzantine women of rank to wear make-up; note Choniates' disparaging comments about Bertha of Sulzbach, Manuel I's German bride, who refused to follow this habit (van Dieten 1975: 53.58–54.64), and the many references in Manganeios Prodromos to the personified and aged City of Constantinople covered in rouge and powder (E. and M. Jeffreys 2001: 110–13).

was white,[83] set in harmonious ranks and appropriate to her lips and were like maidens guarded by her lips. Her entire face formed a perfect circle; her nose held the central place in the circuit, and did I not fear Eros and indeed have my experience to support me I would say – but I shall be silent[84] over the rest so that the lad may not hurl thunder my way again.

[**7.1**][85] I touch her hand and, although she tries to withdraw it and conceal it in her tunic, nevertheless I prevail. I draw it up to my lips, I kiss it, I nibble it incessantly; she pulls away and curls up on herself. [2] I clasp her neck and set my lips on hers and fill her with kisses and exude passion. She pretends to withdraw her lips but bites my lip passionately and steals a kiss. [3] I kissed her eyes and suck all passion into my soul, for the eye is the source of love.[86] Then I find myself at the girl's chest; she puts up a stout resistance, curls up completely and defends her breast with her entire body, as a city defends a citadel, [4] and fortifies and barricades her breasts with her hands and neck and fists and belly; and further down she raises her knees as she shoots off a tear from the citadel of her head, all but saying, "Either he loves me and will be softened by my tears, or he doesn't love me and will shrink from battle." [5] I am rather ashamed to be defeated and so I persist more violently and at length I am almost victorious but find defeat in my victory and am utterly undone. For the moment my hand got to the girl's breast lassitude invaded my heart.

[6] I was in pain, I was in anguish, a strange trembling came over me, my sight was dimmed, my soul softened, my strength weakened, my body grew sluggish, my breath choked, my heart beat faster and a sweet pain poured over my limbs with a kind of tickling sensation and an ineffable, unspeakable, inexpressible passion took possession of me. And I experienced, by Eros, what I had never experienced before.[87] [7] So the girl quickly slipped out of my hands, or it would probably be more appropriate to say that my hands fell away from the girl sluggishly and feebly; and sleep flew from my eyes and, by Eros, I was disconsolate because I had lost such a beautiful dream and had been torn away from my Hysmine and I wanted to go back

83 'chorus of her teeth': cf. Aristophanes, *Frogs* 548.

84 'I shall be silent': Plepelits 1989: 183–84, n. 34 suggests that this omission glides over a reference (cf. *L&K* 1.4.3) to Selene, an embodiment of beauty, which might provoke Eros.

85 3.7.1–7: Cf. *L&K* 1.6.2–5.

86 'eye […] love': a cliché in late antique amatory literature: e.g. *AnthGr* 5.226, 12.91, 92; *L&K* 1.9.4, 5.13.4; Hel 3.7.5.

87 A similarly explicit description can be found in MangProd 14.5–86 (Bernadinello 1972: poem 7) and 147.26–49; see Alexiou 1977.

to sleep again and I wanted to experience the same passionate sensation that I had felt in my sleep.

[**8**.1] But since time and Kratisthenes did not permit this, I return again to the garden, which was in front of the doors of our chamber. I had been entirely bought up by the girl, soul, body, eyes, and I was entirely filled with frenzy from love. [2] Then I come to the picture of Eros painted in the garden, and first of all I do him reverence, as a slave should, and then I abuse the painter because he had not drawn Hysmine in the procession of enslaved maidens, the maiden who is so lovely, so beautiful, breathes such passions, adores Eros so much and is so loved by Eros.

[3] I fix my eyes completely on the painting and I say to Eros, "I am in your power, emperor. I shall never return to Eurykomis; I shall never again be enrolled among the attendants of Zeus. Aulikomis has me as a citizen, recording me in its citizen rolls because of an accusation of passion."[88]

[**9**.1] And Kratisthenes said, "Do you have no respect for the herald's wand? Do you not respect the Diasia, because of which you came as herald to Aulikomis? Have you no respect for your father Themisteus, and for your mother Dianteia whose lot is old age?[89] May you not be unlucky in love. [2] Hysmine is lovely, indeed very lovely and there is no wrong
    in suffering many years for such a woman.[90]
But your father's hopes are based on you; you are the staff of his old age,[91] the warmth for his chills, the breeze in his summer heat. [3] Then, do you not pity your mother, who breathes and speaks for you and rejoices in you and for you forgets the miseries of her old age? No, by the gods, Hysminias, no, by Zeus, as whose herald you came to Aulikomis, no, by Eros, whose slave you have become in Aulikomis. [4] Spare your father's hoary head, spare your mother's tears, spare our country, our peers, our friends, spare the brilliant assembly, spare the brilliant gathering, spare the escorting odes which your father and your country devised together.

[5] Think how your father will lament, think how your mother will wail, how she will mourn, how she will lament so pitiably, so wildly, like a dove

---

88 There is much play in this paragraph with forms of γράφω, πολιτογραφῶ, γραφή, and their multiple meanings ('paint', 'writ', 'enroll').

89 'whose lot is old age': cf. Sophocles, *Ajax* 508 and Basilakes' lament (Pignani 1983: 240.121–22).

90 Cf. *Iliad* 3.156–57, referring to Helen observed by the elders of Troy from the city walls; famously quoted by Psellos in his *Chronographia*, referring to Skleraina, mistress of Constantine Monomachos (Impellizeri 1975: 6.61).

91 'staff of his old age': cf. Hel 1.13.1.

over her lost chicks.⁹² It was not nectar that Hysmine mixed for you, not wine from Aulikomis, but a drug like Helen's that banishes care.⁹³ [6] You have forgotten your father, mother, country, peers, companions, the brilliant company, and what is greatest, the temple of Zeus, god of friendship. O women, who are evil in every respect, and according to the wise man,

> most incompetent in working good,

and most skilled crafters of all evil.⁹⁴

[7] But that famed Odysseus was not a herald but a slave, a stranger, and had gone astray; he judged the smoke of his homeland to be more precious not only than liberty but even divinity itself;⁹⁵ you have become a slave to the fire of passion and you barter away your herald's wand.'

[8] I replied to Krathisthenes, "Look, here is Sosthenes; be quiet; do not make a parade of my passion." Said Sosthenes, "We have everything for the feast well in hand; it is time for dinner, so let us make our way to the table."

[**10**.1] So we sat in our usual place once more and once more we drank; there was little reason for me to eat – not because drink is more preferable to me than food, but because my maiden is pouring the wine, and the maiden Hysmine is sweeter than nectar. [2] And once again Hysmine mixes the wine, and once again I am the lover and once again I kindle my passion; just as wind kindles a spent fire in reeds and grass, even so the eye kindles passion in those who love. [3] Once again Hysmine enflames my soul, once again she draws my eyes entirely to her, once again I see Eros, I shudder at his darts, I fear his fire, I tremble at his bow and embrace his servitude.

[4] The table is bedecked with various dishes; my hand is concerned with these, my eyes with Hysmine, my mind with passion while my limbs were wracked and my fibres torn apart. The variety of dishes on the table occupies my fingers, drink my lips, the girl's charms my eyes and Eros my mind, or to speak more truly, the girl occupies everything – hands, lips, eyes and mind. [5] Thus I am enrolled in a strange servitude to Eros, a servitude which no one else had ever experienced, involving not only the body but also the soul.

---

92 'mother [...] chicks': for the mingled themes of love and death here and elsewhere, see Roilos 2005: 98–102.

93 'drug [...] care': cf. Basilakes' lament (Pignani 1983: 237.47–48).

94 'most [...] evil': cf. Euripides, *Medea* 408–09.

95 'smoke of his homeland': cf. *Odyssey* 1.58; Circe promised divinity to Odysseus if he would remain on her island (*Odyssey* 5.136, 209).

BOOK FOUR

[**1**.1] So the girl mixes the wine in the usual way, and I drink in a way that is not usual, and drinking yet I do not drink and in not drinking yet I drink down passion. So Sosthenes drinks too and I drink third, because Panthia drank before me; and as I drink I squeeze the girl's foot, putting my foot on top of hers. She keeps silence with her tongue but her appearance speaks volumes and she is eloquent in her silence. She bites her lip and pretends to be in pain, [2] she wrinkles her brow, she makes a grimace and sighs gently. My soul is pained by her gestures alone and I immediately remove my foot from the girl's and with my hand return the cup.

[3] Let Kratisthenes pronounce discourses about the delicacies on the table, and any one else about the table; for me the maiden Hysmine was table and food and drink and everything else that goes on tables.[96] As she mixes the wine again, I squeeze her finger; she lets out a gentle whisper, "I am in pain," and the whisper was full of pleasure and brimming with passion.

[**2**.1] After the third and the fourth drink and luxurious dishes the symposium broke up. And Sosthenes said, "Hysminias the herald, today you who have come from Eurykomis to our city now complete the three days which it is our custom to devote to the welcome and honouring of the herald and his message. [2] Now go as usual with this handsome lad," (pointing to Kratisthenes) "and take some rest; tomorrow we will make our way to Eurykomis to sacrifice to the Saviour Zeus."

[3] Having said this he took his customary leave of us, saying "Farewell." I felt, by the gods, that I had been summoned to Hades and was already, as the poet says, tasting chill Hades.[97] I said to Kratisthenes, "What did Sosthenes say to me? Hysmine stays in Aulikomis and I go to Eurykomis? No, by the god in the garden![98] I shall die with Hysmine and I shall live with Hysmine."

[**3**.1] Then I noticed Hysmine in the garden, quite overwrought with passion. Immediately I gathered up the entire garden with my eyes, or rather I strewed them all over the garden and inspected it closely; and seeing that Hysmine was on her own I came close to her and said, "Greetings," and plucked at her tunic. [2] She was silent at first and her only reaction was to resist. When I took her hand, "Respect the herald's wand," she said. When I wanted to kiss her, "Indeed," she said, "do you have no respect for the wreath of laurel and the sacred sandal?" When I was not in the least abashed but

---

96 'for me [...] tables': cf. *L&K* 1.5.3; *H&H* 3.5.4.
97 'chill Hades': cf. Hesiod, *Works and Days* 153; *H&H* 7.11.2.
98 'god in the garden': i.e. Eros, painted on the walls.

continue to press for the kiss, she said, "What will you gain from the kiss?" [3] Said I to the girl with pleasure,

"Even in useless kisses there is a sweet delight."[99]

She gave a little smile and said, "Yesterday you played the virgin, you pretended to be chaste and now you make speeches on behalf of love." [4] I make no reply but kiss her hand, and as I kiss I groan, and as I groaned I wept. She said to me, "Why do you lament?" And I replied, "Because I taste the honey with my tongue only; for your father Sosthenes is escorting me back to Eurykomis." She said, "But I am too," and snatching her hand away ran off.

[**4.**1] I made for the couch as if with winged feet[100] and feigned sleep, for the sound of footsteps had disturbed us. So Kratisthenes appeared, emerging from the myrtle bower where he had been sitting, and pressing my foot, he said, "How long are you going to sleep such a deep sleep? Hysmine is in the garden and are you lying here asleep?" He laughed as he spoke. [2] I said, "Why are you laughing?" He replied, "Because the sound of a servant girl's foot deprived you of the hand of her beloved mistress, a ridiculous bug-a-boo amid such excellent hunting."[101]

I embraced Kratisthenes, saying, "Congratulate me, Kratisthenes. The maiden comes with us to Eurykomis." [3] And then I went into the garden, and tried to catch sight of Hysmine again; when I could not see her (for she had left), I continued to linger in the garden, imagining the maiden. Kratisthenes leads my eyes to the paintings in the garden, and next to my Eros, who was seated on a lofty throne, we see men of foreign races, foreign tongues, foreign birth, all differing from each other in their appearance and conduct.

[**5.**1][102] One was a soldier, a soldier in appearance, a soldier in gaze,

99 'Even […] delight': Theokritos, *Idyll* 3.20, 27.4.

100 'winged feet': cf. *L&K* 7.15.4; *H&H* 4.21.2, 5.20.3.

101 'mistress': often used an amatory sense in *L&K* (e.g. 2.4.4, 2.6.1, 5.20.5, 8.17.3). 'ridiculous bug-a-boo': cf. Oppian, *Hallieutica* 4.575. Once again 'hunting' is adduced in the context of the pursuit of a desirable girl; cf. Ricks 1989; Mackridge 1993.

102 4.5–16: This *ekphrasis* of the 12 months, beginning with March (an outdated liturgical usage) had many antecedents and a long-lasting impact on later Byzantine literature, reappearing in, e.g., *L&R* as well as independently; see discussion, with earlier bibliography, in E. Jeffreys 2005. Note that the 12 months and the Virtues are depicted in Canon Tables in two early twelfth-century Gospel Books (Buchthal 1961; Manion and Vines 1984: 24–26; Ševčenko 2006. For precise allegorical interpretations of these scenes, see Plepelits 1989: 47–54; for a broader contextualization, see Nilsson 2001: 126–36; Roilos 2005: 148–67. Although no examples survive, it is plain from literary evidence that figural scenes with explanatory verses were used to decorate twelfth-century aristocratic houses, as well as monastic establishments; Lambros 1911; Magdalino and Nelson 1982.

a soldier in stature, armed entirely as a soldier[103] – his head, his hands, his back, his brow, his chest, his loins, right down to his feet; [2] thus had the craftsman worked the iron into a covering, or rather had imitated iron with his colours; thus had he armed the soldier as far as his fingernails. [3] He had a quiver round his loins, and a two-edged sword, a long spear in his right hand, a shield was slung from his left. So excellently and artistically were his feet depicted that on looking at him you might declare the man was walking.

[**6**.1] The figure after him[104] was dressed entirely in peasant fashion and entirely as a shepherd. He had his head uncovered, with the hair of his head and beard unadorned, his arms bare to the elbow. The painter had drawn his tunic as far as his knees, his legs below that were left uncovered. [2] The man's chest was hairy, as were all his limbs that had not been covered with paint like a tunic. His legs were sturdy and full of manly muscularity. A goat pregnant with two kids was painted in labour at the shepherd's feet; [3] this giant of a shepherd was acting as midwife to the goat, and was holding the first-born and catching the second. He was preparing his shepherd's flute to pipe a melody for the kids' birth, and seemed to be beseeching Pan for his goats to give birth often and successfully.

[**7**.1] Next there was a meadow with a profusion of flowers, and a man busy about the flowers like a bee.[105] He was not depicted as a gardener but rather like someone wealthy and prosperous, very cheerful and very jovial. The charm of his face had a rival in the beauty of the meadow.[106] [2] His hair flowed over his shoulders, braided elaborately and very carefully. His head was garlanded with flowers, and roses were twined in his braids. His tunic reached to his feet, and looked to be of gold; it was bestrewn with flowers and billowed out. [3] His hands were full of roses and all other plants that delight the nostrils. His feet were clad in sandals, for not even that part of his body was unadorned. And the meadow was reflected in the sandals on his feet as though in a mirror – such charm had the painter bestowed on this figure, even down to his feet and sandals.

[**8**.1] Next to the garden the craftsman had laid out a grassy plain; in the middle of this he painted a man who was equipped entirely as a farmer,[107]

103 The month of March, the 'soldier of Christ' (2 Timothy 2.4); Plepelits 1989: 48. Like the figure of Fortitude earlier (*H&H* 2.4), this figure is envisaged in *kataphrakt* armour (cf. *ODB*, under 'Kataphraktos').

104 The month of April, with Christ the Good Shepherd; Plepelits 1989: 48–49.

105 The month of May. The meadow represents Paradise, and the gardener with his bee-like activities symbolizes Christ and the virgin birth; Plepelits 1989: 49.

106 'The charm [...] meadow': cf. *L&K* 1.19.1; *DigAk* G6.29–37.

107 The month of June. The farmer once again symbolizes Christ; Plepelits 1989: 49–50.

his head garlanded not with roses or flowers but with the light flax which the hand weaves and craft contrives and the farmer uses as an ornament.[108] [2] The craftsman did not let his hair flow down to his shoulders, not did he leave him to cover his neck completely. He drew the tunic inelegantly in rustic fashion, completely like a farmer. [3] Both legs were bare to the knees and both hands were taken up with a sickle whose shape and size was exceptional. The farmer depicted here was deeply preoccupied with cutting grass, his eyes were fixed on the grass and he was completely engrossed in his task.

[**9**.1] The labourer[109] who follows him is bent over in the middle of the corn; he has a sickle in his right hand, and with his left he collects the ears. He is receiving the fruit of his toil, he harvests the rewards of his labours, he gathers the crops from his seeds. [2] He has a covering on his head, a close-fitting cap, in Hesiod's words;[110] he cannot expect to withstand the heat bareheaded. His entire tunic was hitched up around his waist and his entire body was naked, apart from his loins.

[**10**.1] The figure after him was depicted after he had bathed;[111] he was standing at the doors of the bath-house, with a towel wrapped around his loins, but with every other part of his body uncovered; he appeared to be dripping with sweat and quite drenched. [2] On seeing him you might say that the man was panting and had, as it were, collapsed in the heat, so well had the craftsman delineated his form in paint. [3] In his right hand he held a conical vessel which he was conveying to his mouth and from which he was quaffing; in his left hand he held the towel around his navel, so that it should not fall and reveal his entire body.

[**11**.1]   After this man from the bath-house who had bathed and was being consumed by the heat, a man was depicted whose tunic was girded up around his loins but whose legs were entirely bare and who was pouring out an entire fountain of wine before his feet.[112] All his hair was neatly tied behind his back. [2] His left hand mimicked a grape vine and he held a

108 'ornament': following Marcovich's emendation to κόσμον of the manuscripts' τόξον ('bow') and interpreting this as a snare for birds; cf. the equipment for bird snaring in Oppian, *Cynegetica* 1.64 ff. and *Halieutica* 1.31 ff.

109 The month of July, with a reference, according to Plepelits 1989: 50, to the harvesting imagery of Matthew 13.30 and Mark 4.29.

110 'close-fitting cap': cf. Hesiod, *Works and Days* 546.

111 The month of August; Plepelits 1989: 50 points out that λελουμένος, 'bathed', can also imply 'baptized'. On Byzantine attitudes to nudity, see Zeitler 1999; on baths and bath-houses, see *ODB*, under 'Baths'.

112 The scene depicts the month of September; Plepelits 1989: 50 draws a comparison with John 15.1, 'I am the true Vine'.

cluster of grapes that hung from his fingers as if they were twigs; his right hand picked at the bunch and pressed them into his mouth as if into a vat and crushed them with his teeth as though they were feet; and the man that was depicted was vine and harvester, and wine press and fountain of wine.

[**12**.1] The youth[113] that came after him was just growing his first beard, his head was not uncovered but was covered by gossamer-fine linen over both his head and his braids. [2] He has a white tunic, which covers his arms and clings to them, and goes down right to his fingertips. It narrows at the waist and thereafter flows down comfortably and as it were billows out. [3] The craftsman put boots on the youth's legs as far as his knees. He is carrying cages for sparrows and is twisting cords, making traps for birds and keeping a close watch on their flight; he plants an entire meadow, and lets his sparrows out in the meadow but pulls them back often with a light line. [4] The birds do not perceive the trap, they do not understand the trick; they see a pleasant meadow, with sparrows flying round on their line and others chirruping sweetly and delightfully in their cages; they come into the meadow, to the sparrows and are caught in the trap. The fowler who had set the trap catches and kills the birds and mocks their gullibility.[114]

[**13**.1] After this a pair of oxen were depicted with their plough, and a ploughman for whom the craftsman had devised mean sandals,[115] and had painted mean garments on the rest of his body, a mean tunic that was totally ragged (even this he contrived in paint); there was a mean covering on his head, perhaps of felted wool. [2] His face was black, not like an Ethiopian but deeply tanned by the sun.[116] A little of his hair appeared at his back, but his head covering concealed most of it; his beard was long and very thick. [3] His right hand grasped the plough firmly and thrust it into the earth, his left hand held an ox-goad, the farmer's pen which is dipped in ox-blood and inscribes the earth.[117]

113 'The youth': the month of October.

114 'The fowler': Plepelits 1989: 50–51 suggests that the hunting represents the Gospel command to become 'fishers of men' (Matthew 4.19). For twelfth-century fowling techniques, see Manasses' *ekphrasis* of a bird-hunt (Sternbach 1901).

115 This passage deals with the month of November. 'had devised mean sandals': cf. Basilakes' lament (Pignani 1983: 252.373–74).

116 'His face': Plepelits 1989: 51 suggests that the black of the Ethiopian is a reference to the devil while the sun is a symbol of Christ.

117 'inscribes the earth': translating with Conca 1994 and the manuscripts τὴν γῆν rather than πληγήν (Marcovich 2001), though πορφύρεον θάνατον ('purple-hued death') at the equivalent place in Basilakes' lament (Pignani 1983: 243.280–81) gives the emendation some justification. Plepelits 1989: 51 suggests that this image represents the Word of God spread throughout the world

[**14**.1] The figure[118] next to him was similar in appearance, in tunic, sandals, head covering and bodily adornments but was different in body; the colour of his face was black, but not like the last figure, just as the whiteness was not that of the man painted in the garden; but as he was blacker than the one, so he was also more white than the other. [2] His hair came in unruly fashion down to his shoulders; his beard was not disorderly like his neighbour's, but smoothed together and groomed. [3] In his left hand he held a container, and his other hand took corn from it and scattered it over the earth; if the poor were concealed in cracks in the earth and if he scattered seed for them,[119] the craftsman did not let this appear.

[**15**.1] Following these there was depicted a youth with a vigorous body and a bold look, completely mad for hunting and the pursuit of game, with blood-stained hands and seeming to shout to his dogs;[120] for the painter's hand and art, however skilful in other respects, is defeated by sound and is incapable of expressing this with colours. [2] He had gathered all his hair up and tied it back; his tunic was clinging tightly to his upper body and was as if sewn to it but the craftsman had then let it flow to his knees. [3] A tattered cloak covered the rest of him down to his toes, with a cord twined around like ivy. A hare dangled from his left hand and with his right he was fondling the dogs, who were all rolling around at the youth's feet as though playing with him.[121]

[**16**.1] At the end[122] were painted bowls of fire and a flame reaching up from the earth to the sky itself, so that it could not be understood whether the fire came pouring out of the aither to earth or whether it came up from earth to the sky. [2] And an extraordinarily aged man[123] was seated by the flame, completely wrinkled, with completely grey hair and beard, clad in leather from head to loins, the rest of him naked – his hands, his feet and most of his belly. [3] His hands were stretched out and he seemed to draw the flame

118 The month of December. Plepelits 1989: 51 draws a parallel with the Parable of the Sower (Matthew 13.1–43; Mark 4.1; Luke 8.4).

119 'if the poor [...] them': Plepelits 1989: 51 suggests that this recalls Psalm 111.9 and 2 Corinthians 9.9.

120 This scene depicts the month of January. 'shout to his dogs': cf. Euripides, *Hippolytos* 219, *Bacchae* 871.

121 'A hare [...] him': Plepelits 1989: 43, 53 suggests that the hare symbolizes the trembling faithful who flee to the Church, while the dogs stand for spiritual guides and shepherds.

122 'At the end': the series of months ends with February. For fire from heaven, cf. Genesis 19.24.

123 'extraordinarily aged man': Plepelits 1989: 53 suggests verbal parallels with the aged Abraham (Genesis 17.17).

to him and to fan it and completely attract it to himself.[124]

[**17**.1] We look at this spectacle and are amazed by its extraordinary nature, and we were very eager to discover the meaning of the paintings, especially Kratisthenes. For love for Hysmine had me totally in its thrall; and everything else and all the delights of the garden I had found delightful before I had seen Hysmine, or rather, before I was enflamed with love for Hysmine. [2] So I let my eyes wander around the garden, imagining Hysmine, but Kratisthenes saw that there was an iambic line written above the heads of the men painted there. It went as follows:

"When you contemplate these men, you see the whole year."

[**18**.1] Then we debated the appearance of the men in the paintings.

[2] The first, the soldier, indicates the season of year when every soldier sets out on campaign, armed with all his weapons.

[3] The goatherd after him, the goat giving birth at his feet, the pipes that seem to play, show the season when the herdsman brings his flock out after winter, when the goats give birth and the pipes are made ready.

[4] The meadow that was painted full of roses and blooming with flowers, and the man in its midst strewn with flowers, depicts the season of spring.

[5] The plain that was shown covered with grass and the farmer cutting the hay clearly reveals the season in which the hay matures and is ready to be reaped.

[6] The man surrounded by corn who had a sickle and was harvesting the corn delineates the season for harvest.

[7] The man who had bathed, and was naked, drinking and sweating, shows you the hot season, the season of the Dog Star, when the body becomes parched.

[8] The man crushing grapes and gathering them presents to you the season of the vintage and the ripening of the grape clusters.

[9] The fowler who comes after him hints to you of the season in which the birds shiver in the cold and make for warmer climates.

[10] Do you see the labourer with the plough? This is the season when a wise man follows the Pleiades[125] and hones the plough.

[11] The man next to him scattering corn is the sower and reveals though the painting the season for sowing.

[12] Do you see the youth surrounded by dogs, carrying the hare and fondling the dogs? He presents to you the season for hunting; for when the

---

124 'His hands […] himself': Plepelits 1989: 53 sees here an image of mankind drawn in the winter of their soul to the warmth of the monastic life.

125 'follows the Pleiades': cf. Hesiod, *Works and Days* 383–84.

corn and wine and all other things that it is good to collect are gathered into the store-rooms and everything pertaining to agriculture and husbandry for the next season is in good order, then it is the season for relaxation and hunting and the chase.

[13] That greyhaired and wrinkled man who sits hard up to the fire[126] reveals to you the harshness of winter no less than the chill of old age; for winter does not pierce a tender-skinned girl but makes the old man bent.[127]

[**19**.1] Having thus discussed the painting, we made our way back to our chamber, for the time for sleep summoned us. Kratisthenes lay on the couch, but I lingered in the garden, wishing to see Hysmine, and kept my eyes completely on the doorway. [2] For the mind that has been wounded by love constantly creates in itself the beloved object and transfers the eyes to the figure, and seems always to see what it has invented; such is the effect of the fire of love when it attacks the soul and transforms and reconfigures its nature. Kratisthenes got up from the couch and led me to the chamber, saying, "Night has come on, it is good to obey night."[128]

[**20**.1] I said to him, "We have now examined the paintings with our eyes, we have looked at their inscriptions and we have considered their appropriateness to the paintings, and a season was straightforwardly dedicated to heat and cold and spring and all the rest. But Eros is not circumscribed by painting, nor can his colours be changed by art to fit a season; indeed he is appropriate to every season."[129]

[2] Krathisthenes said, "I can ensnare you tightly through my lips, and I have the solution to your queries; for the painting is close by and the painter is not to be ignored. According to the painting and according to you, a season is dedicated to heat and cold and spring, but not in the least to Eros. [3] But if he oversteps the limits,[130] that is the action of a tyrant; if he becomes overbearing and often has control over us, the exception does not prove the rule, for the painter's brush, completely whetted by the paintings' queries, becomes Hermes' javelin[131] for me."

[4] I said to Kratisthenes, "But the javelin will be emasculated by the

---

126 'sits hard by the fire': cf. Hesiod, *Works and Days* 734.

127 'does not pierce [...] bent': cf. Hesiod, *Works and Days* 518–19 and *H&H* 2.4.5.

128 'Night [...] night': cf. *Iliad* 7.282, 293, already used at *H&H* 2.13.1.

129 'season': on the ambiguities of καιϱός, translated here as 'season', see Roilos 2005: 161 with 165 for possible connection to Eros (cf. note at 2.7.3); also Alexiou 2002a.

130 'oversteps the limits': a term derived from athletics, cf. Pollux 3.151; Plato, *Cratylus* 413a 8–9.

131 'Hermes' javelin': that is the validation of the argument; cf. *Hymn to Hermes*, 460 although, in dialogue with Hermes, it is Apollo's javelin by which the validation is made.

colours' hues. Eros has previously been painted as emperor, and all types of men were enslaved to him, especially those men for whom the painter found appropriate seasons. If then everything is in complete servitude to Eros, how can one part escape that servitude? [5] And if every segment of time and space is composed from day or night as its primary matter, and these are in servitude according to the painting and your mystic interpretation, it is quite clear that what is derived from them and through them and everything that is present in them cannot escape servitude but will be brought into servitude[132] against their will."

[6] As I said this I promptly embraced Kratisthenes, saying, "I have defeated you, Kratisthenes." He said, "Very well, you have won; now let us go to our chamber."

[**21.**1] And having done so, we lay down. But a noise in the garden caused me to jump up from my couch, and I see Hysmine by the well; I flew over to her and I called to mind the foot of Eros, which was not like that of men but was altogether winged; [2] and I blessed whoever was responsible for the painting, for Eros put wings on my feet.[133]

Completely unabashed I clasped the girl with both hands and embraced her. She, out of modesty and fear, burst out, "What has come over you? This is shameless for a herald!" "Nothing," I said, "except the bitter-sweet experience of love." [3] And I embraced her again and clasped her again and held her very close to me and quite transported her into my soul and squeezed her with my fingers and nibbled at her and quaffed her with my lips and altogether was wound round her like ivy round a cypress.[134] [4] I was entwined with the girl, I was rooted in her, and I sought to unite our being and I wanted to devour her completely and gulp her down. I pressed her to my lip and I harvested sweet honey on my lips from the hive that was the girl's lip.[135]

[**22.**1] As she is clasped to my mouth she bites my lips, and planted her teeth firmly on my lips; and Erotes grew within my soul, more pugnacious than giants. I was in pain, I compressed my lips and seemed to sigh; she said, "Do your lips hurt? But my soul was pained too when you so precipitously spurned my love at my father's banquet."

[2] And I said to the girl, "Look, could you crush other limbs of mine?

132 'servitude': i.e. to Eros.

133 'wings on my feet': cf. *L&K* 7.15.4; *H&H* 4.4.1, 5.20.3.

134 'entwined like ivy': a common amatory image; cf. Euripides, *Hecuba* 398; *L&K* 1.15.3; *R&D* 6.294–95; *D&C* 1.324, 2.298, 7.230.

135 'honey […] hive': cf. Song of Songs 4.11; *H&H* 7.17.11.

Have a little respect for my lips which are producing the kisses. [3] If you are waving a sting at me like a bee and are guarding your hive and are lashing out at the honey thief, I will take over the hive, put up with the pain from the sting and harvest the honey. For the pain will not deprive me of the honey's sweetness, as the rose's thorns do not turn me away from the rose." [4] And so I kissed her again, and I crushed her once more and I made a more amorous advance. "By Hysmine," she said, "you won't get anywhere with that." "By Hysminias," said I, "I'm not going to give up."

[**23**.1] And so we had a contest between Chastity and Eros, unless you might call Chastity Modesty. For Eros lit cauldrons of fire[136] within me that might have come from the earth's centre, while Modesty dampened the girl with moisture from heaven; [2] Eros emptied all his quivers, Modesty formed a shield of seven ox-hides[137] before the maiden; Eros kindled before my eyes the torch of passion in his hands and tossed the flame towards my soul, Modesty poured out fountains of tears from the girl's eyes. [3] But Modesty's waters could not quench Eros' fire and I am already wearing the garland, and Eros would have conquered Chastity had not someone appeared at the gate – what an unlucky chance! – looking for Hysmine.[138] [4] Being very embarrassed at this we sprang apart, and the maiden (let her still be called this, for thus had Chastity and the gods decreed) went over to the well and sat at its rim among the birds there and played with them.

[**24**.1] I returned to my chamber and immediately lay down, and cleverly feigned sleep, making the pretence out of shame and fear and passion. [2] I had shamed my herald's wand, the garland of laurel, the sacred sandal and the Diasia; I was afraid of Sosthenes, and Panthia, and the whole of Aulikomis, and in my passion I pitied Hysmine more than myself. [3]

The good Kratisthenes got out of bed and went into the garden and since he neither saw Hysmine nor heard any voice from the house (for he could see everything that was going on), he came to me and said, "Your pretence is useless." [4] I jumped up in complete terror and Kratisthenes said, "What a cowardly herald!" But I was still completely terrified and wanted to see Hysmine, saying, "I am done for, Kratisthenes." And Kratisthenes said, "Do be quiet and let us get some sleep,

for it is wise to do what is necessary even in difficult situations."[139]

[**25**.1] And so I was silent, but sleep shunned my eyes and, despite my

---

136 'cauldrons of fire': cf. *H&H* 7.17.5, 10.17 2.
137 'seven ox-hides': used at *Iliad* 7.219–20, 11.545 of Ajax's shield.
138 For this scene of attempted rape, cf. *L&K* 2.10.4.
139 'for [...] situations': Euripides, *Hecuba* 228.

entreaties, fled and I spent the whole night awake, devising all sorts of plans in my mind, and eventually, "I shall never embrace the fair Hysmine again, I shall never clasp her fingers in passion, I shall never be entwined with her like ivy, I shall pour not nectar but a cup of bitterness, [2] I shall never harvest her honey, I shall never be wounded by her sting, nor shall I quaff the girl with my lips – all the passionate games I played so eagerly." I turned these thoughts over in my mind and from my eyes there flowed torrents of tears which flooded my reason and drowned it and then inebriated me and bore me off to sleep.

BOOK FIVE

[**1**.1] And while I lay asleep a whole chorus of dreams thronged around me and made sport of me and sported with me in the way dreams do. One depicted before me Hysmine sporting, being kissed, kissing, nibbling passionately, being nibbled back, being completely embraced by me and embracing me with passion. [2] Another made her lie beside me and displayed a bed strewn with erotic delights, kisses, ticklings, bodies pressed together, arms embraced and the other limbs likewise.

[3] Another of the dreams created a whole bath-house and had me bathing with Hysmine and passionately poured out all delights: my entire mouth was stitched to the girl's breast, biting with my teeth, sucking with my lips, with my tongue conveying the lotus into my soul;[140] all this the girl reciprocated on my neck. [4] Intending to sport passionately, the dream set fire to the bath and, intensifying my thirst and contriving my conflagration, it presented me with the girl's breasts as sweetly gratifying fountains. Pressing these to my mouth it dowsed my soul's heat in the springs of icy pleasure that were sweeter than nectar. And finally it laid us to rest in each other's arms.

[**2**.1] Another set up a bridal chamber, preparing a brilliant bridal procession for the girl, escorting her honourably, and crowning Hysmine together with me magnificently, it sat us down together and spread out a banquet and sang the marriage song and conjured up Erotes dancing around the table and sporting in the way that Erotes do.

[**3**.1] Another most vengeful dream depicts the garden for me and brings Hysmine in and gets me up from my couch and leads me to the girl and

140 'lotus into my soul': referring to the seductive delights of the land of the Lotus Eaters (*Odyssey* 9.82–102).

incites my passion. [2] I draw the maiden to me, at first against her will; but I continue, I hold her, I nibble at her, I kiss her, I embrace her but when I try to become even more passionate the girl would not allow me and I turn passion into conflict.

[3][141] While all this is going on, the girl's mother arrives and, grasping the girl by the hair, drags her off like loot from war-spoils, yelling vituperations and slapping her. I was absolutely thunder-struck, as though I had been blasted by lightning. [4] But that most aggressive of the dreams did not let me remain senseless and turned Panthia's tongue into a Tyrrhenian trumpet[142] which brayed out against me and she cursed my herald's wand. "Alas for your theatricals," she said, "and your play-acting,[143] Zeus and the gods! [5] The herald, the chaste youth who was crowned with laurel, who brought the Diasia to Aulikomis, who was welcomed among us and cherished like a god – he is a fornicator, unregenerate, a rapist, he has come to Aulikomis as a second Paris; he ravages my treasure, he robs me of my heirloom.

[6] But I have got you, you thief, robber, sinner, despoiler of what is most beautiful. All you mothers who conceal your virgin treasures and keep sleepless watch over your treasures, look, I have the traitor who was masked by the laurel crown, the august chiton, the sacred sandal and his office – he put them all on like a lion skin, he invented the whole play.[144] [7] But the sweet zephyr of chastity has blown on him and convicts him of deceit and reveals what had been hidden. So now the herald is no longer a herald but a robber, a brigand, a despot.

[8] Women, let us weave a coat of stone[145] for the despot, let us paint his scenery for him, let us perfect the performance, let us publicly emblazon the

141 5.3.1–3: For this scene of maternal intervention, cf. *L&K* 2.23.4–24.1; see discussion at Nilsson 2001: 224–25.

142 'Tyrrhenian trumpet': the notoriously loud war-trumpet invented by Tyrrhenos, eponymous ancestor of the Etruscans, a common expression in tragedy; e.g., Aeschylus, *Eumenides* 567–68; Sophocles, *Ajax* 17; Euripides, *Rhesos* 988–89, *Heraklides* 830–31.

143 'play-acting': acting and theatricals are a fairly constant reference point for Makrembolites, who also calls his work a 'drama', though the significance of that is not necessarily theatrical (cf. Agapitos 1998 and Introduction, pp. 173–74). Komnenian interest in ancient drama is demonstrated by commentaries (e.g. Tzetzes on Aristophanes) and pastiches (e.g. the *Christus Patiens*, clearly to be attributed to Theodore Prodromos); cf. Püchner 2002.

144 'invented the whole play': the theatrical metaphors continue; Plepelits 1989: 186, n. 61 points out that this alludes to Herakles' traditional costume, as in Aristophanes' *Frogs*; most relevant here are Herakles' abductions, e.g. of Iole in the sack of Oechalia (Apollodoros, *Bibliotheke* 2.7.7).

145 'weave [...] stone': i.e., stone him; cf. *Iliad* 3.57, said by Hektor of Paris.

despot in his tunic so that our actions are an ornament for women, a bulwark for virgins and a crown for Aulikomis.

Did not women destroy the children of Egyptos

and empty all Lemnos of males?[146]

Were not Polymestor's eyes gouged out by women?"[147]

[**4**.1] She said this and instigated an army of women to action and succumbed entirely to a Bacchic frenzy and launched a campaign against my head; I was transfixed by the sight and said to Kratisthenes, "I am done for, Kratisthenes!" [2] Startled by my voice, he springs out of bed and touches me with his hand and shakes the dream from my soul and sleep from my eyes. [3] I thought, by the gods, that I still saw the women, and said to Kratisthenes, "We are done for, quite done for! Panthia is on campaign and the women are her army; but it is Zeus, whose office of herald I have betrayed, who leads the first onslaught."

[**5**.1] And Kratisthenes said, "I think you are still dreaming." I said to him, "I dismiss this nightly vision,"[148] and I told him everything that had happened in my sleep, how the dreams teased me, enticed me, incited me to pleasure [2] and finally I told him about the garden, Hysmine, her chastity, my attack, the struggle, Panthia's intervention as this was going on, the attack on the girl, my scheme, the assault, the violence and above all the army of women. [3] "It was when my soul was terrified by them that I called on you often, good Kratisthenes; and I was afraid that the Divine Being had depicted my future in the dream, for the divinity is accustomed to disclose future events through dreams."[149] [4] Kratisthenes replied, "Dreams are about your daytime preoccupations. These events entered your thoughts when the noise around the door separated us.[150] But already I can see Sosthenes coming towards us rather hastily." I whispered, "I am done for."

[**6**.1] Sosthenes came up and, standing by the door to the chamber, said, "Hysminias the herald, see the entire city of Aulikomis is before your doors. Everyone is looking for the herald. Put the garland on your head, put on your chiton and your sandals, assume your herald's costume so that Poseidon may honour you and offer[151] to Zeus a wind that will convey you to Eurykomis."

146 'Did [...] males?': Euripides, *Hecuba* 886–87.
147 'Were [...] women?': Euripides, *Hecuba* 981 ff. (in vengeance for death of Polydoros).
148 'I dismiss [...] vision': cf. Euripides, *Hecuba* 72.
149 Interest in the psychology of dreams appears also in *R&D* 3.19–42, with several precise Aristotelian allusions; see MacAlister 1990 and 1996: 158–61.
150 Cf. *H&H* 4.23.3.
151 'offer': the phrase is usually used of sacrifices to the gods; cf. *Odyssey* 12.400, 408.

[2] So I, although afraid, in terror and suspecting that Sosthenes' words were fabricated and a piece of play-acting, I put on my herald's garb. When I come into the garden, I see an innumerable host of maidens adorned in every way, with lovely tunics and garlands of laurel, that token of virginity. [3] I looked, and by the despot Eros, I thought I recognized the dream in these events; and I would have all but expired had I not seen Hysmine in their midst, like the moon amid the stars,[152] in all other respects dressed like an empress but with her head crowned like a maiden with laurel. [4] So, gazing intently at the girl and inclining my head, I stole a greeting; she, pretending to adjust her tunic, greeted me in return more openly and smiled rather amorously, and filled my entire soul with ineffable delight and pleasure and made me brim over with boldness.

[7.1] I come to the gate to the garden and I see all Aulikomis preparing a brilliant escorting procession for me with songs, cymbals, torches, flares, roses, flowers, hymns, ululations and everything else that is dedicated to gods, though not to heralds. [2] And so that I do not seem to you[153] to be glory-mongering in my account of my procession, I departed from the lovely Aulikomis, fair in women,[154] Hysmine's homeland, like an Olympic victor who had been victorious in the pentathlon, and – to pass over the intervening stages – I came to my own city of Eurykomis.

[8.1] And once again the city was agog, once again there was a throng awaiting the herald, and once again there was a competition between the cities. It seems to me that the city of Eurykomis, my homeland, is in competition with Aulikomis, Hysmine's homeland, and will not yield the first place for the procession. [2] So I come with such splendour, such honour, such imperial pomp to the altar of Zeus god of strangers, and the entire group that had sailed with me from Aulikomis accompanied me. [3] But my father Themisteus and my mother Dianteia flung themselves upon me in the middle of the brilliant gathering[155] and, surrounded by the throng, they kiss me, hug me, embrace me and drench me with tears of joy and take me home.

[9.1] I said, "But bring Sosthenes too, because he welcomed me with great magnificence and honour in Aulikomis." My father Themisteus listened to my remarks, and went up to him and said, "Welcome, Sosthenes, and thanks

---

152 'all but expired': cf. Basilakes' lament (Pignani 1983: 250.326) and *H&H* 7.17.2. 'moon […] stars': cf. Sappho, fr. 96, 6–9 (Voigt 1971); also Hel 3.6.3 and *D&C* 3.336–37; this is part of the stock-in-trade of amatory vocabulary.

153 'you': a reference to Charidoux who was addressed at the beginning of the text.

154 'fair in women': cf. *Iliad* 2.685, 3.75, 258, 9.447; *H&H* 2.9.2.

155 'gathering': Or 'spectacle'? A *theatron* could be a place or an environment.

are due to you, Zeus god of strangers,[156] for your reception of the herald." [2] And he led him to our house with us, and with Panthia and Hysmine and all those who had sailed with Sosthenes to Eurykomis from Aulikomis.

So we came to the house, and the table was set and we all took our places together. [3] On the side of the table that was by the garden was my father Themisteus and my mother Dianteia, and the third was myself, having completely laid aside my herald's wand. On the other side was Sosthenes, Hysmine's father, and her mother Panthia; [4] next to her mother strict rank placed Hysmine.[157] I inwardly praised the etiquette and thought myself most blessed in this, considering the matter most propitious, and I felt that this line-up,[158] to use the usual expression, showed that love would prosper.

[**10**.1] So the time for drinking sent out its summons and a slight struggle broke out between Sosthenes and Themisteus, our fathers, not a real fight but the sort of contest that serious old men get up to. [2] And so Sosthenes lost and drank first, and after him Themisteus, the victor; for, for them, a victory was what foolish men think a defeat. And after them the women drank in respectful silence since silence is an ornament to women.[159]

[3] After Panthia and my mother Dianteia, Kratisthenes came up to me, carrying the cup, for my father had bidden him to pour the wine.[160] I took it and sipped a little; then, as if changing my mind, I handed it back to him who had offered it, chiding him for his lack of etiquette and for having broken the order of precedence; for strict decorum demanded that the maiden opposite me should drink first.

[4] He obeyed and took the cup to her; she grasped it with both hands, even though – as befits a maiden – she took it with her fingertips only. Understanding the point of this byplay, she thanked me with a gesture, inclining her head slightly in erotic manner, like a cypress gently swaying in a light breeze.[161] Her appearance was full of grace and she was the image of Eros. [5] So we shared the cup, and imbibed together and drank very passionately; thus we mingled our lips in no ordinary manner, sucking the passionate juices of our love[162] and each drawing the other into our souls with our eyes.

---

156 'you, Zeus': omitting, with Conca 1994 and Nilsson 2001, Hilberg's addition of παρὰ, 'from'.

157 'On the side [...] Hysmine': for the meal arrangements, cf. *L&K* 1.5; *R&D* 2.97–105.

158 'line-up': referring to the starting line in athletic contests; cf. Aristophanes, *Acharnanians* 483.

159 'silence [...] women': cf., e.g., Sophocles, *Ajax* 293; *A&K* fr. 107, n.3.

160 For these games with the cup and the stolen kisses, cf. *L&K* 2.9.1.

161 'like a cypress': cf *R&D* 2.209.

162 'sucking [...] love': cf. Basilakes' lament (Pignani 1983: 251.365).

[**11**.1] Once again it was the time to drink, and once again Kratisthenes mixes the wine. Once again Sosthenes drinks first, and after him my father and Panthia in the usual order, and my mother Dianteia; and after her Hysmine, the maiden who breathes out passion. [2] She, in maidenly fashion, took the cup with her fingertips and put it to her lips with maidenly decorum; taking only a small sip from the cup she handed it back completely, maidenly modesty playing its part in the game. [3] And I said to Kratisthenes (for the game had not passed me by as I watched the girl intently, picturing her entirely in my mind and imagining her, for the herald's wand had seared me and left me parched),[163] "Offer me the cup too."

[4] So – what else could he do? – he offered it and, by Eros, I seemed to be drinking down the girl herself. I kissed her lips passionately and, as I kissed, I stole kisses.[164] For the cup was my assistant who conveyed my beloved Hysmine's lips to me. [5] I sipped from the cup and, by the gods, there flowed into my soul what I had sipped from her breasts in my dreams. I gazed deep into the cup, enquiringly, in case a part of the girl's lip had adhered to the lip of the cup. [6] She saw my gesture and glance and my delighted drinking from the cup, and smiled passionately and depicted in her eyes, as if in a mirror, all the graces and Eros himself.

[**12**.1] So, after the luxurious dishes on which I fed delightedly with hand and mouth (for the maiden had, as it were, purchased through passion my eyes and whatever else of my senses was more acute, and these were enslaved to her), Kratisthenes returned again to his duty and, after our fathers and mothers, came to offer the wine to the girl. [2] She once again took a small sip and then whispered to her mother in a maidenly voice, scarcely louder than a zephyr passing over a pine tree, "Mother, I do not want to drink."

[3] Panthia said to Kratisthenes, "My boy, take the cup." He took it away from the girl's hands and placed it in mine. Once again I seemed to take the entire girl and to drink her down entirely. And I received a cup full of kisses which purveyed kisses, and I kissed the kisses. [4] The drink was nectar to me, such as Aphrodite pours and the Erotes drink, and the cup was a mirror conveying into my soul the entire girl with all her graces and all her delights.

[**13**.1] And after the luxurious dishes and drink and all the other things that adorn symposia, the symposion drew to a close. And my father Themisteus and my mother Dianteia took Sosthenes and Panthia and the lovely

---

163 'seared [...] parched': an allusion to the traditional erotic theme of the unquenchable fires of love; cf. *AnthGr* 5.281 (Paul the Silentiary); Musaios 245–46.

164 For this scene, cf. *L&K* 2.9.2.

Hysmine to the chamber that had been set aside for them. Thus we parted from each other, with my mother Dianteia embracing the girl and covering her face with kisses.

[2] But I envied my mother and, by the gods, wished to change my gender; since this was not possible, I kissed my mother's lips and in effect kissed the girl's face, and I enrolled my mother in the service of Eros, conveying kisses to me. [3] I do not know precisely what my father and my mother felt about the girl and how they left her, but I departed with my feet alone for I left my soul and my eyes and my mind with the girl as a deposit, as it were, and as a guarantee.

[**14**.1] And when I came to my couch I was tormented by a thousand thoughts, my soul was under siege and sleep was torn from my eyes like booty in war. [2] I admired Aulikomis for its hospitality, which extended even to its guests' feet. "As for us, it does not even get as far as the hands of those who attend the altar of Zeus, god of strangers, or the festival of the Diasia. [3] Why should not I too wash the girl's feet, as she washed mine with due honour, so that I too may kiss her and squeeze her and massage her passionately, just as she did to me then?"

[4] I was tormented in this way by passion and spent most of the night in erotic thoughts; and my watchful contemplation of the girl was for me both sleep and delight. But Weariness brought sleep to my eyes, and Weariness and Eros had a contest over me, with my eyes in the middle like a city under siege. [5] So sluggish Weariness lobbed sleep at my eyes as if from some catapult while Eros protected my eyes with a barrage of thoughts and warded off the onslaughts. Eventually, after much skirmishing, Weariness won and stole the victory, casting a light sleep over my eyes as if through some small chink in my defences.

[**15**.1] About the third watch of the night my father Themisteus and my mother Dianteia, together with Sosthenes and Panthia and all the others who had accompanied them from Aulikomis, went to the altar with the offerings, to make the sacrifices to Zeus the Saviour and to present the customary dues. Hysmine was left alone in her chamber, since it was not proper for maidens to appear before men.

[2] I, for I was not unaware of what was going on, immediately made for the girl's couch, and kissed her as she lay there sleeping. She was terrified by this unexpected event and jumped up from her bed, saying, "What is happening!" [3] I carried on, and said, "Do not be afraid, my lady; it is I, Hysminias." And as I said this, I kissed her. She asked, "But where are my father and mother?" I said, "At the altar of Zeus god of strangers, to make

sacrifices; [4] shall we not make our own sacrifice to Eros? Let us at least sacrifice virginity itself and ourselves with it." And I embraced the girl and kissed her and fell upon her passionately.

[**16**.1] She embraced me back, but being a virgin she took her kisses surreptitiously out of modesty. I kissed her more passionately, and nibbled at her with my teeth and was fed an erotic food such as Aphrodite offers to lovers. [2] She moaned with delicate passion, and her delicately passionate moan imbued my whole soul with delight.

[3] I entwined myself around the girl entirely, like a vine, and I pressed the unripe grape clusters to my mouth and quaffed with my lips the nectar which the Erotes were squeezing out; and I pressed with my fingers and drank with my lips so that all the nectar could be squeezed out for me into the vat that was my soul – such an insatiable vintner was I. [4] She kissed me in return and embraced me and entwined herself round me like ivy, and thus a myriad Graces danced around us.[165] So, after many embraces and kisses and all the other games that the Erotes teach, I tried to quaff down passion completely and to cease playing and make love in earnest, so that the crows should not croak in an unfinished house.[166]

[**17**.1] But she resisted firmly, with her hands and feet and tongue and tears, saying, "Hysminias, spare my virginity; do not reap the ears of corn before the summer; do not pluck the rose before it bursts from its sheath; do not crush the ripening grape lest you press out vinegar from the cluster instead of nectar. [2] You will reap the ears, but when the field is white for harvest; you will cull the rose, but when the mature bloom bursts from the sheath; you will harvest the grape, but when you see the clusters ripened. [3] I am your unsleeping guardian, inviolable wall and unassailable barrier.

What do you gain by assaulting my chastity? I came to Eurykomis a virgin; what do you gain by my returning to Aulikomis no longer a virgin? [4] I love you, herald, I do not conceal my love. My soul is pierced, I admit the dart; my innermost being is on fire and I cannot deny the fire. But I shall not betray what is most precious: I shall preserve my maidenhood, and I shall preserve it for you."

[**18**.1] So spoke the girl and dissolved into floods of tears. I said to her, "You are the book by which I was dedicated to Eros, because of you I became a slave instead of a free man, because of you I exchanged Zeus god of Friendship for the despot Eros. [2] I no longer have a country, father, mother

165 'myriad [...] around us': cf. Basilakes' lament (Pignani 1983: 237.39).
166 'crows [...] house': cf. Hesiod, *Works and Days* 746–47; see Aelian, *De natura animalium* 3.9 for crows invoked at weddings (LSJ: under κορώνη I.2).

or the great treasure which my father has hoarded up for me, nor any other possession; with you I shall die." So I embraced her and kissed her, and tears flowed from my eyes; and as we embraced we were drenched with tears.

[**19**.1] After a while Hysmine kissed my eyes and as she kissed them she said, "Hysminias, this is your last kiss. For in three days time I will return to Aulikomis with my father; you will remain in Eurykomis, your homeland, and your father will find another girl for you to marry. [2] And you will make the wedding sacrifices, quite forgetting me, your dear Hysmine, and our passionate kisses and our other embraces, which we have enjoyed in vain as if in our dreams. [3] But I will never forget your friendship, not even in Hades,[167] my sweetest Hysminias, and for you I shall keep my virginity inviolate. Not even the kiss of Zeus himself shall I prefer to yours, no, by the fearsome Eros, who has placed my soul in your hands like a bird."

[**20**.1] She said this and, pressing her whole face on to my chest, she drenched me with tears. I said to her, "Maiden Hysmine, my delight,[168] light of my eyes, brimming source of honey, shower of graces, you speak, as you kiss me, of the last kiss – but I am your lover and your slave through Eros, with you I shall die. I too shall preserve my virginity for you. [2] It will not be removed either by parental authority or maternal persuasion, not even if they were to propose Aphrodite herself, no, by Zeus, father of all the gods, whose herald I was when I came to Aulikomis, your homeland, and returned to my homeland Eurykomis, enslaved to your graces." [3] Then, as day began to beam, I embraced the girl and left the chamber, and returned to my couch as if with winged feet, and immediately made my truce with sleep, as if I had found it there.

BOOK SIX

[**1**.1] So my father Themisteus with Sosthenes and our mothers returned from the altar of Zeus, god of strangers, having sacrificed the offerings. And my mother Dianteia approaches my couch, and wakes me up, saying, "My son Hysminias, it is time for luncheon – and have you not yet brushed the sleep from your eyes? Get up, and let us get ready for the meal. [2] For your father Themisteus has sat down with Sosthenes and all the others whom he has summoned for the meal."

---

167 'never forget [...] Hades': cf. *Iliad* 22.389–90 and Basilakes' lament (Pignani 1983: 237.49–50).

168 'my delight': cf. Sappho fr. 126 and Basilakes' lament (Pignani 1983: 238.64–65).

So, going with my mother to the table, we seated ourselves in the usual manner, and once again Hysmine opposite me bedewed me with love through her eyes. [3] I gazed intently at the girl and, leaning over the table, I greeted her, giving her surreptitiously a passionate greeting. She returned this surreptitiously, as usual, inclining her neck in a maidenly fashion. The table was laden in the usual manner with sumptuous dishes, and Krathisthenes pours the wine. Sosthenes drinks first, and after him Themisteus, and then the rest of us as usual.[169]

[2.1] And Sosthenes said, "When you showed us kindness, Themisteus, you were bestowing the kindness not on us but on Zeus, god of strangers.[170] May father Zeus acknowledge your magnificent banquets and other costly displays by preparing for you an appropriate reception in the Elysian Fields and the Island of the Blessed[171] where the heroes are fellow guests. [2] I beg you to join us in our Aulikomis, with Dianteia and this handsome herald," (indicating me with his hand) "for we wish to make celebratory sacrifices for the marriage of my dear daughter Hysmine. [3] The Diasia is consecrated among us as the time for the celebration of weddings, and now that we have made the appropriate sacrifices we shall return to Aulikomis, if Zeus the Saviour so decides.

The young man to whom my Hysmine's marriage bed is dedicated is a fellow countryman from Aulikomis who has mixed a brimming three-fold krater of happiness;[172] [4] he is unparalleled in virtues of the soul, his physical qualities rival those of his soul and strive not to appear inferior; and his other gifts are poured out together into his soul and body and are, as it were, mingled. [5] Such a marriage I and Zeus before me have arranged for this dear daughter of mine; but if you will sail with me to Aulikomis with Hysminias and his mother, I should consider the marriage even more felicitous." [6] My father Themisteus responded, "Now it is Zeus' banquet and the time of the Diasia, and we shall sacrifice the offerings appropriate for the time and the banquet; all else is in the lap of Zeus."[173]

[3.1] Such were Sosthenes' words and such my father's. I, by the gods, found my senses gone from my mind and sat at the table like a statue, with my eyes gazing intently on the girl's face. [2] The maiden's eyes filled with

169 Cf. *H&H* 6.4, below.

170 'you [...] strangers': a reflection of Matthew 25.4 ('whatsoever you do to the least of my brethren, you do unto me')? (Plepelits 1989: 187, n. 71; Burton 1998).

171 'Elysian [...] Blessed': the hereafter as depicted in the literature of classical antiquity.

172 'three-fold krater of happiness': cf. Basilakes' lament (Pignani 1983: 244.200–01).

173 'lap of Zeus': literally 'knees'; a Homeric cliché; cf., e.g., *Iliad* 17.514, *Odyssey* 1.267, 400.

tears and holding her right cheek she wrinkled her brow and sighed bitterly and said to Panthia, "Mother, I have a headache." She said to her, "Go to your chamber."[174]

[3] So she got up immediately from the table and went to her chamber. My mother then said to Panthia, "What has troubled that lovely girl?" She replied, "Her father's remark, which reminded our daughter of her marriage which up till now we have kept the girl from knowing about, for she is a virgin and chaste."

[4.1] Of what happened subsequently at the table I have no knowledge. It was as though my entire head had been struck off by the lightning bolt of Sosthenes' words. If I ate anything, truly – by Sosthenes' terrible voice – I do not know. [2] The good Sosthenes, who had announced to us his daughter's marriage, then spoke once more, "We have had enough of banquets, Themisteus, and a sufficiency of drink and sumptuous dishes spread on the table. Let us go to our slumbers, if you allow us, for night once again summons us to the altar and sacrifices."[175]

[5.1] Thus the symposium came to an end, and I, reclining in my usual way on my usual couch, found my eyes succumbing immediately to sleep and I lay there asleep, with my soul in utter perturbation over the unexpected announcement, and my mind entirely submerged in grief.

[2] Once again there came the accustomed time for sacrifice, and once again my father Themisteus and my mother Dianteia with Sosthenes and Panthia keep vigil at the altar;[176] and once again I rise up from my couch and go to the couch of the girl whom the good Sosthenes would give in marriage in Aulikomis; and once again I kiss the girl. [3] She soaks her mattress with tears, and I kiss her again as I say to her, "Hysmine, what is the matter?" She replies, "My father's remark has destroyed me."

[6.1] I say to her, "You have created an image of my marriage, and you have wooed another girl for me; and I have been condemned by you to forget the many passionate favours which overfilled the cup you poured for me. [2] But I, sweetest maiden, sweeter than honey, I have called the gods to witness that I have not foresworn your love nor abandoned your friendship nor bartered away your love for anything.

174 'I have a headache': cf. Theokritos, *Idyll* 3.52; *D&C* 6.300. On the use of Theokritan allusions in these novels, see Milazzo 1985 and Burton 2003 (at 257 on this quotation).

175 On the blurring of the narrative chronology in *H&H* (noticeable at this point), see Nilsson 2001: 137–39.

176 As noted previously, the night-time vigils are arguably a reflection of twelfth-century liturgical practice, well exemplified in certain poems of Manganeios Prodromos (e.g. poems 67, 68 and 69).

[3] But now your father, Sosthenes, who in all ways is to be respected, has erected for you in Aulikomis a bridal chamber, he has set aside for you a great dowry and prepared a bridegroom, and he will lead you in a brilliant bridal procession and will escort you in a honourable bridal parade. [4] But I, your lover – for I am not ashamed of my love for you – I will bind my head with a virginal wreath and will go in a rich and honourable bridal procession to Persephone and the inhabitants of Hades, who have constructed for me a brilliant and virginal wedding chamber. [5] You will be charged with lack of charity in love, condemned by your erotic favours and those marks which you bear all over your body from my hands and lips. [6] Wealth (Ploutos) will adorn you sumptuously while Pluto[177] will lead me away in a magnificent bridal escort.

But oh, those kisses which we enjoyed in vain! oh, the pressure of our bodies which we endured for naught! [7] oh, the embraces and the entwinings in which we fruitlessly indulged! oh, eyes that gazed to ill purpose and thus mourn gloomily! This hand aided me in passion, and now it will aid me with the sword which I shall thrust into my soul."

[**7**.1] These were my words and, embracing the girl, I kissed her and said, "Truly this is your last kiss;

receive too the last of my pronouncements.[178]

You will return to Aulikomis, to your homeland, a brilliant bride to join a brilliant bridegroom. They will sing for you your wedding song in imperial mode, I will go down to Hades and, gathering up the whole choir of Erinnyes, I will descant upon my misfortune. [2] For you the good Sosthenes will sing a wedding hymn, for me my father will sing a funeral dirge. Your father will sing over you, sweet bride, a sweet melody, my pitiful father Themisteus will strike up a lament over his dead son.[179] The one will dance a wedding ode, my father, most pitiable of all, will chant a lamentable and bitter farewell."[180]

[**8**.1] This is what I said, and I completely soaked the girl with my tears. She said, "You have destroyed me, my sweetest Hysminias. You are my homeland, my father and my mother and my bridal chamber, my bridegroom and my lord through Eros' decree. But – oh, the tears choke my tongue – do not let what has issued from my father's mouth devour the passionate delights which came from my mouth and which we enjoyed together passionately

---

177 'Pluto': god of the underworld.

178 'receive […] pronouncements': Euripides, *Hecuba* 413.

179 'strike up a lament': cf. Basilakes' lament (Pignani 1983: 235.5–6). For a similar set of contrasts, cf. *L&K* 1.13.5.

180 'chant […] farewell': cf. Basilakes' lament (Pignani 1893: 235.11).

but fruitlessly. [2] Do not let the honey, which I collected like an industrious bee but to no avail, be harvested from your mouth. Do not let my father's mouth be so all-devouring that it consumes all the erotic games which we played to no avail, or rather with which the Erotes beguiled us.

[3] Hysminias, you cultivated with passion, like a garden, this girl you call 'your Hysmine'; set a barrier around the garden lest the hand of some passer-by should pluck me.[181] You wish to die, but with that word I also put my soul aside. I shall die with you, just as I shall live with you if you live. [4] And I embrace you and hold you and I share my entire life with you just as I seek to take part in death with you." And so saying she embraced me and as she embraced me she shed a fountain of tears from her eyes and flooded me entirely.

[9.1] I said, "If you wish, let us leave my Eurykomis and your Aulikomis for another country, and let us exchange our homelands, our parents, our wealth and all the other splendours of our homes for a passionate friendship and life with each other. [2] Eros will be our homeland and parents and our domestic luxury and food and drink and clothing."

She, as though summoned to an imperial bridal chamber, responded and said, "You have me, your Hysmine, take me away, I will die with you." [3] And she jumped off the couch and followed me, or rather she dragged me off as she ran. "But not yet," I said, "things are not arranged yet." But she did not want to let go of my hands. [4] With difficulty, by calling on all the gods, I tore myself out of Hysmine's hands and got back to my own couch, to consider the matter. When I found that the complications prevented me sleeping, I got out of bed and dressed brilliantly and made my way to the temple of Zeus, god of strangers, where Themisteus my father and my mother Dianteia and Sosthenes and Panthia were attending to the sacrifices.

[10.1] So after many sacrifices were offered by my father and Sosthenes, Sosthenes and Panthia raised their hands up to heaven and, shedding hot tears from their eyes, said, "Father Zeus, this is our sacrifice to you in honour of the wedding of our daughter Hysmine, whose marriage we wish soon to accomplish." [2] This they said and they placed the sacrifice on the pyre. A huge eagle came shrieking from the clouds and swooped down with whirring pinions and seized the sacrifice and scattered the people by the altar.[182]

181 For the idea of the girl as an enclosed garden cf. Song of Songs 4.12; see in general Littlewood 1979; Beck 1984; Barber 1992.
182 'A huge eagle [...] altar': cf. L&K 2.12.1–2; Nilsson 2001: 222–23. The intervention of an eagle at sacrifices, a major portent, is a common legend, but usually told of the foundation of cities (e.g. Antioch, Constantinople); it also appears in some versions of the Trojan story.

Sosthenes stood there, completely amazed. [3] Panthia fell to the ground and, pulling at her grey locks[183] and tearing at her head, said, "Father Zeus, spare these my grey locks, spare my daughter's youthfulness; she is my comfort, she is my consolation, she is my family's hope; I rejoice in her and forget the cares of my old age. [4] Avert this accursed bird from this my daughter.[184] Father Zeus, do not cut out my eyes, do not extinguish my lamp, do not pluck up my corn by the roots, do not shear the locks of my whole house.[185]

[5] Oh, wretched mother that I am, wretched in the sacrifices, wretched in the omens. Blessed with a lovely child, I came from Aulikomis, my homeland, and now here in Eurykomis I become miserable through my child. I was adorning my Hysmine like a virgin for her bridal procession, and now I lament for her as though dead, and I mourn for her while she still lives.[186] [6] Hysmine, my light, you are torn from my eyes;[187] it is no wedding song that I sing for you but a dirge; these are not wedding libations that I pour for you but funereal streams, and, as the proverb has it, I have found that my treasure is coal."[188]

[**11**.1] So spoke Panthia, and she filled the altar with laments and shrieks, gouging her cheeks, rending her garments, striking her breast with a stone[189] and beating her head. [2] The crowd were perturbed by Panthia's laments and groans (for they were not made of oak or rock),[190] and a bemused cry went up from both men and women. For the women mourned with Panthia and beat their breasts, while the men were astounded and amazed. [3] Some considered the bird ill-omened, others most auspicious; and there were those who thought the whole thing fortuitous. And so people's opinions and

183 'pulling at her grey locks': cf. Basilakes' lament (Pignani 1983: 241.139).

184 'Avert [...] daughter': cf. Euripides, *Hecuba* 96–97.

185 'cut out my eyes': cf. Basilakes' lament (Pignani 1983: 252.384–85). 'extinguish my lamp': cf. Basilakes' lament (Pignani 1983: 239.83–85). 'shear [...] house': cf. *H&H* 10.10.4 and Basilakes' lament (Pignani 1983: 238.72–73).

186 While this has overtones from tragedy (e.g. *Hecuba*), it also has a twelfth-century counterpoint in the laments of the *sevastokratorissa* Eirene for her daughter Theodora (MangProd, poems 22, 47).

187 'light [...] eyes': cf. Basilakes' lament (Pignani 1983: 239.86-7); Psalm 37/38.11; *H&H* 10.7.5.

188 'no wedding song [...] funereal streams': cf. Basilakes' lament (Pignani 1983: 235.2–6); *H&H* 7.17.2. 'treasure is coal': cf. Basilakes' lament (Pignani 1983: 238.70); Lucian, *Zeuxis* 2; Diogenianus 1.52 (Leutsch and Schneidewin 1839–51, vol. 2).

189 'striking [...] stone': cf. Basilakes' lament (Pignani 1983: 241.129).

190 'not made [...] rock': a quasi-proverbial cliché (e.g. *Iliad* 22.126, *Odyssey* 19.163) found in all these novels (*R&D* 8.95–98; *D&C* 4.244; *A&K* fr. 17.2–3).

expressions were confused and varied.

[4] My mother Dianteia with my father Themisteus supported Panthia and took her to our house, rather against her will. I and Kratisthenes (for he was present too) took Sosthenes away, and we returned to the house, where we found Hysmine weeping in front of the doors. For a maid-servant had come running back and told her everything. [5] So once more there were laments and shrieks, the mother raised a lament as if for her daughter that had died while the daughter in her turn bitterly bewailed her mother's laments. And my father Themisteus and my mother Dianteia brought the women to their chamber, subduing the uproar.

[12.1] I and Kratisthenes made for my chamber, where we discussed what had happened since our return from Aulikomis. How etiquette had placed Hysmine opposite me at the banquet, how I took the cup and only set it to my lips and then returned it to the giver, saying that Hysmine should drink before me, [2] and Kratisthenes (for he, on my father's instructions, was pouring the wine) took the cup to Hysmine, how the girl grasped it with both hands, how she gestured her thanks to me, how Kratisthenes with the second cup poured for the girl before me, how she took a small sip and returned the whole [3] while I, pretending to be thirsty, took the cup from Kratisthenes' hands, and all the other erotic games we played as we drank; and our fathers' and mothers' departure to the altar for sacrifice, and our games on the girl's couch, [4] and all the passionate pacts we made, Sosthenes' remark during the second banquet, that he would offer a sacrifice for his daughter's marriage, that he would invite my father and me to that wedding in Aulikomis, our amazement at this unexpected announcement, [5] and everything else that happened at the table, Sosthenes' and Panthia's vigil at the altar for the second sacrifices, the maiden's solitariness, our tears on her couch, and finally the pact which we made and called on the gods to witness.[191]

[13.1] And Kratisthenes said, "I prophesy that the bird is most auspicious for you, and very ill-omened for Hysmine's bridegroom in Aulikomis. If Zeus himself hints at abduction and almost gives you your orders, why are you delaying? [2] Why are you hesitating?" I said to him, "In times of trouble, according to the tragedian, friends are seen most clearly;[192] take care of all this business for me." And Kratisthenes said, "I will be of service to you in this problem." And, "Farewell," he said to me, and set off to organize matters. I went to the chamber.

191 An elliptical account of the events just narrated.
192 'In times [...] clearly': cf. Basilakes' lament (Pignani 1983: 236.21–22) and Euripides, *Hecuba* 1226–27.

[**14**.1] There my father and my mother with Sosthenes and Panthia and the girl were discussing the events at the altar and the sacrifice, and I heard the girl saying to her mother, "Mother, what Themisteus and Dianteia have said to you in truth and not out of mere likelihood is enough to calm the storm in your soul; [2] why are you still so wrought up over the affair and torment yourself so much with laments? Zeus does not approve this wedding, he does not wish me to be led away in marriage; you say that this is what the eagle hints at. [3] The foresight of Zeus! The benevolence! You wished me to marry and to contract an ill-omened marriage. Why, mother, do you mourn so much over such a magnificent omen from Zeus?"

[4] And my father Themisteus commended the maiden, saying, "Congratulations on your perceptiveness, girl, and even more so for your comments." And to Sosthenes he said, "If you like, let us go to the table; it is the time of the Diasia, let us honour the festival so that Zeus may look on us more kindly. [5] Let us share in the food, let us partake of sleep. It is already night and the time of sacrifice approaches, summoning us to the altar."

Panthia said, "I cannot go to the altar again, I shall make no brilliant sacrifice for the high-soaring eagle;[193] [6] I have had enough of sacrifices, enough of laments, I have had a surfeit of this useless taking of auguries. Even if that terrifying and ill-omened eagle is not sated with sacrifices, it is clearly the eagle that gouged out Prometheus' side[194] and fed on his entire liver, and now has utterly gouged out my own belly and has devoured my entrails."

[7] And Sosthenes said, "Do not let your tongue run so precipitously and brazenly in case Zeus is enraged. Let us obey Themisteus." And Panthia said to Sosthenes,

"Restrain yourself, and do not encourage
my obstinacy and heated rage;[195]
for my innermost being is on fire."[196]

[**15**.1] After many things had been discussed, a table was improvised for us in the chamber but the food and drink was without ceremony and with little festivity. While we were dining the good Kratisthenes came, and he sat with us on the ground and on the brilliant marble slabs with which the

193 'high-soaring eagle': cf. *Iliad* 12.201, 219, *Odyssey* 20.243.

194 'Prometheus': Prometheus, as a punishment for bringing fire to humankind, was chained to a rock while an eagle devoured his liver, as vividly depicted in Aeschylus' *Prometheus Bound*; for the phrases, cf. *H&H* 3.4.1.

195 'Restrain […] rage': cf. Aeschylus, *Prometheus Bound* 79–80.

196 'innermost being is on fire': cf. Basilakes' lament (Pignani 1983: 237.51).

chamber had been adorned. [2] At length the business of table and meal, if indeed it could be called such, came to an end.

And once again my father Themisteus spoke to Panthia, "That you are a mother, and mother who loves her child, and are no less the mother of a beautiful child – let the truth be spoken – I will not deny. And that 'for women', according to the tragedy, 'the offspring of travail are wondrous', all mothers would bear witness,[197] and that

the word of truth is simple[198]

all are aware, including you. So sacrifices were made on behalf of your daughter who is entering into marriage but these were all seized by Zeus' eagle. Whether the eagle is ill-omened and the portent not good, I am not a sufficiently accurate soothsayer to tell. But if it seems to you very ill-omened and it really is ill-omened, this is surely a good omen for you.

[4] For if the sacrifice takes place after the ceremony and Zeus disapproves of the marriage and hints at his disapproval through the eagle, your tears would not be untimely; for it was to Epimetheus[199] that useless repentance was granted. [5] But if your sacrifice takes place before the marriage and you seek to know the future and Zeus does not permit the marriage, the god of Forethought looks on you kindly and you are happy over your daughter's concerns. Why, then, do you raise a lament and wailing over such a good omen from Zeus, when you should rather owe a sacrifice of thanks to the Saviour Zeus and a thank-offering for your daughter's safety. If you continue to lament, you will accuse of injustice the one who has saved you from storm and fire, because he has granted you life."

[16.1] Panthia with difficulty accepted my father's comments and, restraining her wailing a little, agreed to lie down and to keep vigil for the sacrifices once more. And so we parted from each other. [2] Kratisthenes accompanied me to my chamber and said, "You have no more time for delay. Zeus, through me, has arranged everything well for you and there is a ship ready to set sail for Syria. And my father has a friend in Syria who will give us hospitality and receive us in a friendly manner."

[3] I said to Kratisthenes, "If your friendship is not a pretence, and if Hysminias is your friend and you think of him as your other self, will you

197 'for women [...] wondrous': cf. Euripides, *Phoinissae* 355.
198 'the word [...] simple': cf. Euripides, *Phoinissae* 469.
199 Cf. Hesiod, *Works and Days* 83–89. Epimetheus ('Afterthought'), brother of Prometheus ('Forethought'), married Pandora who then released misfortunes for mankind from her storage box. This passage is analogous to, but not so lengthy or as ingenious as, the Platonic debate at *R&D* 7.400–515 about the logical necessity of sacrificing the hero.

set sail with us?" [4] He said to me, "I never thought of not sailing with you, of not sharing in your discomforts, or your sufferings and anguish. And it would please me if you did not delay this business." [5] I said to him, "If you like, go down to the seashore for me and see to everything on the ship while I, when it is the time for the sacrifices and Sosthenes and Panthia and my parents are at the sacrifices, I will go to the girl and tell her all the developments in this affair. It will be your task to choose the moment and fetch us down to the harbour and the ship."

[**17**.1] So Kratisthenes left the chamber and I stretched out completely on the couch while I had a whole sea of thoughts heaving through my soul, and I was like a ship tossed around by waves and storms; [2] I despaired, I rejoiced, I was terrified, I grew bold, I was completely full of happiness and fear; the thought of success gladdened my soul exceedingly, the thought of failure dejected me excessively.

[**18**.1] In the midst of these billows, all these seas and storms, sleep overwhelmed my eyes and I see in my chamber an innumerable host of youths and maidens, their heads garlanded with roses, their hands linked in line, and singing a tune such as the Sirens sing.[200] The tune was a hymn to Eros and praises of Aphrodite. The song was like a wedding ode, such as the Erotes sing in a bridal chamber. [2] The throng sang the melody and filled my soul with pleasure and passionate delight. It was as though I was completely in an erotic frenzy.

[3] In the midst of this brilliant, graceful, chaotic throng, in the midst of the garlands and the songs, in the midst of the passionate melodies, I see once again seated on his lofty throne Eros, clad in imperial robes, and leading Hysmine by the hand. I was totally astonished at the sight. [4] He said to me, "Hysminias, see, you have Hysmine," and put her hand in my right hand;[201] with that he flew away from my sight, taking sleep with him.

---

200 'Sirens': seductive maidens who attempted to lure sailors, including Odysseus, on to rocks; cf. *Odyssey* 12.41–45.

201 Cf. *H&H* 3.1–4.

BOOK SEVEN

[**1**.1] So Eros bestowed Hysmine on me in this way, and I seemed in my sleep to possess her completely and I saw Eros wholly. When it was the time for the sacrifices, once again Sosthenes and Panthia, together with my mother and my father Themisteus, took the path to the temple and the sacrifices, and once again I too was concerned with Hysmine, either to sacrifice myself entirely or desiring to receive her as a sacrifice. [2] Once again I kiss and embrace her and am embraced and kissed in return. And I say to the girl, "Eros places you in this hand of mine, and Zeus hints at your abduction."

She says to me, "You do not give heed to Zeus' riddles, and you do not wish[202] to observe the duty committed to you by Eros. [3] You saw the sacrifice, the eagle. Do you want Zeus to stand in front of you and speak to you directly?" And I say to the maiden, "Just now I saw in a dream Eros holding you by the hand and placing you in this right hand of mine." She kissed my right hand, and I promptly kissed hers and we were back to exchanging passionate kisses.

[**2**.1] The girl said to me, "Kisses are all very well, Hysminias, they are very nice indeed and full of pleasure, but the sacrifices will come to an end and Hysmine will have to go back to Aulikomis while my handsome Hysminias stays here in Eurykomis, you the meadow of graces, the hive of Erotes, lord of her you call 'my Hysmine'. [2] But, O light of my eyes, comfort of my heart and consolation of my soul, do not let time and changing circumstances mix for you the cup of forgetfulness, nor – and this is more bitter than death – a maiden from Eurykomis." And once again she kissed me and once again she wept.

[**3**.1] I embraced the girl completely and kissed her all over with passion. I said, "You are presumably not unaware of Kratisthenes, who sailed with me to your homeland of Aulikomis? He is my fellow countryman, my cousin, my other self." She said to me, "I have attended on him too, and mixed wine for him with this hand." [2] "That is the one," I said to her, "and he has got a ship ready for us and equipped it for our flight and he will sail away with us and assist us in the whole affair." And the girl kissed my mouth, saying, "I kiss your mouth and I salute the tongue that announces such good news to me."

[**4**.1] And once again I said to the maiden, "See, Zeus and great Eros

---

202 'do not wish': following the manuscripts and Conca 1994, rather than Marcovich 2001 (deleting 'not').

himself place you in this hand of mine. So why do I not pluck the grape that is ripe and brimming with juice? Why do I not harvest the corn that is bowed down to the ground?" [2] And I tried more passionate actions,[203] and put all of myself into the attempt, squeezing, kissing, embracing, holding her hand more ardently, and doing everything else that arouses passion. But I could not persuade Hysmine. "You will not persuade me, even if you win me over," she said, "for I will not steal the marriage that Zeus has bestowed on me."[204]

[**5**.1] We fought this battle of the passions, yet we sported in earnest. Kratisthenes appeared at the door, saying, "Hysminias." I said to the girl, "Here is Kratisthenes," for I had my ears alert for Kratisthenes' voice and, while my eyes and hands were busy with the maiden, my attention was on him. [2] With shame and delight I jumped off the couch with the girl and we made for the door, saying to Kratisthenes, "Welcome." He said, "This is not the time for sitting still;[205] we must make for the harbour, embark on the ship and leave Eurykomis."

[**6**.1] He said this and started off down the road, while we followed. When we got to the harbour, we raised all our hands to the brilliant heaven itself and said, "Father Zeus, we set off on this journey in accordance with you and your riddles. [2] Your son Eros lays siege to us and takes us as booty from our homeland. You, O Poseidon, blow from behind and not from in front; do not oppose Zeus' fair wind and Eros' Zephyr which would bring us safely to port."

[**7**.1] Having said this and embarked on the ship, we set sail with a fair wind. At first Poseidon was pleasant and sent winds entirely from the stern, billowing out the sail and giving the ship wings and conveying us along delightfully. [2] I had the ship for a couch and the girl's knees as a pillow, and reclining thus I slept sweetly as never before, by Eros. The maiden set her mouth on my eyes and my lips and kissed me noiselessly; and the ship was for us a bridal chamber and couch and pillow and living-quarters.[206] [3] Eros has entered her soul to such an extent and so wholly enslaved her that he induces her to ignore all else and to accommodate herself entirely to him.[207]

203 Cf. the scene at *H&H* 5.16.4–17.4.

204 'You [...] over': cf. Aristophanes, *Ploutos* 600. The reference to 'marriage-stealing' reflects a twelfth-century social preoccupation, which runs through the Komnenian novels (cf. *H&H* 11.6.1; *R&D* 2.400–54 with note 78; *DigAk* G 4.725; and discussion in Laiou 1993 and Introduction, p. 175, and also pp. 60, 229 and 263).

205 'This [...] still': cf. Sophocles, *Ajax* 811.

206 Cf. *L&K* 5.16.3 for similar phrases used in a seduction scene on board ship.

207 Although this may sound like a successful seduction, it is not.

[**8**.1][208] This is what went on at night, but when the sun appeared above the earth and night was nowhere to be found, then Poseidon blows from in front and gusts entirely against our prow [2] and strives to sink the entire ship beneath the waves and submerge it in the deep with its crew, its cargo, its hives of Eros which, full of the honey of passion, were containing the fair Hysmine and me, Hysminias, even if Poseidon was striving to replace the honey with wormwood. [3] But oh, that storm and the double shipwreck![209] The ship was tossed by the opposing winds and battered by the waves, and we all – even before we had descended into the deep – had breathed out our souls into the waves and abandoned them.[210]

[**9**.1] My maiden hung herself entirely around my neck and raised another even more painful and more violent storm for me, with seas of tears pouring out from her eyes[211] and buffeting me completely with her tongue and her embraces and her tears, saying, "Hysminias, save your Hysmine. [2] A dreadful gale is tearing me from your hands; a relentless gale is extinguishing me, the torch of your passion; a great wave from the sea strives to swamp the fire of passion. [3] Neither father, nor mother, nor homeland, nor the comforts of home have been able to deprive me of your support, and now the gale and the waves are tearing me from your hands. Eros put us in servitude to each other and Zeus hinted at the abduction through the sacrifices, but fierce and savage Poseidon raises up mountains of waves and opposes Zeus' riddle and expunges every agreement of passionate servitude with his waves.

[4] I have fled from my father, but I have not fled from shipwreck. I have escaped from my mother, but you, Poseidon, I have not escaped. But, O mother, now your tears are most appropriate. A virgin, I was snatched from your hands, a virgin I descend to Hades. [5] This is what the eagle was hinting to you. The ship is my bridal chamber, the waves my tomb,[212] the howling of the wind my marriage song, and I, the virgin, am the bride. [6] But oh, the strange bridal chamber, the bitter marriage, our miserable flight! Fleeing the smoke, we have fallen into the fire[213] and, overwhelmed by fire,

---

208 For an analysis of this scene, see Nilsson 2001: 215–19

209 Retaining the reading of the manuscripts with Marcovich ('that pitiable storm and bitter shipwreck', Hilberg 1876 and Conca 1994).

210 For a comparable storm, cf. *L&K* 3.2.5.

211 'seas [...] eyes': cf. Basilakes' lament (Pignani 1983: 251.354).

212 'tomb': following Conca 1994 and the manuscripts, rather than Marcovich's emendation to 'marriage',

213 'Fleeing smoke [...] fire': a proverbial expression (e.g. Plato, *Republic* 8, 569 B); cf. *H&H* 8.13.3, 11.15.2.

we will be extinguished in the sea. Oh, fate that relentlessly and savagely blows against us, and kills us with both fire and water!"

[**10**.1] The girl said this, and her eyes were in competition with the waves of the sea, and her tongue with the yet more violent din from the gale, and she quite overwhelmed my soul even before the storm and the deeps of the sea had done so. [2] I said to her, "Maiden Hysmine – for this is the appellation the divinity has bestowed on you – our flight, and everything else that we have planned in vain, is useless. [3] Eros has truly deceived me, and the dreams which he invented for me I see now are truly dreams and are clearly the products of sleep.[214] For the cauldrons of fire which he kindled in the midst of my heart the waves of the sea now strive to extinguish.

[4] But even if I spew forth the entire sea,[215] I shall not extinguish the flame which Eros lit in my soul with Hysmine as its kindling. But I shall embrace you, maiden, and I shall wear a marriage crown with you in the waves, erecting a watery bridal chamber for you. [5] Perhaps Poseidon will take pity on our embrace. Truly this ship is the funerary vessel that conveys us to Hades, truly it is Aphrodite's bridal bower and Persephone's marriage chamber,[216] truly it is the Siren of myth."

[**11**.1] The girl said to me, "My mother's curse raises this tempest against me; my mother's hands lifted up to heaven thrust us down to the deep and overwhelm us completely. [2] Oh, the maternal tongue that drowns us! Oh, her hands that stir up all these seas! Oh, the fever of her soul that seeks to chill ours entirely![217] Already, in the words of the poet, we taste chill Hades.[218] [3] But, O mother, check your tongue, so that Poseidon can check the waves; restrain your hands, so that we can be freed from the waves; spare our souls; stem your tears, so that you can lead us from the squall, from the waves, from the swell and the tempest."

[4] And she said to me, "See, my pact with you reaches its end. I shall die with you, that is my comfort; life is thus undesirable[219] and death is not

214 'dreams': distinctions were drawn between 'waking visions' and visions produced in sleep; for a discussion of Byzantine attitudes to dreams, and the twelfth-century interest in them, see MacAlister 1996: 4–6 and passim; Mavroudi 2002.

215 'spew [...] sea': cf. Basilakes' lament (Pignani 1983: 251.354).

216 'Aphrodite's bridal bower': cf. *L&K* 5.16.4. 'Persephone's marriage chamber': Persephone, daughter, in the Homeric *Hymn to Demeter*, of Demeter, was abducted by Hades, Lord of the Underworld, and compelled to spend part of each year in the underworld.

217 'fever of her soul': The concept of a 'boiling' soul appears in Plato, *Cratylos* 419 E, though with an etymological purpose (Plepelits 1989: 188, n. 91).

218 'chill Hades': Hesiod, *Works and Days* 153; *H&H* 4.2.3.

219 'undesirable': following Dawe 2001: 304 in emending πόθητον ('desirable') to ἀπόθητον.

unpleasing. [5] Thus we share death before death and we convey our souls to Hades, we breathe out our virgin souls, free through their virtue but enslaved by love, vessels full of passion."

[**12**.1] The helmsman said, "Fellow crewmen, men who share in the tempest and imminent death, the gale is fierce, the waves are incessant and reaching up to the clouds. The sail is in shreds, the hull is full of seawater, no longer do I have the strength to withstand such a weight of water, such a violent storm and such contrary winds. [2] I have had enough of battles with the sea. Poseidon is utterly opposed to us. Why do we not follow nautical custom – which is to draw lots – and pour out supplicatory libations and draw lots for a sacrificial victim?"[220]

[3] This is what the helmsman said with tears in his voice, and we were in favour of casting lots, mending a bad situation with a worse. And the fatal lot fell on Hysmine, so here was a fresh fire and an impromptu priest and altar; [4] the sea was the fire, the waves the altar, and the priest the good helmsman who respected nautical custom, the victim (be not shattered, my heart) the maiden Hysmine whom I, the utterly wretched, embraced and clasped and sent to the ship's hold.

[**13**.1] Kratisthenes begged the crew, saying, "Spare the maiden's beauty and youth." But indeed, as the tragedian says, "Sailors' license is mightier than fire"[221] and Kratisthenes too all but went into the waves, and Hysmine was torn from my hands.

[2] The helmsman, making sage comments on others' misfortunes, pronounced, "Chryseis too was torn from the hands of emperor Agamemnon, but the wrath of Apollo was assuaged and the expedition was released from plague;[222] so now let us sacrifice this girl to our god and sink her completely beneath the waves, and let us save our souls from the storm."

[**14**.1] The magniloquent helmsman made his oration from his lofty perch, but the maiden was not torn from my hands, with me intoning "With my shield or on it," like the Spartan mother.[223] The ship was full of strife and a multiform storm. [2] The sea's swell strove to send the ship to the depths and abyss of the sea, the crew were hauling the girl from the ship's hold and

220 Following the word order of Conca 1994.
221 'Sailors' […] fire': cf. Euripides, *Hecuba* 607–08.
222 'Chryseis': a reference to the opening scenes of the *Iliad*, when Agamemnon had retained Chryseis, the daughter of the priest of Apollo, thus goading Apollo into unleashing a plague on the expeditionary force.
223 'With […] it': cf. Basilakes' lament (Pignani 1983: 248.283) and Plutarch, *Lacaenarum Apophthegmata* 241 F (Nachstädt 1935: 222); for this expression, which became proverbial, cf. Suda H 616; Apostolios 8.71 (Leutsch and Schneidewin 1839–51, vol. 2).

these hands of mine; my hands followed the girl like Abradates' daughter[224] and I was being hauled along by those doing the hauling. I begged them to throw me into the deep too and to sacrifice me also to the waves.

[3] But they in their mercy listened to me, or rather, they had mercy on me by not listening. The all-wise helmsman made another pronouncement and another oration, saying, "Poseidon requires the girl; the lot has fallen on her; she is the offering and the atonement for our souls; let her be seized from that youth's hands, let her be torn from his arms, let her be given to the deep and the waves."

[**15**.1] So the maiden is torn from my hands, stripped of her tunic and thrust naked into the helmsman's hands. He, the all-wise, helmsman and priest and unaccustomed sacrificer, took the girl and, turning all eyes to the waves, [2] said, "This, lord Poseidon, is your offering and atonement" (my soul, may you never let such words escape the barrier of my teeth).[225] He hurled the girl from the ship and let her go completely into the waves. I let the whole of my voice and my soul go with the girl, and I strove to sink the entire ship with my tears, saying, "Hysmine, Hysmine."

[**16**.1] But she, as if she had drunk down the whole tempest and then spewed out the entire sea and, like some ebbing tide, had gulped down all the winds, she brought calm to the sea and tranquillity after the swell and the storm. But she churned up my entire soul in fear and confusion. While the crew with their helmsman plucked the sweet spring-time and drank the cup of delight after the intense bitterness of the swell and storm and tempest, [2] I consumed an astringent draught and an entire sea of wormwood, and poured it all out from my mouth and my eyes, and was about to submerge the entire ship and raise another squall and a second tempest. The helmsman could not endure this but, thinking that the lamentation was not a good omen, he brings the ship into land and off-loaded me on to land.

[**17**.1] I sat on the sand by the sea and declaimed laments for my entire sequence of misfortunes, pouring funerary libations for the girl,[226] saying, "Hysmine, Hysmine, light which has vanished from my eyes, bird which has flown from my hands (O bitter shipwreck and pitiful storm, O calm more bitter than a storm); you have been taken away by the heaving swell of the storm, you have submerged my soul, overwhelming it with whole seas of

---

224 'hands […] daughter': cf. Basilakes' lament (Pignani 1983: 250.340), referring to the episode in Xenophon, *Cyropaedia* 7.3.8.

225 'barrier of my teeth': a Homeric cliché; cf. *Iliad* 4.350, 9.409 etc.

226 Hysminias' lament can be compared with that of Dosikles for Rhodanthe at *R&D* 6.264–415. 'funerary libations': i.e. his tears.

lamentations. [2] You have breathed out your virgin soul,[227] all crowned with waves, laments and grief and tears have crowned my head and soul pitiably. The sea is both your marriage chamber and your grave, and I am that chamber's attendant. [3] But I shall not sing a marriage ode for you,[228] I shall not strike up the wedding march but, here on the sand, as if at a cenotaph, I shall contrive for you bitter funeral odes, and summoning the entire choir of Nereids I shall declaim my entire misfortune. [4] O wave from the sea that embitters all my senses, O tempest that submerged the entire wedding chamber and the bride in the waves, O my misfortunes, O fortune that constantly opposes us, O that quiver which Eros emptied into my heart! [5] Alas the fire of passion, from which Eros lit entire cauldrons in my soul!

But, O emperor Eros, most powerful of all the gods, who lords it over souls, who sends out arrows, who entraps souls with eyes, who enflames the innermost being and burns up entire hearts; O emperor of dreams, if not emperor of all then of falsehoods alone, the bold Poseidon condemns you. [6] I saw you under arms and I was wounded with your darts; you were carrying fire and my entire soul was enflamed; you were winged and I could not escape your wings. [7] But now it is time for you to use the nakedness of your body against Amphitrite herself and Poseidon too;[229] they have ravaged the pledge which you bestowed on me, emperor – your Hysmine whom you bestowed on my right hand; they have pillaged my treasure. [8] But lay aside your fire and bow and wings; but if you do not want to do that, gird them on and plunge into the deep and bring back to me Hysmine, the Hysmine whose name alone sets my innermost being on fire and burns up my entire soul.

[9] But oh, the delights in those dreams, the kisses, the embraces, the claspings and all the rest of our passion! Curses on the dreams with which I am entrapped! They are all dreams and sleeping visions, truly a mockery. O Zeus, the most true of the gods, indeed that most ill-omened bird of yours hinted clearly at my whole future; for look, the maiden Hysmine has been torn forcibly from these pitiable hands of mine.

[10] But, girl, I have been false to our contract; I swore to you by the gods themselves to die with you and to share with you in your doom. Now darkness covers you and the wave has pitifully poured over you while I see the light and sit beside the waves. [11] You are in Hades, I am on earth. Your

---

227 'breathed [...] soul': cf. *H&H* 5.6.3.
228 'not sing [...] you': cf. *H&H* 6.10.6.
229 'nakedness [...] Poseidon': cf. *H&H* 2.11.3, and 2.9.3 with note.

mouth, that hive of honey, has grown dumb[230] while my mouth, stretched with pain, sings for you the ode of farewell and swells with anguish as if pierced by your bee's sting. Perhaps you might accuse me of forgetfulness, but I have your memory within me like another soul, I will breathe out that soul together with mine, or rather let us go down together to Hades and to the bowl of forgetfulness itself, lamenting bitterly, pitiably and ineffaceably."

These were my cries, and tears poured from my eyes and flowed like a sea and billowed incessantly and quite overwhelmed me.

[**18**.1] In the midst of this sleep creeps up and falls on my eyes and takes me completely to itself, and once again Eros stands before me in the night as I sleep. [2] And it was truly that Eros who was painted in Aulikomis, and he said to me, "Greetings, Hysminias." And I said, "But I fare badly;[231] for the pledge which you put into these hands of mine, your Hysmine and my maiden, that bold Poseidon has savagely seized from these pitiable hands of mine, stirring up the whole sea, arousing a whole tempest.

[3] But, emperor Eros, I saw all Amphitrite's race[232] enrolled as your slaves and trembling before your nakedness. O emperor, bring back from the deep and the sea Hysmine, the maiden so fair, so lovely, breathing such love, and enslaved to you and enslaving me her lover. [4] Wounded by your darts, emperor, we became migrants from our homeland; with our innermost being aflame from your fire, emperor, we have spent entire nights sleepless.[233] Emboldened by your might, emperor, we embarked on the sea, we ventured across the ocean. [5] But oh, your domination, or rather my misfortune! Poseidon raises up an entire tempest, he empties out all his anger over the sea, he strives to sink the ship completely beneath the waves, and Hysmine – spare her, emperor Eros – alas, with his ever-bold hand he snatches from these my miserable hands. But, Eros, ruler of all things, – "

[**19**.1] He took wing with his feet and darting to the middle of the ocean plunges into the waves and sinks down to the deep and not long after appears before me again, holding Hysmine in his hands, rather damp from the sea and washed by the Graces, and places her in my hands. But I, just as I took hold of Hysmine, in my delight I woke up from my dream. And all this, once again, was but a dream enslaved to Eros.

---

230 'Your mouth [...] dumb': cf. Basilakes' lament (Pignani 1983: 246.241).
231 'I fare badly': cf. Euripides, *Phoenissae* 618.
232 'Amphitrite's race': i.e. fishes; cf. *H&H* 2.8.2.
233 'entire nights sleepless': cf. *Iliad* 9.325, *Odyssey* 19.340.

BOOK EIGHT

[**1.**1] So I rose from sleep with pleasure and delight, and with all my eyes
I sought to find Hysmine, but she was nowhere to be seen. But I see a host
on the seashore, an incalculable host of Ethiopians, savage men, and when I
saw them – oh, the bitter sea of my misfortunes! – I stood bolt upright and
wished I was dreaming. But it was no dream, [2] for they see me and grab
hold of my hair and drag me off savagely, like some hunting trophy, to their
trireme (for it was propped up above the ground with planks and cables).
Taking me to the trireme's hold, they sit me by an oar.

[3] When they push off from land, having drawn in all the cables, they
spread wings on the ship[234] with all those oars in which triremes pride
themselves. On coming to a calm and very lovely harbour, they moor the
trireme and, after partaking in a little food and drink (for they had brought
bread and water with them), they turned to sleep, setting guards who never
slept at both the prow and the stern.

[**2.**1] About the third watch of the night they rise from sleep and again
spread wings on the ship with oars and put out from the harbour. They came
to a small fort and tied the ship up silently; then taking shields in their left
hands and grasping swords firmly in the other and equipping all the rest of
their bodies with arms, they swarmed around the fortress like bees round a
honeycomb.

[2] Generating a barbaric and disorganized hubbub, they made their
murderous attack – armed men falling on unarmed, the alert on the sleeping,
making a savage onslaught like wild beasts, totally tearing the fortress apart;
they looted everything they chanced upon, including women, maidens,
youths, men – everyone whom the barbarians' dagger did not sent to Hades.
[3] Collecting up all their loot on the trireme, the pirates themselves went
on board and left the harbour far behind.

[**3.**1] When they reached the open sea and had the entire ship braced
with cables like a foundation, they share out the spoils. All the men, all the
youths, all the maidens and women they stripped of their tunics and they
were uncovered right down to their private parts and had their whole body
naked.[235] [2] The youths and the men were received by the trireme's hold but
the barbarians' immorality and licentiousness was reserved for the women
while the maidens, by what barbarian law I do not know, were clad in a

---

234 'wings on the ship': cf. *L&K* 8.16.2; *H&H* 8.2.1, 8.8.1.
235 'whole body naked': on Byzantine attitudes to nudity, see *ODB*, under 'Nude, the'.

tattered tunic and no presumptuous hand was laid on them nor was anything barbaric or shameful done to them.

[**4**.1] While these shameful things were happening to the women, the barbarians marshalled themselves chaotically and prepared for dinner. Their banquet was luxurious and not barbaric and quite without seemliness as it had been a short while before. [2] The trireme's hold, as has been said, was reserved for the men, while the area around the prow was kept for the maidens, but the women sat shamefully at the meal with the barbarians.

[3] After the luxurious food, as has been mentioned, and the shameful banquet full of blood, they set the youths (there were few of them) to the oars; those who were somewhat older (woe to the barbarians' pitiless souls) became fodder for the sword, and their heads were hurled mercilessly into the sea. The women lay shamefully with the barbarians, and the trireme became a brothel full of turpitude and a symposium of blood.

[**5**.1] This is what went on at night. When night had vanished (for the sun was over the land) and the longed-for light smiled down on us and brought the day, the barbarians emerged as if from a bridal chamber and were quite intoxicated with their pleasures, making a hideous noise with their barbarian speech as if quarrelling. [2] After a tremendous hubbub of the sort that sailors, and especially barbarian sailors, raise, an alien and unintelligible song saw the trireme adorned with a white sail and the wind that blew from the stern billowed out the sail and the trireme bucked like a horse let loose on the plain.[236]

[**6**.1] To pass over what happened in the meantime, all the barbarians' misdemeanours, all their disgraceful behaviour towards the women and everything else that went on in a barbaric and indecent fashion, we reached Artykomis with a favourable breeze and we see a crowd from Artykomis on the shore. [2] And after many negotiations of the sort that barbarians conduct and which pirates exchange in barbarian manner with those on land, the trireme took hostages on board while the land received the trireme's cargo, which the pirates had looted from the fortress. And there was an impromptu celebration on the seashore. [3] Everything made of silver, gold, bronze and iron and all clothing and anything else that a barbarian band takes as loot, was unloaded from the trireme and all made available for sale. But the loot that consisted of us human beings was not unloaded on to dry land but was put up for sale on board the trireme itself.[237]

236 'bucked [...] plain': cf. Basilakes' lament (Pignani 1983: 249.317); *Iliad* 6.506–07.

237 'loot [...] human beings': on trading in captives, with reference to an earlier period, see McCormick 2001: 244–54.

[**7**.1] Concerning the women and us young men who were captives there was little discussion among the inhabitants of Artykomis – or rather, none; their entire attention was devoted to the acquisition of the maidens. These were much prized by the barbarians and purchased by many of those in Artykomis, following [the test from][238] the bow and spring of Artemis,[239] which Artykomis considers is the Celtic river Rhine.

[2] For there is in Artykomis a famous temple of Artemis; in the middle of this is a golden statue of Artemis aiming a bow with her hands and with a spring bubbling up at her feet and flowing like a raging and turbulent river.[240] [3] On seeing the springs you would say that they are boiling. These – the bow and the spring – test virginity and its loss. If anyone is in two minds about a virgin and wants to test her, they garland the maiden with a laurel wreath and put her in the spring. [4] If the girl who goes into the spring has not lied about her virginity and has not been robbed of her chastity, Artemis does not aim her bow, the water grows calm and the maiden floats comfortably on the water, her head adorned with the garland of laurel. [5] But if a gale from Aphrodite has extinguished the lamp of her maidenhood and Eros has surreptitiously stolen her virginity, Artemis – the maiden goddess – aims her bow against her who is no maiden, who has deceived her, and seems to shoot at her head; the girl shudders at the weapon, dips her head beneath the water and the foaming water takes away her garland.[241]

[6] So all the maidens who had been collected by the barbarians were given laurel wreaths and deposited in the spring. All who did not dip their heads and who did not lose their garlands were sold for a high price; all whose claim of virginity was false were allotted to the trireme and classed with the women, receiving bronze in the place of gold, and a barbarian bridal chamber in place of the virgin's laurel wreath.

[**8**.1] Thus affairs stood at Artykomis, and thus the loot was unloaded from the trireme. Once again the trireme put its accustomed wings in motion[242]

---

238 'the test from': not in the Greek. This is a textually problematic passage (cf. Nilsson 2001a: n. 19); the translation here follows Conca 1994.

239 'bow and spring of Artemis': a mix of mythological motifs involving the river Alpheios which submerges to reappear at Syracuse and a proverbial use of the Rhine as a test for healthy children (Julian, *Ep.* 191 [Bidez 1924]; Apostolios 13.1 [Leutsch and Schneidewin 1839–51, vol. 2]); see Plepelits 1989: 189–90, n. 103. The virginity test parallels Leukippe's ordeal in the Styx in *L&K* 8.12–14; cf. *H&H* 11.17–18.

240 'turbulent river': cf. Basilakes' lament 236 (Pignani 1983: 27–28).

241 The test is arguably a variant on the trial by ordeal (by fire) in *R&D* 1.374–83 (cf. Cupane 1973–74).

242 'wings': i.e. oars; cf. *H&H* 7.7.1, 8.1.3, 8.3.1.

and the barbarian fleet made for another city while we were dragged along, once free men but now the barbarians' slaves. [2] On the third day we put in to another harbour, and when we had hauled the trireme up on to the beach and made it entirely fast with cables, the whole barbarian force poured out and gathered on the shore. They dragged the women out with them and sent up a complete camp by the waves and prepared a lavish banquet. [3] After much eating and drinking and barbarian jests and all the other disgraceful and barbarian activities to which they subjected the women, the barbarians disposed themselves for sleep with the women, immersing their souls completely in pleasure and entirely intoxicated with their passions.

[**9**.1] Thus matters were with the barbarians. We in the ship's hold, emboldened by the barbarians' drunkenness, let ourselves out and were tormented by a thousand considerations, whether we should disembark from the trireme on to the shore or should escape the barbarians' clutches in the trireme itself, or arm ourselves in Hellenic fashion with the many weapons in the trireme and set on the barbarians and either be victorious or fall as we fought.[243]

[2] While we debate this, armed warriors attack the barbarians on land as they all sleep, all debauched with wine and lust; and while the barbarian band was plundered of all its booty,[244] we exchanged servitude to Hellenes[245] for servitude to barbarians and having been slaves became slaves once again, becoming our barbarian masters' fellow slaves, and while in servitude with our former masters were enslaved to Hellenes who spoke our language. [3] And in the middle of the market and city of Daphnepolis, the city sacred to Apollo, the general and his army chant the victory odes over us, and the city applauds and resounds with jubilation. All of us – the booty, the spoils – are dragged pitiably to the shrine of Apollo, which is the wonder of Daphnepolis.

[**10**.1] Immediately everyone gathered by the altar. I clasped the god's feet and, making them completely awash with my tears, said, "Apollo, put an end to this tempest, let a kindly wind blow on my misfortunes. I came from Eurykomis to Aulikomis as herald of Zeus, your father, my wretched

---

243 'either […] fought': cf. Basilakes' lament (Pignani 1983: 247.267); Plutarch, *Lacaenarum Apophthegmata* 231 E (Nachstädt 1935: 186).

244 'barbarian […] booty': translating with Conca 1994 rather than Marcovich 2001 ('the barbarian band as plundered by another army').

245 'servitude to Hellenes': cf. *H&H* 9.10.3; while there is a consciousness of a Hellenic identity that is both linguistic and cultural, the tension between barbarian/Greek, slave/free seems equally important; on evolving twelfth-century attitudes, see Magdalino 1991; Beaton 2007; and Introduction, p. 173 and also pp. 16–17 (on *R&D*).

head crowned with your laurel. But Eros, your brother, crowned me instead with roses. [2] He robbed me of my virginity, or rather transformed it with erotic experiences, setting the maiden Hysmine in these wretched hands of mine, from which and from my very soul Poseidon has torn her, blowing with full blast and a raging sea and tempest.

[3] Bring this tempest to an end and set Hysmine in my hands, or lead me straight to Hysmine herself. I have become a slave instead of a free man, a slave three times over instead of a herald,[246] enslaved first to Eros, then secondly to the barbarians and now for the third time to these Hellenes in your city of Daphnepolis."

[11.1] These were my words, and I was dragged off with the prisoners to the laurel and the tripod,[247] and the oracle and the lot once again made me a slave, and once again I was a slave, and in triple servitude, and I am taken off to the master's house on which the oracle and the lot had bestowed my servitude. [2] My mistress said to me, "Who are you? Where are you from? What is your country and who are your parents?"[248] But I replied, "Mistress, I am your slave; when you ask to know more you are asking for a whole play, a complete tragedy. I am the exemplification of Fate, a ghost from the underworld, the plaything of the gods, the Erinnyes' banquet."[249]

[3] So saying, I fixed my eyes on the ground which I bedewed completely with my tears. She responded, "Tell me all, hold nothing back." [4] My voice failed me, my tongue was stuck,[250] and tears flowed in rivers from my eyes. My master (for he was present too) said, "It is the time for a meal; let us take our places for dinner and at the table, and in the midst of eating let us give some time to our slave's story."

[12.1] So the table was set up and the masters sat while I stood in attendance in servile fashion. Once again the mistress said to me, "Look, now is the time for you to picture your circumstances for us in words." [2] I, at the mere recollection, let out a piteous groan from my heart, and shed many tears from my eyes,[251] saying, "Be sparing with my misfortunes, masters, lest I make the banquet a misery and pour out for you bowls

---

246 'a slave three times over': on the motif of triple servitude, see Nilsson 2001: 117–22. On Byzantium's attitudes to slavery, see Kazhdan 1985; Rotman 2004.

247 'tripod': traditionally the seat of the oracle, especially that of Apollo in Delphi.

248 'Who [...] parents?': a Homeric formula; cf. *Odyssey* 1.170, 10.325, 14.187; 15.264, 19.105, 24.298.

249 'ghost [...] gods': cf. Basilakes' lament (Pignani 1983: 237.57–58). 'Erinnyes' banquet': cf. Basilakes' lament (Pignani 1983: 236.20); *L&K* 5.5.8.

250 'My voice [...] stuck': cf. Basilakes' lament (Pignani 1983: 235.2); *H&H* 11.2.2.

251 'mere recollection [...] tears': cf. Basilakes' lament (Pignani 1983: 236.25–27).

of grief."[252] But my words did not persuade them and, having failed in my persuasion, I said, "Alas, what an evil thing it is to be a slave, to be compelled by force to endure what should not be demanded.[253]

[**13**.1] My home city is Eurykomis, my father Themisteus and my mother Dianteia; whether they are prosperous, whether they hold first rank among the inhabitants of Eurykomis, is not for me to say. It was the time of the Diasia in the city, and the Diasia are celebrated brilliantly. I was garlanded with laurel, robed in a tunic, with the sacred boots, and entirely clad with the herald's accoutrements I came as herald to Aulikomis. [2] And Eros robbed me of my garland, using as his lure the very beautiful maiden Hysmine, daughter of Sosthenes, the most prominent of the inhabitants of Aulikomis. It was as a slave of Aphrodite that I returned to my city of Eurykomis, in the company of the maiden and her father.

[3] What happened next? Sosthenes, Hysmine's father, in the middle of a banquet and an extravagant feast, announces his daughter's marriage to another. We flee from this light-heartedly, but are bitterly entrapped, leaping from the smoke into the flame[254] and from mist into the sea. There was a ship aiding us in our flight, which Poseidon opposes, and he seeks a victim. We cast lots for the victim and the lot fell on Hysmine. [4] She is torn pitiably from my hands and cast into the waves, and the crew escapes from the tempest but leaves me in the midst of a sea and storm of grief and lamentation. The crew cannot bear this and fling me out of the ship on to land, and this barbarian horde, now my fellow captives, takes me captive; and then I was once again made captive at your hands, a former slave now a slave again, three times[255] a slave instead of a herald."

[**14**.1] These were my words and I dissolved into tears; My mistress said to me, "Your affairs are a play in themselves, a complete tragedy; but you are fortunate in that you have us for your masters." [2] I replied, "That I have masters at all is my misfortune." And I said to my mistress,

"Whoever is not accustomed to taste evil
endures it, but suffers pain when the yoke is placed on his neck."[256]

---

252 'Be sparing […] grief': similar sentiments and some shared vocabulary in *R&D* 2.160–65; for the last phrase, cf. Basilakes' lament (Pignani 1983: 235.10).

253 'Alas […] demanded': Euripides, *Hecuba* 332–33; Conca points out that this reading, rejected by modern editors, comes from the MAVL branch of the Euripidean manuscript tradition.

254 'from the smoke into the flame': a proverb used previously at *H&H* 7.10.3.

255 'three times a slave': i.e. once to Eros and captured twice.

256 'Whoever […] neck': Euripides, *Hecuba* 375–76.

[3] And my master said, "If your country is illustrious and your lineage brilliant and your home luxurious, now you have none of those things: [4] you are a slave, and you are our slave. If you exchanged chastity and virginity for Aphrodite and Eros, the virgins' garland of laurel for the rose garland of passion, have nothing more to do with this, but cultivate chastity and love sobriety[257] lest you learn chastity the hard way and find the master's hand a teacher."

[15.1] This from my master. I remained silent and kept my eyes on the ground, all full of tears. Thus the meal came to an end and I, Hysminias, the herald of the Diasia, who had been garlanded with laurel, who had formerly sailed sumptuously from Eurykomis, [2] who had ridden in imperial splendour in a chariot to Aulikomis, who had sat in luxury at Sosthenes' brilliant banquet, now sat at a slaves' table with my band of fellow slaves, and perform a slave's tasks, and am completely a slave, taking on a servile demeanour and functioning as a slave, quite stripped, O Zeus and the gods, of my herald's rank and that of a free man.

[3] This is how my affairs stood and how I carried out my servitude, but not even in the midst of these terrible circumstances did I allow myself to forget Hysmine, my maiden, no, by the awesome Eros, the source of these misfortunes.

[16.1] The time for the Diasia arrived, and even if Daphnepolis does not honour the Diasia and does not hold a festival, it did not escape my attention but kindled my memory and aroused my grief. But my Fate begrudged me even this. [2] I mourned, but it was a surreptitious mourning; I wept, and I concealed my eyes from my masters. I repressed my soul, my voice, my tongue and my tears. The herald who had become a slave held piteous discourse, I held up to my mind Eurykomis, Aulikomis, the herald's wand, Sosthenes' garden, the well within the garden, [3] the birds on it, the golden eagle, Hysmine pouring out the wine, teasing me with passion, playing with my feet, playing with the cups and everything else that we did in our sport (alas for those passionate delights in my dreams); and above all else I whispered softly, "Hysmine, my beloved."

[4] In the middle of all this my mistress suddenly appeared and said, "Why are you so drenched with tears? Look, who is beside you; you have me as your Hysmine, your mistress and your slave in passion." I made no reply but immediately jumped up and respected my love for Hysmine alone, and imagined only her.

---

257 'chastity [...] sobriety': cf. Basilakes' lament (Pignani 1983: 244.209–10).

[**17**.1] How much my mistress sported with me passionately and sat beside me incessantly, and how much she slandered me to my master, and how much she threatened me with her hand and tongue[258] and head, it would not be for me to say in words lest Eros should, unbeknownst to me, corrupt my soul, or even my tongue, which I was keeping for the maiden Hysmine to be full of the passionate graces and the honey of Aphrodite which we devoured insatiably with our tongues alone.

[**18**.1] It was the time of the festival and there was a brilliant celebration in the city of Daphnepolis,[259] and the subject of the festival was the flight of the maiden Daphne and the creation of the plant of the same name.[260] The festival and celebration was all in honour of Apollo. Daphne was a maiden, and a beautiful one; [2] Apollo falls in love with her but the maiden shudders at the god's embrace and refuses his love and seeks help from the Earth. Earth has pity on the girl and conceals her in her flight; she watches over the maiden and transforms her into the plant that bears her name. [3] Apollo makes a garland from the plant and consoles himself for his passion. So close by the plant is an altar, and a city with the same name, the altar is to Apollo and the city is called Daphnepolis.

[**19**.1] So much for that. There was a celebration in Daphnepolis, and heralds in garlands took up the herald's wand according to the oracle. Apollo gives the oracles and pronounced my master herald, a brilliant herald to go to Artykomis. He is garlanded with laurel and given a brilliant escort through the market-place and taken in triumph through the theatre. [2] There was a crowd around the herald and a brilliant and varied procession and everything else that the office of herald had brought to me. I recalled all this in the midst of the brilliant spectacle and the brilliant rite that was full of grace and pleasure, and I was overwhelmed with lamentation and grief and my whole soul was riven by the memory as if transfixed by a thunderbolt.

[3] So, accompanied by such a brilliant, extravagant and honourable escort, the herald, my master, was brought to the house, crowned with laurel, adorned with a brilliant tunic and the sacred sandal. [4] Then, after that brilliant procession which I once (alas for Fate) had led to Eurykomis, the herald, his head garlanded with laurel and a herald from top to toe, sat at a brilliant table with my mistress.

258 'and tongue': retaining this twice with Conca 1994, against Marcovich 2001.

259 'Daphnepolis': perhaps a gloss (Dawe 2001: 304).

260 'Daphne': this myth is used at *L&K* 1.5.5. As noted in the Introduction (p. 171) the issue of 'the same name' is an undercurrent to the novel where hero and heroine also share the same name.

[**20**.1] In the middle of the banquet my mistress said, "Herald, Apollo has garlanded this head of yours, which belongs to me; he sends you as his herald to Artykomis, the herald for Apollo's brilliant festival: may all go well for you on the journey. [2] This slave of ours, whom your spear and noble hand acquired, let him not go with you to Artykomis. For he seems to me to be intelligent and sensible in speech, but he is always frowning and endlessly lamenting and beating his breast. I am afraid that he take some impetuous action against you, since a slave is always hostile to his masters."

[3] My master said, "But, according to the tragedy,
'Their masters' misfortunes afflict
good slaves deeply'."[261]
She responded, "But the tragedy said, 'Good slaves' and this one has a tall tale about having been a herald, and boasts about his family and country, and goes on endlessly about all sorts of other marvels."

[**21**.1] My master said to me, "If you were a herald, as you claimed, was your head garlanded like mine?" I replied, "My master the herald, spare my tongue if it says anything hasty or improper. [2] Truly my feet were adorned and I wore a tunic down to my feet even more splendid than this since I was the herald of Zeus, father of men and gods.[262] Pardon me, master."

[3] My master said to my mistress, "Perhaps he was once a herald and a free man, even if the hand of the barbarian has reduced him to slavery –
'Fate, and not wise counsel, rules men's affairs'.[263]
If he were to accompany me to Artykomis, perhaps he would not be without use to me when I am herald." [4] With these words he left the table and went to perform the rites. Once again the city was astir and once again there was a brilliant procession and once again a celebration and chanting and everything that brings honour to heralds.

BOOK NINE

[**1**.1] So we were conveyed with great brilliance to Artykomis. The herald reached that city, and once again there was a magnificent procession and once again a crowd and a triumphal progress, thronged streets, decorations in the market-place and garlands for the maidens. In this respect Artykomis

261 'The masters' misfortunes [...] deeply': Euripides, *Medea* 54–55.
262 'father of men and gods': *Iliad* 4.68 and elsewhere.
263 'Fate [...] affairs': Chaeremon, Fr. 2.1 (Snell 1986, vol. 1: 217), a much-anthologized phrase; cf. Stobaeus, *Anthologium* 1.6.7.

is fortunate, for it honours virginity and has the altar of the virgin Artemis as its chief adornment. [2] Multitudinous cymbals entranced the hearing, decorated colonnades enchanted the eyes, rose water and all kinds of aromatic perfumes refreshed the sense of smell and a throng of brilliant orators wove the speech of welcome.

[**2**.1] So my master strode forward[264] through this brilliant procession and diverse and extravagant triumph as if Apollo himself were being greeted in triumph; he advanced as if borne above the clouds, with his eyebrows raised to heaven itself. [2] As for me, the recollection cast me down to the pits of Hades and filled my eyes with tears that spilled out into the midst of my soul. [3] The leading citizens of Artykomis sought to have the herald as their guest and each pulled and thrust to have him entirely for themselves, and there was a novel contest and a struggle over hospitality; one might say that

a contest is good for mortals.[265]

[**3**.1] Sostratos wins the struggle and takes him away in his chariot, and brings the herald to his house and cares for him most honourably, as Sosthenes cared for me, Hysminias, most extravagantly, except for the matter of Hysmine. All this struck deep into my soul and I prayed to drink the cup of forgetfulness. [2] The herald laid aside his wand of office completely and a luxurious banquet was prepared, and the maiden Rhodope, Sostratos' daughter, pours the wine, a lovely girl if you compare her with maidens in general but, in comparison with my Hysmine, she was like an ape compared to Aphrodite. There were as many varieties of delicacies on the table as Sosthenes had displayed to welcome the heralds.

[**4**.1] My right eye gave a start at all this,[266] and this was for me a good sign and a most auspicious omen. Whether the wine of Artykomis was sweet in comparison with that of Aulikomis, by the gods, I cannot say. [2] Sostratos did not have, as Sosthenes did, Hysmine to pour it for him, so loses out in this respect, and thus my time as herald had been in this way as much richer than that of my master as it was more unfortunate.

[3] After the delicacies of the table and the extravagance of the symposium and the great munificence, Rhodope mixes the festival's drinking bowl. So the herald, by fate my master, seated brilliantly at this eminently luxurious table, drank with pleasure – I think – while I, who had once been herald and too had been seated at a brilliant table, who had been welcomed with great honour by Sosthenes, and for whom the wine had been poured by

---

264 'strode forward': a Homeric phrase; cf. *Iliad* 3.22, 7.213 and elsewhere.

265 'a contest […] mortals': Hesiod, *Works and Days*, 24.

266 'my right eye gave a start': cf. Theokritos, *Idyll* 3.37.

Hysmine, the mere sight of whom is blessedness, I endure a slave's role and am entirely a servant; [4] and, if the symposium had not come to an end, I would soon have been quite undone. But the herald rose from the table and went to his chamber, and reposed comfortably on a brilliant couch like the one that Sosthenes had once prepared for me.

[**5**.1] Sostratos' daughter, just as my Hysmine had done, came to wash the herald's feet, and three serving girls followed her, to assist in her duties. [2] So Rhodope performed this service, and I, recollecting the caresses given my feet by my Hysmine's hands and lips, gave vent to a great and grievous sigh from the depths of my innermost being, and my eyes filled with tears. [3] And the servant girl who was holding in her hands the towel for the feet moaned gently, as though imitating the echoes of my sigh, and sighed delicately as Hysmine had done when I pressed her foot with mine under Sosthenes' table. I looked at her intently and, by Hysmine, I thought I was looking at Hysmine, and she gazed at me even more intently.[267]

[**6**.1] When Sostratos' daughter had washed the herald's feet and gone away and the attendants had followed her, this girl went with her, and it was as though I myself was looking at Hysmine. [2] I spent the whole night in torment from my thoughts, saying to myself, "Surely it was Hysmine? But she was torn from my hands, and before these pitiable eyes of mine she was hurled into the waves by the hands of the murderous helmsman. [3] But Zeus, but Eros have rescued the girl and now certainly Aulikomis shelters her. They would not have saved her for misery and servitude." [4] I pictured her completely in my mind and, having measured out the night in such mixed debates, I rose from my mattress without sleep having come near my eyelids.

[**7**.1] Day came, and a greater evil is added to those of the night, and misfortune comes upon me in its turn. Once again I, Hysminias, endure a slave's lot and once again am in servitude and suffer indeed a three-fold servitude. Through Eros I am slave to Hysmine, through my eyes I am a slave to my fantasies, and through Fate I am the herald's slave. [2] Once again there is a luxurious banquet, and once again the herald is seated with Sostratos, and once again Rhodope pours the wine, and once again my memory does battle with my soul and lays siege to it entirely and takes me away to Aulikomis, drags me off to Hysmine and revives for me my entire period as herald.

267 For the motif of fortuitous reunion and delayed recognition, cf. *L&K* 5.17.7; *R&D* 8.299 ff.

[**8**.1] In the middle of all this the serving girl once again attends on her mistress, and once again I see the girl, and once again think I am looking at Hysmine. She gazes at me more attentively, and her eyes fill with tears. [2] Leaving the table, I sit down by a dense laurel bush (for Sostratos had prepared the table near the garden) and, with tears filling my eyes, I let out a deep and pitiable groan, saying, "Spare me, Zeus, put an end to my long wanderings, bring calm to my violent tempests. [3] See, once again spirits are playing tricks on me, they conjure up Hysmine, they deck her out erotically, they put her in front of me, and plague my eyes and my mind."

[4] This was my speech, and a serving girl stood before me and said, "This letter is for you from the maiden Hysmine, your beloved and now my fellow slave," and putting the letter in my hand she ran off. I took it and, trembling, opened it. This is what it said:[268]

[**9**.1] "The maiden Hysmine to her lover Hysminias, greetings. Hysminias, son of Themisteus, know that a dolphin rescued your Hysmine from the sea, and that the spring and the bow of Artemis, the virgin goddess, have kept me virgin for you. [2] You must not succumb to forgetfulness either of our many passionate delights in Aulikomis, my homeland, or of those in Eurykomis, your homeland, nor should you forget that because of you I spurned my homeland and my parents and all the comforts of my home and ventured on to the sea and the waves, [3] and because of you I tasted bitter death, and finally became a captive and now a slave, as you see, but through all this I have kept my virginity inviolate. And now I shall sail with you to Daphnepolis as your fellow slave. Farewell, and keeping our vows inviolate, see that you too keep your virginity chastely intact."

[**10**.1] These were the letter's contents, but while I had faith in what was written I could not accept the facts, and while I wanted to have faith in the facts I could not accept the letter. For the letter strove to persuade me that the serving girl was Hysmine and the communication came from her, since it described all our affair, but the novelty and magnitude of the situation did not allow me to believe in the letter. [2] So I read it twice and three times and kissed it all over; I left the laurel bush and returned to the table where I gazed at the servant girl who might have been Hysmine more intently, and wondered at her; she gazed at me in return, and her eyes filled with tears.

[**11**.1] Thus the symposium came to an end. The herald, my master, with us his attendant servants, went to his chamber. Hysmine, in her role of slave, accompanied Rhodope, and so we were separated. [2] Once again a mass of

---

268 For the motif of the letter between enslaved lovers, cf. *L&K* 5.18.

thoughts divided my mind and, once again unfolding the letter, I dug up its sense and meaning like a Lakonian hound,[269] and tracked through the whole missive. [3] So the herald, my master, reclined on a brilliant couch strewn with soft covers, and – comporting himself entirely as a herald, right down to the couch itself – gave himself up to sleep. I lay down on the ground, in the manner of a slave, with my fellow slaves, but my thoughts would not permit me to sleep; the night was for me like day, as far as sleep and wakefulness were concerned.

[**12**.1] On the following day, the herald put on all his official garb and, becoming the herald completely, went to the temple of Artemis. I was left in the chamber, and seated by the door and unfolding the letter, fixed my eyes on the words and washed the whole missive with my tears.

[2] Rhodope, Sostratos' daughter, came into the garden (which was by the door where I was seated) and, seeing me drenched with tears and feeling a kind of pity, said, "What is the matter, boy?" I replied, "It is only, mistress, that I have become a slave after being a free man, and I look on the light of servitude,[270] and find it hard." [3] She wanted to know my family and country, and how I came to be a slave instead of free.

I said to her, "But tears overwhelm my speech,[271] mistress, and hinder my tongue and swamp my soul and inhibit my voice entirely. [4] If you want to observe a Fate that has led to misery, I provide the example in my own person, completely clad in misfortune and transformed into abominable circumstances, a veritable picture of ill luck."

[**13**.1] Rhodope wanted to know more about me, and almost begged me to tell her. I said to her, "My country is Eurykomis, my father Themisteus and my mother Dianteia; they are fortunate in every respect, save in having me as their son; for Eros, Fate and Poseidon have brought me from good fortune to misfortune, from being free to being a slave, and from being a herald into triple servitude.

[2] At the time of the Diasia, I was a herald, and not to any city but to Aulikomis. It would be superfluous for me to describe how the divinity made sport of me, devising brilliant processions and luxurious gatherings. [3] I come as herald to Aulikomis, and to the kindly care of Sosthenes, the leading citizen of Aulikomis. He had a virgin daughter, the nursling of the

---

269 'Lakonian hound': cf. Xenophon, *Kynegetica* 10.4–5 on the qualities of Lakonian hunting dogs.

270 'light of servitude': a Homeric tag: cf., e.g., *Iliad* 6.463, *Odyssey* 14.340 and 17.323.

271 'tears […] speech': cf. Basilakes' lament (Pignani 1983: 235.1).

Graces, Aphrodite's girdle,[272] passion's lure and Eros' ineluctable snare. [4] With this daughter of Sosthenes I fell passionately in love, though without marring our virginity. Her father announces his daughter's marriage with another, a marriage which we flee, not being able to endure even the sound of it, and which we repulse.[273] [5] A ship aids our flight and in a tempest Poseidon and the hand of the helmsman tear that lovely maiden from these wretched hands."

[**14**.1] I said this and, with my soul in distress and myself become quite speechless, I fell pitiably to the ground. Rhodope's serving girls rushed up to me and picked me up and took me off to the chamber and stretched me out on my master the herald's couch. [2] Rhodope sat down by the couch and clasped my hands, wiped away my sweat and wept, completely sharing in my misfortune, and she summoned back my soul by anointing my nostrils.[274] She placed a damp hand on my chest and stimulated the area round my heart.

[3] Finally she dismissed the attendants, except for the serving girl who looked like Hysmine, and, gathering me completely to her, she kissed me and as she kissed me her eyes filled with tears and she sighed deeply, saying, "O Fate, which transforms men's lives and alters their natures; [4] O child of Zeus, the tyrant Eros, who dominates souls, removing freedom and replacing it with servitude." Then she asked my name. But I said, "My lady, the gods have removed even this; [5] they have not spared even my name, but when they made me a slave instead of being a free man and replaced the honey of freedom with the bitterness of slavery and brought darkness in place of light, they also replaced my Hellenic name with a barbarian one, and called me Artakes instead of Hysminias. So now I am a slave entirely, both in name and in deed."

[**15**.1] This is what I said, and I saw the serving girl who looked like Hysmine weeping and quite overcome with tears. Rhodope said, "What is the matter, girl?" She replied, "The young man is my very own brother, mistress."[275] And she embraced me and kissed me and clung to me utterly. [2] I kissed her in return and embraced her, saying, "Hysmine, my sister."

---

272 'Aphrodite's girdle': see note at *H&H* 2.7.3 above.

273 'repulse': following Hercher's emendation for the 'purchase' of the manuscripts, defended in Nilsson 2001a: n. 15.

274 'anointing my nostrils': cf. *R&D* 8.364–66 where Myrilla revives Dosikles with smelling-salts.

275 The motif of hero and heroine pretending to be brother and sister appears also in Heliodoros 1.22.2, 1.25.6, 5.26.3, 7.13.1, 7.26.5 as well as *R&D* 3.328, 3.334–39. There are also biblical precedents (Abraham and Sarah: Genesis 20).

She replied, "My very own brother," and kissed me again. With difficulty we broke off our embrace, trusting in our fiction. And Rhodope embraced me and kissed me, saying, "I kiss for your affection and I embrace you for your brotherly love."

[3] A maid-servant came into the room, saying, "Mistress, your father Sostratos and the herald, this man's master, are returning from the altar." So Rhodope went into the garden with Hysmine, my seeming sister and her slave, following in servile fashion. I took myself off the couch and sat, as was proper, on the ground and the paving stones.

[16.1] My master came in. I got up and we go about our activities, he as master and I as slave. Once again there was a luxurious banquet and once again the herald, my master, attended it and once again I, the slave, subservient to the master, was subservient to the herald. And once again Rhodope pours the wine, and once again I sit beside the laurel. [2] I rejoice that I had seen Hysmine in her proper form, but my soul is grieved and my mind is under siege and I am racked by countless thoughts.

In the midst of these Sosthenes' daughter, Rhodope's slave through Fate, my mistress through Eros and now my sister through a fiction, Hysmine, the light of my eyes, whom my passion had made a slave in Artykomis, comes to the laurel and sits beside me. She kisses me uninhibitedly, laughing as she does so and saying as she laughs, "I kiss you as my brother, I embrace you as my lover. [3] But this kiss is not mine, it is not from me the beloved to you my lover, nor from a sister to her brother; it is from a slave to her mistress's lover.

[4] Rhodope, my mistress, loves you. I am the procuress, and this kiss is her message.[276] Do not measure out my love by my circumstances, do not in your pursuit of freedom become enslaved to the love of the free Rhodope and enslave your soul as you escape from bodily servitude. Do not stray from your love for me, your Hysmine.

[5] For even if my face's beauty were to fade like a Lokrian rose,[277] yet the beauty of my virginity is untarnished. Even if physically I am a slave, my soul's freedom is untrammelled. If I am a slave now because of you, and a prisoner before I was a slave, and before I came into barbarians' hands I was hurled into the sea, my tongue would refuse to mention it."

[17.1] This Hysmine said to me with passion and tears. I said to her,

276 'kiss is her message': cf. *L&K* 2.9.2.
277 'Lokrian rose': cf. Basilakes' lament (Pignani 1983: 283.63–64); *A&K* frag. 80.11 (with note) and 149.4; also Lykophron, *Alexandra* 1429. It has an obscure proverbial history (Plepelits 1989: 191, n. 118).

"Hysmine," and as I spoke I kissed her, and as I kissed her I wept, and weeping I said once again, "Hysmine, I am a slave because of you, and I rejoice that I share servitude with you, because I shared freedom with you in our passion, and I would pray to die a slave with Hysmine rather than be free and immortal with Rhodope. [2] But who rescued you from the depth of the sea? Who brought you to this Artykomis?"

She replied, "But now is not the time for that. I am Hysmine, and alive, even if a prisoner because of you and now a slave, as you see. [3] My mistress, even though she is a mistress, nevertheless suffers from passion and has become your slave through passion, and entrusts her affliction to me, seeking passionately for you Hysminias, the brother of the slave Hysmine. Though a mistress, she is in servitude to the Erotes."[278]

[**18**.1] She said this, and kissed me once again, and once again said, "These are not my kisses but I convey to you kisses from Rhodope, the mistress whom I serve as a slave." I said to her, "You are really my Hysmine. I kiss your lips, even though they belong to my fellow slave, my sister, my beloved. [2] And I kiss the kisses, but not as though they are Rhodope's kisses but Hysmine's, whom Zeus betrothed to me, whom Eros put in my right hand, whom Poseidon tore from me and whom now emperor Eros restores once more. Away with Rhodope and Rhodope's passion and any other maiden whom the Erotes throw in your Hysminias' way!"

[**19**.1] She said to me, "Even if you do not love her, even if you spurn her passion, even if you observe our vows, pretend for my sake to be in love and act the lover for me; and perhaps the deception will not be useless and without results for us. Even if it allows nothing else, I shall be able to converse with you without inhibition as a slave, and embrace you as your sister, and I can convey kisses to you as the procuress."

[2] I said to her, "That I shall not be false to your passion and that I shall preserve those many vows inviolate, let the gods stand as witnesses.[279] See, I follow your pretence and I play the role of your brother, I cease to be your lover and take on the guise of Rhodope's lover. [3] Convey the kisses to me, and anything else more passionate than them. I shall kiss Rhodope on these lips of yours and anywhere else where the grapes of passion are to be harvested, and I shall pluck that entire vine, keeping Hysmine's virginity unsullied and inviolate apart from the kisses." Embracing her and kissing

---

278 A similar play on the tension between master and slave in an amatory context occurs in Romanos' kontakion on Joseph and Potiphar's wife (Maas and Trypanis 1963: 44.12.7–8 and 44.2.5); see Conca 1990.

279 'may […] witnesses': cf. *Iliad* 7.76, *Odyssey* 1.273.

Hysmine all over, I said, "I do not give these kisses to you but I transport them to your mistress Rhodope through your lips."

[**20**.1] She, as if conveying a message, moved quickly away from the laurel and came to Rhodope, and whispered to her. I too left the laurel, after pouring blessings on it, calling it a truly golden laurel, Apollo's seed, earth's offspring, Aphrodite's monument and Eros' solace. [2] So Rhodope used Hysmine as her middle term[280] in her passion and thought that, through her, her passion would make progress. I had her as the whole term in her passion and gathered into the centre of my soul all Hysmine's passion.

[**21**.1] So this is how the banquet proceeded for me, in a passionate manner, and thus the symposium drew to its end. The herald, my master, went to his chamber, and lay down and promptly gave himself up to sleep after the lavish meal. [2] I made for the garden. And once again Hysmine is serving her mistress in her passion and once again comes to her mistress's lover. Once again she embraces her brother, once again she kisses him, once again she acts as the procuress, and once again she conveys kisses. [3] I return the kisses, embrace her, act the brother, pretend to be Rhodope's lover and send reciprocal kisses; I take Hysmine as my assistant, serving her mistress, and I openly steal my secret passion.

[**22**.1] She said to me, "This letter is to you from my mistress Rhodope," and placed it in my hand. I said to her, "Hysmine, you are the only mistress I have, acquired through Eros, I have been sold to your love alone, I am subjected to your bond, and I am Eros' slave. My bond of slavery is bitter-sweet,[281] and cannot be erased. [2] You are the acid by which I am purged of my office of herald, you are the robber who deprived me of my virginity; you are the siege-engine by which I was snatched from my homeland and my parents; so I am a prisoner and now a slave, as you see. All of this I suffer willingly because for me Eros has miraculously rescued you, my Hysmine, once more from Hades. [3] The fiction and pretence of passion for Rhodope I reject; on you alone, Hysmine, and your graces have I bestowed all my eyes."

[4] She said to me, "Even if your kisses are brimming over with passion, even if your mouth is like a bee-hive, even if you drip honey over me, I do not respect passion with words alone, because I hate the profit that brings me a penalty. [5] You from being a herald and free became a slave and unfortunate; that I too am a slave, you can see clearly; if we were previously free, if

---

280 'middle term': a metaphor here and in the next sentence from Aristotelian logic; cf. *Nicomachean Ethics*, 6.9, 1142b 24 (Plepelits 1989: 191, n. 120).

281 'bitter-sweet': a Sapphic echo (fr. 130.2 [Voigt 1971]).

we were previously fortunate, it is in your tongue's power to say. Rhodope is my mistress and can save us and grant us freedom."

[**23**.1] I said to her, "Even if the female sex is more ardent, and more changeable by nature, nevertheless, as the tragedy says,

When she is wronged in the marriage bed,

there is no mind more bloodthirsty."[282]

[2] Her cheeks quivered slightly as she said, "Blessings on men's constancy and their cold good sense in face of passion's fires.

Why should this upset me, when I die in word

but am saved by action, and carry off the glory?"[283]

BOOK TEN

[**1**.1] Hysmine said all this with deep emotion, and clung to me and kissed me, saying, "Hysminias, save your Hysmine, and even before saving her, save my Hysminias." She kissed me again and as she kissed me she begged, "Do what I ask and play the lover, don't let me think you are pretending that you won't." So I do what she wants and open the letter, and this is what it said:

[**2**.1] "The maiden Rhodope, daughter of Sostratos, greets her lover Hysminias. Hysminias, that I am fortunate in my homeland and family and everything else that is considered to bestow good fortune, you have discovered from many indications; indeed, circumstances themselves have revealed this to you. That I have kept inviolate the entire treasure of my virginity, even including that of my eyes, Artemis' spring and bow is my most sure vindication.

[2] You, even though you are a slave (but do not begrudge me that word), have overwhelmed my entire soul with Aphrodite's springs and pierced me through with darts of passion. Even though I am a maiden, and fortunate and of high rank, all this I would exchange for your passionate love and this my glorious land of Artykomis for your Eurykomis, which I have never seen, [3] bestowing freedom on you from my bountiful purse, and this hand of mine, which writes this letter to you. With this letter Hysmine, my servant and your sister, is free. Farewell, as you exchange your slavery for marriage with Rhodope."

---

282 'When [...] bloodthirsty': Euripides, *Medea* 265–66.
283 'Why [...] glory': Sophocles, *Electra* 59–60.

[**3**.1] When I had read the letter's contents, I said to Hysmine, "Whatever you think should be said to please Rhodope, say it as if from me. If she asks to be kissed, kiss her, and give her all the many kisses that my lips have stored on your mouth. [2] And if she is not satisfied with kisses alone and her passion is not assuaged with lips but, like female palm trees,[284] she seeks a shoot from the male palm to penetrate into her innermost soul, I shall demonstrate first with you, conveying this to Rhodope."

[**4**.1] These were my words to Hysmine, and once again I embraced and kissed her. She ran off to Rhodope while I hastened to the chamber where I lay down on the floor in servile fashion and paid my dues to sleep, obeying night's demands.[285] [2] Once again throughout my slumbers I seemed to see Hysmine and to sport with her. For just as a starving man's mind imagines bread, and water fills the thirsty man's dreams, so for a soul in love everything – thoughts, sleeping visions – is directed towards passion. [3] Night passed, sleep followed night, and dreams succeeded to sleep. And once again light came, and the sweetness of day beamed down. I rose from my mattress, busied myself about my master and played the attendant.

[**5**.1] Sostratos arrived and said, "Look, herald, the whole city of Artykomis is at the door asking to sail with you to Daphnepolis. Put on your herald's garb and take up your herald's role." The herald garlands his head, arrays himself in his tunic and sandals, and in the herald's full panoply leaves the chamber. [2] Once again the city is in a hubbub and once again the crowd is dancing and has prepared a magnificent farewell for the herald, as glorious as the welcome that had been offered earlier. To pass over what happened next, going on board ship, we left there and arrived at Daphnepolis.

[**6**.1] The herald, my master, together with those who had joined in the voyage from Artykomis, made for the altar of him who wears the laurel,[286] as is customary for heralds. I, with those of us who had sailed with the herald to Artykomis, went to my master's house. [2] Once again my mistress lusted after me, the slave, and was in a frenzy, as it were, with her passion. She embraced me quite brazenly and strove to kiss me. [3] I covered my face completely out of modesty and was ashamed, by the gods, before my mistress who was so overwhelming me, and before the slave Hysmine, and her chastity.

[4] But my mistress pulled me by the tunic and I, the slave, did not allow

---

284 'female palm trees': cf. *L&K* 1.17.3–5, where, however, it is the female palm that is to be grafted into the male.

285 'obeying night's demands': a Homeric tag used already at *H&H* 2.13.3.

286 'altar [...] laurel': i.e. Apollo Daphnaios, an allusion also to the Daphne/laurel story.

myself to be pulled along, despite being pulled, but I resisted completely. So there was a strange contest between mistress and slave. I, the slave, struggled to keep my chastity free, while my mistress was enslaved to the Erotes and sought to dispose of her freedom entirely.[287] [5] But someone returned from the altar and said, "The master, O mistress," and with that my mistress went to the door and immediately I was thrust from her hands as though from a barbarian's. I recalled these verses, which I declaimed in the appropriate manner,

"O my Cyprian mistress, how can they ever
look on their spouses' countenance?"[288]

[**7**.1] The herald arrived, followed by Sostratos and Sostratos' daughter, leaning on Hysmine's arm. A most exquisite banquet was prepared, and the herald sat down in splendour and luxury, having first removed all his herald's robes; my mistress embraced the herald brazenly and sat down with him. Sostratos took his place with Rhodope.

[2] The meal was luxurious. I, the slave Hysminias, am bidden to pour the wine for my masters and for Sostratos, Rhodope's father. Hysmine offers drink to Rhodope so that her august virginity should not be contaminated even by the cup or the hand. [3] So we were commingled in our passion and had our love so much in common that we also shared our servitude as we performed the same service.

[**8**.1] So my mistress, enrolled in the service of the Erotes, flirted with me over the cup and jested with me, or rather the Erotes flirted with her, using me and the cups. [2] For at one moment she pressed my finger, at another she pulled at my entire hand together with the cup and sported in other ways, or was made a game of by the Erotes. While I tried to escape from this as if from a fire, I too flirted but with my fellow wine-pourer, Hysmine, exchanging games with the mistress for games with the slave. [3] This Rhodope approved and she allowed flirtation with the slave as though she thought she was flirting through her. Understanding this, I felt that Rhodope was rather more Hysmine's slave since she was assisting in her passion. Thus the symposium drew to a close with flirtation, passion and delicious dishes, and our duties came to an end.

[**9**.1] Hysmine followed Rhodope and went away with her and both came to the brilliantly and luxuriously decorated chamber that my master had allotted to Sostratos. [2] I made for the servants' quarters with my band

287 Again hints of the story of Joseph and Potiphar's wife (Genesis 39.6–20), with further instances of a tension between freedom and types of slavery.

288 'O my Cyprian [...] countenance': Euripides, *Hippolytus* 415–16.

of fellow slaves, and took my place with the slaves and dined with them and eventually fell asleep. [3] About the third watch of the night Sostratos, with Rhodope and my masters, went to keep vigil at the altar while Hysmine and I followed our masters in our roles as slaves and came with them to the altar and the tripod and the laurel tree.

[**10.**1] There was a din at the altar and a babble of voices and a confused uproar; weeping and wailing rose through the air. Themisteus, my father, and Sosthenes, Hysmine's father, are leading the lamentations while our mothers are moving even the stone in its line, [2] as they say, to tears[289] – there was nothing they were not saying, nothing they were not doing to rouse pity, to bring compassion; their appearance was pitiable, their words more so, more grievous than the kingfisher, more lamentable than the nightingale, like Niobe in their many tears,[290] competing in their sorrow [3] and both victorious, but both defeated, both rending their garments, both furrowing their cheeks, both beating their breasts, both shearing the hair on their head for mourning locks,[291] and both besprinkled with dust.

[4] "Apollo, Apollo," my mother cried out in anguish, lamenting like a Corybant[292] and in a bacchic frenzy of tears, "Phoibos Apollo, I perish. I have been shorn of my family's locks.[293] [5] My son was a flowery meadow which I tended, but I have been pitiably robbed of him entirely with all the plants, with all the blooms. [6] A spring dripping with honey was my handsome son for me, and I have been quite robbed of it. Now I am totally parched[294] and I am a hive of wormwood, made bitter by circumstances.

[7] A most secure harbour was my son Hysminias for me, and I was like a ship moored in calm waters, untouched by the waves; now the harbour has vanished, and I am like a ship on the open sea, battered by the waves. [8] My son was the sun for me, and now that my son has been lost I am a

289 'moving [...] line': a proverbial expression (cf. Theokritos, *Idyll* 6.18), referring to extreme efforts to achieve an objective.
290 'more grievous than the kingfisher': cf. Basilakes' lament (Pignani 1983: 241.130–31); *Iliad* 9.563. Halkyon (kingfisher), killed by Herakles. Prokne (nightingale), daughter of the Athenian king Pandion: cf. *L&K* 5.3. Prokne and Niobe are also associated at *D&C* 2.327–29.
291 'furrowing their cheeks': cf. Basilakes' lament (Pignani 1983: 214.137). 'shearing [...] locks': cf. Basilakes' lament (Pignani 1983: 131.139–40); Euripides, *Alcestis* 512, *Orestes* 458
292 'Corybant': i.e. like a frenzied participant in a wild oriental cult; Corybants were devotees of the goddess Cybele and notorious for orgiastic behaviour, with references from Aristophanes onwards; cf. *R&D* 1.212–69 for a comparable lament.
293 'shorn [...] locks': cf. *H&H* 6.10.3.
294 10.10.4–9: 'I am totally parched [...] mother': a passage with many phrases with parallels in Basilakes' lament (Pignani 1983: 241.142, 239.98–140.102, 238.77–78, 238.78–80).

mother with no sunshine; I exchange the sunlit delights of Eurykomis for the Cimmerian darkness.[295] [9] My son was a brilliant star for me but he has vanished, and a moonless night has covered me, his mother. My son was my light, but he has been extinguished and now I travel in darkness.

[10] Apollo, your father Zeus crowned him with laurel and sends him as a glorious herald to dread Aulikomis. Once my maternal joy reached as high as the heavens, but now my misery plunges to the very gates of Hades. [11] The herald is a fugitive, the master is a runaway slave, the chaste young man is Eros' prisoner, but above all this I, now childless, lament my child and mourn even more for the mother that I was.

But, my son and herald and master, how shall I mourn for you? How shall I garland you with tears? [12] As a corpse?[296] But perhaps Zeus has kept my son safe for me, your mother, and perhaps you are alive, or perhaps you are a prisoner and a slave to barbarians – you, lover of all things Hellenic, a herald and master of many.

[13] But, O tripod, and laurel, and above all, prophetic Apollo, receive these offerings of mine and in addition these tears for my sufferings, and pronounce an oracle concerning my son. And let this pronouncement be not most inauspicious but most auspicious. [14] Apollo of the unshorn locks,[297] take pity on my pitiably shorn head; Apollo of the laurel, spare my son Hysminias, whose head was once crowned gloriously with your laurel but who now covers my pitiable head with the cap of Hades."[298]

[**11**.1] All this and more Dianteia, my mother, declaimed pitiably in a tragic manner, and was wracked, as it were, with a sea of tears and flooded the entire shrine. Panthia, mother of my Hysmine, sent up her own bitter lamentation, saying incessantly, "Alas, my child Hysmine, you have slipped from these forlorn hands of mine and you have destroyed your mother. [2] Like a fully fledged bird you have flown away and you have fluttered from these pitiable hands of mine.[299] But oh, that wild plumage which has quenched my lamp![300]

---

295 'Cimmerian darkness': the land of the Cimmerians was legendarily full of mist and gloom; *Odyssey* 11.14–19.

296 'how shall […] corpse': cf. Basilakes' lament (Pignani 1983: 235.6–7); *H&H* 10.11.9.

297 'of unshorn locks': cf. *Iliad* 20.39; *Hymn to Apollo* 134; Pindar, *Pythian* 3.14, *Isthmian* 1.7.

298 'cap of Hades': this makes the wearer invisible, like Athena (*Iliad* 5.845) and Perseus (*L&K* 3.7.7).

299 'fully fledged […] mine': cf. Basilakes' lament (Pignani 1983: 241.127).

300 'quenched my lamp': cf. *H&H* 6.10.4.

You were my bridal chamber, the brazen virginal abode,[301] but – alas, my child Hysmine – together with that chamber and that virginal abode I am deprived of you, the maiden. [3] Hysmine, you were to me the high-branching cypress which I planted in the midst of my soul, cherishing it with maidenly dew and all other good things; but a hurricane blasting from Eurykomis tore you up by the roots.[302]

[4] That was no herald but a savage beast,[303] who snatched my Hysmine from these pitiable hands and from my very embrace, and ravaged all my treasure, harvested the corn, culled the grape and plucked the rose. [5] Garlanded, the beast came to Aulikomis, but departed leaving my head unadorned, having taken my garland; he played the chaste youth and secretly made off with my maiden. [6] He sent a dart into my soul and now I am in anguish in my innermost being.[304] An uncouth drone from Eurykomis has taken my Hysmine, my sweet bee, and filled my whole soul with wormwood.[305]

[7] A huge savage eagle snatched from my hands and the pyre, my daughter, the sacrifices offered for you and for me this was not a good omen. Now Zeus' prophecies have come to fruition. [8] You were my fountain of sweetness, sweetening the bitterness of my old age, but a channel from Eurykomis diverts you to a different bitter conduit,[306] and my soul thirsts for you and my mouth searches for you like a fair-flowing spring.

[9] But, my child Hysmine, how shall I mourn for you? How shall I weep for you pitiably? As if you are a corpse?[307] But where are you buried in the earth? And what tomb covers you and conceals the entire fountain of your graces?[308] But perhaps death has spared your youth, I want to know what city holds you, my Hysmine, the maiden, the lovely maiden.[309]

[10] But that tyrant, that audacious youth, who mocked his office of

301 'brazen virginal abode': cf. Sophocles, *Antigone* 944–47, with reference to Danae's imprisonment.
302 'cherishing [...] things': cf. Basilakes' lament (Pignani 1983: 238.73–74). 'hurricane [...] roots': cf. Basilakes' lament (Pignani 1983: 239.99–101).
303 Cf. throughout this passage Manganeios Prodromos' language and sentiments in 1147 on marriage of Theodora, niece of Manuel I, to Heinrich Jasomirgott of Austria (e.g. poem 47.109–30).
304 'in anguish [...] being': cf. Basilakes' lament (Pignani 1983: 238.70–71).
305 'An uncouth drone [...] wormwood': cf. Basilakes' lament (Pignani 1983: 238.74–76).
306 'diverts [...] conduit': cf. *AnthGr* 5.285.3–4.
307 'how [...] corpse': cf. *H&H* 10.10.11.
308 'where [...] covers you': cf. Basilakes' lament (Pignani 1983: 250.328). 'fountain of graces': cf. Basilakes' lament (Pignani 1983: 239.94).
309 'the lovely maiden': Euripides, *Iphigeneia in Aulis* 1574.

herald, and played it false, has ravaged your virginity. O dread and untimely fate, O my misfortune, O protector that failed to protect, O treacherous beast that stole by stealth and abducted by force! [11] But, fountain that gives tongue and laurel that prophesies, and above all Phoibos Apollo, receive these wretched offerings which Panthia, the wretched mother, pours forth on behalf of Hysmine, her wretched daughter."

[**12**.1] Our mothers wailed heartrendingly and most pitiably; our fathers sent up even more pitiable laments and beat their breasts, saying, "O children, you are lost and we are lost with you. [2] Eros has campaigned against you and has laid siege to our hearts. Eros has ravaged the purple[310] of your virginity and we are left broken like the murex shell. [3] Eros has deflowered your roses and has burnt up our souls like a brushwood fence. Eros has consumed the fervour of your youth with his fire of passion and seared your aged fathers to their very depths of their innermost being and incinerated us.

[4] Eros, Zeus' son, campaigns against his father during his festival, in the midst of Zeus' rite, the Diasia themselves; he takes his herald as booty, despoils his virginity and lays siege to the virginal precinct, and loots all our souls. [5] We crowned our children's heads with this laurel of yours, Apollo, but Eros has removed the crowns and crowned our paternal heads with ashes.[311] [6] Apollo, Apollo, have pity on these hoary heads and take our part with the father against this patricidal youth. Accept these supplicatory libations which we, the fathers, pour out to you on behalf of our children lost in the bloom of their springtime, in their unharvested verdure, in the flower of their youth."

[**13**.1] This from our mothers, this from our fathers. All the bystanders were pierced to their souls, their eyes filled with tears, they burst into sobs. I went up to Hysmine and pulled her along by the hand, saying, "Hysmine, do you see?" She said, "But shall we not embrace our mothers?"[312] [2] "Be patient," I replied, "and let us wait for the oracle."

And the water bubbles, the tripod booms, the vatic laurel shudders as though a breeze is passing through it. [3] The ministering attendants are

310 'purple': the costliest form of this colour was derived in Byzantium from a shellfish, the murex; see *ODB*, under 'Purple'.

311 'crowned [...] ashes': Plepelits 1989: 193, n. 134 points out that this is a custom attested both in the Bible (e.g. 2 Kings 13.19) and in Greek literature (e.g. Euripides, *Suppliants* 826–27).

312 There is a similar oracular encounter and reunion of parents with children in *R&D* 9.201–04 and 259–60.

filled with the divine presence, Phoibos prophesies and pronounces his oracle and makes his prediction and predicts the future. The oracle was that he restored us, the children, to our parents and approved our marriage.

At this the bystanders tremble, our mothers wail with pleasure, our fathers dance before the altar and we join hands and prostrate ourselves at Phoibos' feet. [4] Our mothers run up to us, grab at us, embrace us, embrace us again, kiss us, wail and refuse to let us go. Our fathers for their part pull at us, their children, as though dividing our souls between them. [5] Paeans of thanksgiving rise up, hymns of thankfulness are sung, our rescue is applauded. The crowd rejoices, they bless Apollo and we are crowned with laurel.

[**14**.1] The herald, my former master, and Sostratos, Rhodope's father, set upon us. They tear off our garlands, castigating us relentlessly with their tongues and hurling threats at us; [2] they revile the priest, they rant against us, declaring that they had rescued us from a horde of barbarians and had enslaved us according to military law.

The priest who had put garlands on us said to them, "Your legal customs are excellent when you find yourself enslaving Hellenes! And your piety is even greater when you enslave heralds! [3] Apollo gives an oracle and decrees freedom for free men, on whom Hellenic law and nature itself had previously bestowed freedom; you pronounce another oracle and you make other laws by wishing to enslave free men." [4] They replied, "It is not we who make these other laws but the spear and military law has put these people into slavery." And they tried to haul us off, but we would not let go of Phoibos' feet.

[**15**.1] Once again our mothers wailed and our fathers made pleas with tongue and tears. The priest fought with his hands and, when he could not win them over, he took the garland from his head, he removed his tunic and took off his sandals, and ascending the tribunal, he proclaimed in stentorian tones[313] to the crowd, [2] "Why do so many of you rush to the altar of Daphnian Apollo to no effect? Why do you ask the Far-shooter[314] for oracles? You have these august lawgivers to pronounce oracles for you. Enough of your oracles, Phoibos Apollo, enough of your prophecies, enough of your garlands."

[3] The crowd was in an uproar about this, and made for our captors. They promptly seize hold of Phoibos' feet like us, as if they were appealing to him for their souls, and plead with the priest and make supplication to Apollo, saying, "Pardon our folly and words, Apollo." They proclaim that

313 Homeric tag: cf. *Iliad* 5.785; also used at *H&H* 11.17.6.
314 'Far-shooter': a Homeric epithet for Apollo (e.g. *Iliad* 1.14, 96). For similarly ironic arguments, cf. *L&K* 8.8.7–8 and 8.9.9.

we are free, seeking to set their own souls free.

[4] So we are garlanded once more, and are inscribed as free men and restored to our parents. They are totally overwhelmed with joy and delight and offer sacrifices of thanksgiving for the safety and survival of their children. They sing odes of welcome and dance the victory songs. We dance with them and raise the most delightful paean to freedom.

[**16**.1] The time for dinner summons us and we are entertained by the priest, and the banquet is most sumptuous. Hysmine, out of modesty, kept her eyes on the ground and did not pay attention to the dishes, not even with her lips. I, feeling like an Olympian victor in my delight and joy, used both eyes and fingers at the table, I delighted my mouth and throat with the food and feasted my mind with thoughts of marriage.

[2] After many delicious and varied courses, the priest rose from the table and laid aside his tunic and bared his arms and served drink to us, saying, "This is the cup of the Saviour Apollo." [3] So our fathers drank, and after them our mothers, who said, "Thanks be to you, Apollo, for this glorious treasure that you have granted us in our children." [4] And after them he brought the cup to us, saying, "This cup is brought to you by Apollo who approves your marriage in his oracle, bestows freedom on you and bids you hold your lives in common."

[**17**.1] As he said this he took his place again, and spoke once more, "Hysminias the bridegroom – for this appellation Apollo bestowed on you in his oracle – do not shrink from telling us all your adventures from the very beginning to the very end."[315] [2] I said to him, "You kindle for me a bowl of fire and you open up an ant-heap of disasters." He responded, "Do not omit one detail, by Apollo, not one, by your freedom and the brilliant wedding that Apollo prepares for you." [3] I said to him, "Pardon me, master, for my soul is thrown into confusion out of modesty and my mind is totally bewildered. Let me hoard up my story for you until tomorrow."

[**18**.1] I persuade the priest and the symposium comes to an end, and we make for our chambers. The priest had allotted one chamber to Themisteus, my father, and my mother Dianteia and me, and in it had prepared three splendid couches on which we lay down and fell asleep. [2] There was a similar chamber for Sosthenes and Panthia and their daughter Hysmine. As so, separated from each other, we passed that night.

---

315 'from [...] end': cf. Lykophron, *Alexandra* 1–2.

BOOK ELEVEN

[**1**.1] On the following day we were once again at the altar, our heads garlanded with laurel, and we celebrated our freedom, we chanted odes of victory, we intoned hymns to our salvation, sacrificing whole hekatombs[316] to Apollo. [2] The innumerable crowd which thronged around the altar had its eyes fixed on us and pointed us out with their fingers. The story about us, about Hysmine and Hyminias, was on every tongue, and Apollo was praised for his actions on our behalf.

[**2**.1] Once again it was the time for a meal, and once again the priest prepares a splendid dinner, and once again he takes magnificent care of us. When the business of the banquet was brought to a close, the priest who had prepared the dinner sought to know, yet again, about our adventures, and pressed us most persistently. [2] So I, even though I was reluctant and hesitant, nevertheless unwillingly made ready to tell the tale; my voice failed and my tongue stuck[317] – however, I began, with a faltering voice:

[**3**.1] "My father is this Themisteus here, and my mother is Dianteia, whom you are welcoming most hospitably; the city that is my home is Eurykomis, in which is the altar of Zeus Xenios and the rite of the Diasia is celebrated. By lot I was appointed to the office of herald, and being herald not to any city but to Aulikomis, I am crowned with laurel. [2] I come with splendour to the city that had fallen to me by lot, because I am the herald of Zeus and of the Diasia. I am given hospitality by Sosthenes here and received magnificently and welcomed brilliantly. [3] He brings me into the garden, he sets up a table for me in the middle of it, and he prepares my bed near the lawn. Her father Sosthenes instructs his daughter Hysmine to pour the wine, and she obeys her father and does so.

[**4**.1] The banquet came to its end and Hysmine washes my feet, my virgin feet with her virginal hands. I lie down on my bed, in my chastity abandoning myself peacefully to sleep. [2] I arise at daybreak and go into the garden, I admire its ranks of flowers and its other beauties, and I cast my eyes on the wall around the garden and, after observing various paintings, I see a painting of a golden throne, and a naked youth on the throne, with weapons, carrying a torch, with wings on both feet, and a charming face. [3] In servile fashion there were in attendance on this youth emperors, rulers and tyrants, wild beasts and rulers of beasts, every kind of winged creature,

---

316 'hekatomb': a large offering; in the Homeric poems the hekatomb was of a hundred cattle.

317 'my tongue [...] stuck': cf. Basilakes' lament (Pignani 1983: 235.2); *H&H* 6.11.4.

every beast from the sea, and two fantastic women of more than human size, with the wrinkles of age and extreme old age. [4] One was completely white – her face, her hair and tunic, her hands and feet and all the rest of her body. The other was completely black – her face, her arms, from her feet to her head and even down to her nails.

[5] I was disturbed by what I saw, and thought that this strange painting was a figment of the mind and skill of the artist. But above the youth's head were iambic verses, saying that the painting was of Eros seated on his throne and ruling everything as emperor. [6] And I not only abused the painting but also, being chaste, cast aspersions on Eros himself.

[**5**.1] But he appears to me that night as I slept and reproaches me for what I had done during the day and finally penetrates my soul and enrols me among his slaves, entirely transforming me from a herald, from a virgin into a lover. [2] And, placing Hysmine here in this my right hand, he flew away from my sight, taking with him sleep and my virginity and my herald's wand.

[3] And I the herald became a lover, and I the virgin was a virgin no more.[318] Profaning Hysmine with my eyes and tongue and gestures, I transform her into Eros. [4] And thus I return from Aulikomis to Eurykomis, totally enslaved to passion for Hysmine. But not even she could escape the fire and wings and bow of Eros, and my tongue that had been taught persuasiveness by the Erotes.

[**6**.1] So I was in love with Hysmine (and if she reciprocated, let her say) and we vowed to marry each other, a marriage which I would have stolen – let the truth be told – but the girl would not permit me.[319] [2] Sosthenes here, her father, announces in the middle of a banquet and a magnificent feast another marriage for his daughter, which we seek to escape, and Kratisthenes aids us in our escape as does the ship which we boarded to flee from my Eurykomis. We chance upon a favourable breeze and we take flight joyfully.

[**7**.1] But Poseidon churns up the sea and stirs up waves as high as mountains, he attempts to swamp the ship, and the helmsman decrees that a scapegoat should be sacrificed. We cast lots for this and the lot fell on Hysmine. So she is cast into the sea and immediately restores calm to the sea.

[2] Subsequently I see her still alive, how I do not know, by that dreadful storm, by Poseidon and bitter servitude, by Apollo and the sweetness of

318 'virgin [...] more': cf. Euripides, *Hecuba* 612.
319 Marriage-stealing again; cf. *H&H* 7.4.2, and note. Conca 1994: 672, n. 2 points out that γάμος has a double meaning, both sexual union and the legal agreement (cf. *R&D* 1.105).

freedom! [3] I threw the whole ship into confusion with my laments and drowned it in my tears. Neither the helmsman nor the crew could stand this, so they put the vessel in to the shore and take me out of the ship. I poured out my libation of tears[320] for the girl on that cenotaph that was the seashore.

[**8**.1] A trireme suddenly appears, full of barbarians, savage men who set on me unmercifully like wild beasts and brutally drag me by the hair and take me to their trireme and put me to the oar. [2] After a barbaric meal they leave that place and attack a fortress and plunder it, and fill their vessel with the booty. [3] The young men they set to the oars, those who were older they use as exercise for their daggers and throw them into the sea (for it was no inconsiderable number of men that the barbarian band had seized from the fortress). As for the women, they treated them with unbridled lust, but the barbarians made not the slightest improper advance on the virgins.

[**9**.1] And so we came to Artykomis, and the barbarians conducted some form of barbaric negotiation with the citizens of Artykomis. Thus all the loot, apart from the human cargo, was unloaded. The virgins among us were sold for large sums, after having been tested in Aphrodite's spring, but we youths and women were of no value to those in Artykomis.

[2] Once again the trireme received us on board, it was untied and we left the harbour, and put in to another where the barbarians, mooring the trireme with cables, disembarked on to the mainland and dragged the women off. [3] After magnificent food and drink which the trireme had brought in abundance from Artykomis, the barbarians disported abominably with the women and abandoned themselves to sleep, debauched with wine and lust.

[4] In the midst of the sleep and lust, or rather the barbarians' dissolute wantonness, the expedition from Daphnepolis turns up, lays into the barbarians as they slept, gets them all together, slaughters them, loots them and takes us as booty. [5] Then the army holds a triumph over them and over us in this city and finally, following the oracle, makes us slaves and distributes us by lot. So once again I am enrolled as a slave, and the yoke of servitude summons me to this city of Daphnepolis.

[**10**.1] But then there came this present time, the time for Apollo's festival, and the brilliant celebration of the festival and the carnival. Lots are cast for the office of herald, and my master, who yesterday tore from me the crown of freedom, is sent as herald to Artykomis. [2] He comes to the city allotted to him; I follow my master, in my role of slave. We are welcomed by Sostratos, Rhodope's father, who yesterday took away Hysmine's crown.

---

320 'poured [...] tears': cf. Basilakes' lament (Pignani 1983: 235.9–10).

[3] I see Hysmine in servitude to Rhodope. I pretend to be her brother; she plays wholeheartedly at being my sister, and we kiss, with Rhodope herself watching. If Rhodope loves me and uses my sister Hysmine as her go-between in her passion, let Hysmine say.

[4] As for what went on at the altar, you know better than us – our mothers' tears, our fathers' pitiable pleas on our behalf, the oracle, the discovery of the children, the crown of freedom, the crowning, the decrowning, your blessed voice, our crown of freedom and everything else that went on at this great altar of freedom."

[**11**.1] "Thank you," the priest said to me after my speech, as he turns his eyes to Hysmine, saying, "Maiden Hysmine, I have heard from his own tongue what befell this your bridegroom; would you now like to fill out the crescent so that the whole narrative becomes fully illuminated for me?" [2] She said to him, "Spare my tongue, by the Saviour Apollo; for modesty inhibits my maidenly tongue. I would never be so bold as to alarm my father and shock my mother. Silence and sparing speech are a maiden's adornment."

[**12**.1] This the girl said to him modestly, but the priest, who was good in all respects, replied, "Maidenly child, Apollo bestows freedom on you, and joins you in marriage to the handsome Hysminias. [2] Will you not make a sacrifice to Apollo even out of your adventures, so that the narrative persists eternally and the miracle does not fade, which great Apollo wrought so marvellously for you in his oracle?"[321]

[3] She was silent, and only wept. Sosthenes gazed at her intently, casting fierce looks at her, and said, "It is not a silent tongue that is the definition of chastity, but appropriate actions and seemly behaviour. [4] You had no modesty when you behaved so badly, yet you are now ashamed to speak of it. I would pray most devoutly, Apollo, for her to be ashamed to act rather than to speak."

At this, by the gods, I blushed and all but blocked my ears; I was another Proteus, turning a thousand colours,[322] furious at her father's sarcasm. [5] The priest said to him, "Stop this, Sosthenes, do not make the girl leave. Modesty is the child of reproof, actions do not give birth to it." And he said to the maiden, "Do not hesitate to speak."

[**13**.1] She, drenched with perspiration and tears and with faltering tongue and breath catching at her voice, kept her eyes fixed intently on the ground and said, "This man has told you everything that happened as far as

321 Parallel sentiments can be found in many hagiographical texts.
322 'Proteus': a minor sea-god who changed shape to avoid answering questions; cf. *Odyssey* 4.455–58.

the ship, the sea and the storm. [2] When I was cast into the sea, a dolphin takes me on its back as it plunges through the waves and swims on lightly.[323] I, in my nakedness, rode on the wild beast, confused by the waves and made dizzy by the sea, and in my fear of the beast my soul was quite torn apart. [2] The creature was my salvation, yet I thought my benefactor was my enemy; I was terrified of my saviour but loved my enemy and I entwined myself around him as though he were my saviour. [4] Since my saviour was a wild beast, I sought to escape from him, but I dared not trust the waves, and I was buffeted by my thoughts and the waves and the creature.

[**14**.1] When I was on the point of breathing out my soul into the waves, a naked youth appears before me also resting on a dolphin; he stretches out his hand to me and, taking hold of me, brings me to dry land; then, fluttering his feet (for both feet were winged), he flew away from my sight. [2] 'O mother,' I sobbed, 'mother,' as I sat by the waves.

After several days – I cannot tell precisely how many – I see a ship sailing by; I stretch out my hands to it, I make pleas with my gestures, I utter supplications with my cries. [3] The oarsmen bring the ship to the shore; they take me from the land and place me in the ship. They sympathize with my plight, they provide a ragged garment for me, and kindly give me food, altogether commiserating with my misfortune.

[**15**.1] All that night we sail with a favourable wind, with land still just visible, but do not make great speed. As the sun rose, the swell increased and the wind intensified and the sailyards creaked. [2] The helmsman made for land, fleeing the storm, but he went from the smoke into the fire,[324] for the moment he ties the ship up on land he hands us over to savage men.

[3] For there was a trireme in the harbour and a host of men on the beach, with fierce eyes, blackened faces, murderous hands, more like savage beasts than men. They seize hold of us all and slaughter the men pitilessly, and take delight in their prey. [4] As for me, somehow they get me into the ship's hold with shackles on my feet. [5] At daybreak they hoisted the sail and let the ship run with the wind. All that night we were carried gently forward with the fair wind and

when the brilliant sun shone forth,[325]

we see land, and a city on the land.

---

323 'dolphin': for the legend of Arion rescued by a dolphin, see Herodotos 1.24; the story is also used at *L&K* 6.13.2.

324 'smoke [...] fire': a proverb used first at *H&H* 7.9.6.

325 'when [...] forth': an unattributable scrap of tragic verse (Kannicht and Snell 1981: fr. 158; Plepelits 1989: 193, n. 146).

[**16**.1] So the pirates disembarked from the trireme and entered into an agreement with the citizens; they unload the cargo from the vessel and take me out too; they bring me to a spring into whose waters they throw me, after putting a garland of laurel on me. [2] After a while they take me out and inscribe me as a slave to Rhodope, with whom I came to this great altar of freedom; she was my mistress because of the sea, and fate and the slavery imposed by the barbarians."

[**17**.1] When my Hysmine had made her speech, the dinner came to its end, and we immediately made the libation to sleep that follows a luxurious banquet. When night was nowhere to be seen (for the sun was over the earth) and we had completed our libations to sleep, each of us rose from our beds. [2] When the festival's rituals have come to an end, we leave Daphnepolis to go to Artykomis, to assay – as it were – Hysmine with the spring and the bow, like gold in fire.

[3] We come to Artemis' spring and the whole city of Daphnepolis runs out to accompany us. And the people of Artykomis are at the spring and at the bow. They see Hysmine in her garland, they beseech Artemis, they pity the girl, they are in two minds about her virginity, they doubt her chastity, and they are afraid of the test.[326]

[4] I stood looking at the bow, the spring and the garland with all my eyes, and as I looked I wept, and my entire soul was besieged by my thoughts. [5] My Hysmine is garlanded; the crowd howls; she is thrown into the spring. The mob falls silent and not a sound can be heard. The bow does not move, the water does not stir, and the maiden floats lightly on the surface. [6] The mob rejoices, they dance with delight, they clap their approval, and they shout their good wishes, and cry out in stentorian tones, "The girl is a virgin." I faint from delight.

[**18**.1] The virgin is taken out of the spring (no one will be in two minds any more about her status). Her mother embraces her, her father blesses her happily, and she goes to Artemis and is crowned with the victory garland: "The maiden is a virgin and no one can doubt the girl." [2] And so we come from Artykomis to Aulikomis, where we celebrate the wedding magnificently, in the middle of Sosthenes' garden, at that magnificent table and by that well where we had first devised our marriage bower.

[**19**.1] So the whole city of Aulikomis was in a state of excitement, singing, applauding, rejoicing, dancing before the bower, before the bridal

---

326 'they are afraid of the test': Kleitophon in *L&K* 8.13.2–4 is similarly hesitant. See Nilsson 2001: 219–22 for a comparative discussion of this scene as it appears in *L&K* and *H&H*.

chamber, before us the bridal couple, singing the wedding ode, chanting the marriage songs, and creating a glorious marriage scene. [2] Whose muse is so sweet, whose voice so eloquent, whose speech so refined in the Attic style and eloquent in the appropriate manner that he can depict in words the wedding and describe all the participants? [3] That was truly a bower of the gods, Hera's wedding, Aphrodite's bridal chamber.

I rejoiced to be arrayed so brilliantly and honourably for the bridal procession, and even more so because Eros escorted Hysmine for me in splendour and made her sit beside me in imperial magnificence and crowned her with me in glory. [4] But I prayed that the banquet would reach its conclusion and by Eros, I hated the day and sought for night and, changing the words of the comedy a little, I whispered, "O emperor Zeus, how drawn out are day's affairs."[327]

[**20**.1] And so my wedding exceeded the grandiloquence of Homer, every muse and every tongue made eloquent by rhetoric. But, O Zeus, as whose herald I came to Aulikomis, O tyrant Eros, as whose slave I returned to my Eurykomis from Aulikomis, [2] O Poseidon, who took Hysmine as a scapegoat in the storm, O great Apollo, who bestowed freedom on us, O bow of Artemis and spring which adjudged her virginity, do not let an abyss of oblivion overwhelm our adventures, nor the passage of time nor decay nor Hades' bowl that pours out forgetfulness.[328]

[**21**.1] But, O Zeus, if you admire the fraternal love of the Dioskoroi[329] and keep their memory undying in heaven, our fraternal love is greater than theirs since it is life that we share together. [2] If you pitied Herakles for his many hazards and excursions and keep his memory eternally in heaven, were we not prisoners and slaves and vagabonds, and did we not preserve our virginity inviolate throughout? [3] But, alas, I betrayed my herald's wand and exchanged the child Eros for his father Zeus, and Zeus will not place us among the stars and allow memory of us to be preserved in heaven.

[4] But surely you, O Poseidon, if you pity Ikaros and preserve his memory for ever in that sea by bestowing his name on it,[330] will you not

327 'O emperor [...] affairs': Aristophanes, *Clouds* 1–2, where the phrase is 'how drawn out are night's affairs'.

328 While, as Conca 1994: 684, n. 1 points out, these are the sorts of remarks and justifications that one finds in the prologues to histories, similar ideas are also expressed in hagiographical texts.

329 'admire [...] Dioskoroi': cf. Basilakes' lament (Pignani 1983: 237.54–55). The Dioskoroi (Zeus's sons) in Greek mythology were twin sons of Leda and Zeus.

330 'Ikaros [...] it': the Ikarian sea, named for Ikaros, who drowned when his wings, made by his father Daidalos, melted on flying too close to the sun; cf. Apollodoros, *Epitome* 1.11.3.

preserve the memory of our perils by granting our name to the sea and depicting our adventures on the water and conserving them indelibly till the end of time? Yes, indeed. But you are ashamed of defeat and you dread that in depicting our adventures you lay yourself open to mockery.

[**22**.1] You, mother earth, if you have pity on Daphne in her flight, and conceal her and save her and bring forth spontaneously a plant of the same name to preserve her memory, if you make Hyacinth immortal through the plant of the same name,[331] [2] will you not preserve our memory? Will you not grant us plants of the same name, imperishable figures of the perils that befell Hysmine and me, Hysminias, depicting and figuring in the plants all that happened to us, and keeping our memory immortal for those that come after? [3] But Poseidon the earth-stirrer, the earth-shaker will unleash his lion's roar against you and will shatter you, the mother who depicted our adventures and his demeaning defeat by Eros. [4] I love my mother, and I honour my mother and respect her.

So, if Zeus will not place our deeds among the stars, if Poseidon will not inscribe them in the waves, if Earth will not embody them in plants and flowers, our adventures will be set forth on imperishable tablets and slabs of adamant, with the pen of Hermes[332] and ink and a tongue which breathes the fire of rhetoric. And anyone from a later generation will be able to retell these matters and will be able to forge a golden image in words, like an imperishable statue.

[**23**.1] Whatever in mankind is most responsive to passion will appreciate all the charming passion in this story; whatever is chaste and virginal will respond to its restraint; [2] whatever is more inclined to sympathy will pity our misfortunes, and so memory of us will be undying. [3] We will grace this story and adorn this book with erotic charm and everything else that decorates books and beautifies words. And the title of this book will be "The adventures of Hysmine and of me, Hysminias".

331 'Hyacinth': a handsome youth slain by the jealous Zephyr when he preferred the favours of Apollo, and who was then transformed into a plant; cf. *R&D* 6.306.

332 'pen of Hermes': cf. Basilakes' lament (Pignani 1983: 243.175). Hermes is here taken as symbol of writing and rhetoric, rather than of interpretation (despite Plepelits 1989: 194, n. 154). Note also that Hermes and metaphors of writing are much used by Manganeios Prodromos.

CONSTANTINE MANASSES

ARISTANDROS AND KALLITHEA

INTRODUCTION

Author

Constantine Manasses was yet another of the many writers who clustered around the teaching establishments and aristocratic households of mid-twelfth-century Constantinople. There is no clear independent testimony to his birth and death dates, for which the scholarly literature offers a wide range of suggestions on flimsy evidence. His life-span has to be conjectured from his surviving literary works. Of these, the most significant is his verse chronicle, the *Synopsis Chronike*,[1] which contains two firm pointers to its date of composition. The first is that it is dedicated, with lavish thanks for her generosity, to the *sevastokratorissa* Eirene, a noted literary patron, mentioned briefly earlier. Eirene, sister-in-law of the emperor Manuel, was widowed in 1142, her husband Andronikos having briefly been the prospective heir to the empire. On Manuel's accession in 1143 she rapidly fell into disfavour with the new emperor, was imprisoned, and seems to have emerged in around 1145 only to be confined once again in 1148/9. From the silence in the sources she would have died about 1152/3.[2] It is a legitimate question to wonder how during this stormy period she was able to act as a generous patron. The second dating indication comes from lines praising Manuel as a glorious ruler of the empire,[3] thus securely putting their composition after his accession in 1143. Lampsidis, editor of the *Synopsis Chronike*, considers that the emphasis on Eirene's status as wife of Andronikos shows that the dedication was made prior to his death, and so postulates a complex composition process starting before 1142, interrupted to take note of Manuel's accession (and imperial disfavour, possibly extending also to Manasses) and then completed when Eirene emerged from

---

1 Lampsidis 1996.
2 On Eirene, see E. and M. Jeffreys 1994; E. Jeffreys forthcoming a; Varzos 1984, vol. 1: 361–78.
3 *SynChron* 2505–12.

imprisonment.[4] However, Lampsidis has not paid sufficient attention to other works sponsored by Eirene, and in particular those by the poet known as Manganeios Prodromos: in many of these, all of which are securely dated long after Andronikos' death, Eirene's status as his wife continues to be emphasized, as a guarantee – it would seem – of her standing.[5] She had married into the ruling Komnenian family, and that marriage was her sole claim to high status. The case is strong that the *Synopsis Chronike* was written between 1142 and 1152: probably ca. 1145 when Eirene had been freed from confinement. However precocious Byzantine writers may be, it is probably best to assume that Manasses would have been aged at least 20, and probably older, when he attracted his patron's attention and was deemed capable of writing a work as long and intricate as the chronicle. He is likely to have been born ca. 1120.[6]

In the older literature Manasses is stated to have ended his career as bishop of Naupaktos, dying in 1187.[7] Lampsidis has convincingly demolished the case for Manasses' connection with Naupaktos. He is also, with good reason, reluctant to allow that the seal of a Constantine Manasses, bishop of Panion, belonged to the author: Manasses' reasonably extensive oeuvre shows no sign of any episcopal preoccupations and every sign that he was caught up in the secular life of the Constantinopolitan court.[8] Thus once again the only reliable evidence for the end of Manasses' life comes from his writings. In 1160–62 he was sufficiently vigorous, and of high enough standing, to act as an imperial representative on a journey to the Holy Land, as recorded in his *Hodoiporikon*.[9] The latest date that can be given for any other of his surviving works is 1175.[10] Constantine Manasses thus lived between ca. 1120 and some point after 1175.

4 Lampsidis 1996, vol. 1: xvii–xx.

5 As discussed in E. Jeffreys forthcoming a.

6 Lampsidis 1988: 107–08 suggests ca. 1115.

7 As argued by Bees 1930, relying on a letter of Apokaukos and one late manuscript attribution. Manasses' connection with Naupaktos is deeply embedded in the literature: he is, for example, listed by Fedalto 1988, vol. 1: 293 for the see of Panion (Theodosiopolis) in the diocese of Thrace, with a note of promotion to Naupaktos (though his name is not in fact mentioned under the latter heading).

8 Lampsidis 1988: 110–11; see also Magdalino 1997.

9 Horna 1904; cf. Marcovich 1987.

10 Funerary orations for Theodora Kontostephanos (d. 1172/1173; Kurtz 1900) and Nikephoros Komnenos (d. 1173/1175; Kurtz 1910), and an encomium for the victories of Manuel Komnenos in 1173/74 (Kurtz 1906).

Date

The place of Manasses' *Aristandros and Kallithea* in his oeuvre has not received great attention.[11] Horna's suggestion that it was written ca. 1160, based on the use of Aelian in both *A&K* and the *Hodoiporikon*, has not been seriously challenged and is not, for example, disputed by Mazal or Tsolakes in their editions.[12] That this is a fragile line of argument is shown by the fact that Aelian is cited also in the *Synopsis Chronike*, for which a much earlier and relatively secure date has been postulated above. A date ca. 1160 for *A&K* would also have been supported in previous scholarship by the late dating for *H&H* previously current.[13] However, recent work on the Komnenian novels, as discussed elsewhere in this volume, has argued that Prodromos' *R&D* was written before 1138 and Makrembolites' *H&H* in the late 1140s or early 1150s, possibly by 1145.[14] Manasses' *A&K* has more in common with these than the *Hodoiporikon*. Thus, while it is clear that Manasses was active as a writer in the 1160s, a more likely period for the production of *A&K* would be the 1140s, at the time when he wrote the *Synopsis Chronike*, whose dramatic narratives as well as its metre share many of the novel's characteristics.[15] A number of lines appear in both *A&K* and the *Synopsis Chronike*,[16] though it is impossible to draw conclusions from these about the texts' compositional priority. The most striking evidence comes from the epilogue to the novel. This is found in one of the witnesses to *A&K* and partially in one manuscript of the *Synopsis Chronike*, and is – on balance – due to Manasses himself;[17] it refers to Manasses with

11 For general points see Hunger 1978, vol. 2: 126–29.

12 Mazal 1967: 36; Tsolakes 1967: 19 discusses the date for *SynChron* but not for *A&K*.

13 Beaton 1996: 79–80, 211–12; Alexiou 1977; Cupane 1974. Note that, as discussed below, arguments for dating *D&C* to ca. 1156 remain valid.

14 E. Jeffreys 2000a; Agapitos 2000a; Roilos 2005: 7; see pp. 161–65 above.

15 As emphasized by Nilsson 2006.

16 E.g. *A&K* 3.11, cf. *SynChron* 288; *A&K* 23 and 84, cf. *SynChron* 3497–511; *A&K* 54.2, cf. *SynChron* 6155; *A&K* 57.2, cf. *SynChron* 6072, 6074; *A&K* 137.6, cf. *SynChron* 1146; *A&K* 154.2, cf. *SynChron* 3896. Some lines in the WM anthology (= Ma in the headings to the fragments; see Transmission, below) and *SynChron* are identical (WM/Ma 367–69 = *SynChron* 6074–76; 370–71 = 6082–83; 480–83 = 6445–47; 483–87 = 2792–96; 575–89 = 3497–3512; 719–22 = 2529–32; see Mazal 1967: 70–73). Mazal concludes that these have been taken by the compiler of the anthology from *SynChron* and not from *A&K* and so does not include them in his edition; this is slightly illogical since he accepts the epilogue in the WM anthology, which shares some lines with *SynChron*, as deriving from *A&K*. This translation, which follows Mazal's edition, has also not included these lines.

17 Mazal 1967: 152.

a word that suggests he is under, say, twenty-five (*Orpheu neare*, 'young Orpheus').[18] This would place the composition of both texts ca. 1145.[19]

Most of Manasses' literary output known today consists of short pieces, in both prose and verse, written either for sponsors or for self-display.[20] His two most substantial surviving works, the *Synopsis Chronike* and *A&K*, use a metre, the 15-syllable line, that was not favoured by Byzantine *literati* and that Manasses used reluctantly in the *Synopsis Chronike* under compulsion from his sponsor, the *sevastokratorissa* Eirene.[21] This reluctance suggests that *A&K* was also undertaken as a commission from the same sponsor (at a moment when she was free from imperial oppression), although there is little clear evidence for this.[22] It would also be plausible to suggest that Manasses produced *A&K* as part of the literary rivalry endemic at this period in Constantinople, choosing a form to contrast with the iambics of *R&D* and the prose of *H&H*.[23]

Transmission and reception

Unlike the *Synposis Chronike*, which, perhaps supported by its undoubted aristocratic sponsorship and its readability, survives in an abundance of manuscripts[24] and with a fourteenth-century Bulgarian translation,[25] there is no complete extant manuscript of *A&K*, and it survives only as collections of excerpts. In contrast with the other Komnenian novels, it seems to have

---

18　*A&K* 181.2, *SynChron* (Bekker 1837): 286–87; see Mazal 1966: 254.

19　There is also a phrase that suggests that Manasses was involved with teaching (*A&K* 181.5 'address your pupils').

20　For sponsors, e.g. the funerary orations and encomium listed in n. 10 above; for display, e.g. *ekphraseis* on a dwarf (Sternbach 1902) or on works of art (Lampsidis 1991). The *Hodioiporikon*, the longest piece, was perhaps written to establish Manasses' credentials with Ioannes Kontostephanos, in whose entourage he travelled to Jerusalem.

21　*SynChron* 12–17; cf. M. Jeffreys 1974: 158–61.

22　Note, however, that in poem 52 of Manganeios Prodromos (discussed above in connection with *H&H*), largely unedited (a few lines in Miller 1875–81, vol. 2: 771–72), on the wedding in 1145 of Eirene's eldest daughter Maria to John Kantakouzenos, among the wealth of classical allusions there is a clear reference to the central characters of Achilles Tatius' *L&K* (MangProd 52.67). Note too that Eirene's other literary commissions in verse are in the 15-syllable line: Tzetzes' *Theogony*, the poem on astrology probably to be attributed to Manasses, and the copious verse by Manganeios Prodromos; see E. Jeffreys forthcoming a.

23　This of course assumes that *D&C* was written definitively later.

24　Lampsidis 1996: lxxvi–cxlii.

25　Bodgan 1922. The translation was accompanied by illustrations; see Dujcev 1963, and the recent facsimile *Constantin* 2007.

escaped the attention of the thirteenth-century Nicene and Constantinopolitan collectors who gathered up the twelfth-century literary production and
preserved it in omnibus manuscripts such as Oxford, Barocc. 131.[26] It may
be that the 15-syllable metre told against it. At least one other work of fiction
from this period that can be classed with the novels and is in this metre
barely scraped through, and that is *Digenis Akritis*, whose original written
version was produced before 1143, but has survived only in a fractured
manuscript tradition.[27] Something similar may have happened to *A&K*. Be
that as it may, the last known sighting of a full version of *A&K* was in Arta
in 1492, when Janus Lascaris (Ianos Laskaris) noted a copy in the collection
of Demetrios Trivolis.[28]

  A&K is now known from two collections of excerpts. One was made by
Makarios Chrysokephalos (ca. 1300–82), Metropolitan of Philadelphia, who
included 611 lines from *A&K* among the thirty-five or so authors antholo-
gized in his *Rhodonia*; the extracts are presented in sequence, with a note of
the book numbers. Makarios' autograph copy of the *Rhodonia* (later owned
by Bessarion) is now in the Biblioteca Marciana in Venice (as Marcianus
graecus 452). The presence of *A&K* in this manuscript was first brought to
detailed scholarly attention by Villoison in 1781,[29] and the first edition of
the fragments was by Boissonade in 1819, as an appendix to his edition of
D&C.[30] The other collection is anonymous and found in two manuscripts,
in Vienna and Munich.[31] Although mentioned by Krumbacher,[32] this witness
to *A&K* came to serious attention only in 1967 when Tsolakes and Mazal
simultaneously published editions.[33] This set of extracts contains 765 lines,
taken out of sequence and without indication of book number, but with many
passages overlapping those from the *Rhodonia*.

26 As discussed above; see especially Agapitos 1993: 103–07. Oxford, Barocc. 131
includes the prose *H&H*.

27 Also as discussed above (p. 9, n. 41). See E. Jeffreys forthcoming b. The oldest surviving
manuscript, G (= Grottaferrata), is dated to the late thirteenth century.

28 Mazal 1967: 12.

29 Villoison 1781: 75–76.

30 Boissonade 1819, vol. 2: 322–403, using of course only these fragments (as did Hercher
1859; see also Hercher 1873).

31 Vienna, Phil. gr. 306, ff. 1–16v (14th cent.); Munich, Bayerische Staatsbibliothek, Cod.
Cgm 281 ff. 144v–163v (16th cent.).

32 Krumbacher 1897: 380.

33 Mazal's reconstructive edition of 1967 was preceded in 1966 by a preliminary version
of the anthology text alone, in which the manuscripts are referred to as W and M, as they are
occasionally in the notes to the translation in this volume; in the headings to the translated
fragments, they are subsumed under the abbreviation Ma, referring to the 1966 edition.

There are two indirect witnesses to passages from *A&K*. One is a poem on moral topics in a fourteenth-century Paris manuscript (Bibliothèque nationale, 2750 A),[34] with many lines identical to those in *A&K*. Scholarly opinion is divided as to whether the text is to be attributed to Manasses; nevertheless, some passages are included in Mazal's edition, and in this translation.[35] The second witness is provided by prose paraphrases from *A&K* included by Maximos Planudes ca. 1295 in his Συναγωγὴ ἐκλεγεῖσα ἀπὸ διαφόρων βιβλίων πάνυ ὠφέλιμος (*A very useful collection of extracts from a variety of books*), together with excerpts from historians, philosophers and paradoxographical authors (such as Aelian).[36] Planudes seems to have been attracted by the paradoxographical elements, though it should be noted that it was at this time that he was translating Ovid and working on the *Greek Anthology*, and so he may have been interested in *A&K* as a further example of the Greek erotic tradition.

In the ordering of these witnesses, the sequential presentation with book numbers in the *Rhodonia* is key. Mazal's edition is an admirable attempt to slot the other extracts into the same sequence, and to suggest the threads that bind them together, making use of the plot motifs found in the novel tradition as witnessed by the late antique writers and the other Komnenian novels.[37]

The fragmentary and dispersed state in which *A&K* filtered from twelfth-century Constantinople to post-Byzantine Europe has meant that its reception has been muted, and its impact and readership has been limited and in no way comparable to that of, say, *H&H* – though it is included in early nineteenth-century collections of translations of the late antique Greek novels.

Form

As noted above, Manasses uses the 15-syllable line for *A&K*, a flexible metre without a secure ancient model, based completely on the stresses of spoken Greek, and for that reason given little respect by ambitious writers. The standard metre for Byzantine verse was the 12-syllable iambic trimeter, used by Manasses in, for example, his *Hodoiporikon*, and by Prodromos

---

34 Edition: Miller 1875.

35 Mazal 1967a.

36 Cited in the headings to the fragments in Mazal 1967 and in this translation as Plan, from Piccolomini 1874.

37 Note textual comments in Trapp 1969, and remarks in Anastasi 1965 and 1969.

and Eugenianos in *R&D* and *D&C*, respectively. The 12-syllable line often shows respect for the historical quantity of the syllables as well as their number. Since in the *Synopsis Chronike* Manasses uses the 15-syllable line explicitly under protest, as mentioned above, it is a tempting thought that its use in *A&K* is again the result of a commission, quite possibly from the same patron. Manasses' chronicle arguably compensated for the jejune metrical form with inventive coinages, particularly of adjectives.[38] The fragments from *A&K* are too scant to allow much evidence of this, but there are several instances of his use of rare forms (e.g. 8.6). Reasons for the use of verse for an extended fictional narrative are discussed above (pp. 4, 164) in connection with *R&D*. In the case of Manasses, if the influence of a patron is ruled out, its use can perhaps be ascribed to rivalry between the novelists and a wish to demonstrate the potential of another medium beside the 12-syllable line and prose.

Plot summary

The fragmentary state in which *A&K* has survived makes it impossible to be certain of the intricacies of the plot, though educated guesses can be made about its overall shape. The outline that follows is based on Mazal's interpretation of the fragments and his justification for the order in which he placed them in his reconstruction, using the sequence in which the fragments appear in Makarios Chryskephalos' *Rhodonia* and plot parallels from the other Komnenian novels.[39]

Like *R&D*, *A&K* opens when the action of the novel is already under way, with earlier events recounted later in the narrative. In Book 1 it seems that a band of marauding barbarians has captured Aristandros and Kallithea, the central pair. By the end of the book they are still prisoners, have probably met up with a fellow captive and have begun to exchange information. Book 2 would have been largely taken up with the telling of their past experiences. The references to Eros probably concern the separate amatory fates of the prisoners, while the slanderers who are energetically denounced could have played a part bringing them to their present location. Book 3 seems to deal with abrupt twists and turns: a possible suicide attempt by Aristandros after the separation of the lovers, with consolation for him from the companion postulated for Book 1, and another battle. By the end of the book, Aristandros and Kallithea, now reunited, are once again in prison. Aristandros'

---

38 Lampsidis 1971.
39 See Mazal 1967: 85–155; the reconstruction has been followed by Conca 1994.

lament at the beginning of Book 4 lists some of the events and actors in his fate: Nausikrates, presumably the robber chief from the opening of Book 1, Kallisthenes from Tyros, and Bousiris the pirate captain who may be the instigator of the miseries at the end of Book 3. However, the fragments are too disjointed here to suggest a narrative sequence: there is lamentation, and comments on the role of flattery and envy culminating with a diatribe against an evil brigand. Book 5 opens with invective against gold. There is a threat against Kallithea. A reference to Rhodes places the action on the Aegean coast of Asia Minor. The comment on shared sorrows might indicate another recounting of past mishaps, while the reference to great joy might suggest that the pair are reunited. The remainder of the book deals with a suitor's unwanted attentions to Kallithea. In Book 6 these attentions seem to have come to an end. There is a plot and counter-plot of some sort while a reference to eunuchs suggests an aristocratic environment. References to love, Eros and a woman's passion suggest a meeting between Aristandros and Kallithea, while the laments and pleas for death suggest that a new disaster has struck. The fragments from Book 7 do not allow a clear idea of plot development. There are a number of historical analogues, comments on the workings of Fate and observations drawn from natural history; some of these perhaps belong to speeches. A theme appears to be the balance between moderation and excess. In Book 8, the passage on beauty damaged by grief suggests a fresh twist in the plot, while that on friendship again suggests that the central pair have met up with a companion in hardship. There are further comments on treachery and the ineluctable role of fate. In Book 9 can be glimpsed a sub-plot of a lovelorn barbarian woman enamoured of Aristandros. There is a battle involving Egyptians and other Easterners. The reference at the end of the book to merchants perhaps derives from the central pair's inevitable reunion and homecoming.

Further pointers to the place of the fragments in an overall scheme can be found in the notes to the translation.

Characteristics and themes

As discussed above, *A&K* has survived as a series of passages selected for a variety of reasons by three late Byzantine readers (Planudes, Makarios and the anonymous anthologist witnessed in mss W and M). Although it is with ingenuity possible to discern the shape of the text from which these extracts were taken, and although it is clear that *A&K* shares assumptions found in its slightly earlier contemporaries *R&D* and *H&H* and the slightly later *D&C*,

there is much that will have been omitted as not being to the excerptors' tastes or purposes. Any comment on themes in *A&K* is thus rather more a comment on the excerptors' predilections than on those of Manassses.

Not unexpectedly, the largest grouping of passages deals with aspects of love. There are a number of general statements of the power of love, often involving personification of the emotion as Eros: for example, 21, 22, 24, 64, 95, 97, 104, 105.[40] The most elaborate (96) combines personification with physiological analysis (Eros, surprisingly, dwelling in the liver, and Wrath in the heart). Other physiological interpretations, sometimes involving blows through the eyes, can be found at, for example, 41, 90, 106, 112, 113, 115, 118, 119. At 164–66 there is a set of passages on the fury of a woman spurned in love. Related to these are comments on the physiological impact of beauty (e.g. 11, 89), especially that of the heroine (e.g. 5, 6; cf. 116). There are comments on the characteristics of the worthy man (51, 65; cf. 50), a mixed assessment of military men (2, 9, 158, 173), opprobrium of barbarians (7, 40) despite their susceptibility to beauty (42), admiration for the prudent (108, 109), notes on behaviour appropriate to women and girls (107,112), statements that human nature is liable both to low passions (13, 14, 15) and compassion (17, 71, 87), and that offspring reveal their parents' quality (86, 126).

Other passages deal with emotions: the effects of joy (88, 168), suffering (3, 4, 16, 91), grief (121, 122, 123), tears (101, 102, 121), envy and jealousy (48, 114, 129, 169), malice (43, 62), and remarks on the physiology of joy and sorrow (174). There are comments on the nature of flattery (77), treachery (29) and a slanderer's activities and fate (30, 31, 63); noteworthy are remarks on the vileness of eunuchs (80, 110, 161) and the malign lure of gold (23, 84, 133, 178). A passage pleads for moderation (125), others commend the support given by friendship (56, 72, 73, 151).

There is much on the fragility of life (10, 52, 59) sometimes using the image of the wheel of Fortune (49, 54), and the workings of fate (78, 83, 94, 159, 160; with an elaborate personification at 137). The need for justice, sometimes involving the all-seeing eye of God, is notable (e.g. 27, 37, 38, 39, 58, 145, 146, 179); there are comments on the gods and the ineluctable nature of retribution (e.g. 8, 34, 44, 45, 130, 154).

The general misery of life (cf. 69, 70) is apparent in passages on the adverse impact of traitors and slanderers (29, 30, 31, 43, 62), little mitigated by the inevitability of punishment for wrongdoers (32–35, 37, 38, 39, 44,

---

40 References are to fragment numbers.

45). Light relief comes from the paradoxographical passages (largely excerpted by Planudes; e.g. 60, 135, 136, 140, 147, 155, 177).

Signs of the rhetorical show-pieces which (to judge from the other novels) were once a feature of *A&K* have survived the excerptors' knives. Thus some passages can be tentatively ascribed to speeches of consolation (73, 76), to a scene in a law court (79), to an exhortatory speech before battle (158), or to an *ekphrasis* (96). Some may derive from key points in the plot: e.g. an attempted seduction (85) or a crisis afflicting the hero (149). In the comments on school-teachers (25) and the use of an over-refined language (53), there are possible hints of the teaching environment that has been referred to above as an element in the production of texts such as *A&K*. A number of gnomic sayings (e.g. 26, 46, 54, 92) are preserved.

The Olympian deities barely make an appearance in the excerpts, so it is impossible to judge whether any part is played by an equivalent to the Hermes of *R&D*, the Apollo of *H&H* or the Dionysos of *D&C*. Equally it is impossible to discern subversions of twelfth-century Constantinopolitan ecclesiastical processes. However, plot motifs prominent in *R&D* and *H&H* which were taken to reflect aspects of twelfth-century reality are also hinted at here: for example, an interest in dreams (152), and an appreciation of the horrors of captivity (68) and the miseries of slavery (167). Apparently absent, however, is reference to communal meals and banquet etiquette.

Not unexpectedly, in *A&K* the barbarians would seem to be savage, the heroine lovely, the hero noble: all are subject to the arbitrary workings of Eros and Fate. Manasses presents the fickleness of fate and the perfidiousness of companions with a pessimism that is only slightly mitigated by acts of compassion and friendship. How far this is a fair presentation of the novel in its original form is hard to judge: this translation may help readers to refine the arguments concerned.

Manuscripts, editions and translations

Manuscripts[41]
M   Munich, Bayerische Staatsbibliothek, Cmg 281
V   Venice, Biblioteca Marciana, cod. gr. 452, ff. 208-220
W   Vienna, Österreichische Nationalbibliothek, Cod. phil. Gr. 306
Parisinus graecus 2750 A, ff. 89–108 (*Carmen morale*)
Laurentianus LIX, ff. 48r–50r (Planudes' *Very useful collection of extracts from a variety of books*)

41 See also pp. 276–78 and especially n. 33.

Editions
Boissonade 1819, vol. 2: 322–403; Hercher 1859, vol. 2: 533–77; Mazal 1966; Mazal 1967; Tsolakes 1967; Conca 1994: 684–777

Previous translations
Latin: Boissonade 1819, vol. 2: 322–403
Italian: Conca 1994: 689–777

This translation
The translation is based on the edition by Mazal with attention paid to that of Conca; textual points are noted only when these affect the translation. The notes rely heavily on the work of all previous editions: Boissonade, Hercher, Mazal, Tsolakes and Conca in their respective publications. As with Conca's edition and translation, the sequence of excerpts followed here is that of Mazal, while the suggestions in the notes for the connections between the excerpts are based on Mazal's reconstruction.

TRANSLATION

BOOK 1[1]

1[2]   1.1–6 Hr[3] = 248–53 Ma[4]

The orbs of the eyes[5] are very often in error,
with sight naturally dimmed over a distance,
and they exaggerate a crowd of moderate size;
if fear also happens to be present in the soul,
then they consider that rocks and plants and inanimate nature   5
are warriors hung about with weapons.

2   1.7–8 Hr = 254–55 Ma

The soldier is an acquisitive creature
and gluttonous and unjust, if no one restrains him.

3[6]   1.9–11 Hr

Suffering that falls upon a soul numbs and chills it
and presses on the heart like a burdensome rock
and makes even the most talkative mouth silent.

4   1.12 Hr = 247 Ma

Thus grief is able to take even the senses away.[7]

---

1 Book 1: A band of barbarians have captured Aristandros and Kallithea who later encounter a fellow captive and converse with him; Kallithea receives unwanted advances from the barbarian leader.

2 1–2: These passages would fit into a description of an attack on a city of the sort which opens *R&D* and *D&C*, most dramatically in Hel.

3 Hr = Hercher 1859.

4 Ma = Mazal 1966 (= edition of W and M).

5 'orbs of the eyes': a classical and Byzantine circumlocution for eyes; cf. Sophocles, *Antigone* 974; *D&C* 2.177–78.

6 3–4: The sentiments expressed here could be a comment on the capture of Aristandros and Kallithea by the marauders.

7 Cf. *D&C* 8.23 for a similar idea.

5[8] 1–3 Ma

For nature, it seems, which strove to introduce
living beauty of this sort among mankind,
sculpted this young girl as an example.

6 1.13–18 Hr = 4–9 Ma

Beauty that is so vibrant, full of so many graces,
is able to enchant and dominate not only mankind
but also, I think, the sullen lioness, mother of cubs,
and the tusked boar and the bellowing bull.
It is a weapon that lacks iron, but it strikes to the heart   5
and drugs the soul and kills the gaze.

7[9] 1.19–20 Hr = 279–80 Ma

But there was nothing, so it seemed, worse than a barbarian,
not fire, not water, not a savage beast, nor the sea's gulf.

8[10] 1.21–26 Hr = 281–86 Ma

Thus no one can escape the hands of god,
not the impious, not the oath-breaker, not the murderer, not the magician,
even if he had an eagle's wings on his shoulders,
even if he flew to the desert, even if he made for the clouds,
even if he were concealed by darkness, even if he hid beneath the earth;   5
an evil gadfly[11] would drive him back to earth.

9[12] 1.27–31 Hr = 256–60 Ma

It befits a soldier either to act valiantly
or to fall and not to have as witness to his shame the sun

8 5–6: Kallithea's beauty captivates the marauders' leader; cf. *R&D* 1.39–60 and *D&C* 1.120–58 where the capture of the central pair is followed by a description of the heroine's beauty and its impact. In the twelfth century for a statue to appear animate was the ultimate accolade (e.g. *Alexiad* 3.4; *DigAk* G 6.330); in the late antique novels a benchmark of living beauty was to resemble a statue (*L&K* 3.7.2, 5.11.5; Hel 2.33.3; XenEph 1.1.6).

9 Support for the suggestion that the marauders are barbarians; cf. 68 below, where names are given.

10 Perhaps from a speech by one of the prisoners; on the ineluctability of God's omniscience, cf. 137.12 below and Psalm 138/139.710. This sentiment became a cliché; cf. *R&D* 6.88; *H&H* 2.14.5; *DigAk* E 1397–98; *L&Rα* 592-93.

11 'gadfly': a rare Homeric word (*Iliad* 24.532) used by Manasses also at 27.3 and *SynChron* 3605.

12 9–10: Perhaps from a speech before a further battle with the marauders; cf. 65 below for similar thoughts on behaviour befitting a soldier.

and the all-nurturing[13] earth and the moon.
It is a fine memorial for soldiers
when they die as heroes in battle, and not in bed.   5

10   1.32 Hr
Truly nothing is certain for mankind.

11[14]   1.33–42 Hr = 10–16, 17 Ma
Nothing exists that is so likely to enslave even the bold-hearted[15]
as a garden of beauty[16] and a grove of comeliness.
For the conduit for beauty flows through the eyes[17]
and enters the heart and softens the soul,
even if it finds a furnace of wrath and a blazing fire of anger,   5
it quenches the rage and diminishes the anger,
it becomes a salamander and extinguishes the flame;
but it kindles another furnace and fire,
where the Erotes stoke the furnace and Desire pumps the bellows,
sparking the flame with invisible flints.   10

12   18–19 Ma
I do not think it right or proper or fitting
for a young girl to be gossiped about among men of this sort.[18]

13[19]   1.43–45 Hr = 344–46 Ma
There is no wild beast more shameless than the belly,
which compels everyone to be mindful of it

13 'all-nurturing': a word otherwise found only in *SynChron* 30.

14 11–12: These passages presumably refer to Kallithea; the heroine's inflammatory beauty regularly sparks developments in the plot; cf. Charikleia and Thyamis (Hel 1.21), Rhodanthe and Gobryas (*R&D* 3.150).

15 'bold-hearted': a not particularly common word (Euripides, *Hippolytus* 424), taken up by twelfth-century writers including Anna Komnene (*Alexiad* 1.6.3) and Niketas Eugenianos (*D&C* 3.139, 5.117).

16 'garden of beauty': i.e. the heroine; on the Byzantine literary association of nubile girls with gardens, usually walled, see Littlewood 1979; Barber 1992.

17 'conduit [...] through the eyes': for the perception of beauty entering through the eyes, cf. XenEph 1.3.2; *L&K* 1.4.4; Hel 3.7.5.

18 That girls should behave discreetly is a cliché in the novels (cf. Hel 1.21.3; *R&D* 1.119; *DigAk* G 4.808), though often flouted (e.g. *H&H* 1.9.2).

19 13–14: Perhaps from a speech by the prisoners reflecting on their circumstances; on the need to deal with the body at inopportune moments, cf. *R&D* 1.427–30; *D&C* 1.275; with special reference to barbarian marauders, cf. *D&C* 1.159–67.

even in times of danger, grief or torment of the heart.

14   347–51 Ma

There is no wild beast more despicable than the belly
which seeks food endlessly and demands drink,
and indeed turns especially to cups and carousing,
which bring an end to pain for a few and oblivion for grief
but for many are the father of disaster and danger.   5

15[20]   352–54 Ma

Thus a man possessed by an evil spirit is a wretched creature,
falling into error incessantly, unfortunate in every venture
and a plaything of the devil.[21]

16[22]   1.46–47 Hr = 355–56 Ma

The tale of another's suffering can shed
some drops of comfort on one who is faring badly.

17   1.48–54 Hr

Man is a creature that is naturally compassionate.
For it was not a black-hearted rock that gave birth to him,
nor an oak, nor iron, nor a wild beast with ruffling neck.
If members of this species encounter each other
as fellow prisoners or fellow toilers or fellow captives,   5
they share the dangers and disasters with each other,
they groan together, they weep together, and they mourn with each other.[23]

18   1.55–56 Hr = 20–21 Ma

Contemporaries appeal to contemporaries,[24] they say; so a girl responds to
    a girl,
a crone three times older than a crow[25] to a crone and an aged man to an
    old one.

---

20 A comment, perhaps authorial or perhaps from one of the prisoners.

21 'plaything of the devil': a commonplace; cf. Hel 5.4.1.

22 16–18: Sympathetic narration of others' misfortunes, usually in flashback, is a regular element in ancient and Byzantine novels (e.g. *L&K* 7.2.3; Hel 1.9.1; *R&D* 1.132 ff.). These passages suggest that Aristandros and Kaliithea are conversing with a fellow prisoner.

23 Similar sentiments appear in *R&D* 1.144–45, 8.95–96.

24 'Contemporaries': a proverbial expression; cf. Aristotle, *Rhet*. 1.11 (1371b).

25 Crows are proverbially long lived; cf. Pliny, *Nat. Hist*. 10.14.

19[26] Plan[27] §2

That the pankratiast[28] Kleitomachos was so chaste that if anyone made a lewd remark at a symposium, he used to stand up immediately and run off.[29]

20[30] Plan §3

That those bitten by mad dogs see the image of a dog in water.

21[31] 1.57–68 Hr

Eros does not only have power over creatures that swim and fly,
not only over those that traverse the air and the dry land,
but he also controls rocks and plants
and looses his darts against creatures of different species.
Eros even enables a sweet-watered river to cross the sea,   5
for Elian Alpheios fell in love with Arethousa[32]
(Arethousa was a spring in Sicily)
and he crossed the sea and plunged into the waves
and, riding lightly over the backs of the salt water,
he kept his streams uncontaminated by the salty surroundings   10
and offered his fresh water to his beloved,
preserving himself as sweet-streamed bridegroom that had crossed
    the ocean.

21a Plan §4

That Eros does not rule only over the gods in heaven but also those of the sea; and he unites those not of the same species, as he unites Zeus with mortal

26 19–20: These fragments from Planudes' paraphrase precede 21a, whose position is predicated on its derivation from 21, but their relevance to the plot is unclear – perhaps from a speech (if indeed they come from the novel; Mazal 1967: 36–37).

27 Plan = Piccolomini 1874.

28 'pankratiast': a participant in the pankration, in the ancient (but not Byzantine) world a vicious form of wrestling.

29 Cf. Aelian, *De natura animalium* 6.1; the first part of Aelian's statement has been censored.

30 Possibly from a medical text, but cf. Marcus Aurelius 6.57; Glykas, *Annales* 122 (Bekker 1836).

31 21–21a: The powers exercised by Eros are frequently listed in the novels; their inclusion at this point might be part of a discourse between the central pair and one or more fellow prisoners.

32 The river Alpheios flows from the north-west Peloponnese into the Ionian sea near Olympia; Arethousa in legend is a water nymph who escaped from Alpheios to become a fountain in Syracuse in Sicily (Pindar, *Nem.* 1.1; Strabo, *Geog.* 6.2.4). For use of this myth in the novel tradition, cf. *L&K* 1.18.1–2; *D&C* 4.145–46.

women, Aphrodite with Adonis and Anchises;[33] and he makes Alpheios fall
in love with Arethousa, and joins a snake with an eel;[34] and moreover iron
loves magnetic stone and the male date-palm loves the female.[35]

Fragment from Books 1 or 2

22[36]   22–26 Ma

But there did not exist, it seems, a beast or a man or a stone
that is capable of escaping the Erotes' bows,
but the Erotes were lords of all living creatures,
those that fly, those that go on foot and those that dwell in the sea;
none have escaped and none will escape Eros' dart.[37]   5

BOOK 2[38]

23[39]   2.1–2 Hr

<...> with gold that can appease even the gods[40]
and is more effective than all the potions on earth.

24[41]   2.3–6 Hr

Wine plays a part in the mysteries of Eros;
hence wine is called Aphrodite's milk.[42]
The two creatures most difficult to combat on earth are
Dionysos, son of Zeus, and Eros, child of Aphrodite.[43]

33 'Adonis and Anchises': mortal lovers of Aphrodite – Adonis a handsome youth killed by
a wild boar, and Anchises who became father of Aeneas, the Trojan refugee who founded Rome.

34 'snake with an eel': cf. Aelian, *De natura animalium* 1.50, 9.66.

35 'iron [...] date-palm': These examples also appear in *L&K* 1.17.2–3; *D&C* 4.137–41.

36 There is nothing sufficiently distinctive in this passage to suggest whether it should be
assigned to Book 1 or 2, or to any other passage dealing with the effects of Eros.

37 On the ineluctability of Eros' weapons, cf. Longos, Prologue 4; *D&C* 6.367–70.

38 Book 2: Aristandros, Kallithea and their fellow prisoner continue to recount their past
experiences, which will have been emotionally tense and fraught with opposition.

39 The evil influence of gold, both pragmatically and allegorically, is a recurrent motif
in Manasses' work; cf. 84 below, and *SynChron* 3497–515. In this context it may well have
reference to barbarian avarice.

40 The line lacks two syllables.

41 24–24a: Based on *L&K*, this mythological excursus would continue the amatory
expositions of Book 1.

42 For wine as Aphrodite's milk, cf. Aristophanes, fr. 596 (Edmonds 1957), in Athenaios,
Deipnosophistae 10.62.

43 Dionysos was son of Zeus by Semele, god of wine and central figure of Nonnos'

24a   Plan §5

That the poets say that wine is Eros' brother. And hence wine is called Aphrodite's milk; and because of this wine and Eros are the things most difficult
to combat on earth. For they say that when the world was at its beginnings
everything was fine and Eros was pleased with everything; but he selected
the fairest objects, the Morning Star from the stars, the apple from fruits,
the rose from flowers and the vine from plants. He pelts girls with apples as
he teases them,[44] he uses roses like charms, and he adopts wine as his ally.

25[45]   2.7–8 Hr

There is nothing more stupid in life than schoolteachers,
did not the sons of doctors[46] run around on earth.

26[47]   2.9 Hr

Envy, the crafty beast, is the root of evil.

27[48]   2.10–12 Hr = 287–89 Ma

Thus Justice ever pursues the wicked
and torments them on all sides and drives them in all directions,
as a gadfly[49] drives a bellowing bull, as a horsefly does, as flies do.

28[50]   2.13–14 Hr

No one, when there is meat available, eats bitter thyme,[51]
even if he grows turnips and looks like a Pythagorean.[52]

Dionysiaka; Eros, of uncertain paternity, is his mother Aphrodite's constant playful companion,
most notably in the *Anacreontea* (some of 6th cent. CE; West 1993) which are taken up in *D&C*.
For the association of Dionysos with Eros, cf. *L&K* 2.3.3.

44 Apples: cf. *AnthGr* 5.79–80, or Psellos, Letter 84 (Sathas 1876) on being pelted with
apples at a wedding. On apples in Byzantine love poetry, see Littlewood 1974 and 1993.

45 The relevance of this to the plot is obscure, perhaps from a speech, but also possibly
deriving from the circumstances under which the novel was written: cf. 181.5 below referring
to Manasses' pupils, and *R&D* 8.483, 520, also with possible references to teachers.

46 'sons of doctors': i.e. 'doctors' (cf. the patronymic Asklepiades, son of Asklepios = doctor).

47 Again, the relevance of this to the plot is not clear. The pernicious effect of envy is
a recurrent theme in twelfth-century literature; cf. 31 below; *SynChron* 3199–210; Tzeztes,
Chiliades 4.750–54; Reinsch 2007.

48 The agency of Justice is a frequent motif in the novels, e.g. *R&D* 4.69, but its place in
the plot here is not clear.

49 'gadfly': cf. 8.6 above.

50 Perhaps picking up on the gluttony theme of 13 and 14 above.

51 'bitter thyme': a bitter dish eaten by the poor in classical Attica; cf. Aristophanes, *Plutus*
253.

52 'looks like a Pythagorean': i.e. is a vegetarian; cf. Diogenes Laertius, *Lives of*

29[53]   **2.15–22 Hr (2.15–18 = 476–79 Ma)**

Men, a treacherous soul is something dreadful and evil;
it is a serpent as a bedfellow, a scorpion as a house-companion,
a lioness as a partner, a tigress as a companion,
a leopard as a fellow banqueter, a basilisk[54] as a dining companion.
If you have evil within, if you cherish a traitor,   5
though you may have a wall of iron, though you may have towers of bronze,
the fortress is vulnerable, the city is unguarded,[55]
the guards are not guards, the efforts are effort and nothing more.

30   **2.23–32 Hr (2.24–32 = 488–96 Ma) + 497–502 Ma**

And who will evade danger and who will escape the sword,
if an abusive tongue, a bragging slanderer[56]
is considered credible even over matters that have not been examined?
If those who administer justice give ear to the accusers
and accept everything without scrutiny,   5
as if from the tripod of a divine oracle,[57]
will they not end up slaughtering and hewing necks,
flaying, like lambs at the butchers,
whole herds of citizens, peasants and those not peasants,
eminent nobles and those not noble, ragamuffins and scurvy knaves?   10
Come now, those who love Hellenes[58] should not rave in this way;
these are the acts of a Skythian heart, of a savagely barbarian soul;

Philosophers 8.13 on Pythagoras' prohibition on meat-eating.

53 29–31: Passages from one or more speeches of vehement denunciation of slanderers and traitors, whose actions have presumably led to the protagonists' predicaments; cf. *SynChron* 6443 ff. The fanciful analogies derive from paradoxographical collections of natural marvels, such as the *Natural History* of Aelian; cf. 56 below. The pernicious role of slanderers is a recurrent theme in the twelfth century; interestingly, notable examples come from writers closely associated with the *sevastokratorissa* Eirene, e.g. Manganeios Prodromos (her 'household' poet), Poems 43, 108, and Iakovos Monachos (her spiritual adviser), e.g., Letter 39 (E. Jeffreys 2009).

54 'basilisk': a particularly terrifying serpent referred to several times by Aelian (*De natura animalium* 2.5, 3.31, 5.50, 8.28); cf. Hel 3.8.2.

55 'city is unguarded': the phrase appears also at *SynChron* 6450.

56 'slanderer': the slandered also has a role in denouncing the accused in a court case, as in *R&D* 1.160, 321, 371, 400 (Kratandros' account of his trial for inadvertent murder).

57 'tripod of a divine oracle': the apparatus for oracular pronouncements in the classical world.

58 'those who love Hellenes': an ambiguous phrase that opens up issues of nascent national and cultural awareness at the time of writing; cf. Beaton 2007; Kaldellis 2007a: 317–88.

hatred of men belongs to a lioness, madness to a tigress,
rage to a bear's nurse, fury to a leopard;   15
this is the behaviour of a fanged dog, of a wolf,
the behaviour of a tawny serpent, a bristling boar.

31   2.33–64 Hr (2.50–60 = 503–13 Ma; 2.61–64 = 514–17 Ma)

Men, a slanderer is something dreadful and evil.
He destroys cities and overturns houses,
he stirs up a hostile mother against her daughter
and the offspring of his own family against the father;
he is a serpent spewing forth deadly venom,   5
belching terrible man-slaying poison,
a maritime puffer-toad, a fire-breathing katoblepas
and a martichoras,[59] that man-eating Indian beast
which shoots out darts from its mouth's sinews
and like the far-shooters aims most accurately   10
bitter heart-rending words that wound worse than arrows.
A bitter destructive root, a root from the hellebore,
aconite growing in the islands and on the mainland
from the spittle-like juices of a murderous heart;
a wild serpent, a tawny liver-devouring lion,   15
a vulture that does not gouge out eyes nor plunge into entrails
<...> but into the very heart.[60]
If you have a slanderer as a fellow citizen,
you will not escape his venom, you will not evade his goad
even if you become a broad-winged high-soaring eagle,   20
even if you fly high in the air, even if you flee to the aither.
His tongue spouts venom, his heart rage;
he is an accurate archer, he envenoms his darts;
his missiles reach into the heaven and wound;
his dart is not made of bronze, his missile is not made of iron,   25
his bow is not made of horn nor its sinew of ox-gut –

---

59 'katoblepas' and 'martichoras': two fabulous beasts (cf. 77 and 155 below); the katoblepas' head, perhaps based on accounts of a wildebeest, is said to be so heavy it can only hang down: cf. Aelian, *De natura animalium* 7.6; accounts of the martichore's ferocious fangs derive from Ktesias and may well represent a tiger; cf. Aristotle, *Historia Animalium* 2.1 (501a 26); Aelian, *De natura animalium* 4.21.

60 On metrical and sense grounds a lacuna is likely here, perhaps 'into the soul' (Mazal 1967).

but it reaches you and kills, whether you reach for the stars,
whether you soar to the heights of the starless sphere.
Envy that hates the good is the father of slander,
slander is conceived from deeply jealous envy,
the yet more bitter child and offspring of a bitter father,
an appalling tiger-lion sprung from a wrathful viper.

30

32[61] 2.65–67 Hr = 290–92 Ma

Thus he who was mining a pit of death for those close by,
himself plunged into the deeply gaping hollow,
into the inescapable sub-Tartarean abyss.[62]

33 293–94 Ma

Thus the pestilential sorcerer departed thence,
having suffered and been punished rather than taking action and punishing.

34 2.68–70 Hr = 295–97 Ma

Thus no wrongdoing passes entirely unnoticed
either by the eyes of the ever-watchful and all-seeing god[63]
or by most men, I do not say all.

35 2.71–72 Hr = 298–99 Ma

But even death, it seems, fears the wicked
and flees from the criminal and trembles[64] before wrongdoers.[65]

36[66] 2.73–80 Hr

There is a beast from Paionia, and the name of the beast is monops,
in size it somewhat resembles a broad-chested bull.
It feeds on bitter and death-bringing roots;

61 32–35: Passages on the inevitability of due punishment, presumably resolving some complexity in the plot devised by the sorcerer in 33.

62 'sub-Tartarean abyss': in Greek mythology the depths of the underworld, even below Hades, and a place of punishment.

63 'all-seeing eye of God': cf. *SynChron* 4039.

64 Translating τρέμει with Mazal (= ms V) rather than φεύγει ('flees') with Conca (= mss WM)

65 Similar ideas on death and the wicked appear in 81 below.

66 The first of several paradoxographical excurses, here derived from Aelian (*De natura animalium* 7.3). Behind the monops ('one-eyed') probably lurks the European bison or aurochs (extinct in Europe in 1627). Such passages are possibly introduced in *A&K* for their decorative value, but may also serve as a metaphorical comparison (cf. the creatures in 29 and 31 above).

should some big-game hunter pursue it,
it releases a fiery fart of bitter flame;   5
should even a drop of its excrement fall
on a dog, or a man, or any other beast,
it kills it on the spot and destroys it immediately.

37[67] **2.81–92 Hr = 308–19 Ma**
But even the elements as well as fire, earth, rivers
and field-haunting beasts recognize wicked men,
and pursue them from all quarters, loathing their wickedness.
The watchful eye of Justice hunts them out and tracks them down
and follows the impious man everywhere, pursuing him   5
as many-eyed Argos did Inachos' daughter,[68]
even though he leaps over the snowy wastes of Atlas,
even though he hides in the deep chambers of Triton,
even though he plunges into the Ocean and lingers under water,   10
even though, winged like an eagle, he soars over Libya
and the regions beyond the Kaukasos and Gadeira,[69]
even though he flees to the Arimaspoi and to the Massagetai.[70]

38 300–05 Ma
But then I saw the eye of Retribution and Justice,
the punitive and vengeful eye of man-slaying Justice,
I saw the mighty wonder-working hand of god,
the palm that corrects those who have not acted well
and through which you meet god's most dreadful severity;
for he exacts vengeance from evil creatures with many dishonouring afflictions.

39 2.93–94 Hr = 306–07 Ma

67 37–39: On the inescapable power of Justice, cf. 8 above; these passages are perhaps part of a speech.

68 Io, daughter of Inachos, transformed into a white cow by the jealous goddess Hera, was guarded by the monster Argos and pursued by him when maddened by a gadfly (Apollodoros, *Bibliotheke* 2.1.3).

69 'Caucasus and Gadeira': the traditional eastern and western limits of the Mediterranean world.

70 'Arimaspoi': according to Herodotos (4.13), a one-eyed people in the North. 'Massagetai': a nomadic tribe from the borders of the Caspian Sea defeated by Cyrus in 526 BCE (Herodotos 1.202–16); on both, cf. Tzetzes, *Chiliades* 7.677–92.

Thus nothing can endure to bear the impious,
not a river nor a tree nor earth, mother of all.

40[71] 2.95 Hr = 261 Ma

Every brigand is unruly and a bellower and loquacious.

Fragments probably from Book 2

41[72] 27–30 Ma

A man in love, they say, is quick to detect
the love that is prompted by similar emotions;[73]
the heart's yearnings and promptings, they say,
appear in the face as if in a gleaming mirror

42 31–37 Ma

For even a barbarian takes pity on rays of loveliness,
even if he sees a mere flash of beauty, a gleam of comeliness,
he takes pity on the statuesque loveliness that is endangered[74]
and on the god-like visage and the sparkling eye,
even if he is stony-hearted, even if he was born of the sea,   5
even he is the offshoot of that wild and legendary oak,[75]
even if he has the indomitable temperament of a cub-nurturing lioness.

Fragments of uncertain position, perhaps from Book 2 (or from a later book)

43 320–22 Ma

There was indeed nothing more terrible than a heart that bears malice,

71 A comment perhaps derived from a specific episode of confrontation.

72 41–48: These passages from the disorganized anthology in mss WM which are not linked to lines from Makarios' excerpts (which are in book order; see Introduction, p. 277) are not easy to place in the hypothetical plot. 41–42: These deal with the reactions of probably Aristandros but perhaps the villain to beauty, presumably that of Kallithea, and are not event-specific. 43–45: On the expectation of the just elimination of the effects of malice, these lines are likely to come after some reversal to the central pair, in which slander has played a part. 46–48: These passages deal, once again, with reversals of fortune and the malign role of slander.

73 Cf. Hel 6.7.8 for an almost identical expression. Cf. also *L&K* 6.6.2.

74 The idea of the uncouth barbarian responding in kindly manner to a pretty prisoner permeates the novel tradition: cf., e.g., Hel 1.4.3, 5.7.3, 8.9.4.

75 Cf. *Odyssey* 19.163.

not even a vengeful soul and a murderous character
that drinks blood, is bitter and is thirsty for draughts of murder.

44　323–32 Ma

If nothing escapes the eye of god,
if his gaze is all-seeing, if his eye is all-perceptive,
if he loathes the unjust and favours the just,
he will offer us his right hand and he will support us,
and he will wreak justice on the brigands for their evil deeds;　　　　5
and the eye of Victory will smile on us
and the viper's dread twilight will be poured over them;
if he is able to come to the aid of those who have been wronged,
if he chastises and punishes the unjust leaders,
then he will certainly have removed the dread spirits of doom from us.　10

45　333–35 Ma

But behold the eye of god and Retribution and Justice,
how it reveals what is hidden, refutes what is false[76]
and attacks slanderers, even if in the meanwhile it is shut.

Fragments of Book 2 or 3

46　518–19 Ma

There is many a slip between cup and lip,
and mouth and vessel – you know the proverb.[77]

47[78]　520–22 Ma

The crabbed ambiguities of oracles and prophecies,
of dark black-winged dreams
are for the most part unravelled by events.

48　523–27 Ma

But no one, it seems, has existed who has not experienced envy,
who is unscarred by its bitterly piercing goads,
not an emperor or general or he who relies on words;
indeed the emperor in particular, since he is the most powerful,
is the most tormented by envy's thorns.　　　　5

76　Cf. Hel 8.13.4.

77　Cf. Apostolios 14.46 (Leutsch and Schneidewin 1839–51, vol. 2).

78　Dreams have an important role in the novels' plots; this passage (cf. fr. 152) has echoes
of Aristotelian dream theory: see MacAlister 1990: 209–10, and more generally 1996: 156–61.

BOOK 3[79]

49[80]   3.1–8 Hr = 262–69 Ma

Nothing is certain for mortal men, but the wheel of Fortune[81]
frequently rotates and turns intentions
and plans and human fate topsy-turvy.
Even if man's every plan could be accomplished,
mankind would come into rivalry with god.[82]   5
Who then would be able to crack a man's insolence?
But god, it seems, on purpose limits
and overturns deliberations and confuses matters.

50   3.9–11 Hr = 726–28 Ma

If Destiny seizes prematurely one who lives an evil life,
his death is not death, nor his doom doom,
nor his mortification mortification but a cessation of troubles.

51   3.12–14 Hr = 723–25 Ma

It becomes him who has a man's heart and is born of noble stock
and has been reared appropriately either to live a good life
or to quit this life and die befittingly.

52[83]   3.15–31 Hr

You are not unaware, Aristandros, of Fortune's tricks,
you are not unaware that the sea sometimes swells
and is tossed by incessant deeply roaring waves
and then grows quiet again and becomes calm once more
and checks its agitations and heaving energy   5
as a gentle breeze blows mildly.

79 Book 3: The surviving extracts suggest a series of violent swings in the plot, including
Aristandros' despair at the prospect of separation from Kallithea and the prospect of another
battle.

80 49–51: Comments on the instability of human affairs, caused by a jealous deity, and
an individual's reactions suggest that disaster has overtaken the central pair, with perhaps
Aristandros contemplating suicide (51).

81 Cf. 54.2, 159; the wheel of Fortune appears also in *SynChron* 6153–55; it is a motif found
widely in medieval literature; cf. Cupane 1993.

82 'god': translating θεῷ ('god') with mss WM and Conca (cf. 52.7), rather than θεοῖς
('gods') with ms V and Mazal.

83 A consolatory speech to Aristandros, perhaps implying that he and Kallithea have been
separated; in that case the speaker will be a companion and not Kallithea.

Dense clouds do not always occlude and
dim the face of the brightly gleaming sun,
gloom does not always lord it over winter,
the hateful fruit-destroying months do not last forever with
    their falling leaves.   10
The flower-bearing fruitful spring shines forth in due time,
and in due time the fruit-ripening season of summer,
driving away the surly winter cold.
The wrathful demon is not enraged forever,
and does not always cast a grim-looking eye on mortals,   15
but there are times when he smiles and gazes on them
with peaceful countenance and more amiable looks.

53[84] 3.32–33 Hr
In my view boastful and over-refined language
is indicative of a vulgar soul and intellect.[85]

54[86] 357–59 Ma
Thus mankind's whole life is unstable,[87]
thus the wheel of Fortune turns from high to low,[88]
adding unequal and complex burdens.

55 3.34–37 Hr = 360–63 Ma
Thus one should call no mortal happy[89]
till he has crossed the open ocean of life,
the ocean that heaves and rages beyond the brine
of the Atlantic, Sicily and the billowing Pontic Sea.

56[90] 3.38–56 Hr = 38–56 Ma
Tribulation tests the reliability of friendship,
as fire tries the purity of matter,

---

84 Presumably part of the speech from which 52 is taken, but the rationale is not clear.

85 Translating γνώμης ('intellect') with ms V and Tsolakes, rather than γλώσσης ('tongue') with Conca, following an emendation by Boissonade and Hercher.

86 54–55: Probably closing elements to the speech represented in 52.

87 Cf. Hel. 5.4.7, 6.7.3, 6.9.3.

88 Cf. SynChron 6155.

89 A paraphrase of Solon's advice to Kroisos (Herodotos 1.32).

90 56–56a: The friendship is presumably between Aristandros and the companion acquired in captivity (cf. 16–18 above). The disconcerting comparisons have their roots in the paradoxographical tradition; cf. 31, 60.

as a touchstone proves gold;
he is a true friend who, when his friend suffers,
does not flee nor betray him nor turn his back.[91]   5
A friend is a friend in misfortune; for in time of prosperity
god alone is sufficient – who has need of a friend?
But if someone sees a friend being submerged in disaster[92]
and makes his escape, leaving him deserted like some sea-going ship
that has no navigators, no cables, no sails,   10
he is acting like a dolphin or a flea but not like a man.
For a dolphin follows a ship to land,
and if he realizes it is approaching the shore,
he turns deserter and abandons the crew;
and blood-sucking fleas live with the source of blood   15
for as long as they can find channels rich in blood;
but if they lack blood, if they realize that
the flesh and the tissue and the skin have grown cold,
they make their getaway and keep company no longer.[93]

56a   Plan §6

That he who keeps company with his friends in times of good fortune and
deserts them in times of misfortune, acts like a dolphin and a flea but not
like a man. For dolphins frequently follow ships until they approach land,
then they leave them and turn away; fleas feed on the body so long as it is
alive but when it dies they immediately run off.

57[94]   3.57–59 Hr = 364–66 Ma

An airy mind and one that is away in the clouds
cannot bear Fortune's kindliness
which weighs more than lead, more than iron.[95]

58[96]   3.60–63 Hr = 528–31 Ma

The platitude, it seems, is no myth,

---

91 Cf. Euripides, *Orestes* 665–68.

92 Translating συμφορᾷ ('in disaster'), following ms V and Conca, rather than δυστυχῶς
('miserably'), ms WM and Mazal, a dative as opposed to an adverb.

93 Cf. Euripides, *Orestes* 1498–99.

94 Bearing in mind the novels' conventions, these derogatory comments are more likely to
apply to a lesser character rather than Aristandros, the central figure.

95 Cf. *SynChron* 6072, 6074.

96 Cf. 37 for the elements acting together, in that case in hunting out evildoers.

that elements join with each other, they say,
to transmit to each other what is concealed by both;
hence men can communicate everything from mouths without tongues.

59[97]   3.64–66 Hr (= 372–74 Ma) + 375–78 Ma

But what earth-born man will find unmixed good fortune?
For Fate, it seems, holds a grudge against them
and mixes a touch of bitterness into pleasant events.
But the spirit presiding over one's birth seems
always to implant something unwanted into pleasant events,   5
like tares among corn, thorns among roses,
and is resentful of the good and discredits what is lovely.

60[98]   3.67–70 Hr

The mother hen is called 'emperor',[99]
and bustles round her subjects and gathers them in,
the tender unfledged chicks,[100]
and wards off harm and every attack.

61[101]   3.71–72 Hr = 379–80 Ma

When much wine, they say, enters the body,
words bubble out that reveal every secret.

62[102]   381–85 Ma

An oppressed and lowly man would quite easily learn
what is intended against the more lowly,

97 A further comment on the mutability of fate, which seems to have been a prominent motif in this book.

98 A further paradoxographical excursus, possibly from Aelian, perhaps used here with reference to some commander.

99 Cf. Aelian, *De natura animalium* 4.37, 14.7 on the maternal habits of the *strouthos*; Mazal 1967: 112 suggests the reference is to the *trochilos* (Aelian, *De natura animalium* 9.11) but this seems ill-founded.

100 The image of the mother bird and her chicks occurs also in *SynChron* 6365–66.

101 Barbarians are regularly prone to drink in the novels; cf. Harder 1997; Jouanno 1992. This comment may indicate a plot development. For similar sentiments, cf. Theokritos, *Idyll* 29.1; Herodotos 1.212.2.

102 62–63: These indications of a malignant conspiracy could well conclude Book 3. The atmosphere conjured up by these passages is suggestive of the court of Manuel I in the 1140s as revealed by the comments of Manganeios Prodromos and Iakovos Monachos on events involving the *sevastokratorissa* Eirene, Manasses' patron for his Chronicle; cf. E. and M. Jeffreys 2009: xxviii–xxix.

but much escapes the attention of the nobleman, the man of high rank
and of elevated station, and especially when done in darkness
and when attacks are made by his inferiors.   5

63   386–90 Ma

Thus god fends off those of malignant disposition,
thus he who has devised evil for another
brings the injury down on his own head,
he who contrived a pit of death for others
is himself cast hurtling down and flung into the abyss.   5

Fragment not certainly to be included in Book 3

64[103]   57–62 Ma

When the boy Eros, they say, breathes gently,
he instils delight into souls and sports sweetly
like a gently blowing Zephyr over the backs of the waves;
but should he be stern, should he be vehement, should he bring on a squall,
there is no other god so mind-shattering,   5
so tempestuous or so stormy.

Fragments of Book 3 or 4

65[104]   270–72 Ma

It is better, I think, to fall fighting nobly
than to be captured alive like hound-fearing hares
and to succumb to shameful mutilation and bitter torture.

66[105]   Plan §7

That he who rejects his kin and adopts strangers as his own resembles the
serpent in one's bosom that betrays its own flesh; or it is as if someone were
to cut off his foot of flesh and blood and fit a wooden one, or if he were to
cut off his right hand with his left in an outbreak of madness.

---

103 Although its position in the anthology in mss WM suggests that this passage on the
contradictory nature of Eros belongs in Book 3 it is not clear how it fits into the plot.

104 Cf. 9 above. It is not clear with which battle episode these lines are best associated.

105 66–67: The relevance of these passages to the plot is uncertain (66 that adoption is
unnatural, 67 on the nature of anger); their place between Books 3 and 4 is suggested by the
position of Plan §§6 and 9 (= 56a and 73a), confirmed by the anthologies.

67   Plan §8

That anger dwells in men's hearing, like a picket for the heart; if it hears
something pleasant which enters the soul without disturbance, it remains
quiet; but if something oppressive and disobliging enters, it jumps up like
a watchdog.

BOOK 4[106]

68[107]   63–80 Ma

Aristandros groaned, "Oh, woe is me, Kallithea;
once more there are chains and prison, once more there is captivity,
once more gaols and imprisonment, once more gloomy dungeons;
we are bound, we are imprisoned, and the guard is ever alert;
once more we are in captivity, once more we endure the yoke of
    slavery.[108]   5
Kallithea has the earth as her bridal couch and a dungeon as
    her bridal chamber,[109]
and the attendant at the golden girl's[110] bridal chamber bears a sword.
O Fate, wrathful fate, evilly envious spirit,
after that wretched beast Nausikrates
you have placed me in the hands of the leader of the Tyrians.   10
Then after the Tyrian the robber chief Bousiris
took me prisoner again and tried to eat my entrails,
treating me as an a farmyard animal, a grass-eating creature;
Bousiris was not enough, Kallisthenes was not enough,
but there came again a storm, there came again a tempest,   15

106 Book 4: Aristandros' opening lament outlines the couple's previous misadventures,
which then continue, according to the disjointed glimpses permitted by the fragments; an evil
brigand seems to be a prime cause of the difficulties.
107 This passage, with its details of the twists and turns of the central pair's misfortunes,
must precede 69. There seem to have been at least three episodes of captivity at the hands
of Nausikrates (who must be the marauder implied in 5–6 above), the leader of the Tyrians
Kallisthenes (perhaps involved in the battle suggested by 9–10), and Bousiris (perhaps
responsible for the suicidal thoughts of 51); one or more of these episodes are likely to have
been narrated in flashbacks. It is thanks to this passage that the names of Aristandros and
Kallithea are confirmed.
108 Similar laments can be found in XenEph 3.8.6 and *R&D* 7.2.
109 Cf. *L&K* 3.10.5.
110 The heroine in *DigAk* is also golden (E 472) and 'sun-born' (G 4.350, 6.134); cf. the
golden goddesses of classical literature (e.g. *Iliad* 5.425).

there blew again the harsh south-easterly
and stirred up a greater wave that swelled like a mountain,
more troublesome than the poison that had roared out previously.[111]

69[112] 4.1–9 Hr
Into what pool of disasters, into what ocean
is the most miserable race of men thrown
right from the womb, from the first glimpse of light;
and they cannot swim free from misery
until Charon,[113] who escorts the dead, ferries them   5
to the all-receiving prison that welcomes the dead in the nether world,
to other hateful, darkened regions without light
and which the surge of the Acheron and the eddies of the Kokytos[114]
swirl around and enclose in a watery embrace.

70[115] 391–95 Ma
Like a cork tossed in the wind the black wave of misfortunes
was hurled against me, it smote the planks,
it unfastened the plates, it loosed the keel,
it shattered the mast, it shook the sides,
it broke the ribs in the hull.   5

71[116] 396–403 Ma
Common humanity persuades men to share
in the grief and mourning of others who suffer;
this humanity can shame Skythians, Tauroskythians,
the Hippomolgoi, the Arismaspoi and the Kynoprosopoi,
and can make those beyond the Kaukasos and those beyond the Araxes[117] 5

---

111 'roared out': more appropriate for storms than poison.

112 Arguably the disasters are an elaboration of the storms at the end of 68.

113 'Charon': the mythological ferryman of the underworld who conveys the dead to Hades itself.

114 'Acheron', 'Kokytos': rivers in Epirus (north-western Greece), which in Greek mythology flowed into the underworld; cf. *Odyssey* 10.513.

115 Fragment of a first-person speech, probably from Aristandros in the (metaphorical?) storm of 68–69.

116 71–72: Once again an indication that the central pair have acquired a companion in misfortune.

117 A mixture of legendary and genuine distant and barbaric peoples. 'Hippomolgoi': cf. *Iliad* 13.5; 'Kynoprospoi', i.e. dog-faced: cf. Aelian, *De natura animalium* 10.25; 'Araxes': river beyond which the Massagetae were to be found.

sympathize with those who are in trouble and deeply distressed;
for mankind's hearts are not made of iron,[118]
nor are they the offspring of wild beasts or the famed oak of antiquity.[119]

72   4.10–12 Hr = 404–06 Ma
Friendly fellowship between souls and companionship with each other
lightens the great weight of misfortune,
like an awkward burden shared between two.

73[120]   4.13–26 Hr
Wise men, interpreters of the Muses, say:[121]
"If it were possible for all men to gather together
and for each to set out before the others his own miseries
and griefs and constraints on his soul,
and then a herald were to go forth and proclaim distinctly,   5
'Men wrought from mud, men whose form is of earth,
each of you has laid aside his own sorrows
which bow him down and grieve and torment his soul;
now pick up the griefs of the next man',
each of the earth-born would immediately discover   10
how much lighter was the burden laid on him,
how much more easily born when evils were compared;
for no one would be willing to carry another's troubles
once he had cast off his own heart's burdens.

73a   Plan §9
That if it were possible, they say, for all men to gather together and each to
set out in front of the others his own misfortunes, and then a herald were to
go by and say, 'O men, each of you has laid aside his own grief, now take up
in its place the grief of the man next to you', every one would immediately
recognize how much lighter in comparison was the burden he carried, for
no one would want to do what had been proclaimed.

74[122]   4.27–31 Hr = 407–11 Ma
Who is without experience of evil, once they have fallen to earth?

---

118 'hearts': literally 'entrails'; cf. the 'bowels of compassion' of the King James Bible.
119 'oak of antiquity': cf. 42.6 above.
120 73–73a: From a speech of consolation.
121 Cf. Theokritos, *Idyll* 17.115.
122 Again from a consolatory speech.

Or for whom, as they navigated the briny waves of life,
have not misfortunes opened a widely gaping mouth,
like water-spouting, wide-yawning whales
that gulp down sailors, masts and ships and all?   5

75[123]   **412 Ma**
Thus Fortune sports with mortals' affairs.

76[124]   **413–28 Ma**
But it seems that everything has its doom as close kin
which is nurtured with it and remains present and develops with it;
the millipede promptly ravages cabbages
and digs out the roots down below and secretly revels
in the delicate and most tender recent shoots,   5
the tare is planted with the corn and grows with it.
The oak fears thunder, vines hail,
merchants shipwreck, ships waves,
bitter cabbage-eating caterpillars devour cabbages
and browse on the fronds of green-leaved trees   10
and heart-devouring worms cling
to sweet-sapped trees and mortify their roots,
evil undermines virtue and envy the good.
I think that god grows wrathful deliberately[125]
and throws men's affairs into turmoil and humbles them and
    confuses them   15
so that no one can say that they have acquired what is good from
    their own deserts.

77[126]   **4.32–41 Hr = 546–55 Ma**
The platitude is not false, it seems,
that every man who is not endowed with deep-dyed[127] wits,
who does not boast a sharp mind, who does not comprehend what
    is needful,

---

123 Perhaps the conclusion to a consolatory speech.

124 Perhaps also from a consolatory speech, addressed to Aristandros; cf. 49 and 59 above for other comments on the mutability of human affairs.

125 The arbitrary nature ascribed to the deity's interventions are perhaps borderline Christian.

126 On the effects of flattery, possibly part of a character sketch.

127 'deep-dyed': a rare Homeric word (ἀμφιμελαίνας) which appears to mean 'intelligent' (Hesychius A 4069).

delights in being flattered and embraces you
and is glad and thrilled on hearing what he wants to hear;   5
if you tell the truth, if you provoke him with enquiries,
he hates you and reviles you and looks on your words
like daggers, like the venom of a poisonous snake,
like a katoblepas' breath, like a martichore's fangs,[128]
and rushes after a reciprocal irritation – what empty-headedness!   10

78[129]   4.42–44 Hr = 273–75 Ma

But what has been destined defeats, they say, the wits
and leads them away from the path and throws them into the abyss
and pitches them headfirst on to their pates and their shoulders.[130]

79[131]   4.45–65 Hr (45–64 = 429–48 Ma) + 449–53 Ma

A small spark can kindle a roaring furnace,
one mangy beast can destroy a whole herd,[132]
and one caterpillar can made a whole tree leafless;
and one evildoer can disgrace a whole city.
If someone quenches the spark, the fire's seed,   5
the flame will not rise, the furnace will not become incandescent;
if the herdsman removes the suffering beast,
the mange will not affect the remainder, it will not approach the rest;
if the gardener squashes the leaf-eating caterpillar,
the tree will not be covered with its eggs and offspring,   10
and its younger offspring will not eat the leaves;
if the sword cuts the throat of a venturesome man,
no one would be so shameless and rash
as to venture an attack on these evil men,
but will draw back from the bold-hearted venture,   15
having the penalty close before his eyes.
For if a small squealing piglet can panic a heavy-bodied elephant,
if a rooster's call can terrify lions,
how will a sword and an axe not frighten a man,   20
as it hews evil-doing men limb from limb?
If therefore the death of one man can correct an entire city,

128 These monsters also appear in 31 above, with note.
129 Again, possibly part of a character sketch, perhaps with reference to a specific situation.
130 Cf. *Iliad* 5.586.
131 An extract from a speech, probably in a law court or perhaps before an assembly.
132 Manasses (or his excerptor) seems to have an interest in agricultural similes.

away with shamelessness, down with it, do not let
the violent tyrant, the brigand, so-called Brilliant One,[133] remain;
let him become an example to all citizens;   25
the death of one man is preferable to the destruction of the
    whole population.[134]

80[135]   4.66–76 Hr (66–74 = 735–43 Ma)

The most evil man grows old together with his life
and lives long years until his hair is quite white,
and death cannot get the better of him;
indeed death is terrified and flees,
lest the evil man bite him and death dies instead.   5
They say that once a viper, mother of poisons,
managed to bite a eunuch and promptly expired
for it had tasted blood that was much more poisonous
and had overcome even its own deadly venom.
But the good man blooms for a brief time   10
and then shrivels like a Lokrian rose[136] and perishes prematurely.

80a   Plan §10

That it is said that a viper bit a eunuch and expired, having tasted blood that
was deadlier than its own poison.

Fragments of Books 4 or 5

81[137]   454 Ma

This is what the player did, and the demon's dice.

82[138]   455–58 Ma

Thus the winter of grief mortifies hearts
and turns the living element to ice and congeals it and freezes it;

133 'Brilliant One': taking this phrase as referring to a particular individual, perhaps with
a contemporary reference (with Mazal 1967: 119, n. 92).

134 A line that echoes Caiaphas' comments on Jesus (John 11.50).

135 80–80a: A cynical commonplace perhaps referring to a specific character in the plot
(cf. 35). On the mentality of eunuchs, cf. 110 and 161 below where a courtly context seems
probable.

136 'Lokrian rose': a proverbially frail and short-lived flower; cf. Lykophron, *Alexandra*
1429; *H&H* 9.16; *SynChron* 4557 and 149.4 below.

137 On the role of malevolence in the working out of the plot.

138 On the impact of grief.

suffering, winging its way like a tower-shattering rock,
both hacks the soul and shakes the entrails.

83[139]   459–62 Ma

But it is impossible to find unmixed happiness
among any of those caught up in earth's orbit,
even if some attain many possessions, even if they are guided by friends,
even if they are swamped with gold, even if they are flooded with bliss.

83a   556–57 Ma

The word of truth is simple, they say,
and justice has no need of unnecessary verbiage.

BOOK 5[140]

84[141]   5.1–11 Hr = 564–74 Ma

No other worse currency[142] has appeared among mankind
than gold, gold with its aspirations to evil,
the tyrant, the violent hewer of men,
the father of slander, the cultivator of falsehood,
the bitter deceiver of men, the root of evil.   5
It destroys cities and overturns houses;
it destabilizes everything and corrupts and confuses;
it teaches evil and alters minds
and diverts sensible intentions to evil purposes;
it has taught mortals every evil design   10
and every impiety and wicked habit.

---

139 83–83a: Again on the instability of humanity's prospects; cf. 59, 76.

140 Book 5: Troubles continue, perhaps now in Rhodes and perhaps with a new companion with whom to recount past events; passages on joy suggest that Aristandros and Kallithea are reunited, but there may be an aggressive suitor for Kallithea.

141 On the impact of gold, cf. 23. Whether this is a general reflection on gold or motivator for the plot is not clear. Similar sentiments appear in *SynChron* 3497–511.

142 The word translated as 'currency' can also mean 'custom', perhaps a deliberate ambiguity.

85[143]   81–91 Ma

Do you see tall trees during winter storms?
All those that yield to the winds' blasts
keep their branches unharmed and their trunks unshattered,
but each one that tries to resist perishes, root and branch;
thus the oak that refuses to be humble perishes and falls   5
but the reed that bows down escapes destruction;
thus the sailor who, when the wind blows with fierce gusts,
does not submit and slacken off nor set off with lowered sails
but ventures to haul the sheets tight beyond the ship's capabilities,
will be overturned and complete his voyage with up-ended benches;[144]   10
and you, my lovely charmer, do you wish to hold out in opposition?

86[145]   92–102 Ma (102 = 5.12 Hr)

"And breathing out nonsense and much forceful arrogance,
sail away then to Argos and become an islander
and dwell in sea-washed Rhodes instead of Petra."[146]
While he was rattling on about this he added the following too,
"Your father, that Charidemos, was an impoverished show-off   5
of this sort, and empty-headed too,
that creature of servile disposition who begot you;
the offspring knows its own father;[147]
savage things are born of savage parents, insolent from the insolent-
    hearted.
But you should bear this in mind, as you imitate him,   10
that every harsh thought comes to a most shameful outcome."

87[148]   5.13–21 Hr = 590–98 Ma

Hearing the troubles of others
can upset the hearers and move them to grief,

143 Addressed to a girl (line 11) by a suitor, whether unwelcome or otherwise: a frequent motif in the novels: cf. e.g. *L&K* 6 (Thersandros and Leukippe); *R&D* 1 (Gobryas and Rodanthe); *D&C* 6 (Kallidemos and Drosilla).

144 Cf. Sophocles, *Antigone* 712–17.

145 An extract from a speech by a man (cf. the masculine participle in line 4).

146 A deme of Lindos on Rhodes is named Argos (Mazal 1967: 123, n. 101a; PW 2.1 (1895), col. 790 Argos [15]); Petra is a not uncommon place name.

147 Cf. *R&D* 3.51–52.

148 87–88a: Cf. 16 and 17 on humanity's propensity for compassion, with parallels. The passages at this point suggest that there has been a narrative of misfortune, perhaps by one or other of the protagonists whose reunion after separation leads to excessive emotion.

for on the one hand it re-opens their own sufferings
and on the other induces them to pity those of others;
participation in happy events can sometimes lead to envy;   5
but all those who share in similar difficulties
respect their common humanity with their fellow sufferers
and, pitying each others' misfortunes,
drain together the bitter cup of sorrowful friendship.

88   5.22–27 Hr = 558–63 Ma

Thus great joy can bring death,[149]
when in moments of excessive pleasure the elements of life
are slackened and their warmth is exhaled;
great delight seems to intoxicate
those who have been enervated by its ineluctable spells,   5
as heated old wine does those who drink it undiluted.

88a   Plan §11

That great pleasure can kill, when the elements of life are slackened and
their natural warmth is exhaled. Excessive pleasure seems to intoxicate and
enervate, like much wine when drunk undiluted.

89[150]   103–07 Ma

Beauty wounds more sharply than an arrow
and, whistling in through the eyes, it rushes into the soul;[151]
the glance functions as an aqueduct
for Eros' conduits and Desire's streams
and it channels the Erotes' currents into the soul.[152]   5

90   108–09 Ma

Thus the length of one night of brief extent
seems an entire age for those goaded by love.

---

149 Cf. Theagenes and Charikleia in Hel 2.6.

150 89–90: These two passages, of uncertain position, suggest that Kallithea, or another,
has inflamed a lover. Problems are posed by 90 since the central pair of these novels is
conventionally chaste until marriage in the final denouement of the plot: either, despite the
position suggested by the anthology, these lines come from the end or they refer to a sub-plot
and the union of minor characters.

151 For beauty as missile and the eyes as entry points, cf. XenEph 1.3.2; Hel 3.7.5; *L&K*
1.4.4; for the emphatic verb, cf. Nonnos, *Dionysiaka* 48.940.

152 Cf. fr. 11 above.

91[153]   110–15 Ma

Thus nothing, no delicacy, no drink,
even the most choice, tempts the taste-buds or attracts them,
if the heart is not at peace,
if bitterness in the soul restricts the appetite;
for when it is full of unhappiness, the container that is the heart   5
does not admit food, it spits out drink.[154]

92   5.28–29 Hr = 116–17 Ma

Among the living everything is delightful; in the underworld
we shall lie there as bones and earth and a little light dust.[155]

93[156]   5.30 Hr

The honourable delight in honourable companions, the unwholesome in the
despicable.

94[157]   5.31–34 Hr = 118–21 Ma

The gods distribute to mankind nothing that is unmixed
but they mingle together the unwholesome with the good.
On the one hand they bestow gold-gleaming rays of beauty,
but on the other they remove beauty of intellect.

95[158]   5.35–37 Hr = 122–24 Ma

Eros the all-tamer attacks without restraint
and possesses the heart and intoxicates the soul
and equips the lover to be enraged with himself.

96   125–51 Ma

For Eros, they say, is hot and sets the lover on fire;

153   91–92: A comment on a character's reaction to grief, to which 92 is a logical conclusion.

154   A similar effect, but produced by excessive joy, is described at *L&K* 5.13 and *R&D* 9.401–02.

155   Cf. *Anacreontea* 32.9-10 (West 1993).

156   It is unclear how this fits in the plot. For a similar sentiment, of like appealing to like, cf. 18 above.

157   On mixing of pleasant and unpleasant, cf. 59 and 83. The passage could refer either to a man or to a woman but, taken in conjunction with 95–97, would make sense as referring to a captor of Kallithea smitten with her beauty.

158   95–96a: These passages are best interpreted as a comment on the inflammatory impact of the heroine's beauty on her captor with a semi-scientific physiological explanation for the vehemence of passion; cf *L&K* 6.19 (Thersandros and Leukippe).

for as long as he is not despondent of attaining his wishes,
he hovers around the beloved and fawns on him and cultivates him
and consents readily to every request;[159]
but if he despairs and sees there is a danger of failure,   5
there is no raging boar or lion
or sullen leopard that can defeat Eros[160]
in rash deeds, bold ventures and murderous madness.
For he summons Wrath as his fellow campaigner
and in his company he rages with him without restraint   10
and arms himself to take vengeance on the offender.
For Eros and Wrath share the same roof,
they are close neighbours and shield-comrades,
since the seats of the liver and the heart are nearby.
For Eros dwells in the liver and Wrath in the heart,[161]   15
and the current of natural fire is near each,
for innate fire wells up in all viscera;
they are alike in violence but opposite in nature;
for Eros compels love and affection
while the other incites to retaliation and hatred;   20
so if Eros is slighted and spurned,
he without delay summons his neighbour Wrath;
Wrath springs up and responds in neighbourly fashion
and kindles a fire that burns without wood in the heart,
and even if till that moment he had been resting quietly in his own
     domain,   25
he starts the campaign, battles in the front line, breathes together
     with him, fights together with him,
he punishes like enemies those who had previously been loved.

96a   Plan §12

That as long as Eros hopes to achieve his intention, he hovers round the
beloved object and fawns on him; if he despairs, he summons Wrath as
his fellow campaigner in murder and takes up arms for attack. For Eros
and Wrath are neighbours to each other, they are neighbours in the viscera,
that is, they inhabit the liver and the heart. Fire wells up from each of these

----

159 Cf. *L&K* 4.8.5.
160 Translating νικῆσαι with the mss and Conca rather than Mazal's emendation κινῆσαι ('move').
161 *Anacreontea* 33.28 (West 1993).

viscera, similar in violence but opposite in nature; for Eros compels love and affection while the other incites to hatred and retaliation. If Eros is slighted, as has been said, he promptly summons Wrath to take vengeance.

97[162] 152–54 Ma

There is nothing more ready to have his mind
easily distracted than a love-smitten man,
when his desires and passions address him.

98[163] 5.38 Hr

What is done through violence is not culpable.

99 5.39 Hr

Impulsive generosity also has a certain charm.

100 5.40–43 Hr

When the bridal bower is set up and the marriage is being performed,
I think it neither reasonable nor auspicious nor becoming
for the bridegroom's father not to be present
and offer the wedding banquet and join in the festivities.

101[164] 599–614 Ma

If he who weeps is unappealing in appearance,
tears will increase his lack of beauty
and make his ugliness even less bearable.
But if he is handsome, if he is charming, if he is graced with beauty,
if his tint of black[165] is undiluted   5
and he is quietly garlanded with a white complexion,
when he is moistened with tears and filled with dampness
he resembles a fountain's breasts pregnant with water;
when a copious flow of salt tears has poured from the eyes
around the pupils' orbs and watered them,   10

162 This comment could well arise from the situation envisaged in 96.

163 98–100: Cf. Hel 1.21 when the robber Thyamis wishes to marry the heroine Charikleia and prevarication is needed; an analogous situation would provide a context for the reference to an anomalous marriage in 100. Mazal 1967: 128 wishes to argue, not altogether convincingly, that the expression 'bridegroom's father' could be stretched to mean 'parents of the bridal couple'.

164 This passage, based very closely on *L&K* 6.7.1–3, probably refers to Kallithea, as suggested by the reconstruction proposed in 98–100.

165 'tint of black': i.e. in his eyes.

the white is enhanced and appears more white,
the black grows red and changes colour entirely,
so that the white resembles the white-petalled narcissus
while the transformed black resembles the purple-hued violet.
Then the tears laugh and pour out more freely,   15
entangled in the midst of the eyes' orbs.

102[166]   5.44–54 Hr = 155–65 Ma

Thus men's fears are often for many
hindrances to their wicked acts.
Someone who is lurching towards despicable deeds and unlawful actions
like a colt spitting out a fire-tempered bit[167]
with no respect for himself or fear of god,   5
if he has some inbuilt fear, some terror imposed by men,
he refrains from his irregular and shameful lunges,
for he has fear to act like a heavy iron muzzle.
And they say that once a rabid wild dog
terrified a stout-hearted and powerful man   10
and kept him from a bed of adulterous debauchery.[168]

BOOK 6[169]

103[170]   6.1 Hr = 166 Ma

One has unreal images of the things one longs to attain.[171]

104   167–71 Ma

There is an old story that when Eros is unsuccessful[172]

---

166 By analogy with Hel 1.22 (Thyamis dissuaded from marriage with Charikleia) and *L&K* 6.7 (Thersandros' pity for Leukippe), Kallithea may have been able to deflect her captor's intentions on her.

167 Cf. Euripides, fr. 821, 3–4 (Nauck and Snell 1964).

168 For this episode, see Aelian, *De natura animalium* 7.25.

169 Book 6: Kallithea appears to have evaded her suitor, and the scene is probably now moved to an aristocratic setting where perhaps Aristandros and Kallithea come together, though laments suggest a disaster then takes place.

170 103–06: These passages seem to conclude the episode with Kallithea's captor and would-be suitor. 103 is perhaps a comment on the captor's attitude, 104–06 develop ideas of the impact of passion.

171 Cf. *SynChron* 6441.

172 Cf. *L&K* 5.26.2 for a passing comment on the rage of Eros.

his rage and fury is worse than that of a tiger-leopard;
if anyone spurns him he leaps on him violently
and tears the offender apart and devours his flesh,
but he also sets on the messenger who brings ill tidings.   5

105   172–73 Ma
The Erotes bubble away like this among men
and cloud and dim their minds with noxious steam.

106   174–76 Ma
A swooning eye and baleful eyelid,[173]
murky glances and a wasting countenance
can wither even passionate love.

107[174]   6.2–4 Hr (1–2 = 177–78 Ma)
O woman, it is an adornment for women and especially for maidens
not to wear their tongues out on useless matters, but to close their mouths
and not waste time on long and superfluous discussions.

108[175]   6.5–14 Hr = 615–24 Ma
To undertake a great enterprise, they say,
requires great consideration and thought.
If anyone were to be overcome by his urges
and take some bold action recklessly and without due thought
and without having taken into account the element of danger,
sensible people would think he was behaving   6
as though he were balancing his body over the edge of a crag,
like crag-climbing mountain goats,
and over craggy, inaccessible and deep-plunging gorges
or turning somersaults over naked swords.   10

109   6.15–22 Hr = 625–32 Ma
Action which precedes rational assessment
is usually liable to err and be hazardous

173 Perhaps referring to an attempt to diminish Kallithea's beauty, either self-inflicted or by another; cf. XenEph 3.6 (Anthia); *R&D* 8.440 (poison for Rhodanthe).

174 The speaker is male. The content is virtually proverbial; cf. 12 above and *H&H* 5.10.3 with older examples at, e.g., Sophocles, *Ajax* 293; Euripides, *Trojan Women* 654.

175 108–09: It would seem that some drastic plan has been proposed, hence the unknown speaker's counsel for caution. Both passages may come from the same speech; cf. 107.

and disastrous and lead to great injury;
but if one thinks ahead and takes everything into consideration
and stores up the seeds of a plan in his soul,   5
then he achieves both good husbandry and a good crop,
as when he who has used ox-ploughed furrows
reaps an abundant harvest from the richly clodded earth.

110[176]   6.23–30 Hr = 179–86 Ma

The race of eunuchs is by nature jealous;[177]
when entrusted with guard-duty, they do not drowse,
not because they are faithful to their masters or wish them well
but because they are envious, they are jealous and are grudging
   to others;
being unable to perform themselves, they hinder others who can.   5
They say dogs in the manger do the same;[178]
although they cannot eat barley like horses
they do not make way for the horses when they want to eat.

111[179]   187–88 Ma

Bed and night and kisses, embraces and a couch
are balm to the souls of those tormented by love.

112   189–93 Ma

Contact between mouths, and their connection
with each other as they delightfully mingle kisses
and send a stream of pleasure to chests,
entice hearts to the loving-cup
while they drink the bowl that is made nectar with the kiss.[180]   5

---

176 The reference to eunuchs suggests a courtly, or perhaps oriental, setting for this section of the plot; cf. 80, 161. Eunuchs have a place in several novels, e.g., Charit 5.2 ff. (Artaxates); Hel 8.17 ff. (Bagoas).

177 On eunuchs' envious natures, cf. Hel 8.6.2, 9.25.5.

178 For this proverbial fable, cf. Aesop, *Fables* 228 (Halm 1889), and also Proverbs 74 (Perry 1952).

179 111–113a: By the conventions of the novels these passages are unlikely to refer to actual encounters between the central pair (cf. the yearnings of Charikles in *D&C* 8.81 and Dosikles in *R&D* 3.63). The more extensive material preserved by Planudes arguably derives from this area of *A&K*. On the relationship of the *Carmen Morale* to *A&K* see the Introduction, p. 278.

180 Cf. *L&K* 2.8.1–2; *H&H* 1.9.1.

113   Plan §13

That three things flow from the mouth as from a fountain – breath, voice and kisses – which are very important to mankind; we use the mouth to converse with each other and we kiss with the lips; but the fountain of pleasure flows from hearts; contact between the lips and their union, as they mingle kisses, sends the stream of pleasure to chests and summons hearts to the loving-cup. The ancient myths say that when Hephaistos[181] formed man's body after he had mixed earth with water, each of the gods obtained a certain portion by lot: Zeus acquired the head since it was the fortress, Hermes the tongue, Athena the shoulders and hands, Poseidon the chest, Ares the heart, Aphrodite the liver, and Eros the lips since they provide kisses for lovers.

113a   Carmen morale (Cod. Paris. gr. 2750 A), 297–301

Three things flow from the mouth as from a fountain,
speech, breath and kisses, which are very important to men;
with the mouth we send our voices to each other
and we both speak with our lips and kiss with our lips;
but the heart gushes out both what is sweet and what is bitter.

114[182]   6.31–39 Hr = 194–202 Ma

Jealousy is innate in women;[183]
when they are burning in love's furnaces
and their viscera are on fire with that conflagration,
they consider their lovers handsome,
as lovely as statues, tall as plane trees   5
and then they are inclined to be suspicious of their looks, voices,
gait, nods, movements and conversation,
and, irritated by the sores caused by their suspicions,
they behave like jealous and aggrieved women.

---

181 'Hephaistos': for a version of the creation myth that resembles this, cf. Hesiod, *Works and Days* 60–65.

182 114–19: These passages, the first reasonably securely placed from Makarios' *Rhodonia* and the others linked by sense and to some extent by position in the anonymous anthology, involve an amorous encounter, probably between Aristandros and Kallithea. The jealous woman may be Kallithea (the heroine's jealousy is a minor motif in the novels, e.g., Drosilla at *D&C* 5.50; Rhodanthe at *R&D* 9.30), or another woman seeking to usurp Kallithea in Aristandros' affections.

183 Jealousy in women: cf. *D&C* 5.53.

115   203–08 Ma

Since unalloyed desire which has laid hold of a heart
does not permit the lover to be diverted to another,
either to power or a hand full of wealth
or beauteous form or a bloom of comeliness,
it compels him to breathe and imagine   5
and keep before his eyes only the beloved object.[184]

116   209–17 Ma

Thus beauty is a harsh tyrant and master of the heart;
it is a dart not made of iron but it speeds faster than a dart,
it flies more swiftly than a hawk or a falcon;
when it lays hold of the heart, when it enters the soul,
alas the severity of the wounds, alas the pain of the injuries;   5
for the sore oozes a deadly poison
even if he who shoots cannot be seen, even if the dart is not made
      of bronze;
it is a net that cannot be eluded, and it always takes its prey
for it is bird-lime and clutches souls like birds.

117   218–21 Ma

Nothing else in life can make souls
mingle in union and be attached to each other
– not brilliantly woven tunics or the gleam of gold –
as can Eros, the harsh god, the all-powerful, the great one.

118   222–24 Ma

One can conceal all other afflictions,
but not the wounds and intoxication of Eros;
for the gaze betrays both afflictions.

119   225–26 Ma

Every maiden flees the eyes of every stranger
as if from shaggy-necked bears, or tawny lionesses.

120[185]   Plan §14

That vinegar sprinkled on the nostrils shakes off deep sleep.

---

184 Cf. Hel 7.12.6 and 1.2.9 for a lover's immovable focus on the beloved.
185 Positioned here from its place in Planudes' paraphrase, the connection of this passage
to the plot is unclear; Mazal compares Knemon restoring Theagenes and Charikleia to
consciousness with water (Hel 2.6).

121[186]   **6.40–59 Hr = 633–52 Ma**

There are some disasters that go beyond tears;
men's sufferings are by nature of the following sort.
In sufferings that are easily bearable and when in moderate distress
streams of tears flow copiously
and bathe the eyelids and soothe the pupils,   5
as if pouring out from some abundant fountain,
and they alleviate the weight of pain for those in distress
as if they had been relieved of a festering wound.
But in miseries that are hard to endure and pains that are difficult
    to survive
even tears make their escape, betraying the pupils,   10
or rather they retreat to the depths
or sprinkle the face with white blotches;
when gut-devouring grief encounters these
as they struggle to hasten to the eyelids and pupils,
it checks their flow before they emerge,   15
and channels them below as they ooze vigorously;
the tear that is restrained in its path to the pupils
and hindered in its onrush to the eyelids
flows to the soul with a backwards eddy
and makes the wound to the heart more acutely felt.   20

121a   Plan §15

That in moderate disasters tears flow more copiously and much of the grief
is relieved and removed, as from a festering disease; in excessive disasters,
tears remain deep down, abandoning the eyes; grief encounters the tears as
they make for the eyes and checks their flow; these are vigorously channelled
deep down and as they retreat towards the soul they make the wound more
acutely felt.

122[187]   **6.60–65 Hr = 729–34 Ma**

Often an end to life is devoutly to be prayed for
and death that releases from care and causes anguish to cease
is more acceptable than a life of great pain;

---

186 121–121a: Some disaster has precipitated an outpouring of lamentation. On the place
of tears in Byzantine society, cf. Hinterberger 2006: 27–51. 121 is closely modelled on *L&K*
3.11.1–2, where Kleitophon and Leukippe lament their fate at the hands of the Egyptian bandits.

187 A further indication of the magnitude of the disaster.

and certainly for those whose life is weighed down with care and
    full of suffering,
premature death is a benefactor,   5
since it checks agony and obliterates pain.

123[188]   Plan §16

That he who expresses his soul's anguish is refreshed and relieved, for the
smoke of grief is blown out from the mouth as if from a chimney.

BOOK 7[189]

124[190]   7.1–3 Hr = 532–34 Ma

For since the earth is kin to the sun and the stars,
it reveals to them all that is hidden
through silent voiceless tongues[191] and speechless mouths.

125[192]   7.4–30 Hr

If one keeps a bow constantly taut,
it will break, being unable to withstand the strength of the tautness.
If you lessen the force, if you relax the string,
the bow loses its efficiency and the horn becomes soft;
if it is stretched occasionally and slackened occasionally,   5
it is conserved and shoots arrows well,
it places the well-prepared arrows[193] accurately
as well as shots that are neither ineffective nor useless.
If a man achieves a life full of anxiety
and comports himself with a soul laden with cares   10
and wishes to be always preoccupied with business,
he is unwittingly mad, liable to a sudden brain-storm

---

188 This extract sits appropriately at the end of Book 6 as a closure to a scene of grief (cf.
121–22).

189 Book 7: The disjointed surviving passages suggest a number of motifs (the need to
maintain a balance, the destructive role of gold, jealousy and fear), but offer few clues to their
place in plot development; the historical and paradoxographical examples could well have
been set in speeches.

190 For the theme of Nature as all-seeing, cf. 37, 130.

191 'voiceless tongues': cf. Nonnos, *Dionysiaka* 48.290.

192 125–125a: A plea for moderation, prompted, presumably, by the disasters at the end of
Book 6; this passage possibly formed part of a debate or dialogue.

193 'well-prepared arrows': cf. Sophocles, *Philoktetes* 290.

and runs the risk that his soul's tension will snap.
If he becomes excessively effeminate and drinks and gourmandizes
and disports with flute-playing women and makes music with them, 15
handing the reins of his mind entirely over to pleasure,
he will do better than Sardanopolos, he will do better than
  Smindyrides,[194]
he will make himself useless for any task,
he will surpass that delicate Sagaris[195]
who until he was aged and his ancient hair white 20
used to take mashed and chewed food
from his nurse's mouth like a baby
so that he would not hurt his teeth with chewing;
he never put his own hand
below his navel, not even on his genitals. 25
Let there be moderation then in one's pleasures,
as well as in troubles and pain and gloom.

125a Plan §17

That the delicate Sagaris until old age used to take chewed food from his nurse's mouth, so that he would not hurt his mouth with chewing; he never put his hand below his navel.

126[196] Plan §18

That both brambles and vines are produced from the same soil, and both worthwhile and disgraceful people emerge from the same parents. But in the first case the plants' nature is the reason, as well as the quality of the earth and the climatic conditions; in the case of men, their disposition[197] is the sole reason.

126a Carmen morale 539–42

From one and the same yeast of earth,
as well as from the same fountain and arable soil,

---

194 'Sardanopolos': ruler of Assyria and a byword for effeminate debauchery (Diodorus Siculus, 2.23.1–3). 'Smindyrides': from Sybaris in south Italy and renowned for his luxurious tastes (Herodotos 6.127.1).

195 Cited by Athenaios, *Deipnosophistae* 12.40, from Clearchos.

196 126–28: Moralizing comments on virtues and vices, presumably connected with the passage on moderation (125).

197 For the comment on 'disposition', or choice, cf. Aristotle, *Nicomachean Ethics* 3.5 (1113a).

dug and sown by the one man,
there are produced both brambles and corn-bearing ears.

127   Plan §19

That when Kantibaris[198] the Persian worked his jaws while chewing, he used
to gape and aim bread and pieces of meat into his gullet as if into a bucket.

128   Plan §20

That when the Sabine leader honoured him with gold and other precious
objects Manios[199] said he had no need of these things as long as such delicacies existed, pointing to some turnips.

129[200]   7.31–33 Hr = 543–45 Ma

The envious man has debilitating concern as a fellow lodger,
not only through seeing himself in the worst straits
but whenever he perceives another faring well.

130   7.34–36 Hr = 536–38 Ma

There is nothing dim which does not emerge into the light,
there is nothing concealed which does not become known,
even when concealed beneath the deepest roots of the earth.[201]

131   7.37 Hr = 535 Ma

Fear makes even narrow passages broad for those who flee.

132[202]   7.38–40 Hr = 336–38 Ma

But this proverbial saying is true,
that the worthy man cannot change his character
nor escape his inclination to correct behaviour.

198 'Kantibaris': details from Athenaios, *Deipnosophistae* 10.9, again citing Clearchus but
also mentioned in a list of gluttons by Aelian (*Varia historia* 1.27).

199 'Manios': from Athenaios, *Deipnosophistae* 10.13, though also referred to by Plutarch
(*Romanorum Apophthegmata*: Nachstädt 1935: 70 [194F]). Manius Curius was victorious over
Samnites and Sabinces in 290 BCE, and over Pyrrhos in 275 BCE.

200 129–31: These passages may all refer to a single incident in which a wrongdoer is
discovered and pursued.

201 This theme also appears in 8, 34 and 37.

202 Presumably a comment on a consistently upright character in the novel's cast.

133[203]   **7.41–42 Hr = 539–40 Ma**

This common saying is not false, it seems,
that indeed only gold is effective and everything else achieves nothing.

134[204]   **541–42 Ma**

The citron tree, by its natural force, works
both against poisons and attacks from wild beasts.

135   **Plan §21**

That when salt is sprinkled on their holes octopuses immediately come out
of them.[205]

136   **Plan §22**

That guinea-fowl (*meleagrides*) throw their chicks out of the nest as soon as
they leave their eggs, and trample on them.[206]

137[207]   **463–66 Ma + 7.43–51 Hr (= 467–75 Ma)**

How the thread of Fate cannot be spun again!
Such things do not take place without the gods' forethought!
Indeed what the Moirai have spun on their spindles
cannot be unravelled, though one takes a myriad pains!
The Moirai spin man's entire destiny on their threads   5
and what has once been ordained cannot be undone,[208]
the daimon's spool cannot be unwound.
And why, man, do you scheme and plan in vain?
You do not have the strength to alter the daimon's threads,
even if you try everything, even if you take a myriad pains,   10
even if you fly to the heavens, to the height of the aither,
even if you make for the sea's deeps and its harbours;[209]

203 Gold as a motivating force is a recurring motif; cf. 23, 84

204 134–36: A series of exempla from natural history, whose relevance to the novel's plot
is unclear.

205 Cf. Athenaios, *Deipnosophistae* 7.102.

206 On the transformation of the daughters of Meleager into birds, see Antoninus Liberalis,
Metamorphoses 2.7; for chick trampling, Athenaios, *Deipnosophistae* 14.71.

207 137–137a: A rhetorical evocation of the part played by fate in man's life, presumably
after some dramatic twist in the plot. In Greek mythology the Moirai spun threads of life at
each person's birth; they appear intermittently in the novels (e.g. Charit 2.8.5; Hel 8.11.2; *L&K*
1.3.2). On the combination of Tyche and Moira, cf. Pindar, *Olymp.* 12.1. These allusions should
be taken as part of an automatic Hellenizing veneer rather than belonging to a belief system.

208 Cf. Manasses, *SynChron* 1146.

209 Cf. fr. 8 above, with references, and Psalm 138.7.

or is all this false and meaningless poetic quibbling?

137a   Plan §23

That they say about those who devise tricks to evade the future, that if what has just been said is true and the thread has been spun by the Moirai's destiny and cannot be undone however many tricks one tries, all effort will be impossible; if it is false, why does one have an irrational fear of a falsehood?

138[210]   Plan §24

That, of marbles, Karian is white with gleams of purple in it, Thessalian is green; Proconnesian is white with veins of black that are sometimes straight and elsewhere contorted into curves, the Bithynian is unadulterated black, the Pentelian white like milk.[211]

139[212]   Plan §25

That four horses are depicted drawing the sun's chariot since the year, the period of one solar cycle, is made up of four seasons.

140[213]   Plan §26

That bees are small creatures but they accomplish great things. They have an emperor, and these emperors have bodies without stings; the older bees surround the emperors as guards while the younger ones, who have not yet learned how to make honeycombs, are entrusted with the protection of the hives and carry out the dead and expel and kill the lazy drones which eat too much.

141[214]   Plan §27

That when Aristotle compiled his book *On Animals* Alexander presented him with eight hundred talents.

210 138–44: These passages belong in Book 7 since 147a and 147b (Plan §§31 and 32) paraphrase lines from the beginning of Book 8. Their connection to the novel's plot is obscure and their derivation from it might be questioned (given the jumbled nature of Planudes' material, despite a tendency to quote sequentially) but can be justified if these are considered as a series of digressions (digressions being a feature of the novels' style) or exempla decorating a speech.

211 These are among the most renowned types of marble in antiquity, and appear in the novels in lavish *ekphraseis* of buildings.

212 Wall paintings, to which this passage could refer, appear most notably in the novels in *H&H* 2.2–8, 4.5–16.

213 Cf. Aristotle, *Historia Animalium* 9.40 (624b).

214 Cf. Athenaios, *Deipnosophistae* 9.58.

142[215]   **Plan §28**

There is a certain female creature that is talkative and verbose,
and looks after and conceals babes-in-arms;
the babies lack speech and are uninstructed in language,
but nevertheless their utterances exist and are clear;
in the waters of the ocean they can talk to those that they want to,   5
they reach those in the islands and on the mainland;
but many cannot hear them even when they are close by;
the babies lack a sense of hearing.

143[216]   **Plan §29**

There is a certain creature among mortals that at its first appearance is very long in form, as it reaches maturity it grows very short and thick; once it reaches old age it becomes as long as it was infancy.

144[217]   **Plan §30**

I say that that the man who unwillingly carries off the cicadas' prize
will give a great banquet for Epeios, son of Panopeus.

Fragments not definitely from Book 7

145[218]   **339–40 Ma**

If god were to bring about what was wanted and was pleasing,
men's reasoning would become god-stricken.[219]

215 See Athenaios, *Deipnosophistae* 10.73 where the source is Sappho and Antiphanes (Kassel and Austin 1991: fr. 194); the solution first proposed was 'city' for 'female creature' and 'orators' for 'babies', while Sappho's solution was 'epistle' and 'letters' (in words); this riddle is also attributed to Basilios Megalomites (Boissonade 1831: 450–51, no. 39).

216 The solution is 'a shadow'; Athenaios, *Deipnosophistae* 10.75, attributed by Theodektos of Phaselis to Hermippos, a pupil of Isokrates.

217 Epeios was in fact a donkey and the banquet barley. This derives from Simonides (Diehl 1942: 108, fr. 70) via Athenaios (*Deipnosophistae* 10.84): Simonides was training a chorus in a remote island location and water was brought by a donkey; its name was that of the soldier who once carried water for the leaders of the Trojan War, as inscribed on the nearby temple of Apollo; Simonides won the competition ('the cicadas' prize').

218 145–46: The location of these passages in the anthology does not help to fix them in the novel, and the sentiments are also not plot-specific.

219 'god-stricken': translating θεοβλαβεῖς with Conca, Trapp, Tsolakes and the mss, against Mazal's θεοβλαστεῖς (cited as a hapax; Mazal 1967: 141).

146   341–43 Ma

Thus Justice leaves nothing unpunished,
but should it seem to close its eyes briefly,
it will impose a more unpleasant penalty later on the wrongdoers.

BOOK 8[220]

147[221]   8.1–5 Hr

How does the skolopendra,[222] the seafaring creature,
break up when a man puts saliva into its mouth?
And how does the fruit of the willow,[223] when it is crushed and pounded
and put by someone in a man's drink,
destroy and congeal the reproductive and procreative seed?

147a   Plan §31

That when the skolopendra has human saliva put in its mouth it breaks up
like a mass of bubbles.

147b   Plan §32

That the juice of a willow-berry when taken makes the recipient sterile; for
this reason Homer called the willow the 'fruit-loser'.[224]

148[225]   Plan §33

That those who are overcome by shame and fear at the same time, either
through love or some other passion, often appear sometimes pale and
sometimes red, for blood rushes to the surface of the skin when shame
predominates, but when fear has the upper hand, it retreats deep down and
leaves the outer surface as if dead.

---

220 Book 8: The references to disfigured beauty, support from friends and deceptive dreams
suggest that difficult situations have again overtaken the central pair.

221 147–147b: Further paradoxographical passages, perhaps taken from a speech.

222 On the skolopendra, cf. Aelian, *De natura animalium* 4.22.

223 On the effects of the willow, cf. Aelian, *De natura animalium* 4.23.

224 'fruit-loser': *Odyssey* 10.510.

225 Physiological observations on the conflict between shame and fear (cf. *R&D* 4.92,
96–99); these have some connection with 149 but must precede 152 in the novel's structure.

149[226]   **8.6–23 Hr (+ 667 Ma) (6–10 Hr = 662–66 Ma; 667 Ma; 11–16 Hr = 668–73 Ma; 17 Hr; 18–23 Hr = 674–79 Ma)**

For the fog of evil and the twilight of disaster
can darken beauty and disfigure elegance
and the roaring furnace of tribulation
can parch a face like a Lokrian rose.[227]
If you were to have a countenance more radiant than that of Nireus,[228]   5
if you were to rejoice in an elegance more winsome than that of
    Narkissos,[229]
if you were to be endowed with the Nereid's beauty like Achilles[230]
yet the gut-devouring worm of care would eat away at you,
beauty swiftly slips away, the rose withers,
the leaves of the countenance are nibbled by caterpillars,   10
the lily turns yew-green,[231] the brilliant flower becomes dust.
If you should have a giant's strength or the hands of Enkelados,[232]
if you could move all Parnassos or Athos,[233]
if you could carry the pillars of the world like Atlas,[234]
and the winged arrow of tribulation were to touch you   15
and speed and reach to the depths of your heart,
you would not have the strength of a mosquito, or an ant or a gnat;
the weight of evil would oppress you and bow you down,
as a cartwright bends a cartwheel.

226 This passage suggests a crisis point in the novel's structure, where Aristandros, and possibly also Kallithea, have been in some way afflicted.

227 'Lokrian rose': a proverbially beautiful and short-lived rose; cf. 80.11 above.

228 'Nireus': cf. 174.8 below; a Greek warrior second only to Achilles in his beauty; cf. *Iliad* 2.672–74; Lucian, *Dialogi mortuorum* 30.

229 'Narkissos': a handsome youth who in various versions of the legend fell in love with his reflection and perished.

230 Achilles' mother Thetis was a Nereid, a sea-goddess.

231 On the yew as a sign of consumption, cf. Theokritos, *Idyll* 2.88, and scholia (Wendel 1914: 286.4–14).

232 On Enkelados, cf. Apollodoros, *Bibliotheke* 1.6.2.

233 Parnassos, the mountain looming over Delphi and the legendary home of the Muses. Athos, a mountainous peninsula in northern Greece; in legend one of the giants who defied Poseidon, in history the point at which the Persian Xerxes dug a canal in his invasion of Greek lands, and from the tenth century CE site of a large autonomous monastic enclave.

234 Atlas: legendary Titan who supported the heavens; Hesiod, *Theogony* 507; Apollodoros, *Bibliotheke* 1.2.3.

150[235]   8.24–25 Hr = 680–81 Ma

Time can test the character of every man,
as the Lydian stone[236] tests counterfeit and pure gold.

151   8.26–28 Hr

During his friend's misfortunes a friend's friendship is tested,
whether it is feigned or has depth;
and a friend must sympathize with his friend during disasters.

152[237]   8.29–34 Hr

Dreams for the most part produce outrageous fantasies,
fabricating images and depicting figures derived
from things heard or seen during the day;
but often the quality and quantity of food
and excessive digestive juices and sickness and fears[238]   5
can produce disturbing dreams.

152a   Plan §34

That not only do daily cares produce images of themselves in dreams but
also the quantity and quality of food and excessive digestive juice and fear
and sickness cause troubling fantasies.

153[239]   8.35–36 Hr

The heart that is guileless and does not lay snares
cannot comprehend the wiles of a soul with a serpent's disposition.

---

235 150–51: These passages suggest that the plot has reached a critical stage; it is an open
question whether the friend implied here is that of Book 3, though in the other novels the
heroes' companions, once acquired, play a role throughout (e.g. Kratandros in *R&D*). Cf. 56
for the importance of friendship.

236 i.e. a stone taken from Mount Paktolos in Lydia, a source of gold: cf. scholia in
Theokritos, *Idyll* 12.35–37 (Wendel 1914: 257.2–6).

237 152–152a: Dreams play a frequent role in the novels, perhaps most notably in *H&H*;
see MacAlister 1990 and 1996. These passages (cf. fr. 47) sound like a rationalizing attempt
to lessen alarm caused by a nightmare, reflecting Aristotelian dream theory: MacAlister 1990:
209.

238 Cf. *R&D* 3.19–32.

239 Cf. 132 for an earlier reference to an upright man. The formulation here suggests
opposition in the plot between two characters. Some further blow would seem to have struck
the central pair.

154[240]   **8.37–42 Hr = 686–91 Ma**

But neither an iron wall nor a jaw of fire will check,[241]
it seems, the future and what is to be,
no human reason will be able to overturn it;
for the god who touches a man's intellect,
when he mixes a cup of grief for the wretch,   5
does not often allow him to devise what is appropriate.

Fragments from Books 8 or 9

155[242]   **Plan §35**

That the martichoras is an Indian animal, and the hystrix is another; when
they come into conflict with another animal or a man, both of these use their
very stiff bristles as weapons to inflict wounds, the first using bristles from
his tail, the second from the rest of his body.

156[243]   **Plan §36**

That a certain man who pretended to be a soothsayer and that he knew
someone's secrets came forward and announced that he would tell them to
him; so he sat and moved his fingers, as though he was putting pebbles in
order and then disarranging them, and then he produced the secret and was
proved to be a true soothsayer since he had received no information from
anyone.

157   **Plan §37**

That the katoblepas is a Libyan animal that breathes fire.

Fragment from Book 8 or perhaps Book 7

158[244]   **653–61 Ma**

Where Strength is found conjoined with Justice,

240 Cf. 137 for the role of higher powers in mankind's affairs.

241 Cf. *SynChron* 3896; for 'jaw of fire', cf. Aeschylus, *Prometheus* 368, *Choephoroi* 325.

242 155–57: The martichoras (tiger) and katoblepas have been adduced previously (31
above) in a diatribe against a slanderer, which may, with the addition of the hystrix (porcupine),
be their function here against a fraudulent soothsayer.

243 Cf. Kalasiris' very similar behaviour in Hel 3.17.2.

244 This excerpt would seem to come from a speech of exhortation made before a battle:
there is no clear place in the plot as reconstructed for this (though there are possible points
in each of Books 6, 7 and 8) and the position in the anthology between excerpts from Books
6.40–59 (= 121) and 8.6–10 (= 149) does not help.

no other partnership can be more effective;
if Power pulls the yoke of battle on its own
and is not enriched with victory-bearing Justice as its consort,
the general is helpless, his generalship useless,   5
the phalanxes lack strength, the swift hand is sluggish,
the shield-bearer is unprotected, the wearer of the bronze breastplate
    is stripped bare,
the arrow is harmless, the sword is not a sword,
the ally is ineffective, the labourer labours in vain.

BOOK 9[245]

159[246] 9.1–7 Hr = 692–98 Ma

Indeed man is not a heavenly plant or a divine one,
nor a tree tended by god's hand
but god's pastime and the plaything of Fate![247]
Indeed earth nurtures nothing more feeble than man![248]
How unstable is man's whole life and every age!   5
– because mortals' affairs are a shadow;[249] for one day
can revolve and rotate everything like a spinning-top or a wheel.[250]

160 9.8–9 Hr = 682–83 Ma

Nothing is certain, nothing is stable for mankind
but mortals' affairs are like smoke, all is a shadow.[251]

245 Book 9: It would seem that an enamoured barbarian woman pursues one of the male characters; the scene may well have moved to Egypt, or Persia, before a battle leads to the final denouement.

246 159–60: The deep pessimism expressed here chimes in with the gloomy situation that can be deduced at the end of Book 8.

247 On man as a heavenly plant, cf. Plato, *Timaios* 90A; a heavenly plaything, cf. Plato, *Laws* 803 C.

248 Cf. *Odyssey* 18.130.

249 'mortals' affairs a shadow': cf. Pindar, *Pythia* 8.95–96; Sophocles, *Ajax* 125–26.

250 'spinning-top or wheel': cf. 49 (and notes), 54.

251 A variation on theme that mankind's life is the shadow of smoke; cf. Sophocles, *Antigone* 1170, *Philoktetes* 946.

161[252] **9.10 Hr**

Every eunuch is by nature a jealous creature.

162[253] **9.11–22 Hr = 699–710 Ma**

The arrow turns back, they say, into the eyes,
into the face of him who shoots into the depth of heaven;
if someone strives to hurl a jagged rock
and send a bronzed-tipped ash-spear into a brazen target,
his arrow is useless, he who shoots has no force,   5
the spear is ineffective, he aims in vain;
for the spear breaks off and is shattered
and the strength of its tip is dulled;
sometimes the spear is proved blunt and useless and it falls,
fractured in three or four pieces like a brittle pot-sherd,   10
sometimes it turns back and transfixes the shooter's chest
as though propelled from a giant's fist.

163[254] **744–49 Ma**

This garment is not the golden peplos of Helen, wife of Alexander[255]
and of blond Menelaos noble in battle,
nor the famed girdle[256] of Aphrodite,
but a hand-towel for your enslaved hands,
which I offer in servile[257] fashion to you as lord of love,   5
and by which you haul me along in my misery as if by my hair.

252 Cf. 80 and 110. The reference to eunuchs suggests that the plot has again moved to a
court environment, perhaps in a context analogous to Books 7–9 of Heliodoros where Arsake,
wife of the Persian satrap in Egypt, becomes enamoured of Theagenes (Mazal 1967: 146).

253 On the futility of resisting higher authorities, again suggesting that the main characters
are under constraints; probably from a speech.

254 An enamoured woman, perhaps a barbarian, offers a towel to the object of her affections,
perhaps Aristandros. A situation can be envisaged such as that in Book 8 of Heliodoros, where
Kybele attempts to persuade Theagenes to listen to Arsake (cf. 161).

255 'peplos': a form of tunic; for Helen's association with a peplos, cf. the gift she offers
at *Odyssey* 15.124. 'Alexander': i.e. Paris, known as Paris Alexander.

256 'famed girdle': cf. e.g. *Iliad* 2.214–17.

257 'servile': translating δουλικῶς with the mss and Mazal, rather than φιλικῶς ('friendly')
as proposed by Tsolakes (following a ms correction) and accepted by Conca and Trapp.

164[258]   750–57 Ma

Women are clever and daring in these matters
and skilled and inventive in contriving deceits,
but in performing and venturing on other matters they are very fearful,
they are bad at looking on iron, they are terrified when swords are drawn,
they are incompetent in practical matters, runaways[259] in battle;   5
however, when it comes to stitching plots and deceitful conspiracies
and vengeful attacks on a man who has harmed them,
no lioness is more bloodthirsty than they.

165   227–39 Ma

There is nothing that the tyrant Eros does not venture on –
not fire, not water, not snow, not compacted ice,
not poison, not the sword, not Skythian storms,
not the tempestuous ocean, not night, not wild beast, not the sea.
And whoever becomes a slave to Eros' hands   5
thinks nothing terrifying, not the sea, not the abyss below,
not the blade of his enemies' spears, not a swarm of foes.[260]
He thinks wild beasts lambs, chasms bridgeable,
fire is dew[261] and not fire, swords are not swords,
he turns somersaults over swords' double edges,   10
he ventures out over deep-plunging craggy ravines
should he hope merely to glimpse the object of his affections,
should he imagine a kiss, should he merely have this idea.

166   9.23–29 Hr = 240–46 Ma

Every love which is spurned and unsuccessful
rages and snaps like a sharp-fanged rabid dog
and splutters out the froth of madness

---

258 164–66: These passages deal with the fury of a woman spurned, arguably a high-ranking
barbarian rejected by Aristandros (cf. 161); cf. Hel 7.20.4 (Arsake and Theagenes); XenEph,
2.3.5 (Manto and Habrokomes); *D&C* 5.290 (Chrysilla and Charikles).

259 'runaways': a rare Homeric word (*Iliad* 13.102), used of deer but taken up several times
by twelfth-century writers.

260 For a lover's defiance of all dangers, cf. *DigAk* G 4.400–4; also Musaios 293–301
(Leander swimming to Hero).

261 'fire is dew': for the oxymoron, cf. *R&D* 8.225; *D&C* 2.382; and George of Pisidia,
Hexaemeron 1747 (Gonnelli 1998), a phrase with liturgical and hymnographic connotations;
cf. Daniel 3.49–50; Romanos the Melode, Kontakion 46.21(Maas and Trypanis 1963: 390).

and the fumes of anger like Kerberos' icy spittle;[262]
but if it is a woman, and indeed a barbarian, who is rejected,   5
and if fate gives her the power to take revenge,
oh woe, what a vengeful and bloodthirsty character she is![263]

167[264]   9.30–31 Hr

Alas, what an evil thing it is for a man to bear the burden of slavery;
for, overcome by force, he ventures upon what is not proper.

168[265]   9.32–36 Hr = 711–15 Ma

Joy too can become the mother of tears,
when the passages from the heart are unblocked by it
and flow out into the very orbs of the eyes,
as if into water-conveying channels
or into a natural klepsydra[266] full of warmly damp moisture.   5

169[267]   9.37–39 Hr = 276–78 Ma

The devil is jealous of those who are happy
and looks enviously and wrathfully on the wealthy,
and the wise, the handsome and those who are very brave.

170   9.40–41 Hr

The humble and the lowly and the dregs of society are,
it seems, not worthy of the gods' scourges.

171   Plan §38

That the devil is malignant and envious and constantly strives to destroy
the rich and the wise and the handsome. Thus large animals are struck by
lightning but mosquitoes and grasshoppers run off; lofty houses and tall
trees are damaged but small huts and shacks suffer no damage from storms.

262 'Kerberos': the many-headed hound who in Greek mythology guarded the entrance to
Hades; his spittle is icy, as is everything in the underworld.

263 See the list of possible parallels given at the beginning of the note to 164–66.

264 This is presumably to be connected with the situation reflected in 164–66.

265 In terms of the plot, a solution to problems will have been found, perhaps the reunion
of the central pair.

266 'klepsydra': a water clock or device for measuring time, at its simplest draining water
in a regulated flow from one bowl to another; cf. Lewis 2000.

267 169–71: If these passages are taken to apply to Aristandros and Kallithea, the implication
is that they are noble figures, fit to be tested. Manasses would thus be providing a deeper layer
of meaning to the novel, moving beyond a titillating narrative (Mazal 1967: 148).

In tragedies you will see figures like Ajax and Palamedes and Rhesos slain
but never Thersites[268] or anyone of that sort; in democracies Sokrates is
condemned and dies but Mikyllos[269] and those like him suffer nothing
untoward.

172[270]   9.42–43 Hr
Unwitting and unintentional misdeeds
are worthy of pardon both from men and from god.

173[271]   9.44–48 Hr
Those who have been reared with weapons and those experienced in fighting
must either stain their hands with enemy blood
and gird on a tunic bespattered with their slaughter
or fall valiantly and stout-heartedly
after having striven mightily with the opposition.

174[272]   9.49–71 Hr
If a conduit of joy, if drops of pleasure
water the heart's primeval root,
if a honeyed stream of happiness showers down
on the source of life and primal heat,
a sweet flower of brilliance overruns the appearance,   5
the countenance seems to bloom and be renewed,
the face beams like a ruddy rose,
and he who was feeble in physique and dusky in appearance
becomes more brilliantly beautiful than Nireus,[273]

---

268 'Ajax [...] Thersites': cf. Sophocles, *Philoktetes* 496–50. Ajax, Palamedes and Rhesos
are heroic figures, Thersites abusively un-heroic (*Iliad* 2.212–44).

269 'Sokrates [...] Mikyllos': Sokrates is, of course, the renowned philosopher, central to
Plato's dialogues; Mikyllos figures in Lucian's *Kataplous* (*Downward Journey or The Tyrant*)
as the representative 'common man' in the tyrant's underworld trial.

270 A continuation of the scale of moral values suggested in 171.

271 Cf. 175–76 The disasters seem not to have ended since this passage, from some of its
phraseology, would seem to come from a pre-battle speech, cf. 9. There are many parallels
for a battle at the end of the novel, e.g. Iamblichos (Garmos of Babylon against Rhodanes),
Chariton (battles in Egypt and Persia as Chaireas seeks Kallirrhoe) and especially Heliodoros
(the satrap of Egypt against the Ethiopian king); the structure of Heliodoros' last books seems
to have been taken as a model by Manasses.

272 On the physical effects of joy and sorrow; cf. 149. Positioned between passages dealing
with war, this must describe the impact on the novel's events on its characters.

273 'Nireus': cf. 149.5 above.

even if he were a black Erembos[274] or a circlet-wearing Arab.   10
If heart-rending grief ravages the heart,
if bitter sorrow undermines the body's fundamental being
like a wood-devouring worm,
if a conflagration of disasters sets flame to the root,
oh woe, trunk and branch are both burnt up,   15
what was flourishing withers, beauty ebbs away,
the bloom of comeliness cools and fades
and he who used to rival the stars, who radiated beams of beauty,
becomes ashen and sere in hue,
even if he surpassed the beauty of Achilles or Hyakinthos,[275]   20
even if he was nurtured from the loveliest milky breasts,
even if he had just emerged into the light and had bathed
in the streams of the Graces and the fountains of Beauty.

175[276]   **9.72–73 Hr**
In war one needs deeds but not words,
and battle ends with hands but not with chattering.

176   **74–75 Hr**
<...> sagacity is mightier than strength[277]
and sensible advice is more effective than a myriad arms.

177[278]   **9.76–86 Hr**
There is no marble rock or iron club
that can break the bones of a man reared in Egypt;
the reason is that Egyptians shave their heads

274 'Erembos': a legendary people in the southern Mediterranean, cf. *Odyssey* 4.84; Strabo 1.1.3.

275 'Achilles or Hyakinthos': Achilles, of course, is the hero of the *Iliad*; Hyakinthos, a youth whose beauty caused rivalry among the gods that led to his death (see, e.g., Apollodoros, *Bibliotheke* 3.10.3; *D&C* 4.246–51)

276 175–76: These two passages would seem to be related to the battle scene implied in 173.

277 The first half of the line is lost.

278 The details on Egyptians' hard heads derive from Herodotos 3.12; Herodotos is also used by Manasses in his Chronicle (e.g. *SynChron* 714–806, cf. Hdt. 1.107–19; *SynChron* 814–37, cf. Hdt. 1.8–12; *SynChron* 856–71b, cf. Hdt. 3.30). Mazal 1967: 150 suggests that the references elsewhere in the novel to eunuchs and the role of the postulated high-ranking barbarian woman have a context in court either in Persia (cf. Charit) or Egypt (cf. Hel); this passage suggests that a final battle took place in Egypt.

from childhood and strip off the hair;
they make no use of hats or any other form of skull protection,   5
for they leave their heads unprotected from the sun;
so, as the sun's rays beam down fierily,
all the passages in the bone become thicker and more dense
since the impact of the heat affects them directly.
So it is rather rare to see an Egyptian   10
whose hair has fallen out because of baldness.

178[279]   9.87–89 Hr
Hope of profit drives merchants
to venture across rivers and wild seas
and to put their souls in danger for gold.

Fragments not definitely belonging to Book 9

179[280] 684–85 Ma
But god's eyelid and the eye of Justice
did not endure this, but hated and loathed it.

180   716–18 Ma
Those whose minds seethe with the dangers that are underfoot
and whose souls are tormented with fears that exude evil
usually pay attention to such matters and confront them.

Epimetrum

181[281]   758–65 Ma (+ 1–5 codicis R chronici Manassis)
But O Manasses, heart-entrancing mouth,

279 No passage survives that deals with the inevitable reunion of Aristandros and Kallithea with each other and their parents, but these lines may come from the account of their journey home since merchants in the novels tend only to appear when conveying the central pair or their families. If the final scenes are set in Egypt then a return to their homes would be needed.
    280 179–80: Generalized references to unidentifiable episodes.
    281 This epilogue in 12-syllable lines is found in the WM anthology and has some lines in common with the epilogue found in one of the manuscripts of the Chronicle (ms R). Though this is an unusual situation, Mazal (1966: 254) accepts that these lines belong with both texts, and are due to Manasses. However, the presence of these lines in both the Chronicle and the novel add complexity to the arguments over dating of both; see Introduction, pp. 275–76.

young Orpheus[282] better than the old,
tune your sweet kithara once more
and reveal your countenance to your friends
and address your pupils[283] as in the past;[284]   5
for if sweet speech could soften
the deaf hair-stuffed ears[285] of dread Hades,
you would have gone to Hades and accomplished this
since you are the embodiment of charm and sweetness.

282 'young Orpheus': this suggests that Manasses would have been not more than 25 years old at the time of writing.

283 'address your pupils': this suggests strongly that Manasses was involved with teaching, perhaps in a private capacity (cf. Tzetzes) as his name does not appear among those known to have been involved with the patriarchal schools; cf. the comment on school-teachers in 25 above.

284 The summons to re-tune, to appear to his friends and pupils again suggest that Manasses had spent a period out of the public eye, perhaps caught up ca. 1143–45 with the troubles surrounding the *sevastokratorissa* Eirene; her commissioning of the Chronicle from him indicates their association (see Introduction, pp. 273–74).

285 'hair-stuffed ears': a rare adjective, but well embedded in the Byzantine lexika.

NIKETAS EUGENIANOS

DROSILLA AND CHARIKLES

INTRODUCTION

Author

Little is known of the life of Niketas, other than the modest gleanings to be obtained from his writings, which are not voluminous. Works certainly by Niketas are the novel *Drosilla and Charikles* (*D&C*), his most substantial work and the text translated in this volume; and one prose and two verse monodies (laments) on Theodore Prodromos.[1] Other texts transmitted anonymously but now accepted as by Niketas are two verse *epithalamia* (marriage poems) for an unnamed bridal couple;[2] a collection of epigrams;[3] an *epitaphios* (funeral oration) on Stephanos Komnenos, *megas droungarios* (d. 1156/7);[4] and an isolated letter.[5] Niketas is probably also the author of some *schede* (grammatical exercises), one of which deals with material that appears in the funerary oration for Stephanos Komnenos.[6] The case for attributing the *Anacharsis*, a prose satire on twelfth-century Constantinopolitan personalities, to Niketas is attractive, if not completely persuasive.[7] If the *Anacharsis* is accepted as his, then – by the arguments put forward by Christides – so too must the letters that follow in the manuscript

1 Prose monody: Petit 1902; verse monody (in 12-syllable lines): Gallavotti 1935: 222–29; verse monody (hexameters): Gallavotti 1935: 229–31.

2 In 12-syllables: Gallavotti 1935: 233–36; in hexameters: Gallavotti 1935: 232–33.

3 Lambros 1914: 253–58, from Vat., Urb. gr. 134ff. 121v–122r; Niketas' authorship was identified in Pezopoulos 1936 (these are paraphrases of texts in the *Greek Anthology* which are also used in *D&C*).

4 Edited in Helfer 1971; see notes in Sideras 1994: 168–72. On Stephanos, see Varzos 1984, vol. 1: 288–91, no. 57; Varzos is, however, unaware of the funeral oration.

5 Εἰς Γραμματικὴν ἐρωμένην (To Grammatike in love); Boissonade 1819, vol. 2: 6–12, from Florence, Med.-Laur. Plut. XXXI.II, f. 80v. If this letter is to be taken literally, Grammatike has copied and learnt by heart *D&C*.

6 Polemis 1995.

7 Christides 1984: 78–92. Christides' main argument is that the *Anacharsis* shows more affinities with phrases from Eugenianos' writings than with those of other twelfth-century authors; note the sceptical comments of Kazhdan 1985a.

that preserves them; this question remains open.[8] Niketas' authorship for a further monody, by a father for his son, has been proposed but is no longer supported.[9]

From the monody on Stephanos, it is apparent that Niketas had been the young man's tutor. It is this relationship, together with the passages in the anonymous 12-syllable *epithalamium* that have parallels in *D&C*, that form the basis for Kazhdan's proposal that this *epithalamium* should be attributed to Niketas.[10] From the monodies on Theodore Prodromos it is apparent that the two were close friends, with Theodore having possibly been initially Niketas' teacher. In one manuscript of *D&C*, a heading preceding the text claims that the work is written *kata mimesin tou makaritou philosophou tou Prodromou*, 'in imitation of (or, modelled on) a work of the late wise Prodromos'.[11] Niketas was thus another example of those with literary skill who, in mid-twelfth-century Constantinople, found employment in one or more aristocratic establishments, in this case a branch of the Komnenian family, Stephanos' father being Konstantinos Komnenos, also *megas droungarios*.

Date

There are two points that suggest a date at which *D&C* was written. The first concerns the nature of *D&C*. *D&C* lays conspicuous stress on marriage, even more, arguably, than do the other three novels. There are several references to Matthew 19.6 (on the indissolubility of marriage; e.g. *D&C* 3.12, 7.264) and emphasis on the unofficial but still binding marital ties between hero and heroine. The many songs and letters provide a series of amatory variations. The whole reads very much like an extended *epithalamium*, a thought bolstered by the passages shared by Niketas' *epithalamium* for his erstwhile pupil.[12] It is tempting to link the composition of the two, especially as that marriage had generated controversy, requiring a patriarchal judgment,

---

8 Marc. Gr. XI 22, ff. 129r–143v; Christides 1984: 291–328. Grünbart 2001: 32*, under Niketas Eugenianos, expresses mild conviction over Eugenianos' authorship, but does not list the letters under this name (or anywhere, it would seem). The question remains similarly open over the lament from a woman transporting her husband's body home: Christides 1984: 50, 305–06.

9 Sideras 1991: 205–21, from Cod. Pal. (Heidelb.) 18, ff. 3v–4v; but see Sideras 1994: 402–04. This would have provided some details on Niketas' family circumstances.

10 Though see the next section for issues on the identity of the recipients of the *epithalamium*.

11 Paris, BN gr. 2908; see Conca 1990: 8–9, 30.

12 *D&C* 1.121–24. cf. Epithalamium 62, 64; *D&C* 1.134–35, cf. Epithalamium 75–76: Kazhdan 1967: 108.

given in 1156, before it could proceed.[13] The marriage was short-lived, as Stephanos died within a year of its celebration, in the spring of 1156 or 1157.[14]

The second point concerns the manuscript reference to Niketas' imitation in *D&C* of the late Prodromos, with the implication that composition occurred after the death of Prodromos, perhaps to honour his memory. This reference appears in one manuscript only, P (Par. gr. 2908), copied ca. 1500 in Paris by George Hermonymos.[15] It is not present in U and L, the other mss closely linked to P. It is legitimate to ask whether this note, and the slightly sardonic hexameter couplet that accompanies it, was found in his exemplar (and omitted by U and L) or was added by George the scribe himself. In favour of the latter position is the fact that George was an interventionist copyist, frequently adding scholia, particularly when the manuscript was intended for teaching purposes. This was probably the case for P, which has interlinear spaces and ample margins at top and bottom of the page, as well as a number of glosses.[16] However, it is not clear that the term *makarites* ('late') would have been used ca. 1500 of a person deceased some three and a half centuries previously, while the hexameters use vocabulary in vogue in the twelfth century. On balance the heading is probably to be taken as approximately contemporary to the composition of *D&C*. The date of death of Theodore Prodromos is thus relevant. While the older literature puts this at ca. 1170,[17] it is, however, plain that Theodore died around 1156 (the date of his last datable works and when he is referred to by his younger contemporary, Manganeios Prodromos, as having already passed to the next world).[18] There is thus a neat congruence of arguments that would place the writing of *D&C* ca. 1156.

13 Stephanos Komnenos married Eudokia Axouchaina; his cousin had previously been engaged to her elder sister, thus bringing Stephanos and his proposed bride within the limits of consanguinity. On the patriarchal decree, see Grumel 1972: no. 1029. Note that the epithalamium deals with the marriage of a Komnenos groom to a Doukaina bride, whereas Stephanos' bride is otherwise known to be from the Axouch family. Kazhdan's answer, that the reference is to the maternal side of the bride's family, is reasonable: in the prestige stakes, a Doukas would probably always out-trump an Axouch (Kazhdan 1967: 106).

14 From details in the monody on Stephanos: Sideras 1994: 170 (contra Varzos 1984, vol. 1: 289).

15 On Hermonymos see Kalatzi 2010, which supersedes Omont 1885.

16 Kalatzi 2010: 252–53.

17 E.g. Kazhdan and Franklin 1984: 92–100.

18 Last datable works: on Michael Palaiologos, died late 1155 or early 1156 in Bari (Hörandner 1974: nos. 66–67); cf. MangProd 37.27–32; Magdalino 1993: 496. See the discussion in connection with *R&D* (pp. 4–6).

Transmission and reception

D&C is found in four manuscripts, one from the thirteenth century (M), one from the early fifteenth (P) and two from the middle and late fifteenth (U and L).[19] All derive from the same archetype. As discussed by Conca, they fall into two groups, one represented by M alone and the other by PUL; P shows some knowledge of M.[20] This is an adequate, if not large or surprising, manuscript tradition, from which little can be concluded about the extent to which the text circulated in Byzantium, though it does indicate that, unlike *H&H*, *D&C* did not attract the interest of western humanists. It received attention in the late eighteenth century when an edition was prepared (using P and M) but not printed,[21] although this formed the basis for Boissonade's edition that appeared in 1819 (later reprinted in 1856). A further edition was included in Hercher's *Erotici Scriptores* of 1859. No more attempts at an edition of *D&C* were made until Conca's work of 1990 and 1994. An English translation followed (Burton 2004).

Form

Arranged in nine books (as was *R&D*), for by far the greater part of his novel Eugenianos uses the regular Byzantine 12-syllable meter, with no particularly idiosyncratic features.[22] There are three passages in hexameters: 3.263–88, 297–320 (two songs) and 6.205–35 (a lament).

From their presence in all manuscripts, it is plain that *D&C* was always intended to include headings, though their intermittent attestation leaves it uncertain how many may be due to later scribal intervention. Those for which there is the most secure evidence have been included in this translation. For reasons of space these have not been placed in the margin but instead they have been included in the footnotes, introduced by the words 'Marginal gloss'.

---

19 M: Venice, Marc. Gr. 412, ff. 1r–71v, once owned by Cardinal Bessarion. P: Paris, BN gr. 2908, ff. 1r–237v, copied in Paris, as noted above. U: Vatican, Urb. Gr 134, ff.43r–77v. L: Florence, Med. Laur. Aquisiti e Doni 341, ff. 50v–91r. U and L also contain *R&D*.

20 Conca 1990: 7–17.

21 By P. C. Levesque, now in Par. Suppl. gr. 458; see Conca 1990: 22–23.

22 Conca 1990: 19–22.

Plot summary

Book 1 opens with a raid on the city of Barzon by an invading Parthian army. Many captives are taken, among them Charikles and the lovely Drosilla, who had been participating in the festival of Dionysos outside the city walls. After an evening's carousal the Parthian ruler, Kratylos, promises much booty to his men as they set off on the return march, reaching their destination after five days. Charikles is thrown into prison while Drosilla is put in the women's quarters belonging to Chrysilla, wife of Kratylos. Charikles' lament for his and Drosilla's fate is overheard by Kleandros, a fellow prisoner, who attempts consolation. Drosilla laments too, bewailing the separation from Charikles, her bridegroom, though in name only.

Book 2 At daybreak Charikles continues his lament, rousing Kleandros with his weeping. They exchange their past histories. Kleandros, from Lesbos, had fallen in love with the ravishingly beautiful Kalligone, but she was unresponsive to his advances. He sent her a series of inventive letters on the workings of Eros, which he recounts to Charikles. After the fourth letter Kalligone had agreed to a meeting, on the way to which Kleandros sang a lengthy hymn to the moon in anticipation of future delights.

Book 3 When they met, Kalligone revealed to Kleandros that she had experienced a dream in which Eros, responding to Kleandros' tears, had united them. Kleandros proposed immediate flight together, in a ship which happened to be in the harbour. After five days a storm drove them into Barzon, then under attack from the Parthians. Kleandros was taken prisoner but Kalligone eluded capture and Kleandros' ignorance of her whereabouts is now adding to his misery. Charikles then narrates how he, from Phthia, had attended a festival of Dionysos in a delightful grove outside the city walls. His companions at an impromptu picnic devised a sequence of songs commenting, not always kindly, on the girls passing by; the star turn was provided by Barbition. Then there appeared Drosilla, radiant amidst a group of girls. Charikles was immediately smitten and aspired to elope with her. The messenger he used as a go-between arranged a meeting, despite Drosilla being already promised to another. They met, were mutually enraptured, exchanged oaths ratified by Dionysos and promptly set sail, Dionysos having previously in a dream revealed Drosilla to Charikles as his future bride.

Book 4 After four days their ship was overtaken by pirates; escaping with difficulty it put into shore and crew and passengers fled inland, Charikles and Drosilla with them. Eventually they reached a city and, the following day, joined in the festival outside its walls, only to be swept up by the invading

Parthians into their present imprisonment. At this point Kratylos, their captor, has the prisoners brought before him; most he orders to be sacrificed but Charikles is presented to Kratylos' son, Kleinias. Kratylos' wife, Chrysilla, is very taken with Charikles' good looks, while Kleinias is struck by Drosilla's beauty. Kleinias ponders on his passion for Drosilla, expressing his feelings in eloquent song. Charikles intervenes, claiming that Drosilla is his sister and proposing his sympathetic support as a fellow sufferer from the pangs of love. Kleinias gratefully offers Charikles his freedom and high office if he can win him Drosilla as his wife. Disconcerted, Charikles seeks out Drosilla and, finding her asleep in the garden, muses over her beauty and the inexplicable and ineluctable nature of love.

Book 5 Eventually Drosilla awakes and attempts to alert Charikles to Chrysilla's interest in him. He is unconvinced, despite the suggestion (soon to be confirmed) that Chrysilla has poisoned Kratylos: Drosilla, pledged to him by Dionysos, is Charikles' only love. Charikles, however, has to reconcile this with his rash promise to Kleinias concerning Drosilla. In the midst of their despair news comes of Kratylos' sudden death. Though ostensibly mourning for Kratylos, Chrysilla attempts to woo Charikles, and turns to Drosilla as her accomplice. Thunderstruck, Drosilla uses this as an excuse to meet Charikles and bewail their fates. Not two weeks after the death of Kratylos, the Arab ruler Chagos sends his satrap to demand that Chrysilla and the Parthians subject themselves to him. Kleinias rejects the satrap scornfully, whereupon Chagos prepares for war. After appropriate bellicose speeches by leader and men the army sets out, reaching Parthia after eight days. The Parthians prepare for a siege, but the Arabs devastate the surrounding countryside and eventually, despite fierce defence, capture the city. Kleinias falls in battle, and Chrysilla commits suicide. Charikles and Drosilla, together with Kleandros, are captured for the third time.

Book 6 Chagos puts the women prisoners in wagons while the men march on foot. As Drosilla's wagon passes over a rocky cliff, an overhanging tree tips her out into the sea below; she eventually floats to shore. Charikles does not learn of Drosilla's disappearance until evening, whereupon he falls into noisy despair, attracting Chagos' attention. Chagos demands an explanation, which Charikles gives. Moved by their misadventures, Chagos frees both Kleandros and Charikles, at which the pair set off from Arabia, searching for Drosilla as they go. Meanwhile, Drosilla has spent nine days in the desert and has then found her way to a village, where she lingers modestly on the outskirts lamenting for Charikles, whom she assumes is dead. A kindly old woman, Maryllis, gives her shelter and food. Drosilla sleeps and dreams a dream in which Dionysos gives her important information; on waking she asks if there is in the village an innkeeper named Xenokrates. There is, and she is taken to his house, to be confronted by his son, Kallidemos. Kallidemos is amazed by Drosilla's beauty and, when she asks if a young man named Charikles is at the inn, he denies all knowledge of him (although Charikles, in fact, is asleep inside). Drosilla is in despair that the information from Dionysos in her dream has been proved wrong. Kallidemos discourses to her at length, and with many literary examples, about the strength of his passion for her. The old woman supports his courtship. At nightfall she takes Drosilla into her house. Next morning, as Charikles is drowsing in the inn, Dionysos reveals to him that Drosilla is nearby, in Maryllis' house.

Book 7 At daybreak Charikles and Kleandros emerge from the inn. Kleandros is astounded to overhear Charikles' name mentioned as Maryllis is consoling the weeping Drosilla with thoughts of Kallidemos. A rapturous reunion follows. Kallidemos, brooding murder and abduction, is thwarted by a sudden fever. Maryllis asks for an explanation of the situation, which Charikles gives at length, with stress on the role of Dionysos. Drosilla then recounts how she survived her fall into the sea, also with thanks to Dionysos. Maryllis admits that there can now be no impediment to the union of Charikles and Drosilla. She sets up a banquet, and dances grotesquely, to the hilarity of all. At the end of the meal Kleandros and Maryllis take themselves off to sleep.

Book 8 Drosilla explains Kallidemos' role to Charikles, emphasizing that throughout the hazards she had undergone she had remained true to Charikles, retaining her virginity. Charikles urges her to consummate their marriage there and then, but she demurs, since a dream has revealed that they are soon to return to their homeland, where the marriage can be celebrated with their families. Kleandros appears with news of Kalligone's death, brought to him by the recently arrived merchant Gnathon; his laments are consoled by Drosilla and Charikles. They are joined for the evening meal by Gnathon, who quickly recognizes them and reveals that their parents are now in Barzon. The jubilation of Drosilla and Charikles is blighted by the grief-stricken Kleandros' sudden death.[23]

Book 9 At daybreak they bury Kleandros, with Drosilla leading the lamentations until Gnathon urges moderation. After two days, his merchandise sold, Gnathon brings the pair back to Barzon where they find their fathers. Intense rejoicing follows, culminating in a banquet. At dawn Drosilla slips

---

23 This tragic sub-plot has no parallel in the other Komnenian novels.

out to lament over the urn of Kalligone's ashes. Two days later they embark on a ten-day voyage to Phthia, where their mothers greet them with predictable rapture. Amid general rejoicing a priest of Dionysos unites Drosilla and Charikles in marriage.

Characteristics and themes[24]

Like the other authors of these twelfth-century novels, Niketas writes in counterpoint both with his late antique predecessors and his contemporaries.[25] In terms of plot structure, there is – for example – acknowledgement of Heliodoros in the opening *in medias res* with a city under attack (1.1, reflected later in 4.42), in the sub-plots with Dosikles' companion in prison (cf. Kleandros' role in *D&C* and Knemon's in the *Ethiopika*), the presentation of earlier events in flashbacks, the barbarian queen Chrysilla's desire for Charikles (6.389, cf. Arsake and Theagenes in *Ethiopika* Books 7 and 8),[26] but more especially in the frequent appearance of phrases borrowed aptly from many contexts from Heliodoros, of which many are pointed out in the notes to the translation. Achilles Tatius has also been plundered for some scenes and apt phrases, particularly those to do with the physiology of erotic attraction.[27]

Niketas' imitation of, or counterpoint to, Prodromos' *R&D* is an interesting issue. Like *R&D*, *D&C* is in 12-syllable verse and in nine books, but the imitation is not of form alone, for the plot is modelled on that of *R&D*. However, despite extensive lyric passages in *D&C* 2 and 3, the novel as a whole is noticeably shorter than *R&D*, and complexities are truncated (for example, *D&C* 1 covers only the capture of Drosilla and Charikles, their separation in prison and Dosikles' meeting with Kleandros, whereas *R&D* 1 not only deals with these plot elements in connection with Rhodanthe and Dosikles but also includes an account of Kratandros' disastrous attempted abduction of Chrysochroe and his trial; in *D&C* Kleandros' account of his past is postponed to Book 2 and consists of re-telling his letters and songs to Kalligone, etc.).[28] There are many verbal echoes of phrases from *R&D*: a

---

24 For an orientation on *D&C* see discussions in Hunger 1978, vol. 2: 133–36; Beaton 1996: 76–77 and passim; Burton 2003 and 2004; Roilos 2005: 68–79 and passim.

25 As discussed in Svoboda 1935; Deligiorgis 1975; and Jouanno 1989.

26 As indicated in Hunger 1978.

27 See MacAlister 1991: 198–99, using the thwarted seduction scene at *L&K* 2.23 as her case study.

28 Beaton 1996: 76.

number are noted in the translation, and more can be found in the apparatus to Conca's edition; the aptness of these needs further investigation.

By the chronology proposed here, *D&C* would have been written a least a decade after *H&H*, so some awareness by *D&C* of *H&H* would be not unexpected. However, Niketas' relationship with Makrembolites and *H&H* is elusive.[29] There are some shared plot elements; the *ekphrasis* of the meadow at *D&C* 1.77–108 may show influence from Sosthenes' garden at *H&H* 1.4.6, as may the idyllic surroundings of the temple to Dionysos at *D&C* 3.65–100 or Drosilla's garden setting at *D&C* 4.246; the altars and festivals that are a recurrent motif in *D&C* may reflect their dominating presence in *H&H*; the abrupt appearance of Eros at *D&C* 3.6 in a dream may be a parodic reference to the dreams of *H&H*. Some images are found in both texts: e.g. the girl as lovely as the moon (*D&C* 3.337, *H&H* 5.6), the magnet as a symbol of the force of love (*D&C* 4.143, *H&H* 10.3), the sexual connotations of plucking roses (*D&C* 4.274, *H&H* 5.17). Servitude to Eros, a recurrent theme in *H&H* (e.g. 3.9, 5.18), appears at *D&C* 6.339–43, and the notion of a triple captivity is also shared (*D&C* 5.451–52, *H&H* 8.10, 9.13). The eroticism of *D&C* 6.640–43 is perhaps a nod towards the more overt eroticism (albeit in a dream) of *H&H* 3.7.

It is here that the major contrast between *D&C* and *R&D* can be observed. Unlike *R&D*, *D&C* demonstrates an interest in earlier writings on erotic topics: in *D&C* Niketas has taken examples of Hellenistic and late antique erotic poetry and woven them into the texture of his novel. These texts are used with considerable subtlety to make statements about the characters' interaction, which depend on his audience's informed appreciation of the sources. He is more likely to have been prompted in this direction by the attitudes observable in *H&H* than those of *R&D*. The texts thus used in *D&C* are epigrams from the *Greek Anthology*,[30] including the so-called *Anacreontea*,[31] and the *Idylls* of Theokritos.[32] Kleinias, Drosilla's suitor, is made – despite his boorishness – to allude to Heliodoros and Achilles Tatius (6.389–90). Not to be overlooked, however, is the extent to which Niketas

29 See MacAlister 1991: 210, arguing for a textual meshing of *R&D*, *H&H* and *D&C*, with *D&C* as the last in the chain.

30 At e.g. *D&C* 2.125–31, 2.347–55, 3.163–72, 3.174–88, 3.243–50, 3.157–83, 6.617–34, etc.

31 A collection of 60 epigrams of varying degrees of antiquity, all in the Anacreontic metre, contained in the Palatine Anthology; paraphrases appear at *D&C* 2.227–35, 2.327–45, 3.139–51, 4.313–24, 5.131–45, 5.147–55.

32 As demonstrated and discussed in Milazzo 1985 and Burton 2003.

has exploited the eroticism of the biblical Song of Songs (at e.g. 4.222–45).[33]
Despite the frivolous overtones, perhaps more than any of the other novels
D&C – with its reiteration of Matthew 19.6 – emphasizes the strength of
the marriage tie, even though the divinity through whom this bond is to be
assured is the god Dionysos (as it is Hermes in *R&D* and *H&H*).

Manuscripts, editions and translations

Manuscripts[34]
M   Venetus Marcianus graecus 412, ff. 1r–71v
P   Parisinus graecus 2908, ff. 1r–237v
U   Vaticanus Urbinas gr 134, ff.43r–77v
L   Laurentianus Aquisiti e Doni 341, ff. 50v–91r

Editions
Boissonade 1819, reprinted in Hirschig 1856: 1–69 (= Appendix); Hercher
1859: 437–552; Conca 1990; Conca 1994: 305–497

Previous translations
English: Burton 2004 (including Conca's Greek text)
Latin: Boissonade 1819, reprinted in Hirschig 1856: 1–69 (= Appendix)
German: Plepelits 2003
Italian: Cataudella 1988; Conca 1994: 305–497
Russian: Petrovskii 1969

This translation
This translation is based on Conca 1994, with occasional departures recorded
in the notes (e.g. the name Maryllis is preferred at 6.667, and elsewhere, to
Baryllis). As with the translations of *R&D* and *A&K*, although the transla-
tion is in prose it is presented in line lengths corresponding to those of the
Greek verses.

---

33 On the allegorization of the Song of Songs in Byzantium and its use in *D&C*, see Roilos
2005: 205–08, 211–23. Note that Gregory of Nyssa's commentary on the Song of Songs was
used extensively in the 1140s in the correspondence of Iakovos Monachos, the spiritual father
of the *sevastokratorissa* Eirene (E. and M. Jeffreys 2009: xxxviii–xxxix).
34 U and L also contain *R&D*.

TRANSLATION

THE ARGUMENT OF THE WHOLE BOOK[1]

In which is found Drosilla's and Charikles'
flight, wanderings, storms, abductions, violence,
brigands, prisons, pirates, starvation,
dreadful and gloomy dungeons
full of darkness in broad daylight,   5
iron-hammered fetters,
pitiful and miserable separation from each other,
but finally and eventually the bridal chamber and marriage.

FIRST BOOK

Now when the ruler of the stars, the sun that brings the light,[2]
had appeared from the lower hemisphere
bathed with the waters of Okeanos,
and was traversing the peaks
of the great earth that stretched out far and wide,   5
Parthians attacked the city of Barzon,[3]

1 Prologue: This is found only in manuscript P (ca. 1500), where it is preceded by 'The work of kyr Niketas Eugenianos in imitation of the late wise Prodromos. Niketas named for nobility [i.e. Eugenianos] elevating the summit of another labour in the field of heart-gnawing letters.' The latter sentence is a dubious hexameter couplet, whose translation is by no means certain. On the status of the whole passage and the implications of the first sentence for the circumstances of the composition of *D&C*, see Introduction, p. 143.

2 For the opening scene set in a sacked city, cf. Hel 1.1 and *R&D* 1.1.

3 In the probably doomed hunt for geographical precision in these texts, Barzon has been associated with Balzon or Balza between the Halys and Sangarios rivers, mentioned by Theodore Prodromos (Hörandner 1974: 3.43, 42.11) when Kastamon was captured by John Komnenos (Conca 1994: 307, n. 1), and with Anabarzos in Cilicia (Plepelits 2003: 9–10); cf. Boissonade 1819, vol. 2: 19–22.

not to make a formal assault against it,
nor to hurl battlement-breaking stones
at the wall from artillery engines,
nor to knock them down from above   10
by rocks, sappers' tortoises and bronze-tipped rams
– for the city was not easy for them to capture
since a precipice surrounded it in on all sides –
but to abduct those of the men of Barzon
they could capture outside the boundaries   15
and all the possessions they had with them.
And so, fanning out and spreading
at a distance from the walls of the little town,
a band subordinate to the Parthian commander
suddenly plundered the surrounding areas.   20
The barbarians, making an immediate onslaught,
made the area by the gates the Mysians' booty.[4]
Some they put to the sword, wretches
whom they saw trying to resist;
others they took away bound in chains.   25
In their excess they cut down every tree,
although they saw they were heavy with fruit.
   They also plundered those goats and cattle
which had not fled within the walls in time.
They dragged off women who dragged off their infants with them.   30
The unhappy mothers lamented,
and the infants wailed with them:
for they could not suckle easily
since the infant-nurturing flow from the nipples
was turned into a stream flecked with blood.   35
There corn was cut even before the harvest
to feed the barbarians' cavalry
and the firm grape was crushed before the vintage,
miserably trampled by horses' hooves,
as the neighbouring district was laid waste all around   40
by harsh, hostile, alien-tongued Parthians.
What more can be said? All those outside the walls

---

4 A proverbial phrase (Apostolios 11.83 [Leutsch and Schneidewin 1839–51, vol. 2]); cf.
R&D 1.26. In the expedition against Troy, part of the Greek fleet landed in Mysia, on the north-
west coast of Asia Minor, and encountered fierce opposition.

who succeeded in escaping the sword for a time,
alas! placed their necks
under the heavy yoke of unhappy servitude,   45
and were weeping for their terrible fate.
Those who had rushed inside the walls,
fleeing from the Parthian blade,
ran to the secure protection of the lofty wall
and loudly responded to the wailing   50
of their compatriots as they were taken away from their city,
saying, "What malign and savage fate
has again torn apart those of our race?
Alas! what Fury, what vengeful spirit, what fate
makes free men slaves to cruel barbarians?[5]   55
For which of them shall one lament loudly?
For those slaughtered together? For captives put in chains?
For women who are widowed? For maidens without husbands?
For the throng of infants innocent of misdeeds?
For ourselves? Oh the accumulation of disasters!"   60
    These endured their troubles in this way,
and a lament arose, confused, deep and loud,
from men, women, maidens and youths;
but the barbarians were not neglectful of their looting
– they were engaged in thoughts of plunder.   65
For an enemy with a barbarian heart and brutal mind
usually regards it as the height of luxury
to plunder men who have done no wrong.
So it was only when they had fettered their captives together
that they looked at last to indulgence and drinking.   70
    There was also present with them a remarkable prey,
which was bound to them with unbreakable chains
and lamented together with those in fetters
– the handsome Charikles and the even more handsome Drosilla.
Sitting together on the plain,   75
they partook of the meal that was set before them.
    In the midst of the plain was a most delightful meadow,[6]

5 Issues of slavery and freedom are recurrent motifs in the novels, especially *H&H* and
R&D; see discussion in the respective Introductions, p. 17, n. 78 and p. 173.
    6 Marginal gloss: 'Description of the meadow'. 1.77–115: Descriptions of gardens, usually
enclosing the heroine, are a major element in the novels' conventions; cf. Longos 4; *L&K* 1.15;

around which were beautiful bay trees,
cypresses, planes and oaks,
while within it there were delightful fruit trees.   80
There were lily plants and delightful rose bushes
in great numbers, within the meadow.
The buds of the roses, which were closed,
or, more accurately, just slightly opened,
kept the flowers in seclusion like a maiden.   85
One must surely understand the reason for this
to be the warming ray of the sun.
For when it – and this is quite proper –
thrusts its way with its heat into the buds,
they lay bare their rose-scented charms.   90
There was also spring water flowing there,
cold, clear and sweet as honey.
There was a column rising in the middle of the fountain,
carved very skilfully on the inner surface.
It was, as it were, a long tube,   95
through which the liquid rose and flowed.
But an eagle received this –
it was made with careful artistry in bronze and was perched up above –
and made the water flow out from its mouth.
Amidst the white stones of the beautiful fountain   100
there stood a circle of well-sculpted statues:
the figures were creations of Pheidias,
and the work of Zeuxis and Praxiteles,[7]
the best craftsmen in the art of sculpture.
On the right-hand side of the garden   105
outside the wooden fences themselves,
an altar had been constructed to Dionysos,[8]
whose festival the people of Barzon were keeping.
It was during this that the host of lawless barbarians[9]

---

and especially *H&H* 1.4–6, with which this description has much in common and on which it may be modelled. On the symbolism, see Littlewood 1979.

7 Pheidias, Zeuxis and Praxiteles, among the most renowned sculptors of classical Greece, were frequently cited by Byzantine writers as paradigms of artistic excellence.

8 Dionysos provides motivations for the plot development in *D&C*.

9 Military tacticians recommended attacking a city when its inhabitants were outside the walls, celebrating a festival; see, e.g., the tenth-century Heron Byzantinus (Sullivan 2000: 44, §12).

suddenly fell upon the local people   110
when they were outside the protective walls
together with their wives and children,
and were celebrating there the festival
of the god Dionysos, and feasting
within coverings of the tentmakers' craft.   115
It was for this festival that the maiden Drosilla too,
with the girls and maidens who were her companions,
had already left the wall of the city
and started the fair circlings of the dance.
   The girl was like a star-studded heaven,[10]   120
clad, indeed, for the festival
in a golden, shining, white and purple cloak.
Her youthful movements were graceful, her hands white as sardonyx;
her lips and cheeks as crimson as a rose;
her eyes black and well outlined,   125
her cheek flaming, her nose arched, her hair gleaming,
yes, it was lustrous and well groomed;
her lips were a pursed bud, an opening hive,
pouring out the pleasant honey of her speech;
a flashing star of the earth, a rose of heaven;   130
a long neck gracefully poised,
everything was delightful – her curved eyebrows,
flashing fires of white and red colour, radiated
from the torches of her cheeks,
though the rest of the girl's face was snow white;   135
her locks were of gold, her curls
blonde, honey sweet, golden coloured, orderly,
long and redolent of musk;
her jaw and neck were gleaming,
her lip dripped nectar,   140
her breast had the fresh dew of another dawn;
in her youthful vigour she was tall as a young cypress,
her nose was well formed, the setting of her teeth was
like a string of white-hued pearls,
the circular arches of her eyebrows were   145

---

10 Marginal gloss: 'Description of Drosilla'. 1.120–58: Cf. the description of Rhodanthe
(*R&D* 1.39–60).

like the bow of joyful Eros;
she seemed a mixture of milk and roses
and it looked as though nature, like a painter,
had coloured her body white and red;[11]
she was astonishing to the girls who danced with her   150
within the meadow of the temple of Dionysos.
Her fingers and the tips of her ears
were bright with rubies, flaming like fire,
stones set firmly in pure gold.
Her hands flashed with gold,   155
yes, and with them her silvery feet.
Thus was the maiden Drosilla blessed with the grace
of such great and extraordinary beauty.
    When they had enjoyed a long carousal
until sunset and far into the evening,   160
the cruel Parthians, delighting in their plunder
– for the barbarian naturally rejoices in drunkenness
and likes to give himself up to licentiousness and drinking,
especially if he can seize his booty easily,
finding other people's possessions in abundance –   165
with difficulty rose from the table,
whereupon they immediately turned to sleep.
Then Kratylos – for this was the Parthian lord's name –
sobering up briefly from the drunkenness which befuddled him,
spoke as follows to the satrap[12] Lysimachos,   170
"We have now already sated ourselves with food
and drink, and also with intoxication,
which lays sleep on the eyelids.
So it is time, satrap, for us to retire
to sleep, we who have surrendered ourselves to indulgence.   175
But you, a heart truly given to wakefulness,
alone of us all should not join us in slumber.
Take with you also the pick of the army
and ride round the fettered prisoners,
watching, guarding, spying, hustling from all sides,   180
in case they should escape without our noticing

11 A similar concept is found in *R&D* 2.250.
12 'satrap': a term originally used (from 5th cent. BCE onwards) to refer to a Persian provincial governor.

and make us the object of great mockery,
or perhaps they might do something rash
to those of our followers who are happily asleep."
   When the satrap Lysimachos had received 185
this painful message from his lord
he had already shaken sleep far from him,
and he rushed to the guarding of the prisoners.
As the gleaming charioteer, the sun,
lit his torch over all the earth, 190
revealing the brilliant day,
the Parthian lord immediately arose
and, congratulating Lysimachos on his guard-duty,
received the man with enthusiastic words,
fulfilling for him many promises;[13] 195
indeed, he declared that he would himself present
most of the booty to Lysimachos and his men,
"For those whose efforts are greater than others'
must also be rewarded with greater gifts."
   When he had said this, he rose from his bed; 200
and the barbarian tribe also rose,
ready to return home at no tardy pace;
indeed, gathering the plunder they had already won,
the goats, the cattle and the fettered prisoners,
at the command of the ruler Kratylos himself, 205
they set off straight to their homeland.
   They reached there on the fifth day
and consigned the captives to prison,
mixing them with the wretched prisoners
already confined there, the first spoils of war. 210
When they were thrown into the prison,
they fell to the ground and on bended knee
began to bewail their cruel fate;
only one group they called blessed and worthy of praise
– those whom the sword had subjected to slaughter –, 215
calling their murder a benefaction:
for the soul is out of love with life

13 Kratylos had made no promises (not the only such looseness in this novel; Conca 1994: 317, n. 3).

when it falls frequently into boundless grief.
Drosilla, who unfortunately and unluckily
had been separated by vengeful fate   220
from Charikles, her bridegroom in name alone,
was held in Chrysilla's women's quarters,
Chrysilla being the wife of the Parthian Kratylos.
    Charikles, once enclosed
within the prison, as I said, began to lament,   225
saying, "What Fury, Zeus, Lord of Olympos,
has removed Drosilla from the embrace
of her most wretched Charikles?"
Then Charikles cried out even louder:
"Alas, Drosilla, where are you going? Where are you living?[14]   230
To what servile tasks have you been set?
Have you been killed by one of our brutal enemies?
Or do you have a frail hold on life, with a shadowy existence?
Do you weep? Do you laugh? Are you dead? Have you been
        saved from death?
Are you happy or sad or afraid? Do you not fear the sword?   235
Are you in pain or being beaten or suffering? Surely you are
        not enduring rape?
Which chief satrap's bed are you sharing?
Which enemy, now declared your master,
is receiving his wine-bowl from your fingers?
Or perhaps in his advanced intoxication   240
he will strike you with his barbarian fist
for some unwitting offence? Oh, woe upon our fate!
Or perhaps Kratylos here will cast his lascivious eye
on you and envy our marriage?
Before he succeeds, Chrysilla's jealousy   245
will destroy you with a cup of poison.
O child of Zeus, Dionysos, how did you previously
promise me marriage with Drosilla,
when I honoured you then on her behalf with many sacrifices,
you messenger of evil tidings?   250
Do you too have any feeling in your heart,
Drosilla, for your friend Charikles,

    14 Marginal gloss: 'Charikles' lament for Drosilla'. Cf. Dosikles' lament at *R&D* 1.88–131
and that of Rhodanthe at *R&D* 7.17–51; see Roilos 2005: 107–08.

who is grieving and wailing, shut in his prison?
Or have you forgotten the god Dionysos
and the pledge granted Charikles through him, 255
because constraints now stand in your way,
the disaster and suffering of a prisoner of war?"
     While Charikles was composing without restraint[15]
this solemn dirge to Drosilla,
there stood up a fine young man, 260
sweet of voice and noble in appearance,
a fellow prisoner, a foreigner[16] in the same prison,
and, sitting down beside Charikles,
he hastened to console his fellow sufferer,
saying, "Charikles, do put an end your laments.[17] 265
Speak to me, and make a reply,
so that you may relieve the main weight
of despondency by a spontaneous discussion.
For speech is the remedy for all grief,
and certainly the soul would have no other way 270
of quenching the fire of affliction, once it is kindled,
unless it expresses the cause of the affliction to another
who is able to console the afflicted."
     "You are right, Kleandros,"[18] said Charikles,
"Indeed your words to me now are enough 275
on their own to abate most of my suffering.
But now since night has come on, as you see,
and, my friend, I should obey night,[19]
let me be calm and lie down,
in the hope that I may close my eyes for a little sleep, 280
and forget my sufferings for a while.
Tomorrow, when the night has passed,
you will hear of Charikles' disasters."
     While Charikles had thus turned to sleep,

15 Marginal gloss: 'Befriending of Charikles and Kleandros'.

16 The definition of 'foreigner' (ξένος) in this context offers many possibilities, ranging from lack of acquaintance or kinship ties ('stranger') to different ethnicity ('foreigner'); on Byzantine attitudes to 'outsiders', see Smythe 2000.

17 At the comparable point in *R&D* 1.138 the hero's newly found companion embarks on a lengthy narrative of his past.

18 Charikles has in fact not yet heard the young man's name.

19 A Homeric tag (e.g. *Iliad* 7.282, 7.793, 8.502, 9.65), used also in *H&H* 2.13.3.

Drosilla was lamenting bitterly from the depths of her heart   285
as she lay in the maidenly apartments of Chrysilla
– for gentle sleep could not pour over
the girl's eyes and restrain her –,
"Dear heart," she said, "Charikles, my husband,[20]
Charikles, my husband in name only,   290
you are now asleep in some corner of the prison
without the slightest thought in your mind for Drosilla,
but, as a result of your evil situation, you have forgotten
both the pledge willingly exchanged between us
and the god who once joined me   295
to you, Charikles, though only by a promise.
But Drosilla is lamenting loudly about Charikles,
brimming over with tears,
and is reproaching you, and especially Fate,
since you have not remembered her who was pledged to you.   300
And though spiteful Fate may conspire
so unhappily against you, Charikles,
and, before you, against the maiden Drosilla,
so as to break asunder our indissoluble conjunction
and divide us in two   305
– why, malign Fate, have you not been satisfied
with the tortuous circumstances which have already entrapped me
and the punishment which has now overwhelmed me,
but are imprisoning me apart from Charikles?
The darkness of the prison would be better than light   310
if I had been condemned to stay with Charikles,
and yesterday I had entered the prison with him –
so, Charikles, even if Fate strives
so hard to divide friends
and contrives the separation of a couple,   315
and struggles, alas, for the final sundering
of those who breathe as one by a mutual pledge,
you should not succumb nor consign things to oblivion,
but in the face of vengeful Fate
you should show the utmost steadfastness.   320
But you are asleep and are not lamenting Drosilla,

20 Marginal gloss: 'Drosilla's lament'. 1.289–352: See Roilos 2005: 107–08 on intertextual
and ritual aspects of this lament.

while she laments and calls the gods to witness
that she should never be divided from Charikles.
Ivy is inseparable from oak,
for it has been accustomed to its embrace from its first growth   325
and has become incorporated into it and seems to have developed
one body with a double energy;
even so Drosilla with her bridegroom Charikles is
one flesh and mind and a single soul,
though yesterday when the table was set Kratylos   330
was clearly consumed with a terrible passion
and wanting to turn an ill-omened gaze on me.
Alas, Charikles, name I am bound to love,
how will the disasters that have befallen us end?
Thus I now, though separated from you, judge it   335
some consolation just to see
the prison within which you are locked
– yes, just this – and to know at least
where you now live, where you sleep, where you sit.
End your sleep, if you have been able to drowse,   340
think of Drosilla: she laments for you, she weeps for you;
weep with her, lament with her, despair with her.
Indeed, Charikles, you were not born of oak,
and I know that you are lamenting and weeping
and not drowsing in the depths of night   345
as you think constantly of the maiden Drosilla.
Come hither, Sleep, and overcome me a little,
in the hope that a dream may appear and calm me,[21]
by showing me my beloved Charikles;
for those who desire or love often   350
wish, when they do not see each other face to face,
to converse and breathe together in their dreams."
   As the maiden Drosilla was speaking thus,
lamenting bitterly and wailing,
day returned to the captives   355
who were sleeping wretchedly in prison,
although the cell's pitch blackness
prevailed and darkened the day.

---

21 The first of the dreams in this novel; see MacAlister 1990 and 1996, and Introductions,
pp. 16 and 175 for the role played by dreams in *H&H* and *R&D* as well as *D&C*.

SECOND BOOK

As soon as day shone forth
and the giant light-bearing sun
cast a tiny ray through the prison's
narrow constraints on those within,
Charikles alone immediately rose up. 5
Seeing that all were sleeping deeply
he gave a swift groan from the depths of his heart
and said, "Men who are my fellow prisoners,
it is reasonable for you to continue sleeping,
for harsh emotions and the anguish of desire 10
have not possessed the breadth of your heart,
love has not overpowered your souls –
should it surprise me if you embrace sleep
from night's beginning to sunrise?
For Eros usually wings his way by night 15
to penetrate those in love,
since a lover's soul is then relaxed
and, as it were, entirely accessible to him.
You should not, Eros, in your strength
make those moving here on earth fall in love, 20
but when you do so, why do you not grant success
but instead bestow much suffering on many
until they attain the object of their desire?"
    Charikles lamented thus quietly to himself
and shed a flood of tears, 25
for Eros always gives rise to many tears
when he makes a massive onslaught on afflicted souls.
But his weeping did not escape Kleandros' notice;
leaping up he came immediately
to where Charikles had the ground as his couch 30
and said, "Greetings, stranger and fellow prisoner.[22]
Perhaps you might tell me what you promised,
Charikles, your misfortunes and adventures;
then I would sit beside you
and give my attention to your recital.[23] 35

22 Marginal gloss: 'Conversation of Charikles and Kleandros'.
23 'recital' (τραγωδία): a term derived from ancient drama, and used elsewhere in *D&C*

Thus you will lighten your own groans
by revealing to me what grieves you,
and you will also relieve me, your fellow inmate
Kleandros, from my own sufferings.
For you have not entered the prison on your own.   40
Or were you taken captive before this,
with your soul enflamed with love?
Kleandros too was not without experience of love when captured;
he did not make his unfortunate entry into prison
lacking knowledge of love   45
and untouched by the disasters with which Fate
afflicted me when I was entangled in the snares of passion.
Are you in pain? I am in pain too. Do you weep? I weep with you.
Do you feel desire? I feel desire too, and for a beautiful maiden,
Kalligone who has been snatched away from me."   50
    "Kleandros, saviour of my long-suffering heart,"
said Charikles, "which of the Olympian
gods sent you here to comfort me?
Tell me about your circumstances, tell me the suffering we share.
You should speak first since you were imprisoned first,   55
then I, who have been imprisoned with you."
    "Charikles, I had Lesbos as my country;
I came from responsible and respectable parents –
my mother is Kydippe and my father Kallistias.
The maiden Kalligone lived nearby,   60
protected from men's gaze and
guarded in the innermost chamber.
I learnt of her beauty – for I could not behold it –
from those who attended her.
I am not ashamed to say this, Charikles,   65
to one who suffers the same disease.
When, through gifts brought by skilful messengers,
I eventually and with difficulty contrived to see
Kalligone leaning innocently from her window,
I was captured by her tender youthfulness,   70
by her face that was as lovely as widespread rumour made it.

---

with a clear sense of 'lament'. On the ambiguous used of such terms in the novels, see Walden
1894 and, with a different emphasis, Agapitos 1998.

Woe, by Eros' armoury,
alas, alas, by the Graces, you would have said if you saw her
– even you, Charikles if you were not looking at Drosilla –   75
that she was a child whose mother was Selene and father Helios.[24]
She turned onlookers' hearts to stone,
even more she sent arrows through passers-by,
she did not look on those who were gazing out of lasciviousness
but she enflamed everyone with her loveliness.   80
She was a child, a tender child, a maiden.
The sight of her drove even old men,
impotent from excessive age, to passion,
not only lusty fire-breathing youths.
She was the image of Eros, the child of Helios,   85
resembling her father Helios,
or rather rivalling him.
Eros, offspring of savage beasts, you should
have trampled my heart and torn it apart;
indeed you have sucked a lioness's milk   90
and perhaps nuzzled a bear's teats.
So when I saw her, a pang struck my very soul,
ill-fated desire gnawed at me and tormented me,
I struggled, I fell, I was convulsed,
for it was not savage desire alone that possessed me   95
– or rather Eros himself who was wearing me down –
but a deep affection for her childish innocence
and compassion for everything it gives rise to.
One kiss alone would have given me strength
to withstand Eros' slings,   100
for at that time I wanted nothing
more than a kiss from the girl
and this, from compassion alone, would have been a complete cure.
So I addressed her – for I could not restrain myself –,
'I see, girl, a lesser matter that is more important than the main one: 105
kissing your mouth is better than licking honey.'
But the young girl was alarmed by this little speech,
for she was as yet unaware of love.

---

24 i.e. Kalligone's beauty was such that only the moon (Selene) and sun (Helios) could have generated it.

So she promptly hid – alas for the fright I gave her –
and boxed her attendants' ears 110
with a nervous giggle, for embarrassment
had overcome her, and the childish, fragile girl
did not know what to do.
For maidens who are not expecting to be seen
are inclined to turn pale 115
when someone approaches them unexpectedly
or speaks to them somewhat surreptitiously.
    Returning thence to my own home
I abandoned myself to my couch,
finding love's furnace[25] exhausting 120
– for when Eros enters the heart through the eyes[26]
he is not content to set that on fire
but penetrates and enflames every limb –
and I lamented quietly to myself,
    'Let no one fear the sword-edged arrows[27] 125
of desire, even when poisoned,
for Eros in his ravings empties out his entire
quiver full of arrows against us.
Do not be alarmed at the beat of his wings,
for Eros takes possession of my heart 130
as if he were falling into bird-lime, and lays hold of it.
Eros, craven Eros, fire-breathing Eros,
if you had seen my breast set up with a snare,
wretch, you would not have flown down and become enmeshed.
All-powerful, all-daring, all-mighty Eros, 135
you pursue me with bitter vengeance when I have done you no harm.
You do not cut off hands or slice off feet
or gouge out the eyes' pupils,
instead you shoot straight to the heart
and kill me. Strong-armed wretch, 140
you slay, you slaughter, you enflame, you consume with fire,
you strike, you destroy, you poison, you overthrow.
Alas for your strength, winged bearer of fire and bow.'

25 'furnace' (ἀνθρακουργία): a word attested only in *D&C*.
26 Standard physiology of love in the novels; cf. *L&K* 1.6 (Rohde 1876: 161–63; Jouanno 1994).
27 2.125–31: A paraphrase of *AnthGr* 5.268 (Paul the Silentiary).

Thus I pondered in my sorrow,
until I thought that sending a written message   145
to the girl would be a remedy for my disease.
For strange propositions occurred to me,
that perhaps Kalligone had had the same experience
when she caught a glimpse of the handsome Kleandros.
Do not mock my words, Charikles,   150
when you see me downcast by circumstances,
when you see me gloomy and dejected,
shut up in this filthy prison,
for when a soul is tormented by inner grief
and long deprived of what it yearns for,   155
the whole body inevitably responds in sympathy."
    "You are quite right, Kleandros," said Charikles,
"a young man's face blooms and remains handsome
when his soul has found reasons for happiness."
    "So I quickly sent off a letter,"[28]   160
continued Kleandros, "to Kalligone,
trying to find out from her reaction
whether Kalligone had had a similar experience."
    "But may you enjoy Kalligone's passion!"
Charikles said once more to the stranger,   165
"Kleandros, leave nothing unsaid
of what you wrote and sent to the maiden."
"Listen then," Kleandros replied,[29]
        "'Most lovely girl, remembering your desirable
        appearance which overwhelmed me when I saw it,   170
        yesterday when I encountered Charon[30] I asked him a brief question
        since, so he said, he had known you before I had,
        "Wretched Charon, bereft of joy,
        will you miserably snatch away
        Kalligone, best of girls, together with our peers   175

28 Letters sent as part of the hero's courtship of the heroine become a major feature of
the later Greek romances (e.g. the Palaiologan *L&R* and *Ach*); on the role of such letters, see
Agapitos 2006.

29 Marginal gloss: 'Kleandros' first letter to Kalligone'.

30 Charon in classical Greek mythology ferried souls across the river Styx in the underworld;
in the Byzantine world he morphed into an active personification of death, with a prolonged
presence in later Greek folk song; see Alexiou 1978.

and will you destroy that far-famed beauty
and, alas, tear asunder those orbs of her eyes
which have shot at me,
rather than withdraw from gazing at her beauty?"
This is what I said, but the mighty figure,   180
sad, ill-fated Charon, replied, "Yes."
Taking this very badly, I responded,
"Alas, most dreadful of evils, what are you about to do, Charon?"
What next? Nod your assent, Kalligone;
you have me, Kleandros, asking for you.'"   185
"Your letter is short but full of ingenuity,"
was Charikles' reply when he had heard it,
"so that when the girl now thinks of death and of Charon,[31]
who diminishes proud women,
she will incline towards you, who has written to her.   190
But tell me – for you know the answer – what then did Kalligone reply
to Kleandros, how did she respond?"
    "The girl said nothing, Charikles, as was likely.
Either she did not receive that letter
or she was too busy with her playmates.   195
So listen to my second message."
    "Don't begrudge me, my good Kleandros, even
the third message that you sent the girl,"
said Charikles. Kleandros replied,
"Listen then; I will not begrudge you this,   200
for talking to you relieves my sickness.
    'I consider the Sirens' song an invention,[32]
    from the time I saw your face, maiden.
    See, you boast a beauty that is beyond reason,
    you cast an enchantment over me that is beyond nature,   205
    you strike by petrification and allow no means of escape.
    Your braids are golden – gold, be clad in earth again.
    Your gaze is brilliant – farewell, gems' brilliance.

31 It is perhaps a comment on Byzantine religious sensibility that a girl's thoughts should turn to death.

32 Marginal gloss: 'Kleandros' second letter to Kalligone'. The Sirens, sea nymphs who lured sailors with their songs (e.g. *Odyssey* 12.165–200), became in later literature a synonym for a woman seductive through her facility with words as much as her beauty (e.g. Aristainetos 1.1.43)

Your complexion is white – begone, pearls' grace.
When I myself recall, maiden, your appearance   210
that sheds illumination all round,
I am incapable of dowsing the coals
that hostile Eros has lit within me.
And my mind itself contemplates your appearance
and seeks what it possessed, which once I saw.   215
But within my unhappy heart itself
bitter Eros, that serpentine offspring,[33]
insinuates himself into me obliquely, like a snake,
and – alas – devours my breast and my entrails.
It is your task to put an end to the disease.   220
Dowse the coals and cool me
and, maiden, prise off with your spells
the serpent that has encircled me.'"
"Yes, yes, my good Kleandros," said Charikles,
"this is the mark of a man caught with a suffering heart!   225
You have suffered, as you say – that I know from my own experience.
When the throng of Graces[34] bound Eros,
that imperious tyrant over mortals
who has so wasted me away,
they handed the lord   230
to fair-faced beauteous maidens to be their servant.
The Paphian one who roams everywhere[35]
and offers countless gifts in ransom,
seeks her child with great yearning,
and if anyone is found willing to set him free,   235
he will not run away, for he has learnt
submission when in service to the Graces."
   "Listen," said Kleandros, "also to my third
message to the girl, Charikles.

---

33 On these aspects of Eros, cf. Sappho, fr. 130.2 (Voigt 1971); also George of Pisidia, *Hexaemeron* 794 (Gonnelli 1998).
   34 2.227–35: A paraphrase of *Anacreontea* 19 (West 1993). The Graces, usually three, are frequently associated with Aphrodite.
   35 'The Paphian one': Aphrodite, mother of Eros. In Greek mythology Aphrodite was born from the sea, from the foam from Ouranos' severed genitals (Hesiod, *Theogony* 176–206); there were major cult centres on the island of Kythera and also at Paphos on Cyprus.

'Moon, through you I think I see light.[36] 240
Through you I move, I breathe through you, have my being
    through you.
You are my joy but also the dart of my despair.
You are my sickness but also its remedy.
You are my care but instantly my carefree life.
You bring me to life when dead – a strange matter; 245
and you put me to death when living – a miracle. For nature
drew on all her charms[37] for your creation,
when she formed you gleaming with red and white.
O what a star so brilliant and huge
did the Moon, the light-bringing, life-producing mother, 250
bring forth in our times.
You are sick? I am sick too. You rejoice? With you I rejoice greatly.
You are in pain? I am in pain too. You weep? I weep with you.
This one thing is bitter, this one thing gnaws and harasses me –
from the moment I saw you I, miserable wretch, was pierced
    through, 255
but you remain persistently stony-hearted towards me.
For you did not instantly apply a remedy
to my wounded heart,
and now from the gangrenous spot
the maggots have emerged and are devouring me. 260
Eros always aims his bow like this and
slaughters, slays, wounds, lacerates, afflicts,
goads, pierces, kills, cuts short, consumes.
Approach, behold a heart that has been struck
and this breast that is fatally pierced. 265
Pour dew from your bosom to this bosom
like wine, like oil into my wound.[38]
Bring your crystalline fingers here,
touch the whole of my suffering heart,
spread your gossamer robe over me, 270
cleanse me swiftly of the sturdy,
slowly devouring, heart-gnawing maggots.

36 Marginal gloss: 'Kleandros' third letter to Kalligone'.
37 'charms': the word used refers to Aphrodite's magical girdle (*Iliad* 14.214–15; cf. *H&H*
2.7).
38 A distinct hint of the Good Samaritan (Luke 10.34).

In this way may you rejoice in my preservation,
in this way may I rejoice in your great beneficence.
Do this; but may we come under one cloak[39]   275
with fervent desire in our hearts,
contriving a union worthy of praise.'
But, Charikles, if you wish, let me fall silent;
if not, give ear to the fourth message."
   "Do continue, Kleandros," said Charikles.   280
"Listen then to words of anguish
which I sent to Kalligone."
So saying, Kleandros began his dirge:
   'Receive the golden apple[40] that has no inscription,[41]
Kalligone, whose body is entirely graceful.   285
And if it were inscribed, what competition could there be with you?
Receive, fair one, the apple, for you alone are fair;
you are the fairest in the dance of maidens.
Momos[42] himself bears witness,
when he gazed fixedly once with us at the procession   290
as it made its way up and wended back;
and, biting his lip, he was astounded.
Do not knit your brows at me so fiercely:
I have been melted away by Eros' potions,
I have been singed with his coals.   295
Like a wayfarer in the burning sun,
I have found you, my shady tree;[43]
Would that I could be entwined around you all night like ivy
      round an oak.
I must speak the truth: as
spring is far superior to winter,   300
the nightingale to sparrows, a sweet apple to sloes,

---

39 A motif first found in Archilochos, fr. 196a, 29–30 (West 1989); cf. Theokritos, *Idyll* 18.19; *AnthGr* 5.169, 3–4.

40 A reference to the Apple of Discord, inscribed 'To the fairest', presented by Paris to Aphrodite (see, e.g., Apollodoros, *Epitome* 3.2). On the amatory implications of apples, see Littlewood 1974 and 1993.

41 Marginal gloss: 'Kleandros' fourth letter to Kalligone'.

42 Momos, child of Night (Hesiod, *Theogony* 214), is the personification of sarcasm, adduced in similar contexts by Aristainetos (1.1.45–47, 1.12.7).

43 Cf. *R&D* 1.231–31 for this image.

a virgin to thrice-wed wives,[44]
even so is your countenance. Your shadow alone
entranced me yesterday when I glimpsed you intently.
The Kyprian[45] herself, it seems, maiden,   305
has placed her hands on your bosom
and every Grace has beautified you.
The thought came to me that you might be Pandora[46]
whom legendary invention depicts.
But though it is legend that depicts her,   310
it is the manifest word of truth
that presents you to us and reveals
the sun-like, starry being,
you the maiden, the fair Kalligone.'
So, Charikles, unable to resist in any way,   315
I sent a swift exchange of letters.
What next? Wretch that I am, eventually I received a message
that I should come by night to the maiden's quarters
where the sweet one spent her time.
So when evening came,   320
taking my silver lyre
I struck a note with a most pleasing rhythm,
and as I strummed I sang to Kalligone
and – for I despised the Olympians[47] –
I began these delightful songs: 325
  'Moon's torch, give light to the stranger.[48]
    The weeping Niobe was turned to stone,[49]
    unable to bear the loss of her children.
    The child-slaying daughter of Pandion[50]

44 Cf. Theokritos, *Idyll* 12.3–5.

45 'Kyprian': i.e. Aphrodite (from her reputed birthplace, Cyprus).

46 'Pandora': on the creation of Pandora, the first woman, see Hesiod, *Theogony* 560–612 and *Works and Days* 80–105; a complex but ultimately misogynistic myth, and so a double-edged compliment here.

47 Perhaps a reference to archaic contests in the performance of hymns to the gods, e.g. to Apollo at Delphi (Pausanias, *Geography* 10.7.2): this song is not to a god.

48 Marginal gloss: 'Kleandros' song to Kalligone'.

49 2.327–45: A paraphrase of *Anacreontea* 22 (West 1993). Niobe was punished for boasting of the number and beauty of her children by their death; see, e.g., Apollodoros, *Bibliotheke* 3.5.6.

50 Prokne, daughter of Pandion, king of Attica, killed her son by Tereus in revenge for

became a bird when she begged for flight. 330
Moon's torch, give light to the stranger.
  May I become a mirror, lord Zeus,
  so that you may always look at me, Kalligone;
  may I become a many-hued tunic shot with gold,
  so that I can touch your flesh. 335
Moon's torch, give light to the stranger.
  May I become water, so that I may happily
  bathe every part of your face each day;
  may I become perfumed ointment, so that I may anoint
  your lips, cheeks, hands, eyes, mouth. 340
Moon's torch, give light to the stranger.
  Why do I seek great things not easily attainable?
  It would be enough for me to become a golden slipper
  and to exist only to be pounded
  by the imposition of your white-heeled feet. 345
Moon's torch, give light to the stranger.
  In place of fire Zeus provided in this life[51]
  another terrible fire-brand, in the form of woman.
  Would that fire, would that womankind had not
  come to earth and entered this life. 350
Moon's torch, give light to the stranger.
  For fire itself, should it be kindled,
  can swiftly be extinguished,
  but a woman is an unquenchable fire in the heart
  if she brings the fair beauty of a lovely face. 355
Moon's torch, give light to the stranger.
  Should it happen that there are those whom valour in
      battle saved,
  whose heads the sword did not sever,
  whom disease did not make bed-ridden,
  whom a shrewd mind rescued from danger, – 360
Moon's torch, give light to the stranger, –
  whom encircling hazards did not encompass,
  whom chains did not restrain, nor the weight of fetters,

Tereus' rape of her sister Philomela; Prokne was metamorphosed into a nightingale and Philomela a swallow (Apollodoros, *Bibliotheke* 3.14.8); cf. 4.116 below.

  51 2.347–55: A paraphrase of *AnthGr* 9.167 (Palladas); cf. also Hesiod, *Works and Days* 57–58.

and who without preoccupations from the present always
live the bounteous life of Kronos,[52] –   365
Moon's torch, give light to the stranger, –
    these men a woman who talks with charm
    burns up as if with a flaming thunderbolt,
    when her brilliant lightning blazes,
    consuming the flower of young manhood.   370
Moon's torch, give light to the stranger.
    The furnace of your lips, Kalligone,
    kindles terror within those who look on you,
    but it brings at the same time both fire and dew,
    summoning me with the one and turning me away with
        the other.   375
Moon's torch, give light to the stranger.
    He who gazes from afar she enflames,
    but he who approaches your mouth
    or achieves only a kiss
    she receives with a chill drizzle or moistness.   380
Moon's torch, give light to the stranger.
    O cooling fire, O enflaming dew.[53]
    But comfort him who is burning
    and on fire from the coals of your lips,
    and grant him your dew for his refreshment.'[54]   385

THIRD BOOK

"Warbling thus, like a nightingale in spring,
I came, I found, I saw the girl herself
and, 'Greetings,' she said, 'my bridegroom in my dreams',
anticipating me with her speech.
'Eros appeared in the evening of the day before yesterday   5

52 'life of Kronos': a reference to the Golden Age over which, according to some myths, Kronos, son of Ouranos, reigned; cf. Hesiod, *Works and Days* 109–26.

53 This line also appears at *R&D* 8.225; cf. *A&K* fr. 11, 165.9. For the paradox, cf. George of Pisidia, *Hexaemeron* 1793; it is not uncommon in liturgical contexts.

54 As well as an experiment in Anacreontic pastiche, the use of songs and letters could be seen as a deliberately light-hearted variation on the more ponderous *R&D*, or else as an attempt to pad out a thin plot.

and joined you to me, Kleandros, in marriage,[55]
heeding, so he said, the tears which you had shed.
And you must consider, Kleandros, yes, you must consider
how our affairs are to be safely dealt with.
For neither fire or sea or the sword   10
would I fear to achieve union with Kleandros,
for those whom god has joined, who may put asunder?'[56]
   Hearing these words, Charikles,
'Greetings also, Kalligone,' I then replied,
'come quickly, come to the harbour nearby   15
so that we may immediately set sail from Lesbos,
since the lord Eros has made the decision, maiden.'
So hurling ourselves on to a vessel[57]
– for when Eros is aroused he does not brook delays –
we sailed together for five days,   20
and when the sun was setting in the west
and a ship-destroying squall arose,
we were driven against our will into Barzopolis,
where we moored in the harbour,
barely escaping the storm's force.   25
It so happened that baleful Parthians were at that time
encircling the city in a fierce siege
– for they frequently harassed the Barzitai
by attacking them when they were off their guard.
They captured us all together,   30
those who had fled over the sea's expanse,
Kalligone and Kleandros, and the other passengers,
and they burnt the vessel that had been carrying us.
Kalligone, however, was concealed among myrtles
– for they grew densely near the harbour –   35
and so she escaped the Parthian arrogance
while I, to the present day,
from the moment I was separated from her,
dwell in a gloomy dungeon,

55 There has been no hint of this before, and it reads like a parody of the role, and images, of Eros in, e.g., *H&H* 3.1–3, 6.18.3.

56 A clear allusion to Matthew 19.6, but also a reference to Dionysos' role in the plot, as will become apparent.

57 Marginal gloss: 'Flight of Kleandros and Kalligone'.

enduring a fate that is doubly harsh.   40
I am deprived of the maiden Kalligone,
and I am now among the most baleful of enemies.
Now you, Charikles, tell me, as you promised,
of your painful and much-bewailed life."
    "Truly, it is not without tears that you make me speak,   45
Kleandros, of what torments and grieves me,"
said Charikles, beginning to speak,
"nevertheless, since it relieves the heart[58]
to pour out its problems in words,
pay attention, Kleandros, for I do not shrink from speech.   50
My mother was Krystale, my father Phrator,
from a family not lacking in repute, my homeland was Phthia.[59]
I had already reached adolescence,
brought up according to the norms of well-born youths;
I was happy in the company of the young men with whom I associated; 55
I rode, I joined in sports, as is customary for young men,
I hunted hare, I became a skilled equestrian
– for I had highly skilled companions –
but I had as yet no experience of love,
nor had down begun to shadow my chin.   60
When the festival of Dionysos took place,
we went off together to enjoy ourselves
at his altar,[60] which in Phthia was constructed
outside the city from slabs of colourful marble.
    There were in that place dedicated to the god[61]   65
trees that were always blooming as if in spring,
brimming with fruit and with burgeoning leaves.
And the river Melirrhoe[62] flowed out,
sweet to see and even more delightful to drink.

58 Marginal gloss: 'Charikles tells Kleandros about himself'.

59 'Phthia': in southern Thessaly, home also of Achilles and his Myrmidons (e.g. *Iliad* 16.155, 19.14, 23.4).

60 As in *H&H*, altars and festivals are conspicuous elements in the plot.

61 3.65–108: An evocation of a paradisiacal setting, which has its origins in Alkinous' garden (*Odyssey* 7.112–32) and a long history in European literature as a *locus amoenus* (pleasant place), susceptible to metaphorical interpretations; the classic study remains Curtius 1953: 182–303; cf. Sosthenes' garden in *H&H* 1.3–6.

62 'Melirrhoe': i.e. 'Honey-flowing', a fictitious name, probably based on Exodus 3.8 and the promised land flowing with milk and honey.

Most of the cowherds call 70
the sweet Melirrhoe Threpsagrostis,[63]
when they graze their cattle in that area
as it flows peaceably within its banks.
For it is not fed by melted snow
nor do great floods rush down from the mountains 75
and overwhelm the fields with their flow;
it alone of the rivers in Phthia
maintains a constant flow and flows all around.
Every shepherd, every farmer
whose lands are within its streams is fortunate; 80
it is from heaven that the most sweet moisture falls,
which maintains a steady flow.
On its banks a kind of golden plane tree
flourished with vigorous golden leaves.
In comparison with it 85
Xerxes' famed plane tree is nothing,[64]
for the tip of its trunk reaches the aither,
while its leaves shade all the ground round about
which the streams of the Melirrhoe enclose.
A spring flowed out from the plane tree's roots, 90
of the sort that is normally found there.
The soil prospered and nurtured flocks
with the copious abundance of fodder, the surfeit
and the surge from the fair Melirrhoe.
Bleating goats became intoxicated if they drank of it, 95
and frequently skipped around on the green grass.
A temple attendant, recruited in the god's service,
remained to keep watch, maintaining an unwearied vigil
over the sacred plane tree lest
a traveller's careless foot should approach it. 100
    So everyone hastened out of Phthia[65]

63 'Threpsagrostis': i.e. 'Nurturer of farmers'.

64 The ultimate source for Xerxes' golden plane tree is Herodotos 7.27 and 31, but more immediately cf. Theodore Prodromos 18.22–24 (Hörandner 1974). The tree had resonances in the fourteenth-century romances (e.g. *AchN* 793–821; *L&Ra* 686–94), and later; cf. Beaton 1976: 78–81.

65 On the bucolic and pastoral resonances of this scene, particularly in connection with Theokritos and Longos, see Burton 2006.

to the festival of the god Dionysos,
men, women, maidens, young men,
other striplings and young girls.
I, as I attended the feast, was as yet uninitiated   105
in what one might call the erotic onslaught.
Would that I had not gone out
with the noble youths from the gate of Phthia![66]
We, a companionable band of young men, went up
to the guardian of the place and the plane tree   110
and, presenting gifts, found an exceptional place to sit,
which allowed contemplation of maidenly beauty,
that tyrant or avenger of the heart.
For strong-handed Eros,
the aged child,[67] the babe existing before Kronos,   115
is accustomed to attack through the portals of the eyes,
to burn the entrails and enflame the heart,
and to turn the one afflicted with desire into a corpse.
And so, promptly sitting down under the plane tree
with my friends and contemporaries   120
I partook of the multifarious fare,
wretchedly ignorant of what would befall,
that such delight and mirth
would end in floods of tears.
Nevertheless I rejoiced with those with whom I ate: 125
such is the heart which is unaware,
when it rejoices, of future evil.
I listened to amusing erotic speeches
and to even more delightful songs.
One of my companions at the feast   130
began casually to address these words
to the maidens who had hastened thither
or to the varied groups of women
who were making their way in one direction or another:

66 Phthia has now become a city, rather than a region, and, as in Book 1, the festival takes place outside the city precincts.

67 The concept of the old age of Eros can be found in, e.g., Plato, *Symposium* 178 B–C; cf. also Longos 2.5.2, and later the three ages of Eros in *L&Rα* 481–92.

'Yesterday a fiery thirst seized me, and taking water[68]   135
– for I happened to be passing along the road –
I drank to satiety, as if quaffing ambrosia.
Remember yesterday, for it was you who gave it to me.
But the winged one, the uniquely bold-hearted,[69]
Eros the archer who is hard to face,   140
disguised himself as a mosquito and slipped into the cup,
and I drank him down and, wretch that I am, am tickled
in my heart with his wings,
and up to this very minute – oh, the grief, the pain –
he scratches me and bites me, and I am in a dreadful state.   145
Now, relenting belatedly and with reluctance,
Eros, the cruel lord of mortals,
sends me to you, who alone can heal
the wound and the bite and my heart;
he sends me, so take me into your embrace,   150
without any reluctance; yes, take me, take me.'
Another promptly responded after him,[70]
'O woe, what is this? That starry girl,[71]
who once was a riot of beauty
like the Corinthian Lais of olden times,[72]   155
is now worn down by a miserable disease – O evil disease;
her well-nourished flesh, as far as I can see, is fading.
May this not happen, indeed may it not; flesh, resume your strength;
may every wasting indisposition perish,
for it is not one woman's flesh that perishes,   160
but with her such a great throng of friends.'
Then another glanced at another girl and replied,
'You look down, girl who desires and is desired,[73]
when the one you love often passes by,
and you try to conceal your breast and face   165

---

68 Marginal gloss: 'Symposium's first epigram'.
69 3.139–51: A paraphrase of *Anacreontea* 6 (West 1993).
70 Marginal gloss: 'Symposium's second epigram'.
71 'starry girl': cf. Eugenianos, *Epithalamium* 5.61 (Gallavotti 1935).
72 'Lais': a famously expensive courtesan (4th cent. BCE); cf. Plutarch, *Nikias* 15.4; Pausanias, *Geography* 2.2.5. For Lais' regrets for lost beauty, cf. *AnthGr* 6.18 and 20 (the prefect Julian), and also 5.271 (Makedonius the consul), paraphrased here in 3.154–56.
73 Marginal gloss: 'Symposium's third epigram'. 3.163–72: A paraphrase of *AnthGr* 5.253 (Irenaeus referendarius).

and you are constantly fiddling with the ends of your girdle,
and with your delicate toes
you make marks in the dust on the ground.
Is this respect for modesty? But this is inappropriate:
the Kyprian one does not recognize modesty nor Eros shyness.   170
But if you want to respect modesty so much,
at least bestow on me your nod.'
Another youth let out a shrill cry in his turn,
    'How I give a thousand thanks to the grey-haired hag.[74]
She judges well and always passes sound judgments;   175
she is an advocate for the Kyprian,[75] in my view,
driving haughty girls to passion.
She who exults in her elegant curls
sees that the long plait has vanished,
the once blonde locks have turned to white;   180
she whose brows were lofty and arrogant
has now lost all the grace of her beauty.
The breast that formerly jutted out in front of the girl
now droops: time has destroyed it.
Alas, old lady, your voice is elderly;   185
your lips which were previously moist have become dry;
your brow has sunk, it brings disgust;
all your beauty, woman, has gone.
What is left for you? Come on, become a procuress.
You used to give insults; be insulted now, thrice-wretched.   190
You used to pass me by; now I reciprocate.
You used to strike me, you know; now be struck in your turn.
You are in distress? I was in distress before. You take this badly?
    I used to too.
Having suffered and learnt, as the saying goes,[76]
teach all the other maidens to submit speedily to their lovers.'"   195
"Oh, Charikles, what mirth comes to me
from your honeyed stories!"
said Kleandros, "oh, the evils that are foretold!

---

74 Marginal gloss: 'Symposium's fourth epigram'. 3.174–88: A paraphrase of *AnthGr* 5.273 (Agathias).

75 'Kyprian': Aphrodite.

76 Originally from Aeschylus, *Agamemnon* 177–78, then becoming proverbial; cf. *R&D* 9.148.

But I now see that you are smiling,   200
yet you said at the beginning of your story
that you could not tell it without tears."
    "I omit," said Charikles, "the long story
which another of the worthy symposiasts told me."
"Do not do so, by Drosilla," replied Kleandros.   205
"Listen then to his honey-sweet words:
    'You prefer effeminate men, as I have heard,[77]
    you raving Maenad,[78] insolent, wretch, old maid.
    Have no worries for your womb, for you won't become pregnant
    even if you lie with thousands of men,   210
    even if you slept with Herakles,[79] woman,
    or even with Priapos[80] whose lechery is legendary.
    Childless, though once you bore many children,
    childless you will remain. For Pluto[81] summons you to the world below.
    Stop this juvenile behaviour; push the boat out.'   215
This is what he said, and he said immediately to another girl:
    'Goodness me, how that old story was wrong.[82]
    They say that there are three Graces, but one eye of yours,
    girl, boasts a myriad Graces.[83]
    Alas, you turn me to ash in the furnace of desire   220
    and you burn up my entrails and my heart.
    O abominable girl, is this the mark of great love?
    Don't raise your brows, tremble before Kypris;
    acknowledge those who love you, have moderate thoughts.
    A girl's vehement threats   225
    I have realized are often in themselves Kypris' messengers,[84]
    while the various prevarications of her behaviour
    and her silence are a curiously reciprocal response.[85]

77 Marginal gloss: 'Symposium's fifth epigram'.

78 'Maenad': though usually referring to a maddened devotee of Dionysos, this can also refer to a prostitute.

79 'Herakles': Greek mythic hero of, among other achievements, legendary sexual prowess; cf. Apollodoros, *Bibliotheke* 2.7.8.

80 'Priapos': ithyphallic fertility god of noted ugliness and potency.

81 'Pluto': god of the underworld; in ancient Greek cult the beneficent aspect of Hades.

82 Marginal gloss: 'Symposium's sixth epigram'.

83 Cf. Musaios, *Hero and Leander* 64–65; Eugenianos, *Epigrams* 3.1–2 (Lambros 1914).

84 Cf. Musaios, *Hero and Leander* 130–32.

85 Cf. Musaios, *Hero and Leander* 164–65.

And as for you, you who are unyielding, this
for me is an excellent sign. Greetings, my heart!   230
Alas for your delectable conversation, maiden.
Your inexorable rejection may
move even rock itself to pain.
What could anyone suffer? But, Eros the archer,
you alone have been able to heal my wound.   235
For you I will traverse the sea's flooding tides
and pass through fire to be able to approach you.
Give me a gracious acknowledgement, and all is mine.
Do not strike out, do not exhaust yourself – you will achieve nothing –
against Eros' labyrinthine snares.'   240
When he had been declaiming thus, in the meantime
another youth began another declaration to another girl:
      'Your eye is heavy and full of desire,[86]
      profound pallor disfigures your cheeks.
      You look in need of sleep, woman.   245
      If you have been indulging in gymnastics all night,
      how fortunate is that blessed mortal
      who laid his hands on your flesh.
      But if Eros has aimed his fire at your liver and consumes you,
      may you instead be on fire for us.   250
      You are now Achilles; you look on Telephos,[87] woman;
      yes, put an end, since you caused the wound, to the liver's pangs;
      but if this does not please you, aim another dart at me;
      leave my liver and also my heart.'[88]
As the young men were jesting in this way,   255
one of their regular companions joined them,
Barbition, outstanding for his sweet voice;
he sat down nearby and said,
'Friendship always arrives unbidden, my friends.'[89]
Carefully setting in order the lyre that was in his hands   260
and skilfully preparing to play,

86 Marginal gloss: 'Symposium's seventh epigram'. 3.243–50: A paraphrase of *AnthGr* 5.259 (Paul the Silentiary).

87 Telephos, cured of his wound by Achilles, is used as an example in the erotic tradition: cf. *AnthGr* 5.225.5–6 (Makedonios) and 291.5 (Paul the Silentiary).

88 A paraphrase of *AnthGr* 5.224 (Makedonios).

89 A proverbial expression (e.g. Diogenianus 1.60 [Leutsch and Schneidewin 1839–51, vol. 1]).

he began to sing a charmingly tuneful song of love:[90]
   'Fall in love with Barbition, fair-complexioned lady Myrto.[91]
      Rhodope once paid no heed to foam-born Kypris[92]
      and all through every year preferred to live with   265
      Artemis, desiring dogs, deer and horses,
      girt with her bow and arrow-shafts as she strode over the lofty
         peaks.
   Fall in love with Barbition, fair-complexioned lady Myrto.
      Kypris frowned; she set her son on her
      with his bow on his shoulders, and armed him against her.   270
      Rhodope was wielding her spear against a mountain-ranging
         deer;
      Kypris' son drew his accursed bow at Rhodope.
   Fall in love with Barbition, fair-complexioned lady Myrto.
      She was confident, but she was struck; Eros' spear is swifter.
      The deer was hurt in its shoulder, it ran off into the depth
         of the wood;   275
      Rhodope was hurt in her heart and the very centre of her being,
      where Eros planted his deadly and unendurable dart.
   Fall in love with Barbition, fair-complexioned lady Myrto.
      She was hurt, she groaned, she lurched towards desire.
      She fell in love with Euthynikos; he too was smitten   280
      for the lad shot him and drove him to desire for her;
      they beheld each other, but Eros had kindled the fire.
   Fall in love with Barbition, fair-complexioned lady Myrto.
      The deed was done, and both reached desire;
      she renounced her unendurable virginity under Eros'
         compulsion.   285
      You too should respect Kypris, recognizing indeed the
         violence of her actions;
      do not reject her but be swayed by my words.
   Fall in love with Barbition, fair-complexioned lady Myrto.'
'You have delighted us, amiable Barbition,'
we said immediately, 'but come and join   290

---

   90 3.263–88, 297–322: These passages demonstrate Eugenianos' command of hexameter verse.

   91 Marginal gloss: 'Barbition's song in hexameters'.

   92 On the fateful encounter of Rhodope with Euthynikos, see *L&K* 8.12. 'Kypris', or the Cyprian one, refers to Aphrodite and her connections to Cyprus.

your companions' abundant banquet.'
He was persuaded and ate until he reached satiety;
and then, setting his lyre in order a second time,
he rested his right elbow on the ground
– for he was accustomed to play with his left hand –   295
and he sang a sweet and melodious air:
    'Who has seen the girl I desire? Sing to me, dear comrade.[93]
        There was once a charming and winsome girl, Syrinx,[94]
        a maiden, tamer of souls, fair-complexioned, with feet of silver.[95]
        Pan saw her and ran after her, his heart pounding.   300
        The brave girl fled before him, he the stronger came after
            her in pursuit.
    Who has seen the girl I desire? Sing to me, dear comrade.
        Syrinx reached a reed-bed in a meadow,
        earth took the maiden into her bosom.
        But Pan was in a frenzy, for he had lost the girl Syrinx.   305
        Yet he grasped the foliage and cut some reeds.
    Who has seen the girl I desire? Sing to me, dear comrade.
        He bound them with wax, he adapted them for his sturdy lips,
        he kissed them and breathed into them; the breath traversed
            the reed
        and produced a sweet melody that is love's remedy.   310
        And do you hate me who loves you, and do you not desire me
            who desires you?
    Who has seen the girl I desire? Sing to me, dear comrade.
        I have suffered dreadfully; why do you cast off your lover?
        Would that you could become for me a reed or a flourishing
            laurel,
        oh high-soaring cypress with far-reaching shadow,   315
        with which Phoibos[96] once strove to be united against her will.
    Who has seen the girl I desire? Sing to me, dear comrade.
        And refreshing some day my suffering mind as it groans
            deeply,

93 Marginal gloss: 'Barbition's second song'.

94 For the myth of Syrinx, the half-goat god Pan and the making of pan pipes, cf. especially *L&K* 8.6, 7–10 and Longos 2.34.

95 'feet of silver': normally an attribute of a goddess, e.g. Thetis (*Iliad* 1.538), but sometimes of a girl, e.g. *AnthGr* 5.60,1 (Rufinus).

96 'Phoibos': an alternative name for Apollo, alluding to his grandmother, the Titaness Phoibe.

I would make a continuous melody from the reeds clad in
    flesh
or, wearing a garland, I would have you slake the flames of
    love.   320
It is a force like this that keeps you encircled in my being.[97]
    Who has seen the girl I desire? Sing to me, dear comrade.'
Having sung this, he stood up
and said, 'Come, let us watch the girls
as they dance with entwined fingers   325
and contrive a supple circle.'
    As he spoke the young men followed him,[98]
first among them being the stranger who is addressing you,
Charikles who is in such peril.
What do you think my wretched heart   330
suffered, friend Kleandros, my fellow prisoner,
when it was struck with erotic songs?
So I made a move, then I ran forward
so that I could find a suitable position from which to see
the girls who were at that moment dancing together.   335
There I saw a moon that had come to the earth below,
circled about by the stars themselves[99]
– that was Drosilla with the girls dancing round her.
And knowing from what I had just heard,
that those in love take on a burden of grief,   340
I said to my mind , 'It would have been good, Drosilla,
if you had not come to Charikles' attention.
But since this was Dionysos'
wish – what? Kleandros, do you not weep with me? –
it is no reproach to you, maiden,   345
for Charikles, your bridegroom bestowed by the god,
to suffer long and to endure flight or danger,
or even your abduction before he wins you in marriage,
and whatever other dreadful thing
the evil thread of vengeful Fate might spin for me.'[100]   350

---

97 The poet is to imitate Pan by playing on reeds (Syrinx), and Apollo by wearing a laurel
crown.

98 Marginal gloss: 'Where Charikles first saw Drosilla'.

99 The same image appears at *H&H* 5.6.

100 In Greek mythology personified Fate (here Τύχη, generally Μοῖρα) spun the thread of
a child's destiny at birth: cf. *Iliad* 16.334, 24.49, 24.209.

Saying this calmly to myself,
I returned to the ancestral precinct
where I gazed at the statue of Dionysos,
and, flinging myself at his feet   355
a breathing living corpse, I cried out:
    'O child of Zeus, remember now the sacrifices
and the incense offered up to you of old,
and come to my aid over Drosilla's marriage
to me, Charikles, newly snared by passion.
Should I achieve my desire,   360
I will not neglect further sacrifices to you.
I came out here, child Dionysos, for your sake
and my recompense for coming was a bitter dart,
for there feeds in my heart a fire
which a kiss will quench, not water.'[101]   365
    When I thus addressed the god Dionysos,
I was prepared to abduct the girl,
whom I hastened to greet with both hands
and to escape her attendants by stealth;
for the heart that is in love vows   370
to seize as soon as possible the day when
it can delight in the beloved object.
Considering the situation and estimating my confidence,
realizing that I could not otherwise
achieve my aim easily and unhindered   375
unless the girl became my confederate,
I made my passion plain to the maiden,
I revealed my purpose and what was to be done,
and I indicated the abduction that I had in mind.
But when she received the messenger[102]   380
– a woman skilled in such matters –
she was promised to another by the laws of marriage:
the girl declared this to her with grief.
So I looked to my second device,
in which I would use my friends as accomplices   385
and win my beloved without danger.

101 Cf. *AnthGr* 9.420 (Antipater), on the ineffectiveness of water.
102 The messenger has not previously been mentioned; perhaps a lacuna should be
postulated, or faulty plotting.

But she, anticipating this too,
revealed the lineaments of her suffering soul
through a messenger sent then to me;
she proclaimed her heart's secret suffering,   390
that she had seen me, that she suffered, that she was captured,
that she too was wounded through seeing Charikles,
and wanted to take me in lawful marriage.
So I sent a message appointing a time
at which I could engage in discussion with the girl.   395
I came, I found her, I saw her with delight,
I spoke and exchanged words,
we were bound with reciprocal oaths.
Dionysos ratified the agreement,
being summoned as witness by us with oaths of surety.   .   400
And to the harbour of Drakon
– for so it was named by the locals –
I hastened with the maiden Drosilla
and, seeing a ship that was setting sail,
and which was already casting off the cables at its prow,   405
we installed ourselves on it
and sailed away with a most favourable wind,
under the guidance of the god Dionysos.
For it was he who led the girl to me in bridal procession,
he who appeared to me in the guise of a dream,   410
before we had exchanged words.

FOURTH BOOK

"Thus we voyaged in the vessel
over the watery path of the low-waved sea,
until the evening of the fourth day,
and the thrum of the oars of the pirate fleet
fell upon us as we sailed ahead, and beat   5
the wits and not merely the hearing
of us who were within the vessel I mentioned.
As evening grew dim everywhere
with the descent below ground of the mighty light-bearer,[103]

103 i.e. the sun; cf. Theodore Prodromos 3.1 (Hörandner 1974).

we could not see each other clearly;   10
but they, capable of greater speed
and extending their hands and also their feet
so that the triremes sped more swiftly,
drove the oars with all their strength,
thrashing the sea's back   15
with sturdy forearms stripped for fair-sailing,
and as they neared our vessel
they bared their own swords.
So those who were with us, being excellent seamen,
although they were a small, easily numbered group   20
against those bold wielders of swords,
bravely took up their shields
and they fought the sword-wielders on the sea;
they slaughtered and were slaughtered, not fearing
their disproportionate odds against so many pirates;   25
they dyed the water red
and kept up a valiant resistance until nightfall.
But eventually they pulled the ship away from the conflict,
since so many had fallen in battle,
and put in, weakened, to the shore.   30
Leaving the ship with its cargo on board
though bereft of its captain,
they fled to the ravines and the depths of the mountains.
As they sought safety in flight
I, emerging wounded from the battle,   35
followed them with the maiden Drosilla.
I hastened, I pressed on, I dragged the girl,
I guided her to precipitous places
until we found a dense thicket
where we flung ourselves down in concealment.   40
When on the morrow day dawned,
we peered over the mountains[104] and saw down below
a conflagration reaching up on high;
we conjectured that those robbers,
exulting over their plunder, were burning the vessel,   45
now beached and empty of its contents.
As hither and yon in our bewilderment

---

104 A scene reminiscent of the opening of the *Ethiopika* (Hel 1.1).

we cast our eyes, which bring illumination,
we immediately spied a well-fortified crag,
dimly and vaguely – for it was far distant from us.   50
So we both hastened towards the city
and reached it late and with difficulty,
travelling from first light until evening;
we slipped into it together, having escaped
the robbers' sea-borne cruelty,   55
even though the city was destined to put Charikles,
like Kleandros, into Parthian hands
and, although I had escaped the sea's dangers,
to impel me towards other painful constraints
with – ye gods – my dearest Drosilla.   60
When the inhabitants came out of the city,
we too slipped out again while there were celebrations
for the brilliant festival of Zeus' birth.
As for the accursed Parthian tribe,   65
I do not know whence it came, but it swept us up
and taking us to its own territory,
brought us to the present prison."
    Occupying themselves with these many speeches,
the young men indulged in mutual grief,
Kleandros and Charikles, the foreigners.   70
The barbarian Kratylos, with arrogance
seated beside Chrysilla in the morning,
also had with him his son Kleinias.
Those who had been imprisoned by the laws of captivity
he bade him bring from gaol.   75
The prisoners were brought out and drawn up.
The barbarian's wife, Chrysilla, suffered pangs in her breast
as she suddenly saw Charikles
and was smitten by passion's dart.
For he was a golden-haired, ruddy-complexioned youth,
        his cheeks smooth,   80
his back broad, with golden curly locks[105]
reaching his waist;
his arms were slender, with white fingers,

105 Marginal gloss: 'Description of Charikles'.

and the immeasurably radiant stars
he dimmed with his beauty and the brilliance of his countenance.   85
The Parthian ruler contemplated them as they stood there
and some he distributed to the satraps under him,
"Accept, Parthian leaders," he said,
"bounteous gifts in return for your participation."
Some he dismissed to gaze on the light of freedom,[106]   90
others he returned miserably to prison,
to be freed by gifts from their begetters.
Many he doomed to the sword,
thinking that the foreigners' blood
would be a sacrifice acceptable
to the saviour gods who gave him constant aid.   95
He bestowed Charikles on Kleinias,
not because he had asked for him
– for his mind was fixed on Drosilla,
most comely of all women –
but as a generous gift from a father to his son.   100
For of all those who had been imprisoned previously
he was handsome to look on, the fairest of the fair.[107]
Having made these arrangements, he rose up from his throne
and offered brilliant sacrifices to the gods.
    So, wounded in the depth of his heart,   105
Kleinias, son of the barbarian Kratylos
– for he was taken captive by the captive maiden –
murmured many things quietly to himself,
making a dirge of his sufferings:
"All passion is a dreadful thing; if it is for a beloved girl,   110
it is doubly dreadful; if it is for a young girl,
the goad is triple; if she is brimful of beauty,
the evil is worse; if it leads to marriage,
an inner fire nourishes the heart itself.
There is no strength that can escape the archer,   115
the winged one who kindles fire;
with his wings he catches up with me, with his flame he sets me on fire,
he shoots me in the heart with his bow.

106 'light of freedom': a phrase repeated below (8.206) and also at *R&D* 6.284; cf. *Iliad*
6.455.
107 Marginal gloss: 'Kleinias' love for Drosilla'.

Nectar, the drink of the gods, seems mythical to me
in comparison with your strange sweetness, you of the crystal breast.   120
For if I look on you as a ripening cluster of grapes,
should one press your chest like a sweet grape
or pour out a nectar-like flow of a pleasant new vintage
or a comb of aromatic honey?
Your face seems to me a meadow, maiden,[108]   125
most comely slave of my mother Chrysilla.
Your delightful complexion is that of a narcissus,
the bloom of your cheeks is that of a red-hued rose,
your two eyes are like a dark-gleaming violet,
your curling locks are entwined ivy.   130
Oh, how can I drag my eyes away[109]
from your beauty, the vision of your face?
But my eyes pause, drawn in contrary directions,
not yielding to what is not permitted.
For Eros seems to control plants,   135
and iron and stone, not men alone.
For iron runs towards the magnet,[110]
seeming to me to contain an inner fire of passion;
it inclines towards it, it moves, it hastens along a strange course,
this seems to me to be a kiss between the two,   140
the lover and the beloved; oh, strange relationship.
One plant often loves another;
a palm tree is unwilling to take root in the earth[111]
unless you plant its mate close by.
And the ocean knows of the marriage of Arethousa,[112]   145
approached by the sweet, sinuously flowing
broad Alpheios, whose waters, as they joined,[113]
their union did not permit to mingle.
Listen, stone-breasted one, heart of bronze,
and allow me to partake in your incomparable beauty."   150

108 4.125–30: Cf. *L&K* 1.19.1.
109 4.131–34: Cf. *L&K* 1.4.5.
110 4.135–48: The erotic parallels (magnet, palm, the rivers) are to be found in *L&K*
1.17.1–18.2; and also in later romances, e.g. *L&Ra* 173–84.
111 Marginal gloss: 'About the palm tree'. Cf. *H&H* 10.3.2.
112 'Arethousa': see *A&K* 21–21a, and note; also *AnthGr* 9.362 and 683; *L&Ra* 182–84.
113 Marginal gloss: 'About Arethousa and Alpheios'.

Suffering thus from an onset of passion, Kleinias
turned swiftly to a musical mode,
producing with his delicately white fingers
this utterance and harmonious beat,
from the clear sweet notes of the lyre: 155
    "O Drosilla, how you burn up Kleinias![114]
        Kypris used to call out loudly in the middle
        of the streets to Eros, her offspring,
        'If anyone catches the errant boy
        either in the narrow alleys or in the centre of the road,   160
        the messenger will receive a great reward from me:
        he will snatch Kypris' kiss as his recompense.[115]
    O Drosilla, how you burn up Kleinias!
        But understand that my son is an archer,
        the runaway Eros, the mischief-maker,   165
        and take care that he does not wound you mortally.
        Listen to him and learn his ways.
        If you glimpse him with a charming smile,
        he is most likely to strike and want to kill.
    O Drosilla, how you burn up Kleinias!   170
        If you catch him and find he wants to sport with you,
        he will aim at you and shoot you. So listen and pay attention;
        if he comes up to you and wants to embrace you heartily,
        make your escape: he will enflame you and consume you.
        He is a child, he has fire, a bow and wings;   175
        he does not come with invisible pinions.
    O Drosilla, how you burn up Kleinias!
        Eros burns, wounds, pursues and seizes;
        and he smiles while remaining wild at heart,
        and he appears to joke while playing a savage game,   180
        the bold, fire-bearing archer.
        Whoever finds him, catches him and tells me,
        would be gratified with the reward I spoke of.'
    O Drosilla, how you burn up Kleinias!
        The story has it that there sprang into existence   185
        the girl Pallas Athena, daughter of Zeus,

114 Marginal gloss: 'Kleinias' love song to Drosilla'.
115 4.157–83: A paraphrase of Moschos, *Runaway Eros* (*AnthGr* 9.440).

fully armed and as a sentient maiden;
but Eros, however, paints you in greater beauty
as he placed his fingers on your mother's womb,
applying a two-fold colour, milk white and rose red.   190
O Drosilla, how you burn up Kleinias!
And yet he paints you without weapons,
for he does not grant you a bow, nor a sharp sword,
the better to direct you to manslaughter;
for he makes your arched eyebrows into bows,   195
the shafts from your eyes into bitter arrows,
with which you shoot me through the heart.
O Drosilla, how you burn up Kleinias!
How well aimed is that bow, maiden,
how well fitted is its point. I have been struck, I feel it.   200
How bitter is the wound, and how large.
How new is the experience, and how strange.
The dart does not kill – what a concept –
as it pierces, it sets up a disintegration that lasts forever.
O Drosilla, how you burn up Kleinias!   205
But look, night seems to be coming on, girl,
and I have still long roads to travel;
either accept your fellow banqueter as your bedfellow
or, if you do not want this, with a responsive word
kindle a torch from your lips   210
– for I know that you can do this if you want –
O Drosilla, how you burn up Kleinias!
and illuminate this present evening for me
and lighten the wearisome darkness for me
and allow me, O radiant lantern, to make haste   215
homewards without losing my way or stumbling.
I suffer from inflammation of the brain and madness;
do not begrudge me the remedies that end the pain.
O Drosilla, how you burn up Kleinias!"
So Charikles, realizing that his master was in love,[116]   220
approached him, saying in a kindly way,
"You are in love, I realize this, Kleinias, my master,

116 Marginal gloss: 'Charikles consoles Kleinias'.

you are in love with the maiden my sister,[117]
you are in love with the lovely, the very lovely Drosilla.
Why should this be unusual? Even your servant,   225
the humble, the unfortunate Charikles, the miserable stranger,
was once utterly entrapped by a delicate girl.
I did not have the courage to address her,
although I longed to – for I could not look at her,
just as you cannot look at Drosilla –   230
with difficulty I glimpsed her as I peered out of windows
into a garden burgeoning with roses and flowers
and saw her who was always present in my mind,
shedding gentle balm among the basil
and bedewing the balsam with the roses' exhalation,   235
and lotuses, hyacinths and a throng of plants,
and white lilies, saffron and narcissus,
and a great host of sweet-smelling flowers.
There I saw her arms half-uncovered,
with which not even snow could compete,   240
there I saw her crystalline fingers,
which could compete with white milk.
As I saw her I was entrapped by her abundant beauty,
for I was not made of oak or born of rock.
Entrapped as I was I addressed her, not being able to hold back:[118]   245
   'Greetings, gardener to so many flowers:[119]
why do you not open the door to me?
Do you have in mind Narkissos' anguish,[120]
when he flung himself into the well for love?

117 The motif of the hero declaring his beloved to be his sister has a long history, from Abraham and Sara (Genesis 20.2) onwards; cf. also Hel 1.22; *R&D* 3.335; *H&H* 9.14–16 (though Hysmine claims to be Hysminias's sister). Here the biblical, and highly erotic, Song of Songs is probably more relevant: see Roilos 2005: 211–23 for the extent to which this text permeates *D&C*.

118 Charikles demonstrates to Kleinias that even the initially tongue-tied (4.229) can eventually overcome their hesitations.

119 Another example of the metaphorical use of a garden for a nubile girl's protected virginity; cf. *H&H* 1.4.4; Littlewood 1979; Barber 1992; and Roilos 2005: 214–23, with special emphasis on the allegorical overtones.

120 Marginal gloss: 'About Narkissos'. Narkissos, endowed with extreme beauty, became enamoured of his own reflection: Pausanias, *Geography* 3.19.7–9.

Do you recall the lad Hyacinth[121]   250
and his unlucky discus-throws,
how he endured envy through the envy
of the love-smitten Zephyr?
Do you have in mind Kypris of old,[122]
who dyed the rose's white hue red   255
with the blood flowing from her feet
that were wounded from the thorns
when she learned of Adonis' savage death
as he succumbed to Ares? O evil envy,
that often causes the death of lovers.   260
The garden is full of joy and tears;
it takes pride in the lovely maiden that is its gardener,
yet it is laden with lovers' misfortunes;
you seem to be unaware of the strange things you are hearing.'
    Thus I addressed the girl,   265
and she swiftly replied:
'How you have sweetened my aching heart.
You are a cunning enchanter, I see, wretch;
you turn despair into content.
Scoundrel, what do you say? Pass through the doors,   270
admire the garden,[123] behold the couch
and regale me with your tales,
since you have learned from experience how great an evil is desire.
Pluck roses from my rose bush;[124]
recline I will join you.   275
Will you eat something, scoundrel? There is no fruit;
even if there is no ripe apple in the garden,
accept my breast in place of an apple;
if it pleases you, miserable one, bend down and eat.
If there are no ripe grapes on the vine,   280

---

121 Marginal gloss: 'About Hyacinth'. Zephyr, the west wind, jealous of Hyacinth's preference for Apollo, blew the discus off course, killing Hyacinth: cf. Pausanias, *Geography* 3.1.3;
Apollodoros, *Bibliotheke* 1.3.3. Narkissos and Hyacinth, with their flowery transformations,
are often listed together in the ancient mythological handbooks.
122 Marginal gloss: 'About Adonis and Aphrodite'. Adonis, lover of Aphrodite (Kypris),
was gored by Ares (Aphrodite's former lover) in the guise of a wild boar; cf. Apollodoros,
Bibliotheke 3.14.4.
123 4.271–85: The suggestive imagery is based on the biblical Song of Songs.
124 On the sexual connotations of plucking roses, cf. *L&K* 1.8.9; *H&H* 5.17.

squeeze the clusters from my firm breast;
take a pleasant kiss from me instead of the honeycomb.
Instead of the twining around tree and branches,
which anyone who wants to gather fruit knows,
I am the tree; come, embrace me;   285
you have my arms in place of branches.
I am the tree; ascend me,
harvest the fruit that is sweeter than honey.'
　So entrust all your affairs to me,
and you will see from my deeds that I am a faithful servant."   290
　"Not a captive nor a slave, as you said,"
responded Kleinias, the barbarian's son,
"but a free man, a fellow countryman, a friend,
and partaking in the rank of satrap
will you indeed become, and lord of a great property,   295
if only it comes about that Kleinias
can be joined to Drosilla with your assistance.
But, Charikles, when you meet with the maiden,
tell her of my trouble.
Disease wastes me away; understand this brief speech;   300
Hades makes off with me before my time,
that brilliant light-bringer that rules the stars
is setting for me while it sheds rays on all others.
Let river-water flow upwards;
for I die as is my doom, but before my time.   305
Let the bramble bloom with sweet-scented roses,
may everything happen contrariwise in life[125]
when Kleinias dies, unless your determination,
Charikles, is able to save him."
　"As for Drosilla, Kleinias, be confident,"   310
said Charikles, "don't be despondent,"
adding another charming story to his remarks.
"Once Eros, son of Aphrodite born from the sea,[126]
did not notice a bee sleeping among the roses;
he was wounded in the middle of his finger   315
and, in his astonishment, flew off in haste
to his mother, saying, 'Mother, I am dying;

125　Cf. Theokritos, *Idyll* 1.131–35.
126　4.313–24: A paraphrase of *Anacreontea* 35 (West 1993).

a little winged snake has bitten me,
the sort that farmers call a bee.'
But the lovely Kytherean one laughed daintily   320
at the wounded boy and then replied,
'If the bee's sting hurts you,
how much do you think those who are struck
by your wretched arrows suffer, Eros my son?'"
    This is what Charikles said to Kleinias,   325
and, having pledged marriage with Drosilla,
he withdrew quickly for a short distance to consider,
not how he might unite Drosilla with Kleinias,
but how he could urgently get out of his foolish plan.
He wanted to see her privately,   330
so that he could grieve with her over their misfortune,
and he found her lying alone in a meadow,
sleeping deeply because of her worries,
rivalling the white roses' blooms,
and seeming to smile as she listened   335
to the honeyed cries of the lovely swallows.
Oh, what astonishment and what awe[127]
took hold of Charikles all at once
when he saw her drowsing in the garden,
glittering like the sun   340
when it radiates a glowing light on mankind in the springtime.
Seating himself by Drosilla
– for courtesy prevented him from waking her –
he said, gazing at her intently:
    "Here, my beloved, the Graces   345
surround you gently as you sleep,
watching lest some foul accident
befall you from ill-omened fate.
Oh, how lightly you draw breath, girl;
oh, how sweetly you seem to smile now,   350
you whose lips and cheeks nature once dyed red,
so that they seem to nurture a flame,
and whose locks, which not even gold can rival,
she drew out to your waist.
Everything falls silent when you are silent, maiden;   355

---

127 Marginal gloss: 'Charikles' speech to the sleeping Drosilla'.

no sparrow may chirp, no wayfarer make haste,
no one may utter a word, no serpent slither by;
even the winds' breath has ceased, I think,
out of respect for the sleeping girl's beauty.
Oh, how every twittering sparrow has now fallen silent.   360
Only the brooks babble on, my beloved,
to bring you even sweeter sleep.
And their flowing waters are a voice, saying to you,
'O you who are girt with all beauty,
you are silent; the cool air is silent for you.   365
You are asleep; the tribe of winds are slumbering too;
only the brooks murmur on for your sake.'
Then, since they do not have you to sing in response,
the Muse-loving tribes of birds fall silent.
But do not prefer the sleep of oblivion to me,   370
for you would grieve the nightingales, it would seem,
whom your most sweet voice rivals.
For you utter sounds that drip honey, maiden.
But, dear comrades and companions,
goodly Graces, pearl-breasted maidens,   375
guard and keep safely
the breast and back of the sleeping girl,
warding off the inquisitive breed of flies.
There is no other strange cure for Eros
except a song and music that is a respite from suffering.[128]   380
For even Polyphemos once, when wounded
in the breast by man-shooting Eros
and nurturing a deep passion for the Nereid,
found no other cure for his sickness
than a song, pan-pipes, an enchanting tune,   385
and a rocky seat, from which he could gaze at the sea.
For I suppose – and this is surely right –
that stones would grow wings and fly through the air
and adamant would be split with a sword
before Eros would cease from his archery here below,   390

128 4.380–86: A paraphrase of Theokritos, *Idyll* 1.1–20 (*The Cyclops*); Burton 2003: 253. Polyphemos, the savage one-eyed giant Cyclops from the *Odyssey*, is presented more sympathetically by Theokritos in *Idylls* 6 and 11 as a shepherd in love with Galatea, the water-nymph (Nereid).

so long as beauty exists and eyes have sight.[129]
The sea eventually brings its squalls to an end,
the winds' gusts draw to a close,
and a fire that has been lit can be dowsed again,
but the squalls and fire never cease   395
for those whose breasts are pierced by Eros' bow,
for he can melt – as fire melts wax –
those he entraps in his furnace.
Eros the archer is a vexatious creature;[130]
clinging like a swampy leech   400
he sucks every drop of blood. Oh, the magnitude of the disease!
How you ignite those you capture, Eros, Eros,
you burn, you enflame, you consume, you sear;
so that from those who have been charred previously
anyone can kindle a huge lamp.   405
You often make a lover seem to carry around
in his bosom the girl he loves.
Thus everyone who is in love – and what an ineluctable thing is passion –
is entrapped in Eros' snares,
like a mouse that has fallen into a pot of sticky resin.[131]   410
Anyone who can slip past and escape
the winged tyrant Eros
seems to me able to measure out the stars above."[132]

FIFTH BOOK

All this and much more like it
he sang quietly to himself
until the moment that Drosilla roused.
She remained speechless for a long time
when she saw Charikles beside her,   5
her soul loving the passionate heart,
and she lightly wiped away with her fingers
her sweat that was dripping like pearls.

129 Cf. Longos, Proemium 2.
130 Cf. Theokritos, *Idyll* 2.55–56.
131 Cf. Theokritos, *Idyll* 14.51.
132 Cf. Theokritos, *Idyll* 30.25–27.

If anyone had seen her then, as she abandoned sleep,
he would have said, "Zeus, father of the Olympians,   10
everything that is delightful in life brings delight –
songs, luxury, a dazzling banquet and drink,
a great mansion, gold, silver, precious stones,
and all other wealth in money and possessions;
yes, these things bring delight – who would gainsay this? –   15
but not so much as a rosy-complexioned girl,
when she wakes up at midday
with drops of sweat flowing off her,
like grass in spring with the morning dew;
if anyone were to attempt to kiss her chin   20
shedding light drops of sweat,
he would dampen the fire and quench the flame
that burns within his heart,
unhappy and fire-consumed,
as if indeed it were charred by love;   25
with the ember with the ember from girl's lips
he would dowse the ember in his heart."
     Eventually she said to Charikles:[133]
"You, Charikles, you seem to be standing beside me.
Is it you yourself who are now close by Drosilla   30
or does the reflection of your image wish to trick me?
Place your lip on mine, clasp my fingers;
touch my neck and chin.
Allow me, Charikles, to reciprocate the love of him who loves me;
as long as you in your heart of hearts do not want to love me,   35
I think I possess only half of the life I desire.[134]
How is it sensible to grieve the girl who loves you?
Put a nest on a branch
which can be easily reached by
neither a winged bird nor slithering serpent.   40
Be ashamed when you listen to her who loved you first;
do not put me in second place to Chrysilla,
do not prefer the hag to the girl.
Eros the winged marksman, learn this;
how can a woman past her prime   45

133 Marginal gloss: 'Drosilla's dissembling speech to Charikles'.
134 Cf. Theokritos, *Idyll* 29.5.

catch the attention of a swift-winged archer?"
    Charikles replied, jesting a little in response,
and not looking in anticipation to the future
– for he was unaware of what Drosilla was hinting,
Chrysilla's terrible passion for him: 50
    "Such taunts you contrive against me!"[135]
I am not unaware, being experienced in passion,
that womankind is inclined to jealousy;
it knows how to produce fictitious arguments,
always inclined to think that previously devised   55
figments of the imagination are actuality,
for they believe that they are hypostaseis of the essences.[136]
But when mocked I endure what has to be endured;
prudently spurning all other women,
I desire one alone; you have possession of the whole of my life."[137]   60
    But Drosilla responded, "Yes, Charikles,
I would concur with your arguments,
had not Chrysilla hastened to do away
with her spouse Kratylos by poison,
since she is in love – alas, alas – with the handsome Charikles."   65
    "Oh woe," Charikles intervened,
"Drosilla, what is this you are saying?" He immediately continued,
"What you are saying is a combination of delight and grief.
The death of the tyrant Kratylos would be
a stroke of good fortune for us miserable slaves.   70
Perhaps we might free our necks from this yoke,
giving little thought for Kleinias.
But that the wrinkled Chrysilla
should nurse an anguished passion for Charikles,
does this not seem disgusting? No, by Themis,[138]   75
no, no, by Eros' malicious coals,
you will not be united to me, miserable old woman, in my heart,
a savagely murky sea of anguish.
Your kiss is a punishment in itself, woman;

135 Marginal gloss: 'Charikles' dissembling speech to Drosilla'.
136 'hypostaseis of the essences': terms familiar from orthodox theology and undoubtedly used deliberately (if tautologically; both have the sense of 'existence').
137 Marginal gloss: 'Ignorance of Chrysilla's love for Charikles'.
138 'Themis': a personification of Justice.

your lips are harsh and your mouth is dry. 80
Time has made your jaw protrude through your skin;
you are bleary-eyed already, even if you have mascara everywhere;
yes, you are sallow, even though you have larded on the cosmetics.[139]
And even if Chrysilla, loathsome as she is now,
will become once more lovelier than Artemis, 85
what, oh what, Drosilla, will Charikles do with his sworn oaths
once he is united with the barbarian woman?
Be ruined, tyranny; be accursed, satrapy;
riches, be torn from Charikles.
I shall not prefer fame to chastity. 90
Passion for Drosilla is embedded in me;
may I not be deprived of you, maiden.
Do you see, Zeus' fair-formed grandson?[140]
You pledged to me marriage with Drosilla,
and now a savage old barbarian woman 95
is trying to separate Charikles from her.
You see the anguish which she brings, you see the sickness.
Slay Kratylos and Kleinias,[141]
yes and kill yourself too, lady Chrysilla.
In that way you would please your servant Charikles, 100
in that way you would delight your servant Drosilla.
Let this be the gods' concern, maiden;
but as for our master Kleinias' passion,
where in our dread fate can we place it?
Do make a brief reply, for I have been sent on my own 105
to unite you and to make all the arrangements."[142]
    At this the girl wept a little[143]
and said, "Olympian Zeus, lord of the heavens,
why do you allow me still to live in misery,
the exile, the foreigner who has abandoned her homeland? 110

139 Cosmetics for eyes, face and hair were a normal part of Byzantine life, in spite of intermittent ecclesiastical objections; cf. *R&D* 8.257; *ODB*, under 'Cosmetics'.
    140 i.e. Dionysos.
    141 Marginal gloss: 'Ignorance of Kleinias' love of Drosilla'.
    142 Though the underlying sentiment is undoubtedly medieval misogyny, the emphasis on the beautification of elderly women (here negative) is reminiscent of the imagery (positive) on the personified Constantinople in the poems from the time of the Second Crusade; cf. E. and M. Jeffreys 2001.
    143 Marginal gloss: 'Drosilla's lament'.

Why did the sea's expanse not swallow me up?
Why did the barbarian sword not slaughter me?
Since you wish me to continue living unhappily,
why did you not turn me to stone?
Why did you not give me wings,   115
like the grandchildren of Attic Pandion?[144]
Why did not some savage and bold-hearted lion
rush out from a thicket[145] and swiftly tear me to pieces,
when I was in flight to the marshes and ravines
away from the robbers' insolence?   120
It would have been better, ye gods, for me to have died then,
and to have found release from my sufferings,
than to live an endlessly mournful life in the land of the barbarians.
But, beloved eye and dear countenance,   125
all these things are very agreeable; do not weep for me,"
– for knowing that she had endured this for him,
he was shedding a tear out of shame –
said Drosilla, and Charikles responded,
gazing at some swallows' nests: 130
    "You, flitting around in the spring days,
fair swallow,[146] with your tripping melody,
and preparing one nest for your twin fledglings,
when winter comes, you flee;
but Eros, the winged archer,   135
endlessly weaves a lodging in my heart.
One Desire generates sturdy plumage,
and another already proclaims the conception,
another runs around outside the egg
and all the while my sad heart within   140
is harassed by the cheeps of the gaping nestlings;
for young creatures are brought forth from those who have been
        reared already.
But what solution is there for my heart?
It cannot endlessly produce, vivify, bear
and nurture young Erotes.   145
It is dreadful to love, but more so not to love;

144 'grandchildren': i.e., Philomela and Prokne; cf. 2.329 above.
145 Cf. *R&D* 1.226–27.
146 5.131–45: A paraphrase of *Anacreontea* 25 (West 1993).

I consider it the worst of all evils[147]
that lovers do not always meet with success.
Nature endowed bulls with horns,[148]
horses with hoofs, timorous hares   150
with fleet footedness, a pride of lions
with the sharp gouging strength of their claws,
the dumb tribe of fish with the ability to swim,
birds with flight, mankind with intelligence.
To Drosilla, since Nature had now no other gifts,   155
she gave beauty in place of any shield
or dart or many spears;
beauty conquers well-whetted iron
and all-devouring fire that is burning fiercely.
Drosilla, I pledged to my master Kleinias   160
a prosperous marriage with you,
not because I wanted this to happen – may it never take place! –
but to offer a brief respite to calm
the barbarian's enraged heart
and to enable us to consider what would be best.   165
But it is now time and we must consider
how we might contrive to quench the love
of Chrysilla and of her son Kleinias."
    So they were occupied in this way
– chaste love was their mutual bond –   170
Charikles himself and the maiden Drosilla,
when a disturbing rumour began to circulate,
that Kratylos had succumbed to a sudden disease.[149]
Then they tore themselves away from each other
and went back to their masters   175
to learn what had happened, comporting themselves mournfully.
And all the subordinates came rushing together,
men, women, satraps and barbarians;
when they were gathered and Kratylos was laid out,
Chrysilla wailed in the midst of them all,   180
ostensibly concerned for her husband,
but in truth preoccupied with Charikles:

147 Cf. *Anacreontea* 29.1–2 (West 1993)
148 5.149–59: A paraphrase of *Anacreontea* 24 (West 1993).
149 Marginal gloss: 'Death of Kratylos'.

"You have departed, before your wife and child,
Kratylos my husband; they have been miserably abandoned.
It was not the hand of the chief satrap that slew you, 185
holding out a dagger in time of battle,
nor was any other enemy able to act against you,
but the providence[150] of the Olympian gods
has sent you to the chill abode of Pluto.
Who will succeed to your rule? 190
Who will reign over my Chrysilla?[151]
Who will display paternal affection
for those around your Chrysilla and your son Kleinias?"
    While uttering these laments she sent to Charikles
a message full of bitterness 195
to the young people, Charikles and Drosilla:
    "You can move, I know – I speak the truth – [152]
even bronze statues of maidens
to inescapable love, wretched Charikles.
But consider that the dead have no hope; 200
there is hope among the living but not among the dead.[153]
Honey-sweet Siren, enchant the wayfarer,
petrifying mortals and vivifying rocks;
rocks sing to the sound of your feet.[154]
O brilliant star, shine also on me the stranger. 205
Sing, swallow, repeat an entrancing tune,
for the Muses themselves pour nectar into you
and sweeten your honeyed mouth.
But what is all that to me? Learn my purpose.
A drought is disastrous to rivers and snow to trees, 210
a snare to sparrows and disease to the body,
and love of young men to women.[155]
Why, when I gaze at you with genuine pleasure,
do you knit your brows and scowl back?
A cicada is dear to cicadas, a shepherd to shepherds, 215

150 Again a Christianizing term used in the context of the Olympian deities.
151 The control and affection is presumably intended in a legal sense.
152 Marginal gloss: 'Chrysilla's message to Charikles'.
153 Cf. Theokritos, *Idyll* 4.42.
154 Cf. Theokritos, *Idyll* 7.25–26.
155 Cf. Theokritos, *Idyll* 8.57–59.

an ant to ants[156] – but for me there is you alone.
Eros is blind too, not only Wealth.[157]
The wolf pursues the lamb, the goat green grass,
dogs hunt hares, the wild bear the young lamb,
the sharp-clawed hawk the sparrows' chicks;   220
I increase my love for you alone.
But you are still unresponsive to me;
in defeat you do not think as frogs do;
for those who gape wide in the water
they feel no envy or spite; neither should you.   225
You have absolutely no reason for fear, Charikles,
now that my husband, as you see, is dead;
use my possessions and their mistress;
rule, be satrap; receive great honour;
instead of a captive become lord of all   230
my hoarded wealth, my property;
look on your maiden sister, Drosilla,
free from me and ruling with you,
married to whichever satrap she pleases.
Who would begrudge me such blessedness?   235
Since you are receiving so much, promise me marriage in return,
Charikles, my husband, my renowned bridegroom."
    This is what she said, and gladly –
for she employed the maiden as her messenger –
she took Drosilla in her arms and said,   240
"Be my accomplice in the marriage to Charikles,
beloved above all women;
for you have learned of the pledges that guarantee
what is to be given; what need have I of further words?"
    As she comprehended these bitter words,   245
a thunderous bolt of lightning obliterated the maiden.
She was split apart, contending
with two mutually conflicting thoughts.
"I do not wish," she said, "to report now
this barbarian woman's scheme to Charikles;   250
he would not be able to restrain himself if I told him;

156 Cf. Theokritos, *Idyll* 9.30–31.
157 Cf. Theokritos, *Idyll* 10.19–20.

but it gives me an excuse to meet Charikles.
I will cheerfully go to talk to him."
    So she went in search of Charikles,[158]
just as the sun was preparing to set.   255
Kratylos had been buried by his own men
according to the barbarian custom.
She spoke, she made her announcement gloomily;
she shattered the soul within Charikles
with the mental sword of dismal tidings,   260
and he said, "Alas for this present day.
O sweet light, O maiden Drosilla,
what a bitter sound you have brought to me.
Alas, alas, swallow that should only utter sweet sounds,
you have embittered my soul with your words,   265
O golden honeyed mouth with subtle speech."
    "Alas, alas, Charikles, the inhuman fate
that oppresses me with far-reaching cares!
What will be the conclusion to our dangers
and multiform hazards?   270
Which of the gods – and at what time –
will bring an end to our misadventures?
How long will you continue, enraged Fate,
to stir up multiform tricks against us
and subdue us with endlessly repeated pain?"   275
    While they were thus lamenting greatly together,
not yet twice nine days had passed
since the demise of the barbarian Kratylos,
and the satrap of the Arab ruler Chagos
sent a letter to Chrysilla, demanding subjection.   280
Chrysilla heard this and was cast down
when she saw Mongos (for this was the satrap);
she was horrified at the sight of the satrap,
she was appalled and summoned her son Kleinias
to her, and took the letter   285
which contained the following sentences:[159]
    "I, Chagos the thrice-great, lord of the Arabs,

---

158 Marginal gloss: 'Speech of Drosilla and Charikles'.
159 Marginal gloss: 'Letter of Chagos, ruler of the Arabs, to Chrysilla'.

demand tribute and command it
from Chrysilla, wife of the Parthian lord,
and from the Parthian tribe subject to her. 290
Choose then one of two paths,
either to be enrolled among those who provide
the lord Chagos with annual tribute,
and acquire without delay
my prompt goodwill if you obey me, 295
or indeed to see Chagos' forces
trampling over you for your disobedience."
    When Kleinias heard these words
– he was an foolhardy young man and eager for battle –
he tore the letter in half 300
and with insults compelled
Mongos, Chagos' satrap, to turn back.
    On reaching his home country,
the satrap Mongos recounted all this to his lord Chagos;
he spoke and filled Chagos with wrath. 305
When the army commanders had quickly gathered
and had been incited to mount a counter-offensive
through their lord's exchange of letters,
Chagos positioned himself on horseback in the midst of the army,
which was drawn up on foot in an extensive circle. 310
Bursting with pride and full of plans,
he was also to be seen raising a large trophy,
carrying on his left side a golden shield,
which had depicted on it in a manner befitting a general,
Herakles slaying the Lernaian Hydra,[160] 315
urging the heart and mind on to battle.
It was right, oh it was right for a graphic craftsman
to depict on the shield of a stoutly corseleted warrior
the greatest feat of mighty Herakles.
Such was the brilliant horseman Chagos as he stood there, 320
equipped with bow, quiver and sword,

160 The second labour of the hero Herakles, in which he was assisted by Iolaos; the hydra, a nine-headed water monster, sprouted two heads in the place of each one that was chopped off. See Apollodoros, *Bibliotheke* 2.5.2. This is a nod in the direction of the Shield of Achilles memorably described at *Iliad* 18.478–608.

saying, "Generals and commanders of the phalanxes,[161]
who rejoice in the rites of Ares' feats,
Mongos, your fellow general, was despatched by my majesty
yesterday to the Parthian insignificance[162]   325
which is now controlled by the son Kleinias,
together with his mother Chrysilla.
Mongos demanded tribute and bade
the Parthians to render service immediately to the Arabs,
but he was not allowed to wait even a short time,   330
neither in the presence of Chrysilla nor of Kleinias,
but was indeed sent away with contumely.
What then is your response," Chagos stood and asked,
"gathering of great achievers and sword-bearers?"
      "Blessed lord," replied the commanders,   335
"before whose power tremble the ends of the earth,
every army, every barbarian kingdom
and leading satrap of the Persian lords,[163]
and every enemy, every lord, every satrap,
it would bring destruction on us and great mirth   340
to those far from us, to those round about and to those nearby,
if we were to be spurned by the Parthian satrapy
when we do not even need your presence
to put them to flight, with the gods' assistance.
Now we on our own must embark on a campaign,   345
encouraged by your great might,
and make an onslaught on the enemy,
for it is not against them, unarmed peasants,
who live in robber fashion from their booty,
that your ever-terrifying might should be set in motion."   350
      "I praise you for your great manliness,"
replied Chagos, lord of the Arabs,
"my fellow warriors and kindred shield-bearers,
indigenous dwellers of a prosperous horse-rearing land.
But indeed Epaminondas, who was a noble creature,   355

---

161 Marginal gloss: 'Chagos' oration'. As at *R&D* 5.115–414, a general's exhortation to
battle stands at the centre of the novel.
    162 A typical Byzantine circumlocution.
    163 Kazhdan 1967: 109 suggests that this may be a reference to the Seljuk Turks.
Alternatively, perhaps a reference to the alliances resulting from the Second Crusade.

on seeing an army teeming with bravery
but lacking a general,
said, 'This is a great beast but it has no head.'[164]
So it is proper for me to set out with you,
my fellow warriors and dear compatriots."   360
   Thus spoke the lord of the Arabs
and he inspected his own expeditionary force.
The main body of the Arab army
acclaimed their ruler in their speeches,
but lingered without yet mounting,   365
accustoming the cavalry to the sound of the trumpet
and the bray of the cornet, cleaning their helmets
and exercising their fingers for battle.
   The commander bade the trumpets sound;
the entire Arab force rode out,   370
and on the eighth day of their expedition
they reached the unhappy land of Parthia.
They set up camp in the middle of the plain,
with the river Saros[165] flowing close by.
The wretched Parthian tribe   375
had no confidence in a battle with the Arabs in open country,
since the satrap's cavalry force was large;
so, shutting the gates skilfully,[166]
they topped the walls with stone copings
and stone-hurling machines with quadruple flanges;   380
they stationed up there to operate them
armed men who were accurate stone-throwers
and infantry slingsmen who were experienced in archery.
They erected secure wooden towers;
they surrounded the towers with armfuls of rushes;   385
they suspended from the walls
protective structures like cedar-wood bulwarks;[167]

164 'Epaminondas': Theban general (410–362 BCE), whose campaigns broke Spartan hegemony in the Peloponnese. The source of this saying not known (Boissonade 1819, vol. 2: 273 quotes a similar Spanish phrase à propos Cardinal Mazarin's incompetent brother, a general).

165 'river Saros': the Seyhan river that runs through Adana (in Cilicia).

166 Marginal gloss: 'Parthians' safety'.

167 'cedar-wood bulwarks': there are textual problems here, as discussed by Conca

they fortified their entire city
against the Arabs' penetrative onslaught.
But the myriad shield-bearing[168]   390
Arab phalanxes that hurled themselves against the city
violently ravaged the regions round about.
Some of the forts they overcame;
others they were not able to capture immediately with their arms,
but the surrounding land and the peasants who dwelt there,   395
they enslaved, they put to the torch, they consumed with fire;
thus much dreadful slaughter on the inhabitants
was wreaked by the long-speared Arabs.
The next day they positioned their bronze-mouthed equipment[169]
close by the gates themselves;   400
they wove a great wall from rushes
and made a covering for their rock-hurling machines
to ward off the Parthian stone attacks.
The Arabs sent stones against the wall;
the archers aimed at them accurately,   405
those who were struck fell from the walls,
taking with them their bows and their stones.
Stones rattled against the bulwarks;
they struck, they shattered them accurately.
But the Parthians contrived some nocturnal scheme   410
against the Arabs' machines
(for the Parthian tribe is skilled
at contriving devices and finding tricks
that destroy their opponents).
Standing aloft and peering down   415
to aim their darts on the rushes
providing the Arabs with protection,
they let loose heated iron
and burned the barbarians' equipment;
as the rushes' leaves were dry   420

1994: 409, n. 21; Dawe 2001a: 18 proposes κνώδοντας ('sharp-edged') for the κεδρίνους
(translated here) or κώδωνας of the manuscripts. Sense and practicality would demand
'leather' or 'matting', both of which are recommended by the military manuals as effective in
warding off missiles.
  168 Marginal gloss: 'Arabs' attack against the Parthians'.
  169 Marginal gloss: 'Description of the Arab siege'.

and ready to burst into flame the moment a spark appeared,
they were burned up; and so they set fire easily
to all the defensive equipment.
Then there arose shouts and the clashing of cymbals
from Parthians in exultation. 425
But when the third day arrived[170]
the Arabs armed themselves and in fury
encircled the entire city with their weaponry;
a violent battle broke out
and the Parthian fortification was captured. 430
There Ares with the brazen tooth,
as he stood between the Parthians and the warrior Arabs,
could find no fault while battle raged.
So Chrysilla, when Kleinias fell[171]
– for he was slain in the heat of battle – 435
seized a well-whetted dagger
and, thrusting it into her very heart,
miserably spewed forth her soul together with it.
Drosilla, though surrounded by death
– for swords grow feeble before beauty[172] – 440
remained unwounded in the midst of swords,
but the dagger's edge[173] received most of those guarded within.
    Utter destruction overwhelmed
the wretched Parthian tribe;
Charikles with the girl Drosilla, 445
yes, indeed, and with them the foreigner Kleandros,
were constrained with chains, indeed unbreakable ones,
and having escaped the Arab dagger,
alas, the three were condemned for the third time 450
to undergo a third captivity.[174]

---

170 Marginal gloss: 'Arabs' victory'.
171 Marginal gloss: 'Chrysilla's suicide over Kleinias' corpse'.
172 Cf. Euripides, *Orestes* 1287.
173 Cf. Luke 21.24.
174 The theme of triple captivity appears also in *H&H* 8.10.3, 8.11.1, 8.13.4, 9.7.1, 9.13.1; Introduction (*H&H*), p. 173.

SIXTH BOOK

So Chagos, the mighty lord of the Arabs,
decreed that all the women – out of pity, perhaps –
and all moveable goods[175]
should be placed in covered wagons
and, separating the male captives from the women,   5
he ordered them to march on foot on their own.
He pressed on then swiftly to his homeland.[176]
And while they were traversing a craggy area,
densely shaded with thick woods,
a branch brushed against Drosilla's arm,   10
dragging her easily from the wagon,
and tipped her headlong from her seat.
At first the sea's savage wave
battered her against the shore's rocks
– for the sea at the mountain's foot   15
did not have sand strewn on its coast,
but craggy black rocks and plunging depths –
then a brief moment later
the long dry trunk of an oak tree bobbed up,
on which she floated safely   20
towards a desolate land as evening closed in.
Charikles did not realize this,
for the dense wood prevented him from seeing
that Drosilla had fallen from her seat
– indeed he would have promptly flung himself over the cliff   25
and joined her in the deeps of the sea.
But a small tender-hearted boy
sitting on his own with Drosilla
in a wagon shouted out
when he saw her falling into the sea's depths.   30
From him, when the day had run its course,
Charikles learnt of Drosilla's fall.
His heart shattered to its core,

---

175 Though there are textual issues here over the word translated as 'goods' (ἀνθύπαρξιν),
the sense is clear.
   176 Marginal gloss: 'Drosilla falls into the sea'.

he called out, "Oh heart-rending disaster,[177]
oh how wretched you are, Charikles, how wretched.   35
Were you destined after so many wanderings,
evil, wretched, vengeful Fate,
after imprisonment and captivity,
after multiform dangers at sea,
after the shedding of so many tears,   40
after the robbers' terrible pitilessness,
after the yoke of slavery in thronged battles,
were you destined to hurl more severe danger
which Charikles cannot endure?
Were you destined, alas, to sunder finally   45
the indivisible union,
the entirely appropriate concord?
You have added fire to fire and flame to flame,[178]
committing the girl to the watery deep
while preserving me, Charikles, among the living.   50
It is not cowardice, nor procrastination, nor lethargy
that have prevented me from dying happily with Drosilla;
so why have you in your indignation deprived
the wretched Charikles of this benefit?
I have wanted either to look on Drosilla while she lives, 55
or not to look on myself when she is dead to me.
Oh, you who are my only beloved in this life,
my eye and light and breath and heart,[179]
you are quenched, you have vanished, ceased to exist and suddenly
    expired.
How fortunate I was a short while ago, maiden,   60
when you shared my good cheer.
Like a wayfarer fleeing the burning sun,
I sank into the shade of your embrace,[180]
my lovely golden plane tree, fleeing
the heat of despondency and the weight of grief.   65
You lie there, a great and youthful tree,
except that you are already dry and dead, no longer living,

177 Marginal gloss: 'Charikles' lament for Drosilla'.
178 A proverbial phrase (Diogenianus 6.71; Leutsch and Scheidewin 1839–51, vol. 1: 281)
179 Cf. *R&D* 6.322.
180 Cf. Theokritos, *Idyll* 12.8–9.

a piteous sight for those nearby
if ever the sea's surge
casts you up on the shore;[181] I see you lying there,   70
the cause of my deluge of tears.
I am bewildered; I am astounded;
how, tree, could you expire in the midst of the water?
How could you become withered, sweet-smelling rose?
If, alas, I were to depart from mortal men before you,   75
I would perhaps be alive in my death, even if there were no
    compulsion to live.
Even a partial separation from the maiden
who is my very breath is quite unendurable.
Woe, woe, you have preceded me, and I wish to accompany you.
Alas, you have been wickedly torn from me,   80
like some twig violently broken from its conjoined stem.
O dear kindred breath and life,
union and harmony of two souls,
one spirit, one mind, one reason and one intellect,
one thought perpetually in two hearts.   85
What swimmer's mouth has closed over you?
What massive sea-creature has gulped you down,
or what shoal of fish engulfed you?
Was it in the sea that you reached the end of your life,
or did a beetling crag dim your eyes, girl,[182]   90
and do you lie stretched out as a corpse,
pitiably providing dismal fodder for wild beasts?
O where are you now? I cannot run
to seek you out, maiden, laden as I am with chains."
    Heeding these words, Chagos[183]   95
– for sleep had not yet taken hold of his eyes –
bade Charikles to come before him,
softened by pity and grieving in his heart.
He heard and came with mournful mien.
    Chagos said, "Who are you? Whence do you come? Why do you
    weep?"   100
    Charikles replied, "I was Kratylos' captive,

181 Cf. *R&D* 6.482–84.
182 An untranslatable play on words between the two meanings of κόρη ('girl' and 'eye').
183 Marginal gloss: 'Chagos' questions to Charikles'.

now I am your slave; my homeland is Phthia.
I lament for my sister, of whom I was deprived
when she fell, alas, into the watery deep;
I loathe life and no longer wish to look on the light." 105
    "Since you are not a Parthian, being from Phthia,"
said Chagos, "how did Kratylos have hold of you?"
    "Kinsmen lured me to the plain of Karia
with Drosilla," I responded, "with their speeches.
As we sailed away towards them we encountered, 110
alas, a vessel-destroying pirate fleet,
I and Kleandros, who were fellow slaves,
and Drosilla, my sister, as I said;
this we escaped with difficulty
as we skilfully pulled our vessel away, 115
and came against our will to Barzopolis;
the wretched Parthian expedition
restrained us by the law of captivity,
and until your fortunate arrival,
with our necks set to the yoke, 120
we endured successive pains;
for events did not afflict us so much
when we saw that we were forcibly overcome
as did our grief for Drosilla,
who was a woman, and young and a maiden. 125
And now, because of her we loathe looking on the light,
we lament, wailing and grieving."
    "You have spoken well," Chagos replied,
"Where is this Kleandros? Let him come forward quickly."
    He was brought forward, full of tears, 130
for he considered as his own
Charikles' devastating plight;
for a soul that has its private grief
is inclined to weep
when others are talking and lamenting loudly 135
of their own most wretched fates.
So looking at them as they grieved, he felt pity,
struck by their beauty,
for the youths were somewhat alike.
So, sympathetically, he spoke these words: 140

"Since you were previously restrained by Kratylos' band[184]
when you barely escaped the battle at sea,
since prison even before you fell to Chagos
had held you as wretched captives
– and especially as you are good friends –   145
you may go free with my best wishes.
May Chagos never slip so far
from the accustomed pattern of sympathy
that he continues to keep in burdensome chains
captives who have done no wrong,   150
who have not resisted the Arab might,
strangers who have been long shown to be unfortunate
– and thus transgress the laws of nature.
Indeed I offer a *mina* of gold[185]
for Drosilla who is mourned,   155
who, if she is preserved by the gods among the living,
will be a talisman of Chagos' brilliant fortune.
And may you too keep her safe in freedom
wherever the gods wish to rescue her from the world below."
    So Charikles and Kleandros the foreigners[186]   160
bowed their necks before Chagos' feet
and flooded the earth with their tears.
With difficulty Kleandros stood up and replied,
for Charikles had not yet ended his tears:
    "May the lord Zeus bestow on you,   165
Chagos, mighty lord of the Arabs,
every wish that is appropriate to your soul,
may he give you a long and flourishing period to your life
and subdue every enemy to your power."
    To this Charikles added the following response: 170
"May you fare well, Chagos, blessed ruler of the Arabs,
may grief not take possession of your heart
after your actions in now setting free through your generous disposition
these long-suffering and thrice-afflicted brothers."
    So, released from Arabia,   175
they both set out on their return journey,

---

184 Marginal gloss: 'Chagos' decision'.
185 '*mina*': ancient Greek weight and unit of currency, worth 100 *drachmai*.
186 Marginal gloss: 'The young men's freedom'.

making a very careful search
for the maiden Drosilla,
expecting to find her lying dead –
for they thought that she could not have survived her fall.   180
But she had fallen and been saved
and spent the period of three days
plus six in the desert,
for she lacked strength to venture forth
because of the bruising to her limbs and bones   185
that she had endured from the cliffs;
with grass from the earth her only nourishment,
together with fruit from wild trees,
she was able to make her way with difficulty to a village
which possessed copiously the wherewithal for life.   190
In that place there was an abundance of crops
and a superabundance of all kinds of harvests,
women, men, children to outnumber the stars,
and an inn that welcomed strangers.
Seeing the village from a distance,   195
she was reluctant to approach on her own;[187]
nevertheless, running up to the boundaries of the place
and, with great trepidation and fear,
she lingered within a house that lacked a roof;
she ate nothing apart from groans and pain,   200
she drank nothing except the cup of tears;
in her ignorance of Charikles and his affairs
she uttered a horrendous lament,
thinking that he had been executed and was dead:
    "I, the thrice-accursed by her own kin,[188]   205
I, greatly weeping, endure incurable sorrows.
I lie wasting away, lamenting ceaselessly;
for when the ill-named black Doom snapped [its thread],[189]
it had not yet brought the day of wrath to an end.

187 The reaction of a well-brought-up Byzantine girl; cf. Rhodanthe at *R&D* 2.74–75, or the Girl at *DigAk* G 4.809–11, E 1043–46; see Laiou 1993 for legal issues, and for literary interpretations, Garland 1990; Burton 2000.

188 Marginal gloss: 'Drosilla's lament over Charikles, in hexameters'. 6.205–35: Another hexameter showpiece.

189 For the thread, to be coterminous with its life, spun at a child's birth by Fate (here μοῖρα), cf. 3.350 above, with note.

But he on whom I previously gazed in relief   210
from the sufferings induced by love,
he whom I desired unceasingly, Charikles, lies of necessity
swathed in the desolate mists of death,
he lies a corpse beyond the aid of my vision;
and him the evilly named, ever-indestructible Doom,   215
the black one, the pain-bringer, has deprived of light by the
     Arabian sword.
Those desirable lips, which I have often kissed,
raging fire has seized and turned to ashes;
ever-weeping darkness has covered his brightly beaming eyes;
black filth has defiled his sunny locks.   220
Woe is me, the all-hapless, the ever-toiling Drosilla.
I contrived an unlooked-for flight from my parents;
I traversed afar the deep-surging billowing sea;
I fled brigands ranging far over mountains;
alas, alas, in tears because of the lad Charikles,   225
I saw the day of slavery; I was struck violently
and fetters, the smith's plaything,[190] girt me around;
then I fell from the wagon on the high-soaring mountain,
approaching the billows and coastal rocks
of the sea's wasteland and its arduous eddies: 230
an oak's trunk which chanced to be there saved me.
O woe for my burden of tears because of you, Charikles,
for when I gazed on you previously my days were blessed,
but now that you are lost I suffer unending anguish,
not wishing to look on the light-bringing star that is the sun."   235
     As she was weeping thus from the depths of her soul,
a good-hearted old woman discovered her;
she came up, found her, saw her and stood beside her;
she groaned, she clasped her and embraced her
and took her into her own house   240
and allowed her to share her victuals.
She ate a little and turned herself to slumber
– for darkness had already taken possession of night –
and, reclining on a low-slung couch,
she dreamed a pleasant dream and had a surfeit   245
of pain-releasing sleep, the remedy that puts an end to grief.

190 A word that apparently is found only here.

Light came, and darkness moved aside;
she arose and, "Old woman," she said, "blessed mother,
my deepest thanks for your hospitality
and this low-slung couch   250
on which a sweet dream came to me,
comforting my suffering heart.
But can you tell me if there is here
a good man, an innkeeper named Xenokrates?"
    "Yes," said the old woman, "and why do you want to know this?"   255
    "Indulge me in this, I beg you,"
said Drosilla, "for I want to see
whether the dream that appeared to me was deceitful."[191]
    The old woman yielded and, taking the girl,
brought her to Xenokrates' house;   260
standing in front of the doors to the house
and with the girl wishing to wait there,
she called to Kallidemos to come out to her
(he was Xenokrates' son),
summoning the young man with a wave of her hand.   265
He came out and asked the girl,
"Who are you and where are you from? Who is your father and
    what your city?"
The moment he saw her he was amazed,[192]
overwhelmed by her beauty.
    Drosilla promptly replied,   270
"Let me be, Kallidemos, but tell me this,
whether there is a youth inside from foreign parts,
called Charikles, handsome in appearance."
    But he, falling in love with this good-looking maiden,
and clearly taken with her incomparable beauty   275
and envying Charikles this girl,
caused Drosilla a myriad pains
and denied even knowing the name,
whether such a person as Charikles existed.
    "Why, Kallidemos, do you not strike me   280
with the sword and destroy me? Why do you not give me to the sea?

---

191 The dream has told her where Charikles is, but this development is revealed very
obliquely and the reader has been given no prior knowledge of it.

192 Marginal gloss: 'Kallidemos' love for Drosilla'.

Why do you not slay me, proving yourself a murderer?"
she replied, weeping amidst her groans,
"Because now, greeting me with bitter words,
you offer me, alas, immoderate affliction."   285
     "If you have lost Charikles, girl,
do not be troubled, do not be upset, do not be downcast",
said Kallidemos to Drosilla,
"do not prefer death to survival.
Many among us are superior to Charikles,   290
and provoke jealousy among the girls who see them."
     These were his remarks; and the maiden
Drosilla smiled a little and said
– for even if one is constricted by grief
one can often smile unexpectedly,   295
as if happiness had intervened, as well as weep –
"When my fellow countrymen are handsome young men from the city
how, Kallidemos, son of Xenokrates,
can foreign villagers be superior?[193]
I have a headache,[194] Kallidemos, and   300
for the time being I cannot talk to you any more."
     Meanwhile Charikles, within Xenokrates' house,[195]
was dozing lightly in ignorance,
weighed down by exhaustion and grief and cares.
Drosilla, gasping a little,   305
sat down far away from Xenokrates' abode,
saying and lamenting, "O son of Zeus,
where will you take me now, wretch that I am,
to find Charikles? Not to Xenokrates' house;
or are you completely deceiving me with visions?   310
You should have come to my aid in my misery;
you should have released me from my misfortunes
and burdens and lengthy moans;
you should have led me to where I shall prosper,
you should not have added oppression to oppression,   315
deceiving me with visions in my sleep.

193 A Constantinopolitan viewpoint.
194 Cf. Theokritos, *Idyll* 3.52 and *H&H* 6.2.2; Burton 2003: 257, emphasizing the frequency of Theokritan allusions in this section of *D&C*; also Milazzo 1985.
195 This is the first indication of Charikles' presence.

But if you are a god and scion of Zeus,
tell me whether Charikles still lives;
for appearing last evening
you revealed that he was alive and had been freed   320
by Chagos, together with the foreigner Kleandros,
and had been welcomed at Xenokrates' inn.
But your prediction has been proved untrue.
And now, since I do not find Charikles there
alive and he is not at liberty,   325
he has either departed this life through the sword
or chains chafe his neck
and he lives a painful and pitiable life."

   Kallidemos was standing close by her
and heard her sorrowful words   330
and, being unable to restrain himself, said,[196]
"Your beauty has proved, girl,
that we were conquered the moment I said 'Greetings'.
But I myself, the thrice-unreasonable, expected,
by corrupt reasoning, to remain unaffected by beauty,   335
although lacking experience in lovers' discourse, and unaffected
    by desire;
I despised lovers' pains,
and instantly rejected their marriage.[197]
But now I am trapped as a miserable slave,[198]
by force I am totally in servitude to Eros;[199]   340
the former bloom has fled my cheek,
the fire of my gaze is quenched
by tears as though by a torrent of water.
So I cannot endure the anguish,
and I reproach Homer's Kalliope,[200]   345

196 6.332–558: On the complexities of this passage, which sets out, and reprises, amatory themes that are central to the novel, with allusions to Heliodoros, Longos, Musaios and Theokritos, see Roilos 2005: 73–79 (an *ethopoiia*, with playful contrast between the rustic villager and his rhetorical and literary sophistication); Burton 2003: 255–59.

197 6.334–38: Cf. Hel 3.17.4.

198 Marginal gloss: 'Kallidemos' amorous oration to Drosilla'.

199 6.339–43: Cf. Hel. 3.19.1. The theme of servitude to Eros also prominent theme in *H&H*, e.g. at 3.9, 5.18.

200 6.345–49: Cf. Hel 4.4.3, with *Iliad* 3.636–37. 'Kalliope': the Muse who inspired Homer's *Iliad* and *Odyssey*.

who said that there can be a surfeit of everything of this world,
and even of affection, which can have no limit, in my opinion;
for love does not seem to bring satiety,
whether pleasure is achieved, or whether it is spoken of.
I will cast overboard, then, as the ancient saying has it,   350
my last anchor in time of danger,[201]
and set sail on my second voyage[202] – what will happen to me? –
and address you, who are desirable in every respect;
for I know that silence nurtures disease.[203]
O you who are blessed with beauty's every grace,   355
and who pierce every part of my heart,
you boast lips that are softer than roses[204]
and a mouth that is sweeter than honeycomb;
and your kiss, like a bee's sting,
brings a bitter death, it poisons painfully.   360
Your mouth is, as it were, full of poisons,
even if it is smeared with honey on the outside
and, when I have apparently achieved a kiss,
alas, alas, I acquire even greater anguish.
My chest aches, my heart pounds,[205]   365
my body and wits seem turned upside-down.
No one can escape, even if he thinks he has,
the tyrant Eros armed with his bow,
so long as light and beauty remain on earth
and mortals' eyes turn towards these.   370
For Eros himself, the bold, the archer,[206]
is depicted in myth as a divine and handsome young man,
he is endowed with a bow and bears a quiver.
He delights above all in young people;
wherever there is beauty, he pursues and reaches it,   375
and agitates the mind and heart;
no one alive has found the antidote to him,
except in embraces and sweet marriage.[207]

201 A proverbial expression, but cf. Hel 8.6.9.
202 Another proverbial expression, cf. Plato, *Phaedo* 99c and Hel 1.15.8.
203 Cf. Hel 4.5.7.
204 Cf. Longos 1.18.1.
205 Cf. Longos 1.17.2.
206 6.371–76: Cf. Longos 2.7.1.
207 Cf. Longos 2.7.7.

I have quickly found you to be a severe god, Eros,
I have discovered you are an oak's sprig, a wild beast's scion.   380
You are savage, feigning charm in vain.
Listen then and learn and comprehend,
pearl-breasted girl who are now before us,
and on whom nature has bestowed a mane of fair curly hair,
comprehend how great is the wave, the storm, the tempest.   385
I beseech you to call to your mind
those who in the past were united by love into one soul;
remember among those of old
Arsake's love for Theagenes,
Achaimenis' passion for Charikleia;[208]   390
if you do not wish to think of these since they are improper,
then consider those who were chaste in their love,
whom their very oaths hedged around when under duress
and warded off disgrace and brought legitimately
to the safe union of lawful marriage.   395
Passion is no different from intoxication;
but Drosilla is for me a precious stone that prevents intoxication.[209]
Passion can kindle a flash of fire
but I have you as my precious Indian 'pantarbe',[210]
and fire will shun me when I carry you.   400
For the pain that wears me down draws[211]
my eyes with it to the earth's surface, girl,
but the sight of your graces draws them back.
I lack the strength to be chaste when gazing on you,
and I am tempted to cease gazing   405
so as to prevent desire's flame increasing,
since the sight of you is its very fuel,
so inescapable is the net of desire

208 A knowing literary reference to Heliodoros' *Ethiopika* (Books 7 and 8) where, in a parallel to the present situation, the hero Theagenes becomes the object of passion for the Great King's sister Arsake, while the heroine Charikleia is unsuccessfully desired by the slave Achaimenis; cf. *DigAk* E 709–19 for an appeal to lovers from the past. See Introduction, pp. 342, 350 for the emphasis placed in *D&C* on the strength of marriage ties.

209 An untranslatable pun on 'amethyst', literally 'not intoxicating'.

210 'pantarbe': a stone that protects from fire; cf. Hel 4.8.7, 8.11.2 and Philostratus, *Life of Apollonius* 3.46 as well as twelfth-century writers, notably MangProd 42.306, 66.247, 62.251.

211 Cf. Hel 1.2.3.

that you have thrown from your eyes over me, your prey.[212]
Your mouth is full of coy phrases,   410
your hand is reluctant to rescue quickly
the man who has been trapped in the strange net.
Thus you control the man you have found suspended;
you neither want him to be brought down to the ground,
nor do you save him immediately from his predicament.   415
What device can I invent and where[213]
can I in my misery find love spells,
so that I can persuade you and compel you to suffer
through heart-turning spells of enticement?
For you are a woman – know your own nature –   420
a woman lovelier than all those among us,
a wondrous creation of extraordinary nature,
a superlative example of womankind,
as is the moon among the other stars.[214]
Grant everything; do not respond with words alone,   425
for you seem to conceal your soul's suffering
and turn to me with negative responses.
Using then a measure of goodwill,
you told me previously, when you were annoyed,
that your head pained you and was in distress,   430
that head of yours which is so dear to me.
And this is nothing strange, O maiden Drosilla;
for, coming to an unknown village
and appearing before a large group of strangers,
you have probably attracted the evil eye;   435
however, today I want you who are my sickness
to be released from this troubling sickness,
but may my sickness hasten towards health,
lest we both fall miserably ill.
But that lad Daphnis and Chloe[215]   440
united themselves in marriage thrice blessedly;
that sweet Daphnis, only a shepherd,

212 Cf. Hel 2.25.1.
213 Cf. Hel 2.33.6.
214 Cf. Hel 3.6.3.
215 Marginal gloss: 'About Daphnis and Chloe'. Longos' *Daphnis and Chloe* is the next source used for persuasive amatory examples.

untamed by love's arrows,
yet being loved and in turn loving even more,
though still ignorant of anything other than love;   445
for the passionate infant, her fellow shepherd, was linked
to the maiden Chloe from the cradle.
For long he loved the fair Chloe,
Chloe that as yet unformed maiden,
whose glance was fire for the youth,   450
whose words were bows and her embraces darts.
In matters of love the generation that is past was a golden one,
for he who was loved responded greatly;[216]
this present generation of bronze is incapable of that
for, when beloved, it does not wish to respond.   455
O what is the reason, what the event and what the natural force
that allows passionate maidens to rule over us
when they have been smitten by a heart-gnawing reaction to love?
Or perhaps the maidens are not in love with us?
They are passionate, but they are full of coyness;   460
they are in love, but they wear out those whom they love,
they make their hearts waver,
they melt away, alas, alas, their flesh before its time,
they shoot right into the soul itself;
this is like a noose and the end of life   465
for those who endure love's wound.
Woe, how much time has passed
and yet I have not won over the iron heart;
how often have I made advances but the maiden,
unyielding and rock-hearted, has not heeded me.   470
Wretch that I am, I perish, in my misery I am lost
unless these pleas soften your heart.
The patient Leandros of old, who was enamoured of Hero,[217]
alas, was found dead, drowned in the sea,
woe, when the lamp had been snuffed out by the wind.   475
Abydos knew of this, as did the city of Sestos.[218]

216 On the idea of a golden age of love, cf. Theokritos, *Idyll* 12, 15–16.

217 Marginal gloss: 'About Hero and Leander'. Cf. Musaios, *Hero and Leander* 327–30.

218 In legend, as recounted by Musaios, until the last fatal evening Leander regularly swam by night across the Hellespont from Abydos to visit the priestess Hero in the temple of Aphrodite in Sestos.

But when the sea became his tomb,
he also had his beloved as its fellow occupant
for she flung herself from the wall into the water;
those whom passion has joined in a union,   480
passion drives to share a tomb.[219]
That was a tragic end to life,
but in another way it could be seen as blessed,
for a harmony of souls shared the tomb,
one love, one mind in two bodies.   485
O breeze that snuffed out two rays;
the lamp was snuffed out and with it was snuffed out desire.
O breeze that cast down two stars,
Hero and Leandros, into the abyss.
Pain at the memory enters my vitals,   490
my chest is aflame with the fire of suffering.
That was his condition; I in my misery
do not struggle by night, I do not sail across the sea,
yet I am in danger of drowning, my dearest,
from the tempest of desire that possesses me,   495
unless you manage to offer me your dear right hand.
Consider what has been done, keep in mind my desire.
You are well aware that pain is the offspring of desire.
Open the gates of your heart to me[220]
while subduing the tempest of passion,   500
and make welcome the sea-tossed wanderer
in your embrace, as if in a harbour.
You are not unaware that of old[221]
the famed Kyklops,[222] in love with Galateia,
attempted to entice the unwilling girl,   505
for she greatly loathed the shaggy monster
and fled from her lover;[223] yet she loved him,
for she aimed only little apples at the great creature.
However, he made strange promises in return,
for he said in his desire for her   510

219 A parody of Matthew 9.16; see Introduction, p. 342.
220 Cf. *AnthGr* 12.167 (Meleager).
221 Marginal gloss: 'About Kyklops and Galateia'.
222 The Kyklops is best known as the one-eyed giant whom Odysseus blinded (*Odyssey* 9).
223 Cf. Theokritos, *Idyll* 1.30–31.

that he would throw his hands and feet and belly into the fire
to turn the shaggy hair into ashes,
and if possible his very heart,
should this please his beloved,
and also the one illumination he had,   515
his wide, great eye, drawn like a circle.[224]
In this way, being in love, he enticed her. Kyklops begged
Galateia to enter the cave
where he declared he reared young fawns,
skittish calves, lambs, other flocks   520
and many savage wolf-slaying dogs;
and he declared that he had sweet grapes
and cheese in winter and in the summer season[225]
pails brimming full of milk,
more than six hundred bee-hives   525
and cleverly carved drinking-cups[226]
and countless tanned deerskins.
Kyklops enticed Galateia with all these things,
singing melodiously, gazing at the sea,[227]
holding well-crafted pipes to his lips;   530
he enticed her with these and begged her
to choose the hearth in his cave
and abandon her life by the sea.
You neither make a gesture nor signal your thoughts,
but neither do you wish to join in the game.   535
You have no apple, no sweet laugh
like the Nereid had in the past;
you expect a huge smile
to be a recompense for my many words,
I thank you for the recompense, girl;   540
let the poor scavenging crow, as the proverb has it,[228]
when need drives, find – the wretch –
his food from stinking entrails.
Agree to come inside with him who is making these requests of you,

224 Cf. Theokritos, *Idyll* 11.51–53.
225 Cf. Theokritos, *Idyll* 11.34–36.
226 Cf. Theokritos, *Idyll* 1.27–30.
227 Cf. the scene at 4.386 above.
228 For this proverb, cf. Zenobios 4.56 (Leutsch and Schneidewin 1839–51, vol. 1).

and you will see that the living 545
Kallidemos is finer that the famed Kyklops.
Xenokrates is the chief man in the village;
Kallidemos is not unpleasing to look on,
he is one of the noble and prosperous,
marriage to whom you would not regret, 550
Drosilla, ornament of women.
Do you want me to make this clear to Xenokrates?
The wedding of Kallidemos and Drosilla
he would celebrate with brilliant marriage bowers.
Why do you smile as you gaze quietly at the ground?[229] 555
O good old woman, wise old woman, modest old woman,
win over the unyielding maiden,
and receive a great reward from Kallidemos."
   Xenokrates' son took pleasure in his remarks,
and the old woman made a brief intervention 560
in Kallidemos' speech to the girl and said,
"Unless Drosilla errs in her vision,
Kallidemos, son of Xenokrates,
she will see no one else on earth more handsome than you."
   But he made a further response to the girl, 565
"When you are seen you bring unbelievable sweetness,
but when you are concealed you bring inexpressible hurt.
Merely by being seen you become a meadow teeming with grace;
yet everywhere you seem to bring with you a barrier wall.
And now, you are ripe to be harvested, girl, 570
like the very topmost shoot of the tree's lusty fruit;
so open the garden's portals for me[230]
and allow yourself to be devoured and consumed to satiety.
Who was it among those striving below
who was skilled in the smith's craft, who took the flame 575
and kindled a new Hephaistian furnace[231]
and seized your heart with his tongs and
indicated that he had placed a bronze figure amidst the coals?

   229 Re-punctuating, with Ruth Harder (personal communication), so that 6.555 refers to
Drosilla and 6.556 to the old woman.
   230 This highly suggestive language is once again based on the Song of Songs and is also
part of a literary tradition that goes back in Greek to Archilochus and Sappho.
   231 Hephaistos in Greek mythology was the god of fire and of metal-working.

Who was it that tempered you, that steeled in the flame
your already hardened heart?   580
Oh, the clumsy fingers of that craftsman!
Alas for the miserably wretched tools,
oh, the right hand that has crafted burdens for me,
that has forged in bronze your breast and heart.
He was bold, a second Kyklops,   585
weighty, strong, blood-stained, all-devouring,
who – unique wretch among men –
wrought you to be my great pain.
Who is able to make the dead live?
Who says that he who drinks a cup of poison   590
shares in a song of enchantment?
Behold the living corpse. And what more?
You have thus rejected me who loves you.
How stonily immovable is your heart!
Eros, wretched Eros, fire-breathing Eros,   595
your bitter arrows, alas, burn me like coals.
Woe, woe, does not your bow bring fire?
Truly it does; but what will you be able to do?
Not even Herakles could win against two, so the proverb goes;[232]
and you, a little lad who cannot outwit   600
three stout-fingered Graces,
are constrained to run here and there
and suffer like a slave and wait around;
and even if you spread your wings as you run all over the earth,
performing your duties wherever beauty is found,   605
the Graces aim their bow at you;
they arm you, their slave,
they have the runaway as a faithful servant,
they see you the fugitive now awaiting them.
How wild you are even when you smile sweetly, Eros;   610
I see you brandishing inescapable chains.
You are mad with passion, even when you seem to sport willingly.
Since you have hands that are alert to take aim,
you strike unsparingly; not even she who bore you
has escaped your bow's darts.   615
A peasant saw Niobe weeping

232 For this proverb, cf. e.g. Plato, *Phaedo* 89c.

and said, 'Oh, how can rock shed tears!'[233]
And now, girl, your breathing rock
does not wish to pity us even a little as we sigh.
You appeared suddenly like a bow with me in your sights,   620
you who surpass the maidens in the village.
Should a competition be established over your beauty,[234]
Kypris would not win the first prize again,
even if the judge were he who had made that judgment,
love-smitten Paris with the tawny locks.   625
Soft is your kiss, your braided locks,[235]
your intertwining limbs, everything of yours,
but your soul is unyielding and spiritually adamantine.
I agonize between the Paphian one and Pallas;
who can endure the thirst of Tantalos?[236]   630
And now I am left to accuse Zeus[237]
of lacking love, for not transforming himself
before this girl of ours, who is more lovely
than Leda, Danae, Ganymede and Europe.[238]
Your wrinkle that comes eventually with the passage of time[239]   635
is preferable to the juice of youth, in my judgment;
your autumn is better – how else can I express this? –
than another's spring, your winter is lovelier
than the temperate fruitfulness of another's summer.
But strip off to your very skin   640
and let naked limbs lie against each other;
for your light garment seems to me like
Semiramis' wall.[240] May this happen to me!"
   So saying, he turned towards his house,
beseeching the attending crone with gestures   645

233 Cf. *AnthGr* 5.229.1–2 (Makedonios). See Burton 2003: 261–62.
234 6.622–25: Cf. *AnthGr* 5.222.5–6 (Agathias).
235 6.626–30: Cf. *AnthGr* 5.246 (Paul the Silentiary).
236 6.629–30: Cf., in addition, *AnthGr* 5.272 (Paul the Silentiary).
237 6.631–34: Cf. *AnthGr* 5.257 (Palladas).
238 In Greek mythology Zeus approached Leda in the form of a swan, Danae in a shower of gold, Ganymede as an eagle and Europe as a bull.
239 6.635–59: Cf. *AnthGr* 5.258 (Paul the Silentiary).
240 6.640–43: Cf. *AnthGr* 5.252 (Paul the Silentiary). Semiramis, legendary queen of Babylon, walled the city (Diodorus Siculus 2.9). The eroticism at *H&H* 3.7 or MangProd 14.5–86 (Bernardinello 1972: poem 7) is more overt.

to persuade the girl to yield.
She took the girl and escorted her away,
for night compelled them to make their way back.
   So Charikles remained in Xenokrates' house
and towards dawn he complained to the swallows,   650
"I have been awake all night;[241]
if dawn brings a brief moment of sleep,
the swallows twitter and do not let me be.
Be quiet, most abominable species of abominable birds.
It was not I who cut out Philomela's tongue[242]   655
in fear that she should talk of her rape.
But, yes, go and lament Itys' fate for me
in some harsh and loathsome desert,
so that I can get a little sleep and while I am drowsing
a dream may come to me, perhaps wishing   660
to enfold me, in my desire, in the hands of my beloved.
Tithonos, you have grown old; your Dawn, your dear bedfellow,[243]
you have driven from your couch."
   As he was drooping once more towards sleep,
the handsome form of Dionysos came near   665
and revealed that Drosilla was in the village,
in the dwelling of old Maryllis,[244]
and granted him conversation with her.

---

241 6.651–61: Cf. *AnthGr* 5.237 (Agathias).

242 On the fate of Philomela and her sister, cf. 2.326 above, with note, and 5.116.

243 Cf. *AnthGr* 5.3 (Antipater). Dawn (Eos) requested from Zeus immortality for her lover Tithonos, son of Laomedon of Troy, but omitted to include eternal youth (*Hymn to Aphrodite* 218–38); in debilitated old age he was eventually transformed into a cicada.

244 'Maryllis': this is the form found in all but one of the mss and most editions; Conca chose to follow M (the oldest ms) and printed Baryllis (cf. Giusti 1993: 222, n. 16); Maryllis, however, given the extent of the references to Theokritos in *D&C*, provides a piquant intertextual contrast with the Amaryllis of Theokritos, *Idylls* 3 and 4 and is preferred in this translation.

SEVENTH BOOK

Already it was morning and saffron-hued day,
and lustrous light had poured everywhere over all creation
from the great translucent star
that rose from the ocean,
as learned poetry wisely puts it,[245]   5
and from the highest mountains it shed warmth even-handedly
over the peaks and densely shaded foothills
to produce fertile offspring and a joyous life.
Charikles too rose from sleep
and came out of Xenokrates' house,   10
bringing with him his friend Kleandros.
    Meanwhile the old woman had been trying to comfort[246]
the girl who had been weeping since daybreak,
and said, "Come, child, tell me;
where do you come from and who is your father and what your city,   15
and who is this Charikles on whom you call and for whom you lament?
You mourn ignobly and weep senselessly,
for you have not accepted marriage with Kallidemos
who exceeds all the inhabitants here
in beauty and burgeons with gold.   20
You do not make a good choice, poverty-stricken stranger,
if you now consider that Kallidemos, a noble youth,
is not fit to be united with you."
    As Drosilla began to speak,
"Since you want to learn, mother, from me, the foreigner,   25
about what happened to me and to Charikles,"
Kleandros heard this and stopped in his tracks,
for the sound of Charikles' name checked him
as he was running ahead of Charikles himself,
and, "Charikles, give assurances of joy   30
to me, Kleandros, who shares your troubles,"
said he to Charikles, as he turned to him.
Charikles was astounded by these words,
he was amazed by the mere sound of them.

---

245 A nod towards Homer's 'rosy-fingered dawn' (e.g. *Iliad* 8.1.1, 19.1).
246 Marginal gloss: 'Maryllis asks Drosilla about herself'.

Then, clasping each others' hands,[247]   35
they immediately burst into that abode
within which the kind-hearted old woman
was conversing sympathetically with Drosilla.
Then there was speech hovering between joy and tears,
clapping of hands, the reverberation of smacking kisses,   40
an immeasurable storm flooding from eyes,
cries of thankfulness to Semele's son,[248]
kind words from Charikles to the old woman
for her hospitality to Drosilla,
many thanks to Kleandros   45
from that best of maidens, Drosilla,
for his having shared Charikles' hardships.
Such was the hubbub among the four of them,
truly a mixture of joy and tears.
But Kallidemos was not unaware of these developments.   50
While he was contemplating frantically within himself
performing a murderous deed against Charikles,
a deed that was without a wound, that was not too gory,
so that he could achieve marriage with Drosilla,
he was unaware that he was preparing the noose for himself.   55
When he realized that Charikles was aware
of the girl's arrival in the village
before he had completed his projected plan,
emboldened by love-inspired madness
he embarked on an abduction more suited to a brigand.   60
For frequently love knows no shame.[249]
So he planned in the desert-wastes of night[250]
to fall unexpectedly on the young men,
having with him comrades of his own age,
in order to abduct the girl   65
– for he had prepared a vessel for their departure.
But instead of the flame which his desires had kindled,
the fire of a tertian fever gripped him;
instead of a vessel sailing away,

247 Marginal gloss: 'Charikles and Drosilla recognize each other'.
248 i.e. Dionysos.
249 Cf. 3.170 above.
250 Marginal gloss: 'Kallidemos' plot against Drosilla'.

it was a couch of suffering that claimed him;   70
instead of a speedy departure to another village,
he discovered protracted immobility for his limbs.
    But Charikles could have no surfeit
of Drosilla's refreshing kisses;
for if anyone has an opportunity to kiss his beloved,   75
his heart is insatiable
and he easily soaks up the flow of pleasure;
his lip is no longer parched,
for it has attained sweetness without limits,
and pleasure is emptied into his being.   80
When they broke off from their kisses,
old Maryllis sobered up and said,
"Charikles, my child, you have come here now opportunely,
and you have found Drosilla who was rescued by the gods
and who till now has not stopped weeping   85
and uttering mournful laments for you;
since you have come opportunely – great is our gratitude to the gods
who have brought you to us safe and sound
and reunited you with your beloved –,
since you have come opportunely, child, it is now your opportunity
        to tell us   90
how the two of you came to your union,
what is your homeland, and what the origins of your passion,
and who is this foreigner Kleandros,
what was the reason for your separation
and for your finding each other once more.   95
The maiden was starting to tell me
and was about to explain all this,
yes, and to recount it all in sequence,
before you arrived at the house."
    "Painfully and with groans   100
– how else?", said Kleandros, "but your suggestion is good."
    "Since, oh golden fate, you have come under my roof,
guided by some god,
so that the girl who weeps night and day
might briefly pause in her wailings,   105
you could to us explain your arrival here
and Eros' mystic boldness

with great pleasure and joy.
What is it that grieves Drosilla still,
or what is that troubles her, now that you, Charikles, have arrived?   110
For since she moaned when you were absent, shrieked,
cried bitterly, wailed grievously,
now that you are present and joy once instituted
holds sway, oh saviour gods,
the story should follow an appropriate path.   115
You would delight the girl even more
if you opened your sweet mouth
and she hearkened to its sound.
You will also encourage me to sympathize with troubles I understand,
from which till now she has suffered woefully."   120
    "How indeed I would like first,
my dear Maryllis, to ask the girl,"
said Charikles, "by what means she was saved although on her own,
when she fell into the sea from the high mountain.
Indeed I am still somewhat bemused and wonder   125
whether I see Drosilla in a vision;
but since it is your wish, old mother, that we should tell
of our huge periods of suffering
in exchange for your hospitality,
listen; for how can we spurn   130
the cause of so much happiness
for me, Drosilla, and Kleandros, the foreigners?
Know then that our homeland is Phthia,
my mother is Krystale and my father Phrator,
Drosilla's parents are Myrtion and Hedypnoe.   135
While a holy festival was being celebrated
in honour of Dionysos, son of Semele and Zeus,
Drosilla came out beyond the gates of her home city
in the company of tender maidens;
I saw her and was overcome. You will not blame me, woman,   140
as I saw the vision of her countenance,
for in the great crowd that was gathering together then
none could be seen more beautiful than Drosilla.
Once overcome I addressed her and, addressing her, I begged her
to join with me in flight.   145
She consented, for she too was experiencing a strange reciprocal love.

We found a ship about to sail off
and, abandoning our parents and country,
we embarked together on the vessel.
But after we had sailed a little way in fair conditions,   150
we came unexpectedly upon men
who rejoice in banditry by sea,
whose clutches we escaped eventually and with difficulty,
and fled, taking refuge in a wood,
and we slipped into the city of Barzon in haste.   155
When we left there together while a great celebration
for Zeus was in progress,
we fell in with the Parthian expedition
as a new prey; and with necks bound
we were brought to their city.   160
There many circuits of days
we measured out with so many groans,
and we encountered the good Kleandros whom you see, woman,
who had been captured previously by the barbarian band
and was an excellent companion in slavery   165
– for we saw in prison against expectation
the life of slavery, alien lords,
and loves that were so ill fated.
Then for the third time we fell prisoner together,
to the Arabs when the Parthians were routed.   170
So, having become captives, we were led away
to traverse a path that was perpetually confined
by dense and overhanging woods
and we were in distress, each supporting the other,
with the just and reasonable fear   175
that we might slip from the crags
and find our grave in the sea.
Which is what befell this maiden here,
whom I see living, O Zeus and all the gods.
So the ruler of the Arabs, lord Chagos,   180
finding me lamenting at night for the girl,
immediately set me free together with Kleandros here,
out of pity for our suffering.
So, having demanded all that is expedient for life
from the gods' providence,   185

we were freed from the burden of slavery's yoke.
At the twelfth dawn we approached
with difficulty the abode of Xenokrates,
and we were planning today
shortly to leave the village and hasten elsewhere   190
– for we have spent three circuits of days in Xenokrates' house
in respite from our ordeal –
had not a dream been sent from the gods,
or rather, not a dream but the appearance of
the fair-formed son of Zeus and Semele,   195
who restrained us, saying, 'Go no further
until you find Drosilla, whom you want to see alive
and who is weeping in the village.'
  So now you have discovered, woman, all about us,
as you asked; but for the rest of the story,   200
I beg you to ask the maiden herself,
how – after being hurled into the sea – she managed
nonetheless to reach you here,
who have proved a second Hedypnoe to her."
  "As for me, Charikles, even if the malignant thread,"   205
said Drosilla, "of vengeful fate
always wishes to spin a grievous destiny,
yet the providence of the saviour god
which we have been fortunate to have
as our ally in our love – but do not cease, lord,   210
from protecting, as you wish, her who abandoned her country –
that providence always wishes to bring the best outcome.
That providence, when I fell – oh, the abominable branch
which caught my arm at the elbow
and threw me into the abyss from my perch –,   215
saved me when my breast and guts and elbows
were thoroughly battered on the rocks."
– And bending over the girl as she spoke,
Charikles with tears kissed
her red and white crystalline fingers. –   220
"Who placed in those hands which you now kiss and embrace
that tree trunk, and gave me
such a broad and substantial log
that swiftly brought me safe to land?

Oh many thanks, Dionysos, lord of the earth,   225
who saved me from many dangers
and bestowed on me a gift greater than any other.
He whom I placed among the dead I see among the living."
    And embracing in the pause in her speech
like ivy clinging to an oak, they kissed each other gladly.   230
So difficult was their embrace to bring to an end
that it occurred to Maryllis
that the two had indeed become one body,
who in speech had become one soul.[251]
Thus it is with every lover who is redolent with desire;   235
for when after a long time he sees her whom he desires,
he kisses her insatiably until his desire is assuaged.
    As soon as Charikles had with difficulty sobered up, he said,
"O you who have endured so much that you cannot recount,
O longed-for light, O breath and heart,   240
how did you travel such a long path
and come to this village here?"
    The girl replied once more, "He
who led me to the village was he
who had saved me from the ocean's watery wastes   245
and allows me now to look on a living Charikles."
    At this Maryllis demonstrated her delight,
saying, "What a novel sight I see, strangers!
For I am an old woman and advanced in age,
and I have had experience of much good and evil,   250
but I have never known such desire,
nor have I seen such a handsome couple
coming to their union so pitiably and so young
from such unendurable mutual anguish.
That she, oh Zeus, a protected virgin   255
and yet many times forced into slavery,
should escape raving passions,
and that he who, before the barbarians' naked swords,
fell like summer grass
should be among the living and united with the girl,   260
after having previously been sundered from her,
you say this is the work of a god, and you say rightly,

---

251 Cf. *DigAk* G 3.277–87 for a clinging embrace between reunited lovers.

chaste Drosilla. Let Kallidemos go hang.
Those whom a god has joined, who may separate?"[252]
    These were her remarks, and she set up a table in their midst,[253]   265
saying, "I rejoice with you, strangers,
today. Keep me company,
and I will dance in honour of the god Dionysos
who has firmly united those who had suffered pitiably."
    So they then busied themselves   270
and delightedly consumed food and drink,
and the old woman – for she was good-hearted – [254]
gave herself over to the festivities and the drinking.
Then she got up from her seat
and, being already prepared for this,   275
took a napkin in both hands[255]
and began a somewhat Bacchic dance,
producing a small snuffling sound,
which initiated festivity and instigated mirth.
However, the constant gyrations quickly   280
tripped Maryllis up in her movements
and so the poor wretch fell over
with her legs in a tangle;
she promptly lifted her feet over her head
and pushed her head into the ground.   285
The symposiasts let out a huge guffaw.
Old Maryllis lay where she fell
and farted three times,
because she could not bear the pressure on her head.[256]
She did not get up – the poor wretch   290
said she could not, and lying there
she held out her hands to the young men.
But Kleandros could not contain himself;
he collapsed with laughter and on his own
lay there half-dead, panting hard.   295

252 Matthew 19.6 again.

253 Marginal gloss: Maryllis' banquet'.

254 Marginal gloss: 'Here the old woman dances'.

255 Cf. Nausikrates' 'somewhat nautical dance' at *R&D* 2.110. On the carnivalesque aspects of this scene, including the grotesque role of the old woman Maryllis, see Roilos 2005: 288–96.

256 The Byzantine sense of the ridiculous focused on bodily functions and slapstick; see Garland 1990; Haldon 2002.

What about Charikles? Amidst the mirth,
thinking he had found an excellent opportunity,
he had bent over Drosilla's neck
to laugh at the good Maryllis,
and he could not get enough kisses,   300
with their lips glued together.
But Kleandros picked himself up and with difficulty
got the old woman upright again,
afraid, I think, after what had already happened,
that she might go one better and foul herself,   305
or batter her head as she lay there,
and as a reward for her hospitality
have this crushing headache.
But she sat with the young people and said,
"By the gods, my children, just look at me.   310
From the time that the good Chramos, Maryllis' son,
was buried – and that was eight years ago –
I have not laughed or danced;
I have this to thank you for.
They say that even an old man runs when fooling with lads."   315
    "By your son,' responded the young men,
"you have given us great pleasure, decorous Maryllis,
in many ways, including your food and drink.
And your dancing and skilful gyrations,
and the abundant movements of your feet,   320
and the speed of your subtle contrapuntal motions,
have delighted us more than food, more than drink,
more than the most luxurious banquet,
more than the most overflowing cup.
And you have done nothing strange, mother;   325
even if we were old men three times over,
we would not have been afraid of sharing your experience,
since the gods always grant what is agreeable."
    The youths addressed these words to the old woman,
and with the table taken out of the way,[257]   330
Kleandros lay down to sleep
while the old woman took herself off too.

---

257 Permanent arrangements for dining were not the norm in Byzantine houses; cf.
Oikonomides 1990; Parani 2003: 173–76; cf. *R&D* 2.55.

EIGHTH BOOK

Then Charikles gave his hand to the maiden[258]
and immediately went out with her into the garden
that was nearby. Advancing a little he looked quizzically
at the trees, the fruit, the medley of flowers,
a handsome sight that delighted the onlookers.   5
Then, seated beneath a myrtle tree,
they addressed themselves to conversation.
And said Charikles, "Who, my dear beloved,
is the Kallidemos whom the old woman mentioned in her cups?
Surely malignant fate has not permitted   10
some vicious bully and savage tyrant
to enjoy your beauty and marriage with you?
Surely no one has been able to quench the fire
which you have in the depth of your soul for Charikles?
O, O desired eye, conceal nothing,   15
for you speak to Charikles and not to a stranger."
    "What do you mean? Be silent," responded
the maiden Drosilla to Charikles,
"Charikles, my husband. Yes, you alone are
my husband; this is no false saying.   20
Wit and judgment have deserted you
because of the lengthy troubles that have beset you,
for distress befuddles the mind too.
Indeed, father Zeus and the assembly of the gods,
if Drosilla had not kept her virginity until now,   25
the fact would have become apparent of its own accord.
What a word, excellent Charikles, my husband,
has escaped the barrier of your teeth![259]
I will explain to you, and may there stand as witness to my statement
Zeus' son, who the day before yesterday in my sleep   30
revealed to me as he stood beside me when I lay slumbering,
that you were sheltering in Xenokrates' house.
Obeying his command – for how could I not? –
and full of joy, I asked the old woman

258 Marginal gloss: 'The young people in the garden'.
259 A Homeric cliché (or formula); e.g. *Iliad* 4.350, *Odyssey* 5.22.

if there was an innkeeper in the village.   35
When she indicated Xenokrates to me,
I followed her to his dwelling.
She was acquainted even before your maiden was
with Kallidemos, son of Xenokrates,
and she begged the young man to come to us,   40
so that she could find out about your arrival here.
For the two of us did not enter his abode,
and this is a demonstration of my decorous behaviour.
But would that I had entered the dwelling!
I would have found bliss more speedily,   45
and what abundance would I have possessed
when I recognized the magnificent treasure that is Charikles!
Kallidemos, whom I have just mentioned, promptly[260]
when he saw us came out of his house
and by dreadful ill fortune begrudged me   50
your happy presence here
and denied, Charikles, knowledge of your name.
He stood close by me, from head to feet
he measured me and, gazing at me intently,
seemed to have lost his breath.   55
For if beauty is often capable of attracting
men past their prime,
how much more can it attract a youth in his prime?[261]
What speeches he made in vain,
how many promises he recited,   60
it is impossible to recount, Charikles, even if I wanted to;
and how could I, since I paid not the slightest attention.
This one thing I know – and the old woman is witness to my suffering –
that when I heard the heart-rending denial
of your arrival – alas, alas, the envy –   65
my heart seemed to have been torn from me,
I was forced to vomit forth my soul,
I was spiritless, speechless, nothing but a statue,
I blamed, woe, the gods in their entirety,
shedding copious floods of warm tears,   70

---

260 Marginal gloss: 'Drosilla explains Kallidemos' love to Charikles'.
261 Cf. Longos 3.13.3.

lamenting bitterly for my true husband.
For whom? Alas, alas, for the handsome Charikles."
    To this Charikles responded. "Thanks be to you,
O son of Zeus, greatest of the gods,
who removed the jealous inclination   75
which Kallidemos felt for Drosilla,
and who led Charikles
to the abode of old Maryllis.
For if Kallidemos had not begrudged us our passion,
he would not have undergone this disease sent from the gods."   80
    And bending over her neck
and kissing her three times, he grasped her by the elbow
and asked her to give a womanly recompense,
saying, as he pointed with his finger, "You see the trees,[262]
how many birds' nests with their nestlings there are in them;   85
there regularly the sparrows celebrate their marriages;
the tree is a bridal bower, the branch the bridal chamber,
which has its leaves as the bridal couch;
yes, the great bridal hymn is sung
by the winged creatures fluttering around the garden.   90
Grant me, Drosilla, marriage with you,
for which I have undergone a myriad pains,
for which I have endured flight, slavery, captivity,
for which I have shed groans and oceans of tears.
Oh loving bonds and interwoven arms   95
and entwined fingers and linked feet.
I know, I know, Ares, from what happened,
that not even you were inappropriately aggrieved
when you were caught by the iron chains, Hephaistos' wiles,[263]
as you slept blissfully with the sea-born one.   100
But, O dear one,[264] do not hinder me.
Eros, aid me by inspiring the maiden;
no one running on foot will escape the winged creature.[265]
O my light, warm my heart too;

262 Marginal gloss: 'Charikles' charming speech in the meadow to Drosilla'.
263 *Odyssey* 8.266–366. Hephaistos, lame iron-working son of Zeus, cast a metal net over his wife Aphrodite, caught sleeping with Ares, god of war.
264 'dear one': Drosilla.
265 Cf. *AnthGr* 5.59 (Archias).

ungracious beauty pleases but does not hold one,   105
like a hook without a barb.[266]
Hera and the unwed Pallas, on seeing you,
said, 'We no longer strip as we did before;
one judgment from a shepherd is quite enough.'[267]
Would that I were a zephyr, maiden,   110
and you, seeing me blowing mildly,
would bare your breast and take me in.[268]
You, blessed Selene gleaming palely,
beam down, guide and illumine the stranger;
Endymion lit up your heart.[269]   115
Away with silver and brilliant gems
and gold that mocks hearts;
perdition on all those things, wealth, infinite happiness,
which was once pledged by Chrysilla;
you are all these things to me, chaste maiden.   120
You pride yourself on your fair hair; away with the weight of gold;
you have a white complexion; farewell, the charm of pearls;
your embrace ornaments a neck,
a gleaming ruby is enfolded in your lips.
Marriage with you is not entirely without adornment;   125
nightingales sing as they flutter around in a circle,
swallows chorus in response.
All this is your bridal ode; grant me marriage.
The sparrow can make love, it can have a marriage;
but we who are in the throes of passions, can we not be united?"   130
    He addressed many such remarks to the girl,
for every lover who gazes on his beloved
and pours out all his attention on her
thinks nothing of the rest of his life.
But although Drosilla held the handsome Charikles   135
and kissed the young man,
she welcomed him only with embraces

---

266 Cf. *AnthGr* 5.67 (Capito).
267 Cf. *AnthGr* 5.69 (Rufinus). A reference to the Judgement of Paris.
268 Cf. *AnthGr* 5.83 (author unknown).
269 Cf. *AnthGr* 5.123 (Philodemos). Selene (the moon) was enamoured of Endymion, for whom she requested endless sleep, thus preserving his beauty; cf. Apollodoros, *Bibliotheke* 1.7.5–6.

and the honeyed sweetness of kisses.
For she said, "O Charikles, my heart,
you are not going to achieve union with Drosilla.   140
Do not struggle, do not force me, do not make pointless efforts;
it is not right for a girl who is chaste
to behave in an unseemly manner.
I love you; how could I not? For what reason?
I love Charikles and I desire him more than anything else,
but I will not betray my virgin state like a courtesan   145
without the consent of my kin, my mother and my father.
Be confident in the gods' providence;
for I call to witness heaven and earth and the stars
that I shall be given in marriage to no one
other than Charikles. Listen to why this is going to happen.   150
Understand that from the night
in which the dream came revealing, husband,
that you were staying here, thrice-beloved heart,
I have been confident that with the god's assistance
I shall in due time see my fatherland   155
and Myrtion and dear Hedypnoe,
and I shall dance with the dear maidens who are my companions
at the altar of the god Dionysos,
and I shall drink from the streams of the lovely Melirrhoe,
and I shall join, Charikles, in marriage with you.   160
It would be impossible, and I could not endure to hear it said,
that I could not remain chaste, especially in foreign regions."
    "Oh how chaste is your disposition and how good your sense,"
Charikles responded to Drosilla,
"how well your golden mouth makes its pronouncements,   165
how well your thrice-blessed tongue gives utterance.
All this would be very sensible and very proper, maiden,
unless, as we travel to Phthia,
we should be obstructed once again by Fate.
That there may be bandit raids in mid-journey,   170
and savage-hearted barbarians' daggers,
and the sea's savage surface,
you are not likely to be unaware;
we cannot forget the dreadful events inflicted on us by Fate.
What if – but be merciful, hostile Fate,   175

and cease at last your fury against us –
we should succumb once again to a different
variety of evil captivity,
or be parted from one another? Respond."
"But, O Charikles," replied the girl, 180
"it is not Drosilla but the savage Eros
whose charming role you seem to have embraced."[270]
While these two were conversing[271]
Kleandros came up to make the third, groaning quietly
and saying, "Alas, Kalligone is dead." 185
And, "Who, dear Kleandros, brought
this bitter news?" asked the young people.
"A certain Gnathon arrived, a merchant from Barzon,"
replied Kleandros, but "Oh, how dreadful,"
they responded once more, shedding tears. 190
And so, as Kleandros began to lament,
the two once again wept with him.
He recounted amidst innumerable groans
such pitiable and random happenings
that the late hour did not permit him 195
to complete his prolonged lament.
"Woe, woe, woe for this present day,[272]
on which I, the only wretch among mankind,
learn of your death, Kalligone.
I deprived you of your home once, 200
becoming, alas, slave to crooked-minded Parthians;
I had a small life-nurturing hope
that you would have escaped the barbarians' hands
and I would be able once more to look on you, maiden.
And now I was beginning a more modest exultation, 205
since – O gods – I had chanced to see the light of freedom,
for I had it in my mind to search for you when I returned.
And now you, my light, have been dimmed completely.
How shall I make my journey? How shall I reach my destination alone?
I should not – O earth, fire, water, air, mist 210

270 On the savage Eros, cf. e.g. *AnthGr* 5.177 and 178 (Meleager) and also Plato, *Phaedo*
81a (Roilos 2005: 218–19).
271 Marginal gloss: 'Arrival of Gnathon and death of Kalligone'.
272 Marginal gloss: 'Kleandros' lament for Kalligone'.

and all-receiving globe and light of the sun –
I should not have emerged from the womb and proceeded towards life.
If there was a pressing need for me to have been born from my mother,
those ominous fates should have
destroyed me and turned me to ash　　　　　　　　　　　　215
before I achieved full perception
and before I saw the present day.
Alas, alas, I mourn you who have died, as it were harvested
like an unripe grape or an immature ear of corn
in the field by Charon's hostile fingers.　　　　　　　　220
How can I bear this abominable fate,
as disaster after fresh disaster in succession
encompasses my head?
You escaped from the hands of barbarian men,
but not from Charon, the slayer of men.　　　　　　　　225
The hope that till now nurtured me has perished,
Kleandros has perished like Kalligone.
O unfortunate Barzon, you wretched city,
in which we were separated from each other by force.
It would have been better for me to have died with the maiden　　230
than to live feebly and groan deeply,
inhabiting the earth like a shadow that has movement.
All the former hopes have vanished.
I did not address you in your final breath,
Kalligone, my wondrous, revered maiden.　　　　　　　　235
Oh how my wits find it astonishing
that the incessant squalls of disaster
have not swayed to pity and compassion
the Fate that, alas, is so hostile to us."
　As the youth bewailed thus,[273]　　　　　　　　　　　240
the young people wept with him and comforted him
with beguiling and cheerful words.
When night came on as the day concealed itself,
they went together to Maryllis'
dwelling and, finding the table prepared,　　　　　　　245
took their places.[274] The old woman once more

273 Marginal gloss: 'The young people console Kleandros'.

274 'took their places': literally, 'reclined'. On dining practices in these novels and the vocabulary used, see the notes at *R&D* 2.95 and *H&H* 1.6, and Grosdidier de Matons 1979.

set out food and wine before them.
The stranger sat down with them,
for he came as messenger with a double announcement,
bitter for Kleandros but sweet for Charikles.   250
Setting their hands to the meal,
they urged the old woman to bend her knee and sit;
but she, being busy with the lamp,
delayed a little as she lit it carefully
and said, "Children, you Kleandros and Gnathon,   255
and you Charikles and the maiden Drosilla,
the four of you must gladly consume my banquet,
– for I love you like Chramos
who was my son, the only son whom I bore,
whose graces I enjoyed but briefly   260
and for whom I grieve for so long –
the four of you must gladly consume my banquet,
the four of you must quaff my wine,
for my food is the sight of you."
    When Gnathon heard the portentous names of[275]   265
Drosilla and Charikles from Maryllis,
he made a move as if to speak, but then checked himself.
But looking at them intently,
and realizing clearly from their reactions to each other
that he had met up with the fugitives,   270
he said vehemently in his joy,
"O Zeus and the gods, what an excellent day is this.
I can receive from two men
the greatest recompense for their joy.
Rejoice, Phrator and you too, Myrtion,   275
I will proclaim to you that your children live."
    "Your mouth is dipped in honey, Gnathon,"
they said as they questioned the stranger,
"How Phrator is present and Myrtion also
and how you recognized that we two   280
are their children you must sweetly reveal."
    "I will explain this to you in your bewilderment,"[276]
said Gnathon to them as he joined the banquet,

275 Marginal gloss: 'Gnathon recognizes Charikles and Drosilla'.
276 Marginal gloss: 'Gnathon's announcement about the parents' arrival'.

"for, strangers, these men whom I mentioned,
whom I saw and with whom I entered into conversation,   285
have recently come to the city of Barzon,
sent, they said, by dreams;
they were carrying a great burden of gold
and made much mention within the city
of Drosilla and Charikles.   290
The old men were extremely upset,
saying that the son of the god Zeus
had sent them from Phthia to Barzon
and they were seeking for their children.
Since they had not yet discovered you,   295
'As for us,' they said, '– for where can we go?
And how can we go wandering? How can we catch up with them? –
we will remain here in obedience to the god;
perhaps they will eventually reach the city.
He who brought us to this place   300
will compel them to take refuge here
and to bring an end to their wanderings.
But you, our good friend, Gnathon from Barzon'
– for they saw that I was loading my donkeys
and was making haste to come to the village –   305
'keep those wanderers in mind,
in case with the gods' help you happen to find them.
And when you bring the news, you will receive ten *minai* of gold.'
And now good fortune has accompanied me
and has led me, as you see, to recognize you."   310
    "Kalligone, the fair-formed maiden,[277]
has died; alas, alas, the inhumanity of Fate",
Kleandros uttered his final words
and with these words so he released his spirit.
For the onset of piercing grief can often   315
slay more effectively than a well-sharpened sword.
Thus around Drosilla and Charikles
Fate's hostility did not cease
scattering the debris of disaster
and painfully mingling distressing events with happier ones.   320

277 Marginal gloss: 'Death of Kleandros'.

NINTH BOOK

It was already dawn and the light of day
gleamed brilliantly everywhere over the earth from the east.[278]
Weeping copiously, as is customary for friends,
they burned the body in the convention of the Hellenes,[279]
offering up libations of roast meats   5
together with flowing milk and honey.
There gathered together every shepherd, every peasant,
every compassionate man at the stranger's grave,
and every long-suffering woman,
among whom was Maryllis, leading the mourning.   10
For him there mourned oaks and rocks,[280]
rivers in valleys and heavily shaded glades,
for Kleandros was capable at that moment
of arousing pity even in unyielding rocks.
Drosilla, although still a maiden,   15
mourned then more than all the women.[281]
For just as, when the sea rises in a southerly gale,
the constant swell of the waves
overturns the ship that has been trapped in the blast,
however stable the keel and well constructed the vessel;   20
waves billow incessantly one after the other,
without pause or limit to their size,
unless the foolish Koroibos[282] has
a son who has his father's wits,
and tries pointlessly and in vain   25
to measure the immeasurable sequence of waves

278 Marginal gloss: 'Burial of Kleandros'.

279 There are several implications in Eugenianos' use of the term 'Hellenes' (see pp. 16–17); here the 'convention of the Hellenes' is that of a Homeric funeral, far removed from the rites of the twelfth-century Byzantine church.

280 Marginal gloss: 'Mourning for Kleandros'. Compassionate nature is a topos, especially in bucolic poetry; cf. Theokritos, *Idyll* 1.69–85; Moschos, *Epitaphios for Bion* 1–2. On the multiple layers of allusion in this passage, see Burton 2003: 263–67.

281 i.e. laments over the dead were for married women to perform; Roilos 2005: 89–91. See Alexiou 2002: 39–44 for echoes of Byzantine practice in mourning customs in rural Greece in the 1960s.

282 'Koroibos': proverbially foolish, noted particularly for attempting to count waves (Zenobius 4.58; Diogenianus 5.56]Leutsch and Schneidewin 1839–51, vol. 1]).

when, in the season of mellow fruitfulness,
Poseidon stirs up the south wind,
and the south wind raises the sea in response
while the sea harasses the ships 30
and ships harass the hearts of those sailing;
even so there poured forth without measure a myriad
of squalls of torrid and unending disasters
and washed over Drosilla's wits,
like a mighty wave sweeping over a ship with no ballast.[283] 35
  She cried out as she wept over the youth,[284]
"Alas, Kleandros, who is the strong-armed demon,
the vengeful demon that swoops down at a time of misery
and attacks us fiercely and in anger?
It brings disaster upon disaster, 40
and always the fresh disaster outdoes the old.
Why is this, Fate? When will this come to an end?
What limit is there on our tears?
O sweet Kleandros, my fellow prisoner,
fellow slave, fellow worker, fellow youth, 45
fellow in captivity, fellow in freedom, stranger,
you have departed before your time, corn that is handsome but not yet ripe,
not even addressing your own father
as you breathed out your last breath.
O twig from a sturdy Lesbian branch,[285] 50
you were born sturdy and handsome and sweet
but little by little, as if shrivelled by a strange flame,
you slipped away to your destruction.
Yesterday you were among us, but now you are with those below;
yesterday you were speaking to me, today you cannot hear; 55
you conversed with me yesterday and brought me happiness,
now you are speechless and bring me misery.
There is no surfeit to our sufferings.
And how much further can we progress in misery?
Oh how unfortunate you are, unfortunate Kallistias. 60
For your child, Kleandros, the stranger,

---

283 'a ship with no ballast': a traditional expression, e.g. Plato, *Theaetetus* 144a; cf. also *R&D* 2.318. 9.17–35 is a version of a Homeric simile.
  284 Marginal gloss: 'Drosilla's lament for Kleandros'.
  285 An allusion to Kleandros' homeland (cf. 2.57), and also to Sappho, fr. 115 (Voigt 1971).

flying like a bird from the paternal embrace
lies here, fallen pitiably in foreign lands.
Oh where did you nurture, wretch, high hopes
of finding your son and welcoming him from his wanderings,   65
and lighting the fire and the wedding torches,
and setting up festivities and dances and a bridal chamber,
while her friends rejoiced with Kydippe
at the return of the handsome Kleandros?
But, learning at last of your wits' error,   70
and the incoherent force of your reasoning
and discovering that your son had fallen in a foreign land
– for time instructs about events –
you will both weep greatly and groan deeply,
compelled to shed an abundant flood from your eyes   75
in addition to your previous tears.
Earlier, perhaps, a restrained hope had restricted
the flow of unrestrained tears,
but little by little you will waste away through time
and the coals of grief, like snow in the sun.   80
Alas, alas, fellow captive, fellow wayfarer.
If ever Charikles by some unlucky chance
should run the risk of being deprived once again
of me, the long-suffering and thrice-afflicted Drosilla,
who, who could offer him consolation for the weight of grief?   85
Who would provide a respite for his pain
with honeyed words and comforting manner?
Spiritual relief, salvation,
all-comforting support would have vanished for me.
What light breeze and flame-destroying coolness   90
would quench the unceasing fire and leaping blaze
of my sufferings that know no rest?
What cessation and end to pain would there be?
And would my mind be at peace after the storms of suffering?[286]
Oh who, Charikles, would comfort you,   95
if Drosilla should suffer some grievous fate?
Deep night and the darkness of late evening
and murky dust – oh evil combination –

286 A proverbial expression; cf. Aeschylus, *Prometheus* 1015; Charit 3.2.6.

contain, alas, alas, Kleandros' heart.
Oh how will you bring honour to your mother Kydippe   100
when you are buried so sadly in a foreign land,
and how will you delight with garlands and glorify
the loins from which you came to this light,
and how would you be the rod and staff
for your begetter when with the passage of time he reaches old age?   105
O light that is joy's candle, your family's lantern,
you have been snuffed out, shattered, destroyed, concealed."
    While Drosilla thus wailed over the stranger,[287]
"Enough of this excessive tumult over the corpse
and immoderate tears and lamentation,"   110
said the foreign merchant Gnathon, as he stood among them;
"If some unexpected painful event that grieves the mind
takes place in the midst of joy,
the sensible man gives precedence to joy;
when the grief is unmitigated,   115
then no one can be reproached for excessive tears;
but if benefits are mixed with what is distressing,
then – I think – the more favourable aspects of fate should be preferred.
For what is unfavourable predominates over the favourable,
there is more that is miserable in life than pleasant.   120
Therefore consider your afflictions carefully,
in case any benefit may be derived
unexpectedly from them by chance.
For expected events do not bring as much joy   125
to those about to undergo pleasant experiences
if they are awaiting them
as does the good that happens unexpectedly
and assuages the soul and relieves the heart;
it drives all previous distress   130
from the furthermost reaches of the mind
and hidden places of reason,
and enables those who have suffered to recreate themselves,
while it smooths the appearance of those in distress
so that they acquire another shape and a new condition,   135
and it tints the appearance of their countenances

---

287 Marginal gloss: 'Gnathon stops the lament'.

in a quite beautiful form.
But do cease at last your lengthy lamentations,
and allow yourself to recover, girl.
And you too, Charikles, leave the mourning;   140
take hold of yourself lest anything worse befall,
for one must endure whatever happens with nobility."
    Thus they overcame their distress.
Two days had not yet gone by,
and all the goods he had brought Gnathon   145
had sold to the local peasants;
so, taking the loving couple with him,
he travelled with the speed of wings to Barzon.
When they reached the entrance gate,
Charikles and the maiden Drosilla   150
saw their own wretched fathers
seated on a rock, a well-polished seat,
and they were amazed and quite appropriately ashamed.
But Gnathon went ahead and preceded them[288]
and embraced both the old men   155
and, announcing the arrival of their children,
received in return a gift of ten *minai* of gold.
But when they clasped their children,
I cannot describe their joy
as they saw this handsome couple   160
unexpectedly treading the soil of Barzon.
First they wept, as is habitual in old age,
then they kissed their heads delightedly,
they rejoiced, they grieved, they were happy, they were despondent,
they laughed, they cried, they burst into loud applause.   165
Tears of joy flowed abundantly,
laments of happiness were raised even more.
The entire population of Barzon appeared on the streets,
for they had learned of the event from messengers running through
        the town;
they emerged rejoicing from their houses,   170
children, old women, strapping lads, maidens,
young striplings, women, frail children and aged crones,

---

288 Marginal gloss: 'The fathers recognize the young people'.

all thronged closely round the young people.
Lamentation pierced the tumult,
but joy put an end to mourning;   175
thus the entire city joined with the fathers
in their grief and also in their celebration.
Phrator embraced the maiden Drosilla,
and addressed her as his child,
"Rejoice, children, who have been restored safely to your parents;   180
you have brought happiness to two fathers
as we also have found happiness in our children.
How welcome is the conclusion of your wanderings;
how fortunate is the cessation of our tears.
May you prosper and be preserved for your marriage,   185
you whom the gods, your marriage sponsors, have united."
   When they had occupied themselves with long conversations
with each other till nightfall,
they turned their attention to dinner. Gnathon took his seat
and asked Phrator to sit beside him.   190
Phrator yielded to Gnathon's request
and asked Myrtion to take his place by him,
as Myrtion did to the bridegroom Charikles,
and Charikles to the maiden Drosilla.
The three were seated on the left,   195
while on the right was the loving couple,
that is, Charikles and the maiden.
Charikles thought Gnathon deserved not mild reproaches
but rather insults and jeers
for being the cause of the undesirable seating plan,   200
because he had not put Drosilla opposite Charikles
when his eyes were melting with love,
and Myrtion, the girl's father,
was in the place close by his seat,
so that throughout the entire banquet   205
he could look directly at the girl.
He even envied – how can this be phrased? –
the cup that so excellently touched
the maiden's delicious lips;
he was jealous of the draught of wine   210

that came near Drosilla's mouth.[289]
Thus the banquet took its course.
Black-footed night flowed around the strangers
and, relaxing the tension of their brows,[290]
brought sweet sleep to their eyes.   215

    But towards dawn the lovely, the very lovely
daughter of aged Myrtion
took Kalligone's urn
and showered it with yet another bath of tears.
For womankind is easily moved,   220
and is ready to mourn for the sufferings even of strangers,
and is ever inclined to weep.[291]
For it is not only in time of disaster
that women like to mourn and to weep at length,
but even more so if anyone has completed his life;   225
constantly as the years sweep by,
they weep for the recollection of past evils.
So that maiden in her compassion
slipped past the four as they slept,
Gnathon, Myrtion her begetter,   230
and yes indeed Charikles and his father,
and she cried out as she bent over Kalligone's urn,
she smote her breast and cried out again
with groans and a flood of tears,
"O malignant one, O hostile Fate,[292]   235
you are not satisfied with all the previous
dreadful events that lie bitterly in Drosilla's heart,
but now you add even more to them.
You brought death to the maiden Kalligone.
Kalligone slew Kleandros;   240
but Kleandros does not put his kin
to death with him, though in their hearts
he releases the bitterness of great grief.
So I mourn for you, Kalligone,
fellow maiden; it is I who weep for you, buried in the earth,   245

289 Cf. *R&D* 2.127–28, and Eugenianos, *Epigrams* 1.7–8 (Lambros 1914).
290 Cf. *AnthGr* 42.3 (Dioskorides) and *R&D* 8.2.
291 Cf. *R&D* 1.149–50, 2.361–62.
292 Marginal gloss: 'Drosilla's lament for Kalligone'.

instead of Kleandros who has departed,
who shared our exile in foreign lands;
I weep for you who are deprived of your mother and father,
and who, alas, died far from your homeland;
yet I never saw you, never entered into conversation with you,   250
did not greet you and embrace you in time of joy,
nor have you as a consolation in time of disaster.
Would that I had never seen Kleandros
and shared food and tears with him.
But receive my lamentation,   255
which I have now poured out for you like a mourning libation."
    She finished her speech and, with modest propriety,
she returned once more to Gnathon's abode
where Gnathon had offered hospitality to the old men
and their children since the first day.   260
They did not wish to stay longer,
and finally he approached them and addressed them pleasantly
and gave the men a hearty embrace
and on the second day sent them to their homeland.
As the sea had became smooth   265
and no ship-destroying gale was blowing
nor were the waves heaving,
they encountered a pleasant and calm voyage
and made their way to their beloved country.
When they had sailed for ten days   270
they eventually arrived at their homeland
and set foot on the longed-for territory;
then Phrator, begetter of Charikles,
tried to take Myrtion to his house,
while Myrtion, progenitor of Drosilla,   275
tried in turn to take Phrator to his home,
while the mothers of the young man and the girl,
Hedypnoe and, with her, Krystale,
as soon as they learnt what had happened, immediately
ran there, embraced the young people   280
and soaked them with tears of joy.
The affectionate family group,
the throng of fellow countrymen, the fellow citizens,
all joined in the applause, they rejoiced, they celebrated hugely,

they were more delighted than one can express. 285
    So this is the state they were in; then there arrived one
of their leading men, the priest of Dionysos,
with the intention of taking
the entire crowd with all speed to the temple,
so that he could unite the bride Drosilla[293] 290
in matrimony with Charikles.
    He made his pronouncement and promptly,
holding out two branches from a vine to the bridal pair,
he led them to the temple, together with the crowd.
And what happened next? There was united in marriage 295
the bride Drosilla with her bridegroom Charikles,
and she was taken to the parents' house
with crowns and applause and cymbals;[294]
and the girl who in the evening was a virgin,
arose from her bed in the morning a woman.[295] 300

---

293 Marginal gloss: 'Union of Drosilla and Charikles'.
294 Cf. *R&D* 9.479–84.
295 Cf. Musaios, *Hero and Leander* 287.

BIBLIOGRAPHY

Agapitos, P. 1992. *The Study of Medieval Greek Romance: a reassessment of recent work* (Copenhagen)

Agapitos, P. 1993. 'Ἡ χρονολογικὴ ἀκολουθία τῶν μυθιστορημάτων *Καλλίμαχος, Βέλθανδρος καὶ Λίβιστρος*', in N. G. Panayotakis, ed., *Origini della letteratura neograeca*, vol. 2 (Venice): 97–134

Agapitos, P. 1993a. Review of Marcovich 1992, *Ἑλληνικά* 43: 229–36

Agapitos, P. 1998. 'Narrative rhetoric and "drama" rediscovered: scholars and poets in Byzantium interpret Heliodorus', in R. Hunter, ed., *Studies in Heliodorus* (Cambridge): 125–56

Agapitos, P. 2000. 'Der Roman der Komnenenzeit: Stand der Forschung und weitere Perspektiven', in Agapitos and Reinsch 2000: 1–18

Agapitos, P. 2000a. 'Poets and painters: Theodoros Prodromos' dedicatory verses of his novel to an anonymous Caesar', *JÖB* 50: 173–85

Agapitos, P. 2004. 'Genre, structure and poetics in the Byzantine vernacular romances of love', *Symbolae Osloenses* 79: 7–54.

Agapitos, P. 2006. 'Writing, reading and reciting (in) Byzantine erotic fiction', in B. Mondrain, ed., *Lire et écrire à Byzance* (Paris): 125–76

Agapitos, P. 2006a. *Ἀφήγησις Λιβίστρου καὶ Ῥοδάμνης. Κριτικὴ ἔκδοση τῆς διασκευῆς α* (Athens)

Agapitos, P., and D.-R. Reinsch, eds. 2000. *Der Roman im Byzanz der Komnenenzeit* (Frankfurt am Main)

Alexiou, M. 1977. 'A critical reappraisal of Eustathios Makrembolites' *Hysmine and Hysminias*', *BMGS* 3: 23–43

Alexiou, M. 1978. 'Modern Greek folklore and its relation to the past: the evolution of Charos in Greek tradition', in S. Vryonis, ed., *The 'Past' in Medieval and Modern Greek Culture* (Malibu): 221–36

Alexiou, M. 2002. *The Ritual Lament in Greek Tradition* (2nd edn, Oxford)

Alexiou, M. 2002a. 'Eros and the "constraints of desire" in *Hysmene and Hysminias*', in M. Alexiou, *After Antiquity: Greek language, myth and metaphor* (New York): 111–26

Anastasi, R. 1965. 'Per una nuova edizione del romanzo di Constantino Manasse', *Helikon* 5: 1–20

Anastasi, R. 1969. 'Sul romanzo di Constantino Manasse', *Rivista di cultura classica e medioevale* 11: 214–36

Aubreton, R., and F. Buffière. 1980. *Anthologie grecque, deuxième partie. Anthologie de Planude, tome XIII* (Paris)

Barber, C. 1992. 'Reading the garden in Byzantium', *BMGS* 16: 1–19

Beaton, R. 1976. 'Dionysios Solomos: the tree of poetry', *BMGS* 2: 161–82

Beaton, R. 1989. *The Medieval Greek Romance* (Cambridge)

Beaton, R. 1996. *The Medieval Greek Romance* (2nd edn, London)

Beaton, R. 2000. 'The world of fiction and the world "out there": the case of the Byzantine novel', in Smythe 2000: 179–88

Beaton, R. 2007. 'Antique nation? "Hellenes" on the eve of Greek independence and in twelfth-century Byzantium', *BMGS* 21: 76–95 (repr. in Beaton 2008, no. 2)

Beaton, R. 2008. *From Byzantium to Modern Greece: medieval texts and their reception* (Aldershot)

Beck, H.-G. 1984. *Byzantinisches Erotikon: Orthodoxie, Literatur, Gesellschaft* (Munich)

Bees, N. A. 1930. 'Manassis, der Metropolit von Naupaktos, ist identisch mit dem Schriftsteller Konstantinos Manasses', *Byzantinisch-neugriechische Jahrbücher* 7: 119–30

Bekker, I. 1836. *Michaelis Glycae Annales* (Bonn)

Bekker, I. 1837. *Constantini Manassis Breviarum historiae metricum* (Bonn)

Bekker, I, 1838. *Theophanes continuatus, Ioannes Cameniata, Symeon Magister, Georgius monachus* (Bonn)

Bernard, F. 2010. 'The Beats of the Pen' (unpublished PhD thesis, University of Ghent)

Bernardinello, S. 1972. *Theodori Prodromi De Manganis* (Padua)

Bodgan, J. 1922. *Die slavische Manasses-Chronik* (Bucharest)

Bidez, J. 1924. *L'empereur Julien: oeuvres complètes,* vol. 1.2 (Paris)

Boissonade, J. 1819. *Nicetae Eugeniani narrationem amatoriam et Constantini Manassis fragmenta,* 2 vols (Paris)

Boissonade, J. 1831. *Anecdota Graeca,* vol. 3 (Paris)

Bowie, E. L. 1985. 'The Greek novel', in P. E. Easterling and B. M. W. Knox, eds, *Cambridge History of Classical Literature,* vol. 1 (Cambridge): 683–99

Browning, R. 1962. 'An unpublished funeral oration on Anna Comnene',

Proceedings of the Cambridge Philological Society 188 (n.s. 8): 1–12 (repr. in *idem, Studies on Byzantine History, Literature and Education*, London, 1977: no. 7)

Buchthal, H. 1961. *An Illuminated Byzantine Gospel Book* (Melbourne)

Burton, J. 1998. 'Reviving the pagan Greek novel in a Christian world', *GRBS* 39: 179–216

Burton, J. 2000. 'Abduction and elopement in the Byzantine novel', *GRBS* 41: 377–409

Burton, J. 2003. 'A reemergence of Theocritean poetry in the Byzantine novel', *Classical Philology* 98: 251–73

Burton, J. 2004. *A Byzantine Novel: Drosilla and Charikles by Niketas Eugenianos* (Wauconda, IL)

Burton, J. 2006. 'The pastoral in Byzantium', in M. Fantuzzi and T. Papanghelis, eds, *Brill's Companion to Greek and Latin Pastoral* (Leiden): 549–79

Burton, J. 2008. 'Byzantine readers', in Whitmarsh 2008: 272–81

Carani, L. 1550. *Gli amori d'Ismenio composti per Eustathio filosofo* (Florence; repr. Venice, 1560, 1566)

Carile, A. 1968. 'Il cesare Niceforo Briennio', *Aevum* 42: 429–54

Cataldi Palau, A. 1980. 'La tradition manuscrite d'Eustathe Makrembolitès', *Revue d'histoire des textes* 10: 75–113

Cataudella, Q. 1988. *Niceta Eugeniano, Le avventure di Drosilla e Charicle* (Palermo)

Cesaretti, P. 1991. *Allegoristi di Omero a Bisanzio: ricerche ermeneutiche (XI–XII secolo)* (Milan)

Chalandon, F. 1912. *Jean II Comnène, 1118–1143, et Manuel I Comnène (1143–1180)*, 2 vols (Paris)

Christides, D. 1984. *Μαρκιανὰ ἀνέκδοτα* (Thessalonica)

Ciccolella, F. 2000. *Cinque poeti bizantini: anacreontee dal Barberiniano greco 310* (Alessandria)

Collande, Marquis de. 1785. *Les amours de Rhodante et de Dosicle* (Paris)

Colletet, G. 1625. *Les aventures amoureuse d'Isméne et d'Isménie* (Paris)

Conca, F. 1990. *Nicetas Eugenianus de Drosillae et Chariclis amoribus* (Amsterdam)

Conca, F. 1990a. 'Guiseppe e la moglie di Putifarre', in I. Gallo, ed., *Contributi di filologia greca* (Naples): 143–58

Conca, F. 1994. *Il romanzo bizantino del XII secolo* (Turin)

Conca, F. 1994a. 'Osservazioni al testo del romanzo di Teodoro Prodromo', in U. Albini and others, eds, *Storia, poesia e pensiero nel mondo antico: studi in onore di Marcello Gigante* (Naples): 137–47

Constantin Manasses 2007. *Constantin Manasses Synopsis Chroniki /Cod. Vaticano Slavo 2, 1344–45* (no ed.; Athens: Militos)

Cooper, C. 2007. 'Forensic oratory', in I. Worthington, ed., *A Companion to Greek Rhetoric* (Oxford): 203–19

Cottone, M. 1979. 'La tradizione manoscritta del romanzo di Teodoro Prodromo', *Miscellanea* 2 (Istituto di studi bizantini e neogreci, University of Padua): 9–34

Cupane, C. 1973–74. 'Un caso di giudizio di Dio nel romanzo di Teodoro Prodromo (I 372–404)', *Rivista di studi bizantini e neoellenici* 10–11: 147–68

Cupane, C. 1974. ''Ερως βασιλεύς. La figura di Eros nel romanzo bizantino d'amore', *Atti dell'Accademia di Scienze, Lettere e Arti di Palermo*, ser. 4, vol. 33, pt. 2: 243–97

Cupane, C. 1984. 'Natura formatrix: Umwege eines rhetorischen Topos', in W. Hörandner, ed., *Byzantios. Festschrift für H. Hunger* (Vienna): 37–52

Cupane, C. 1992. 'Concezione e rappresentazione dell'amore nella narrativa tardo-bizantina. Un tentative di analisi comparata', in A. M. Babbi, A. Pioletti, F. Rizzo Nervo and C. Stanoni, eds, *Medioevo romanzo e orientale. Testi e prospettive storiografiche* (Messina): 283–305

Cupane, C. 1993. 'La figura di Fortuna nella letteratura greca medievale', in N. Panagiotakis, ed., *Origini della letteratura neograeca*, vol. 1 (Venice): 413–37

Cupane, C. 2000. 'Metamorphosen des Eros. Liebesdarstellung und Liebesdiskurs in der byzantinischen Literatur der Komnenenzeit', in Agapitos and Reinsch 2000: 25–54

Cupane, C. 2003. Review of Marcovich 2001, *BZ* 96: 302–05

Curtius, E. R. 1953. *European Literature and the Latin Middle Ages*, trans. W. Trask (New York)

Darrouzès, J. 1970. *Recherches sur les ὀφφίκια de l'église byzantine* (Paris)

Darrouzès, J. 1970a. *Georges et Dèmetrios Tornikès, Lettres et Discours* (Paris)

Dawe, R. D. 2001. 'Some erotic suggestions. Notes on Achilles Tatius, Eustathius Macrembolites, Xenophon of Ephesus, Charito', *Philologus* 145: 291–311

Dawe, R. D. 2001a. 'Notes on Theodore Prodromus *Rodanthe and Dosicles* and Nicetas Eugenianus *Drosilla and Charicles*', *BZ* 94: 11–19

Deligiorgis, S. 1975. 'A Byzantine romance in international perspective: the

Drosilla and Charikles of Niketas Eugenianos', *Neo-Hellenika* 2: 21–32

Des Places, E. 1971. *Oracles chaldaiques avec un choix de commentaries anciens* (Paris)

Diehl, E. 1942. *Anthologia Lyrica Graeca*, vol. 2 (2nd edn, Leipzig)

Dolezal, M.-L., and M. Mavroudi. 2002. 'Theodore Hyrtakenos' *Description of the Garden of St. Anna* and the ekphrasis of gardens', in A. Littlewood, H. Maguire and J. Wolshke-Bulmahn, eds, *Byzantine Garden Culture* (Washington, D.C.): 105–58

Dölger, F., and P. Wirth. 1995. *Regesten der Kaiserurkunden des oströmischen Reiches*, vol. 2, *Regesten von 1025–1204* (rev. edn, Munich)

Doody, M. A. 1996. *The True Story of the Novel* (Piscataway, NJ)

Dostalova, R. 1993. 'Zur Bildekphrasis des Eros im Roman des Eustathios Makremvolitis', *Acta Universitatis Carolinae, Philologica 2; Graecolatina Pragensia* 14: 45–52

Downey, G., and A. F. Norman. *Themistii orationes*, vol. 2 (Leipzig)

Dujcev, I. 1963. *Letopista na Konstantin Manasi* (Sofia)

Edmonds, J. M. 1957. *The Fragments of Attic Comedy*, vol. 1 (Leiden)

Eideneier, H. 1991. *Ptochoprodromos. Einführung, kritische Ausgabe, deutsche Übersetzung, Glossar* (Cologne)

Fedalto, G. 1988. *Hierarchia ecclesiastica orientalis*, 2 vols (Padua)

Gallavotti, G. 1935. 'Novi Laurentiana codicis analecta', *Studi bizantini e neoellenici*, n.s. 4: 203–36

Garland, L. 1990. '"Be amorous but be chaste …" Sexual morality in Byzantine learned and vernacular romances', *BMGS* 14: 62–122

Garland, L. 1990a. '"And his bald head shone like a full moon …": an appreciation of the Byzantine sense of humour as recorded in historical sources of the eleventh and twelfth centuries', *Parergon* 8: 1–31

Garland, L. 2006. *Byzantine Women: varieties of experience 800–1200* (Aldershot)

Garland. L. 2006a. 'Imperial women and entertainment at the Middle Byzantine court', in Garland 2006: 177–91

Garzya, A. 1969. 'Intorno al *Prologo* di Niceforo Basilace', *JÖBG* 18: 57–71

Garzya, A. 1984. *Nicephorus Basilaca Orationes et Epistolae* (Leipzig)

Garzya, A. 1993. Review of Marcovich 1992, Κοινωνία 17: 226

Gaulminus, G. 1617. *Eustathii De Ismeniae et Ismenes amoribus libri XI* (Paris; reprinted 1644)

Gaulminus, G. 1625. *Theodori Prodromi philosophi Rhodanthes et Dosiclis amorum libri IX* (Paris)

Gautier, P. 1972. *Michel Italikos, Lettres et discours* (Paris)

Gautier, P. 1975. *Nicéphore Bryennios, Histoire* (Brussels)

Gautier, P. 1985. 'Le typikon de la Théotokos Kécharitôménè', *REB* 43: 5–165

Giusti, A. 1993. 'Nota a Niceta Eugeniano', *Studi italiani della filologia classica* 11: 216–23

Godard de Beauchamps, P. F. 1746. *Les amours de Rhodante et de Dosiclés* (Paris; repr. 1797, and *Bibliothèque universelle des dames*, vol. 8, Paris, 1786)

Godard de Beauchamps, P. F. 1729. *Les amours de Hysmène et d'Isménias* (Paris; repr. 1797)

Gonnelli, F. 1998. *Giorgio di Pisidia, Esamerone* (Pisa)

Gouma-Peterson, T., ed. 2000. *Anna Komnene and her Times* (New York)

Grosdidier de Matons, J. 1979. 'Note sur le sens médiéval du mot κλίνη', *TM* 7: 363–73

Grossschupf, F. 1897. *De Theodori Prodromi in Rhodantha elocutione* (Leipzig)

Grumel, V. 1972. *Les regestes des actes du Patriarcat de Constantinople*, vol. 1 (2nd edn, Paris)

Grünbart, M. 1996. Review of Marcovich 1992, *Anzeiger der Altertumwissenschaft* 49: 93–96

Grünbart, M. 2001. *Epistularum byzantinarum initia* (Hildesheim)

Häger, O. 1908. 'De Theodori Prodromi in fabula erotica Ῥοδάνθη καὶ Δοσικλῆς fontibus' (unpublished dissertation, Göttingen)

Hägg, T. 1983. *The Novel in Antiquity* (Oxford)

Haldon, J. 1999. *Warfare, State and Society in the Byzantine World, 565–1204* (London)

Haldon, J. 1999. 'Chapters II. 44 and 45 of *De Cerimoniis*. Theory and practice in tenth-century military administration', *TM* 13: 201–352

Haldon, J. 2002. 'Humour and the everyday in Byzantium', in G. Halsall, ed., *Humour, History and Politics in Late Antiquity and the Early Middle Ages* (Cambridge): 48–71

Halm, C. 1889. *Fabulae Aesiopicae collectae* (Leipzig)

Harder, R. 1997. 'Diskurse über die Gastlichkeit im Roman des Theodoros Prodromos', in H. Hofmann and M. Zimmerman, eds, *Groningen Colloquia on the Novel, VIII* (Groningen): 131–49

Harder, R. 2000. 'Religion und Glaube in den Romanen der Komnenzeit', in Agapitos and Reinsch 2000: 55–80

Hausrath, A. 1959. *Corpus fabularum aesopicarum*, vol. 1, rev. H. Hunger (Leipzig)

Heiberg, I. L. 1921. *Paulus Aegineta*, vol. 1 (Leipzig)

Helfer, B. 1971. 'Nicetas Eugenianos, ein Rhetor und Dichter der Komnen-zeit. Mit einer Edition des Epithaphios auf den Grossdrungarios Steph-anos Komnenos' (unpublished dissertation, Vienna)

Hercher, R. 1859. *Eroticorum scriptorium Graecorum*, vol. 2 (Leipzig)

Hercher, R. 1873. 'Zu den Romanfragmenten des Constantinos Manasses', *Hermes* 7: 488–89

Hilberg, I. 1876. *Eustathii Macrembolitae protonoblissimi De Hysmines et Hysminiae amoribus libri XI* (Vienna)

Hill, B. 1999. *Imperial Women in Byzantium 1025–1204* (Harlow)

Hinterberger, M. 2006. 'Tränen in der byzantinischen Literatur', *JÖB* 56: 27–51

Hirschig, G. A. 1856. *Erotici scriptores* (Paris; repr. 1885)

Hörandner, W. 1974. *Theodoros Prodromos, Historische Gedichte* (Vienna)

Horna, K. 1903. 'Die Epigramme des Theodoros Balsamon', *Wiener Studien* 25: 165–217

Horna, K. 1904. 'Das Hodoiporikon des Konstantinos Manasses', *BZ* 13: 313–55

Howard-Johnston, J. 1996. 'Anna Komnene and the *Alexiad*', in M. Mullett and D. Smythe, eds, *Alexios I Komnenos* (Belfast): 232–302

Hunger, H. 1972. 'Byzantinische "Froschmänner"?', in R. Hanslik, A. Lesky and H. Schwabl, eds, *Antidosis: Festschrift für Walther Kraus zum 70. Geburtstag* (Vienna): 183–87

Hunger, H. 1978. *Die hochsprachliche profane Literatur der Byzantiner*, 2 vols (Munich)

Hunger, H. 1980. 'Antiker und byzantinischer Roman', *Sitzungsber. Heidel-berg. Akad. der Wiss.* 3: 5–34

Hunger, H. 1998. 'Die Makrembotliten auf byzantinischen Bleisiegeln und in sonstigen Belegen', in N. Oikonomides, ed., *Studies in Byzantine Sigillography* 5 (Washington, D.C.): 1–28

Hyland, A. 1994. *The Medieval Warhorse from Byzantium to the Crusades* (Stroud)

Impellizeri, S. 1984. *Imperatori di Bisanzio, Cronografia, Michele Psello*, 2 vols (Milan)

Jacoby, D. 2008. 'Silk production', *OHBS*: 421–28

Jeffreys, E. 1980. 'The Comnenian background to the *romans d'antiquité*', *Byzantion* 50: 455–86

Jeffreys, E. 1998. *Digenis Akritis: the Grottaferrata and Escorial versions* (Cambridge)

Jeffreys, E. 1998a. 'The novels of mid-twelfth-century Constantinople: the literary and social context', in I. Sevcenko and I. Hutter, eds, *ΑΕΤΟΣ*.

Studies in Honor of Cyril Mango (Stuttgart): 191–99

Jeffreys, E. 2000. 'Akritis and outsiders', in Smythe 2000: 189–202

Jeffreys, E. 2000a. 'A date for Rhodanthe and Dosikles?', in Agapitos and Reinsch 2000: 127–36

Jeffreys, E. 2003. 'Nikephoros Bryennios reconsidered', in V.N. Vlysidou, ed., *Η αυτοκρατορία σε κρίση (;), Το Βυζάντιο τον 11ο αιώνα (1025–1081) (Empire in Crisis? Byzantium in the 11th Century (1025–1081))* (Athens): 201–14

Jeffreys, E., 2005. 'The Labours of the Twelve Months in twelfth-century Byzantium', in E. Stafford and J. Herrin, eds, *Personification in the Greek World: from antiquity to Byzantium* (Aldershot): 309–24

Jeffreys, E. 2009. 'Why produce verse in twelfth-century Constantinople?' in P. Odorico, P.A. Agapitos and M. Hinterberger, eds, *«Doux remède ...» Poésie et poétique à Byzance* (Paris): 219–28

Jeffreys, E. forthcoming a. 'The sevastokratorissa Eirene as patron', *Wiener Jahrbuch für Kunstgeschichte* 60

Jeffreys, E. forthcoming b. 'The afterlife of Akritis', in P. Roilos, ed., *Byzantine Fictional Narrative* (Cambridge, MA)

Jeffreys, E. 2013. 'Byzantine romances: eastern or western?', in M. Brownlee and D. Gondicas, eds, *Renaissance Encounters: Greek East and Latin West* (Leiden)

Jeffreys, E. and M. 1994. 'Who was Eirene the sevastokratorissa', *Byzantion* 64: 40–68

Jeffreys, E. and M. 2001. 'The "Wild beast from the West": immediate literary reactions in Byzantium to the Second Crusade', in A. Laiou and R. Mottahedeh, eds, *The Crusades from the Perspective of Byzantium and the Muslim World* (Washington, D.C.): 101–16

Jeffreys, E. and M. 2009. *Iacobi Monachi Epistulae* (Turnhout)

Jeffreys, M. 1974. 'The nature and origins of the political verse', *DOP* 28: 142–95

Jouanno, C. 1989. 'Nicétas Eugénianos: un héritier du roman grec', *RÉG* 102: 346–60

Jouanno, C. 1992. 'Les barbares dans le roman byzantin du XIIe siècle: fonction d'un topos', *Byzantion* 62: 264–300

Jouanno, C. 1994. 'L'oeil fatale. Reflections sur le role du regard dans le roman grec et byzantin', *Pris-Ma* 10: 149–64

Jouanno, C. 1996. 'Sur un *topos* romanesque oublié: les scènes de banquets', *RÉG* 109: 157–84

Jouanno, C. 2002. 'Les jeunes filles dans le roman byzantine du XIIe siècle', in B. Pouderon, ed., *Les personnages du roman grec* (Tours): 229–46

Jouanno, C. 2005. 'A Byzantine novelist staging the ancient Greek world: presence, form and functions of antiquity in Macrembolites' *Hysmine and Hysminias*', in S. Kaklamanis and M. Paschalis, eds, *Η πρόσληψη της αρχαιότητας στο βυζαντινό και νεοελληνικό μυθιστόρημα* (Athens): 15–29

Jouanno, C. 2006. 'Women in Byzantine novels of the twelfth century: an interplay between norm and fantasy', in Garland 2006: 141–62 (French version: Pouderon 2001: 329–46)

Kalatzi, M. 2010. *Hermonymos: a study in scribal, literary and teaching activities in the fifteenth and early sixteenth centuries* (Athens)

Kaldellis, A. 2007. 'Historicism in Byzantine thought and literature', *DOP* 61: 1–24

Kaldellis, A. 2007a. *Byzantine Hellenism* (Cambridge)

Kannicht, R., and B. Snell. 1981. *Tragicorum Graecorum Fragmenta*, vol. 2 (Göttingen)

Kassel, R., and C. Austin. 1991. *Poetae Comici Graecae*, vol. 2 (Berlin)

Kazhdan, A. 1967. 'Bemerkungen zu Niketas Eugenianos', *JÖBG* 16: 101–17

Kazhdan, A. 1985. 'The concept of freedom (eleutheria) and slavery (duleia) in Byzantium', in G. Makdisi, ed., *La notion de liberté au Moyen Age: Islam, Byzance, Occident* (Paris): 215–26

Kazhdan, A. 1985a. Review of Christides 1984, *Hellenika* 36: 184–89

Kazhdan, A., and S. Franklin. 1984. *Studies on Byzantine Literature of the Eleventh and Twelfth Centuries* (Cambridge)

Kirk, G., J. Raven and M. Schofield. 1983. *The Presocratic Philosophers: a critical history with a selection of texts*, 2nd edn (Cambridge)

Kleinbauer, W. E. 2004. *Hagia Sophia* (London)

Krumbacher, K. 1897. *Geschichte der byzantinischen Litteratur* (Munich)

Kühn, C. G. 1826. *Claudii Galeni opera omnia*, vol. 12 (Leipzig)

Kurtz, E. 1900. 'Dva proizvedeniya Konstantina Manassi', *VV* 7: 630–45

Kurtz, E. 1906. 'Eshche dva neizdannykh proizvedeniya Konstantina Manassi', *VV* 12: 88–98

Kurtz, E. 1910. 'Evstathiya Thessalonikiskago i Konstantina Mannasi monodie na konchinya Nikifora Komnina', *VV* 17: 302–22

Labarthe-Postel, J. 2001. 'Hommes et dieux dans les *ekphraseis* des romans byzantins du temps des Comnène', in Pouderon 2001: 347–71

Laiou, A. 1992. *Mariage, amour et parenté à Byzance aux Xie–XIIIe siècles* (Paris)

Laiou, A. 1993. 'Sex, consent and coercion in Byzantium', in A. Laiou, ed.,

Consent and Coercion to Sex and Marriage in Ancient and Medieval Societies (Washington, D.C.): 109–221

Lambert, J. A. 1935. *Le roman de Libistros et Rhodamné* (Amsterdam)

Lambros, S. 1911. 'Ὁ Μαρκιανὸς κῶδιξ 524', *NH* 8: 3–18

Lambros, S. 1914. ''Επιγράμματα ἀνέκδοτα', *NH* 11: 353–58

Lampanitziotis, P. 1791. *Εὐσταθείου τὸ καθ' Ὑσμήνην καὶ Ὑσμηνίαν δρᾶμα* (Vienna)

Lampsidis, O. 1971. 'Τὸ λεξιλόγιον τοῦ Κωνσταντίνου Μανασσῆ ἐν τῇ Χρονικῇ Συωόψει', *Platon* 23: 254–77

Lampsidis, O. 1988. 'Zur Biographie von K. Manasses and zu seiner *Chronike Synopsis*', *Byzantion* 58: 97–111

Lampsidis, O. 1991. 'Der vollständige Text der ἔκφρασις γῆς des Konstantinos Manasses', *JÖB* 41: 189–205

Lampsidis, O. 1996. *Constantini Manassis Breviarium Chronicum*, 2 vols (Athens)

Lane Fox, R. 1986. *Pagans and Christians* (Harmondsworth)

Latte, K. 1953–2009. *Hesychii Alexandrini lexicon*, 4 vols (Copenhagen)

Laujon, P. 1770. *Ismene et Ismenias, tragédie en trois actes* (Paris)

Le Bas, P. 1822. *Aventures de Hysminé et Hysminias par Eumathe Macrembolites,* Collection de romans grecs, vol. 14 (Paris; repr. 1828)

Le Bas, P. 1856. *Eumathii philosophi De Hysmines et Hysminiae amoribus fabula,* in W. A. Hirschig, *Erotici Scriptores* (Paris): 523–97

Le Moine, L. H. 1788. *Ismene and Ismenias, a novel* (London)

Leone, P. A. M. 1972. *Ioannis Tzetzae epistulae* (Leipzig)

Leutsch, E. L., and F. G. Schneidewin. 1839–51. *Paroemiographi graeci,* 2 vols (Göttingen)

Lévêque, P. 1959. *Aurea Catena Homeri. Une étude sur l'allégorie grecque* (Paris)

Lewis, M. 2000. 'Theoretical hydraulics, automata, and water clocks', in O. Wikander, ed., *Handbook of Ancient Water Technology*, vol. 2 (Leiden): 343–69

Littlewood, A. 1974. 'The symbolism of the apple in Byzantine literature', *JÖB* 23: 33–59

Littlewood, A. 1979. 'Romantic paradise: the role of the garden in the Byzantine romance', *BMGS* 5: 93–114

Littlewood, A. 1993. 'The erotic symbolism of the apple in late Byzantine and meta-Byzantine demotic literature', *BMGS* 17: 83–103

Louveau d'Orleans, J. 1559. *Les amours d'Ismenias composé par le philosophe Eustatius* (Lyons)

Maas, P., and C. A. Trypanis. 1963. *Sancti Romani melodi cantica: cantica genuina* (Oxford)

MacAlister, S. 1990. 'Aristotle on the dream: a twelfth-century romance revival', *Byzantion* 60: 195–212

MacAlister, S. 1991. 'Byzantine twelfth-century romances: a relative chronology', *BMGS* 15: 175–210

MacAlister, S. 1994. 'Ancient and contemporary in Byzantine novels', in Tatum 1994: 308–23

MacAlister, S. 1996. *Dreams and Suicides: the Greek novel from antiquity to the Byzantine empire* (London)

Mackridge, P. 1993. '"None but the brave deserve the fair": abduction, elopement and marriage in the Escorial *Digenes Akrites* and Modern Greek heroic songs', in R. Beaton and D. Ricks, eds, *Digenes Akrites: new approaches to Byzantine heroic poetry* (London): 150–60

Magdalino, P. 1991. 'Hellenism and nationalism in Byzantium', in P. Magdalino, *Tradition and Transformation in Mediaeval Byzantium* (Aldershot), no. 14

Magdalino, P. 1992. 'Eros the king and the king of *amours*: some observations on *Hysmine and Hysminias*', *DOP* 46: 257–74

Magdalino, P. 1993. *The Empire of Manuel I Komnenos, 1143–1180* (Cambridge)

Magdalino, P. 1997. 'In search of the Byzantine courtier: Leo Choirosphaktes and Constantine Manasses', in H. Maguire, ed., *Byzantine Court Culture from 829 to 1204* (Washington, D.C.): 141–65

Magdalino, P. 2002. 'The medieval empire (780–1204)', in Mango 2002: 169–213

Magdalino, P. 2008. 'The empire of the Komnenoi (1118–1204)', in J. Shepard, ed., *The Cambridge History of the Byzantine Empire c. 500–1492* (Cambridge): 627–63

Magdalino, P., and R. Nelson. 1982. 'The emperor in Byzantine art of the twelfth century', *Byzantinische Forschungen* 8: 123–83

Maguire, H. 1999. 'The profane aesthetic in Byzantine art and literature', *DOP* 53: 189–205

Maguire, E. and M. 2007. *Other Icons: art and power in Byzantine secular culture* (Princeton)

Maiuri, A. 1914–19. 'Una nuova poesia di Teodoro Prodromo in greco volgare', *BZ* 23: 397–407

Majercik, R. 1989. *The Chaldean Oracles: text, translation, and commentary* (Leiden)

Mango, C. 1980. *Byzantium: the New Rome* (London)

Mango, C., ed. 2002. *The Oxford History of Byzantium* (Oxford)

Manion, M., and V. Vines. 1984. *Medieval and Renaissance Illuminated Manuscripts in Australian Collections* (Melbourne)

Marcovich, M. 1987. 'The *Itinerary* of Constantine Manasses', *Illinois Classical Studies* 12: 277–91

Marcovich, M. 1991. 'The text of Prodromus' novel', *Illinois Classical Studies* 16: 367–401

Marcovich, M. 1992. *Theodori Prodromi de Rhodanthes et Dosiclis amoribus libri IX* (Leipzig)

Marcovich, M. 2001. *Eustathius Macrembolites, De Hysmines et Hysminiae amoribus libri XI* (Munich)

Markopoulos, T. 2008. 'Education', *OHBS*: 784–95

Mavroudi, M. 2002. *A Byzantine Book on Dreams: the Oneirocriticon of Achmet and its Arabic sources* (Leiden)

Mazal, O. 1966. 'Neue Excerpte aus dem Roman des Konstantinos Manasses', *JÖBG* 15: 231–59

Mazal, O. 1967. *Der Roman des Konstantinos Manasses: Überlieferung, Rekonstruktion, Textausgabe der Fragmente* (Vienna)

Mazal, O. 1967a. 'Das moralische Lehrgedicht in Cod. Par. gr. 2750A – ein Werk eines Nachahmers und Plagiators des Konstantinos Manasses', *BZ* 60: 249–68

McCormick, M. 2001. *Origins of the European Economy: communications and commerce A.D. 30–900* (Cambridge)

Meineke, A. 1836. *Ioannis Cinnami Epitome rerum ab Ioanne et Alexio Comnenis gestarum* (Bonn)

Meunier, F. 1991. *Les amours homonymes* (Paris)

Meunier, F. 2007. *Le roman byzantin du XIIe siècle. À la découverte d'un nouveau monde?* (Paris)

Milazzo, A. 1985. 'Motivi bucolici e tecnica alessandrina in due "Idilli" di Niceta Eugeniano', *Studi di filologia bizantina* 3: 97–114

Miller, E. 1875. 'Poème moral de Constantin Manasses', *Annuaire de l' Association pour l'encouragement des études grecques* 9: 23–75

Miller, E. 1875–81. *Recueil des historiens des Croisades: historiens grecs*, vol. 2 (Paris)

Miller, E. 1884. 'Lettres de Thédore Balsamon', *Annuaire de l'association pour encourager les études grecs* 18: 8–19

Miller, T., and J. Nesbitt, eds. 1995. *Peace and Warfare in Byzantium: essays in honour of George T. Dennis, S.J.* (Washington, D.C.)

Mioni, E. 1973. *Bibliothecae Divi Marci Venetiarum codices graeci descripti*, vol. 3 (Rome)

Moennig, U. 2010. 'Biographical arrangement as a generic feature and its multiple use in late-Byzantine narratives: an exploration of the field', *Phrasis* 1: 107–47

Moreno Jurado, J. A. 1996. *Teodoro Prodromo, Rodante y Dosicles* (Madrid)

Nachstädt, W., and others. 1935. *Plutarchi Moralia*, vol. 2 (Leipzig)

Nauck, A., and B. Snell. 1964. *Tragicorum Graecorum Fragmenta* (Hildesheim)

Nilsson, I. 2001. *Erotic Pathos, Rhetorical Pleasure: narrative technique and mimesis in Eumathios Makrembolites' 'Hysmine and Hysminias'* (Uppsala)

Nilsson, I. 2001a. Review of Marcovich 2001, *Bryn Mawr Classical Review* http://bmcr.brynmawr.edu/2001/2001-08-35.html (accessed 15 December 2011)

Nilsson, I. 2006. 'Discovering literariness in the past: literature *vs.* history in the *Synopsis Chronike*', in P. Odorico, P. Agapitos and M. Hinterberger, eds, *L'Écriture de la mémoire: la littérarité de l'historiographie* (Paris): 15–31

Nispen, A. van. 1652. *De Grieksche Venus, vertoonende de beroemde vryagien van Klitophon en Leucippe, Ismenias en Ismene, Leander en Hero vyt't Griecksch vertaald* (Dordrecht)

Odorico, P. 1989. 'La sapienza del Digenis: materiali per lo studio dei *loci similes* nella recenzione di Grotteferrata', *Byzantion* 59: 137–63

Oikonomides, N. 1990. 'Contents of the Byzantine house from the eleventh to the fifteenth century', *DOP* 44: 205–14

Omont, H. 1885. 'Georges Hermonyme de Sparte, maitre de grec à Paris et copiste de manuscrits', *Bulletin de la société de l'histoire de Paris et de l'Ile-de-France* 12: 1–38

Parani, M. 2003. *Reconstructing the Reality of Images: Byzantine material culture and religious iconography (11th–15th centuries)* (Leiden)

Perry, B. E. 1952. *Aesopica: a collection of texts relating to Aesop or ascribed to him or closely related with the literary tradition that bears his name* (Urbana, IL)

Petit, L. 1902. 'Monodie de Nicétas Eugénianos sur Théodore Prodrome', *VV* 9: 446–63

Petit, L. 1903. 'Monodie de Théodore Prodrome sur Étienne Skylitzes', *Izvestija Russkogo Archeologiceskago Instituta v Konstantinopole* 8: 1–14

Petrovskii, F. A. 1969. *Τῶν κατὰ Δρόσιλλαν καὶ Χαρικλέα βιβλία θ* (Moscow)

Pezopoulos,E.1936. 'Νικήτας ὁ Εὐγενειανὸς ποιητὴς τῶν ἐπιγραμμάτων τοῦ κώδικος Urbin. 134', *ΕΕΒΣ* 12: 426–32

Piccolomini, E. 1874. 'Intorno ai collectanea di Massimo Planude', *Rivista di filologia e d'istruzione classica* 2: 101–17, 149–63

Pignani, A. 1983. *Niceforo Basilace, Progimnasmi e Monodie* (Naples)

Plepelits, K. 1989. *Eustathios Makrembolites, Hysmine und Hysminias* (Stuttgart)

Plepelits, K. 1996. *Theodoros Prodromos, Rhodanthe und Dosikles* (Stuttgart)

Plepelits, K. 2003. *Niketas Eugenianos, Drosilla und Charikles* (Stuttgart)

Polemis, D. 1968. *The Doukai: a contribution to Byzantine prosopography* (London)

Polemis, I. D. 1995. 'Προβλήματα τῆς βυζαντινῆς σχεδογραφίας', *Hellenika* 45: 277–302

Polyakova, S. V. 1965. *Evmathii Makremvolit 'Povest ob Isminii i Ismine'* (Moscow)

Polyakova, S. V. 1969. 'K voprosu o datirovke romana Evmatija Makrembolita', *VV* 30: 113–23

Poljakova, S. V. 1971. 'O chronologiceskoj posledovatelnosti romanov Evmatija Makremvolita i Feodora Prodroma', *VV* 32: 104–08

Pouderon, B., ed. 2001. *Les personages du roman grec* (Lyons)

Pryor, J., and E. Jeffreys. 2006. *The Age of the Dromon: the Byzantine navy ca. 500–1204* (Leiden)

Püchner, W. 2002. 'Acting in the Byzantine theatre: evidence and problems', in P. Easterling and E. Hall, eds, *Greek and Roman Actors* (Cambridge): 304–24

Reardon, B., ed. 1977. *Erotica Antiqua: Acta of the international conference on the ancient novel (Bangor 1976)* (Bangor)

Reardon, B., ed. 1989. *Collected Ancient Greek Novels* (Berkeley, CA)

Reinsch, D.-R. 2007. 'Die Palamedes-Episode in der Synopsis Chronike des Konstantinos Manasses und ihre Inspirationsquelle', in M. Hinterberger and E. Schiffer, eds, *Byzantinische Sprachkunst* (Berlin): 266–76

Reinsch, D.-R. 2001. *Annae Comnenae Alexias*, 2 vols (Berlin)

Reiske, E. C. 1778. 'Hysmene und Hysmenias', in *Hellas*, vol. 1 (Mitau): 101–206

Ricks, D. 1989. 'The pleasures of the chase: a motif in Digenes Akrites', *BMGS* 13: 290–95

Rohde, E. 1876. *Der griechische Roman und seine Vorläufer* (Leipzig)

Roilos, P. 2000. 'Amphoteroglossia: the role of rhetoric in the medieval Greek learned novel', in Agapitos and Reinsch 2000: 109–26

Roilos, P. 2005. *Amphoteroglossia: a poetics of the twelfth-century medieval Greek novel* (Cambridge, MA)

Rotman, Y. 2004. *Les ésclaves et l'ésclavage de la Mediterranée antique à la Mediterranée médiévale VIe–XIe siècles* (Paris)

Sargologos, E. 1964. *La vie de Saint Cyrille le Philéote, moine byzantin* (Brussels)

Sathas, C. 1876. *Bibliotheca medii aevi*, vol. 5 (Venice)

Schirmer, G. 1663. *Ismenens und Ismeniens Liebesgeschichte ... aus dem Lateinischen in insre hochteutsche MutterSprache übersetzet* (Leipzig)

Schissel, O. 1942. 'Der byzantinische Garten: seine Darstellung im gleichzeitigen Romane', *Sitzungsberichte der Akademie der Wissenschaften in Wien, Philosophisch-Historische Klasse* 221, Bd. 2

Ševčenko, N. 2006. 'Spiritual progression in the canon tables of the Melbourne Gospels', in J. Burke et al., eds, *Byzantine Narrative* (Melbourne): 334–44

Sewter, E. R. A., trans. 2009. *Anna Komnene, Alexiad*, rev. P. Frankopan (London)

Sideras, A. 1991. 25 ἀνέκδοτοι βυζαντινοί ἐπιτάφιοι. *Unedierte byzantinische Grabreden* (Thessalonica)

Sideras, A. 1994. *Die byzantinischen Grabreden: Prosopographie, Datierung, Überlieferung, 142 Epitaphien und Monodien aus dem byzantinischen Jahrtausend* (Vienna)

Smith, O. L. 1999. *The Byzantine Achilleid: the Naples version* (Vienna)

Smythe, D., ed. 2000. *Strangers to Themselves: the Byzantine outsider* (Aldershot)

Snell, B. 1986. *Tragicorum Graecorum Fragmenta*, vol. 1 (Göttingen)

Spatharakis, I. 1985. 'An illuminated Greek Grammar manuscript in Jerusalem: a contribution to the study of Comnenian illuminated ornament', *JÖB* 35: 231–44

Spyridakis, G. K., ed. 1962. *Hellenika demotika tragoudia* (Athens)

Sternbach, L. 1901. 'Analecta Manassea', *Eos* 7: 180–91

Sternbach, L. 1902. 'Constantini Manassae ecphrasis inedita', in *Symbolae in honorem Ludovici Cwiklinski* (Lemberg): 6–20

Sullivan, D. 2000. *Siegecraft: two tenth-century instructional manuals by 'Heron of Byzantium'* (Washington, D.C.)

Svoboda, K. 1935. 'La composition et le style du roman de Nicétas Eugenianos', in B. D. Filov, ed., *Actes du IVe Congrès international des études byzantines: Sofia, septembre 1934*, vol. 1 (Sofia): 191–201

Swain, S., ed. 1999. *Oxford Readings in the Greek Novel* (Oxford)

Tatum, J., ed. 1994. *The Search for the Ancient Novel* (Baltimore, MD)

Teucher, H. 1792. *Eustathii De Ismeniae et Ismenes amoribus libellus* (Leipzig)

Thomas. J., and A. C. Hero. 2000. *Byzantine Monastic Foundation Documents*, 5 vols (Washington, D.C.)

Trapp, E. 1969. 'Textkritische Bemerkungen zum Roman des Konstantinos Manases', *JÖB* 18: 73–77

Trapp, E. 1995. Review of Marcovich 1992, *JÖB* 45: 361–62

Treu, M. 1893. *Eustathii Macrembolitae quae feruntur aenigmata* (Programm des Friedrichs-Gymnasiums Breslau)

Trognon, A. 1822. *Amours de Rhodanthe et Dosiclès* (Collection de romans grecs, vol. 8; Paris)

Tsolakes, E. 1967. *Συμβολὴ στὴ μελέτη τοῦ ποιητικοῦ ἔργου τοῦ Κωσταντίνου Μανασσῆ καὶ κριτικὴ ἔκδοση τοῦ μυθιστορήματος του «Τα κατ᾽ Ἀρίστανδρον καὶ Καλλιθέα»* (Thessalonica)

Tsoungarakis, D. 1995. *Strategikon, Kekaumenos* (Athens)

Van der Valk, M. 1971–97. *Eustathii Archiepiscopi Thessalonicensis commentarii ad Homeri Iliadem pertinentes*, 5 vols (Leiden)

Van Dieten, J. J. 1975. *Nicetae Choniatae Historia* (Berlin)

Varzos, K. 1984. *Ἡ γενεαλογία τῶν Κομνηνῶν*, 2 vols (Thessalonica)

Vassis, I. 1993–94. 'Graeca sunt, non legunter. Zu den scheodographischen Spielereien des Theodoros Prodromos', *BZ* 86–87: 1–19

Villoison, J. B. C. d'Ansse de. 1781. *Anecdota graeca e regia parisina et e veneta S.Marci bibliothecae deprompta*, vol. 2 (Venice)

Voigt, E.-M. 1971. *Sappho et Alcaeus Fragmenta* (Amterdam)

Vogt, A. 1967. *Constantin VII Porphyrogénète, Le Livre des Cérémonies*, 4 vols (2nd edn, Paris)

Walden, J. W. H. 1894. 'Stage terms in Heliodorus' *Aethiopica*', *Harvard Studies in Classical Philology* 5: 1–43

Welz, C. 1910. *Analecta byzantina carmina inedita Theodori Prodromi et Stephani Physopalamitae* (Leipzig)

Wendel, K. 1914. *Scholia in Theocritum vetera* (Leipzig)

Wendel, C. 1948. 'Tzetzes', *Paulys Real-Encyclopädie der classischen Altertumswissenschaft: Supplement* 7A: 1959–2010

West, M. L. 1989. *Iambi et elegi graeci*, vol. 1 (Oxford)

West, M. L. 1993. *Carmina Anacreontea* (Leipzig)

Whitmarsh, T. 2008. *The Cambridge Companion to the Greek and Roman Novel* (Cambridge)

Zeitler, B. 1999 '*Ostentatio genitalium*: displays of nudity in Byzantium', in L. James, ed., *Desire and Denial in Byzantium* (Aldershot): 185–201

GENERAL INDEX

INDEX OF PERSONS AND PLACES

Drosilla and Charikles